Praise for the authors of *Cowboy Country*

Praise for #1 *New York Times* bestselling author Linda Lael Miller

"Miller tugs at the heartstrings as few authors can."
—*Publishers Weekly*

"Miller's name is synonymous with the finest in Western romance."
—*RT Book Reviews*

"Linda Lael Miller creates vibrant characters and stories I defy you to forget."
—#1 *New York Times* bestselling author Debbie Macomber

"Miller is one of the finest American writers in the genre."
—*RT Book Reviews*

Praise for *USA TODAY* bestselling author Delores Fossen

"Clear off space on your keeper shelf, Fossen has arrived."
—*New York Times* bestselling author Lori Wilde

"Delores Fossen takes you on a wild Texas ride with a hot cowboy."
—*New York Times* bestselling author B.J. Daniels

"You will be sold!"
—*RT Book Reviews* on *Blame It on the Cowboy*

"In the first McCord Brothers contemporary, bestseller Fossen strikes a patriotic chord that makes this story stand out."
—*Publishers Weekly* on *Texas on My Mind*

LINDA LAEL MILLER

DELORES FOSSEN

COWBOY
Country

HQN™

HQN™

ISBN-13: 978-1-335-06296-3

Cowboy Country

Copyright © 2017 by Harlequin Books S.A.

The publisher acknowledges the copyright holders of the individual works as follows:

The Creed Legacy
Copyright © 2011 by Linda Lael Miller

Blame It on the Cowboy
Copyright © 2016 by Delores Fossen

Recycling programs for this product may not exist in your area.

CONTENTS

THE CREED LEGACY

Linda Lael Miller

For Nicole Blint, with love.

CHAPTER ONE

Lonesome Bend, Colorado

RANCHING, BRODY CREED THOUGHT, shifting in the saddle as he surveyed the sprawling range land from a high ridge. *It can mend a broken heart, this life, and then shatter it all over again, in a million and one different ways and twice that many pieces.*

There were plenty of perils. Cattle starved or froze to death when a hard winter came around, which averaged once a year up there in the high country. Spring calves and colts fell prey to wolves and coyotes and sometimes bears, hungry after hibernating through the coldest months.

It was now May, and all was well, but come summertime, wells might dry up for lack of rain, and turn the grass to tinder, ready to blaze up at the smallest spark. He'd seen wildfires consume hundreds of acres in a matter of hours, herds and houses and barns wiped out.

Year-round, good horses went lame and pickup trucks gave up the ghost, and every so often, somebody drowned in the river or one of the lakes.

On the other hand, Brody reflected, the beauty of that land could heal, take a man by surprise, even though he'd called the place home all his life. That day, for instance, the sky was so blue it made Brody's heart ache, and the aspens, cottonwoods and pines lining the landscape were shimmering splashes of green, a thousand hues of it, ranging from silvery to near-indigo. The river wound like a ribbon through the valley, clear as azure glass.

After a few moments, Brody adjusted his hat and sighed before giving the gelding a light nudge with the heels of his boots. The buckskin, long-legged with a black mane and tail, picked his way cautiously down the steep slope that led to the water's edge.

Behind them and a hundred yards farther along the riverbank, in a westerly direction, hammers clacked and power saws screeched, and Brody glanced back, pleased, as always, to see the steel-and-lumber skeletons of his house and barn rising.

Not so long ago, there had been a campground and RV park on the site, owned by Tricia McCall, now his sister-in-law and therefore a Creed. The picnic tables and the concrete fire pits were gone, along with the public showers and electrical hookups for trailers. Only the log building that had once served as the office remained; Brody had been baching in it since last Thanksgiving, when he'd moved out of the main ranch house.

The peace between him and twin brother, Conner, could be a fragile one at times, and they both benefited by a little distance.

Now, ready to get moving, Brody clucked his tongue and gave the gelding, Moonshine, another tap with his heels.

"Come on, now," he told the buckskin, his tone reasonable. "The water's shallow here, and it's real calm. If we're going to be working livestock on both sides of this river, then you've got to learn how to cross it."

Moonshine, recently acquired at an auction in Denver, was young, and Brody hadn't had a chance to train him in the ways of a cow pony.

No time like the present, he figured.

Brody was about to get down out of the saddle and lead the horse into the water, which lapped gently at the stony shore that used to be a swimming beach, back when the River's Bend Campground was a going concern, when Moonshine suddenly decided he was willing to get wet after all.

He plunged into the water, up to his chest, making a mighty splash in the process. Brody, gripping the barrel of that horse hard between his knees, just to stay in the saddle, laughed out loud before giving a whoop of pure delight.

His boots filled, and within moments his jeans were soaked to the tops of his thighs, but he didn't care. Moonshine swam that river like he had Olympic aspirations, his powerful legs pumping, his head high and his ears pricked up.

"Good boy," Brody told the horse, with gruff appreciation. "You're doing just fine."

Reaching the other side, Moonshine bunched his haunches for the effort and bunny-hopped up the steepest part of the bank, water pouring off him in sheets. Once he'd gained level ground, the animal shook himself like a dog and Brody laughed again, for no other reason than that life was good.

He was home.

And, for the most part, he was happy to be there.

Drenched, he got down from the saddle to pull off his boots, empty them and yank them back on over his sodden socks. When he got to the main house, he'd swap his wet duds for dry ones from Conner's closet.

Having an identical twin brother had its advantages, and one of them was access to a whole other wardrobe.

There'd been a time when Conner would have groused about Brody's tendency to borrow his stuff, but last New Year's Eve, Brody's "little brother," born a couple of minutes after he was, had taken a wife. Conner was happy with Tricia, and these days it took more than a missing shirt or pair of jeans to get under his hide.

They were on a perpetual honeymoon, Conner and Tricia, and now, with a baby due in three months, they glowed, the both of them, as if they were lit from within.

Brody mounted up again and reined Moonshine toward the home-place, feeling a mixture of things as he considered his twin's good fortune.

Sure, he was glad things were working out so well for Conner, but he was a little envious, too.

Not that he'd have admitted it to anybody.

Tricia was beautiful, smart and funny, and she'd taken to ranch life with surprising ease, for a city girl. Essentially a greenhorn, she'd gone horseback riding almost every day since the wedding, when the weather allowed, anyway—until her pregnancy was confirmed. Then Conner had put a stop to the pursuit.

No more trail rides until after the baby's arrival.

Period, end of discussion.

Brody grinned, recalling how adamant his brother had been. For the most part, the marriage appeared to be an equal partnership, but this time, Conner had laid down the law. And Tricia, normally the independent type, had capitulated.

That was just common sense, to Brody's mind, though a lot of country women continued to ride when they were expecting a baby, herding cattle, rounding up strays, checking fence lines. Conner's strong opposition was a no-brainer—Rachel Creed, Conner and Brody's mother, had continued to enter barrel-racing events long after she learned she was carrying twins. There hadn't been a specific incident, but soon after giving birth to Brody and Conner, Rachel's health had begun to go downhill.

She'd died when her infant sons were less than a month old.

Blue Creed, their father, hadn't lasted much longer. Overwhelmed by the responsibility, he'd brought the babies home to the ranch, right around their first birthday, and handed them over to his brother, Davis, and Davis's wife, Kim. Soon afterward, Blue himself had been thrown from a horse and broken his neck. He'd been in a coma for six weeks, and then died.

Now, crossing the range between the river and the two-story house Conner and Tricia had been sharing since they got hitched, the grass rippling around him like a green sea, Brody did his best to ignore the clammy chill of wet denim clinging to his legs—and the old, deep-seated sorrow rooted in his soul. He did take some consolation from seeing the cattle grazing all around, most of them Herefords, with a few Black Anguses to break the red-brown monotony. Two dozen broncos, specially bred for the rodeo, and six Brahma bulls completed the menagerie.

Clint and Juan and a couple of the other ranch hands wove in and out among the different critters on horseback, mainly keeping the peace. Brody touched his hat brim to the other men as he passed, and those who were looking his way returned the favor.

By then, Moonshine was restless, trying to work the bit between his teeth, so Brody gave him his head. That cayuse might be skittish when it came to crossing rivers, but he sure did like to run.

Brody bent low over the buckskin's neck, holding his hat in place with one hand and keeping a loose grip on the reins with the other.

And that horse ate up ground like a jet taxiing along a runway before takeoff.

Brody was enjoying the ride so much that the corral fence sprang up in front of them as suddenly as a line of magic beanstalks.

Moonshine soared over that top rail as if he'd sprouted wings, practically stretched out flat, and came in for a magnificent landing about one foot short of the place where Conner stood, looking like he'd had rusty nails for breakfast instead of bacon and eggs.

Brody gazed down into a face so like his own that the sight of it even took *him* aback sometimes, and he was used to being pretty much an exact duplicate of his brother.

Conner was scowling up at him, through swirls of settling dust, and he looked as though he'd like to grab hold of Brody, haul him off that horse and beat the holy bejesus out of him. So much for personality improvements resulting from wedded bliss!

"Oops," Brody said cheerfully, because he knew that would piss off Conner and he still enjoyed doing that now and again, even though they'd been getting along well for a respectable length of time. "Sorry."

He swung down and faced Conner, who was taut with

annoyance, his shoulders squared, his fists clenched and his attitude contentious.

"Damn it, Brody," he growled, "am I having one of my invisible days, or are you going blind? You darn near ran me down, and it'll take me the better part of the morning to get this mare calm enough to work with again!"

Prior to the leap, Brody hadn't noticed his brother *or* the pinto mare, now nickering and tossing her head over on the far side of the corral, but he didn't think it would be smart to say as much. Instead, he decided to come from a place of helpfulness.

"You starting horses yourself these days, instead of letting one of the wranglers do it?" he asked, bending to pick up the lightweight saddle the mare must have tossed when he and Moonshine came over the fence.

Conner grabbed the saddle and jerked it out of Brody's hands. "Yes," he snapped in response. "You dropped out for a decade, Davis broke both legs the last time he rode a bronc and Clint and Juan are downright creaky at the hinges. Who the hell did you *think* was starting the horses?"

"Whoa," Brody said, recoiling slightly and still grinning. "What's chewing on you? Did you have a fight with the little woman or something?"

"No!" Conner yelled.

Brody chuckled, adjusted his hat and then turned to get Moonshine by the reins. After the river crossing and the hard run over the range, not to mention that spectacular jump, he figured the horse deserved some stall time, free of the saddle and bridle. "Well, what's the matter, then?" he asked reasonably, starting toward the side door of the barn.

"Nothing," Conner bit out, setting the dusty saddle on the top rail of the fence and turning to the mare.

"Something is," Brody insisted calmly, pausing.

Conner looked at Brody then, through the haze of slowly settling corral dirt, and sighed. "Tricia and I might have had words," he said grudgingly.

"Trouble in the vine-covered cottage?" Brody teased, knowing it couldn't be anything serious. He'd never seen a man and a woman more deeply in love than his brother and Tricia were.

"She says I'm overprotective," Conner said, taking off his hat and swatting his thigh with it before putting it back on.

Brody flashed a grin. Rubbed his beard-stubbled chin with one hand. "You?" he joked. "Overprotective? Just because you'd wrap the lady in foam-rubber padding, if she'd let you, so she wouldn't stub her toe?"

Conner glared, but there was a grin to match Brody's brewing in his blue eyes. He held it off as long as he could, but then it broke through, like sunlight penetrating a cloud-bank.

"Put your horse away," Conner said. "I might as well turn the mare out to graze for the rest of the day, now that you and that gelding scared her out of three years' growth."

Brody led Moonshine into the barn, put him in a stall and gave him a couple of flakes of hay. When he left by the main door, Conner was waiting for him in the yard, throwing a stick for the Lab-retriever mix, Valentino.

In Brody's opinion, that was a prissy-assed name for a ranch dog, but the poor critter had already been saddled with it when Conner and Tricia took up with each other. Conner had tried calling him "Bill" for a while, but the former stray wouldn't answer to that, so Valentino it was.

Brody looked around. There was no sign of Tricia, or the Pathfinder she drove.

"She's gone to town to help Carolyn at the shop," Conner said. He usually had a pretty fair idea what Brody was thinking, and the reverse was also true. "The woman is pregnant out to here." He shaped his hands around an invisible basketball, approximately at belly level. "What would be so wrong with staying home for one day? Taking it easy, putting her feet up for a while?"

Brody chuckled and slapped his brother on the shoulder. "She's running a small-town art gallery, Conner," he said, "not bungee-jumping or riding bulls in a rodeo."

Conner's face tightened momentarily and, once again, Brody knew what was on his twin's mind because they so often thought in tandem.

"There's no connection between our mom's pregnancy and Tricia's," Brody added quietly. "Stop looking for one."

Conner sighed, managed a raw kind of grin. Nodded.

It struck Brody then, though not for the first time, of course, just how vulnerable loving a woman made a man. And after the baby came? It would be way worse.

Brody shivered, momentarily swamped with recollections.

"What happened to your clothes, anyhow?" Conner asked, looking him over. He tended to get around to things in his own good time.

"Moonshine got a little overenthusiastic crossing the river," Brody replied.

They headed into the house, the dog trotting behind them, and Brody ducked into the laundry room to swipe a pair of jeans, a T-shirt and some socks from the folded stacks on top of the dryer. After a quick shower to thaw out his bone marrow, he dressed in the room he and Conner had shared as kids, with their cousin Steven joining them in the summertime, and emerged to find his brother still in the kitchen, brewing a cup of coffee with one of those fancy single-shot machines designed for the chronically caffeine-deprived.

"How's the new place coming along?" Conner asked, holding out a steaming mug, which Brody took gratefully.

"It's a slow process," he replied, after a sip of java. "The builder swears up and down that it'll be move-in ready by the middle of August, though."

Conner gave a snort at that, retrieved a second cup from under the spout of the shining gizmo and raised it slightly, in a little salute. "Nice clothes," he observed wryly. "I once owned some just like them."

CAROLYN SIMMONS held her breath as she watched her very pregnant friend and business partner, Tricia Creed, making her wobbly way down from the top of a ladder. Tricia had just hung a new batik depicting a Native American woman weaving at a loom. The work of a local artist, the piece wouldn't be in the shop long, which was possibly why Tricia had placed it so high on the wall. No doubt she reasoned that if the picture wasn't within easy reach, she and Carolyn could enjoy it for a while before some eager buyer snatched it up.

With her long, dark braid, loose-fitting cotton maternity clothes and attitude of serene faith in the all-around goodness of life, Carolyn thought Tricia resembled the weaver a little.

Taller than Tricia, with artfully streaked blond hair, Carolyn wore her usual garb of jeans, boots and a fitted T-shirt. Tricia liked to joke that if an opportunity to ride a horse came up, Carolyn was determined to be ready.

"What were you doing on that ladder?" she asked now, propping her hands on her hips as she regarded Tricia. "I promised Conner I'd keep an eye on you, and the minute I turn my back, you're teetering on the top rung."

Tricia dusted her hands together and smiled, stepping back a little way to look up at the batik. "I was nowhere near the top rung," she argued cheerfully, her face glowing in the sunlight pouring in through the big front window. She sighed. "Isn't she beautiful?"

Carolyn, following Tricia's gaze, nodded. Primrose Sullivan, the artist, had outdone herself this time. The weaver was indeed beautiful. "I think some of our online customers would be interested," she mused. "I'm not sure it would photograph all that well from this angle, though—"

The hydraulic squeal of brakes interrupted.

Tricia moved to the window and peered through the antique lace curtains. "It's another tour bus," she said. "Brace yourself."

The business, a combination boutique and art gallery, filled the first floor of Natty McCall's venerable Victorian house—Carolyn lived upstairs in Tricia's former apartment, along with her foster cat, Winston. The items the two women sold ranged from goats' milk soap and handmade pincushions to one-of-a-kind dresses and near museum-quality oil paintings.

"I'm braced," Carolyn confirmed, smiling and taking her customary place behind the counter, next to the cash register.

Tricia straightened an already straight display of handmade stationery.

The shop wasn't going to make anyone rich, but for Carolyn, it was a dream come true. In Lonesome Bend, she had a comfortable place to live—not a small thing to a person raised in no fewer than fourteen foster homes—and an outlet for the various garments, decorative pillows and retro-style aprons she was constantly running up on her sewing machine. Formerly a professional house sitter, Carolyn had been selling her designs online for years. Her online business brought in enough extra money to build a small savings account and buy thread and fabric for the next project she had in mind, but that was the extent of it.

The little bell over the front door jingled merrily, and the busload of customers crowded in, white-haired women with good manicures and colorful summer clothes, chatting good-naturedly among themselves as they thronged around every table and in front of every shelf.

The store, loftily titled Creed and Simmons—Tricia's great-grandmother, Natty, said the name sounded more like a law firm or an English jewelry shop than what it was—barely broke even most of the time. Tour buses heading to and from Denver and Aspen and Telluride stopped at least twice a week, though, and that kept the doors open and the lights on.

For Tricia, having sold property inherited from her father for a tidy sum and then having married a wealthy rancher to boot, the place was a hobby, albeit one she was passionate about.

For Carolyn, it was much more—an extension of her personality, an identity. A way of belonging, of fitting into a community made up mostly of people who had known each other from birth.

It *had* to work.

Without the business, Carolyn would be adrift again, following the old pattern of living in someone else's house for a few days or a few weeks, then moving on to yet another place that wasn't hers. House-sitting was a grown-up version of that old game musical chairs, only the stakes were a lot higher. Once or twice, when the figurative music stopped unexpectedly, Carolyn had been caught *between* houses, like a player left with no chair to sit in, forced to hole up in some cheap motel or sleep in her car until another job turned up.

Thankfully, there were plenty of opportunities around Lonesome Bend—movie stars and CEOs and high-powered political types kept multimillion-dollar "vacation homes" hidden away in private canyons, on top of hills and at the ends of long, winding roads edged with whispering aspen trees.

Carolyn still did some house-sitting now and then, for longtime clients, but she much preferred the cozy apartment above the shop to those enormous and profoundly empty houses, with their indoor swimming pools and their media rooms and their well-stocked wine cellars.

In the apartment, she was surrounded by her own things—the ceramic souvenir mugs she'd collected from cities all over the country, a few grainy photographs in cheap frames, her trusty laptop and the no-frills work-horse of an electric sewing machine that had been a parting gift from her favorite foster mom.

In the apartment, Carolyn felt substantial, *real,* rooted in one particular place, instead of some ethereal, ghostlike being, haunting lonely castles.

For the next forty-five minutes, Carolyn and Tricia were both so busy that they barely had a chance to look at each other, let alone speak, and when the tour bus pulled away at last, it was almost time to close up for lunch.

The cash drawer was bulging with fives, tens and twenties, and there was a nice pile of credit card receipts, too.

The shelves, racks and tables looked as though they'd been pillaged by barbarians, and the air still smelled of expensive perfume.

"Wow," Tricia said, sagging into the rocking chair near the fireplace. "*That* bunch just about cleaned us out."

Carolyn laughed. "That they did," she agreed. "Bless their hearts."

Tricia tilted her head back, sighed slightly and closed her eyes. Her hands rested protectively over her bulging stomach.

Carolyn was immediately alarmed. "Tricia? You're all right, aren't you?"

Tricia opened her eyes, turned her head and smiled. "Of *course* I am," she said. "I'm just a little tired from all that hurrying around."

"You're sure about that?"

Tricia made a face, mocking but friendly. "You sound just like Conner. *I'm fine,* Carolyn."

Frowning slightly, Carolyn went to the door, turned the Open sign around, so it read Closed, and turned the lock. She and Tricia usually had lunch in the downstairs kitchen at the back of the house, and sometimes Tricia's husband joined them.

Tricia was still in the rocking chair when Carolyn got back.

And she'd fallen asleep.

Carolyn smiled, covered her friend lightly with a crocheted afghan and slipped away to the kitchen.

Winston, the cat, wound himself around her ankles when she entered, purring like an outboard motor. Like the house, Winston technically belonged to Natty McCall, Tricia's great-grandmother, now a resident of Denver, but because he stayed with Carolyn whenever his mistress was off on one of her frequent and quite lengthy cruises, she loved him like her own.

Apparently, the feeling was mutual.

Or he just wanted his daily ration of sardines.

"Hungry?" Carolyn asked, bending to stroke the cat's gleaming black ears.

Winston replied with a sturdy meow that presumably meant *yes* and leaped up onto a sideboard, where he liked to keep watch.

Smiling, mentally tallying up the take from the power-shopper invasion, Carolyn went to the fridge, got out the small bowl of sardines left over from the day before and stripped away the covering of plastic wrap.

She set the bowl on the floor for Winston, then went to the sink to wash her hands.

Winston came in for a landing squarely in front of his food dish and, at the same time, a knock sounded lightly at the back door.

Conner Creed pushed it open, stuck his head inside and grinned at Carolyn, flashing those way-white teeth of his.

Her heart skipped over a beat or two and then stopped entirely—or at least, that's the way it felt—as he stepped into the house.

Because this *wasn't* Conner, as she'd first thought.

No, siree. This was *Brody*.

Carolyn's cheeks burned, and she barely held back the panicked "What are *you* doing here?" that sprang to the tip of her tongue.

The grin, as boyish and wicked as ever, didn't falter. Clearly, their history didn't bother Brody at all. It shouldn't have bothered Carolyn, either, she supposed, since almost eight years had passed since they were *together*-together. And what they'd shared amounted to a tryst, not an affair of the heart.

Be that as it may, every time she encountered this man—a recurring problem now that his brother was married to one of her closest friends—she wanted to flee.

"Is my sister-in-law around?" Brody asked, well aware, Carolyn would have bet, that he'd rattled her.

Carolyn swallowed hard. Once, when she'd been on a trail ride with Conner and Tricia and a number of their friends and neighbors, Brody and his now-and-then girlfriend, Joleen Williams, had raced past on horseback, their laughter carried by the wind. Carolyn, taken by surprise, had played the fool by bolting for the barn, without so much as a goodbye to the other members of the party, and she'd been kicking herself for it ever since.

"Tricia is in the front," she replied, in a remarkably normal tone of voice. "We had a busy morning, and she fell asleep."

Brody closed the door behind him, crossed to the cat and crouched, extending a hand.

Winston hissed and batted at him with one paw.

"Whoa," Brody said, drawing back.

Carolyn chuckled, relaxing a little. Clearly, Winston was a good judge of character, as well as an expert mouser and a connoisseur of fine sardines.

Having made his position clear, the cat went back to snarfing up his lunch.

Meanwhile, Brody rose off his haunches, still holding his hat in one hand, and looked disgruntled. Being drop-dead gorgeous, he probably wasn't used to rejection—even when it came from an ordinary house cat.

"Animals usually *like* me," he said, sounding baffled and even a little hurt.

Carolyn, realizing she'd been gawking, turned away, suddenly very busy getting a can of soup, a box of crackers and a loaf of bread from the pantry.

Glancing back, she saw Brody approach the inside door, push it open carefully and peer into the next room.

He turned, with a kind of brotherly softening in his eyes, and put his index finger to his lips.

"Shh," he said.

"I didn't make a sound," Carolyn protested, in a whisper.

Why didn't the man just *leave* now, if he didn't want to disturb Tricia?

Instead, he lingered, one-hundred-percent cowboy, with his hat in his hands and his mouth tilted sideways in a grin.

"We don't have to be enemies, you know," he said quietly.

Carolyn, in the middle of slapping a slice of bologna onto a piece of bread, opened her mouth and then closed it again.

"Do we?" Brody persisted.

Carolyn recovered enough to reply, though the words came out in a terse little rush of breath. "Tricia is my friend and business partner. You're her brother-in-law. Therefore, we have to be civil to each other."

"Is it that hard?" Brody asked. "Being 'civil,' I mean?"

Suddenly, all the old feelings rose up inside Carolyn, nearly overwhelming her. Tears stung her eyes and she turned her head quickly, bit down hard on her lower lip.

"Carolyn?" he said.

He was standing right behind her by then; she felt the heat and hard masculinity of him in every nerve in her body.

Just go, she thought desperately, unable to risk turning around to face him.

Brody Creed had never been one to leave well enough alone. He took a light hold on her shoulders, and Carolyn found herself looking up into the treacherous blue of those trademark eyes.

"I'm sorry for what I did, way back when," he told her, his voice a gruff rumble. "I was wrong. But don't you think it's time we put all that behind us and stopped walking on eggshells every time we happen to be in the same room?"

He was *sorry.*

As far as Carolyn was concerned, *sorry* was the emptiest, most threadbare word in the English language. People hurt other people, said they were *so sorry* and then, in her experience at least, turned right around and did the same thing all over again.

Or something worse.

Carolyn glanced nervously in the direction of the inside door, afraid of upsetting Tricia. When she spoke, her voice was a ragged whisper. "What do you want me to say, Brody? That I forgive you? Okay, for what it's worth, I forgive you."

Brody's expression was bleak, but his eyes flashed with frustration. He was famous for his temper, among other things.

"You'll forgive, but you won't forget, is that it?"

"I might conceivably forgive a rattlesnake for biting me," Carolyn responded. "After all, it's a snake's nature to strike. But I'd be worse than stupid if I forgot and cozied up to the same sidewinder a second time, wouldn't I?"

A muscle bunched in Brody's cheek. He was already sporting a five o'clock shadow, a part of Carolyn observed with a strange detachment. Or maybe he hadn't shaved at all that morning.

Oh, hell, what did it matter?

"You think I'm asking you to 'cozy up' to me?" Brody almost growled. His nose was an inch from Carolyn's, at most. "*Damn* it, woman, I can't avoid being around you, and you can't avoid being around *me,* and all I'm suggesting here is that you let go of that grudge you've been carrying for seven-plus years so we can all move on!"

Carolyn would have loved to slap Brody Creed just then, or even throttle him, but suddenly the door to the next room opened and Tricia peeked through the opening, stifling a yawn with a patting motion of one hand.

"Have you two been arguing?" Tricia asked, her gaze shifting from one of them to the other.

They stepped back simultaneously.

"No," Carolyn lied.

"Everything's just *great*," Brody added, through his teeth.

CHAPTER TWO

MISCHIEF LIT TRICIA'S blue eyes as she studied Brody and Carolyn, the pair of them standing still in the middle of Natty McCall's kitchen.

Just looking at her took the edge off Brody's irritation. He'd always wanted a sister, after all, and now he had one. He felt a similar affection for Melissa, his cousin Steven's wife, but he didn't see her practically every day, the way he did Tricia, since Steven, Melissa and their three children lived in Stone Creek, Arizona.

"Did Conner send you to check up on me, Brody Creed?" Tricia asked in a tone of good-natured suspicion, tilting her head to one side and folding her arms before resting them atop her impressive belly.

Out of the corner of his eye, Brody saw Carolyn turn away. Her streaky blond hair swung with the motion, brushing against her shoulders, and just that fast, she was busy thumping things around on the counter again.

"Brody?" Tricia persisted, while Brody was untangling his tongue.

"It was my own idea to look in on you while I was in town," Brody finally answered, grubbing up a crooked grin and turning the brim of his hat in both hands, like some shy hero in an old-time Western movie. "I don't figure Conner would object much, though."

Tricia smiled broadly, flicked a glance in Carolyn's direction.

The can opener whirred and a pan clattered against a burner.

Brody sighed.

"Join us for lunch?" Tricia asked him.

Carolyn's backbone went ramrod-straight as soon as Tricia uttered those words, and Brody watched, at once amused and confounded, while she jammed slices of bread down onto the beginnings of two bologna sandwiches. She used so much force to do it that the things looked like they'd been made with a drill press.

Deciding he'd stirred up enough ill will for one day, Brody shook his head. "I'd better get back to the ranch," he said. "We're replacing some of the wire along one of the fence lines."

"Oh," Tricia said, as if disappointed.

She moved slowly to the table, pulled back a chair just as Brody went to pull it back *for* her and sank onto the seat.

"Hey," Brody said, concerned. "Are you feeling all right?"

Tricia sighed. "Maybe I'm a little tired," she confessed. "It's no big deal."

At that, Carolyn stopped flinging food hither and yon and turned to look at Tricia. "I think you should go home and rest," she said. "This morning was crazy, and we've been taking inventory for a couple of days now."

"And leave you to straighten up the shop and restock the shelves all by yourself?" Tricia asked. "That wouldn't be fair."

"I can handle it," Carolyn said. She spoke in a normal tone, but Brody could feel her bristling, all over, like a porcupine fixing to shoot quills in every direction. She didn't deign to glance his way, of course. "And, anyhow, I'd like to close the shop early today. That way, I could catch up on the bookkeeping, then put the finishing touches on that gypsy skirt I've been working on and get it posted on the website."

Brody neither knew nor cared what a gypsy skirt was. He was feeling indignant now, standing there on the fringes of the conversation as if he'd either turned transparent or just disappeared entirely.

He cleared his throat.

Tricia didn't look at him, and Carolyn didn't, either.

The cat fixed an amber gaze on him, though, and Brody was affronted all over again. He'd never met a critter that didn't take to him right away—until this one.

"Tell you what," Tricia finally said to Carolyn, after a few moments spent looking happily pensive. "I'll take the afternoon off. *If* you promise not to stay up half the night stitching beads and ribbons onto that skirt."

"I promise," Carolyn said quickly.

Most likely, by her reckoning, persuading Tricia to go home was the best and fastest way to get rid of *him,* too.

Brody felt his back teeth mesh together.

"All right, then," Tricia conceded. "I guess I *could* use a nap." With that, she headed off into the other room, probably on the hunt for her purse, and thus Brody and Carolyn were left alone again, however briefly.

On the stove, soup began to boil over the sides of the saucepan, sizzling on the burner and raising a stink.

Brody automatically moved to push the pan off the heat, and Carolyn did the same thing.

They collided, sideways, and hard enough that Carolyn stumbled slightly. And Brody grabbed her arm, an instinctive response, to steady her.

He actually felt the charge go through her, arc like a bolt of electricity from someplace inside Carolyn to someplace inside *him*.

Instantly, both of them went still.

Brody willed his fingers to release their hold on Carolyn's arm.

She jerked free.

And Tricia was back in the kitchen by then, taking it all in.

Although he and Carolyn were no longer physically touching each other, it seemed to Brody that he'd been fused to her in some inexplicable way.

The very air of the room seemed to quiver.

"I'll drive you home," Brody managed to tell Tricia, his voice a throaty rasp.

"I'll drive *myself* home," Tricia countered, friendly but firm. There'd be no more use in arguing with her than with any *other* Creed. "I don't want to leave the Pathfinder behind, and, anyway, I *told* you—I feel just fine."

Carolyn favored her friend with a wobbly smile. "Take it easy, okay?" she said.

Tricia nodded on her way to the back door. She noted the spilled-over soup on the stove and, with the smallest grin, shook her head.

Brody happened to see her expression because he'd just leaned past her, to take hold of the knob. Where he came from—right there in Lonesome Bend, as it happened—a man still opened a door for a lady.

And this particular lady was trying hard not to laugh.

Brody's neck heated as he stood there, holding the

door open for his brother's wife, all too aware that she'd drawn some kind of crazy female conclusion about him and Carolyn.

He clamped his jaw down tight again and waited.

ONCE BRODY AND TRICIA were gone, and far enough along the flagstone walk to be out of earshot, Carolyn let out a loud, growl-like groan of sheer frustration.

The sandwiches were smashed.

Most of the soup—tomato with little star-shaped noodles, her favorite—coated the stove top. The rest was bonded to the bottom of the pan.

All of which was neither here nor there, because she wasn't the least bit hungry now anyway, thanks to Brody Creed.

Winston, having finished his sardine repast, sat looking up at her, twitching his tail from side to side. His delicate nose gleamed with fish oil, and out came his tiny, pink tongue to dispense with it.

Comically dignified, his coat sleek and black, the cat reminded Carolyn suddenly of a very proper English butler, overseeing the doings in some grand ancestral pile. The fanciful thought made her laugh, and that released most of the lingering, after-Brody tension.

Carolyn frowned at the catch phrase: *After Brody.* In many ways, that simple term defined her life, as she'd lived it for the past seven years. If only she could go back to *Before Brody,* and make a different choice.

A silly idea if she'd ever heard one, Carolyn decided.

Resolutely, she cleaned up the soup mess, filled the saucepan with water and left it to soak in the sink. She wrapped the flattened sandwiches carefully and tucked them away in the refrigerator. When and if her appetite returned, she'd be ready.

Winston continued to watch her with that air of sedate curiosity as she finished KP duty and returned to the main part of the shop.

Winston followed; whenever Carolyn was in the house, the cat was somewhere nearby.

She tidied the display tables and put out more goats' milk soap and handmade paper and the last of the frilly, retro-style aprons that were so popular she could barely keep up with the demand.

That task finished, she stuffed the day's receipts into a zippered bag generously provided by the Cattleman's First Bank, double-checked that the front door was locked and there were no approaching customers in sight and went upstairs to her apartment.

Every time she entered that cheery little kitchen, whether from the interior stairway, like now, or from the one outside, Carolyn felt a stirring of quiet joy, a sort of lifting sensation in the area of her heart.

She rented the apartment from Natty McCall for a ridiculously nominal amount of money—nominal was what she could afford—so it wasn't *really* hers. Still, everything about the place, modest though it was, said *home* to Carolyn.

Sure, she was lonely sometimes, especially when the shop was closed.

But it wasn't the same *kind* of loneliness she'd felt when she was constantly moving from one house to another and her address was simply General Delivery, Lonesome Bend, Colorado.

The irony of the town's name wasn't lost on Carolyn. She'd ended up there quite by accident, a little over eight years ago, when her car broke down along a dark country road, leaving her stranded.

Her unlikely rescuers, Gifford Welsh and Ardith Sperry, both of them A-list movie stars, had been passing by and stopped to offer their help. In the end, they'd offered her the use of the guest house behind their mansion-hideaway three miles outside of town. After a series of very careful background checks, the couple had hired Carolyn as nanny to their spirited three-year-old daughter, Storm.

Carolyn had loved the job *and* the child. Most of the time, she and Storm had stayed behind in the Lonesome Bend house, while Gifford and Ardith crisscrossed the globe, sometimes together and sometimes separately, appearing in movies that invariably garnered Oscar nominations and Golden Globes.

Although Carolyn had never given in to the temptation to pretend that Storm was her own child, strong as it was some of the time, she and the little girl had bonded, and on a deep level.

For Carolyn, life had been better than ever before, at least for that single, golden year—right up to the night Gifford Welsh had too much to drink at dinner and decided he and the nanny ought to have themselves a little fling.

Carolyn had refused out of hand. Oh, there was no denying that Welsh was attractive. He'd graced the cover of *People* as the World's Sexiest Man, not just once, but twice. He was intelligent, charming and witty, not to mention rich and famous. She'd seen all his movies, loved every one of them.

But he was married.

He was a father.

Those things mattered to Carolyn, even if he'd temporarily lost sight of them himself.

After fending off his advances—Ardith had been away on a movie set somewhere in Canada at the time—Carolyn had resigned, packed her belongings and, once a friend had arrived to pinch-hit as Storm's nanny, left that house for good.

Within a few months, the property was quietly sold to the founder of a software company, and Gifford, Ardith and Storm, reportedly having purchased a sprawling ranch in Montana, never set foot in Lonesome Bend again.

Even now, years later, standing in the kitchen of her apartment, Carolyn remembered how hard, and how painful, it was to leave Storm behind. The ache returned, like a blow to her solar plexus, every time she recalled how the little girl had run behind her car, sobbing and calling out, "Come back, Carolyn! Carolyn, *come back!*"

Before that—long, long before that—another little girl had frantically chased after another car, stumbling, falling and skinning her knees, getting up to run again.

And that child's cries hadn't been so very different from Storm's.

Mommy, come back! Please, come back!

"Breathe," Carolyn told herself sternly. "You're a grown woman now, so act like one."

Indeed, she *was* a grown woman. But the child she'd once been still lived inside her, still wondered, even after twenty-five years, where her mother had gone after dropping her daughter off at that first foster home.

"Reow," Winston remarked, now perched on the

kitchen table, where he was most definitely not supposed to be. "Reow?"

Carolyn gave a moist chuckle, sniffled and patted the animal's head before gently shooing him off the table. He immediately took up residence on the wide windowsill, his favorite lookout spot.

Being something of a neat freak, Carolyn moved her portable sewing machine aside, replaced the tablecloth beneath it with an untrammeled one and washed her hands at the sink.

The gypsy skirt, the creative project of the moment, hung on the hook inside her bedroom door, neatly covered with a plastic bag saved from the dry cleaner's.

Carolyn retrieved the garment, draped it carefully over the side of the table opposite her sewing machine and silently reveled in the beauty of the thing.

The floor-length underskirt was black crepe, but it barely showed, for all the multicolored, bead-enhanced ribbons she'd stitched to the cloth in soft layers. She'd spent days designing the piece, *weeks* stitching it together, ripping out and stitching again.

It was exquisite, all motion and shimmer, a wearable fantasy, the kind of original women like Ardith Sperry wore to award ceremonies and premieres.

Carolyn hadn't sized the piece for a movie star's figure, though. It was somewhere between a ten and a twelve, with plenty of give in the seams, allowing for a custom fit.

Carolyn, a curvy eight since the age of seventeen, had deliberately cut the skirt to fit a larger figure than her own, for the simple reason that, if she could have worn it, parting with it would have been out of the question.

She'd been making purposeful sacrifices like that since she'd first learned to sew, in her sophomore year of high school. Once she understood the basics, she hadn't even needed patterns. She'd sketched designs almost from day one, measured and remeasured the fabric, cut and stitched.

And she'd quickly made a name for herself. While other kids babysat or flipped burgers for extra money, Carolyn whipped up one-of-a-kind outfits and sold them as fast as she could turn them out.

That made *two* things she did well, she'd realized way back when, with a thrill she could still feel. Carolyn had an affinity for horses; it seemed as though she'd always known how to ride.

Over the years, most of her foster homes being in rural or semirural areas, where there always seemed to be someone willing to trade riding time for mucking out stalls, she'd ridden all kinds of horses, though she'd never actually had one to call her own.

Now, determined not to waste another second daydreaming, she shook off the reflective mood and picked up the skirt again, carefully removing the plastic wrap and holding it up high so she could admire the shift and shiver of all those ribbons, the wink of crystal beads.

It was silly, she supposed, but she *coveted* that skirt.

Aside from the money the sale would bring in, which, as always, she needed, where would she even *wear* a garment like that? She lived in blue jeans, cotton tops and Western boots, and for good reason—she was a cowgirl at heart, not a famous actress or the wife of a CEO or a cover model for *Glamour*.

With a sigh, Carolyn put the skirt back on its hook on the bedroom door—out of sight, out of mind.

She crossed to the small desk Tricia had left behind when she moved to the ranch, and booted up her laptop. While the magic machine was going through its various electronic thumps, bumps and whistles, Carolyn heated a cup of water in the microwave to brew tea.

Winston, still keeping his vigil over the side yard from the windowsill, made a soft yowling sound, his tail swaying like a pendulum in overdrive. His hackles were up, but his ears were pitched forward instead of laid back in anger. While Carolyn was still trying to read his body language, she heard someone coming up the outside stairs.

A Brodylike shape appeared in the frosted oval window at the door, one hand raised to knock.

Before he could do that much, however, Carolyn had yanked the door open.

"I don't believe this," she said.

Over on the windowsill, Winston expressed his displeasure with another odd little yowl.

"What is that cat's problem, anyway?" Brody asked, frowning as he slipped past Carolyn, graceful as a billow of smoke.

Carolyn shut the door. Hard.

"Winston," she said stiffly, "is a very discerning cat."

Brody sighed, and when Carolyn forced herself to turn around and look at him, he was gazing at Winston with an expression of wounded disbelief on his handsome face.

"Does he like Conner?" Brody inquired.

Carolyn hesitated. Brody threw an emotional wrench in the works every time she encountered him, but she didn't hate him. Not all the time, that is. And she didn't enjoy making him feel bad.

"Yes," she replied, eventually. "But you shouldn't take it personally."

"Easy for you to say," Brody answered.

"Tricia's okay, isn't she?" That was it, she decided. He was there because he had bad news. Why else would he have come all the way back in from the ranch, where he was supposed to be stringing new fence lines with Conner and the crew?

Brody must have seen the alarm in Carolyn's eyes, because he shook his head. Holding his range-battered hat in one hand, he ran the other through his shaggy, tarnished-gold hair.

Sighed again.

In a searing flash, it came back to her, the feel of that mouth on her skin.

"As far as I know, she's taking a nap." Another grin flickered in Brody's eyes and twitched at one corner of his amazing mouth. "As soon as Tricia turned in, Conner decided he was a little tired, too. That was my cue to make myself scarce."

Carolyn's cheeks were stinging a little, but she had to smile. "Probably a good call," she agreed. And then she waited. It was up to Brody to explain why he'd come back.

His remarkable blue eyes seemed to darken a few shades as he looked at her, and the gray rim around the irises widened. "I know the word doesn't mean much," he said, at long last, "but I meant it before, when I told you I was sorry about the way things ended with us."

Suddenly, Carolyn wanted very much to cry. And this was a sign of weakness, an indulgence she rarely allowed herself. All her life, she'd had to be strong—as a matter of survival.

She swallowed painfully and raised her chin a notch. "Okay," she said. "You're right. We'll just…let it go. Act as though it never happened." She put out her hand, the way she might have done to seal a business agreement. "Deal?"

Brody looked down at her hand, back up at her face. "Deal," he said hoarsely. And in the next moment, he was kissing her.

Carolyn felt things giving way inside her and, as good as that kiss was, she wasn't about to surrender so much as an inch of the emotional ground she'd gained after the cataclysm that was Brody Creed.

She wrenched herself back out of his arms, put a few steps between them and then a few more.

Brody merely looked at her, with his mouth upturned at one corner, a bemused *I thought so* gleaming in his eyes.

Stunned, not only by his audacity, but also by what he made her feel, Carolyn touched her lips, as if relearning their contours after a long absence from her own body.

"Don't you dare say you're sorry," she muttered.

Brody chuckled as he opened the door to leave. "Oh, believe me," he intoned. "I'm not the least bit sorry—not for that kiss, anyhow." His gaze shifted to Winston, who watched him from the windowsill, ears laid back, fur ruffled. "So long, cat," he added. "For now."

In the next moment, Brody was gone—so thoroughly gone that Carolyn felt as if she might have *imagined* the visit, at the same time certain that she hadn't.

After that, her concentration was shot.

She waited until Brody had had plenty of time to drive away. Then she logged off her computer, pulled on a lightweight blue corduroy jacket and retrieved her purse and car keys.

Sewing was out of the question, and so was doing the bookwork. She was too jumpy to sit still, or even stay inside.

So she drove to the Creed ranch, taking the long way around, following the back roads and bumpy logging trails to avoid running into Brody.

After some forty minutes, she reached Kim and Davis's place, parked beside the barn and then stood next to her car for a few moments, debating with herself. She and Kim were good friends; she really ought to knock on the door and say hello, at least.

The sprawling, rustic house had an empty look about it, though, and besides, Carolyn didn't feel like chatting. Kim was perceptive, and she'd know something was bothering her friend just by looking at her.

Because she had permission to ride any of the Creeds' horses anytime she wanted—with the exception of the rescued Thoroughbred, Firefly—she could go ahead and saddle up one of the cow ponies without asking first.

Firefly, a magnificent chestnut, was "too much horse" for anybody but an experienced jockey, according to Davis. When they'd learned that the animal was about to be euthanized because his racing days were over and, being a gelding, he couldn't be put to stud, Kim and Davis had hitched a trailer behind their truck and driven all the way to Kentucky to bring him home.

Passing the corral, an enclosure as large as many pastures, Carolyn stopped to admire Firefly, who had the area to himself that cool but sunny afternoon. He towered against the blue of the sky, and his beauty all but took her breath away.

She stood still as he tossed his great head and then slowly approached her.

Carolyn reached up to pat his velvety nose. Normally, if she planned to ride, she stuffed a few carrots into her jacket pockets before leaving home. Today, though, she'd made the decision impulsively as, let's face it, a knee-jerk reaction to Brody's kiss.

"Sorry, buddy," she told the former racehorse. "No carrots today, but I'll be sure to remember them next time."

Firefly nodded, as if to convey understanding, and Carolyn's spirits rose a little. For her, there was something therapeutic about horses—even as a kid, cleaning stalls and stacking bales of hay to earn riding privileges, she'd felt better just for being around them.

"Wish I could ride you," she told the former champion, "but you're off-limits."

He stretched his long neck over the top rail of the fence, and Carolyn patted him affectionately before moving on.

Besides coming there to ride when the mood struck and time allowed, she'd spent a lot of time in that place, house-sitting and looking after the horses while Davis and Kim were off on one of their frequent road trips, and everything about the barn was blessedly familiar. In fact, Carolyn figured if she ever went blind, she'd still be able to go straight to the tack room, collect the saddle and bridle Kim had given her and get the pinto mare, Blossom, ready to ride.

The horse knew every trail on that ranch by heart. Blossom would cross the creeks without balking, too, and she was as surefooted as a Grand Canyon mule in the bargain. Snakes and rabbits didn't spook her, and Carolyn had never known her to buck or run away with a rider.

Blossom, standing in her stall, greeted Carolyn with a companionable whinny.

Five minutes later, the two of them were out there under that achingly blue sky. Carolyn tugged at one stirrup, to make sure the cinch was tight enough, and then mounted up.

Once she was in the saddle, her jangled nerves began to settle down. Her heart rate slowed and so did her breathing, and her mouth curved into a smile.

She reined Blossom toward the green-festooned foothills, headed in the opposite direction from the main ranch house and away from the range as well, still wanting to avoid Brody if at all possible, but beyond that, she allowed the mare to chart her own course.

Blossom strolled along at a leisurely pace, stopping to drink from the icy, winding creek before splashing across it to the high meadow, one of Carolyn's favorite places to be.

Here, wildflowers rioted, yellow and pink, blue and white, and the grass was tall and lush. From the ridge, Carolyn could not only see the river, but also Lonesome Bend beyond it.

Brody's new house and barn, both sizable buildings, looked like toys from that distance. The workmen were no bigger than ants, moving over the framework, and the sounds of construction didn't reach her ears, though the horse might have heard them.

Blossom grazed contentedly, her reward for making

the climb to high ground, and Carolyn stood in the stir-rups, in order to see even farther.

There was the highway that led to Denver and points beyond.

Immediately after Brody's return to Lonesome Bend the year before, Carolyn had considered loading up her things and following that road wherever it might lead—like in the old days, she'd had no particular destination in mind.

Just somewhere *away.*

But her stubborn pride had saved her.

She'd loved Lonesome Bend and its people.

She'd had friends, a library card, a charge account at the local hardware store. Not a lot by most folks' standards, Carolyn supposed, but to her, they were important. Leaving would have meant starting over some-where else, from scratch, and the idea of that had galled her.

She'd decided to stand her ground. After all, Brody was bound to take off again, sooner or later, because that was what Brody did.

He took off.

Looking out over the landscape, Carolyn sighed. Trust that man to break his own pattern by staying on this time, buying the land that had belonged to Tricia's father, Joe McCall, making it part of the family ranch.

Still, staying out of Brody's way hadn't been very difficult at first, as small as the town was. No doubt, he'd been doing his best to steer clear of *her,* too.

Then Tricia and Conner fell in love, and everything changed.

As Tricia's friend and eventually her business part-ner, Carolyn was included in every gathering at the

Creed ranch and, since they were a sociable bunch, tending to go all out for holidays or anything that could possibly be construed as a special occasion, it happened often. Even in the rare month without a red-letter day on its calendar page, it seemed there was always a picnic, a barbecue, a trail ride, a potluck or some kind of party.

Most of the time, Carolyn attended the shindigs and did her best to have fun, but Brody was inevitably somewhere around, seldom speaking to her, or even making eye contact, but *there,* nonetheless, a quiet but dynamic presence she had to work hard to ignore.

And just doing *that* much required a level of concentration tantamount to walking barefoot over hot coals, like a participant in some high-powered seminar.

Frankly, Carolyn resented having to make the effort but, besides pulling up stakes and leaving town herself, she didn't seem to have any options.

She kept waiting to get over Brody.

Get over the hurt.

Get over caring about him.

So far, it hadn't happened.

Carolyn drew the scenery into her mind and spirit the way she drew breath into her lungs.

A hawk soared overhead, riding an invisible current of air.

Small animals rustled through the grass.

And beneath it all, Carolyn heard the steady *tick-tick-tick* of her biological clock.

At thirty-two and counting, she wasn't getting any younger.

How long could she afford to wait around for fate to make her dreams of a home and a family come true?

She leaned forward to pat Blossom's long, sweaty neck. Shook her head in silent answer to her own question.

She'd wasted enough time waiting around for the proverbial prince to ride up on a snow-white steed and whisk her away to Happily-Ever-After Land.

Okay, sure, she'd hoped a grand passion would be part of the package. But she'd *had* that with Brody Creed, hadn't she—for a whole week and a half?

And where had it gotten her? *Heartbreak Hotel, that was where.*

Obviously, love wasn't going to just *happen* to her, like in all those fairy tales she'd lost herself in as a child. It happened to some people—Tricia and Conner and a few others—but those were probably flukes.

Bottom line, she could wish all she wanted, but the fulfillment of said wishes was her own responsibility. Nobody was going to wave a magic wand and make things happen *for* her.

It was time to do something, time to *take action*.

Gently, she drew back on the reins so Blossom would stop grazing and continued the solitary trail ride, thinking as she went.

She'd been resistant to the idea of signing up for one of those online dating services, afraid of attracting, oh, say, a serial killer, or a bigamist, or some sort of con man set to make an appearance on *America's Most Wanted*. In light of a statistic she'd recently come across—that twenty percent of all romantic relationships begin via a matchmaking website of some sort—she was willing to reconsider.

Or, more properly, she was *willing to be willing* to reconsider.

Denver was probably full of nice men looking for

a partner. Maybe there were even a few eligible guys right there in Lonesome Bend.

It wasn't as if she needed a doctor or a lawyer. She'd settle for a mature man, a grown-up with a sense of humor and a steady job.

The word *settle* immediately snagged like a hook in the center of her chest.

She drew a few deep breaths as she and Blossom started back toward Kim and Davis's barn, traveling slowly. She wasn't signing up to be a mail-order bride, she reminded herself. Posting her picture and a brief bio online wasn't a lifelong commitment, but just a way of testing the water.

"You can do this," she told herself firmly.

Now, all she had to do was start believing her own slogan.

CHAPTER THREE

BRODY GAZED WISTFULLY toward his half-finished house—the barn had stalls and a roof roughed in, so Moonshine had shelter, at least—and swung down out of the saddle.

It was twilight—the loneliest time of all.

In town and out there in the countryside, where there were a dozen or more farms and ranches, folks were stopping by the mailbox, down at the road, or riding in from the range after a day's work, to be greeted by smiling wives and noisy kids and barking dogs. Dishes and pots and pans clattered cheerfully in kitchens, and the scents of home cooking filled the air.

At least, that was the way Brody remembered it, from when he was a boy.

Back then, Kim baked bread and fried chicken in honest-to-goodness grease. She boiled up green beans with bacon and bits of onion, and the mashed potatoes had real butter and whole milk in them. Usually, there would be an end-of-the-day load of laundry chugging away in the washer, in the little room just off the kitchen, since "her men"—Davis, Conner and Brody and, in the summer, Steven—went through clean clothes like there was no tomorrow.

With a sigh, Brody led Moonshine into the partially completed shelter, placed him in one of the twelve stalls and removed the saddle and bridle and blanket. He filled the feeder, and made sure the waterer was working right, and took his time brushing the animal down, checking his hooves for stones or twigs. The overhead lights weren't hooked up yet, but he didn't need them to do this chore. Brody had been tending to horses and other critters all his life—he probably could have performed the task in a catatonic state.

He patted Moonshine on one flank before leaving the stall, making his way back to the doorway, which was nothing more than a big square of dusk framed in lumber that still smelled of rawness and pitch, and took off his hat so he could tip his head back and look up at the sky.

It was deep purple, that sky, shot through with shades of gray and black and navy blue, the last fading line of apricot light edging the treetops. A three-quarter moon, the ghost of which had been visible all afternoon, glowed tentatively among the first sparks of stars.

Something bittersweet moved in Brody's chest, both gentle and rough, a contrary emotion made up of sorrow and joy, and a whole tangle of other feelings he couldn't name.

He wondered how he'd ever managed to stay away from Lonesome Bend, from this land and its people, for so many years. His soul was rooted in this land, like some invisible tree, tethered to the bedrock and pulling at him, pulling at him, no matter where he wandered.

This was the only place he wanted to be.

But that didn't mean *being here* didn't hurt sometimes.

Figuring he was getting a little flaky in his old age, he grinned and put his hat back on, raised the collar of his denim jacket against the chill of a spring night in the high country and surveyed the house he'd been building in his head for as long as he could remember—he'd drawn the shape of this room or that one a thousand times, on a paper napkin in some roadside café, on the back of a flyer advertising some small-town rodeo or a stock-car race, sometimes even on paper bought for the purpose.

And now, here it was, a sketch coming to life, becoming a real house.

The question was, would it ever be a *home,* too?

Brody looked around, taking a mental tally of what was finished and what was yet to be done. The underfloor had been laid throughout, the walls were framed in and the roof was in place. The kitchen—the heart of any country house—was big, with cathedral ceilings and skylights. There was space for one of those huge, multiburner chef's stoves. The massive double-sided fireplace, composed of stones from the fields and pastures around Lonesome Bend, and from the bans of the river, was ready for crackling fires, except for the hardware.

He moved on, into what would become the combination dining-and-living room. He paused briefly to examine that side of the fireplace. In this part of the house, the skylights were still covered in plastic, turning the shimmer of the moon murky, but the bowed windows overlooking the river would brighten things up plenty during the daylight hours.

There were five bedrooms in that house, besides the master suite, and almost as many bathrooms. Brody planned on filling those bedrooms with rambunctious little Creeds, ASAP, but there *was* the small matter of finding a wife first. He was old-fashioned enough to want things done in their proper order, though, of course, when it came to babies, that first one could come along anytime, as Davis liked to say, whenever there was a wedding. Invariably, he'd add that the others would take the customary nine months, and Kim would punch him playfully in the arm.

Kim and Davis had a solid marriage, the kind that lasted. The kind Brody wanted for himself, only with kids.

He smiled to himself, there in the gathering darkness of his new house. If she could have heard that thought, Kim probably would have said they'd *had* kids—him and Conner and Steven.

They'd been a handful, Brody reflected. Most likely, keeping up with two boys year-round, and a third when the school term ended, had been plenty of mothering for Kim. Either way, she'd never complained, never withheld love or approval from any of them, no matter how badly they behaved, but she'd been strict, too.

Chores and homework and church on Sunday were all nonnegotiable, and so was bedtime, until they all reached their teens. Scuffles were permissible, even considered a part of growing up country, but they had to be conducted *outside*.

Of course, Davis usually refereed, though he was always subtle about it.

Bullying, either among themselves or out there in the bigger scheme of things, was the biggest taboo. It was the one infraction that would guarantee a trip to the woodshed, Davis told them.

None of them had ever wound up there, but they'd sure gotten their share of skinned knuckles and bloody noses interceding when kids at school picked on somebody.

Brody roped in his thoughts. Quieted his mind. Carolyn Simmons popped into his brain. She had a way of doing that.

Which was a waste of thinking power, since that woman had about as much use for him as a stud bull had for tits.

And who could blame her, after the way he'd done her?

He leaned against what would be a wall, someday, and took off his hat. Lowered his head a little.

He'd never set out to hurt Carolyn, and he'd meant it when he apologized. He'd been young back then, and foolish, and when the call from his most recent girl-friend, Lisa, came late one night, her voice full of tears and urgency, he'd panicked.

It was as simple as that.

"I'm pregnant," Lisa had told him. "The baby's yours, Brody."

After she'd calmed down a little, she'd gone on to say that she wasn't cut out to raise a baby by herself, and she wasn't about to hand an innocent child over to a rodeo bum like him, either. No, sir, she wanted her child to have a mom and a dad and grow up in one house, not a series of them. If he didn't marry her, pronto, she knew an attorney who handled private adoptions.

Brody hadn't discussed the matter with Conner, or with Davis and Kim, because he'd been estranged from all of them during those years. In fact, he'd made damn sure they weren't around before he showed up on the ranch, badly in need of a hideout, a place to lick his wounds.

And he sure as hell hadn't brought the subject up with Carolyn. He hadn't known what to say to her. So he'd simply packed up his gear, within an hour after hanging up with Lisa, and loaded it into his truck.

Carolyn, still flushed from their lovemaking earlier in the evening, had been smiling in her sleep when he leaned over and placed a kiss as light as a whisper on her forehead. Except for a note, hastily scrawled and left next to the coffeemaker on the counter beside the back door, that kiss was all the goodbye he could manage.

There was no way to sugar-coat it, then or now. He'd skipped out on her.

End of story.

All during the long drive to San Antonio, where Lisa was living at the time, though, it had been Carolyn haunting Brody's heart and mind, not the woman he was heading for in that beat-up old truck, not the life they would make together, him and Lisa and the baby.

Before Lisa's call, he'd been this close to telling Carolyn he loved her, that he wanted to marry her. Start a family as soon as they were settled.

He'd planned to make up with his kin, too, and, if they'd have him, make a home right there on the ranch.

Fortunately, Brody reflected, remembering his long-ago honorable intentions, he'd had enough sense to override that particular impulse, on the grounds that he and Carolyn had only known each other for about ten days, and that flat-out wasn't long enough for anything real to get started.

Reaching San Antonio, he'd driven to Lisa's tiny rental house, hoisted her few belongings into the back of his truck and the two of them had headed straight for Las Vegas. Within a couple of days, they were man and wife, setting out to follow the rodeo.

They'd been happy enough together, Brody supposed. Especially after the baby came.

Marriage hadn't cured Brody's penchant for Carolyn,

though. He'd been with Lisa for about a month, when, one night in a seedy bar, after guzzling too much beer with some of his bull-riding buddies, he'd tracked down the pay phone and punched in Davis and Kim's number, without a hope in hell that Carolyn would answer.

By then, she'd surely have finished her house-sitting stint and moved on, but he had to try. If Kim answered, he'd ask her how to reach Carolyn. Beyond that, he had no clue how to get in touch with the woman he still loved.

Miraculously, though, Carolyn *did* answer the phone. His aunt and uncle were on the road again, she'd said, and then she'd fallen silent, waited for him to explain himself.

He'd meant to, but it didn't happen. Brody was thrown and then hog-tied by his own tongue and, in the end, all he said was that ever-inadequate phrase, *I'm sorry.*

Carolyn had hung up on him then, and justifiably so. Brody had stood in the corridor of that dive of a bar, with his hand still on the receiver and his forehead against the graffiti-covered wall, feeling as though he'd been gut-punched.

After that night, Brody had kept his alcohol consumption to a minimum. He knew Lisa loved him, and he'd made up his mind, then and there, to love her back. Even if it killed him.

It had taken some doing, but he *had* come to care for his pretty young wife, especially after their son, Justin, was born. One look at that kid, and Brody would have done anything—*given up* anything—for him.

And he *had* given up things he'd once believed he couldn't do without.

Carolyn.

The old and tired dream of going home, setting things right with his family, settling down to a rancher's life. He wanted to show Justin off to the folks, but he was scared shitless of running into Carolyn, so he stayed away.

He'd regret that particular choice forever, probably, because three weeks before he would have turned two, Justin was killed in a car wreck, along with Lisa.

The pain of remembering that time was as fresh as ever, and it nearly doubled Brody over, even now. He'd quit the rodeo after the accident, and stayed drunk for a solid year.

Eventually, he sobered up, but he stayed mad at the world, and he stayed ashamed. More in need of his home and family than ever, he'd denied himself both—as a sort of self-punishment, he supposed.

If he hadn't been off riding bulls, after all, he'd have been driving that snowy night, not Lisa. He might have been able to avoid the drunk driver doing ninety on the wrong side of the freeway.

And if he'd brought his wife and son home, where they belonged, the greatest tragedy of his life might never have happened.

It was all about choices, Brody reflected, forcibly hauling himself back into the present moment again. The past was over. A man made choices, and then he had to live with the consequences, whether they were good, bad or indifferent.

Brody squared his shoulders, walked on toward the small log structure where he'd been bunking for too damn long.

He switched on the lights as he stepped over the

threshold, but two of the three long fluorescent bulbs in the ceiling fixture were burned out, the third flickering ominously, and the ambience was just plain gloomy.

The original furnishings were gone, except for the long counter that had served as a sign-in place for campers, when Joe McCall was still running River's Bend, and the ancient woodstove. Brody slept on a roll-away bed he'd borrowed from Kim and Davis, never made up now that he and Joleen were in an "off" stage of the on-again-off-again thing they had going. He'd had a shower installed in the small rest room, and he did his laundry either at the Wash-and-Go on Main Street or out at the ranch. He owned a double-burner hot plate and a minifridge with a microwave the size of a matchbox sitting on top, and his desktop computer served as TV, DVD player and general, all-around communication device. He used a cell phone when he had something to say to somebody, or he went to see them in person, face-to-face.

What a concept.

Tricia's dad had always referred to the shack as a lodge.

Brody called it a log cabin—or a shit-hole, depending on his frame of mind.

That night, despite his best efforts to alter his attitude, it was a shit-hole.

HE'D *KISSED* HER.

Try though she might, even after the ride on Blossom and the meandering drive back to town, Carolyn could not get past the fact that Brody Creed had had the nerve, the unmitigated *gall,* after all he'd done to her, to haul right off and *kiss her.*

"Unbelievable," she told Winston in the apartment kitchen as she set his nightly kibble ration down in front of him. "The man is *unbelievable*."

"Reow," Winston agreed, though he went straight to his food dish.

Carolyn shoved up one T-shirt sleeve, then the other, still agitated. She was hungry, but not hungry enough to cook. Remembering the flat bologna sandwiches from lunch, she went downstairs, retrieved them from the refrigerator in Natty's former kitchen and pounded back up the inside steps.

She tossed one wrapped sandwich into her own fridge—maybe she'd have it for breakfast—and slowly removed the plastic from the other one.

Winston was still noshing away on his kibble.

Carolyn washed her hands and then plunked down in a chair at the table, along with her sewing machine, the day's mail and a rapidly cooling cup of herbal tea.

"I'm talking to a *cat*," she told the cat.

Winston didn't look up from his bowl. "It's pathetic," Carolyn went on. She took a bite out of her sandwich, and it was soggy, tasteless. The crusts of the bread were curling a little, too, and none of that even slowed her down. The meal wasn't about fine dining, after all. It was about making her stomach stop grumbling. "*I'm* pathetic. And do you know what, Winston? I'm no closer to achieving my goals than I was last year, or the year before that, or the year before *that*—"

Winston paused at last, gave her a disapproving glance for talking with her mouth full and finished off the last of his supper.

Carolyn offered him part of her sandwich, but he

wasn't into people-food, except for sardines, and he'd already had his daily ration of those.

"You tried to warn me, didn't you?" she prattled on, dropping the remains of her supper into the trash and then washing her hands again. She squirted a dab of lotion into one palm and then rubbed the stuff in with vigor. "You made your opinion of Brody Creed absolutely clear, but did I pay attention? Did I keep my defenses up?"

"Reoooooow," Winston said wearily.

"This is ridiculous," Carolyn said, addressing herself now, instead of the cat. Was talking to herself better than talking to a pet? Seemed like six of one thing and half a dozen of another. "I've got to get a grip. Do something constructive."

Winston, curled up in his cushy bed now, yawned, wrapped his tail around himself with typical feline grace and dozed.

"Am I boring you?" Carolyn asked sweetly. Then, getting no answer, naturally, she laughed, flung her hands out from her sides and let them slap against her blue-jeaned thighs. "I'm certainly boring *myself.*" She approached the laptop, drew back the chair and sat down. Pressed the on button and waited.

Maybe she could find a helpful website. Say, getalife.com, or something along those lines.

She checked her email first—nothing much there.

Then she went to the online banking site and posted the day's sales receipts.

"Look at that," she said, squinting at the screen, though she knew Winston wasn't listening. "If we have many more days like today, Tricia and I are in serious danger of *making a profit.*"

There was more bookkeeping to do—there was *always* more bookkeeping to do—but, being in a low-grade funk, even after a horseback ride, Carolyn decided not to do today what she could put off until tomorrow. Things were usually slow in the shop on weekday mornings and, besides, she'd be fresh then. Capable of left-brain pursuits like balancing debits and credits in a virtual ledger.

She'd brew another cup of herbal tea and sew, she decided. Let her ever-energetic right brain run the show for the rest of the evening.

It couldn't hurt to just *look* at the online dating services, though, she mused, still sitting at the desk and sinking her teeth into her lower lip as she entered a request into her favorite search engine.

The number of choices, as it turned out, was mind-boggling.

There were sites for people who wanted a same-religion partner.

There were sites for dog-lovers, cat-lovers, horse-lovers and just about every *other* kind of lover. A person could sign up to meet people who enjoyed the same hobbies, political beliefs, movies, foods and wines, books, etc.

Hooking up by preferred profession was an option, too. Just about every legal vocation—and a few that were distinctly iffy—was represented by not just one website, but *dozens* of them. If she wanted to meet men with a certain first name, or a particular sign of the zodiac, no problem.

It was overwhelming.

It was also intriguing, especially for a woman who'd eaten a squashed bologna sandwich for supper and carried on an impassioned and fairly lengthy discourse with a cat for her only audience.

Reminding herself that fortune favors the bold, not the lily-livered, Carolyn settled on one of several sites based in Denver, and serving the surrounding area. The main page was tastefully designed, and the questionnaire for trial members was short and relatively nonintrusive—some of the sites required enough personal data to trace a person's ancestors back to the Ice Age.

Well, *practically* that far.

The first two weeks of the proposed trial period were free, giving her plenty of time to pull out, and all she had to do was post one photo of herself and give her first name, age and a few minor details.

Carolyn decided to call herself Carol for now. She uploaded a recent picture, taken at the town's Independence Day picnic, admitted that she'd hit the big 3-O, and then—well—*lied.* Just a little.

She loved to bowl, she wrote, in the little panel labeled Little Tidbits About Me, and she worked in a bank. She had two rescued dogs, Marvin and Harry, and she'd been married once, when she was very young.

Reading over what she'd entered, Carolyn sighed, propped an elbow on the desk and sunk her chin into her palm. None of this was true, of course, but she couldn't help being creative—it was in her nature. Besides, she was starting to like the fictional Carol.

She sounded like a good person.

Reassured by the certainty that prospective dates could contact her only through an assigned email address connected with the site, Carolyn moved the cursor to the little box in the lower right-hand corner of the screen, marked Go For It!, and clicked.

Dater's remorse struck her in the next second, but it was too late now. She was *out there* in cyberspace, albeit under an assumed identity, and it was kind of exciting, as well as scary.

She'd taken a step, after all. Made a move, however tentative, toward her heart's desire: a home and family of her own.

Carolyn slumped back in her chair, glumly scanning the Friendly Faces web page for a button that would allow her to back out of her trial membership—what had she been thinking?—but the best she could come up with was the Contact Us link.

That would have to do. She'd send a brief message, say she'd changed her mind about online dating and that would be that.

But then a message popped up.

Someone likes your friendly face! it crowed, in letters that appeared to be dancing across the screen. Click on the heart to get acquainted!

Carolyn hesitated, amazed and curious and wishing she'd worked on the gypsy skirt as planned, instead of surfing the Net.

She thought about Tricia, happily married and expecting a baby.

She thought about Brody Creed, who apparently believed he could just go around kissing women he'd dumped.

Dumped? He hadn't even had the decency to do that. He'd just boogied, abandoned her in the middle of the night, while she was sleeping.

She clicked on the pulsing heart icon.

A photo of a nice-looking—as in, he looked as though he was probably nice—man popped up immediately. Hi, the message bar read. My name is Darren.

Darren wore a mild expression on his roundish face, and his hairline was receding, just a little. He was a dentist, divorced with no kids and he loved dogs and bowling and computer games.

At least appearance-wise, he was *nothing* like Brody.

A point in his favor, for sure.

Carolyn drew a deep, shaky breath, let it out slowly, and clicked on the chat button. Hello, she told him. I'm Carol.

Darren, in addition to his other talents, was a speedy typist. He flashed back with an immediate, Wow. That was fast. Hi, there, Carol.

Carolyn felt a pang of guilt. She'd been acquainted with the man for two seconds, and she was already lying to him. *Lying* to a divorced dentist, with no kids, who loved dogs.

What kind of person was she, anyway?

A careful one, she thought.

Hi, there, Darrell, she wrote back.

Darren, he corrected.

Carolyn stifled a groan. Sorry. Darren. I haven't had much experience at this, as you've probably guessed. *And my name isn't Carol, it's Carolyn. I don't work in a bank and I'm looking for a husband to father my children. Anybody who isn't a Creed and doesn't have a criminal record will do.*

Darren replied with an LOL and an animated smiley face that was winking. Everybody was new here once, he added, in his rapid-fire, e.e. cummings style. On the

Friendly Faces site, I mean. It's a great way to meet new people. Very low-key.

It's a virtual singles bar, Carolyn thought but did not type. *And the secret password is probably* loser.

Really? Carolyn wrote in response. Have you met a lot of people through the site? *And if so, why are you still trolling the web for prospective dates?*

Sure, Darren answered. I'm making friends right and left. So far, it's just been dinner and a movie, but, hey, at least I'm doing something besides filling cavities and begging patients to floss. Ha ha.

Darren had a sense of humor, then.

Sort of.

Carolyn sat with her fingers poised over the keyboard, and no earthly idea what to say next.

Carol? Darren asked. Are you still there?

I'm here, Carolyn replied.

You're shy, Darren said.

Carolyn blew out a long breath, making her bangs tickle her forehead. Not really, she answered. There, she'd said something honest. She *wasn't* shy. She was merely cautious. Sensible.

It finally occurred to her that if *she* was stretching the truth, Darren might be, too. Maybe his name was Dave, and he was married and not a dentist at all. Maybe he owned the Friendly Faces website, and this was his way of making people think they were in for some action.

Nice "talking" to you, Darren, she wrote. But I should be going. Lots to do.

Wait! Maybe we could meet for coffee? he replied.

Maybe, Carolyn said.

Your picture is great, Darren hastened to add. Promise we can chat again, at least?

Carolyn sighed. We'll see, she wrote.

She logged off the computer, pushed back her chair and stood. Stretched, enjoying the pull in her muscles, and turned around. There was the sewing machine, the plastic box full of ribbon scraps saved from various projects, her quilted-top basket, where she kept scissors, thimbles, needles and other notions.

Sewing, like horseback riding, had long been a refuge for her. She could lose herself in either pursuit... usually.

But tonight was different.

All because Brody Creed had kissed her.

The bastard.

The good-looking, sexy *bastard*.

Carolyn squared her shoulders, spun around on one heel and marched herself back to the desk, and her computer.

She switched on the laptop and waited impatiently for the system to reboot.

Then she went online and clicked her way straight to the Friendly Faces website.

Who knew? Maybe Darren—Darrell?—the dentist was still hanging around.

Carolyn's eyes widened when she spotted the message-box counter. "Carol" had over a dozen emails waiting.

After pushing her sleeves up again, Carolyn plunged in.

BRODY TIPPED what was left of his microwave-box dinner into the trash and looked up at the last of the functioning lightbulbs. Might as well change them out, he figured. It wasn't as if he had anything better to do.

He rustled up the extras he'd bought days before, but never gotten around to installing, and vaulted up onto the counter to take out the dead bulbs first. The job was tricky—he'd seen these thingamajiggies shatter into a jillion tiny, razor-sharp shards for no sensible reason—so Brody took his time.

He'd just finished, his eyes still a little dazzled by the glare of three fluorescent tubes, when he heard what sounded like a thump, or maybe a scratch, at the door.

He got down off the counter. Listened.

That was when he heard the whimper. It was faint, and almost human.

A chill trickled down his spine. He sprang to the door and wrenched it open, half expecting to find a person on the other side, injured and bleeding, looking for help.

Instead, his gaze fell onto the skinniest, dirtiest, most pitiful dog he'd ever seen. It was just sitting there, looking up at him with a sort of bleak tenderness in its eyes.

Brody, a sucker for anything with four legs and fur, crouched down, so he wouldn't be looming over the poor critter like a grizzly or something.

"Hey, buddy," he said huskily. "You selling something? Spreading the Good News?"

The dog whimpered again.

Brody examined the animal. No collar, no tags.

Fleas were a sure thing, though, and maybe something worse, like ringworm.

Brody stood up, slow and easy, and stepped back. "Come on in," he said to the dog. "Nothing to be afraid of—you're among friends."

The stray just sat there for a few moments, as though he might have heard wrong. He was obviously used to fending for himself.

"Come on," Brody repeated, speaking gently and giving the dog room.

Slowly, painfully, the wayfarer limped over the threshold and right into Brody Creed's heart.

CHAPTER FOUR

THE DREAM WAS disturbingly vivid.

Carolyn was in a supermarket, surrounded by dozens, if not hundreds, of eager suitors. There were men of every size and shape, color and type, a regular convention for fans of the Village People.

They nudged at her cart with theirs.

Some of them carried signs with her modified name printed on them in ransom-note letters, and one wore a sandwich board that read Marry Me, Carol! and Have Free Dentistry for Life!

"Carol," all the others chanted, in creepy unison, "Carol, Carol, Carol!"

Carolyn's feet seemed to be glued to the floor, but she looked wildly around for an escape route anyway. The freezer aisle was completely blocked, in both directions. She was trapped. Cornered.

Heart-pounding panic set in, washing over her in sweeping, electrified waves. A man with an elaborate wedding cake teetering in his shopping cart pushed his way past the others, to the forefront.

Carolyn recognized Gifford Welsh. He smiled his big movie-star smile, and his piano-key teeth sparkled cartoonishly, like something out of an animated mouthwash commercial.

"You're already married!" she said, turning her head

when Gifford tried to stuff a handful of cake into her mouth. Then, pressing back against the cold door of the ice-cream freezer, she shouted, "I don't want to marry *any* of you! You're not—you're not—

"Brody." She started awake at the name. Could still feel its singular weight on her lips.

Winston, curled up at her feet, made a halfhearted hissing sound. There was no telling whether the noise was a comment about Brody or annoyance because she'd awakened him from a sound sleep.

Carolyn's heart thumped against the back of her rib cage, and her breathing was fast and shallow. She lay there, in her dark bedroom, looking up at the ceiling and fighting tears.

Don't be a crybaby, she heard one of her long string of foster mothers say. *Nobody likes a crybaby.*

Carolyn had subscribed to that belief ever since, and she blinked until the sting in her eyes abated a little.

Going back to sleep was out of the question, lest the dream go into rewind, so she got out of bed and padded into the kitchen, barefoot. She was wearing flannel pajamas she'd sewn herself, covered in a puppy-dog pattern, and the fabric was damp against her chest and between her shoulder blades. Perspiration.

The nightmare had been a doozy, then. Normally, dreams didn't cause her to sweat.

But, then, this hadn't *been* a normal dream, now, had it?

You're not Brody. The words still reverberated through her mind.

She took a mug from the cupboard, this one a souvenir of Cheyenne, Wyoming, filled it with water, added an herbal tea bag and stuck the works into the microwave to heat.

A dog, she thought peevishly, would have gotten up when she did, to keep her company, lend silent reassurance. Winston, by contrast, did not put in an appearance, sympathetic or otherwise.

That was a cat for you.

Not that Winston was *her* cat—he was a frequent boarder and no more. Just passing through.

Somebody else's cat.

Somebody else's house.

Everything in her life, it seemed, belonged to somebody else.

Including Brody Creed. Whenever Joleen Williams blew into town, she and Brody were joined at the hip. It was probably only a matter of time before Joleen roped him in for good.

He was building a house, wasn't he? A *big* house, obviously not meant for man to live in alone.

The bell on the microwave dinged, and Carolyn carefully removed the cup. Took a sip.

The tea had the usual placebo effect, and she calmed down a little.

In need of something to occupy her mind, but scared to log on to the computer again, lest more men should pop up, in search of her alter ego, Carol, she flipped on the light at the top of the inside stairway and made her way down the steps.

The shop looked magical in the moonlight. Like some enchanted workshop, where elves ran up ruffly cotton-print aprons on miniature sewing machines and made more goats' milk soap whenever the supply was low.

Carolyn gave a little snicker at the thought.

She made the aprons, and they bought the soap from a woman who ran a small goat farm a few miles out of town. A few elves would certainly come in handy, though, even if it *wasn't* Christmas.

She loved the shop; it grounded her, like sewing and riding horseback usually did, and she loved the twinkling quiet surrounding her.

A shaft of silvery light struck the batik of the Native weaver, high on the wall, illuminating the image as though to convey some message.

There was no message, Carolyn thought. Not in the picture, at least.

The dream, now? That had clearly been a manifesto from her subconscious mind.

As usual, she wanted what she couldn't have.

Right or wrong, for better or worse, she wanted Brody Creed.

She gave a loud sigh of frustration, set her mug of tea down on the glass top of the handmade-jewelry display and shoved all ten fingers into her hair, pulling just a little.

Why couldn't she just *let go?* It had been over seven years, after all, since that awful morning when she'd awakened in a guest-room bed at Kim and Davis's place to find Brody gone.

At the time, she'd figured he was merely out in the kitchen making coffee, or even whipping up some breakfast. He was a fair cook, and he seemed to enjoy it.

She'd gotten out of bed, pulled on a robe and headed for the kitchen, in search of the man she loved.

Instead, she'd found the note.

Have to go, Brody had written. *Something came up.*

That was it.

Have to go, something came up.

The tears that had threatened before, after the dream, sprang up again. Carolyn hugged herself, chilled, and gazed at her own woebegone face, reflected in the big mirror behind the counter.

"Nobody likes a crybaby," she told her image.

And then she cried anyway.

"WHERE'D YOU GET the dog?" Conner asked the next morning, with affable interest, as Brody carefully lifted the bathed, brushed and still-skinny critter down from the passenger side of his truck, onto the grassy stretch of ground between the main ranch house and the barn.

"His name's Barney," Brody replied. He'd hung that handle on the stray after taking him by the vet's office that morning for a checkup. And he'd been so glad over the dog's clean bill of health that he'd named him after the doctor. "He showed up at my door last night, in pretty sorry condition, so I took him in."

Conner grinned and crouched to look the dog in the eyes, much as Brody had done the night before, when Barney turned up on his doorstep.

"Well, hello there, Barney," Conner said, putting out his hand.

To Brody's mingled amazement and irritation, the dog laid a paw in Conner's outstretched palm.

Man and dog shook hands.

"I'll be damned," Brody muttered, impressed, then worried. Maybe whoever had taught Barney to shake hands was out combing the countryside for him, right now. Maybe somebody loved him, wanted him back.

Conner, meanwhile, stood up straight again. "I guess

Doc must have checked for a microchip and all that," he said.

"First thing he did," Brody replied. "No chip, no identification of any kind."

"You gonna keep him?" Conner ventured, as Valentino trotted out of the back door, joined the group and sniffed Barney from head to tail.

"Yeah," Brody said. "I'll keep him. Unless his original owner tracks him down, anyway. Doc's assistant took his picture, and she'll upload it onto several lost-pet websites, just in case…"

"But?" Conner prompted.

"But my gut says he's in need of a home."

"Mine, too," Conner agreed. He had been frowning until then, but suddenly, the grin was back. "It'll be good for you," he preached. "The responsibility of looking after the poor critter, I mean."

The words, though he knew they were well-meant, raised Brody's hackles a little just the same. Was he going to be the Irresponsible One for the rest of his life, while Conner got to play the Good Brother?

Before he could figure out a way to answer, Davis came barreling down the hill in his truck from his and Kim's place. Kim rode beside him, her smile visible even through the dusty grunge covering the windshield.

"Kim's pinch-hitting for Tricia today at the shop," Conner said.

Brody felt a pang of alarm, remembering how tuckered out his sister-in-law had seemed the day before. "Tricia isn't having trouble, is she?"

"No," Conner replied, raising a hand to greet the new arrivals. "She just enjoyed yesterday so much that she wanted today to be just like it."

Brody chuckled, partly amused and partly relieved.

An instant later, though, the worry was back. Women were fragile creatures, it seemed to him. Lisa, for instance, couldn't have weighed more than a hundred and ten pounds sopping wet; she hadn't stood a chance against two tons of speeding steel, not driving that little car of hers.

He'd always had access to his inheritance and his share of the ranch profits, even when he was staying as far away from Lonesome Bend as he could. Why hadn't he gotten her a sturdier rig to drive?

"Brody," Conner said suspiciously. "Where's your head right now?"

"You know where," Brody replied, as Davis parked the truck and he and Kim got out of the vehicle and started toward them. Kim was wearing a lightweight sweater with big pockets, where her impossibly small dogs, Smidgeon and Little Bit, were riding.

Barney whimpered and moved behind Brody, leaning against the backs of his legs. He could feel the animal trembling.

Seeing that, Kim smiled, crouched down and set the two Yorkies on the ground. Ignoring Valentino, who was probably considered old news by now, they wagged their stumpy little tails and one of them growled comically.

"Now, come on out here," Kim cajoled, addressing Barney. "Smidgeon and Little Bit aren't going to hurt you."

Kim definitely had a way with animals, and Barney's reaction was proof of that. Probably drawn by her gentleness, as well as his own curiosity, he came out of hiding to stand at Brody's side. His plume of a tail wagged once, tentatively.

The Yorkies nosed him over and then lost interest and tried to start a game of tag with Valentino. They were absolutely fearless, those two. Or maybe their brains were just so small that they couldn't grasp the difference between their size and Valentino's.

"Come have supper with us tonight," Kim told Brody, when she was standing upright again. "You look a little ribby to me, like this dog."

Brody's mouth watered at the mere suggestion of Kim's cooking, not to mention a chance to avoid another lonely evening.

"Is this a setup?" he asked good-naturedly. It didn't take a rocket scientist to figure out that everybody was hoping he and Carolyn would get together.

"Of course it is," Kim replied with a laugh, looking at Brody but slipping an arm around Davis's waist and giving him a brief squeeze. "Why fight it?"

Brody laughed, too, despite the little thrill that quickened in the pit of his stomach at the thought of being in the same house with Carolyn. He folded his arms and countered, "Why not?"

Kim punched him. "You're just like your uncle," she said.

Whatever that meant.

That he was a stubborn cuss, probably.

The quality came free with the Creed name, one to a customer but guaranteed for life.

Conner and Davis, meanwhile, moved off toward the house, where Tricia surely had a pot of coffee brewing.

Smidgeon, Little Bit and Valentino ambled along

after them, leaving Brody and Kim in the yard, with Barney.

"Carolyn's probably wise to your tricks, Kim," Brody ventured, serious now, his voice a little husky. "She'll know you've invited me to supper, and she'll think of some excuse to get out of it."

Kim, still a striking woman in her mid-fifties, shook her head and mimicked his stance by folding her own arms. "Could you *be* any more negative, Brody Creed?" she asked. "You and Carolyn are perfect for each other. Everybody seems to know that but the two of you."

Brody recalled kissing Carolyn the day before, and an aftershock went through him. When it was over, she'd looked as if he'd slapped her, and he'd made some smart-ass remark about not being sorry for doing it.

Oh, yeah. He was zero-for-zero in Carolyn's books, no doubt about it.

Kissing her had only made things worse.

He just hadn't been able to resist, that was all.

"Brody?" Kim prompted, evidently reading his face.

He smiled, laid a hand on Kim's shoulder. "I'm all right," he told her. "Stop worrying about me, okay?"

"Okay," she said, in a tone of bright irony. "Are you coming to our place for supper tonight or not?" Not waiting for an answer, Kim added, "Six-thirty, on the dot and don't be late." She looked around, parodied a frown. "If Davis Creed thinks he gets to keep Smidgeon and Little Bit with him while I'm in town, covering for Tricia at the shop, he's got another think coming."

With that, she turned and headed resolutely for the house.

Brody watched her go, one side of his mouth quirked up in a grin. It was anybody's guess whether Carolyn would accept Kim's supper invitation or make up some excuse to get out of it, but he sure hoped it would be the former.

He wanted to see Carolyn again, even though the idea pretty well scared the crap out of him.

"Women," he told Barney ruefully.

Barney gave a little yip of agreement.

Brody chuckled, bent to ruffle the dog's ears and the two of them started for the house, where the others were gathered and the coffee was on.

"You have dark circles under your eyes," Kim announced, the moment she stepped over the threshold at the shop. "Aren't you sleeping well?"

Carolyn smiled as her friend took the pair of tiny dogs from her sweater pockets and set them down carefully on the floor, where they proceeded to romp like a couple of kittens.

Winston, long since resigned to the occasional presence of the canine contingent, ignored them.

"I slept just fine, thank you very much," Carolyn lied, in belated reply to Kim's question. She'd eventually managed to get to sleep again the night before, but she'd promptly tumbled right back into a variation of her dream. This time, with the added fillip of Brody riding through a conglomeration of suitors and shopping carts on horseback, reaching her side and then leaning down to hook an arm around her and haul her up into the saddle in front of him.

The dream hadn't stopped there, either. With no noticeable transition, Brody and Carolyn were alone in a forest, both lying naked in a stand of deep, summer-fragrant grass, making love.

She'd awakened in the throes of a very real orgasm, which was downright embarrassing, even if she *was* alone at the time.

"I don't believe you," Kim said, moving behind the sales counter to put away her purse.

Smidgeon and Little Bit were rolling across the center of the floor now, in a merry little blur of shiny fur and pink topknot ribbon.

Carolyn, thinking of the spontaneous climax, was blushing. "Would I lie to you?" she retorted, with an attempt at a light tone.

There weren't any customers in the shop yet, and she'd been keeping her mind off the nightmare/dream by catching up on the bookkeeping on the store's computer.

"Depends," Kim replied mischievously. "How about joining Davis and me for supper tonight? I'm thawing out a batch of my world-famous chicken-and-pork tamales."

A bar of that old song "Suspicion" played in Carolyn's head. "Hard to resist," she admitted. Kim's tamales were fantastic. "Are Conner and Tricia coming, too?"

Kim nodded, but she averted her eyes and was busying her hands rearranging costume jewelry in the glass case.

"And Brody?" Carolyn asked, rather enjoying herself, despite all her nerves being on red alert.

"Maybe," Kim said, her manner still evasive. "Did you know he adopted a dog? Brody, I mean? It's a very good sign. He really *is* serious about settling down in Lonesome Bend—"

"Dogs travel pretty well," Carolyn said, amused and, at the same time, wickedly excited over the perfectly ordinary prospect of sitting across a supper table from Brody Creed.

The bastard.

Kim straightened, looked at her directly. Her smile was a little weak. "You think he's planning to leave again? Even though he's building that big house and a fancy barn to go with it?"

Carolyn's casual shrug was, in reality, anything *but* casual. "He could always sell the house and barn, if he wanted to move on," she reasoned. In truth, though, she didn't like the idea of Brody going back to his other life any more than Kim did, and that surprised her. The prospect *should* have been a relief, shouldn't it?

Kim's gentle blue eyes filled with tears. "Brody's had a tough time of it," she said.

Carolyn needed a few moments to recover from that tidbit—she'd always imagined Brody whooping it up, as the cowboys liked to say, riding bulls and winning gleaming buckles and bedding a different woman every night.

"How so?" she asked, finally, in an oddly strangled voice.

Kim sniffled, squared her shoulders and straightened her spine. "I can't say," she told Carolyn, in a forthright tone. "I'm not supposed to know what Brody went through, and neither is Davis. He'd be furious if he knew Conner had told us."

"Oh, boy," Carolyn said.

"He'll tell you himself, one of these days," Kim said, with new certainty. "And that's the way it should be."

Just then, the bell over the front door jingled and Smidgeon and Little Bit ran, yapping, to greet whomever was there.

Kim rolled her eyes and chased after them. "Little devils," she muttered, with abiding affection.

Carolyn smiled, but on the inside, she was shaken.

She knew better than to go to supper at her friends' place, since it was a given that Brody would be there. Just being around him was playing with fire, especially in light of that stolen kiss—and last night's dream.

She'd be there, just the same.

Maybe she'd take in the gypsy skirt—just baste it to fit temporarily—and wear that.

BRODY WATCHED with a combination of affection and envy, that evening, in Kim and Davis's kitchen, while Conner and Tricia flirted like a pair of teenagers.

It was enough to make Brody roll his eyes.

Get a room, he wanted to say.

Davis, sitting beside him at the unset table, nudged him with one elbow. "You remember how it was with those two?" Brody's uncle asked, keeping his voice low. "When they first noticed each other, I mean?"

"I remember," Brody said, grinning a little. A stranger would have given odds that Conner and Tricia would never get together, but everybody who knew them wondered when the wedding would be.

Was Carolyn going to show up for supper or not?

He hoped so.

He hoped not.

"You and Carolyn remind me of them," Davis said, with a twinkle in his eyes.

That got Brody's attention, all right. He swiveled in his chair to look at his uncle with narrowed eyes. "What's that supposed to mean?"

"Just what I said," Davis replied, undaunted. "You know me, son. If I say it, I mean it."

Tricia snapped a dish towel at Conner, who laughed, and the dogs all started barking, while an apron-wearing Kim tried to shush the lot.

It was happy chaos.

It was a *family*.

Again, Brody felt that bittersweet sense of mingled gratitude and loneliness.

"Give things a chance, boy," Davis told him, pushing back his chair and heading for the back door. His uncle had always been able to read him and, clearly, that hadn't changed.

Brody hadn't heard the car drive up, what with all the barking and shushing, dish-towel snapping and laughing, but Davis must have.

He opened the door just as Carolyn was raising one hand to knock.

She looked shy and sweet standing there, wearing black jeans and a gossamer white shirt. Her sun-streaked hair was pulled back in a French braid and, unless Brody missed his guess, she had on just a touch of makeup, too.

"Hi," she said to Davis, with a little wobble in her voice, shoving a large plastic food container into his hands and not sparing so much as a glance for Brody. "I brought pasta salad. It's from the deli at the supermarket, but I'm sure it's good."

"That's fine," Davis said, in that Sam Elliott voice of his, sounding amused. "Come on in and make yourself at home."

Conner and Tricia knocked off the prelude to foreplay to greet Carolyn—Conner with a smile, Tricia with a hug. When Kim joined in, it was like something out of a reality-show reunion.

All Brody could do was wait, though he did remember enough of his manners to stand in the presence of a lady.

Carolyn finally forced herself, visibly, to look at him. Pink color pulsed in her cheeks and hot damn, she looked good.

"Hello, Brody," she said.

"Carolyn," he replied, with a nod of acknowledgment.

Brody immediately grew two left feet and felt his tongue wind itself into a knot.

It was junior high school all over again.

Only worse.

In junior high, it had been all about speculation. As a man, he knew, only too well, what it was like to kiss this woman, to make love to her.

Stand in a puddle and grab hold of a live wire, he thought.

That's what it's like.

"Kim says everything's fine at the shop," Tricia told Carolyn, with a sparkling little laugh. "I was hoping I'd be missed a *little bit,* though."

Carolyn smiled, no longer looking quite so much like a doe poised to run after catching the scent of a predator on the wind. "Oh, you were definitely missed," she said.

"Absolutely," Kim agreed cheerfully, opening one of the big double ovens to check on the tamales.

They smelled so good that Brody's stomach rumbled.

Things settled down to a dull roar over the next few minutes—Carolyn and Tricia washed up at the sink and began setting the table, while Davis pulled the corks on a couple of bottles of vintage wine.

It came as no surprise to Brody—and probably not to Carolyn, either—that they wound up sitting side by side at the huge table in the next room. The others made sure of it, the way they always did.

Brody and Carolyn were so close that they bumped elbows a couple of times. The scent of her—some combination of baby powder and flowers and a faint, citrusy spice—made him feel buzzed, if not drunk, which was weird because he let the wine bottle go by without pouring any for himself.

Tricia passed on it, too, of course, being pregnant.

Carolyn, by contrast, seemed uncommonly thirsty. She nibbled at the salad, and then the tamales and Kim's incomparable Mexican rice and refried beans, but she seemed to be hitting the wine pretty hard.

"So, anyway," Kim said, her voice rising above the others. "Carolyn signed up for Friendly Faces—that dating website—and she's practically *under siege,* there are so many men wanting to meet her."

Out of the corner of his eye, Brody saw Carolyn go pink and then mauve. Obviously, she hadn't expected Kim to spill the frijoles in front of God and everybody.

Brody wanted to chuckle. He also wanted to stand on Carolyn's front porch with a shotgun and make sure no other man got past him.

"Oops," Kim said, widening her eyes. She'd let the news slip on purpose, and everybody knew it, but since the horse was already out of the barn, so to speak, that was that. "Sorry."

Davis gave his wife a look.

Carolyn looked down at her lap, still red and making no pretense of eating.

Casually, Brody leaned over, took hold of the nearest wine bottle and refilled her glass. She glanced at him with an expression of mingled desperation and gratitude and practically drained the thing in a few gulps.

Brody bit back a grin. Well, there was *one* bright spot to the situation, he reflected. Now he had the perfect excuse to drive Carolyn home, because she was obviously in no condition to get behind the wheel.

An awkward silence fell, broken only by the clinking of silverware against colorful pottery plates.

"I think it's wonderful," Tricia piped up, breaking the verbal stalemate. "The dating service thing, I mean. More and more people are meeting their soul mates online these days. Why, the statistics—"

Carolyn looked so utterly miserable by then that Brody felt downright sorry for her. She swallowed hard, raised her chin and bravely interrupted, "It's only a trial membership. I was curious, that's all."

"She's *swamped* with guys wanting to get to know her," Kim said, warming to the topic all over again.

Another wine bottle was opened and passed around.

Carolyn sloshed some into her glass, avoiding Brody's eyes when she shoved the bottle at him to keep it moving.

"Are you sure you ought to…?"

At last, Carolyn looked at him. She flashed like a highway flare on a dark night, because she was so angry.

Because she was so *beautiful*.

"I'm of legal age, Brody Creed," she said, slurring her words only slightly.

The others were talking among themselves, a sort

of distant hum, a thing apart, like a radio playing in the next house or the next street, the words indistinct.

"Besides," Carolyn went on briskly, before he could reply, "I've only had two glasses."

"Four," Brody said quietly, "but who's counting?"

"It's not as if I normally drink a lot," she informed him, apropos of he wasn't sure what.

"Have another tamale," Brody counseled, keeping his voice down even though they still seemed to be alone in a private conversational bubble, him and Carolyn, with the rest of the outfit someplace on the dim periphery of things.

"I don't *want* another tamale," Carolyn told him.

"You're going to be sick if you don't eat something," Brody reasoned. He didn't think he'd used that particular cajoling tone since Steven and Melissa's last visit, when he'd been appointed to feed his cousin's twin sons. He'd had to do some smooth talking to get them to open up for the pureed green beans.

"That's my problem, not yours," Carolyn said stiffly.

"Around here," Brody said, "we look out for each other."

She made a snorting sound and tried to snag another passing wine bottle, but Brody got hold of it first and sent it along its way.

That made her furious. She colored up again and her eyes flashed, looking as if they might short out from the overload.

Brody merely held her gaze. "Eat," he said.

She huffed out a sigh. Stabbed at a tiny bite of tamale with her fork. "There," she said, after chewing. "Are you satisfied?"

He let the grin come, the charming one that sometimes got him what he wanted and sometimes got him slapped across the face. "No," he drawled. "Are you?"

It looked like it was going to be the slap, for a second there.

In the end, though, Carolyn was at once too flustered and too tipsy to respond right away. She blinked once, twice, looking surprised to find herself where she was, and swayed ever so slightly in her chair.

"I want to go home," she said.

Brody pushed his own chair back and stood, holding out a hand to her. "I think that's a good idea," he replied easily. "Let's go."

Kim and Davis, Conner and Tricia—he was aware of them as a group, rimming the table with amused faces but making no comment.

"I guess I have to let you drive me, don't I?" Carolyn said.

"I reckon you do," Brody said. "We'll take my truck. Somebody can bring your car to town later."

Carolyn, feisty before, seemed bemused now, at a loss. "But what about washing the dishes and…?"

"Davis and Conner can do the cleaning up." Brody slid a hand under her elbow and raised her to her feet, steered her away from the table and into the kitchen, Barney sticking to their heels like chewing gum off a hot sidewalk.

He squired her to the truck and helped her into the passenger seat, careful to let her think she was doing it all herself.

Barney took his place in the backseat of the extended cab.

Once he was behind the wheel, Brody buzzed his

window and Carolyn's about halfway down. She was going to need all the fresh air she could handle.

"You're going to hate yourself in the morning," he said easily, as they drove toward the gate and the road to town.

He'd only been teasing, but Carolyn's sigh was so deep that it gave him a pang, made him wish he'd kept his mouth shut.

"It might not even take that long," she said sadly. "I'm—I'm not used to drinking and I—well, I'm just not used to it, that's all."

Brody reached over, gave her hand a brief, light squeeze. "That's pretty obvious," he said gently.

"I feel like such a fool," Carolyn lamented, refusing to look at him.

"Don't," Brody said.

She looked down at her hand, where his had been rested for a second, and frowned, seemingly surprised to discover that he'd let go.

"You probably think I'm pathetic," she went on, staring straight through the windshield again.

"Nothing of the sort," Brody assured her gruffly.

"Getting drunk. Signing up for a dating service—"

Before he needed to come up with a response, she turned to look at him, straight on. And she was pea-green.

"Stop!" she gasped. "I'm going to be—"

Brody stopped, and she shoved open the door and stuck her head out.

"Sick," she finished.

And then she was.

CHAPTER FIVE

If she'd deliberately *set out* to make a lasting impression on Brody Creed, Carolyn thought wretchedly, as she stared at her wan image in the mirror above her bathroom sink later that evening, she couldn't have done a better job.

First, being the proverbial bundle of nerves, she'd had too much wine at supper. Then, with ultimate glamour and grace, she'd *thrown up*, right in front of the man. Just stuck her head out of his truck door and hurled on the side of the road, like somebody being carted off to rehab after an intervention.

"Very impressive," she whispered to her sorry-looking one-dimensional self.

With the spectacle playing out in her mind's eye, Carolyn squeezed her eyes shut, mortified all over again. Brody had reacted with calm kindness, presenting her with a partial package of wet wipes and following up with two time-hardened sticks of cinnamon-flavored chewing gum.

She'd been too embarrassed to look at him afterward, had hoped he would simply drop her off at home and be on his way again, with his dog, leaving her to wallow privately in her regrets.

She couldn't be that lucky.

Instead of leaving her to her misery, he'd told Bar-

ney to stay put, insisted on helping Carolyn down from
the truck and escorting her not only through the front
gate and across the yard, but also up the outside staircase to her door.

"I'll be all right now," she'd said, when they reached
the landing, still unable to meet his eyes. "Really, I—"

Brody had taken her chin in his hand; sick as she
was, the combination of gentleness and strength in his
touch had sent a charge through her. "I believe I'll stay
a while and make sure you're all right," Brody had replied matter-of-factly.

Though she was painfully sober by then, Carolyn
didn't have the energy to fight any losing battles, so
she merely unlocked the door and allowed him to follow her inside.

Winston, perched on the windowsill, greeted him
with raised hackles and a hiss.

"Whatever, cat," Brody had said, with desultory resignation. "I'm here, like it or not, so deal with it."

Carolyn had hurried into the bathroom to wash her
face and brush her teeth, following up with a mouthwash swish and two aspirin from the bottle in the medicine cabinet. Then she'd slipped into her room and
changed her T-shirt.

And here she was back in the bathroom again, trying
to work up the courage to go out there into the kitchen,
thank Brody for bringing her home and politely send
him packing.

He was moving around out there, running water in
the sink, carrying on a one-sided chat with Winston,
his voice set too low for her to make out the words. The
tone was chiding, but good-natured.

Most likely, Brody was bent on winning over the cat.

The idea made Carolyn smile, but very briefly, because even *smiling* hurt.

How would she feel when the actual *hangover* kicked in?

Sobering thought. *That's what you get for drinking,* she told herself grimly. *You* know *you're not good at it.*

All this self-recrimination, she realized, was getting her nowhere, fast. So Carolyn drew a deep breath, squared her shoulders, let the air whoosh out of her lungs and forced herself to step out of the bathroom and walk the short distance to the kitchen.

Brody was leaning against one of the counters, sipping what was probably coffee from one of her three million souvenir mugs.

This one bore the image of a famous mouse and was painted with large red letters trumpeting Welcome to Orlando!

"You have quite a collection," Brody observed, raising the mug slightly for emphasis.

"I've been everywhere," Carolyn said, in a lame attempt at normality. Some of the mugs were from thrift stores and garage sales, actually, but she saw no point in explaining that sometimes she liked to pretend she'd purchased them on family vacations over the years.

Which was pathetic, because to take a family vacation, one needed a *family.*

Brody gave her that tilted grin, the one with enough juice to power a cattle prod, his eyes as soft as blue velvet but with a twinkle of amusement, too. Moving to the microwave, he took out a second cup, this one commemorating some stranger's long-ago visit to the Alamo, in San Antonio.

Carolyn had always wanted to visit the Alamo.

She caught the soothing scent of mint tea with just the faintest touch of ginger. Her throat, still a little sore from being sick, tightened with some achy emotion.

"Good for what ails you," Brody said, setting down the tea on the kitchen table. "Have a seat, Carolyn. I'm not fixing to bite you or anything."

She dropped into a chair, wishing she'd put the sewing machine away before she'd left for Davis and Kim's house to have supper and campaign for fool of the year. Now Brody would probably think she was a *slob* as well as a shameless lush.

Brody waited a beat, then sat down across from her. Watched in easy silence as she took a sip of the tea, sighed at the herbal goodness of the stuff.

"You've been very…kind," Carolyn managed to say, after more tea. She was recovering in small but steady increments. "Thank you."

Brody's eyes smiled before his mouth did. "You're welcome," he said. He'd finished his coffee, but he appeared to be in no particular hurry to leave.

"I'll be fine on my own, now that I've had some aspirin and this tea," Carolyn told him, hoping he'd take the hint and hit the road.

Hoping he wouldn't.

He lingered, watching her. "I'm sure you will be," he agreed.

"And your dog is all alone, down there in your truck."

Brody chuckled. "Barney's fine," he replied.

Carolyn let her shoulders slump, and her chin wouldn't stay at the obstinate angle she'd been maintaining since her kitchen reentry. "I'm so embarrassed," she said, in a near whisper, without planning to speak again at all.

"Don't be," Brody said. "It's obvious that you can't hold your liquor, but that's not such a bad thing."

Carolyn bit down hard on her lower lip and forced herself to look Brody Creed directly in the eye. Before, she'd spoken without meaning to—now, she couldn't seem to get a word out.

"You probably should have some soup or something," Brody said mildly. What was it like to be so at ease, so at home, in his own skin? Was this what came of belonging somewhere, being part of a tribe? Even with all those years away, Carolyn reflected enviously, the man's roots went deep into the Colorado soil, curling around bedrock, no doubt. "Might settle your stomach down a little."

Carolyn shook her head quickly. The *thought* of putting food in her mouth—even soup—threatened to bring on a new spate of helpless retching.

"I couldn't," she managed to croak.

"Okay," Brody said.

Oddly, his unflappable solicitude made her feel even more vulnerable to him than that infamous kiss had.

Carolyn steeled herself against what was surely a perfectly normal human need to be reassured, cared for, looked after—normal for other people, that is. Foster kids, no matter how good the homes they were placed in, had to be strong and self-reliant, tough to the core.

Always.

"You could leave now," she suggested carefully.

Brody chuckled again. Sat back in his chair and folded his arms. "I could," he agreed, showing absolutely no signs of doing so anytime soon.

"And as for what Kim said at supper, about my signing up for a dating service…"

"Who said anything about that?" Brody asked, when her voice trailed off.

"If I'd known she was going to tell everyone," Carolyn said, "I wouldn't have mentioned it to her in the first place."

"Kim didn't mean any harm, Carolyn," Brody offered quietly. "Anyway, you're a grown woman, sound of mind and…body—" He paused, and once more that special *something* sparked in his eyes. "And if you want to date potential con artists, that's your business."

On one level, Carolyn knew full well that Brody was baiting her. On another, she couldn't resist taking the hook. "*Potential con artists?* Well, *that's* cynical," she accused, and never mind the fact that she'd had similar thoughts herself, right along.

"If you're in the market for a man, Carolyn, it's your call how you go about roping one in. All I'm saying is that you ought to be careful. There are some real head-cases out there."

"In the market for a man?" She leaned forward in her chair, incensed. *"Roping one in?"* Being incensed felt like an improvement over being embarrassed, at least.

"Will you stop repeating everything I say?" Brody intoned. A tiny muscle bunched in his cheek, then smoothed out again.

"Who else would want to date me, right?" Carolyn ranted, stifling her voice so she wouldn't yell and scare Winston. Or the neighbors. "Only a *head-case* loser who couldn't get a woman the normal way?"

Brody laughed. *Laughed.* He didn't lack for nerve, that was for sure.

Or sex appeal, damn him.

"There you go again, putting words in my mouth," he

said, all relaxed and affable. His gaze dropped ever so briefly to her breasts and then returned to her flushed face. "Take a breath, Carolyn. If you want to sign on with Funky Faces, or whatever that outfit calls itself, go for it."

"*Friendly* Faces," Carolyn corrected, hating that she sounded so defensive. Why couldn't she, just once, get the upper hand in one of these sparring matches?

"Whatever," Brody said dismissively, pushing back his chair—at long last—and rising. "You sure you're all right?"

"I'm sure," Carolyn insisted, hugging herself and not looking at him.

Funny, though. Even with her eyes averted, the man was an onslaught to her jangled senses. She was aware of Brody Creed in every part of her; he made everything pulse.

She felt angry triumph at the prospect of his leaving and, underlying that, a certain quiet dejection.

Go, she thought desperately. *For God's sake, Brody, just* go.

Instead of heading straight to the door, however, Brody stepped around the table, paused behind Carolyn's chair and then leaned down to place the lightest of kisses on the top of her head.

"See you around," he said gruffly.

Carolyn clamped her molars together, so she couldn't ask him to stay.

To cajole her about soup and hold her.

She'd said and done enough stupid things for one day, met and exceeded the quota.

A few seconds later, Brody was gone.

The apartment, once her refuge, felt hollow without him.

She sat still in her chair, listening to the sound of his boot heels on the outside stairs, waiting for the roar of his truck engine, the sounds of driving away.

Only then, when she was sure he wasn't coming back, did Carolyn push her teacup aside and bend forward to thump her forehead lightly against the table in frustration.

Once, twice, a third time.

Winston jumped down from the windowsill and padded over to wrap himself around her ankles, purring and offering general cat-comfort.

She bent, scooped him onto her lap and petted his silky back.

Since there was no one but the cat around to see, Carolyn finally gave in and allowed herself to cry.

"OKAY, SO I WAS a buttinski," Kim allowed, with a sheepish glance at Brody.

The two of them were standing in the ranch-house kitchen.

"Ya think?" Brody retorted.

In the time he'd been out, Tricia and Conner had gone back to their place—they were probably having slow, sleepy sex at that very moment—and Davis had retreated to his saddle shop, where he was working on a custom order.

Little Bit and Smidgeon must have gone with him, because there was no sign of them.

Except for the lingering scent of homemade tamales, all signs of supper were gone. Dishes washed, leftovers wrapped and put away, counters clear.

Kim Creed ran a tight ship.

Too bad she didn't exercise the same control over her mouth.

"I'm sorry," Kim said, reaching into the laundry basket on the table and pulling out a towel to fold. "I just thought you should know that Carolyn is...well... *looking.*"

"Why?" Brody asked. "In what universe is that my business, Kim? Or yours, for that matter? Carolyn was nervous in the first place—my guess is, that's why she was swilling wine like she was. And then you had to make everything worse by blurting out something she probably told you in confidence."

Kim stopped folding, and tears brimmed in her eyes.

Brody ached when any woman cried, but with Kim, it was the worst. She was, for all practical intents and purposes, his mom, and he loved her accordingly.

"It seemed like a good idea at the time," she admitted with a sniffle. "I'll apologize to Carolyn tomorrow."

Brody put his arms around Kim, gave her a brief squeeze. "Maybe you could lay off the matchmaking, too, for a while, anyway," he suggested, taking a towel from the basket and folding it.

"Trust me," Kim said, "I've already had this entire lecture from Davis. If you and Carolyn are both too thickheaded and stubborn to see that you're meant for each other, well, it's out of my hands, that's all. You're on your own."

"Thank you," Brody said, smiling. "I'll take it from here."

Kim's eyes widened, and her hands froze in mid towel-folding. "What do you mean, you'll take it from here? Are you...?"

Brody held up one index finger and shook his head, grinning as he turned to head for Davis's shop to bid the man good-night before heading back to the cabin at River's Bend.

The spacious room smelled pleasantly of leather and saddle soap and the wood fire that crackled in the Franklin stove, the flames casting a dancing reflection on the worn planks in the floor. Davis stood at one of several worktables, tooling an intricate design into a strip of cowhide.

At Brody's entrance, he looked up and grinned. Set the rubber mallet and the awl aside and dusted off his hands on the sides of his jeans, a gesture of habit more than necessity.

"Carolyn still feeling peaky?" Davis asked, evidently to get the conversational ball rolling.

"She'll be all right," Brody replied, looking around and recalling when he and Conner were kids, always getting underfoot in their uncle's first shop, a much smaller room than this one, connected to the barn at the other place. Back then, they'd believed nothing and no one could hurt them if Davis was around. They'd grown up feeling safe, and that had fostered self-confidence.

Or arrogance, depending on how you looked at it.

Davis tilted his head to one side, studied his nephew in silence for a few moments, then went back to his worktable, picked up a chamois and began polishing the piece he'd been tooling before.

"How's that fancy house of yours coming along?" Davis asked, at some length. He wasn't a man for chatter.

Brody spotted the little dogs under one of the tables, snuggled up in a bed made to look like a plush pink slipper, and smiled. Dragged back a wooden chair and sat astraddle of it, resting his forearms across the back.

"Slowly," he replied, eliciting a bass note of a chuckle from Davis.

"Pretty big place for one cowboy and his dog," Davis commented. Barney had wandered in behind Brody by then, and lay down at his feet.

"Don't start," Brody warned, leaning to ruffle the dog's floppy ears so the critter would know he was welcome.

"Don't start what?" Davis asked, though he knew damn well what.

Brody merely sighed.

Davis chuckled, shook his head. "My wife did stir something up at supper tonight, didn't she?" he said, polishing away at that hunk of leather.

"You might say that," Brody said dryly.

Davis paused in his work, gave Brody a mirthful assessment before going on. "Conner and Tricia turned out to be a good match," he observed. "Kim put her foot in it, sure enough, but she just wants you to be as happy as your brother is, that's all."

"I know," Brody answered, on a long sigh. Then, presently, he added, "Here's the thing, Davis. Something happened between Carolyn and me, a long time ago, and she'd sooner throw in with a polecat than with me. We're never going to get together, she and I, no matter how much you and Kim want that."

"Is that right?" Davis asked, with his customary note of charitable skepticism. He'd finished with the polishing, and now he was wiping his hands off on a shop towel.

"Take it from me," Brody said. "If it came down to

me or a polecat, the polecat would win, hands down. Carolyn wants no part of me, and I can't really say I blame her for it."

Davis laughed. "Is it just me, or was there something mournful in your tone of voice just now, boy?" Smidgeon and Little Bit tumbled out of their slipper-bed and rushed him, scrabbling at Davis's pant legs so he'd bend down and pick them up.

Which he did.

"Mournful?" Brody scoffed, a beat or two too late. "Not me."

"You're taken with Carolyn," Davis said quietly, standing there with a froufrou dog in the crook of each elbow. "Nothing wrong with that. She's a beauty, and a hand with a horse, too."

Brody chuckled ruefully. Saying somebody was "a hand with a horse" was high praise, coming from a Creed—better than a good credit score or a character reference from a VIP. "Well," he said, "I kind of messed things up with her."

Davis put the little dogs down gently, and they scampered off, probably in search of Kim. Then the rough-and-tough cowboy pulled up a chair for himself and sat down, regarding Brody solemnly, but with a crook at the corner of his mouth.

"I've messed up with Kim more times than I care to recall," Davis said, once he was settled. "And here we are, married thirty-five years as of next October."

A companionable silence fell; they both sat listening to the fire in the stove for a while, thinking their own thoughts.

Brody's throat tightened a little. "Did you and Kim

ever regret not having kids of your own?" he asked, the words coming out rusty.

"We *had* kids," Davis pointed out, with a smile. "You and Conner and Steven."

"Of your own," Brody persisted. Davis's marriage to Steven's mother hadn't lasted.

Davis thought a moment, and there was a twinkle in his eyes when he replied. "We'd have liked to have had a girl," he allowed. "But now that Melissa and Tricia have married into the family, why, Kim and I feel like we've got everything anybody could rightfully ask for."

Brody stayed silent.

Davis reached out, laid a hand on his nephew's shoulder, squeezed. "I know I've said it before," he told Brody, "but it's better than good to have you back home where you belong, boy. We all missed you something fierce."

With that, the conversation appeared to be over.

Davis stood up and went to the stove to bank the fire.

Brody told Barney they'd better get on the road, stepped into the corridor outside the shop, then remembered what he'd come for and stuck his head back in.

"'Night, Davis," he said.

His uncle nodded, smiled. "'Night," he replied. "You drive carefully now, because we can't spare you."

Brody nodded back.

He didn't run into Kim on his way out.

Twenty minutes later, he pulled up at River's Bend, near the unfinished barn, and parked the truck. He and Barney went inside to make sure Moonshine was settled for the night—he was—and headed for the cabin.

Brody flipped on the lights and went straight to his computer to log on.

While he was doing that, Barney drank loudly from his water bowl on the floor and then curled up on his dog-bed to catch up on his sleep.

Once he got online, Brody skipped his email—he often went days without checking it—and called up his favorite search engine instead.

Hunt-and-peck style, he typed *Friendly Faces*.

Something like ten thousand links came up.

He narrowed the search to dating services, blushing a little even though nobody was ever, by God, going to find out he'd stooped to such a lame-assed thing.

There it was, the website Carolyn evidently hoped would land her a husband.

Brody's back teeth ground slightly; he released his jawbones by deliberate effort.

Finding her took some doing, but eventually, Brody came across Carolyn's profile. She was calling herself Carol, he soon discovered.

For some reason, that made him feel a little better.

He decided to send her a message.

To do that, he had to sign up for the free trial membership, which was very much against his better judgment.

Having no stock alias to fall back on, as Carolyn evidently did, he used his own name. Since he didn't keep pictures of himself on hand, he uploaded a snapshot of Moonshine instead.

That made him grin. According to Kim, no self-respecting woman would take up with a cowboy unless she'd seen his horse.

He completed the few remaining cybersteps, and the way was finally clear: he could send Carolyn a message.

Right off, Brody hit a wall. Now that he'd gone to all that trouble, he couldn't think of a darn thing to say.

Feeling mildly beleaguered, he sighed, sat back in his chair, frowning at the screen as if something might materialize there if he concentrated hard enough.

Well, slick, he taunted himself silently, *where's all that smooth talk and country charm you've always relied on?*

Brody sighed again. Rubbed his chin pensively.

This was ridiculous.

A simple howdy ought to do, even if there *was* some bad blood between him and Carolyn.

Only *howdy* wasn't going to pack it.

"For a good time, call Brody" sprang to mind next, and was mercifully discarded.

He decided on Hope you feel better, and he was tapping that in when the instant message popped up.

Hello, stranger, Joleen wrote. What luck to catch you online—is there a blue moon or something? Anyway, I wanted to give you a heads-up—I'll be back in Lonesome Bend in a few days.

Brody went still. And cold.

Joleen had hit the road weeks ago, swearing she'd stay away for good this time.

"Shit," he muttered. Timing, like luck, was never so bad that it couldn't get worse.

Hello? Joleen cyber-nudged.

Hi, he responded.

Joleen was faster on the draw, when it came to keyboards. I was hoping I could stay at your place. Mom and Dad have room, but they're not too pleased with me these days.

Brody let out a ragged breath. Sorry, he wrote back,

using only the tip of his right index finger. Quarters are too tight for a visitor.

Still mad over that little spat we had? Joleen inquired, adding a row of face icons with tears gushing from their eyes.

It isn't that, Brody replied laboriously.

Joleen's reply came like greased lightning. Are you dumping me, Brody Creed?

Brody sighed again, dug out his cell phone and speed-dialed Joleen's number.

"Hello?" Joleen purred, like she couldn't imagine who'd be calling little old her.

"I just think it's time we called it quits," Brody said, seeing no reason to bother with a preamble. "The sleeping-together thing, I mean."

"So you *are* dumping me!" Joleen chimed. To her credit, she sounded cheerful, rather than hurt. One thing about Joleen—she was a good sport.

"Okay," Brody said. "Have it your way."

"If I had things my way," Joleen immediately retorted, "we'd be married by now. With a bunch of kids."

Brody closed his eyes. He could envision the kids all too clearly, but they were all dead ringers for Carolyn, not Joleen.

"We had a deal," he reminded Joleen gruffly. "We agreed from the first that we wouldn't get serious."

Joleen laughed, but the sound had a bitter edge to it. "So it's finally happened," she said, after a lengthy silence. "Some filly has you roped in, thrown down and hog-tied."

"Nice image," Brody said, without inflection. "And for your information—not that I owe you an explanation, because I sure as hell don't—*nothing* has happened."

"Right," Joleen scoffed. "Well, I'm coming back anyway. If you get lonely, I'll be at my folks' house, trying to convince them that I'm a good girl after all."

"Good luck with that one," Brody said, sensing a letup in the tension, however slight. He'd never loved Joleen, and they'd had some wild fights in their time, but he liked her. Wanted her to be happy.

"You and me," Joleen mused, surprising him with the depth of the insight that came next, "we pretty much just use each other to keep everybody else at a safe distance, don't we?"

"Yeah," Brody agreed presently. "I think that's what we've been doing, all right."

"Huh," Joleen said decisively, as though she'd come to some conclusion.

"And it's time we both moved on," Brody added. *You go your way, and I'll go mine.*

"Just tell me who she is," Joleen urged.

"There isn't a specific *she,* Joleen."

"The hell there isn't, Brody Creed. I *know* you, remember? You've been on this path for a while now, coming back to Lonesome Bend, making up with Conner and Kim and Davis, building a house—" She made a moist sound then and, for one terrible moment, Brody feared Joleen was either already crying or about to. "Silly me," she finally went on. "I thought all that talk about not getting too serious was just that—talk. We go way back, Brody."

Brody shut his eyes for a moment, remembering things he'd been doing his best to forget right along. Joleen had been Conner's girlfriend, back in the day, and with plenty of help from him—Brody—she'd driven a wedge between the brothers that might have kept them estranged for a lifetime, instead of a decade.

And a decade, to Brody's mind, was plenty too long to be on the outs with Conner.

"I'm sorry if you misunderstood," Brody said quietly, when the air stopped sizzling with Joleen's ire. "But I never gave you any reason to think whatever it was we had together was going anywhere, Joleen, and I'm not responsible for what goes on in your imagination."

She sighed, calming down a little. "Is this the part where you say we'll always be friends?" she asked, at long last.

"That's up to you, Joleen," Brody said, wishing he could ask her not to come back, at least not right away, because things were complicated enough already. Trouble was, Lonesome Bend was as much her home as his, and she had every right to spend time there. "We can be friends, or we can steer clear of each other for a while and let the dust settle a little."

"I could make trouble for you, you know," Joleen reminded him mildly.

Was she serious or not? He couldn't tell.

"You could," he allowed.

"You might as well tell me who she is, Brody," Joleen went on reasonably, ignoring what he'd said. "I can find out with a phone call or two, anyway."

"Up to you," Brody reiterated. "Goodbye, Joleen."

She paused, absorbing the finality of his words. Gave another sniffle…and hung up on him.

Brody closed his phone and stood there looking at it for a few moments, frowning.

Barney, snugged down over by the stove, raised his

head off his muzzle and regarded his master with something resembling pity.

He was probably imagining that part, Brody decided.

"Women," he told the dog, before turning back to the computer and the message he'd been trying to write to Carolyn. "There's no making sense of them, no matter how you try. They say one thing when they mean another. They cry when they're sad, and when they're happy, too, so you never know where you stand."

Barney gave a little whimper and settled back into his snooze.

Grimly, Brody glared at the message box on the screen in front of him. Hope you're feeling better was as far as he'd gotten, as far as he was likely to *get,* if inspiration didn't strike soon.

There didn't seem to be much danger of that.

He rubbed his chin again, aware that his beard was growing in. He'd shaved just that morning—hadn't he?

Brody tried to round up his thoughts, get them going in the same direction, but it was hard going. He was mystified to find himself so confused and at a loss for words. He'd been a smooth talker all his life, he reflected, but when it came to Carolyn Simmons, it seemed, he was about as verbal as a pump handle. Presently, Brody gave up and hit the delete key, logged off of the computer and turned around in his chair.

The bed was still unmade, and there was still no woman in it.

The microwave and the minifridge, inanimate objects posing as some kind of kitchen, presented a sad image of the bachelor life.

The only bright spot in the whole place, Brody decided glumly, after mulling it all over, was the dog.

CHAPTER SIX

DENIAL, CAROLYN DECIDED, as she went through the motions of opening the shop for business promptly at nine the next morning, would be the watchword of the day.

All she had to do was pretend. That she hadn't gotten tipsy on wine at Kim and Davis's tamale supper, in front of Brody Creed.

That she hadn't leaned out the door of a hot guy's truck and thrown up on the side of the road.

That she hadn't made an utter and complete idiot of herself.

Like hell she hadn't. She'd done all those things and more, and the worst part was, she didn't know *why*. It wasn't like her to drink at all, let alone overindulge. She simply didn't have the capacity to assimilate alcohol, never had.

Now, confounded as well as queasy, Carolyn looked up at the Weaver, the art piece gracing the high place on the wall, seeking wisdom in all that quietness and color, but all she got was a crick in her neck and the conclusion that her longtime coping mechanism had failed her.

Without denial to fall back on, she'd be stuck with reality.

Yikes.

There were positive sides to the situation, though. She *had* slept through the night, at least, and two more aspirin, with a water chaser, had made her head stop pounding.

She hadn't been able to manage coffee, though, or even herbal tea.

Breakfast? Forget about it.

Her stomach was still pretty iffy.

So she'd fed Winston, taken a shower and gotten dressed for the day, choosing faux-alligator flats, black pants and a rather prim-looking white shirt over her usual: jeans, T-shirt and Western boots. She applied makeup—without blusher, she'd have had no color at all—and even put her hair up in a sort of twisty do she hoped looked casually elegant, then donned her one and only pair of gold posts.

She wanted to look…well, businesslike. A woman of substance and good sense.

But she'd settle for looking *sober*.

Tricia breezed in at nine-fifteen, wearing sandals and a soft green maternity sundress and carrying two mega-size cups of coffee from the take-out place down the street. She glowed like a woman who'd spent the night enjoying great sex with her adoring husband.

Carolyn felt a stab of envy. Great work, if you could get it.

Casting a glance at Carolyn before she set the cups on the display counter, Tricia smiled warmly, taking in the slacks and the shoes and the fussy shirt.

"Well, look at you," she observed finally. "All dressed up like somebody about to head over to the bank and ask for a big loan. Or apply for membership in a country club."

Carolyn sighed, and the truth escaped her in a rush. "I think I was trying to change my identity," she said.

The scent of the coffee, usually so appealing, made her stomach do a slow tumble backward. "Become somebody else. Lapse into permanent obscurity, disappear forever. Create my own one-woman witness protection program."

Tricia laughed. "You've got it bad," she said forthrightly. "And I'm not talking about the flu, here."

Carolyn's cheeks burned, and she felt her chin ratchet up a notch. "If you mean the hangover, thanks for reminding me. I already feel like four kinds of a fool, after everything that happened last night."

Tricia picked up one of the cups and held it out, and Carolyn shook her head, swallowed hard.

"You had a little too much wine," Tricia said gently, with a shrug in her tone. "It's no big deal, Carolyn—we've all done that at one time or another. And if you do have a hangover—your word, not mine—it doesn't show." She paused while she went behind the counter and stuck her purse into its usual cubbyhole. Then, straightening, she went on. "I was referring, my prickly friend, to the bare-socket electricity arcing between you and Brody all evening. I'm surprised all our hair didn't stand on end, and our skeletons didn't show through our skin."

Carolyn had to laugh, though the sound was hoarse and it hurt her throat coming out. "*That* was visual," she said. "And what an imagination you have, Tricia Creed. If there was anything 'arcing' between Brody and me, it was hostility."

"Sure," Tricia agreed smoothly, and a little too readily, fussing with a display of sachet packets beside the cash register. Unless a tour bus came through unexpectedly, they probably wouldn't be very busy that day, and

Carolyn's heart sank at the prospect of long hours spent making work where none existed.

"I'll check for internet orders," Carolyn said, desperate to change the course of their conversation before it meandered any deeper into Brody Territory. They kept the shop computer in their small office, a converted bedroom, off the living room. "Maybe we've sold a few more aprons online."

"Maybe," Tricia said, shooting another glance at Carolyn as she was about to turn and walk away. Then she came right out with it. "How come you didn't mention signing up for cyberdates to me, but Kim knew?"

Carolyn wanted to lie, but she simply couldn't. Not to Tricia, one of the first real friends she'd ever had. "I wasn't planning on telling *anybody*," she admitted ruefully, folding her arms. "Kim and I were upstairs, having lunch, and this message just popped up on my laptop screen." She drew in a breath, huffed it out again. "That website—Friendly Faces, I mean—is a little scary. The thing *talks*. If the computer is on, and a message comes in, it just pipes right up with the news. 'Somebody likes you!'" She threw her arms out wide, let her hands slap against her sides. "When that happened, Kim was onto my secret and I had no choice but to explain."

Tricia smiled. "Relax," she said. "It's a new world. Lots of people connect online before they meet in person."

"Easy for you to say," Carolyn pointed out. "You don't have to resort to desperate measures—*you're* already married."

Tricia gave a dreamy sigh. "Yes," she said. "I am most definitely married."

Carolyn barely kept from rolling her eyes.

Tricia came back from the land of hearts and flowers and cartoon birds swooping around with ribbons in their beaks and studied Carolyn with slightly narrowed eyes. "I just have one question," she said.

"Of course you do," Carolyn said, resigned. This was the troublesome thing about friendships—they opened up all these private places a person liked to keep hidden.

"Why go online and meet strangers when the perfect man is right in front of you?"

Carolyn pretended to look around the surrounding area in search of this "perfect man" of Tricia's. Arched her eyebrows in feigned confusion and set her hands on her hips. "He is? I don't see him."

"You know I'm talking about Brody," Tricia replied, going all twinkly and flushed again. She might have been talking about Brody, but it was a good bet she was *thinking* about Conner.

Carolyn reminded herself that Tricia meant well, just as Kim did. She *was* being prickly with her friend, and she regretted it.

"I'm sorry," she said.

"For what?" Tricia wanted to know.

"I might have been a little snappish."

"And *I* might have been meddling," Tricia said. Another long pause followed, then she added, "Was it really so bad, whatever happened between you and Brody?"

Carolyn opened her mouth, closed it again, stumped for an answer.

Tricia touched Carolyn's arm. "There I go, meddling again."

"Could we not talk about Brody, please?" Carolyn asked, after a long time. She realized she was hugging herself with both arms, as though a cold wind had blown through the shop and chilled her to the bone.

"Of course," Tricia said, her eyes filling. "Of course."

Carolyn turned on her heel and marched off to the bedroom-office, keeping her spine straight.

Was it really so bad, whatever happened between you and Brody?

Yes, answered some voice within Carolyn, too deep to be uttered aloud. *He was the first man I ever dared to love. I gave Brody Creed everything I had, everything I was and ever planned to be. I thought he was different from all the others—Mom, the social workers, the foster families—so I trusted him. In the end, though, he threw me away, just like they did. He left and I watched the road for him for months, hoping and praying he'd come back, and he stayed gone.*

So much for hope and prayer. When had either one of them ever done her any good at all?

Reaching the office, Carolyn booted up the computer, only to be rewarded with an all-too-familiar greeting as soon as she went online.

"Somebody likes you!"

"Imagine that," she muttered.

Why was this happening? She hadn't signed on to Friendly Faces through this computer; she'd used the laptop upstairs.

It was creepy.

On an annoyed impulse, Carolyn clicked on the Show Me! icon.

And there was a picture of a buckskin horse.

Give me a chance, read the message beneath the photo.

It had been posted in the middle of the night, and it was signed, Brody.

Carolyn put a hand to her mouth. Then, in a shaky voice, she called out, "Tricia?"

Her friend appeared almost immediately. Tricia was light on her feet, for someone so profoundly pregnant.

"Is something wrong?" she asked, from the doorway.

"Am I seeing things?" Carolyn countered, gesturing toward the screen.

Tricia crept forward and peered at the monitor. "That's Brody's horse," she said, very quietly. "Moonshine."

"Apparently," Carolyn quipped, "Moonshine is looking for action."

Tricia giggled, but it was a nervous sound. "*Brody* sent you a message through Friendly Faces?" she marveled. "Wow. He must *really* like you."

Carolyn felt a crazy thrill. "Yeah," she retorted. "That would be why he's hiding behind his *horse*."

"He knows you like horses," Tricia reasoned. It was a weak argument.

"Oh, for Pete's sake," Carolyn scoffed.

"You registered as 'Carol'?" Tricia asked, frowning a little.

"Never mind that," Carolyn said briskly. "What do I do now?"

"Go out with Brody?"

"Oh, right."

"What can it hurt? The two of you go out for a bite to eat, maybe take in a movie? Harmless fun."

"Nothing about Brody Creed is harmless," Carolyn said, with conviction.

"True," Tricia agreed, wide-eyed. "But is that the

kind of man you really want? Somebody *harmless,* who makes zero impact?"

"He scares me," Carolyn admitted. The words were out before she'd had a chance to vet them as something she actually wanted to say out loud. And Brody *did* scare her, because no one, not even her feckless mother, had ever had as much power to hurt her, to crush her, as he did.

"One date," Tricia negotiated. "You set the terms. How bad can that be?"

"Trust me," Carolyn said, "it can be *really* bad."

"He must have done you a number," Tricia ventured, meddling again and showing no signs of apologizing for it. "You can *tell* me, Carolyn."

"Like I told Kim?"

Tricia made the cross-my-heart motion with her right hand and then held it up in the oath position. "I will tell *no one.* Not even Conner."

Carolyn sighed. She turned to Tricia and, against years of conditioning, took a chance. "Brody was passing through Lonesome Bend," she said wearily, like an old-fashioned record player on slow speed. "It was years ago. I was house-sitting for Kim and Davis, and he— well, he just showed up on their doorstep. Something happened. Then something *else* happened. The next thing I knew, we'd been sharing a bed for a week and I was crazy in love with Brody Creed. We were making plans for a future together—babies, pets, a house somewhere on the ranch, the whole thing. Brody was going to reconcile with Conner, and with his aunt and uncle, and we were going to get married. Then, one morning, I woke up and found a note. 'Something came up,' he said, and he had to leave. That was it. He was gone."

"Oh," Tricia said, absorbing the story like an impact. "You didn't hear from him again?"

"He called me a month later, drunk out of his mind. It was worse than not hearing from him at all."

"I'm so sorry," Tricia whispered, looking so broken that Carolyn immediately forgot her own pain.

"Don't," Carolyn said. "Don't agonize over this, Tricia. It's ancient history. But you know what they say about history—those who fail to learn from it are condemned to repeat it."

"I love my brother-in-law," Tricia said, "but right now, I could wring his neck."

"The last thing I want is to turn you against Brody," Carolyn told her friend. "He's your husband's brother, Tricia. Your baby's uncle. It would be so, so wrong if what I've told you caused problems within the family. I couldn't bear that—families are precious."

Tricia hugged her, briefly but hard. "Don't worry about me," she said. "You need to do what's right for *you,* Carolyn. When was the last time you put yourself first?"

Carolyn searched her mind, then her soul, for an honest reply. "Always," she said. "And never."

Tricia was quiet for a long, long time. Then she said, "In the beginning, when I was first attracted to Conner, I mean, I resisted my feelings with every ounce of strength I could muster. I was *so* afraid. Nothing in my life had ever prepared me to believe in happy endings—not my parents' brief marriage or, after I was grown up, my own relationships. Nothing worked. Ever. Somewhere along the line, I decided that true love was something that happened in books and movies, and to other, luckier people, and that I was better off alone, because that way, I couldn't be hurt." She stopped, her eyes searching Carolyn's. "Pretty stupid, huh? Only one thing hurt worse than I thought loving and losing Conner Creed would, and that was not *allowing* myself to take the risk. And you know what? No matter what the future holds—even if, God forbid, Conner dies in his prime, or he leaves me, or whatever else the fates might throw at us—it would be worth it, because once you've loved someone the way I love Conner, once someone has loved you the way he loves me..." Tricia's blue eyes brimmed with tears again, and she swallowed before going on. "Once you've loved, and *been loved,* that way, nothing and no one can ever take it away. Whether it lasts five minutes or fifty years, that love becomes a permanent part of you."

Carolyn studied her friend. "It's that way for some people," she said, at some length.

"It can be that way for *you,*" Tricia insisted quietly.

"Not with Brody Creed, it can't," Carolyn replied. And she turned back to the monitor, clicked on the appropriate icon and replied to his message, fully intending to turn him down flat.

Instead, she found herself typing Nice horse and then clicked Send.

AFTER NUKING A frozen breakfast in the microwave, going out to the barn to feed Moonshine and walking the dog, Brody finally logged on to his computer at around nine-thirty. All the while, he was telling himself it didn't matter a hill of beans if he'd heard from Carolyn, aka Carol.

Barney, having chowed down on his kibble, sat at

Brody's feet, waiting patiently for whatever was next on the agenda and probably hoping he'd get to participate.

Brody grinned down at the mutt and flopped his ears around gently, by way of reassurance. "We ought to be on the range already," he confided to the animal. "Davis and Conner will be biting the heads off nails by now, and complaining to each other that some things just never change."

Barney opened his mouth wide and yawned.

Brody laughed and turned back to his computer just as an electronic voice chirped, "Someone likes you!"

"I sure as hell hope so," Brody told the dog, who, by that time, had stretched himself out for a spur-of-the-moment nap.

And there it was.

Nice horse, Carolyn had written.

Brody sighed. It wasn't a yes, but it wasn't a no, either.

He rubbed his hands together and thought hard.

Once again, inspiration eluded him.

Thanks, he finally wrote back. Want to go riding with me?

Brody sighed again, heavily this time, and shoved the fingers of one hand through his hair in frustration. He was a regular wiz with the ladies, he chided himself.

The truth was that he had *lot* to say to Carolyn Simmons, starting with "I'm sorry," but he'd sooner have his thoughts posted on a billboard in the middle of town than send them over the internet.

His cell phone rang.

Distracted, Brody hit Send, and immediately wished he hadn't.

"Hello," he said into the phone.

"What kind of outfit do you think we're running over here?" Conner demanded. "This is a working ranch, Brody—operative word, *working*—and it would be nice if you could drop by and do your part sometime before noon."

Brody laughed. "Now, Conner," he drawled, because he knew slow talking made his brother crazy, "you need to simmer down a little. Take life as it comes. The cattle have a thousand acres of grass to feed on, and the fences will get fixed—"

"Brody," Conner broke in tersely, "this is as much your ranch as it is mine. We split the profits down the middle, and *by God* we're going to do the same with the work!"

"What got up your backside?" Brody asked. "For a man getting regular sex, you're pretty testy."

He could literally feel Conner going from a simmer to a boil on the far end of that phone call.

"Enough of your bullshit," Conner almost growled. "Get over here, unless you want me coming after you."

"Maybe you're *not* getting regular sex," Brody speculated.

"Brody, I swear to God—"

"Okay, okay," Brody relented affably, logging off of the computer, pushing back his chair and rising to his feet. "Don't get your bloomers in a wad. I'm on my way."

Barney scrambled upright, with a lot of toenail scrabbling against the plank floor, and Brody didn't have the heart to leave him behind. He decided to give Moonshine a day off and drive out to the ranch in his truck.

It was big, that fancy new extended-cab truck, painted a bluish-silver color, and it had all the upgrades, from GPS to video screens in the backs of the front seats. For all the flash the rig had, Brody still missed his old pickup, the one he'd driven right down to the rust.

He hadn't had to worry about denting the fenders or scraping up the bed of the previous truck with feed sacks and tools. And it would have gone anywhere.

Unfortunately, it had finally breathed its last, a few months before, and Brody had been forced to sell it for scrap.

He opened the rear door on the driver's side and Barney leaped through the air like a movie dog showing off for the paparazzi. Settled himself on the far side and stared eagerly out the window.

Chuckling, Brody took his place behind the wheel and started up the engine. He should have been thinking about downed fences and stray calves and generally staying on Conner's good side, but his mind was stuck on Carolyn.

Nice horse? What the devil was *that* supposed to mean?

Fifteen minutes later, he and Barney pulled in at the main ranch house.

He let Barney out of the truck, watched as he and Valentino met in the driveway and sized each other up.

Conner strode out of the barn while the dogs were still getting to know each other, his face a thundercloud with features.

He started right in, tapping at the face of his watch with one index finger. "Damn it, Brody, do you have any idea what time it is?"

Brody didn't wear a watch. Hadn't for years. He went to bed when he felt like it and got up when he was darned good and ready, and old habits were hard to break.

"No," he replied smoothly, "I *don't* know what time it is, and if I did, I probably wouldn't give a rat's ass anyway."

Conner glowered at him, hard, but when it came right down to it, he couldn't sustain his bad humor. Hoarsely, and entirely against his stubborn Creed will, Conner laughed.

Brody grinned and slapped his brother on the shoulder. "That's better," he said. "You're going to be somebody's daddy one day soon, little brother, and that means you've got to stop stressing out about everything. What good will you be to that kid if you keel over from a heart attack?"

Conner shook his head, took his hat off and then plunked it back in place again. Shoved out a loud sigh. "You're impossible," he finally said.

"So they tell me," Brody replied lightly. "What's on the schedule today, boss?"

Conner let the word *boss* pass without comment and arched one eyebrow. "The usual. There are strays to round up, calves, mostly. Davis spotted half a dozen of them down by the river, but he didn't go after them because that gelding of his threw a shoe, and he had to head home to fetch another horse."

"We running low on horses these days?" Brody asked, with a pointed glance at the barn, and the surrounding corral and pasture area. He counted eight cayuses right there in plain sight.

"You know Davis," Conner said. "He wants to ride the roan, and it's up at his place, in the pasture. He's pigheaded and set in his ways, our uncle."

Brody grinned. "You'd think he was a Creed or something," he said.

Conner laughed again, started back toward the barn. "Let's ride, cowboy," he replied. "Calves aren't known for their intelligence, and we'll have a hassle on our hands if any of them take a tumble into the river and get swept off by the currents."

The possibility was real enough; they'd lost plenty of cattle, a few horses and a handful of people to the falls. The plunge was better than a hundred feet, and there were boulders directly below, in the white water.

This probably explained Conner's sour mood earlier, during that phone call.

Brody and Conner saddled their horses at the same pace, with the same motions, and when they rode out, they were side by side.

Barney and Valentino kept up.

Brody enjoyed that ride, enjoyed being with Conner, on horseback, and out in the open air.

But once the brothers reached the ridge overlooking the river, where a narrow trail ribboned off the dirt road and down the steep side-hill to the stony bank, the fun was over.

Five yearling calves bawled in loud dismay at edge, and a sixth was already in the drink, struggling in vain to regain its footing and get back to shore.

"How's this horse in the water?" Brody asked Conner, with a nod to his own mount, resetting his hat as he spoke.

"He's good," Conner said, with grave reluctance. "Brody, maybe you oughtn't to—"

But Brody cut him off with a whooping "Yee-haw" and headed straight down that hill, Snowy-River style, unfastening the leather strap that secured his coiled rope as he went.

Conner yelled a curse after him and followed.

Having gotten a head start, and with the trail barely wide enough for one horse, forget two, Brody reached the riverside first. He and the gelding he'd saddled back at the main barn splashed into the water at top speed.

Back in his rodeo days, Brody's event had been bronc riding, but he was a fair roper, as well. He looped that lariat high over his head, shot a wordless prayer heavenward and flung.

The rope settled around the calf in a wide circle of hemp, and Brody took up the slack. The yearling beef bawled again and paddled furiously, being too stupid to know he'd already been helped.

The current was strong, though, and it was work, for man *and* horse, hauling that noisy critter back to the riverbank.

Conner was mainly dry, except for a few splashes on his shirt and the legs of his jeans, and he'd corralled the other calves into a loud bunch, his well-trained cow pony expert at keeping the animals together.

Brody, of course, was soaked, but he laughed as he brought that calf out of the water, out of sheer jubilation.

"Looks to me like your horse is doing all the work," he called to Conner, swinging down from the saddle to grab hold of the rope and pull that calf along.

"You damn fool," Conner retorted, messing with his hat while that pony danced back and forth, containing the calves in a prescribed area, "you've been away from this ranch—and this river—for too long to go taking chances like that!"

Brody grinned, removed the lasso from around the calf's neck and prodded it toward the herd.

The poor critter didn't need much persuading and, for a bit, the cacophony got louder, while the baleful tale was told.

This time, Conner was in the lead as they drove that pitiful little herd back up the trail to high ground. Valentino and Barney waited up top, their hides dry and their tails wagging.

It just went to show, Brody figured, that they were the smart ones in this bunch.

"What is it with you and rivers, anyhow?" Conner grumbled, as they walked their horses slowly along the dirt road curving along the edge of the ridge.

Brody sighed, took off his hat and wrung the water out of it, leaving it a little worse for wear. "First you bitch because I wasn't here at the crack of dawn, punching cattle. Then, when I get a little wet pulling one out of a river, you complain about *that*. Damned if I know what, if anything, would make you happy."

Conner shook his head. "You always were a grandstander," he accused, though not with much rancor.

"Oh, hell," Brody groused back, "you've just got your tail in a twist because *you* wanted to show off your roping skills."

Conner let loose with a slow grin. "I can outrope, outshoot and outwrestle you any day of the week," he said, "and you know it."

Brody laughed at that. His clothes felt icy against his skin, and his boots were full of water—again. At this rate, he'd need a new pair every payday. "Keep telling yourself that, little brother, if it'll make you feel better."

"You could have roped that calf from the bank," Conner pointed out, almost grudgingly, after tugging his hat brim down low over his eyes because they were riding straight into the sun. "Instead, you risked your life—and the life of a perfectly good horse—to pull a John Wayne."

"I was safe the whole time," Brody replied, "and so was this horse. It was the *calf* that was in a fix, and I got him out of it. Seems like you ought to be glad about that, in place of griping like some old lady whose just found muddy footprints on her carpet."

Conner's jaw tightened and he looked straight ahead, as though herding six yearling calves along a country road required any real degree of concentration. When he did speak up, Conner caught Brody off-guard, as he had a way of doing.

"I reckon Carolyn's out to find a husband," he said, with a hint of a smirk lurking in his tone. "And she's not too picky about her choice, as long as she doesn't get you."

The words went right through Brody's defenses, as they'd no doubt been meant to do. Heat surged up his neck, and he glared over at Conner. The two dogs were traveling between them now, both of them panting but otherwise unfazed by the morning's adventure.

"If you're looking for a fight, little brother, you've found one," Brody said. "As far as I'm concerned, we can get down off these horses right now and settle this discussion in the middle of the road."

Conner smiled without looking at Brody and rode blithely on. The main part of the herd was up ahead, grazing on spring grass.

The stray calves seemed to know that, too, because

they picked up speed and quit carrying on like they were being killed.

Conner didn't speak again until they'd reached the edge of the range, where the view seemed to go on forever, in every direction.

Even with his hackles raised, Brody couldn't ignore that scenery. The land, the trees, the mountains and the sky, the twisting river—all of it was as much a part of him as his own soul.

Conner raised his hat and swung it in a wide arch, as a greeting to the mounted ranch hands on the far side of that sea of cattle.

Then he turned to look Brody's way. "You'd better get on home," he said. "Get out of those wet clothes before you come down with something."

Brody just sat there, breathing in his surroundings, letting it all saturate him, through and through. "I'm already half-dry," he argued, "and not the least bit delicate, for your information."

Conner laughed. "I got to you, didn't I?" he said, in quiet celebration. "I do like getting a rise out of the great Brody Creed."

"Why don't you go to hell?" Brody suggested mildly.

Again, Conner laughed. It seemed there was no end to his amusement that morning. "Are you just going to stand back and watch Carolyn order up a husband online?" he asked, a few moments later.

"She can do what she wants," Brody bit out, more nettled than he would have cared to admit.

"What do *you* want, Brody?"

"Me?" Brody asked. "What do I want?"

"That was my question, all right, " Conner replied, implacable and amused.

"Fine," Brody answered, nudging his horse into a trot, figuring the dogs had had time to rest up a little by then. "I want you to stay the hell out of my business, *that's* what I want."

CHAPTER SEVEN

IT WAS TIME to take action, Carolyn thought, a wicked little thrill going through her as she reread Brody's response to her message earlier that day.

Want to go riding with me?

She bit her lower lip.

Brody had asked her to go riding with him, and she was actually considering it. A sad commentary on her level of intelligence, she figured, since she'd been burned, and badly, the *last* time she played with fire.

And she'd be doing exactly that if she spent any time alone with Brody Creed, no doubt about it.

That was that, then.

She wasn't getting any younger, and if she ever wanted a home and a husband and children, if she ever wanted to take *real* family vacations, instead of buying souvenir mugs at garage sales and pretending she'd been somewhere, she had to do something, take matters into her own hands.

Prince Charming, if he'd ever been headed in her direction in the first place, had obviously been detained.

"Carolyn?" Tricia appeared in the office doorway, a merciful if temporary distraction from her troubling thoughts. True to Carolyn's prediction, they hadn't had a customer all morning, or since lunch, and the apron orders from the website were wrapped and ready for shipping. "I'm going now. Do you want me to drop the packages off at the post office before I head for home?"

Not wanting Tricia to see that she'd been checking Friendly Faces, Carolyn turned to face her friend with a wide smile, blocking the computer monitor from view.

She hoped.

"That would be great," she said brightly. *Too* brightly, probably. "Thanks, Tricia."

Tricia eyed her curiously, maybe even a little suspiciously. "You'll be okay working alone for the rest of the day?" she persisted.

I've been working alone my whole life. Why would today be any different?

"I'll be fine," Carolyn promised cheerfully. "I'm just tying up a few loose ends online, then I'll go upstairs and start sewing. We're going to need more aprons soon, and I'd like to finish the gypsy skirt before I die of old age."

Tricia hesitated a moment, then smiled and left the doorway. "See you tomorrow," she called, in parting.

"'Bye!" Carolyn sang out, all merry innocence.

Then she turned back to the computer, and Brody's brief message.

If she agreed to go anywhere with this man, even for a horseback ride, she needed her head examined.

In the first note, he'd asked for a second chance.

A second chance to hurt her, to rip her heart out and stomp on it? Was that what he'd meant? Or was she being too cynical? Suppose the man simply wanted to be friends?

That would make sense, wouldn't it, given the way they were always running into each other at social functions, both in town and on the Creed ranch? Maybe

Brody was as tired of those awkward encounters as she was.

He'd said as much, just the other day, but then he'd gone and kissed her and confused the issue all over again.

And then there was the fact that Carolyn never felt freer, or more alive—or lonelier—than when she was on a horse's back, riding through wide-open spaces.

To have someone riding alongside her out there on her favorite trails, someone who knew horses and was comfortable around them, well, that would make the experience close to perfect.

Adrenaline jolted through Carolyn's system when she made the reckless decision: she would accept Brody's invitation. It was, after all, a horseback ride, not an elopement, or a wild weekend in Vegas, whooping it up in the buff.

Heck, it wasn't even a date, really.

Still, the idea made her nerves leap around under her skin like tiny Cirque du Soleil performers determined to outdo themselves.

What she needed, as she'd already concluded, was some sort of emotional *insurance,* protection against Acts of Brody, and there was only one way to get that— by going out with other guys. As many other guys as she reasonably could.

Not only would they insulate her, create and maintain a safe distance between her and Brody, but she also might actually fall for one of them and forget him entirely.

What began as a defense mechanism could turn out to be the kind of true and lasting love she'd always dreamed of finding.

And wouldn't *that* be something?

Yes, she would make a definite and honest effort.

She finally entered a reply to Brody's note, a lackluster okay and flashed it off to his mailbox.

She checked her new messages then.

It was sort of gratifying to know she was popular on Friendly Faces—five different men wanted to get acquainted with her, three from Denver and its close environs and two from right there in Lonesome Bend.

Forehead creased with the effort to place the pair of locals, Carolyn studied their photos, one after the other, and came up with no clear recollection of either of them.

Both were moderately attractive, in their thirties.

Richard was tall, if his bio could be believed—wasn't she living proof that people stretched the truth, calling herself Carol?—with dark hair and brown eyes. He was a technical writer, divorced, with no children, and he'd moved to Lonesome Bend only a month before. Since he worked at home, he hadn't made many friends.

He liked to cook, loved dogs, but was violently allergic to cats.

Carolyn, mindful of Winston, gently dispatched Richard to the recycle bin.

The other candidate was named Ben, and he, like Richard, was a fairly recent transplant to the community. He was a widower, with an appealing smile, a nine-year-old daughter and a job that took him all over the western states, fighting forest fires.

He looked like a nice guy, which didn't mean for one second that he couldn't have made the whole story up, invented the daughter, the adventurous career, the dead wife. Stranger things had happened, especially when it came to online dating.

Still, if she was going to have any chance at all against Brody Creed and his many questionable charms, assuming he even meant to turn that effortless dazzle on her anyway, she had to do *something,* get the proverbial ball rolling, here.

After drawing and releasing a very deep breath, Carolyn responded to Ben's friendly inquiry with a short, chatty missive of her own. Not wanting to give away too much information—Lonesome Bend was, after all, a small town—she chose her answers carefully.

Ben's response was immediate. Did the man have nothing better to do than hover over his computer, waiting for his trial membership in Friendly Faces to pay off big?

Hi, Carol, he'd written. Nice to hear from you. So to speak.

Carolyn reminded herself that what *she* was doing could conceivably be described as hovering, and she certainly had better things to do, so she'd better get off her high horse, and answered, I like your picture.

I like that you didn't bail out on your daughter after your wife died.

If you even have a daughter.

If there isn't a current wife, very much alive, innocently cooking your favorite meal or ironing one of your shirts at this very moment, unaware that you're flirting with other women online.

Carolyn reined in her imagination then, but it wasn't easy, and she didn't know how long she could keep it from running wild again.

I like yours, too, Ben responded. I'm new at this computer-dating thing. How about you?

Brand-new, Carolyn confirmed. It's awkward.

Tell me about it, Ben answered.

Carolyn drew another deep breath, rubbed the palms of her hands together. What brought you to Lonesome Bend?

That seemed innocuous enough.

I wanted to raise Ellie in a small town, and my late wife's family lives nearby.

That's nice, Ben. Where did you live before?

Down in L.A. I'm not scared of a wildfire, but the traffic on the 405 is another matter, especially when Ellie's in the car.

Carolyn smiled. Ben was a conscientious father, and he had a sense of humor. She began to warm up to the conversation a little, though she was still wary of the man. I'm not crazy about crowded freeways myself, she replied.

Ben came back right away with Have you always lived in Lonesome Bend?

Carolyn hesitated. I came here eight years ago, she wrote. Before that, I traveled a lot.

You're mysterious, Ben replied, adding a winking-face icon.

Hardly, Carolyn typed. I'm not a woman with a past or anything exciting like that.

Unless, of course, my week-long, red-hot affair with Brody Creed makes me a woman with a past.

The thought of Brody, even in that context, gave Carolyn a twinge of guilt, but she shook it off quickly. It wasn't as if she was cheating on him, for heaven's sake.

So why did it feel that way?

Ellie just came in, Ben told her, and she's trying to get my attention, so I'd better find out what's up. Hope we can chat again soon, Carol.

Me, too, Carolyn wrote in response.

Liar, accused the voice in her head, the one she was always telling to shut up. *You're interested in* using *this guy to keep Brody at arms' length, nothing else. And, admit it, Ben's* other *main attraction is that he has a young daughter.*

"Shut up," Carolyn told the voice.

Then she logged off, wrote a hasty note for any customer who might happen by and taped it to the front door.

Working upstairs today. Just ring the bell, and I'll be right down to let you in, she'd printed, in large letters.

Always better off when she was busy, Carolyn felt pretty chipper as she turned the handle on the dead bolt and headed for the staircase.

Winston, who seemed to be in an unusually circumspect mood that day, scampered after her and, when she entered the kitchen, leaped gracefully onto his usual lookout perch, the windowsill.

Carolyn fussed over him a little, scratching behind his ears and nuzzling his silky scruff once, and washed her hands at the sink, prior to fixing them both lunch.

Winston had his beloved half tin of water-packed sardines, eating off a chipped china saucer right there on the windowsill, while Carolyn nibbled her way through a peanut butter and jelly sandwich, breaking all the food rules by foregoing a plate and standing up while she ate.

Actually, she could have argued that there were sensible reasons for her choice.

Number one, her sewing machine was on the table, and she'd be working there in a little while, and a stray drop of jelly might stain a piece of fabric. Furthermore, who *really* ate sandwiches off a plate?

In any case, the sandwich was soon gone, rendering the whole subject moot. Carolyn washed her hands again, fetched the gypsy skirt from the hook on the other side of her bedroom door and took a few sweet moments just to admire the creation.

It really *was* gorgeous, she thought, loving the way the gossamer ribbons shimmered and shifted. The reds, golds, blues and greens seemed to ripple, like liquid light.

Not for the first time, Carolyn was seized by a crazy urge to *keep* that skirt, alter it to fit her own figure and never let it go. She held it close against her chest for a few moments, as though prepared to defend it against a crazed mob.

"You're being silly," she murmured aloud.

Still, the skirt was so pretty, almost animate with all that subtle motion going on, a true work of art. *Her* art, born of her dreams and her imagination and all the fairy-tale hopes she'd cherished as a lonely child.

She ached to hold on to this one piece, this glorious thing woven with strands spun in the deepest places of her own heart.

Practicality took over quickly.

She'd been over this with herself before, hadn't she? A garment like this should be worn, seen, enjoyed. Where would she, Carolyn Simmons of Lonesome Bend, Colorado, wear such a thing?

Horseback riding?

Sure, there were parties now and then, and she was

always invited, but the occasions were never formal—people held cookouts in their backyards, and bingo was big on Wednesday evenings, in the basement of the Moose Lodge, and every year, on the weekend closest to the Fourth of July, there was an amateur rodeo and a visiting carnival.

The closest Lonesome Bend ever got to glamour was when the lodge sponsored a dance the third Saturday of every other month. The music was live, always country-western, and good enough that people came all the way from Denver to dance to it.

Most of the women wore jeans to the gathering, with a slightly fancier shirt than they might ordinarily don, and they fussed with their hair and makeup, too, but that was pretty much the extent of it.

Carolyn would have looked like a fool, just about anywhere she ever went, showing up in that skirt.

She sighed, put the skirt back on its hanger and then back on the hook behind the bedroom door. She'd finish it another day, when she wasn't feeling so much like Cinderella left behind to sweep floors on the night of the prince's ball.

Resolutely, she brewed a cup of herbal tea and got out a stack of fabric purchased on a recent shopping trip to Denver. By then, she'd made so many aprons—frilly ones, simple ones, ones for kids as well as adults—that she no longer needed to measure.

She chose a bluish-lavender calico from the pile, smiling at the small floral print and the tactile pleasure of crisp and colorful cloth ready to be made up into something useful. She decided to stick with the retro designs that sold so well through the online version of the shop and pictured the end result in her mind's eye.

Then, after eyeballing the fabric once again, Carolyn took up her sewing shears and began to cut.

Sewing, like riding horses, always consumed her, drew her in, made her forget her worries for a while. She got lost in it, in a good way, and invariably came away refreshed rather than fatigued.

The apron came together in no time, a perky, beruffled thing with lace trim stitched to the pockets.

Delighted, Carolyn set it aside, to be pressed later, and delved into her fabric stash again. This time she chose a heavier weight cotton, black and tan checks with little red flowers occupying alternate squares.

She went with retro again, savoring the whir of the small motor, the flash of the flying needle and the familiar scents of fabric sizing and sewing machine oil.

When the doorbell rang downstairs, just as Carolyn was finishing up apron number two, she was so startled by the sound, ordinary as it was, that she jumped and nearly knocked over her forgotten cup of tea, now gone cold.

She glanced at the clock above the stove—three forty-five in the afternoon, already?—and, remembering the note she'd stuck to the front door, in case some prospective shopper happened by, shouted from the top of the inside staircase, "Coming!"

The bell rang again, more insistently this time.

Skipping the normal protocol by not looking out one of the flanking windows first, Carolyn opened the door.

Brody was standing on the porch, his expression so grim that Carolyn felt alarmed, thinking Tricia had gone into premature labor or someone had been in an accident.

She gulped, fumbled with the hook on the screen

door that separated them. Through the mesh, she noted Brody's wrinkled clothes, mussed hair and disturbing countenance.

"Brody...what—?"

He'd taken off his hat at some point, and now he slapped it once against his right thigh. "Can I come in?" he bit out. Then, almost grudgingly, "Please?"

Carolyn's concern eased up a little then, as she realized Brody was frustrated—maybe even angry—but not sad, as he surely would have been if he were bearing bad news.

She gave one slightly abrupt nod instead of speaking, not trusting herself to be civil now that Brody's irritation had sparked and spread to her, like wildfire racing over tinder-dry grass.

Once the door was open, Brody practically stormed over the threshold, giving Carolyn the immediately infuriating impression that if she didn't get out of his way, she'd be run over.

So she stood her ground, and that proved to be a less than brilliant choice, because they collided and the whoosh of invisible things reaching flash point was nearly audible.

"What?" Carolyn demanded, and found herself flushing.

His nose was half an inch from hers, if that, and fierce blue flames burned in his eyes, and his words, though quiet, struck her like stones. "I. Don't. Like. Games."

Carolyn felt several things then, not the least of which was a slow-building rage, but there was a good bit of confusion in the mix, too, and a strange, soft, *scary* kind of excitement.

"*What* are you talking about?" she asked tartly. It would have been prudent, she supposed, to take a step or two backward, out of Brody's force field, but for some reason, she couldn't move.

"I'm *talking*," Brody all but growled, after tossing his hat in the general direction of the antique coat tree that dominated the entryway, "about this whole Friendly Faces thing. You trying to scare up a husband online. It's all wrong—"

Carolyn's temper, mostly under control before, flared up. *"Wrong?"* she repeated dangerously.

Brody sighed, but he was still putting out the same officious vibes. "Okay, maybe *wrong* wasn't the best word," he said.

"Maybe it wasn't," Carolyn replied succinctly, folding her arms and digging in her heels.

"I hate to break this to you," Brody spouted, leaning in again—she kind of liked it when he did that, even though it *was* infuriating—"but you can't just go around trusting people you've never even met. *Men tell lies,* Carolyn."

Carolyn widened her eyes in mock surprise. "Really?" she trilled, as though she just couldn't conceive of the possibility.

She saw his jaws clamp down, watched with some satisfaction as he relaxed them by a visible effort.

"Men tell lies," she repeated, amazed. Then she stabbed a finger into his chest and said, "Oh, yes, *that's right,* Brody. I remember now. *You* lied to me, through your perfect white teeth!"

"I did not lie to you," Brody lied.

"Oh, no? You said you cared about me—you wanted to stay and make things right with your family. Settle down and start a family. And then you left, vanished, flew the coop!" Carolyn realized she was perilously close to tears, and she was damned if she'd cry in front of the man who had broken her heart so badly that even after more than seven years, she wasn't over it.

So she turned away from Brody, not wanting him to see her face.

He caught hold of her shoulder, his grasp firm but not hard enough to hurt, and made her look at him again.

"I meant everything I said to you, Carolyn," he said evenly.

He had *not,* she recalled, with a terrible clarity, said he loved her. Not in words, anyway.

"But then *something came up,* as you put it in that note you left me, and you hit the road and left me alone to wonder what I did wrong," Carolyn accused, in an angry whisper.

Getting mad, in her opinion, was a lot better than bursting into tears. And it wasn't just Brody she was furious with. She blamed herself most of all, for being gullible, for loving and trusting the wrong man and maybe missing out on the *right* one because she'd wasted all this time loving him. Because she'd so wanted to believe what Brody told her. What his body told hers.

"I regret leaving like I did," Brody said. "But I had to go. I flat-out didn't have a choice, under the circumstances."

"And what would those *circumstances* be?" Carolyn asked archly. "Another bronc to ride? Another buckle to win? Or was it just that some formerly reluctant cowgirl wannabe was willing to go to bed with you?"

Brody closed his eyes for a moment. He looked pale,

like a man in pain, but when he opened them again, the frustration was back. "If that's the kind of person you think I am," he snapped, "then it seems to me you ought to be *glad* I took off and saved you all the trouble of putting up with me!"

"Who says I *wasn't* glad?" Carolyn demanded. Who *was* this hysterical person, speaking through her? Was she *possessed?*

"You're not going to listen to one damn thing I say, are you?" Brody shot back.

"No," Carolyn replied briskly. "Probably not."

"Fine!" Brody barked.

"Fine," Carolyn agreed.

"Reoww!" added Winston, from the top of the stairs. His hackles were up and his tail was all bushed out and he looked ready to pounce.

On Brody.

Guard-cat on duty.

"It's all right, Winston," Carolyn told the fractious feline. "Mr. Creed is just about to leave."

Brody made a snorting sound, full of contempt, swiveled around and retrieved his hat from the floor next to the coat tree, where he'd flung it earlier.

He wrenched open the front door, looked back at Carolyn and growled, "We're still going on that horseback ride."

Carolyn opened her mouth to protest, but something made her close it without saying the inflammatory thing that sprang to her mind. She didn't like to use bad language if she could avoid it.

"You agreed and that's that," Brody reminded her tersely. "A deal is a deal."

With that, he was gone.

The door of Natty McCall's gracious old house closed hard behind him.

Carolyn got as far as the stairs before plunking herself down on the third step from the bottom, shoving her hands into her hair and uttering a strangled cry of pure, helpless aggravation.

Winston, having pussyfooted down the stairs, brushed against her side, purring.

Carolyn gave a bitter little laugh and swept the animal onto her lap, cuddling him close and burying her face in the lush fur at the back of his neck.

Being a cat, and therefore independent, he immediately squirmed free, leaped over two steps to stand, disgruntled, on the entryway floor, looking up at her in frank disapproval, tail twitching.

"You've decided to *like* Brody Creed after all, haven't you?" Carolyn joked ruefully, getting to her feet. "You've gone over to the dark side."

"Reow," said Winston, indignantly.

Carolyn made her way upstairs, determined not to let the set-to with Brody ruin what remained of the day. She had tea to brew—that would settle her nerves—and aprons to sew for the website and the shop, a *life* to get on with, damn it.

Instead of doing either of those things right away, though, Carolyn went instead to her laptop.

She turned it on and waited, tapping one foot.

Practically the moment the computer connected to the internet, the machine chimed, "Somebody likes your picture!"

"Good," Carolyn said.

While she'd been offline, six more men had taken a shine to her—or to Carol, her recently adopted persona, anyway—and while five of them were definite rejects, the sixth was a contender, right from the instant Carolyn saw his photo.

His name was Slade Barlow, and he hailed from a town called Parable, up in Montana. For the time being, he lived in Denver. Like Ben, the firefighter, he was a widower, with a child. His eleven-year-old-son, Brendan, attended a boarding school there in Colorado but spent weekends and holidays with him.

"Hmm," Carolyn said aloud, clicking on the response link. Tell me about Brendan, she typed into the message box.

Slade apparently wasn't online, but Ben was, as she soon learned, when he popped up with a smiley face and a hello.

Carolyn, jittery but determined, responded with a hello of her own.

How about meeting me for a cup of coffee? he asked. Page After Page Book Store, on Main Street, five o'clock this afternoon?

Carolyn's first impulse was to shy away, but her most recent run-in with Brody was fresh in her mind, too. The *nerve* of the man, showing up at her home and place of business the way he had, and *announcing* that she *would* go horseback riding with him, simply because she'd made the mistake of agreeing to his invitation.

She consulted the stove clock, saw that it was four-thirty.

She would, she decided, *show* Brody Creed that he couldn't go around dictating things, like he was the king of the world, or something.

Okay, she wrote. Page After Page, five o'clock. How will we recognize each other?

Ben replied with a jovial LOL—laugh out loud—and another of those winking icons he seemed to favor. *I look just like my profile photo,* he responded. *Hopefully, so do you.*

Right, Carolyn answered. *Was there a computer icon for scared to death? See you there.*

Half an hour later, having refreshed her makeup and let down her hair, Carolyn arrived at Page After Page. The bookstore was, at least, familiar territory—she spent a lot of her free time there, nursing a medium latte and choosing her reading matter with care.

She spotted Ben right away, sitting at a corner table in the bookstore coffee shop, a book open before him.

As advertised, he looked like his picture. He was a little shorter than she'd expected, but well-built, with a quick smile, curly light brown hair and warm hazel eyes that smiled when he spotted her.

"Carol?" he asked, standing up.

Good manners, then.

Guilt speared Carolyn's overactive conscience. "Actually," she said, approaching his table slowly, "my name is Carolyn, not Carol."

He laughed, revealing a healthy set of very white teeth, extending one arm for a handshake. He wore jeans, a long-sleeved T-shirt in a dusty shade of blue and an air of easy confidence. "And mine is Bill, not Ben."

The confession put Carolyn at ease—mostly. She managed a shaky smile and sat down in the second chair at Ben's—*Bill's*—table. "Do you really have a nine-year-old daughter named Ellie?" she asked.

"Yes," Bill replied, sitting only when Carolyn was settled in her own chair. "Do you really work in a bank, have two dogs and like to bowl?"

"No," Carolyn admitted, coloring a little. "I lied about my job, my hobbies and my pets. Is that a deal-breaker?"

Bill chuckled. His eyes were so warm, dancing in his tanned face.

And as attractive as he was, he wasn't Brody.

Too bad.

"What's the truth about you, Carol—*yn?*" he asked, smiling.

"I sew a lot, I look after a friend's cat and I'm in business with a friend," Carolyn confessed, after a few moments of recovery. She blushed. "And I can't remember the last time I was so nervous."

Ben—*Bill*—smiled. "I don't sew, I'm strictly a dog-person and I fight fires for a living, just as I said in my bio. That said, I'm amazed, because despite all the prevarications, you look just like your picture. You're beautiful, Carolyn."

At that, the blush burned in Carolyn's face. She looked down. "Flatterer," she said.

Bill smiled. "What can I get you?" he asked.

"I beg your pardon?" Carolyn countered, a beat behind.

"Coffee?" Bill said, grinning. "Latte? Café Americano? Espresso with a double-shot of what-the-hell-am-I-doing-here?"

Finally, Carolyn relaxed. A little. "Latte," she said. "Nonfat, please."

Bill smiled, nodded, rose and went to the counter to order a nonfat latte.

Carolyn, desperate for something to do in the meantime, checked out the book he'd been reading when she approached.

You could tell a lot about a person by what they liked to read.

A Single Father's Guide to Communication with a Preteen Girl.

Well, Carolyn thought, trust her to meet up with a guy who was both sensitive and masculine *after* she'd been spoiled for functional relationships by Brody Creed.

Presently, Bill returned with her latte, looking pleasantly rueful. "Confession time," he said, with a sigh, as he sat down again. "I'm on the rebound, Carol—Carolyn. I didn't mention that in my profile."

"No," Carolyn said, oddly relieved. She reached for her latte, took a sip. It was very hot. "You didn't."

"Her name," Bill told her, "is Angela. We're all wrong for each other."

Carolyn considered the foam on her latte for a long moment. "His name is Brody," she said. "Two people were never more mismatched than the two of us."

A silence fell.

"Well, then," Bill finally said. "We have *something* in common, don't we?"

"Are you in love?" Carolyn asked, after a very long time and a lot of latte. "With Angela, I mean?"

"I don't know," Bill replied. "One minute, I want to spend the rest of my life with the woman, the next, I'd just as soon join the Foreign Legion or jump off the Empire State Building."

Carolyn wanted to cry. She also wanted to laugh. "Love sucks," she said, raising her latte cup. Bill touched his cup to hers.

"Amen," he said. "Love definitely sucks."

CHAPTER EIGHT

IF CAROLYN HAD had any say as to whom she fell in love with, she would definitely have chosen Bill Venable, brave fighter of forest fires, devoted father of a nine-year-old daughter, all-around good-looking hunk of a guy.

Alas, she *had* no such influence in an unpredictable universe, but she knew early on that she'd found a valuable ally in the man who bought her a latte.

"So, tell me more about Angela," she said, stirring her latte and avoiding Bill's gaze. "Does she live in Lonesome Bend?"

Bill cleared his throat, looked away, looked back. Finally nodded. "She teaches third grade at the elementary school," he said.

"I see," Carolyn answered, without guilt, because in many ways, she *did* see. "So what's the problem between the two of you?"

"She doesn't like my job," Bill answered, after pondering a while. "Firefighting, I mean. Too dangerous, keeps me away from home too much, et cetera."

"Yikes," Carolyn observed. "How does Ellie feel about Angela?"

"She adores her," Bill admitted. "And the reverse is true. Ellie thinks Angela would make the perfect stepmother. It's a mutual admiration society with two members. Trust me, this is not my daughter's usual reaction to the women I date."

"So the fundamental problem is your job?" Carolyn inquired, employing a tactful tone. While she understood Bill's dedication to his work, she sympathized with Angela, too. Love was risky enough, without one partner putting his life on the line on a regular basis.

Bill thrust out a sigh. "Yeah," he said.

"Maybe you could look into another kind of career," Carolyn suggested, already knowing what his answer would be.

Bill shook his very attractive head. Too bad he didn't arouse primitive instincts in Carolyn the way Brody did, because he was *seriously* cute. "I *love* what I do," he replied. "Flying an airplane. Putting out fires. It is a definite high."

"But...dangerous," Carolyn said.

"Well," Bill affirmed, "*yes*. But I'd go crazy doing anything else. The boredom—" He fell silent again, his expression beleaguered. Obviously, he'd been over this ground a lot, with Angela and within the confines of his own head.

Carolyn waited a beat, then went ahead and butted into a situation that wasn't any of her darn fool business in the first place. "What about your daughter, Bill?" she asked gently. "How does Ellie factor into this whole job thing?"

He sighed, shook his head again, aimed for a smile but missed. "I love that child with all my heart, and I want to do what's best for her," he said. "Keep her safe and happy and healthy. Raise her to be a strong woman, capable of making her own choices and taking care of herself and, if it comes to that, supporting a couple of kids on her own. But—"

Again, Bill lapsed into pensive silence.

"But?" Carolyn prompted quietly, after giving him a few moments to collect his thoughts.

"But," Bill responded, managing a faint grin, "like I said before, I love what I do. Doesn't that matter, too? And what kind of example would I be setting for Ellie if I took the easy route, tried to please everybody but myself?"

Carolyn toyed with her cup, raising and lowering her shoulders slightly in an I-don't-know kind of gesture. It was remarkable, connecting so quickly with another person—a *male* person, and someone she hadn't known existed until she signed on at Friendly Faces.

They were so simpatico, she and Bill, that anyone looking on would probably have thought they'd been close friends for years.

Too bad there was no buzzing charge, no *zap,* between them, like there was between herself and Brody and, it was a sure bet, between Bill and his Angela.

"No," she said, in belated response to his question. "Of course you can't live to please other people, not if you hope to be happy, anyhow." Carolyn paused before asking, "Does Ellie worry about you, when you're away fighting fires, I mean?"

Bill gave a raspy chuckle. "Probably," he acknowledged. "Ellie never lets on that she's scared something might happen to me—she just tells me to be careful. The thing is, even though she's only nine, she seems to get where I'm coming from better than Angela does."

Carolyn took a sip of her coffee, which was finally cool enough to drink without burning her tongue. Now, she thought, with the inevitable rush of reluctance, it was *her* turn to open up.

Sure enough, Bill ducked his head to one side and a quizzical little quirk tugged at the corner of his mouth. "You're a beautiful woman, Carolyn," he said. "Half the men in the county, if not the state, must be trying to catch your eye. What prompted you to sign up with an online dating service?"

"Curiosity?" Carolyn speculated, blushing a little.

He smiled, settled back in his chair, watching her. "Are you looking for friends, a good time, or a partner for life?" he asked.

There was nothing offensive in his tone or manner, and he positively radiated sincerity. Bottom line, Bill was easy to talk to, perhaps *because* he was a virtual stranger and, therefore, the two of them had no issues, no shared baggage, nothing to get in the way of friendship.

"It's not a new story," she replied, quietly miserable. "I fell for the wrong man, I got hurt—fill in the blanks and you'll probably have it just about right."

Bill arched an eyebrow, waited. On top of everything else working in his favor, the man was a good listener. And all she could drum up was a walloping case of *like*.

He was the big brother she'd never had.

The pal.

And he wasn't even gay, for Pete's sake.

Carolyn squirmed on her chair, not sure how much more she ought to say. This *was* their first meeting, after all, and as genuine as Bill Venable seemed, it certainly wasn't out of the realm of possibility that she was totally, completely, absolutely *wrong* about him.

It had happened before, hadn't it?

Once, she'd been convinced that she knew Brody Creed, through and through. After a long string of shallow, going-nowhere-fast relationships, she'd believed in him, been convinced he was The One, taken the things he said and did at face value, only to be burned in the back draft of all that passion when he showed his true colors and lit out.

And there was that other lapse in judgment, too—when she'd thought she'd hit her stride by becoming a nanny. She'd trusted her movie-star boss implicitly, admired his down-to-earth manner, his apparent devotion to his wife and small daughter.

Until he'd come on to her, forcing her to abandon a job—and a child—she'd loved.

Carolyn closed her eyes, remembering—*pummeled by*—the rearview mirror image of little Storm running behind her car, screaming for her to come back.

Come back.

Without saying a word, Bill reached across the table and took her hand in a brotherly way. Squeezed it lightly.

Carolyn opened her eyes again, smiled weakly. Enough, she decided, was enough. For now, anyway.

"I should be getting home," she said, bending to fumble under the table for her purse. "My cat will be wondering where I am."

Bill sighed, glanced at his watch and nodded. "I'm sure Ellie's perfectly happy at her grandparents' house," he said agreeably, "but it'll be suppertime soon, and when I'm in town, I try to make sure we're both sitting at the same table for at least one meal a day."

"That's nice," Carolyn said, feeling awkward now.

Supper, for her, was usually a lonesome affair, something she did to stay alive.

She and Bill rose from their chairs at the same moment.

He walked her to the door, opened it for her, waited until she stepped out onto the sidewalk.

It was a balmy May evening, shot through with the first faint lavender tinges of twilight, and there were lots of people out and about, just strolling, or talking to each other under streetlamps that would come on soon, glad to be outdoors.

Winter was long in Lonesome Bend, and good weather was not only savored, it was also celebrated.

Friends smiled and waved, their expressions both kindly and curious as they took note of Carolyn's escort, a man few, if any of them, actually knew.

By the time she went to bed that night, she thought, with a little smile, word would be all over town. Carolyn Simmons was *seeing someone,* and that someone *wasn't* Brody Creed.

Since her car was parked on the street, in plain view of at least a dozen fine citizens, she felt no compunction about letting Bill walk her to it and open the door for her.

"I had a great time," he said, his gaze direct as he waited for her to get settled behind the wheel.

"Me, too," Carolyn said, fastening her seat belt and sticking her key into the ignition.

"Friends?" he asked, with a wry grin.

"Friends," Carolyn agreed.

Bill stepped back, waved and watched from the sidewalk as she drove away.

"WHO IS HE?" Tricia demanded eagerly, when she entered the shop the next morning.

She hadn't even put away her purse yet.

Carolyn, smiling to herself, pretended a keen interest in unpacking the most recent delivery of goat-milk soap.

"And don't say you don't know what I'm talking about," Tricia warned, waggling a finger. Her eyes sparkled with mischievous affection. "Three different people called the ranch last night to ask about the hunk you had coffee with."

Carolyn chuckled. "His name is Bill Venable," she said, "and he fights forest fires for a living. Flies one of those airplanes that spray chemicals on the hot spots."

"Like in that old Richard Dreyfuss movie?" Tricia asked. She was having a hard time bending far enough to stow her purse on its usual under-the-counter shelf. The baby bump seemed to get visibly bigger from one day to the next. "What was it called?" She stopped to stretch her back, her hands resting on either side of what had once been her waist. "I remember. It was *Always*. And Dreyfuss's character went out in a blaze of glory, didn't he?"

"I don't recall," Carolyn lied, still stacking neatly wrapped bars of soap on the counter. The truth was, being a classic movie buff, she'd long since picked up on the similarities.

"Did you meet him through that website?" Tricia persisted. "Friendly Faces?"

"Yes," Carolyn said, making a production of removing the now-empty carton the soap had arrived in and heading toward the storage room. It was company policy to recycle cardboard boxes, among other things.

Tricia was waiting when she came back. "Do you like him? Are you going to see him again?"

Carolyn laughed. "Yes, I like him," she said, with exaggerated patience, "and I wouldn't be surprised if he asked me out at some point."

Tricia's beautiful blue eyes widened. It was hard to tell if she was excited or alarmed by the prospect.

Probably, she was both.

"Will you go? If he *does* ask you, I mean?"

"I haven't really decided," Carolyn said, with breezy nonchalance. She was looking up at the batik of the Weaver now, trying to absorb some of its serenity. "I must say, I was pleasantly surprised by how *normal* Bill turned out to be."

"Normal," Tricia echoed, her tone making it clear that she wasn't planning on dropping the subject anytime soon. "What did you *expect* him to be like, Carolyn?"

Carolyn tilted her head to one side, studying the Weaver, wishing she could afford to buy the piece and keep it forever. There was something so soothing about the thing, about the figure of a woman drawn with indistinct lines, strokes of color and shapes that were hardly more than suggested.

"Carolyn?" Tricia persisted, standing beside her now, giving her a poke with one elbow. Since just about everything on Tricia's body was rounded into soft curves, it didn't hurt. "Talk to me."

Carolyn sighed and turned to look at her friend. "I guess I thought there was the outside chance he might be another Ted Bundy," she confessed.

Tricia rolled her eyes, and then laughed, and then looked serious, all in the space of a few seconds. "Brody isn't going to like this one bit," she said. Tricia wasn't normally given to mood swings, but there were a lot of hormones splashing around in there.

A flash of...*something*—resentment? Triumph?—plucked at Carolyn's heartstrings. "Too bad for Brody," she replied.

Tricia studied her face. "Unless, of course, that's *exactly* why you're thinking about going out with this Bill person. To make Brody jealous."

Carolyn's mouth dropped open. She felt an indignant sting race through her, even as she recognized a disturbing quality of truth to Tricia's words. She *hadn't* set out to stir up Brody's envy, not consciously anyway, but there was no denying, in retrospect, that the idea gave her a delicious little thrill.

She gasped, horrified by the insight, and put a hand to her mouth.

Tricia smiled. "Oh, relax," she said, patting Carolyn's upper arm briefly, in a demonstration of feminine solidarity. "I know your intentions were honorable." She paused, looked speculative again. "But what *were* your intentions, exactly?" she asked, her tone and expression kind.

Carolyn sighed, her eyes burned and she swallowed hard before answering, in a small voice, "I just want to—to *get over* Brody Creed. Move on. Have a home and a family of my own."

Tricia gave her a quick, impulsive hug. Awkward business, with that pumpkin-shaped tummy of hers. "Listen to yourself, Carolyn," she said. "You want to *get over* Brody? *You still care for him.* Doesn't that mean something?"

"It means I'm dysfunctional," Carolyn replied

briskly, swiping at her cheeks with the back of one hand even though, as far as she knew, she hadn't actually started to cry. "Codependent, a basket case—whatever."

"Poppycock," Tricia said, with a dismissive wave. "*Dysfunctional. Codependent.* Those are just labels, buzzwords, and in my opinion they are overused in our society. You're a smart, strong, talented woman, Carolyn, not some psychological train wreck of a person. Give yourself a little credit, will you?"

Carolyn gave a wavering smile. "And you, Tricia Creed, are a very good friend."

"I'm also right," Tricia said, smiling back.

Having tacitly agreed on that, they both went to work then.

After an hour or so, two vanloads of middle-aged women sporting red hats and purple outfits showed up, and a shopping frenzy ensued.

One of the ladies seemed particularly taken with the Weaver. "That's lovely," she said, looking up at the batik.

Carolyn, busy ringing up purchases at the register, heard the remark even over the cheerful din of oohs and ahhs bubbling up around the shop as the other red-hats examined the merchandise.

So, apparently, did Tricia.

A glance flew between her and Carolyn.

"Isn't it?" Tricia said, edging over to stand alongside the woman who'd spoken first.

"I can't see the price from here," the woman said.

"I'm afraid the piece is already spoken for," Tricia replied quickly, a pink flush rising to her cheeks. "The artist is very prolific, though. I'd be glad to give you her contact information if you'd consider commissioning something—?"

Carolyn frowned. The Weaver was spoken for? Since when?

Several people had admired the batik, but they'd all sighed and shaken their heads when they were told how much it cost.

Tricia gave her another look, as if she thought Carolyn might contradict her.

Carolyn pointedly returned her friend's gaze, though she didn't speak up. She simply turned her attention back to the task at hand.

It was almost lunchtime when the red-hat ladies climbed into their vans and left, leaving the shop pleasantly denuded.

Carolyn was about to ask Tricia why she'd said the batik was sold when the shop door opened again, and Conner strode in, with Brody right behind him.

Carolyn's breath caught, though she tried to look as though she hadn't noticed the man.

Not noticing Brody, she reflected, was like not noticing a meteor big enough to wipe out the dinosaurs.

Still, she had to try. It was a matter of principle.

Conner greeted Tricia with a resounding kiss and then picked her up and swung her around once, in a small, gentle circle, making her laugh ring out like church bells on Easter morning.

Distracted by these goings-on, Carolyn didn't see Brody approach.

He was just *there,* all of a sudden, standing on the other side of the counter.

Carolyn started; every last nerve in her body jumped.

Brody favored her with a slow, unperturbed smile.

Either he hadn't heard the gossip about her coffee date with Bill—this option seemed highly unlikely given the nature of small towns—or he simply didn't care.

"That picture up there," he said, indicating the Weaver with a motion of one thumb. "Is that one of Primrose Sullivan's?"

Carolyn cleared her throat, in a way she hoped was subtle, and nodded. "Yes, but—"

Tricia sidled over. Bumped against Brody from one side. "Are you in the market for art?" she asked.

Conner, standing a few feet away, stared at his wife with an expression of baffled wonder on his handsome face. Clearly, to him at least, Tricia was a brilliantly colored butterfly in a black-and-white world.

"I might be," Brody said. "A lot of wall space is going to need filling, once my house is finished."

Carolyn reminded herself to breathe. Told her heart to start beating again, pronto, and no more of that Bambi-on-ice business. After all, this was a perfectly ordinary conversation.

"Primrose would be thrilled if the Weaver found a home right here in Lonesome Bend," Tricia said brightly. "You know how sentimental she is."

Carolyn frowned at her business partner, confused. "Didn't you say it was already spoken for? The Weaver, I mean?"

Tricia smiled. "I was lying," she said, with no apparent qualms whatsoever.

Carolyn opened her mouth, closed it again. Frowned harder.

Brody, meanwhile, got out his wallet, extracted a credit card and set it down on the counter. "I'll take it," he said.

"Don't you want to know how much it costs first?" Carolyn asked.

He gave her that smile again. She was powerless against that smile.

Did Brody know that?

"I reckon I can probably afford it," he said easily.

Carolyn blushed, embarrassed and clueless when it came to the reason. "Okay," she said, and stated the price.

Brody didn't bat an eye. He glanced down at his credit card, and Carolyn recovered enough to swipe it through the machine and push the necessary sequence of buttons.

Conner and Tricia were in the kitchen by then. Carolyn heard their voices, and the sounds of lunch being assembled.

The credit-card machine spit out a slip, and Brody signed it.

"I'll just get the ladder," Carolyn began nervously. "I can have the picture down off the wall and wrapped in no time."

Brody hadn't moved, after putting away his card and wallet. "We're on horseback," he said.

Carolyn blinked. "You're what?"

"Conner and I," Brody said, and she could feel his grin like sunshine against her skin, even though she was still being very careful not to look at him directly. "We rode our horses into town."

"Why?"

He chuckled, and she had to look at him then. He drew her eyes the way a magnet draws metal shavings. "It's what cowboys do," he said simply.

"Oh," Carolyn said, wishing she could shrink, like

Wonderland's Alice after a swig from the drink-me bottle, or just fall down any old rabbit hole.

"It would be sort of awkward, hauling that big picture over to my place on a horse, so I'm hoping you'll be so kind as to deliver it for me."

She stiffened her spine. Raised her chin. "I'm sure Tricia would be happy to drop it off for you," she said.

"She can't be carrying heavy things in her condition," Brody answered, with a faint note of disapproval in his voice. He looked around. "Where's that ladder?"

Carolyn told him where the ladder was, and he went and fetched it.

He came straight back, jackknifed that ladder open with a purposeful squeak of metal hinges and climbed nimbly up to the top rung. Lifted the framed batik off its hook and brought it down when he descended, the muscles in his back moving gracefully beneath the fabric of his shirt.

Blood pulsed in Carolyn's ears.

Tricia and Conner were laughing now, their joy in life and in each other bursting out of them between silences. She heard the fridge door open and close, and plates clattering, as if from some great distance, or from fathoms under the sea.

Carefully, almost reverently in fact, Brody laid the Weaver on the round table where Carolyn and Tricia normally displayed handmade papers. She watched his face as he studied the image and knew it would hang in his new house one day soon, a thing he was proud to own.

"You'll bring it by the lodge, then?" he asked, his voice hoarse, as if he'd gone a long time without speaking.

"You could always stop by with your truck," Caro-

lyn said, because it seemed important—if pointless—
to stand up to him.

"I could," Brody agreed. "But I'd like to show you
my house, and you did seem taken with Moonshine's
friendly face. Here's your chance to say howdy to him
in person."

"Moonshine?"

"My horse," Brody said, with a ghost of a grin. "I
think he gets pretty lonesome, out there in that unfinished barn. He'd probably like a visitor."

Carolyn thrust out a sigh. She might be able to resist
Brody, albeit not with anything resembling ease, but she
could not resist a horse. "All *right*," she said. "I'll bring
the picture over. What's a good time?"

"I'm usually there in the evenings," Brody replied.

*Of course you are. And what big teeth you have,
Grandma.*

"I like to sew in the evenings," she said.

Brody was facing her again—and the counter between them wasn't wide enough to suit Carolyn. The
whole state of Colorado wouldn't have been wide
enough.

He let his eyes drift over her, and she'd have sworn
he left her clothes in smoldering rags, just by looking
at her.

"And then there's that ride you owe me," he said,
his voice low.

Carolyn's face flamed—even after all the talk about
horses she managed to misunderstand him right from
the get-go—and then he laughed, the sound low again,
and raspy.

"The *horseback* ride," he drawled.

Carolyn gulped. "Why are you pushing this?" she

whispered angrily, leaning toward him without thinking and then wishing she hadn't.

His mouth was within kissing distance of hers and she couldn't pull back out of reach. She couldn't *move*.

"You said yes when I asked you to go riding with me," Brody reminded her, very quietly, "and that makes it a matter of honor. Either your word is worth something, Carolyn Simmons, or it isn't."

That freed her from the spell he'd cast over her.

Carolyn snapped her head back and glared. She gripped the edges of the counter so tightly that her knuckles ached. "You're a fine one to talk about honor," she told him, her voice ragged with fury, "after what you did. Furthermore, *my* word has never been in question here. Yours, on the other hand—"

He had the audacity to grin, to raise both hands, palms out, in an ingenuous bid for peace that made her want to slap him silly.

"Carolyn," he said slowly, "you are a hard woman. You are a *stubborn* woman. And you sure do know how to hold a grudge."

"Count on it," Carolyn practically snarled.

They glowered at each other for a long, silent moment.

Then Tricia pushed open the kitchen door and poked out her head, like a turtle peering out of a shell.

"Are you two joining us for lunch or not?" she asked sunnily.

"I'm not hungry," Carolyn said.

"Me, either," Brody agreed.

"Okaaaaay," Tricia replied, singing the word and ducking back into the kitchen.

Carolyn rounded the counter, stormed past Brody

toward the front window and dragged a lace curtain aside to look out at the street.

Sure enough, there were two horses, a buckskin and a bay, saddled and standing untethered at the picket fence. They were systematically devouring the leaves of Natty McCall's century-old lilac bush.

Carolyn turned on Brody, full of challenge. And heat.

And things it was better not to identify.

"Two people, two horses," she said tautly. "Let's take that ride right now, Mr. Creed, and get it over with."

"'Get it over with'?" Brody sounded amused—and a little insulted.

"I didn't promise to like it," she reminded him. "All I said was that I'd go." Carolyn indicated her jeans, boots and long-sleeved T-shirt. "And I want to go *now*."

"Fine," Brody said, inclining his head toward the fence, where the horses waited. "We'll go now."

Carolyn didn't even pause to tell Tricia that she was leaving the shop, because then she'd have had to explain *why* she was leaving, and she wasn't willing to do that. Steam would probably shoot out of her ears if she tried.

So she strode to the door, wrenched it open and crossed the threshold, then the porch.

"Take the bay," Brody told her, when, reaching the gate, she finally hesitated. Ire had carried her this far, but now she was at a loss.

"Great," she bit out.

She gathered the bay's dangling reins, stuck one foot in the stirrup and mounted with an expertise born of outrage as much as long experience.

Brody was standing on the sidewalk one moment, and sitting easy in the saddle the next. Holding the buckskin's reins loosely across one palm, he said, "One hour, Carolyn. Anything less than that doesn't amount to a ride, unless you're on a pony at the carnival."

On the ground, Carolyn was uncertain about a great many things.

In the saddle, she ruled. Her confidence, once she was on the back of a horse—any horse—was complete. Unshakable.

This was something she knew, something that came as easily to her as her breathing or the beating of her heart.

"Let's go," she said.

"See if you can keep up," Brody taunted, with another grin.

"If I don't, it will be this horse's fault, not mine," Carolyn replied, pressing the words through her teeth.

Brody laughed, an exultant, whooping sound, and he turned that buckskin in the general direction of the ranch and took it from a trot to a gallop to a full run in the space of half a dozen strides. The animal fairly flew along that unpaved road, like a butter-colored Pegasus, with Brody bent low over its neck, the two of them melded into one magnificent creature.

Pride swelled in Carolyn, and some emotion fiercer and more intense than joy, and she let Conner's horse have its head. The two geldings ran neck-and-neck then, over vacant lots and across dirt roads, over railroad tracks so long unused that the rails had rusted, and through breast-high brush.

When they both splashed into the river, Carolyn gave a shout of startled jubilation and held on as the waters filled her boots, soaked her jeans from the knees down and then saturated the denim covering her thighs.

Brody turned his head to look at her, and in his eyes

she thought she saw the one emotion she'd never expected to inspire in him: respect.

By the time they reached the opposite bank, the horses were wearing out, slowing down. They plodded up the steep bank, laboring for high ground.

Gaining the road that edged the ridge above the river, Brody and Carolyn let the horses set their own ambling pace.

Carolyn knew this road from her own rides on Blossom, knew the direction they were taking would bring them to the main ranch house.

She was wet, and breathless, and thoroughly exhilarated. Only one thing was better than a full-out, hell-bent-for-election ride like the one she and Brody had just shared, and that was the kind of shattering orgasm he'd brought her to, so easily and so often, back when they were lovers.

A shiver went through her, but it had nothing to do with the chill of the river water.

At last, Brody deigned to break the silence. Cocky bastard.

"Tricia probably has some clothes that will fit you," he said. "You need to get into some dry duds, and the sooner, the better."

She looked at him, which was a concession in and of itself. "Did you *plan* that plunge into the river?" she asked. She wouldn't have put it past him—what better way to get her out of her clothes?—but, on the other hand, he probably hadn't, because he couldn't have known whether or not she'd be able to rise to the challenge.

And whatever else she might have believed about

Brody, she *didn't* believe he'd deliberately put anyone at risk for any reason.

"Nope," he said, with another easy grin. He was as wet as she was; even his hat was soaked. He leaned to pat Moonshine's neck affectionately. "I should have seen it coming, though. This horse loves the water." He studied her, a grin in his eyes and playing around, but not quite settling on, his mouth. "You all right, cowgirl?" he asked.

Something in his voice, in the way he sat that horse and the way he looked at her, touched Carolyn in a deep and inexplicable way.

"I'm all right," she confirmed.

"You ride," he said, "like a Comanche."

It was a compliment, and Carolyn took it in. Owned it. Knew she'd bring it out, in future lonely hours, and turn it over and over in her mind, savoring it like some precious heirloom passed down through generations of forbearers.

"So do you," she replied, as they rode slowly toward the ranch house.

"Thanks," he answered.

After that, the horses picked up their pace, probably expecting a rubdown and a flake or two of grass-hay once they got to the barn.

Once there, Carolyn and Brody dismounted, led their tired mounts into waiting stalls and worked in easy concert with each other, grooming the animals carefully, filling their feeders and finally meeting up again in the breezeway.

"Let's get you into some warmer clothes," Brody said, extending his hand.

Like a sleepwalker, Carolyn accepted the offer, let

him lead her out into the bright sunlight of early afternoon.

She'd expected Conner and Tricia to be around—they'd had plenty of time to drive from town to the ranch in Tricia's Pathfinder—but there was no sign of them.

Brody tightened his grasp on Carolyn's hand, but only briefly and only slightly.

Entering the house, they were immediately greeted by two dogs, Valentino and Brody's Barney.

"I thought Conner and Tricia would be here," Carolyn said.

Brody smiled. "And miss a chance for some alone-time in that big Victorian house?" he teased. "The place has a lot of meaning for them. By now, they're probably making love."

Carolyn blushed again. Looked away, to avoid Brody's knowing gaze. "I should—" She hesitated, bit down on her lower lip. "I should be getting back to the shop. Would you mind giving me a lift into town?"

"Later," Brody said, taking her hand. He led her across the kitchen, through a doorway into a long corridor. Pushing open a door, he gestured for her to enter.

Carolyn was already in so deep that there was no going back. She stepped into the full bathroom that linked two small guest suites.

Brody had to know he had the advantage, an advantage he could have pressed, but he remained in the hallway, watching her with a sort of grave amusement. "While you shower, I'll rustle up something for you to wear," he said.

Carolyn *was* cold, and the thought of a hot shower was enticing.

Still, to take a shower, one had to get naked. And getting naked in the same house with Brody Creed was asking for trouble. Especially in her present mood.

For whatever reason, Carolyn wasn't her usual self.

"Tricia keeps extra robes for company," Brody went on, as calmly as if the situation were—well…a *non-*situation. "They're in the closet next to the linen cabinet." He inclined his head, indicating the huge antique wardrobe behind her. "Help yourself."

With that, he walked off down the hall.

Carolyn shut the door quickly, then she turned the lock. *Then* she scurried to make sure the doors leading into the adjoining guest suites were locked, too.

It was silly, she knew, as, shivering, she started the water running in the shower and began peeling away her soggy clothes.

Whatever his other faults might be, Brody wasn't one to force himself on a woman.

But, then, it wasn't what *Brody* might do that worried her.

It was what *she* might do.

CHAPTER NINE

BRODY HID OUT in the laundry room at the main ranch house, keeping his voice down as he spoke into his cell phone.

"Tricia," he growled, feeling his neck turn warm, "cut it out. This isn't funny. Carolyn needs to borrow some of your pre-pregnant clothes *because she got wet while we were crossing the river.*"

"I absolutely believe you," his sister-in-law chimed sunnily on the other end of the call he hadn't wanted to make. "If Carolyn had taken off her clothes for any *other* reason, she would simply put them back on when necessary."

Brody had called for permission to pilfer Tricia's wardrobe, not for a ration. Helping himself to Conner's stuff when he needed it was one thing, and pawing through Tricia's dresser drawers and closets was another.

Tricia went prattling on, without waiting for him to talk again, which was a good thing, because he didn't have a clue what to say. He'd stated his business, and now all he could do was wait.

"One minute," Tricia chirped, in a to-sum-it-all-up kind of tone, "Carolyn was right here in the shop, perfectly dry. The next, she's racing away on a horse and winds up drenched to the skin—"

"Tricia," Brody interrupted hoarsely, getting desperate.

She laughed. Paused to repeat Brody's earlier request to Conner, making *him* laugh, too.

It didn't help one damn bit that his brother's easy, rumbling chortle had a distinctively *satisfied* quality to it. Brody, being Conner's identical twin, and therefore wired the same way, right down to the double helix, knew what that sound meant.

Sure enough, Conner and Tricia had just made love.

Conner, you lucky SOB, Brody thought, too distracted to catch the irony.

Silently, Brody seethed, his body taut with the anticipation of something that wasn't going to happen. Not that he couldn't have had Carolyn—he knew he could. He'd sensed her vulnerability, and the biochemical signals had definitely been traveling both ways.

The lovemaking wasn't going to happen, though, because he wasn't going to *let* it happen. Not yet. It was too soon, the situation was delicate, and while he hadn't learned all his life lessons, or probably even a fraction of them, he *had* learned that one.

Carolyn wanted him, but she wasn't ready.

Oh, she'd respond, all right—she was a responsive woman, as spirited as a wild mare—but when the effects wore off, when the afterglow went out like yesterday's fire in the woodstove, she'd hate him.

Worse, she'd hate herself, too.

So Brody meant to wait—no matter what it cost him.

He shoved a hand through his river-dampened hair—*one* dunk in the water hadn't been enough to do him for a whole day. He'd had to get wet *twice.*

Serve him right if he came down with pneumonia.

While he was thinking all these thoughts, Conner and Tricia were still enjoying the hilarity of it all.

At his expense. And here he was, being freaking *noble,* too.

He deserved better.

At last, Tricia took pity on him. "My skinny clothes are in boxes at the back of the walk-in closet in Conner's and my room," she said, very sweetly. "Feel free to plunder."

Brody had to smile then, even though he was still feeling pretty darned grumpy, all things considered. "Thanks," he said. "I appreciate it." He paused. In the distance, he could hear the water running in the downstairs bathroom. He pictured Carolyn naked, her trim body sluiced with soap suds and spray, and got so hard that the ache practically doubled him over. After a moment spent recovering, he cleared his throat. "You two will be coming home soon, right?" he asked.

Say yes.

Say no.

"Wrong," Tricia said happily. "Conner is taking me out for a very romantic dinner. Would you mind feeding Valentino for us? And the horses?"

"Sure," Brody said, thrown by what ought to have been a perfectly ordinary turn of events. "I mean, no, I wouldn't mind feeding the critters for you. Have fun at dinner."

"We will," Tricia said, and he didn't need to see her smile, because he could feel it, hear it in her voice. This, he dimly recalled, was how a woman sounded, when she was in love. "We'll see you hours—*hours and hours*—from now."

Brody chuckled, shook his head. *If only.* "Suit your-selves," he said.

Goodbyes were exchanged, and the call ended.

Brody rubbed his stubbled chin, sighed as he set the cell phone aside on a counter. Obviously, Tricia thought he and Carolyn were going to spend those "hours and hours" making up for lost time, getting it on.

He was going to have the name without the game, and so was Carolyn.

It just plain sucked.

CAROLYN STEPPED OUT of the shower, dried off with a thirsty towel and appropriated one of the guest robes from the exquisitely carved antique wardrobe against the long wall. Fleece-lined, the garment brushed against her skin like a whole-body caress.

Don't go there, she admonished herself silently. *Do not think about skin and caresses. You are in deep yogurt here, lady. Out of your depth.*

She padded over to one of the two sinks set into the counter, with its custom-painted ceramic sinks, and stared at her image in the mirror, combing her hair with splayed fingers and making eye contact with that other Carolyn.

"Well," she began in a whisper, though she didn't really think Brody had his ear stuck to any of the bath-room doors, "you have done it this time. You are in a real fix, and it won't be easy to get out of this one."

If you even want *to get out of here without giving in to the overwhelming urge to have sex with Brody Creed.*

Carolyn flushed, indignant. "Of *course* I want to get out of here without having sex with Brody," she muttered. She often had these kinds of conversations with herself—what the rest of the world didn't know wouldn't hurt them.

Do you want to make love with him or not?

"Well," Carolyn admitted, deflating a little as she sighed, "*yes*. What healthy, red-blooded woman in her right mind *wouldn't* want to have sex with Brody Creed?" She drew in a deep breath, raised her chin and squared her shoulders under the sensuous fabric of that ridiculously luxurious robe. *"But,"* she went on, "I'm *not* going to give in to temptation. Period. I've already been down this road once, remember, and once was more than enough."

She must have made her case because after that, the argumentative little voice in her head was silent.

A rap sounded at the door leading into the hallway.

"Yes?" Carolyn asked, with only the slightest tremor, finger-combing her hair again.

Brody's low-pitched chuckle penetrated the thick wood of the door. "I've got some of Tricia's things here," he said. "I'll just set them down on the floor and back away real slow."

A smile crooked Carolyn's mouth, but she quickly subdued it. This was a serious situation, she reminded herself, and if she wasn't very, *very* careful, all her drummed-up resolution to take the high road would go right down the old drain.

"Thank you," she called back stiffly.

She waited until she heard Brody walk away, then waited a few moments longer, for good measure. Once she was sure the proverbial coast was clear, she unlocked the door, bent to grab up the untidy stack of feminine garments from the floor and locked herself in again.

Sitting down on the edge of the humungous bathtub because, all of a sudden, her knees had gone squishy, holding the borrowed blue jeans and white cotton shirt on her lap, she considered hiding out in that bathroom until Tricia and Conner got home.

That would be silly, though.

And boring. Who knew how long they'd be gone?

So, with another sigh, Carolyn put on the jeans and the shirt, sans underwear because her own bra and panties were still wet and no self-respecting woman borrows *or* lends lingerie, fluffed out her hair with her fingers one more time and marched out into the corridor.

She found Brody in the kitchen, fiddling with the coffee machine. He'd showered, too, and changed into jeans and a blue chambray shirt, Western-cut with snaps. His boots were old and scuffed, which completed the singularly appealing look.

With a frown, he glanced in her direction. "Do you know how to work this thingamajig?" he asked. "I cannot for the life of me figure out why people can't be satisfied with an ordinary coffeepot."

The question relaxed Carolyn slightly, neutralized some of the charge in the atmosphere. Tricia loved gadgets, and Carolyn had been with her when she bought the machine. They'd given it a trial run at the shop, studying the instruction book and finally mastering the thing.

It was, in a world thick with enigmas, a problem she could solve.

"Like this," Carolyn said, popping a pod into the top, setting a clean cup under the spigot and pushing the buttons. It was only after the java began to brew that she realized closing the gap between herself and Brody might not have been the smartest thing she'd ever done.

Brody didn't move. Why should he? He'd been there first.

Carolyn didn't move, either. It wasn't pride, or stubbornness, that made her stay put. It was some strange, thrumming kind of centrifugal force.

Brody cleared his throat, an affable sound, but raw at the edges. "Just so there are no misunderstandings," he said, finally, and Carolyn had to strain to hear him over the beat of her heart, "I can't remember when I've ever wanted a woman the way I want you. Fact is, if my conscience would allow it, I'd do my cowboy-best to seduce you, right here and right now."

Carolyn gave a twittery little laugh. "You have a conscience?"

Lame.

The single shot of fresh coffee had long since finished processing itself, but neither of them paid any attention to it.

Brody's mouth kicked up at the corner, but the expression in his eyes was soft. "Believe it or not," he replied, "I do indeed have a conscience. And it's telling me not to screw up." A pause, another quirk of his mouth. "So to speak."

Color flooded Carolyn's face, and heat suffused her traitorous body. "Gee, thanks," she said, somehow keeping her tone level, despite what felt like a million tiny universes colliding within her.

His grin went full-throttle then.

It wasn't the least bit fair.

"A while back," Brody went on, mercifully lowering the wattage on his grin, "I asked you for a second chance.

I meant it, Carolyn. Even if this doesn't go anywhere—whatever it is that's happening between you and me—I think we should explore it."

Carolyn couldn't speak. Couldn't even swallow past the lump in her throat. So she just looked up into Brody Creed's damnably handsome, deceptively earnest face, powerless against him. Hoping and praying he hadn't already guessed that.

Fat chance.

He curved his right index finger under her chin, lifted ever so gently, so their gazes locked with an almost audible click, like the tumblers in a lock.

"Carolyn?"

"I'm listening," she whispered. And she was. With her whole being, body, mind and spirit.

Again, the wicked grin flashed. He nodded once. "So do you have an opinion?" he teased. "And, if so, how about letting me in on it?"

"There is—" Carolyn had to stop, clear the frog from her throat, before she could go on. "There is *apparently* something…well…*going on,* here. And I think, most definitely—maybe—we ought to find out what it is. Sometime."

Mischief danced, cornflower-blue, in Brody's eyes. He arched one eyebrow and waited, calm as a seasoned fisherman with a trout on the hook.

"But not *immediately,* mind you," Carolyn clarified. "I mean, the sensible thing to do would be to forget the whole stupid idea and pretend we never had this conversation. But—"

"But…?" Brody prompted, his voice husky.

He was still standing too close.

"But I'm not feeling very sensible at the moment," Carolyn admitted, on a rush of breath.

"Me, either," Brody said, and the twinkle was back in his eyes. "But one of us has to be strong, here. Somebody has to be responsible. So I'm telling you flat out, Carolyn Simmons—no matter how badly you may want me, I'm not available."

Carolyn smiled wryly, calm on the outside, every nerve jangling on the *inside*. "Thanks for straightening me out on that score," she said, pleasantly surprised that she was able to strike a breezy note. "What happens now?"

"We do the thing up right," Brody said, sounding confident. "Starting with a few ground rules."

"Ground rules?"

"Yeah," Brody told her. "No sex, for the time being, anyhow. And both of us can see other people if that's what we want to do."

Carolyn hoped the pang that last stipulation gave her didn't show on her face. She was *sort of* seeing Bill Venable, and sort of *not* seeing him, but she already knew he'd never be more than a friend to her, nor she to him.

Bill loved Angela.

And she, God help her, was still hung up on Brody.

"What?" Brody asked, when she didn't say anything.

"If you want to go out with Joleen Williams," Carolyn said loftily, "that's certainly your prerogative."

The twinkle in Brody's eyes turned to temper. "Did I, at any point in time, say I wanted to date Joleen?"

"You didn't have to," Carolyn said. She folded her arms. "It's quite obvious."

"I don't know how you figure that," Brody said, clearly irritated. "Do you see Joleen standing around here somewhere, waiting for me to help her on with her coat or pin a corsage to her party dress so we can go out on the town?"

It just went to show a person, Carolyn thought, how quickly a spring breeze could turn into an ill wind. Not more than a minute before, she and Brody had had all they could do not to have sex right there in his brother's kitchen. *Now* they were practically at each other's throats.

"You're the one who wanted to keep their options open when it came to dating," Carolyn pointed out, proud of being—okay, *sounding*—so collected and reasonable.

"And *you're* the one who's *already dating,*" Brody bit out.

So he *did* know about Bill. She'd wondered.

"Look at that," Carolyn retorted, flinging her hands out from her sides because she had to do *something* with the buildup of energy that wouldn't constitute felony assault. "I was already playing by the ground rules before I even knew there *were* any!"

Brody glared at her.

Carolyn glared back.

One of the dogs gave a mournful little whimper, as though the poor creature had just spotted a mushroom cloud billowing on the horizon.

"What kind of guy is so hard up for a date that he joins an outfit like Friendly Faces?" Brody finally demanded. That familiar muscle in his cheek was bunched up again.

"One like you, I guess," Carolyn took great delight in saying. "Or are you going to claim it was your *horse* who signed up for a membership?"

Brody leaned in, his nose nearly touching hers. "*This* is why we need ground rules," he said.

"I think we need a *referee*," Carolyn replied. "Why don't we just call it a day, Brody? Why don't we cut our losses and run?"

That was when he rested his hands on her shoulders, bent his head and kissed her, lightly at first, then hard and deep, with tongue.

The effect was tectonic, and she was literally breathless when the kiss finally ended.

"*That's* why we're not going to *cut our losses and run*," Brody all but growled. "Get your things, Carolyn. I'm taking you home."

She should have been glad about that, but, oddly, she was stung instead.

She did return to the bathroom, however, collect her original clothing, now rolled up in a soggy clump, and stomped back to the kitchen, where Brody was waiting, with his truck keys already in hand.

Talk about anxious to get rid of somebody.

Carolyn squelched a crazy urge to cry and marched out through the back door, which Brody obligingly held for her.

The two dogs followed, eager, like all their species, for any chance to go *anywhere*.

When Brody reached his truck, he went immediately to the passenger side and opened the door. Once Carolyn was in, he hoisted the dogs, one at a time, into the rear part of the extended cab.

Carolyn fixed her gaze straight ahead, silently noting that the windshield needed washing.

Brody got behind the wheel, slammed his door shut

and cranked the key in the ignition, causing the starter to make an ominous grinding sound.

"This is going to keep happening," he told her tersely, "until we go to bed and get each other out of our systems."

Carolyn shifted in the confines of her seat belt and would not look at him. "Way to sweep a girl off her feet," she snapped. "Take me home, Brody. *Now*."

The truck made another odd noise when he shifted it into gear. "Fine," he replied. "I'll be *glad* to take you home. Of course, there's always the possibility that Conner and Tricia are swinging naked from the chandeliers or something, but I guess that's a risk you'll just have to run."

Carolyn blushed so hard it hurt. What if Tricia and Conner *were* still somewhere in Natty McCall's wonderful old Victorian house, thinking they had the place to themselves and, well, *whooping it up?*

In the next moment, though, Brody's words took root and blossomed into an image—Tricia, six months pregnant, swinging nude from one of the light fixtures, like the daring young girl on the flying trapeze.

Carolyn laughed. She couldn't help it.

Out of the corner of her eye, she saw that Brody was grinning. "What?" he asked.

"I was just thinking about the chandelier thing," Carolyn admitted.

That made Brody chuckle. "It brings one hell of a picture to mind, all right," he agreed. "My guess is, my brother and his lovely bride are probably behaving themselves again by now. Tricia mentioned that they were headed out to dinner."

"Are we crazy?" Carolyn asked, very softly and after

long consideration. Every silence that fell between them seemed to throb with things that wanted saying and *couldn't* be said. "The way we go from being this close to having sex to fighting like a pair of feral cats in a back alley—what *is* that, Brody?"

He thought before he answered. Finally said, "I think they call it passion."

With that, he reached over and gave her thigh a squeeze, about midway between her knee and her hip.

Carolyn tilted her head back, closed her eyes and offered up a silent prayer that Brody didn't know he'd turned her insides to molten lava with a single touch.

HE'D MEANT TO GO straight to the shop—Brody would always think of the place as Natty McCall's house, no matter what they turned it into—but darned if his truck didn't turn in at River's Bend of its own volition.

Carolyn didn't protest, or comment. She just turned her head toward the rising house and since Brody couldn't see her face, he was left to guess at what might be going on inside her head.

The construction crew was finished for the day, loading toolboxes into the backs of pickup trucks, calling to each other, laughing.

For some reason, the sight stirred up some lonesome feelings inside Brody.

That sensation of being on the outside looking in was getting old.

Or maybe it was this confounding woman sitting in the seat just across the console, determined to say as little to him as possible.

The workmen all waved and smiled, and Brody greeted them with nods as he drove up what would one day be a paved driveway. For now, though, it was still a dirt road, thinly peppered with gravel.

"Tricia mentioned that you mean to go on calling the property River's Bend," Carolyn said, her head still turned toward the house, her tone bemused, or maybe wistful. "She seemed pleased by that."

"River's Bend is as good a name for the place as any other," Brody said. "Besides, I liked Tricia's dad. Most everybody liked Joe McCall."

"Tricia misses him," Carolyn observed, finally looking at Brody. He couldn't read her eyes, but it didn't matter, because she was so damn beautiful, in the late afternoon light, a gilded creature wearing somebody else's clothes.

This nobility crap, Brody decided glumly, was overrated. By now, if he'd pressed his advantage earlier, in the ranch-house kitchen, they'd probably be recovered from round one and ready to move on to round two. Or even three.

"That's natural," Brody said, in belated reply to Carolyn's remark.

"Do you miss your dad?" Carolyn asked, as he parked the truck in front of the partially completed three-car garage and shut off the engine.

She sure did have a way of coming out of left field, this woman.

Brody sighed, shook his head. "I never really knew my father," he answered honestly. "Conner and I were just babies when he died, and our mother didn't live long after we were born. When I think of parents, I think of Kim and Davis, and I'm sure my brother does, too."

He opened the truck door and would have gone around to help Carolyn out of the rig—he'd been raised to treat a lady with respect and courtesy, as had Conner and their cousin Steven—but she was over the running board with her feet planted firmly in the rocky dirt before he could get there.

He took Valentino and Barney from the back and let them circle, as dogs will do when they've been confined for a while, sniffing the ground and looking for a likely place to let fly.

"What about you, Carolyn?" he asked.

"What about me?" she challenged, but mildly, shading her eyes from the sun with one hand.

"You asked me about my dad. I'm asking you about yours."

"Never knew him," Carolyn said, like it didn't matter.

This seemed important, though Brody wasn't sure why. Important enough to press the issue, in fact.

"What about your mother?"

She met his gaze then, and the expression he saw in her eyes was so bleak that he felt it like a punch in the gut. "Just a memory of somebody driving away and leaving me behind," she said.

Brody hadn't wept since the day Lisa and Justin were buried, side by side, in a windswept little graveyard up in Montana, but he wanted to then.

Didn't, though.

They were both quiet for a few moments, neither one moving.

"This is quite a house," Carolyn said, at long last.

Brody rummaged around inside himself and came up with a flimsy grin. He was proud of that house, saw its conception and construction as the first really grown-up things he'd ever done, and showing it to Carolyn made him feel good.

"Yes, ma'am," he agreed. "It will be, if it's ever finished."

"Show me where you plan to hang the Weaver," Carolyn said, her still-wet boots making a squishy crunch in the gravel as she approached the front door.

He was a few moments remembering what she meant by the term, but then it came to him that she was referring to Primrose Sullivan's picture, the one he'd bought at the shop and insisted she deliver. He'd have to keep it over at the cabin for a while, of course, but he did have a spot picked out for it.

The doors and locks had been installed, and Brody found the key among the others on his ring.

The inside of the house smelled like fresh lumber and new masonry, and the windows were all glassed in. He flipped a switch, expecting nothing, and the track lighting high over their heads came on, throwing the massive living room into an oddly forlorn relief.

He was going to be lonely here, he realized. He was lonely *everywhere*.

Brody shook off the thought, smiled at Carolyn and gestured toward the space over the living room fireplace.

"There," he said. "That's where the picture's going to wind up."

Carolyn seemed to see the piece hanging there. She smiled, albeit a little wanly, her hands resting on her hips. "Perfect," she said.

Brody cupped a hand under her elbow, loosely, wanting her to look at him, not wanting her to turn skittish and spook. "Now that we've established the ground rules," he began, pausing once to clear his throat, "there's the part that comes after."

She held his gaze, and she deserved credit for that, because it was so obvious that she wanted to look away instead. "You're a persistent man," she said, very softly.

Brody had never wanted to kiss a woman—Carolyn or anyone else—as badly as he wanted to now.

At the same time, he knew it might be the mistake of a lifetime if he went ahead and did it.

"*Persistent* doesn't begin to cover it," he said, when he figured he could trust himself to speak. "You've never met a man with more stick-to-it in him than I have, except for Conner, maybe, and he's taken."

"Yes," Carolyn agreed, almost in a murmur, her whole attention focused, it seemed to Brody, on his mouth. Her voice was dreamlike, almost sleepy-sounding. "Conner is definitely taken."

Brody wondered, momentarily, if Carolyn had had a thing for Conner, before he married her best friend. Wondered if by chance her attraction to him was a case of transference.

But that was crazy. Before Lisa's call that fateful night, seven years back, Carolyn had been in love with *him,* Brody—hadn't she?

This is me *standing here,* he wanted to say. *This is me, Brody Creed. Not Conner.* Brody.

But, of course, he didn't, though the decision couldn't be chalked up to good sense; he was just plain thunderstruck by the possibility.

"What comes after the ground rules, Brody?" Carolyn asked quietly. "After the no-sex pact, and the freedom to see other people if we want to, what happens then?"

At last, Brody found his voice. He even rummaged up a passable grin, one that might even have masked all the catastrophic things happening in the core of his being.

"Maybe," he said, struck by sudden inspiration, "we could start with dinner and a movie?"

CHAPTER TEN

Dinner and a movie.

With Carolyn.

Sounded like a good start to Brody. But *no sex? Had he actually been the one to stipulate that? Was he out of his ever-lovin'* mind *or* what?

"Dinner and a movie," Carolyn repeated thoughtfully, mulling his invitation over. She looked wicked-hot, standing there in the middle of what would one day be his living room. The borrowed shirt was a little too tight across her breasts and a little too short in the bargain, revealing a tantalizing glimpse of stomach skin whenever she moved just right.

Brody shifted uncomfortably, and he was just about to jump in and try to renegotiate the whole no-nooky thing when Carolyn rocked him with a tiny smile and announced her decision.

"A tame enough evening, I think," she said, and was quick to add, "As long as we don't have to sleep together, of course."

Tame? Was that how she saw him—as *tame?*

Brody gulped. "Of course."

But he was thinking, *You and your big mouth. Brody Creed, you are five known kinds of fool, and a few that haven't been discovered yet.*

"When?" Carolyn asked.

Brody just stood there for a moment, stumped by the question, simple as it was. Then he untangled his tongue and said, "Tomorrow night? I promised Tricia I'd feed their horses and these dogs tonight, and it's getting pretty late, anyhow."

Carolyn bit her lower lip, thinking again. Was it really *that* hard to make the decision?

"Tomorrow night isn't good," she said, with a little shake of her head. "I have other plans. How about Friday or Saturday?"

"Saturday would work," Brody suggested, cagey now. Carolyn was probably playing hard to get, and two could ride in *that* rodeo. The only reason he didn't go for Friday instead was that he didn't want to seem too eager.

"Great," she said, looking around. "Is there more?" she asked, with a quirky little grin. "To the house, I mean?"

"Yeah," Brody replied, oddly relieved even though, by his reckoning, Saturday was on the yonder side of forever. He offered his hand, letting her decide whether to take it or not.

She did.

By then, the dogs were already off on an expedition of their own, checking out other parts of the house.

Brody showed Carolyn the kitchen first, with its big stove and center island and its many windows, then the room he planned on using as an office, then the guest quarters and the family bedrooms and, finally, the master suite.

"Big place," Carolyn said, hesitating in the double doorway of the main bedroom.

"Carolyn," Brody teased, shaken and, at the same

time, buzzed, "it's okay to go inside. There isn't even a bed in here yet."

She blushed a little, stooped to pet Barney when he doubled back briefly to brush against her before taking off again. After that, like a person wandering in a dream, Carolyn moved to the middle of the room. Putting her hands out from her sides, she tilted her head back, closed her eyes and did a slow, graceful pirouette.

In that moment, Carolyn seemed impossibly beautiful to Brody, like a sprite or a fallen angel or a fairy queen. He wouldn't have been all that surprised if she'd sprouted gossamer wings. When she stopped moving and met his gaze again, she looked embarrassed.

He wanted to tell her it was okay, that he could watch her dance like that for the rest of eternity and be perfectly happy, but he'd sound like a damn idiot if he did, so he held his tongue.

"What do you think?" he asked, just to break the silence. "Of the house, that is?"

She smiled a real smile, practically lighting the place up. "It's *wonderful,* Brody. Did you design it yourself?"

People made plans for houses all the time, but Carolyn made it sound as though he'd personally drawn up the blueprints for Stonehenge, and that made him feel half again his normal height.

He nodded, suddenly modest.

That would have cracked Conner up for sure—his twin brother acting modest. Conner and a lot of other people besides.

"I did," he confirmed belatedly, feeling the backs of his ears heat up. "Got me through a lot of long nights, figuring out the overall floor plan and then the details."

She was silent for a few minutes, absorbing that statement.

"I should be getting home," Carolyn said next, standing in a shaft of silvery moonlight spilling in through the skylights.

For as long as Brody could remember, he'd wanted to be able to lie in his bed at night and look right up through the ceiling and the roof at the stars. In a couple of months, he'd get his wish.

But what about a woman to share it all with?

Looking at stars could be lonely business without a partner. Made a man think how small he was, how small the whole planet—the whole *galaxy*—was, specks of dust in all that vastness.

"Okay," he said, finding his voice again. It came out in a husky rasp, and he hoped he hadn't caught a cold, crossing and then recrossing the river. That would be a hell of a note. "Let's go."

He whistled for the dogs and they came promptly, so he sort of herded them toward the front of the house. Stepping around Carolyn, Brody grabbed hold of a fancy brass knob and opened the door for her.

Valentino and Barney, neither one a gentleman, bounded out ahead of her to sniff around in the grass, nearly knocking her off her feet and, at the same time, making her laugh.

Brody loaded them up first, in case they had a mind to take off in all their excitement, and then waited until Carolyn was settled in the passenger seat before he sprinted around the back of the truck and jumped in behind the wheel, not because he was in any hurry to come to a parting of the ways with Carolyn, however

temporary, but because he suddenly felt energized, electrified, wired for action, like the dogs.

Carolyn didn't say anything as they drove back to the
main road, the one that would take them the rest of the
way into town, but this time, she didn't seem annoyed
with him. She was relaxed, and maybe a little pensive.

Brody drove her home to Natty's place, noticed right
away that Tricia's Pathfinder wasn't parked in the driveway and, knowing that meant his brother and his wife
were nowhere around, briefly considered trying to seduce Carolyn after all.

It would have been a fine thing to peel away those
clothes she was wearing, lay her down somewhere soft
and warm and lose himself in her, but common sense
intervened.

They'd made an agreement, and a deal was a deal.

No sex.

Yet.

Brody parked the truck at the curb, told the dogs to
behave themselves and walked Carolyn all the way up
the outside stairs to her door.

He waited, his hands wedged into the pockets of his
jeans—*Conner's* jeans, anyway—until she'd unlocked
the door, stepped over the threshold and switched on
the kitchen lights.

While he was still trying to work out whether or not
he ought to follow her in, give kissing her a try, that
cantankerous cat purred and wound itself around her
ankles. Anybody would have thought it had a halfway
decent personality, that critter, but Brody knew better—
it was demon spawn.

Carolyn smiled fondly down at the animal, said a

quick, soft "Good night, Brody," and shut the door in his face with a gentle click.

Well, that settled the kiss question.

Brody gave an inward shrug, turned and descended the stairs.

He had chores to do at the ranch, and the dogs would be getting antsy soon, shut up in the truck like they were.

Despite these concerns, he took a little detour on the way home, drove past the ticket booth and the snack bar at the erstwhile Bluebird Drive-in Theater and parked, looking up at the peeling hulk of a movie screen.

He'd been meaning to have the thing bulldozed ever since the last of the snow finally melted off back in mid-March, along with the two buildings on the property, but what with the new house and barn going up and his responsibilities on the ranch, he hadn't gotten around to making the arrangements. And, like most residents of Lonesome Bend and the even smaller towns surrounding it, he had fond memories of the place.

He still intended to clear these neglected acres, put in fences, and have it seeded for grass so he could run cattle and horses here, but in the meantime, well, it seemed to him that the Bluebird Drive-in deserved a last hurrah.

Carolyn wanted dinner and a movie?

Coming right up.

AFTER THE VISIT TO Brody's house, the apartment seemed not only small to Carolyn—once, she would have said "cozy"—but also out-and-out *cramped*.

"Ingrate," she scolded her reflection in the door of the microwave as she stood at the counter, scraping

Winston's half-tin of sardines into one of the several chipped china bowls reserved for his use.

"Reow," Winston said, sounding moderately concerned.

"I didn't mean you," Carolyn told him, setting his dinner on the floor and watching with affection as he gobbled up the stinky fish he loved so much. She washed her hands at the sink, her movements quick with pent-up exasperation. "*I'm* the ingrate around here. I have everything I need, everything anybody could ask for, right here in this apartment." She paused, remembering. "But, Winston, you should *see* that house. It's *huge.* But it's not one of those mansion wannabes, either, it's—it's *homey.* I couldn't help imagining what it would be like to live there." She threw her hands out from her sides, let them fall back. "How crazy is that?"

Winston, busy with his fine dining experience and, after all, *a cat,* naturally didn't reply.

Carolyn, used to carrying on one-sided conversations, didn't let that slow her down. "You're right," she said. "It is *totally* crazy." She dried off her hands, went to the refrigerator, yanked open the door and took out a carton of cottage cheese, the kind with little chunks of pineapple mixed in. After squinting at the expiration date, she decided it would be relatively safe to eat the stuff and lobbed some onto a salad plate with a serving spoon. "The man *cons* me into going for a horseback ride with him, and I end up soaked to the skin and squeezed into clothes that belong to a woman who is at least two inches shorter than I am, and a size smaller, and I'm ready to *get it on* with Brody Creed. I swear, if he hadn't made that speech about responsibility and setting ground rules, I probably would have jumped his bones—"

The landline rang, interrupting her discourse.

Probably for the best, she figured, reaching for the receiver.

"Hello?" she almost snapped. She needed to eat her questionable cottage cheese, put on her own clothes and get her head together, not necessarily in that order—*not* stand around talking on the phone.

She recognized Bill's chuckle immediately. "Am I calling at a bad time?" he asked.

"Who is that?" Carolyn heard a little girl's voice chime in, at the other end of the line. "Is that Angela? It had *better* be Angela."

Carolyn smiled. She remembered what it was to be nine years old. What she *didn't* remember was having a father who, like Bill, was devoted to her.

She'd never met her father. Didn't even know his name, or if he was alive or dead, or if she looked anything like him.

"This is a private call, Ellie," Bill told his daughter kindly, but firmly. "Beat it. Go do your homework or bug your grandmother or something."

"Maybe I'm the one who should be asking if it's a bad time," Carolyn said, still amused. She loved kids, even when they were difficult. *Especially* then. She'd been a handful herself; just ask any one of her fourteen foster families.

"Have dinner with me?" Bill said. "Here, at our place? We'll barbecue on the patio, and Ellie's grandparents will join us, so we shouldn't give rise to a local scandal."

Carolyn felt warm inside. Unfortunately, it wasn't

the same kind of warm she felt when she was around Brody, or even thought about him.

Brody.

She'd lied to him, saying she had plans for the following night, simply because she'd needed a chance to catch her breath, regain her perspective, before she stepped into the lion's den a second time by being alone with a man who could melt her with a look, a touch, a word.

"You haven't been in Lonesome Bend long," she joked, "if you think my coming to your place, even for an outdoor meal with your in-laws present, wouldn't be fuel for gossip."

Bill sighed. "Is that a no?"

She watched as Winston licked his bowl clean and then strolled regally away, tail high. "I'd love to come over for a barbecue," she said. If she was going out with Brody, even for an innocuous evening of food and film, it was only reasonable to see other men, too. That way, she'd be in less danger of losing her head and doing something rash.

Keep your options open.

Always know where the exits are.

The foster-kid credo of life.

"Would tonight be too soon?" Bill teased.

"Yes," Carolyn said, with a rueful glance at her cottage cheese. "It would be. Tomorrow night?"

"Perfect," Bill said.

"What shall I bring?"

"Your beautiful smile and all the charm you can muster. The in-laws will be friendly, but Ellie—"

"I can handle Ellie," Carolyn said, with kindness and humor. *Because I* was *Ellie, once upon a time, except that I didn't have adoring grandparents and a first-class father.*

"Okay," Bill responded, sounding relieved. "Tomorrow night, six o'clock if that's not too early. Casual dress, of course." He gave her the address, and Lonesome Bend being Lonesome Bend, she knew right where it was. Two-story brick house with green wooden shutters, surrounded by a wrought-iron fence, a block and a half southeast of the public library.

"I'll be there," Carolyn promised, wondering at her bravery.

She could count the dates she'd had, post-Brody, on one hand. And most of them had been at been mediocre at best, disastrous at worst.

The ones in between were highly forgettable.

"Good," Bill said. "I'll be looking forward to seeing you again."

After that, there didn't seem to be much to say, so they exchanged goodbyes and ended the call.

Carolyn exchanged Tricia's clothes for an oversize pair of cotton pajamas, ate the cottage cheese and prayed she wouldn't get food poisoning.

She wasn't much of a cook, it was true. She simply couldn't see the point in fixing elaborate meals when she'd be the only one around to eat them.

The subject of food brought Brody's incredible soon-to-be kitchen to mind; she'd noticed the gigantic professional stove, with its many burners and a space for grilling indoors, noticed the subzero refrigerator, the special built-in cooler for wine, the two oversize dishwashers and the extra sink and ceramic stove top set into the granite covering the island in the middle of the room.

It was the size of Kansas, that island.

All of which meant that Brody either liked to cook and entertain crowds, or expected any woman he took up with to do the same...or both of those things.

Smiling to herself—except for helping out with the chili feed/rummage sale last fall, she'd never whipped up any dish more ambitious than macaroni and cheese, the kind that comes in a box—Carolyn went downstairs to make sure everything was in order in the shop. Whatever *else* Tricia had done that afternoon, once she was alone with Conner, she'd remembered to lock up, shut off the computer and wrap the Weaver for delivery to Brody's place.

Carolyn paused, the shop in semidarkness now, at the base of the inside stairs, already missing the Weaver. Like the gypsy skirt, though, it was a luxury she not only couldn't afford, but also had no real use for.

At Brody's, the magnificent batik would be seen and appreciated, as it should. Perhaps it would even be passed down, a cherished heirloom, through generations of Creeds, the house surrounding it becoming more and more of a testament to family continuity with every passing year. Just like its much older counterpart on the ranch.

Carolyn climbed the stairs slowly, with her head slightly lowered, her heart filled with a sort of bereft enjoyment of the thought.

From her place of honor above Brody's living room fireplace, the Weaver would see newborns brought through the wide front entrance, see those same babies grow up, fall in love, marry and bring home children of their own. She would be a silent witness to whole lifetimes, that woman of wax and paint, there for the joys and the sorrows and the millions of ordinary moments in between those extremes.

Carolyn had coveted many an artwork in her time, but this was the first time she'd ever *envied* the piece itself.

Oh, to *be* the Weaver.

Reaching the top of the stairs, she put the back of one hand to her forehead, checking for fever. There was none, so why was she delirious?

That made her smile again.

She was suffering, she concluded, with glum humor, from a bad case of Brody-itis.

All the more reason to hedge her romantic bets.

ONCE HE GOT BACK to the ranch, Brody took the dogs inside and fed them, then headed out to the barn to tend to the horses. He planned on leaving Moonshine right there with the others until morning, when he'd figure a way to get him home to River's Bend.

When he stepped outside, the stars were spilling across the dark sky, and the three-quarter moon looked magnified, hovering just above the rims of the mountains, like it had dipped too low somehow and gotten itself snagged on a tree or the craggy face of a cliff.

Brody sighed and lifted his hat briefly, just long enough to shove a hand through his hair, and stopped right there in the yard to admire the handiwork of a God he wasn't sure he believed in.

God or no God, he figured, and daunting as the expanse of it could be, being there, awake and a part of the whole thing, even for what amounted to the blink of the cosmic eye, was a miraculous gift.

Lisa sure hadn't gotten to stick around long, though,

he thought sadly, and little Justin, his boy, hadn't lived long enough to have see two candles blazing on his birthday cake.

Just like that, Brody's throat twisted itself into a painful knot, one he could barely swallow past.

It was true that he wanted a family of his own, wanted to marry a sweet-tempered woman and fill that house at River's Bend with their kids and pack its barn with their ponies, but when he was tired, or felt particularly lonely, like tonight, the idea scared the hell out of him.

Nothing had ever—*ever*—hurt the way losing Lisa and Justin did. What if history repeated itself? What if he had to bury *another* wife, another *child*?

He was Creed-tough, thanks to all those sturdy forbearers of his and a graduate degree from the school of hard knocks, but he'd gone stark-raving crazy after that double funeral in the chapel of a mortuary in a little Montana town. He'd taken to drinking way more than too much, been on the lookout for a reason to fight, 24/7, cut himself off from the people he'd needed most— Conner and Steven and Davis and Kim.

Brody tried to shake it off, this sorry mood, made himself get moving again. Inside the house, he made sure Valentino had all he needed, told Barney it was time they headed for home and led the way out under all those stars again.

Since it was just the two of them, he let Barney ride shotgun instead of consigning him to the backseat, and drove straight to River's Bend.

There, he remembered that he hadn't eaten, and poked around in his minifridge for a minute or so, hoping something tasty might have created itself out of the ether.

Nothing had.

He got out the milk carton, took a sniff to make sure it hadn't soured and was just shaking cold cereal into a bowl when he saw headlights—beams of dusty gold—sweep across the front window.

Barney, having just settled himself on his bed over by the unlighted stove, gave an anxious little whine and perked up his ears.

A car door slammed.

Footsteps crunched along the dirt path leading up to the lodge.

A knock sounded.

"Oh, hell," Brody told Barney, setting his cereal bowl aside on the counter with a bad-tempered thump. "She's back."

Just then, the door opened and Joleen poked her head inside, beaming in the unfounded expectation of a warm welcome. This month she was a blonde, and her contacts turned her eyes an unlikely shade of purple.

Brody had trouble recalling what her real coloring was—Joleen was a chameleon, constantly searching for that perfect look.

"It's me!" she sang, quite unnecessarily, strolling right in and setting a suitcase down on the floor.

"Damn it, Joleen," Brody grumbled, "I *told* you not to come here—"

"It would just be for one night," Joleen chimed, as though that made everything different. "And what kind of welcome is that, anyway, after all we've been to each other?"

"We've been bed partners, and that's about it." Stubborn, Brody folded his arms across his chest. Hardened his jawline. "You're not staying, Joleen."

Joleen tried the hurt expression that had always stood her in such good stead, not just with him, but probably with scores of men. "You know I can't stay with my folks," she said, her mouth pouty and her eyes luminous with on-demand tears. "Mrs. Collins promised I could rent that room over her garage, but it won't be ready until tomorrow and I— It's been a long drive and I'm worn out, Brody."

He took out his wallet, extracted several bills and shoved them at her. "Then I guess you'd better check in over at the Sunset Motel," he said.

"But that's *miles* from here," Joleen practically wailed.

"It's *three* miles, Joleen, and it's not as if you have to hike over there. You have your car."

Joleen eyed the fan of twenties Brody was holding out, hesitated and then took them with a quick, snatching motion, folded them and stuffed them into the pocket of her tight jeans. "I'm almost out of gas," she persisted.

"And I'm almost out of patience," Brody replied.

The threat of tears had subsided, Joleen having figured out that it wouldn't work, but there was a flash of temper behind those tinted lenses. Evidently, she was a member of the contacts-of-the-week club.

"If you won't let me stay here," she said, "then give me the keys to the new house. I'll camp out over there tonight."

"No," Brody said bluntly. "If you don't want to go home to your folks' place or stay with a friend, you can either sleep in your car or check in at the Sunset Motel. Your choice, Joleen."

For a second there, he thought she might throw a hissy fit. Instead, though, she reached down and grabbed the handle of her suitcase again.

"I thought *you* were my friend," she said, sounding not just accusatory but genuinely wounded.

Brody didn't take the bait. In fact, he didn't say anything at all.

"It's Carolyn," Joleen said, with a note of furious triumph. "You're fooling around with Carolyn Simmons. *Again.* Did you think I wouldn't find out, Brody? I have eyes all over this town!"

"I'm not 'fooling around' with anybody—not that it would be any of your business if I were. The point is, *you're not staying here,* Joleen, tonight or any other night, and since you've already been here too long, I'd really appreciate it if you'd get out."

Her lower lip wobbled, and her eyes narrowed to mean slits. "You *bastard,*" she said. "You've been *using* me, all this time, and now that your fancy house is almost ready to live in, and you're planning on settling down with a wife, having some kids, *starting a life,* you have the nerve to throw me over for that—that movie star's *castoff?*"

Brody went around Joleen, pulled open the door, was grateful for the cool breeze that blew in from outside. His temper was at flash point.

"Get out," he said.

Joleen crossed the threshold with her suitcase, stood with stiff pride on the step and glared back at Brody over one shoulder. "If my car runs out of gas and I get murdered by some serial killer because I'm forced to

walk in these shoes, *in the dark,* it will be *your fault,*
Brody Creed."

"You have a cell phone," Brody reminded her. "And
a hundred dollars of my money. If you get stranded on
the road, call the auto club."

With that, he closed the door.

He heard Joleen give a furious, strangled scream of
frustration on the other side.

But then she stomped away.

Her car door slammed again.

The motor started with a roar.

Brody flung a meaningful look at Barney, who was
calm again, now that Hurricane Joleen had changed
course.

She laid so much rubber getting out of there that
Brody could smell burning tires, even through the
closed door and the walls.

"I have always had a way with women," he told Barney.

Barney lay down, shut his eyes and dozed off.

Well, at least *somebody* would get some sleep that
night, Brody thought.

CAROLYN ROOTED THROUGH her closet the next morning
until she found a breezy pink cotton sundress she'd made
years ago, in one of her I-enjoy-being-a-girl moods.

The garment was wrinkled, from hanging for so
long, and it could use freshening, too.

Carolyn took it downstairs to the laundry room,
tossed it into the machine, added a little soap and set
the washer to the gentle cycle, with cold water.

She had a date that night, after all, and even if Bill
had said to dress casually, she wanted to look her best.

She nearly tripped over Winston, who had trailed her from upstairs.

"What?" she asked archly, meeting the cat's thoughtful amber gaze. "I *do* wear dresses sometimes, you know. Of course, this means I'll have to shave my legs—"

"Reoww," Winston said, stepping out of her path.

"I know," Carolyn replied. "It's a major bummer."

"Hello?" The voice was Tricia's, coming from the main part of the house, where the shop was. "Carolyn? Are you here?"

Carolyn crossed the kitchen and pushed open the door leading into the shop. "I'm here," she confirmed cheerfully, with a glance at the antique clock on Natty's front-room mantel. "And you're early. We don't open for another hour, remember?"

"Oh, we'd better open right now," Tricia said, stashing her purse under the counter and smiling at Winston, who went purring to greet her. "Primrose Sullivan called me while I was making breakfast. She wanted us to have a heads-up—seems she spotted three tourists' buses in the parking lot out at the Roadside Diner."

"Yikes," Carolyn said. There went a new batch of goats' milk soap. Then, speculatively, "Maybe they'll just go right on past."

"Nope," Tricia answered matter-of-factly, picking up the telephone receiver to check for voice mail. For a watermelon smuggler, she looked very businesslike, especially after she popped her reading glasses on and began scribbling down notes. "You know Primrose. She stopped and snagged one of the travelers and asked where they were headed. Ultimately, the casino up at Cripple Creek, but the next stop? Us. Primrose is rush-

ing over with a few new pieces just in case there are
some big spenders in the crowd."

Carolyn looked at her friend in wonder. How could
she listen to voice mail, carry on a conversation *and*
take down names and call-back numbers, all at the same
time?

"Don't just stand there," Tricia commanded good-
naturedly. "Thank heaven there were some deliveries
from our suppliers yesterday afternoon, so we'll be able
to stock the shelves properly. I had Conner stack the
boxes in the small parlor."

Said parlor stood just to the left of the front door.

Carolyn hurried in that direction and, when she got
there, immediately started ripping open cartons. She
and Tricia sold handcrafted items from all over the
United States, made by talented people they usually
referred to as "cottage industrialists."

Today, there were chenille bedroom slippers in one
box, and Victorian tea cozies in another.

Tricia arrived to help, unpacking exquisitely made
art dolls, personal journals and all manner of scented
bath salts.

Primrose showed up with a pair of canvases, both
mixed-media abstracts in colors that roused a yearning in Carolyn.

"Oh, Primrose," Tricia said, stopping to look at the
pictures. "Those are *lovely.*"

Primrose, bespectacled, with gray curly hair and
owner of the largest and most colorful collection of
muumuus that side of Hawaii, beamed with pleasure.
"They're not batiks, like the Weaver, but—"

"They'll be sold in no time," Carolyn said, almost
sadly.

Tricia and Primrose both looked at her with curious concern, but neither one commented.

For the next twenty minutes, which was all the time they had before the first of the three jam-packed buses pulled up outside, the three women were far too busy to chat.

CHAPTER ELEVEN

BY THE TIME the third tour bus pulled away, an hour and a half later, Carolyn and Tricia were so low on merchandise that they had to close the shop in order to regroup.

Primrose's two new works of art had been sold immediately, as had the last of the aprons, the most recent batch of goats' milk soap and the contents of most of the boxes they'd unpacked earlier.

"That was *incredible*," Tricia marveled, sitting wearily at the table in the downstairs kitchen, a cup of tea steaming in front of her. "Like a plague of locusts, but in a good way."

"Beyond incredible," Carolyn agreed happily. "Of course, we still have to pay all our consignment people, cover basic expenses and all that, but—drum roll, please—*we definitely turned a profit!*" She'd just taken her pink dress out of the washer and was about to hang it outside, on the clothesline.

Tricia was focused on the dress. "That's pretty," she said. "Is there a special occasion coming up?"

Pleased, Carolyn nodded. "I have a date tonight," she confided.

Interest sparked, Tricia asked hopefully, "With Brody?"

Carolyn paused at the back door, shook her head.

"Brody and I are going out Saturday night," she said, blushing a little.

Tricia's face lit up. "Really?"

"It's only dinner and a movie," Carolyn said. Then, with a gesture of one hand that meant "hold on a moment," she dashed outside, pegged her sundress carefully to the line and drew in a breath of that thin high-country air, full of blue sky and budding flowers and freshly cut grass.

When she returned to Natty's kitchen, Tricia went right on, as though there had been no interruption in the conversation. "But you *are* going out with Brody?"

Carolyn got out a cup and poured tea into it from the china pot on the counter. Sat down at the table, across from Tricia.

"We have ground rules," she said, treading carefully. *"Responsibilities."*

"Who does?" Tricia asked, raising one eyebrow.

"Brody and I. For one thing, we have agreed not to have sex."

Tricia twinkled as she smiled. "Is that a ground rule or a responsibility?" she teased.

Carolyn made a face at her.

Tricia laughed. "And tonight?"

"Bill invited me over to his place for a barbecue," she said.

"Bill?" Tricia pretended to muse over the name. "That would be Mr. Coffee, right? The death-defying firefighting pilot?"

Carolyn sighed. "Yes," she said.

"Does Brody know?"

"He does."

"I love it," Tricia enthused. "My brother-in-law must be beside himself."

"He was actually pretty unconcerned," Carolyn recalled, concerned.

"Maybe he wanted you to *think* he was," Tricia said, with utter confidence in her own powers of discernment.

Carolyn wished she could be that sure of herself and her perceptions, but certainty didn't seem to be part of her personal makeup.

She stiffened, reminded of the original conversation with Brody, in Tricia and Conner's kitchen, when the whole situation had come dangerously close to circuit-blowing, spark-throwing overload. "You didn't hear him setting his stupid ground rules," she said, revealing more than she'd ever intended by that statement.

"No sex?" Tricia asked, visibly battling back a laugh.

"*And* we can both see other people if we want to."

Tricia's expression changed in an instant. "Brody said that?"

Carolyn nodded.

"That stinker," Tricia muttered.

Carolyn peered at her in a don't-stop-there kind of way. "If you know something I don't, Tricia Creed, you'd better tell me," she challenged.

"There's probably no connection," Tricia said.

"Spill it," Carolyn persisted, her tea entirely forgotten.

"Well," Tricia replied, squirming a little, "Joleen is back in town, that's all."

Joleen is back in town—*that's all?*

Although she knew she had no right to bristle at this news, Carolyn did indeed bristle. Like a porcupine.

Tricia smiled again and reached over to pat Carolyn's hand. "I'm sure one thing has nothing to do with the other," she said.

Carolyn just looked at her.

"Joleen grew up in Lonesome Bend," Tricia explained quickly. "Her family is here. I'm sure that's the reason she came back—and you know she never stays around for long."

"I should have known what he was up to," Carolyn said. "In fact, I *did* know, but I chose the luxury of denial."

This time, it was Tricia who didn't respond. She seemed to be at a complete loss for words.

"Brody knew Joleen was on her way," Carolyn went on. "*That's* why he said what he did about both of us seeing other people. I wonder if *he and Joleen* have set any ground rules? No sex? I doubt it!"

Tricia looked pained. "Carolyn—"

"If that's the way Brody wants to play the game," Carolyn interrupted, *"fine."* She pushed back her chair, stood up again. "As a matter of fact," she continued, "I think I'll go upstairs, log on to my laptop and check my mailbox at Friendly Faces."

"Carolyn, you shouldn't— Brody wouldn't—" She fell silent, after uttering a long sigh, and covered her face with both hands.

Carolyn left her friend sitting at the table and practically sprinted toward the inside staircase.

She was behaving like a crazy person, she knew that.

It was just that knowing didn't seem to make much difference.

While the laptop booted up—it was old and therefore slow—Carolyn paced back and forth across the kitchen. Winston, meowing, kept weaving his way back and forth between her feet.

She finally sank into the chair in front of her desk to wait for the computer to grind through all its mysterious electronic sequences. Better to sit down than to squash the cat, or trip over the fool critter and break her neck.

Spookily, the Friendly Faces website opened on its own.

Carolyn's eyes widened. The mailbox icon—a yellow one, rural-style, with a red flag—pulsed like a heart. Cartoon letters spewed from its opening in bursts like erupting fireworks.

She drew a deep breath, let it out slowly and clicked on the mailbox.

Robert, from Telluride.

Buck, from Colorado Springs.

Sam, from Aspen.

All in all, there were an astounding forty-three messages.

Rattled, Carolyn looked down at Winston, who was now sitting on the floor next to her chair, as attentive as ever.

"It wasn't even a very good picture of me," she complained to him.

Downstairs, she could hear Tricia moving around Natty's kitchen.

Carolyn sighed, got up from her chair and went back down to find her friend.

"I'm sorry," she said, from the kitchen doorway. "For the way I acted just now, I mean."

Tricia, having washed their teacups and set them in the drainer to dry, turned to smile at her. "Breathe, Carolyn. Everything will be all right."

Carolyn hunched one shoulder, let it fall again. "I

have forty-three messages on my Friendly Faces page," she said weakly. "*Forty-three.* Tricia, what am I going to do?"

"Read them?" Tricia asked mildly, rehanging the hand towel she'd just used. "Answer some and delete others?" She pressed her hands to her back, stretched contentedly. "It's an embarrassment of riches, Carolyn. *Enjoy* it. You might meet the perfect man for you." A pause, accompanied by another smile. "Of course, there are those among us who believe you already *have* met the perfect man for you and can't bring yourself to admit it."

"What do you want from me?" Carolyn asked, in a burst of friendly frustration. "I'm going out with Brody on Saturday—against my better judgment, I might add."

Tricia's eyes danced. "Ah-ha," she said.

"I didn't name names, Tricia," Carolyn pointed out. "I didn't say *Brody* was the perfect man for me. If there even *is* such an animal."

"I didn't name names, either," Tricia said, her tone sunny. "Interesting that you made the leap, though. From *perfect man* to *Brody.*"

"Stop it," Carolyn said. "Nobody made any *leaps* here."

"Whatever you say," Tricia replied, heading for the shop. Taking a sheaf of receipts from the drawer of the cash register, she waggled them at Carolyn. "I'll do the books this time," she said. "Do you want me to order more goats' milk soap? And those beeswax candles went fast, too, especially for this time of year—"

Carolyn felt a surge of affection for her friend. "It's a lot of paperwork, Tricia. It might take all evening—"

Tricia extracted her purse from under the counter

and shouldered it on, like one of those old-fashioned plow harnesses. "Carolyn," she said, "it's the least I can do. Aren't you always sewing aprons and filling orders from our website? Excuse me, but even *you* can't do everything."

With that, she waddled over, kissed Carolyn on the cheek, bid Winston a fond farewell and headed for the back door.

Carolyn followed her.

The pink dress looked like a swath of cotton candy, billowing in the fresh breeze.

"What am I supposed to do for a whole afternoon, if you're taking all the work home with you?" Carolyn called, as her friend opened the door of her Pathfinder to get behind the wheel.

"Get ready for your date?" Tricia responded merrily. "Soak in a bubble bath. Give yourself a facial. Take a nap. You're an intelligent woman—you'll think of something."

Carolyn wanted to offer a parting protest, but she didn't have one ready.

There were, however, plenty of things to keep her occupied for the rest of the afternoon, she soon realized, even without Tricia's decadent suggestions.

She could work on the gypsy skirt.

She could make more frilly aprons, with zigzag trim and ruffles.

She could deal with all those emails in her Friendly Faces box.

She could even shave her legs.

"So," CONNER SAID, as he and Brody and Davis hoisted a sick calf off the ground and into the bed of one of the work trucks, "I hear Joleen blew back into town last night."

Once upon a time, Joleen had been a sore subject—a *real* sore subject—between the brothers. Now she was just another way for Conner to get under Brody's hide. He couldn't seem to go more than fifteen minutes without making the attempt.

"Is that right?" Brody asked, dusting his hands off on the thighs of his jeans. "I hadn't heard."

The mama cow was bawling her head off, worried over her baby being hauled away. Davis patted her flank and said, "We'll fix your little one up for you, Bessie. Good as new."

The range cattle didn't have names, as such, but Davis called all cows Bessie, and all bulls Ferdinand.

Conner cocked a grin at Brody as he stepped up onto the running board of the pickup, about to get behind the wheel. "You're a pretty bad liar for somebody with a rascal's history," he joked. "Word is, Joleen went straight to your place and you threw her out with a hundred dollars and a speech about taking the moral high road."

"Drive slow," Davis advised, hoisting himself up onto the tailgate to ride with the calf. "Bessie here will be following after us, and I don't want her worn out from trying to keep up."

Conner nodded—he'd been through this process many times, and so had Brody and Davis—and Brody got in on the passenger side.

"Small-town gossip is one of the few things I *didn't* miss while I was away from Lonesome Bend," Brody said immediately.

Conner chuckled, checked the rearview mirror to

make sure Davis was ready to roll and put the truck in gear. "Folks talk about you," he said. "It means they care, that's all."

"It *means,* little brother, that they have small minds and too much free time."

That made Conner laugh.

Bessie ambled behind them, still carrying on like a sinner on his first day in hell. Even over the roar of that old truck's old engine, she was audible.

Back at the barn, they'd settle Bessie and the calf in a stall, keep an eye on the little one for a day or two, bring the vet if necessary. They'd found the calf lying with his head downhill, probably suffering from sunstroke and mild dehydration, but the worst danger— being vulnerable to predators—was over.

Usually in these cases, a little TLC did the trick.

Bessie and her baby boy would be back out on the range, with the rest of the herd, in no time.

All of a sudden, his jocular mood vanished, and Conner turned serious as all get-out. "Be careful, Brody," he said. "Carolyn is a good woman, and she's had a hard row to hoe almost since the day she was born. It wouldn't be right to hurt her."

Again.

Conner hadn't actually said the word, but it hung in the air between them.

"You think I *want* to hurt her?" Brody asked, nettled. He shifted around on the seat, which was cracked leather, with springs and stuffing showing in places. Davis believed in using equipment until it disintegrated back to the particle state.

"I didn't say that," Conner replied, shifting again. "Didn't mean to imply it, either."

Brody heaved a sigh. "I know," he said. "Maybe I'm a little touchy when it comes to Joleen. She's got some wild hair about my being involved with Carolyn, and I'm afraid she's going to make trouble."

"Did she say she would?"

"In so many words," Brody answered wearily, "yes."

Conner considered for a while before asking, "Are you, Brody? Involved with Carolyn, I mean?"

Brody glanced over at his brother, at the profile so remarkably like his own that he might have been looking into a mirror. "Let's just say I'd *like* to be," he finally said. "But she doesn't trust me, and I can't blame her for that."

"Amen," Conner agreed.

They were quiet for a while, except for the truck engine and old Bessie.

"What did you mean before," Brody ventured, "when you said Carolyn has had a hard time from when she was little?"

Conner was silent for so long that Brody didn't think he was going to answer. "She grew up in foster homes," he said. "There are a lot of good ones out there, caring people trying to make a difference in kids' lives, but there are also a few whose hearts just aren't in it. From what Kim and Tricia have told me, Carolyn got more than her share of the second variety."

Brody pictured Carolyn as a skinny, coltish little girl, tall for her age, with freckles and clothes either handed down or bought cheap, probably smarter by half than the other kids in her class, and the image bruised the underside of his heart. The secondary emotion, though, was anger.

"Was she abused?"

"More like neglected, from what I gather. And then there was the thing with that movie star, after you left."

Something quickened inside Brody at the reminder. What had Joleen called Carolyn last night?

A movie star's castoff.

"What happened?" Brody asked carefully. The barn was in sight now; soon, poor Bessie could relax, and the calf could start recovering from whatever ailed it.

And that god-awful caterwauling would stop.

"Don't know," Conner said, turning his head long enough to give Brody the kind of level look that always meant he was telling the truth. "There were lots of rumors flying around at the time, of course. Carolyn was the live-in nanny, and some people said she was having an affair with Gifford Welsh while his wife was away on some movie set."

Brody's back molars clamped together, unclamped again. As the lifelong resident of a glass house, he couldn't go around throwing stones, but it galled him, just the same, to think of another man—*any* other man—touching Carolyn in all the intimate ways he once had.

And wanted to again.

"If you had to hazard a guess as to whether or not the gossips had it right," he began, watching Conner, who was watching the bumpy range trail by then, "what would you say?"

Again, Conner was thoughtful. He liked to take his time when he answered a question, especially one he considered important. "I'd say," he finally replied, "that Carolyn wouldn't take up with a married man, and not just because she'd figure it to be wrong. She's got too much pride for that."

Brody laughed, out of relief and not because anything was funny, and reached over to clasp his brother briefly by the nape and give him a good, squeezing shake.

"Bull's-eye," he said. "Give the man a Kewpie doll."

"A what?" Conner asked, with a frown that made Brody laugh again. And this time, it *was* funny.

"Figure of speech, little brother," he said, when his amusement had ebbed away a bit. "Back in the day, when somebody won a prize at a carnival booth, they'd get a Kewpie doll."

"Whatever," Conner said, comically indignant.

By then, they were home, with the task of unloading the sick calf before them, and poor Bessie panting and huffing from the exercise.

"Everything will be all right now, girl," Brody heard his uncle tell the cow. "Your baby is safe, and so are you."

LEGS SHAVEN, hair clean, Carolyn stepped out of the shower and wrapped herself in a towel.

Winston sat on the lid of the toilet, waiting for her to emerge from what probably seemed, to him, to be a chamber of horrors.

"See?" Carolyn said, patting his head. "It *is* possible to get wet and survive."

"Reow," Winston objected, and leaped down off the commode, tail fluffed out in annoyance. The top of his head was damp where she'd touched him.

Carolyn laughed. "Okay," she said, waiting for the fogged-up mirror over the sink to clear up so she could apply moisturizer. The makeup—she didn't plan on wearing much—could wait. "That's two things off the predate checklist. Legs shaved, hair washed. Now, for the facial."

She opened the medicine cabinet and peered inside.

A box of stick-on bandages. A bottle of mouthwash, nearly empty. Toothpaste, a brush, a box of cotton swabs and three tampons trying to escape from their paper wrappers.

Not one single component of a facial.

Oh, *well*.

That left the nap.

Carolyn left the mirror to defog on its own and went into her bedroom. Flung herself down on the bed and lay there, spread-eagle.

Nope.

Sleep was not going to happen.

She was too keyed up to get any shut-eye and, anyway, it was the middle of the day.

And it was too early to take the pink dress from the clothesline, give it a quick spritz of spray starch and a few licks with a hot iron.

She arose, with a sigh, and put on her bathrobe, but that was too warm, so she replaced it with an oversize T-shirt.

For now, that would have to do.

Carolyn took the gypsy skirt down from its hook on her bedroom door and held it out for inspection. She'd expected to be over wanting to keep it by now, but she definitely was not over it.

She could fit it to her own dimensions in a trice, but that was beside the point. The skirt definitely would not work at a backyard barbecue—or when Brody took her out on Saturday night, either.

There was only one movie theater in that part of the

county, and it was in the next town, Wiley Springs. The nearest fancy restaurant, where one might presumably wear a magical concoction of ribbons and beads, was just outside of Denver.

Carolyn put the skirt back on its hook, suddenly dispirited. She'd planned to fuss with it a little, but now the prospect had zero appeal.

There were always the aprons. They could barely keep up with the demand.

Yee-haw, she thought sourly. Aprons.

Carolyn decided to give the nap another shot.

This time, it worked.

When she woke up to the cold, nuzzling nose of a cat wanting his supper, it was after five o'clock.

Hurriedly, Carolyn doled out Winston's sardine ration, then rushed downstairs, still in the T-shirt, to collect the pink dress from the clothesline.

The smell of the fabric was delicious.

Back upstairs, she wielded the iron, keeping one eye on the kitchen clock the whole time, and then went into the bathroom to put on mascara, minimal foundation and lip gloss to match the dress.

Since she'd gone to sleep with her hair still damp from the shower, it stood out around her head like the mane of a lion named Frizzy, and bringing it under control practically called for a whip and a chair.

Pinned into a loose knot at the back of her head, it looked passably good, Carolyn decided. Although there might well be wide-spread injuries if it escaped its pins at an inopportune moment.

"Now you're just being silly," Carolyn told her reflection, in the fog-free mirror. "Get a grip, okay?"

Carolyn's reflection looked indignant.

"Well," Carolyn told the familiar image, "it's your own fault for not blow-drying before you took your nap."

"Reow," said Winston, now sitting in the bathroom doorway, licking his chops.

Nothing like a good sardine.

Carolyn laughed, at the cat and at herself.

She was going to a barbecue in Bill Venable's back-yard. His late wife's parents would be there, along with his nine-year-old daughter.

What was there to be nervous about?

Plenty, as it turned out.

When Carolyn pulled up in front of Bill's very nice house, in her very old car, a child who had to be Ellie was waiting on the sidewalk.

With a big sign, hand-lettered in colorful markers and stapled to a stick.

It read "Go Away. We Don't Want You Here Unless You're Angela."

The greeting gave Carolyn pause, of course, and so did the glower on the child's face. She was as pretty, this kid, as a Victorian rendering of *Alice in Wonderland*.

And if looks could kill, Carolyn would have been incinerated on the spot.

She was debating—go or stay—when Bill suddenly appeared, bursting through the front gate and gently but firmly taking the sign from Ellie's hands before pointing a stern index finger toward the house.

Ellie obeyed, shuffling her feet, her head lowered.

Bill tossed the sign into the yard, summoned up a sporting smile and approached Carolyn, opening the car door for her.

"Maybe this isn't a good idea," Carolyn fretted. Despite the child's behavior, she'd taken an instant liking to Ellie. The munchkin definitely had spirit.

"Nonsense," Bill said. "It's a *great* idea. Come along—the steaks are on the grill, and I want to introduce you to Ellie's grandparents, Charlie and Stella. They're excited to meet you."

Privately, Carolyn doubted that. Most likely, Charlie and Stella were Angela supporters, like Ellie. They, being grown-ups, would just be a bit more subtle about it, that was all.

"I don't know—"

"Carolyn," Bill said, smiling, "it's *supper,* not the coronation of King William."

Carolyn laughed, reminded of how much she liked this man.

If only she could muster up something more.

Bill offered his hand. "Let's go," he said quietly. "I promise you, Ellie isn't a monster. She just acts like one sometimes."

"Don't we all," Carolyn responded, her smile genuine now, comfortable on her face.

Bill led her around the side of the big house and into a wonderful, shady backyard, with flowers and an arbor and a swinging bench.

Charlie and Stella were both attractive, a well-matched couple in their sixties. As Bill and Carolyn approached, Charlie, a big man with a full head of snow-white hair, rose from his seat on the bench at the picnic table. Stella, also white-haired, looked like a slender pixie, and her smile was warm.

Bill made the introductions and, once Carolyn was settled at the picnic table, with a glass of fresh lemonade, excused himself to duck into the house, presumably to deal with Ellie.

Stella, seated beside her handsome husband, watched Bill disappear through the back door, a wistful smile lingering on her lips but not quite reaching her eyes. "I take it our granddaughter has been acting up again," she remarked.

Carolyn chuckled, took a sip of the tasty lemonade and set her glass down on the red-and-white checked oilcloth covering the top of the picnic table. "She certainly doesn't lack for imagination," she replied.

Charlie raised bristly white eyebrows. "What happened?"

Carolyn hesitated, then described the sign incident.

"Oh, dear," Stella breathed.

"It might have been an imaginative thing to do," Charlie began, "but it was also rude. Bill needs to stop fooling around and get married again, give that child a mother to guide her before she turns into a complete mess."

Stella elbowed him in the ribs. "Charlie!" she scolded, but there was so much love in her voice that Carolyn choked up a little, just hearing it. What a beautiful thing it was, the two of them growing older together, and still frisky.

Charlie ignored his wife, but his love for Stella, like hers for him, was clearly visible to Carolyn, who was feeling oddly detached from the scene now, an observer, not really part of things.

"Don't get me wrong," Charlie went on, quietly earnest. "We love our granddaughter. Ellie's a force of nature—the spitting image of her mother, our daughter, Connie—and we wouldn't want to see her change too much." He paused, sighed. "However, it *will* be a relief when the brat phase passes."

"Ellie," Stella said firmly, "is *not* a brat."

At that, the screen door swung open, and the little sign-bearer stepped out onto the back porch, looking like a recalcitrant angel in her pink cotton shorts, matching top and purple flip-flops.

Bill, standing behind her, gave her a little nudge to the shoulder. "March," Carolyn heard him say.

Ellie sucked in a dramatic breath and let it out as a huge and wobbly sigh. She looked back at Bill.

Bill gave a brief nod, part encouragement, part impatience.

Carolyn, looking on, felt another sweet stab of affection for little Ellie Venable.

Stalwartly, Ellie faced forward again, high-stepped it down the porch stairs and walked over to stand near the picnic table, next to Carolyn.

Putting out one small and probably sticky hand, the child said, with an utter lack of conviction, "I'm sorry for being impolite. After all, you can't help it if you're not Angela."

Muted groans from the other adults greeted this pronouncement.

But Carolyn merely smiled and took the small hand, shook it. Sure enough, it was sticky.

"You're right," she replied, after a moment, "I have my hands pretty full just being *Carolyn* these days."

Ellie narrowed crystalline blue eyes, studying Carolyn. "Are you willing to start over?" she asked.

Carolyn was struck by the wisdom of that question, especially coming from a nine-year-old. "I'd like that," she said.

The little girl indicated that she wanted to sit down, and Carolyn scooted over to make room.

"My dad says when I grow up, I'm either going to be the first woman president or the head of my cell block," Ellie said, quite seriously. The tiniest smile peeked out from the clouds of caution veiling that lovely little face, and she dropped her voice. "My dad kids a lot. He doesn't *really* expect me to wind up in prison."

"I don't know, kiddo," Charlie teased, grinning at his grandchild from the opposite side of the picnic table. "It seems to me that you're developing criminal tendencies."

"My grandpa makes jokes, too," Ellie confided to Carolyn.

"I *am* a retired cop," Charlie insisted, with a twinkle, picking up the lemonade pitcher and pouring a glassful for Ellie. "I know a troublemaker when I see one."

"All you have to do is look in the mirror," Stella supplied, singsonging the words and, at the same time, beaming at Ellie like a golden sunrise. "You'll be *president*," she told the child, without a hint of doubt.

"I'm not sure I'd want the job," Ellie replied, with the solemnity of a very intelligent and precocious child. "No matter what the president does, somebody pitches a fit about it. I'd rather fly airplanes and put out big fires that cover whole states, like Dad does."

Bill, who had been turning steaks on the grill until then, joined the others at the table, sitting at Carolyn's right, not too close, but not too far away, either.

Yet again, Carolyn silently lamented her lack of passion where he was concerned. Why couldn't she have these brotherly feelings toward *Brody,* and want Bill with an intensity that was getting harder and harder to deny with every breath she drew?

It was *perverse,* that was what it was.

She did enjoy the remainder of the evening, though. The steaks were delicious, Bill was attentive without coming on too strong, Charlie and Stella were chatty and cordial, without asking any questions more intrusive than, "Did you grow up in Lonesome Bend, Carolyn?"

Even Ellie warmed up considerably, though it was clear that she still had her reservations about her father's new friend.

When the air got chilly and the mosquitoes came out, it was generally agreed that the party was over.

Carolyn offered to help clear the table and carry in the leftovers and the dirty dishes, but Stella and Charlie insisted that this was their job. Ellie could be their assistant.

Bill walked Carolyn back to her car, stood on the sidewalk looking down at her with an expression of friendly regret in his eyes.

"This airplane isn't going to lift off the runway, is it?" he asked.

Carolyn sighed, smiled up at him and shook her head. "No," she said. "I don't think so."

"Can we still be friends?" Bill wanted to know. "Because here's the thing, Carolyn Simmons—I really *like* you."

"I like you, too," Carolyn said truthfully.

He lowered his head then, and brushed his lips lightly against hers, but there was no charge.

Both of them sighed in resignation.

"I had to try," Bill told her, smiling when she laughed.

"I understand," Carolyn replied, feeling sad but kind of relieved, too. "Did you mean what you said just now, about our still being friends?"

"I meant it, all right," he said.

Carolyn rocked back on her heels slightly, something she did when she was thinking. "It would have to be take-out food or something," she mused, "because I don't cook very well. But I'd love it if you'd come over to my place for dinner one night soon."

Bill's expression was one of pleased surprise. "Sounds good," he said. "But if we're not going anywhere, the two of us—?"

Carolyn's smile broadened. "If we're not going anywhere," she finished for him, "we can relax and have fun."

"I like that idea," Bill said. "How would you feel about taking a spin in my airplane?"

CHAPTER TWELVE

"I'M GOING TO BE a little late getting to the ranch today," Brody said into his cell phone.

"What else is new?" Conner retorted from his end of the call, but there was a grin lurking in his voice. "You're about *ten years* late already, not that I've been keeping track or anything."

"Of course you haven't," Brody said wryly. He stood outside the old snack bar/projection house at the Bluebird Drive-in that sunny May morning, watched as his contractor and another member of the crew unloaded the gas-powered generator that would, hopefully, provide the necessary juice to run the movie on Saturday night.

The original projector was useless; over the years, it had been converted to a mouse-and-spider condominium complex. Brody had rented the necessary equipment from an outfit in Denver, and a friend of his, a film distributor by profession, was overnighting a couple of first-run movies. An electrician was due any minute to check the antiquated speaker boxes, on their rusty poles, and run a line out to whichever one worked best.

If *any* of them worked.

Inwardly, Brody sighed.

"Brody?" Conner prompted. "Usually, when people are on the phone, they *talk* to each other."

Brody chuckled. "Yeah," he agreed. "Guess that's an indication that the call is over. I've said my piece, and I have things to do."

"What things?" Conner wanted to know. Usually the classic man of few words, impatient with telephones, he was being downright chatty.

"Who pulled your string?" Brody countered, giving the contractor and his helper a thumbs-up when they were ready to set the generator down.

Conner sighed. "It's like you to be late," he said. "It *isn't* like you to call and explain. What's going on, Brody?"

"It's none of your business, little brother," Brody replied affably, "but I'll tell you anyway. I'm getting ready for a big date."

Silence.

Now it was Brody's turn to do the prompting. "Conner? You still there?"

"I'm here," Conner said. "What *kind* of 'big date,' Brody?"

"How many kinds are there?" Brody countered, amused.

Conner didn't say anything right away, but the two-way twin radar was functioning just fine, and Brody knew what he was thinking.

"I'll tell you all about it later," Brody assured his brother. "Provided you don't keep me on this damn phone all day, that is. In that case, I'll be rolling out there sometime tomorrow."

Conner broke down and gave a raspy chuckle then. "See you when I see you," he said. "Davis and I will be on the range for most of the morning, rounding up strays, if you want to look us up."

Brody grinned. "*Goodbye,* Conner," he said pointedly, before shutting down the call. They'd had their share of long conversations, he and Conner, back when they were boys, yammering on about everything from girls and fishing tackle to what their lives might have been like if their folks had lived to raise them.

They'd traveled their own separate broken roads for a long time after that, though, and, despite all the progress they'd made, opening up to each other still took an effort.

Maybe, Brody thought, his throat tightening even as his spirits rose, the worst was over, and those winding roads were finally going to converge.

CAROLYN HAD THE SHOP all to herself that morning, except for Winston, of course. Tricia was at home resting. Over the phone earlier, she'd insisted she felt fine, and there was nothing to worry about—it was just that her ankles were swollen, she felt like an elephant and she was *so tired*.

Carolyn couldn't help worrying, at least a little bit, because Tricia was her friend, but she kept herself busy, and that helped.

Not that there were a lot of customers, because there weren't.

Primrose brought in more art pieces—she apparently had a stockpile of them stashed in her home studio—and she and Carolyn decided on prices and hung the series of small batiks, all featuring Native American women, on one wall of the shop.

After Primrose had gone, Carolyn took digital pictures of the arrangement and posted the best images on the website, since a lot of their business came via the internet.

More boxes full of merchandise were delivered, thankfully, and Carolyn made the necessary changes to the inventory list she and Tricia kept on the downstairs computer, ignoring the pesky little blitzes from Friendly Faces—*somebody likes your picture!*—as best she could, given how intrusive they were.

Once that was done, and the items had been tagged with prices and set out on shelves and display tables, it was lunchtime.

Upstairs, in her apartment kitchen, Carolyn shared a couple of hard-boiled eggs with Winston and contemplated the long afternoon that lay ahead. To be followed, alas, by an even *longer* evening.

Determined to make good use of what would otherwise be idle time—she didn't want to close the shop early again that day, lest it become a habit—Carolyn lugged her portable sewing machine downstairs and set it up on one of the display tables. She carted down stacks of fabric next, along with various sewing notions, and settled in to run up a new supply of aprons.

Two local women came in around 3:00 p.m., looking for birthday gifts for a friend, and bought up the pair of aprons Carolyn had just finished making, sending her happily back to square one.

It looked like the rush was over, as far as customers were concerned, and Carolyn, with tiny threads stuck to her clothes and eye strain setting in, decided four-thirty wasn't too early to close.

She was at the door, in fact, just about to turn the dead bolt, when she saw someone step up onto the porch, hesitate and then reach for the knob.

Carolyn swung the door open, never one to turn away a potential sale, and nearly gasped.

The woman standing on the other side of the threshold was about her own age, and outlandishly beautiful, with copper-blond hair and striking brown eyes. Except for her modern clothing, a trim tan pantsuit, she might have stepped out of a Renaissance painting, she was that regal.

Instantly, Carolyn knew who she was.

"Angela?" she said, stepping back and holding the door open wide.

"How did you know?" Angela asked, after a short and rather nervous nod of acknowledgment.

"Wild guess," Carolyn said, with a smile. "Come in."

"I—I didn't really come here to shop. I just wanted—"

Carolyn touched the woman's arm. "Come in," she repeated. "I'll make tea."

Angela finally stepped into the entryway, and was instantly greeted by a purring Winston.

The Botticelli face lit up, and she bent to pet the cat. "Hello, there," she said.

Winston, the diplomat, Carolyn thought, with a tender twist to her heart. Except when it came to Brody, the animal was a one-cat welcoming committee.

"This way," Carolyn said, and moved through the entryway, then through the shop and into Natty's big kitchen.

Angela followed, politely reluctant. She was probably wondering what had possessed her to drop in on the woman Bill Venable was dating, though she gave no outward indication of that.

Carolyn liked to brew tea the old-fashioned way, especially when she had guests, and she warmed the china pot with hot water while putting the kettle on the stove to boil, got out the canister of fresh tea leaves.

Angela, meanwhile, took a seat at the table.

"I'm so sorry," she said, after long consideration and a shake of her head. She wore her hair in a tidy, up-swept style, accented with a braid across her crown. That probably accounted for the Renaissance look. "I never do things like this."

"Things like what?" Carolyn asked, determined to put her visitor at ease.

"I needed to see what you look like," Angela confessed, in a little burst of self-exasperation.

Carolyn laughed softly, mindful of her blue jeans, baggy T-shirt and the coating of tiny threads clinging to her clothes and probably her hair, too. She spread her hands, while waiting for the tea water to boil, and joked, "Here I am. Are you impressed?"

A little smile flicked at one corner of Angela's Cupid's-bow mouth, but her eyes were sad. "Actually," she said, "yes. I *am* impressed."

Carolyn didn't know what to say to that—"thank you" wouldn't sound right—so she went to the break-front, another of Natty's belongings, passed down to Tricia, and took out china cups and saucers. Silver teaspoons. And where were the sugar bowl and the little milk pitcher?

"I shouldn't have come here," Angela said.

The teakettle began to wobble on the burner.

Carolyn crossed to the table and sat down across from Angela. Trying to project friendly receptivity, she simply waited for the other woman to speak again.

Tears swam in Angela's eyes, but she quickly blinked them back.

Ah, Carolyn thought, *another tough cookie, like me, holding it together.*

"Bill has a perfect right to go out with other women," Angela announced.

Carolyn let her mouth quirk at one corner, but held her peace. The ball was, after all, still in Angela's court.

"Do you like him?" Angela's voice was small now, almost timid.

"Yes," Carolyn said. *Not in the way you think, but, yes, I definitely like Bill Venable. I like him a lot.*

Angela gave a little sigh. "Help me out, here," she said, her eyes glistening again. "Please?"

"What do you want to know, Angela?"

The teakettle came to a whistling boil.

Great timing.

Carolyn hurried to the stove, took the kettle off the heat and poured hot water into the china pot, over the waiting leaves of orange pekoe, left the works to steep for the requisite five minutes.

"Is it serious?" Angela asked. "Between you and Bill, I mean?"

Carolyn considered her answer carefully. Obviously, Angela cared for the man, whatever her reservations might be concerning his work as a flying firefighter, but this was dangerous ground.

She meant to tread lightly.

"I guess that depends on your definition of *serious,*" she said, at last.

"I know I don't have any right to ask," Angela said, shaking her head and looking baffled, as if she just didn't understand herself sometimes.

God knew, Carolyn could relate to *that* feeling.

"I like Bill," she reiterated, albeit gently, "but I wouldn't feel right trying to explain *his* feelings. If you have questions, Angela, you need to ask him."

Angela was quiet, thoughtful. But, thank heaven, no longer tearful.

Carolyn brought the teapot to the table, giving her unexpected company a few moments to collect herself. She poured for Angela, then for herself and shushed Winston, who was lobbying for his sardine ration. Not trusting the milk she had on hand, she retrieved the sugar bowl but not the matching creamer.

Angela, somewhat recovered, actually smiled—and went from beautiful to dazzling. "Ellie was right," she said. "You're a 'nice lady,' Carolyn."

"I try," Carolyn said, spooning sugar into her tea. Silver rattled against the inside of her cup. And, of course, the conversation lagged. To get it going again, Carolyn added, "I hear you teach school."

"Third grade," Angela said, with pride.

"Is Ellie in your class?" Did nine-year-olds go to third grade? Carolyn couldn't recall.

Angela's hand trembled slightly as she lifted her teacup to her mouth, took a sip and shook her head, but she was more relaxed than before.

Not that that was saying a whole lot.

"She was last year," Angela replied. "That's how—" She paused to blush. "That's how Bill and I met. At a parent-teacher meeting."

"I see," Carolyn said.

Angela spoke reluctantly. "Did Bill tell you about me?"

"Yes," Carolyn answered, in a tone that said she'd

go that far, but no further. As she'd told Angela before, if she wanted to know how Bill felt about her, she was going to have to ask *him*.

Angela sighed. "There I go again," she said. "You must think I'm on the short list for my own reality show—they could call it *The Real Crazies of Colorado*."

Carolyn laughed. She liked Angela, hoped they might become friends at some point. "Do you like teaching?" she asked. "I used to want to be a teacher, once upon a time."

Again, Angela lit up. "I *love* teaching," she said. "Make that, I love *children*. The job itself can be really discouraging—the pay is bad, and the parents can be impossible. But the kids, well, they make it all worthwhile."

Carolyn had been blessed with several insightful, compassionate teachers while she was doing her best to grow up, and their kind guidance had made all the difference. They'd told her she was bright, and talented, and she could be anybody she wanted to be, if she was willing to put in the effort.

"What stopped you?" Angela asked, breaking into her thoughts, bringing her back to the here and now.

Carolyn must have looked puzzled, because Angela immediately clarified her question. "From being a teacher, I mean."

"I didn't go to college," Carolyn said, off the top of her head.

"Oh," Angela said, and took another sip from her elegant teacup. Now *she* was the one doing the waiting.

"Which means," Carolyn went on presently, "that I didn't want to teach badly enough to go the scholarship, student-loan route. When I did manage to take a few night courses, they were all design-related. Color theory. Perspective. Things like that."

"You're an artist?" Angela asked, with genuine interest.

"No," Carolyn hastened to say. "I sew a little, that's all."

She thought of the gypsy skirt, hanging on its hook upstairs, behind her bedroom door, and she felt a twinge of guilt, as though she'd been disloyal to a trusting friend.

"Sewing is an art," Angela said.

To Carolyn, sewing was a craft, not an art, but it was also sacred. There was no magic quite like making something useful and pretty from a bolt of cloth; for her, the process was almost mystical, a form of active prayer. "I guess for some people, that's true," she said. "I've seen some quilts that belong in museums."

Angela nodded in agreement. "I'd like to see something you've made," she said. Then she blushed. "I'm not good at sewing myself. I could never set a sleeve, or put in a zipper that didn't look as though it was the work of a chimpanzee."

Carolyn, smiling, thought of the aprons she'd been working on, but immediately dismissed the idea. She had the oddest desire to show Angela—a woman she barely knew—her masterpiece, the gypsy skirt. So far, only Tricia had seen it.

She bit her lower lip, thinking.

"I've overstepped," Angela said. "Again."

"Wait here," Carolyn told her, pushing back her chair. Before she could change her mind, she hurried upstairs, grabbed the skirt and brought it back down to Natty's kitchen.

Shyly, she held the garment up for Angela to look at.

Angela's eyes widened. "Oh, *my,*" she said, setting her teacup in its saucer with a little rattle. "You *made* that?"

Now that she'd done the deed, Carolyn was suddenly flustered, even a little embarrassed. The skirt probably seemed gaudy, with all those shimmering beads and ribbons.

Oh, but the way they captured the light, those beads and ribbons. The sight made Carolyn's breath catch in her throat, just like always.

"It practically makes *music,*" Angela said, with what sounded like wonder. She stood up, approached and examined the skirt carefully, though she was careful, Carolyn noticed, not to touch it.

It practically makes music.

Carolyn felt quietly joy-stricken by the comment.

"You *are* an artist," Angela pronounced, her voice taking on an insistent note now. "Do you take orders? For custom-made things, I mean?"

Carolyn was thrown by the question, which was really strange, considering that she'd been making clothing for other people since that first sewing class in high school. "I...yes, sometimes," she managed to reply.

"Of course, something like this would cost the earth," Angela said, looking thoughtful. She sighed. "But a girl can dream."

That remark sealed it. Friends. She and Angela were going to be *friends.*

And that was bound to complicate things.

"I know what you mean," Carolyn said. "I can't afford this skirt, either."

That made Angela laugh. "But you *made* it," she

said, after a few moments. "You don't have to buy your own work."

Oh, yes, I do, Carolyn thought. "I need to recover the cost of supplies," she said, feeling very young all of a sudden, and very *poor.*

For Carolyn, that was a watershed moment. It was time to stop fiddling around with the skirt, finish it and put it up for sale. Holding on to the thing, wishing she had a place and a reason to wear it, was just a way of putting off the inevitable.

It was getting too painful.

"I guess you could make another one to keep for yourself," Angela said, faltering. She was reaching for her purse, preparing to leave.

Carolyn shook her head. "I couldn't duplicate it, even if I tried," she said, thinking how peculiar it was that Angela had come here to size up a rival, and Carolyn, famously independent, had ended up confiding in her.

A virtual stranger.

"I suppose not," Angela agreed sadly. "It's definitely one of a kind." She smiled. "Thank you for the tea, Carolyn, and for showing me this amazing work of art and, especially, for overlooking the fact that I acted like a maniac by coming here in the first place."

"I'm *glad* you stopped in," Carolyn said warmly, draping the skirt over the back of one of Natty's kitchen chairs, wishing there was more she could say, or do, to reassure Angela that things would work out for her and Bill.

Unfortunately, that might not be the case, given the impasse the two of them had reached over the perils of Bill's job.

"I think you really *are* glad I came over," Angela

said, in good-natured surprise. "You're a hard woman to hate, Carolyn. I can see why Bill is taken with you—not that I like the idea."

Carolyn wished she could tell Angela that Bill loved her but loved his job, too, and wouldn't feel like himself without it. Since this would amount to a betrayal of Bill's confidence, though, she would do no such thing.

"I hope you won't work too terribly hard at hating me," Carolyn said, with another smile, accompanying Angela as she started toward the front door.

Angela held her reply until they reached the entryway. "You'll be patient with Ellie?" she asked quietly. "She's a wonderful child, bright and funny and every other good thing. It's just that she had her heart set on Bill and me getting together."

Carolyn nodded. "Ellie," she agreed, "is a delight."

Angela opened the door, stepped over the threshold and onto the porch and would have gone down the steps and along the walk to the gate—her car was parked at the curb—except that Carolyn stopped her with a word.

"Angela?"

Angela paused, turned to look back at Carolyn. Waited.

"Talk to Bill," Carolyn said.

Angela's brow knitted with pretty puzzlement, and the nod she gave was hesitant. With that, she walked away.

Carolyn watched her for a few moments, then closed the door, turned the lock and returned to the kitchen.

It was time to serve up Winston's plate of sardines.

THE CALF THEY'D BROUGHT in off the range the day before was back on its feet, Brody was glad to see, when he and Barney arrived at the ranch early in the morning and headed straight for the barn.

"He's lookin' good," Brody said to Davis, after inspecting the calf in the stall it shared with Bessie. Conner was probably around somewhere, but he wasn't in sight at the moment.

Davis, having backed one of the ranch trucks in at the rear entrance to the barn, was standing in the bed of the pickup, about to start unloading sacks of horse feed. He grinned and gave Brody a thumbs-up. "Bessie and her boy will be ready to go back to the herd in another day or two," he said.

Brody approached the truck and reached in for a feed sack. The things weighed fifty pounds, and he didn't think Davis ought to be doing such heavy work at his advanced age, but he wasn't stupid enough to say as much. "Where's Conner?" he asked.

The unspoken subtext was, *And why isn't he out here helping unload this truck?*

"Tricia's feeling a mite flimsy," Davis replied, hoisting another bag and waiting to hand it down to Brody. "Conner's been checking on her at regular intervals. Truth is, he's probably driving her crazy, running in and out like that, but he's a Creed, after all, and that means you can't tell him a damn thing."

Brody took the second bag and stacked it in the storage room while Davis picked a new one up. "Tricia's all right, though?" he asked, worried.

"She told Kim she was fine, and we see no reason not to take her at her word," Davis replied. Then, probably not the least bit fooled by Brody's attempt to be casual, he added, "Pregnant women get tired, Brody. That doesn't mean they're ailing, or about to lose the baby. But Tricia's got a genuine human being taking shape inside her, and that takes some doing."

The past had a way of ambushing Brody when he least expected, and suddenly, his knees wanted to buckle and he felt as though he'd had the wind knocked out of him.

"Babies die, Davis," he told his uncle, without looking at him. "And so do their mothers."

Davis, in the process of handing down another sack of feed, stopped, gave a low whistle of exclamation through his teeth.

Barney, busy smelling every corner of the barn he could get to, paused at the sound, and trotted to Brody's side.

Brody acknowledged the dog with an ear-rub, but he looked up at Davis, who was standing motionless in the bed of the pickup, watching him.

"Can we just forget I said that?" Brody asked. He'd tried for levity, but the words came out sounding husky and a little raw, just the same.

"Nope," Davis replied, in his taciturn way, after climbing down out of the truck to stand facing Brody. "We can't."

"I'm not sure I'm ready to talk about this, Davis," Brody said.

Davis squeezed his shoulder briefly, then vaulted himself up to sit on the extended tailgate of the truck. "I'll wait," he said, with a kindly twinkle and a brief quirk of a grin.

Brody sighed, and then laughed. At least, he'd *meant* to laugh—the sound came out sounding like something else. "I wasn't born yesterday," he told his uncle grimly, and with another failed attempt at humor. "I know Con-

ner told you and Kim about my wife—my *late* wife—
and the baby boy we had together."

"Whatever Conner did or didn't say, he had the best
of intentions," Davis replied, in the same deep, solid
voice he'd used to tell three young boys they'd be all
right when they'd scared the hell out of themselves
watching rented horror movies for hours on end. After
all that on-screen blood and gore, a summer thunder-
storm or mice in the rafters had them instantly convinced that they were about to experience wholesale
slaughter, right there in their ranch-house bedroom.

Davis had always been able to put those fears to rest,
though, just by reminding them that he was right there,
under the same roof. His presence was enough, though
his words were a comfort, too. It went without saying
that anything or anybody out to hurt any member of his
family would have to get past Davis Creed first, and
that would take an army or two.

These days, Brody's demons didn't come from any
movie. They came from the hidden caverns of his heart,
from the darkest parts of his mind, lying in wait until
something triggered them to spring.

True to his word, Davis waited.

Brody tried to reach past him, unload another feed
sack, go on as if nothing had been said, but his uncle
stopped him by taking a hold on his upper arm. Davis
might have been in his fifties, but he still had a hell of
a grip.

Just then, Conner stepped into the barn. Brody didn't
see or hear his brother—he just felt a tug on that unseen
cord that connected them to each other.

Davis had let go of Brody's arm by then—he'd only
been out to make a point by taking hold in the first

place—and there was a silent message in his eyes as he looked past one nephew to the other.

"Is Tricia okay?" Brody asked, without turning around.

Conner was silent for a charged moment before he responded gruffly, "She claims she'll be fine if I just let her alone long enough to close her eyes for an hour or two."

Brody nodded, but still didn't move to face his brother.

"Is this what I think it is?" Conner asked, stepping up to stand next to Brody. He'd brought his dog along, and Valentino and Barney, evidently nonplussed by all that human drama, trotted through the rear entrance to the barn and disappeared into the dazzling sunshine.

"Now, what the hell kind of lame-assed question is *that?*" Brody wanted to know, glaring sidelong at his twin and hoping the subject would change course, like some river blasted into a new direction with dynamite.

"Brody, here," Davis drawled, looking at Conner, "is about to jump right out of his own hide. Make no mistake about it, though—he *doesn't* want to talk about the wife and the little boy."

Conner moved to lay a hand on Brody's shoulder, and then, wisely, thought better of the gesture. "I told Davis and Kim what you told me," Conner said, quietly forthright and with no trace of regret or apology. "About Lisa and Justin, and the way you lost them."

It was no good pointing out that he'd told Conner the story and trusted him to keep it a secret. On some level, Brody had known Conner would confide in their aunt and uncle, if no one else. Maybe he'd even hoped, somewhere down deep, that his brother *would* let the cat out of the bag. That way, Davis and Kim would know the bitter truth without Brody having to tell them what happened.

Feeling cornered, Brody looked from Davis to Conner and back again. "If you already know," he began tautly, reasonably, "what's the point of my repeating it all?"

"Because you need to," Davis said, solemn and certain. "It's festering inside you like a wound, son. Holding that secret corralled up inside you kept you away from your home and your people and a lot more for too long. Don't you think it's time you turned it loose?"

Brody shoved a hand through his hair, barely noticing that he'd knocked his hat to the floor in the process. He didn't move to retrieve it.

"Lisa said she'd put the baby up for adoption if I didn't marry her," Brody said, sounding, in his own ears, like a man ranting from the depths of some consuming fever. He didn't see Davis, didn't see Conner—just a blurry rush of scenes from years gone by. "If I'd let her, if I hadn't bailed out on Carolyn in the middle of the night and rushed off to put a golden band on Lisa's finger, then Justin would still be alive, a growing kid with parents and maybe brothers and sisters—"

Brody's voice ground to a painful stop. It was as though the gears running his speech had rusted and then seized up.

"I used to think my brother, Blue, would have lived," Davis said evenly, "if I'd done some small thing differently the morning your dad tried to ride that crazy horse. If only I'd called him out of bed a few minutes later, or stretched breakfast by another cup of coffee or two, or even started some kind of row with him. *Any-*

thing to keep him off the back of that stallion. But he was bent on making that ride, Brody, and if he hadn't gotten himself thrown that day, he'd have done it some *other* day. What I'm trying to get at here is that folks seem to come into this life with a list of things they need to get done while they're here inscribed on their souls. Old or young, when their work is done, they leave."

After that, nobody said anything.

There was no need for words.

CHAPTER THIRTEEN

CAROLYN HAD SLEPT fitfully the previous night, and she was awake early, feeling jittery, rather than rested.

She fed Winston, brewed herself a cup of instant coffee and peeked out at the beginnings of a blue-gold day in May. In the neighbor's yard, as well as the distance, the ever-lovely cottonwood trees shimmered and shifted, like the ribbons on the gypsy skirt.

Of all the places she'd lived, she liked Colorado best. Especially when spring evolved into summer so quickly, as it seemed to be doing this year.

With her head cloudy from lack of sleep and hectic dreams she couldn't quite remember, Carolyn imagined herself on horseback, riding the crooked trail on the rim of the ridge on the Creed ranch, or along the banks of the river. The air was thin there in the high country, but once a person got used to it, every breath of fresh air was exhilarating.

Carolyn bit her lower lip, pondering her options.

Today was a workday, and she had to open the shop by nine-thirty at the latest, but that still left her with a couple of hours of freedom. If she hurried, she could drive out to Kim and Davis's place, saddle up old Blossom and quite literally head for the hills.

Or the trail that followed the wandering line of the river.

A ride would clear the cobwebs from her brain and maybe even ease the anxious little ache in her heart, the one she'd awakened with some tattered remnant of dreams forgotten.

Or denied.

Hastily, before she could change her mind, Carolyn showered, dressed in the usual jeans and T-shirt and, because of the inevitable morning chill, a long-sleeved flannel shirt. She donned socks, hauled on her boots and said goodbye to Winston, promising she'd be back soon.

The drive to the Creed ranch was refreshing in itself—Carolyn kept her car window rolled halfway down and listened to a Keith Urban CD while she drove. By the time Davis and Kim's rambling house and barn came into view, she was singing along at the top of her lungs.

Kim came out of the house when Carolyn pulled in, smiling a warm welcome, the little dogs frolicking at her feet.

"Come in and have coffee," Kim called. "I have something to ask you."

Kim Creed was a dear and treasured friend, but Carolyn didn't want to sit and drink coffee—she wanted to ride.

"I was hoping to take Blossom out for a little spin," she answered, pausing to smile at the comical antics of the dogs. "What did you want to ask me?"

Kim scooped the Yorkies up into each hand and walked over to where Carolyn was waiting. "Davis and I have a hankering to head down to Stone Creek for a week or two, and spoil our grandchildren," Kim said. "Run interference for Steven and Melissa a bit, so they can go off somewhere by themselves for a couple of days. We need somebody to stay here and look after the house while we're away, though. Can you do it?"

"I'd be glad to," Carolyn said, pleased. As much as she loved her apartment on the second floor of Natty McCall's house, she enjoyed a change of scene once in a while, too. And while other people's houses usually left her feeling rootless and more adrift than ever, this was the Creed Ranch; for whatever reason, she'd always felt at home here. "Would it be okay if I brought Winston along?"

"That would be fine," Kim answered, nuzzling the top of one tiny dog's head and then the other. Early as it was, Smidgeon and Little Bit's carefully trimmed coats were already brushed to a high shine, their topknots tied with little yellow ribbons. "Brody will stop by twice a day to tend the horses—just call him or Conner if there's any sort of emergency. You're more than welcome to ride Blossom anytime, but Davis doesn't want you going near that Thoroughbred. Firefly's too dangerous."

The *Thoroughbred* was dangerous?

He couldn't hold a candle to Brody when it came to making trouble.

"Kim Creed," Carolyn reasoned, in fond irritation, "if Brody is set to take care of your horses, why can't he simply sleep here at night, too, and keep an eye on the property?" She paused, enjoying her friend's sheepish expression. "Is it just my imagination, or are you trying to throw the two of us together?"

Again.

Kim's cheeks were pink, but her eyes smiled even before her mouth did. "Would I do a thing like that?" she challenged.

"In a heartbeat," Carolyn said, with smiling conviction.

Kim was not only thinking fast, she was thinking *visibly*. The gears behind that still-lovely face were turning for sure. Finally, she drew a deep breath and huffed it out.

"Brody can't stay here because he's got to take care of his own place, the new construction, I mean. There's always a chance of theft or vandalism, you know, particularly after the sun goes down."

Carolyn laughed and rolled her eyes, wondering if Kim knew about the Saturday night date she and Brody had scheduled.

She decided not to mention it, in case the gossip hadn't reached Kim's ears yet. There was no sense in pouring fuel on the fires of speculation, especially when the evening with Brody would probably turn out to be a nonevent.

Or the mother of all rows.

When it came to herself and Brody, there seemed to be no middle ground.

"You'll do it, then?" Kim persisted. "Stay here at the house while Davis and I are in Stone Creek? I know you have the shop to run, but other than that—"

Silently, Carolyn completed her friend's sentence. *Other than that, you have no life.*

"I'll be here, Kim," she said gently. Kim and Davis had always been kind to her, and their trust was something she prized. She couldn't have refused the request without a much better reason than her compulsive need to avoid Brody whenever possible. "When are you leaving for Stone Creek?"

"Sunday morning," Kim answered, with a glance in

the direction of the barn and a crooked little smile. "Go ahead and saddle Blossom. I know your time is limited, and I won't insist on the coffee klatch."

On impulse, Carolyn hugged Kim, being careful not to squash the little dogs.

"What was that for?" Kim asked, blinking even as she smiled.

"You're a good friend, Kim," Carolyn answered, turning to walk away, but looking back over one shoulder. "And I'm grateful to you and *for* you."

The majestic Thoroughbred, king of all he surveyed, nickered a greeting to Carolyn as she moved past the corral fence, heading for the barn.

"Good morning, handsome," she told the gigantic gelding. What an amazing creature he was, standing there with his head high and his ears pitched forward, his whole frame rimmed by morning sunlight.

A few moments later, Carolyn reached the door of Blossom's stall.

The little mare seemed ready for an excursion and submitted happily to all the customary preparations— saddle blanket, saddle, bridle, cinch-tightening and, finally, a quick check of her hooves.

"You're getting fat from standing around in this barn or out in the pasture all the time," Carolyn told the animal, leading her out into the unusually warm morning air. "Let's get some exercise."

Carolyn chose the route that led along the ridge, as opposed to the one next to the river, mainly because she didn't want to look over the waters and see Brody's fabulous house, nearer to completion with every passing day.

Would he end up marrying Joleen?

Or would it be some other woman who wasn't even on the scene yet?

Brody had taken out a trial membership on Friendly Faces—and even though he'd posted his horse's picture instead of his own, he wouldn't lack for prospective dates—or *mates*. He was, after all, a real catch— young, single, good-looking and financially secure, if not downright rich.

Strangers might not know these things, but plenty of available Lonesome Bend women *would,* and they wouldn't hesitate to lobby for a date.

What if Brody fell for one of them?

Then he *fell for one of them,* Carolyn thought, in rueful answer to her own silent question.

She stuck a foot into the stirrup and swung herself up onto Blossom's wide back. A glutton for punishment when it came to Brody Creed, Carolyn imagined a wedding, crowded with well-wishers. A beautiful bride, with one hot groom—Brody—promising to love, honor and cherish.

One thing led to another. She pictured the two of them—Brody and the faceless woman—leaving on their honeymoon.

In her mind's eye, she witnessed their return to Lonesome Bend. Brody would carry his new wife over the threshold of that amazing house—she could probably even *cook,* the bitch—and there would be a baby on the way in no time at all.

Carolyn, leaving Blossom to choose their path, blushed at the thought.

The new Mrs. Creed would probably stop by the shop often—after all, she'd be Tricia's sister-in-law and, therefore, need no excuse to visit—and Carolyn would have to watch as the woman's belly swelled with Brody's child...

"Stop it," she told herself out loud.

Blossom, no doubt thinking Carolyn was speaking to her, stopped and looked back in comical equine curiosity.

"I'm sorry," Carolyn told the horse gently, patting the mare's neck. "I wasn't talking to you."

Blossom, seemingly satisfied, plodded on.

Carolyn, in the meantime, went right on daydreaming, paying no attention when Blossom left the ridge trail and meandered through a copse of cottonwood trees to the banks of Hidden Lake.

Hidden Lake.

Carolyn's heart almost stopped when she realized where they were. She'd been careful to avoid the place since her last visit, years ago—with Brody.

They'd camped on the shore, sharing a single sleeping bag inside an insulated pup tent made for one.

They'd fished, and fried the catch over a fire in the open air.

And, oh, how they'd made love.

Carolyn had never been happier, before or since.

"Let's get out of here," she said to the horse, tugging lightly on the reins.

But Blossom waded into the water instead, lowered her head and began to drink noisily of the crystal-clear water.

With a sigh, Carolyn backed the mare onto the shore and dismounted to walk around a little, and work the kinks out of her legs. Lately, she'd gone too long between horseback rides, and she felt the omission in the insides of her thighs and in her lower back.

Blossom waded in again, bent her head to satisfy her thirst.

Carolyn looked around, stricken anew by the beauty of the place. With the trees filtering the light of the sun and causing it to dance with leaf shadows on the surface of the lake, it seemed sacred, almost cathedral-like.

It was ridiculously warm, for a morning in May, and she shed the flannel shirt, draping it over a nearby boulder, and enjoyed the feel of soft heat on her shoulders and arms. She shouldn't be dallying out here, she thought—the shop was supposed to open in an hour, and she'd need another shower and a change of clothes before then.

But the silence, the trees, the muted birdsong, all of it was solace to her soul.

Eventually, the sensual pull of the water proved to be more than she could resist. Carolyn, so rarely impulsive, resolutely kicked off her boots, peeled away her socks and waded into the sky-tinted waters of Hidden Lake.

The water was warm, and soft as liquefied silk.

Carolyn rolled her jeans up to her knees and waded in deeper. The lake bottom was covered in tiny, smooth stones, and those stones worked the flesh on the bottoms of her feet like the fingers of a gifted masseuse.

Tilting her head back and closing her eyes, Carolyn gave herself up to sensation—peace, the deliciousness of water, the smooth caress of the little rocks under her soles, the sunshine spiking between the branches of the cottonwoods that arched overhead like great pillars supporting the sky.

For all the things she would have changed about her past, her present and her future, if that had been possible in the first place, in the here and now, Carolyn counted only the good things.

She was young, she was healthy and she loved her life.

She loved working in the shop. She loved sewing, and riding horses, and taking care of Winston. She loved her friends and her modest apartment and the town of Lonesome Bend, Colorado, which *felt* like a family, even if it wasn't.

She was blessed among women.

Blossom nickered, attracting Carolyn's attention.

She turned, watched as the mare moved farther up the sloping bank to graze happily on sweet grass, the reins still looped loosely behind the horn of the saddle.

The urge to strip to the skin and swim in that lake came over Carolyn suddenly, and it was all but overwhelming.

Carolyn got out of the water, intending to get back on Blossom and ride away, but instead, she found herself peeling off her clothes, piling them on the dry boulder, with the flannel shirt she'd doffed earlier. She plunged back into the lake, gasping at the initial chill but adapting quickly. She swam out into deeper water and then turned onto her back to float and gaze up at that painfully blue sky.

It was a time out of time; she'd drifted, somehow, into a magical world, parallel to the one she usually inhabited.

Then she heard the sound—another horse, somewhere very nearby.

Heart pounding, Carolyn stopped floating to tread water, her eyes narrowed as she scanned the trees for any sign of an intruder.

All was silent now—even the birds had stopped singing.

Carolyn was convinced of it: she had *definitely* heard a horse, and it hadn't been Blossom. The mare was still grazing.

"Who's there?" Carolyn called, somewhat shakily, as terrible headlines flashed through her mind.

Woman Found Dead Near Remote Lake...

Local Shop-owner Perishes in Brutal Attack...

There it went again, that imagination of hers.

She'd probably heard a deer, or, since livestock ranged all over the Creed ranch anyway, a cow or a horse.

Then Brody appeared, riding through the cottonwoods and swinging down off the back of his buckskin gelding, Moonshine. He smiled, took off his hat and hung it on the saddle horn. Soothed a fretful Blossom with a muttered word and a few pats on the neck.

Carolyn's heart seized and moved up into her throat. Things like this only happened in books, or in old movies.

They did *not* happen to her, not in real life, anyway. There might have been a fantasy or two, but those were just—well—*fantasies*.

"These your clothes?" Brody asked mildly, inclining his head toward the boulder and the pile of discarded garments.

Carolyn felt a surge of true annoyance and her cheeks burned. "Who *else's* clothes would they be?" she demanded. "And what are you doing here? Did you follow me?"

"Davis sent me out to ride the fence lines," Brody replied, kicking off one of his boots. "That's one of his prescriptions for a case of what he calls 'the moody blues.' Hard work or a long ride. I happened to spot you and Blossom leaving the trail, so I decided to follow, make sure the both of you were all right."

Off went the other boot.

Carolyn was gripped by memories of the last time she and Brody had been here, together. It had been too cold to swim then; now, she was surprised the lake didn't start to simmer.

"What are you doing?" she snapped, still treading water but moving away from shore, away from *Brody*.

"It's a nice day," he said, neatly evading the question, tossing his hat down on top of his boots. "Unusually warm for May, wouldn't you say? Perfect for skinny-dipping."

"Brody Creed, don't you dare—"

He hauled his shirt off over his head, tossed it.

His chest was sculpted, sprinkled with gold; time had been good to Brody Creed.

Damn it.

"It's a free country," he told her, his belt buckle making a jingling sound as he unhooked it. "And this lake *is* on Creed land."

"I'll leave," Carolyn said, on a rush of breath. "Just turn your back, so I can get out of the water and put on my clothes, and I'll be gone—"

Brody unfastened his jeans.

That was no answer, Carolyn thought frantically.

Or was it?

She squeezed her eyes tightly shut, trying to think. Her breath was shallow, and her heart was thudding against her rib cage.

She wanted to be anywhere but here.

She wanted to be *nowhere* but here.

There was a splash, and Carolyn felt a subtle, sensual movement in the water, and when curiosity forced her to open her eyes again, Brody was right in front of her.

Crystal beads glimmered in his eyelashes, and his grin was as obnoxiously winsome as ever. Maybe more so.

From the neck down—Carolyn *did* try not to look— he was a moving shadow. Sunshine, filtered by cottonwood leaves, glimmered in his tarnished-gold hair and that grin—well, *that grin.*

"Relax," he drawled, his blue eyes percolating with mischievous delight—and something else that might have been desire. "I'd never force you or any other woman to do anything you didn't want to do."

This, Carolyn knew, was a perfectly true statement. It was also no comfort whatsoever.

"Don't," she murmured, not knowing if she was addressing that single desperate word to Brody, or to herself.

He raised one eyebrow. "Don't what?"

He knew damn well *don't what.*

But did she?

With a great sigh of lusty contentment, Brody tilted his head back, closed his eyes, breathed in the blue-sky air with the same relish Carolyn had earlier.

Carolyn, though still flustered, used those few stolen moments to admire him—the strong line of his jaw, the long eyelashes, the hair bejeweled with droplets of lake water.

When he opened his eyes again, and caught her looking at him, she actually gasped, startled.

That made Brody chuckle, and Carolyn blushed.

"Remember the last time we were here?" he asked, his tone slow and almost sleepy. "It was a lot colder than it is now, and we kept the bonfire going long into the night. Not that we needed it to keep warm."

Now it was Carolyn who closed her eyes, tangled in the vision like a fish in a net. They'd *hadn't* needed a fire—their lovemaking had set them both ablaze.

"I remember," she murmured softly.

"Carolyn," Brody said, "open your eyes and *relax*. I'm not trying to seduce you, here."

"You could have fooled me," Carolyn protested, getting angry again. "Taking off your clothes and jumping right into this lake when I *specifically* asked you not to—"

He laughed—threw back his head and *laughed.* He certainly didn't lack for nerve.

Carolyn seethed.

When Brody's amusement abated a little, he said, "You were naked when I got here, remember? How was I to know you weren't *hoping* I'd show up and seduce you?"

If the water hadn't limited her momentum, Carolyn swore she would have broken all her personal rules about violence and slapped him, hard.

"How was *I* to know," she countered, quietly furious, "that you were *following* me, like some—some *stalker?* Do you honestly think I would have *taken off my clothes* if I'd had the faintest glimmer that *you* were going to show up?"

This time, Brody didn't laugh. His gaze was solemn, with just the faintest sparkle of mischief, as he regarded her. "I wouldn't have thought you'd take off your clothes for *any* reason," he drawled. "Especially to take a swim in a mountain lake that doesn't generally warm up until the middle of August."

When had he gotten closer? Carolyn wondered distractedly, moving back a little, scanning the lakeside for Blossom

No Blossom.

The mare must have wandered off at some point.

Which was just terrific, because now Carolyn wasn't just naked and embarrassed and alone with Brody in what basically amounted to the Blue Lagoon. She was all of those things *and* stranded.

"Blossom!" she called out, going around Brody and heading for shore, but pausing when she realized she was about to reveal herself in the altogether. "Blossom, where are you?"

Nothing.

Brody appeared beside her.

Carolyn crouched a little and crossed her arms in front of her breasts. Her nipples felt hard and tight, and it wasn't just because there was a slight nip to the water.

"That's one thing about Blossom," Brody said easily, evidently enjoying this new development in an already impossible situation. "She's always been kind of flighty. As likely as not, she's halfway home by now."

"Don't say that," Carolyn sputtered. "Don't even *think* it."

"You and I can ride double, on Moonshine." He paused, sighed. "We'd better get going. Kim will freak out when that horse trots into the barnyard with her saddle empty."

"I *have* to get my clothes first," Carolyn said. All she needed was for Kim to call Davis when Blossom came home without a rider, and the two of them to come searching for her.

Brody chuckled again, but very slowly he turned his back. "I won't look until you tell me it's all right," he promised.

Tugging dry clothes over wet skin, especially in a hurry, had frustration singing through Carolyn's veins by the time she was decent.

"Okay," she said begrudgingly.

Brody turned around and started out of the water, no more concerned with his own nakedness than Adam in the Garden.

Carolyn whirled to give him her back and folded her arms tight against her chest.

Brody muttered the occasional cheerful curse as he dressed himself, and when he was ready, he whistled for Moonshine.

The buckskin came right to him, docile as a dollar-a-ride pony at the state fair.

"Need a boost?" Brody asked, his voice like the flick of a feather across the sensitive skin at her nape.

Carolyn cast one last look around for Blossom, didn't see a sign of that fickle critter, and climbed into Moonshine's saddle like the skilled horsewoman she was.

For a second or so, she actually considered riding off and leaving Brody to *walk* home from Hidden Lake, but of course she couldn't do it. The Code of the West went way back and ran deep. And one of its tenets was that you never took off on somebody else's horse and left them afoot.

Even now, in this modern day and age, there were too many bad things that could happen to a stranded rider.

Brody chuckled, reading her expression accurately,

it would seem, and sprang up behind her, nimble as a
Native warrior. "I knew you weren't a horse thief," he
teased, leaning around her, *into* her, to take up the reins.

"H-how?" Carolyn asked. Damn Brody for suggesting that the lake was too cold to swim in at this time
of year. Now her teeth were starting to chatter, and she
could feel a wicked sneeze building up in her sinus
passages.

He nudged Moonshine into a fast walk. "Well, for
one thing," he replied, "you're missing the big handle-
bar mustache."

Carolyn did not—*would* not—laugh.

But she wanted to, and Brody probably knew that.

They rode out of the cottonwoods and onto the trail,
picking up speed as they went.

Carolyn tried not to notice that Brody felt as hard-
chested as a statue behind her, that the heat of his body
was leaching past the chill of her damp flesh, warming
her, making her heart race a little.

She should have been relieved that they hadn't made
love, she supposed, and she *was,* mostly. She was also
somewhat disappointed.

Like before, he seemed to know what she was thinking.

Which just went to prove how arrogant he was.

And how right.

He bent his head, touched his tongue to the back
of her neck, made a chortling sound when she reacted
with a little groan.

"Back there at the lake," he told her, his voice throaty
and almost hypnotic, but audible even over the clatter
of Moonshine's hooves on the hard-packed dirt of the

trail, "I wanted to lay you down in the grass and have my way with you. Know why I didn't try?"

A tremor, as involuntary as the groan, shuddered through Carolyn. "You didn't try," she managed to reply, "because you knew I'd scratch your eyes right out of your head if you did."

Brody laughed. "I didn't try," he said, "because I didn't have a condom handy."

Carolyn was still in way over her head, lake or no lake, but she *had* had the presence of mind to wonder why Brody hadn't even attempted to make love to her, when he had the chance.

"You wouldn't have succeeded anyhow," she said stiffly, and maybe a beat too late.

"Are you challenging me?" Brody wanted to know. Managing the horse, even with another rider in front of him, required no discernible effort on his part. He might have been part of the animal, he was so at ease. "If you are, I'm up to it—so to speak."

Hard need went through Carolyn's entire being in that moment. She was half again too stubborn—and too rattled—to come up with a response.

Brody laughed, and one of his hands rose to slip inside her loose-fitting flannel shirt to cup her breast. Even with a bra and a T-shirt in between, he must have felt her nipple tighten against his palm.

It took all of Carolyn's considerable self-control to grab his wrist and jerk his hand away. "We have an agreement, Brody," she reminded him tersely. "*No sex.* Remember?"

"That might have been a little rash of us," he said. "Deciding to save ourselves, I mean." His breath brushed her right ear, and then he nibbled briefly at the lobe.

Carolyn bit back another groan. Gave him a quick jab with her elbow. "*Stop it,* Brody," she said.

He sighed again. By then, Moonshine was traveling at a smooth lope, and the motion of that horse, and Brody at her back—well, it was beyond sensual. It was very nearly climactic.

"Is this agreement of ours...open-ended?" he finally asked.

Up ahead, Carolyn spotted Blossom, placidly munching on grass alongside the trail.

"Wh-what do you mean?" Carolyn asked, glad to see the runaway mare within catching distance, and unhurt.

"I mean," Brody almost breathed, making no comment on Blossom's reappearance, though he'd surely seen her, "that the no-sex deal isn't working for me. We need to discuss it, Carolyn."

"*Discuss* it?" Carolyn echoed. "That isn't what you mean at all, and you know it."

They drew up alongside Blossom, and Carolyn swung one leg over Moonshine's neck and jumped to the ground while Brody leaned to take hold of the mare's bridle strap in case she took a notion to run off again.

"What *do* I mean, then, since you seem to know?" Brody countered, wielding that grin again. He let go of the bridle when she was mounted on Blossom, but he didn't make Moonshine turn, didn't give her so much as an inch of space, so his left leg was pressing into her right.

"It's working fine for me," Carolyn said, ignoring the question.

"What's working fine for you?"

She flushed. "The no-sex agreement," she said. She pointed Blossom toward home and gave the animal a light nudge with her boot heels to get her going.

Brody kept up. "Now, that is a peculiar statement, Carolyn," he observed mildly, "because the nooky-ban obviously *isn't* working any better for you than it is for me—which is to say, not at all."

"Nooky-ban?" Carolyn shot back. "Isn't *that* colorful?"

"Oh, I just ooze *colorful*," Brody teased.

"Shut up, Brody."

He didn't, of course. "Why can't you just admit it, Carolyn? Wherever else we might have dropped the ball, we had a real good thing going in bed."

Even she, the queen of denial, couldn't refute that one. "Not good *enough*, obviously," she said, glaring over at him. "It didn't keep you in Lonesome Bend, now did it?"

Now that they'd recovered Blossom, and Kim and Davis wouldn't be sending out a posse to look for her, Carolyn had time to be mad at herself.

She should be at the shop right this minute, have the door unlocked and the Open sign facing the porch.

Instead, Tricia was probably there by herself, wondering where the heck Carolyn was.

She was so engaged with this thought, and others like it, that she didn't immediately notice the strange stillness that had descended over Brody.

A glance in his direction verified the intuition.

His jawline was tight, his backbone was straight as a ramrod, and he was looking directly ahead, between

Moonshine's ears. Both horses were ambling along at an easy pace now.

"Like I said before," Brody went on, without looking at her, "it's time we talked."

"I'm not sure we have anything to say to each other," Carolyn said, hoping those words hadn't come out sounding as sad as they *felt*.

At last, he caught and held her gaze. His expression was grim. "I have plenty to say to you, Carolyn," he answered, "and I mean to get it all said."

Panic took wing behind Carolyn's rib cage, like some crazed little bird. "Brody, I have to get back to the shop—I never planned on being gone this long and—"

"Later will be fine," he said, when she finally fell silent. "Your place or mine?"

Your place or mine?

Risky business, either way.

Still, Brody wasn't going to let her put him off, that much was plain.

"How about the coffee shop?" she asked, too brightly. "We could meet after I close the shop at five."

"Too public," Brody said, looking as though he'd never grin that trademark grin of his again, he was so solemn.

Carolyn tried to think. If they "talked" at Brody's place, he'd have condoms handy, so why not go ahead and seduce her? Essentially, she'd be helpless against him, and he knew that.

If, on the other hand, they got together at the apartment, all he'd have to do was kiss her, or cup her breast in his hand again, and she wouldn't *care* whether or not they used a condom.

"My place," she finally said. "Six o'clock?"

Brody nodded, and Kim and Davis's barn came into view, and the conversation was over—for the time being, anyway.

CHAPTER FOURTEEN

IN FRONT OF Kim and Davis's barn, Brody dismounted and left Moonshine at the hitching rail to take hold of Blossom's bridle strap. Carolyn was still in the saddle, flustered and so delicious that just looking at her sent a whole new charge of desire grabbing its way through him like wildfire.

"I'll tend to the mare," Brody told her quietly. "You go on into town and do whatever it is you figure you should be doing right now."

Carolyn bit her lower lip, nodded once, got down and practically sprinted to her car. Next thing he knew, she was speeding down the driveway in the proverbial cloud of dust.

One corner of Brody's mouth quirked up at the sight, but there wasn't much juice behind that grin. If only he hadn't run off at the mouth before about how he and Carolyn oughtn't to have sex, he might be making love to the woman in the tall grass back there at Hidden Lake right now—condom be damned—instead of watching her rush off like the devil himself was on her trail.

He heard the creak of screen-door hinges, and Kim stepped out of the house, sans her usual yappy little sidekicks, to stand on the side porch, shading her eyes from the sun with one hand. "Brody?" she called, casting a concerned look in the direction of Carolyn's still-billowing dust-plume. "Did something happen?"

"Nothing happened," Brody replied.

And I mean nothing. *Damn it all to hell.*

He led Blossom inside the barn, hoping Kim would leave him in peace, so he could unsaddle the mare, give her a flake of hay and a quick brushing and get on with his day.

No such luck.

"It's not like Carolyn to rush away like that," Kim said, standing in the breezeway now, watching him over the door of Blossom's stall. "She didn't even say good-bye."

She'd always been as light-footed as a Sioux scout, Kim had. Back when he and Conner and Steven were kids, she'd had an uncanny way of showing up out of no-where, without any sound to warn of her approach, just when they were about to get into some kind of mischief.

"She's in a hurry to open the shop," Brody said off-handedly.

He'd spilled his guts to Davis and Conner, back at the other barn, going over all that bitter ground, and he meant to do the same thing all over again when he went to see Carolyn at her place, later in the day. In the meantime, he preferred to enter into as little conversation as possible.

"You made Carolyn mad again, didn't you?" Kim persisted.

Inwardly, Brody sighed, wondering if the whole universe was out of whack, or if it was just him. There had to be *some* reason why nothing had gone his way since he'd opened his eyes that morning.

"No," he said, returning the grooming brush to the

high, rusty nail where it was kept, dangling from a small leather loop. "I didn't."

Kim narrowed her eyes at him as he opened the stall door and eased through the gap to stand there in the aisle, facing her. "*Something* upset her," she said.

Brody ducked his head, rubbed the back of his neck. It wasn't until then that he realized he'd left his hat in his truck, down at the main ranch house. These days, he figured, he probably would have forgotten his right arm if it wasn't hooked to his shoulder.

"Carolyn doesn't need me to upset her," he said reasonably. "She can handle that one all on her own."

Kim sighed and folded her arms. She was dressed about normal for her, in a pink Western-cut shirt with pearly snaps, worn jeans and boots. "Maybe you ought to go after her. The two of you could talk…"

"We've already made plans to do that," Brody answered, willing to give Kim that much information but no more.

Kim opened her mouth, closed it again, evidently deciding she had nothing more to say. It was a rare phenomenon, but it happened.

Brody grinned, kissed her on the forehead and headed for the barn door.

Moonshine, ever patient, waited at the hitching post. Brody released the loose slipknot he'd made with the reins and hauled himself up into the saddle.

Kim, on her way back to the house by then, waved a farewell.

Passing the corral on Moonshine, Brody paused to look over at Firefly, the Thoroughbred Kim and Davis had adopted sometime before. While he understood their concern about the animal's welfare, he had serious reservations where Firefly was concerned.

This was no ordinary saddle horse. The Thoroughbred was fifteen hundred pounds of raw power, with the blood of champions running hot in his veins. He was still sound physically, but famously temperamental—according to Davis, even the most seasoned jockeys in the business had refused to ride him, there at the end of his mostly unremarkable career.

Brody was a cowboy, not a jockey, and for that very reason, he was tempted to throw a saddle and bridle on that gelding and see for himself just how fast the sucker could run.

Of course, Davis would kill him if he tried. Provided the horse didn't kill him first, that is.

Still, the idea burrowed into Brody's already beleaguered brain, germinated and took root there, like a magic bean.

But he was, as Davis would say, burning daylight; he had fence lines to ride, if he didn't want a lecture from his uncle about pulling his weight on the ranch.

At the moment, Brody didn't want a lecture from *anybody.*

WHAT HAVE I DONE? Carolyn asked herself, as she drove toward town.

Well, duh, that self answered. *You practically offered yourself to Brody Creed on a silver platter,* that's *what. You invited him to your apartment, knowing full well what's going to happen.*

A smile broke over Carolyn's face, and a thrill went through her, lodging squarely between her pelvic bones. "God, I hope so," she said, right out loud, the announcement rising, it seemed, from the very ground of her being, as though her body had somehow summoned all its resources to be heard over the voice of common sense.

Brimming with crazy emotions she couldn't begin to untangle, let alone name, Carolyn wondered if she really *was* losing her mind.

When she arrived at the shop, Tricia was there, as she'd expected.

What Carolyn *hadn't* expected was a store full of customers.

Where had they all come from? She hadn't seen a bus outside, or even a car.

"Glad you could make it," Tricia told her sweetly, looking her over with an expression of knowing amusement frolicking in her eyes.

Carolyn, unprepared for a crowd, blushed. She smelled like a horse, her hair probably looked like a fright wig, and her friend seemed to know precisely what she'd been up to that morning, up at Hidden Lake.

Or *almost* up to, anyway.

Probably impossible, she thought, with considerable relief. Tricia was smart, but she wasn't psychic, for pity's sake.

"I'll be right back," she told Tricia, racing for the inside stairs.

Reaching her apartment, Carolyn took the world's fastest shower, threw on fresh clothes, blow-dried her wild tresses into a semblance of submission and practically broke her neck getting back down to the shop.

All the shoppers had gone by then, and Tricia, perched on a high stool behind the counter, eyed Carolyn with good-natured suspicion.

"And where have *you* been, pray tell?" she asked warmly.

Carolyn knew what Tricia was thinking—that she'd been out the whole night and not just for part of the morning—and she teetered on the edge of protesting too much.

"Out," she replied pleasantly, as Winston meowed and curled himself around her ankles. "Where did all those *people* come from?"

"Around," Tricia said airily. "Word seems to be getting out that we carry unique merchandise. Two of them had seen the gypsy skirt online, and they wanted to know if they could make offers. I told them they'd have to go to the auction site and bid."

Carolyn felt the usual pang at the thought of selling the skirt. It would be better if it went to a stranger, though, someone who lived far away from Lonesome Bend. Seeing some local woman wearing it would be like catching regular glimpses of a child she'd given up for adoption in the company of another mother.

"Good call," Carolyn said, and began straightening a display table. She needed, in that moment, to look busy.

"Carolyn," Tricia said firmly, but quietly.

Carolyn stopped cold, like a Londoner during the Blitz, hearing the telltale whistle of a dropping bomb.

"We need to talk," Tricia told her.

Brody had said pretty much the same thing, just that morning.

Why did everyone suddenly want to *talk?* Whatever happened to leaving well enough alone?

"O-o-okay," Carolyn said warily, stretching out the word. She stopped pretending to work and turned to meet Tricia's gaze. "You start."

Tricia sighed. "You've probably noticed that I've been leaving the shop early a lot lately," she began. "And I don't think that's fair to you. We're supposed to be partners."

"Tricia," Carolyn reminded her friend softly, "you're *expecting a baby*. I don't mind covering for you once in a while."

"That's just it," Tricia answered, "it hasn't *been* just *once in a while*. I feel perfectly fine—honestly, I do—but some days I just feel so *tired*. My doctor says that's pretty much normal, but that doesn't change the fact that you're doing more than your share." Another sigh. "Which means something has to give."

Carolyn swallowed hard, suddenly aware, and keenly, of what was coming. She should have anticipated that Tricia would want to quit the business, she supposed, but she hadn't. The decision made sense—while Tricia would have lots of help at home after the baby came, the new arrival would take up more of her time and energy, not less.

"I'm not asking you to buy me out," Tricia went on. "I know that isn't possible right now. Maybe, once the baby is older—"

When the baby was older, Carolyn thought, with a mixture of understanding and affectionate envy, there would probably be *another* baby. If not several.

"Carolyn," Tricia urged, "*say* something."

Carolyn rummaged up a smile. "Everything has to change sometime," she said, looking wistfully around at the shop, with all its colorful and many-textured hand-made offerings. It was a haven of grace, a virtual celebration of creativity, and Carolyn hadn't realized how much she loved the place until now. "But it was good while it lasted."

Tricia eased down off the stool then and sort of waddled over to Carolyn. A worried frown creased her forehead. "While it lasted?" she echoed. "Are you saying you don't want to keep the shop open?"

Carolyn spread her hands wide for a moment. "How would I do that, Tricia?" she asked. "I can't afford to hire help, and running this place alone would be too much, considering all the sewing I need to do in addition to stocking shelves, keeping the books, waiting on customers and all the rest."

"Carolyn," Tricia said, her voice taking on a note of quiet urgency, "I don't think you understand what I'm saying here, and it's no wonder, I guess, given all I've left out." She drew a deep breath, let it out and rested her hands on the sides of her protruding belly. "I was hoping to become a sort of silent partner—you know, pump some cash into the business and maybe help out in an advisory capacity once in a while. Track down new artists online. If I invested in the shop, well, then you *could* hire some help—maybe a couple of part-timers?—and still have more time for the creative stuff."

Always wary of anything that sounded too good to be true, Carolyn plunked her hands on her hips, in an unconscious reflection of Tricia's stance, and considered the situation. Finally, she blurted out, "Is this charity?"

"Oh, for heaven's sake," Tricia replied, "*of course* it isn't charity. It's a business proposition." She looked thoughtful for a long moment. "I suppose I could buy *you* out, though, and hire a manager and some salespeople—but what would be the use in that? It's things like those aprons you're always whipping up, and your eye for unique merchandise, that sets us apart from other stores and galleries."

"No," Carolyn said, very quickly, and then blushed.

"Huh?" Tricia asked, clearly confused.

"What I meant was, I don't want you to buy me out," Carolyn explained, with a nervous laugh and a shake of her head. "Kim asked me to house-sit for her and Davis, this coming week, while they're in Stone Creek visiting the grandchildren, and if I put the word out, I could probably get right back into the groove with all my former clients—"

"But you love this shop," Tricia interrupted. "And the apartment. And what would happen to Winston?"

"Winston," Carolyn reminded her friend tenderly, "belongs to your great-grandmother. And once Natty gets all this world travel out of her system, she'll want him back."

"Natty is *never* going to get world travel out of her system," Tricia argued. "When her time comes—and that won't be for a long while, God willing—she'll probably be in a state room on some cruise ship, or riding a camel or shopping for exotic spices in some distant marketplace. She knows Winston is happy with you, Carolyn, and she doesn't plan on reclaiming him. Why do you think she charges you so little rent for the apartment?"

Carolyn, busy wondering how she'd ever bear being parted from that silly, spoiled, sardine-eating cat, was brought up short. She simply looked at Tricia, at a loss for words.

"And besides," Tricia went on, evidently suffering no such difficulty, "Natty's planning on signing the house over to me ahead of time, on the advice of her lawyer—something about avoiding probate when she passes—which means, for all practical intents and purposes, that *I'm* your landlady. And I'm lowering your rent—to zero."

"That *would* be charity," Carolyn protested.

"No," Tricia replied pointedly, but with a hopeful little smile, "it would be good business sense. Part of the compensation package for running the shop while I concentrate on giving this baby the best possible start in life. Think of it as just another house-sitting job, if it makes you feel better."

Carolyn's eyes widened, even as her throat constricted. "You don't have to do this, Tricia," she almost whispered. "Really. I'll be fine. I can make my own way—"

"Stop being so stubborn and so proud and listen to me," Tricia said. "Right now, I want to be at home. I want to be Conner's wife and this child's mother, full-time. But I'm still *me,* Carolyn. I still love arts and crafts, and I want to promote them—the world needs beautiful things that don't come in blister packs. *Please,* say you'll stay. Say you'll keep Creed and Simmons going." She stopped long enough to draw breath. "Don't you want to see what our little company could become? I know I do."

Carolyn blinked. She'd had a few thoughts along those lines herself—fanciful ones, about expanding the selection of merchandise, building a stronger presence on the internet, maybe even trying mail order—but she'd never taken them very seriously.

But she could start small, virtually on a shoestring. Carry greeting cards and regional cookbooks and the like. And what about scrapbooking supplies and whimsical rubber stamps?

It was even possible that Primrose, along with other talented locals, might be willing to teach art classes, share their knowledge and skill.

All these thoughts were still tumbling into Carolyn's mind when Tricia's face, plump with pregnancy, lit up with excitement. She took both Carolyn's hands in hers and squeezed. "You're seeing it, aren't you?" she guessed, with amazing accuracy. "You're seeing all the wonderful possibilities, just like I do."

Carolyn's eyes burned then, and pride dictated that she had to turn away, sniffle. "Suppose it's all a big mistake?" she murmured.

There was nothing wrong with Tricia's hearing. "Everything worth doing involves risk, Carolyn," she said.

Everything worth doing involves risk.

"I'll think about it," Carolyn said, very carefully, and then, after squaring her shoulders and straightening her spine, she headed for the small office where the shop's computer lived.

She logged on, ignoring another onslaught of enthusiasm from the Friendly Faces website, and clicked over to the auction page, where she'd put the gypsy skirt up for sale.

What she saw there nearly took her breath away.

The bidding was over the four-figure mark already and, judging by the number of people competing for the item, it was bound to go higher still.

That was when Carolyn began to imagine what it would mean, having help around the shop, so she could spend more time on creative work, like designing and sewing *other* one-of-a-kind wonders.

Maybe, she mused, her heart beating a little faster, Tricia was right.

Maybe it was time to stop being so careful and take a chance on something.

And some*one*.

THE EXPRESS PACKAGE was waiting on Brody's doorstep when he and Barney got back to the lodge at River's Bend, around five o'clock that afternoon, and he picked it up, smiled at the return address and bounced it once in his hand before tossing it onto the counter.

The DVDs he'd cadged from his film-distributor friend had arrived, with time to spare. When Saturday night rolled around, and it was finally time for his drive-in movie date with Carolyn, he'd be ready.

He shoved a hand through his hair, got out some clean clothes and made for the bathroom, where he took a very quick, very hot shower, shaving and washing the dust and sweat out of his hair while he was under the spray.

Once he was dressed again, Brody fed Barney, made sure his water bowl was full and fresh and walked to the door. Barney, exhausted from playing ranch-dog with Valentino all day, out at the other place, went straight to his bed and collapsed onto it with a contented sigh.

Brody locked up, glanced over at the new house to note any visible progress and climbed into his pickup. He was due at Carolyn's place at six, and it was almost that now, but she was probably still in the process of winding down from the day anyhow, so a few more minutes probably wouldn't matter.

He pulled into the lot at the supermarket, hurried inside, bought two dozen bright pink roses and a box of condoms and hurried out again.

Fortune, he reminded himself, with a grin, *favors not only the bold, but also the well-prepared.*

When he pulled up in front of the McCall house, Tricia was just coming down the porch steps. They met in the middle of the walk, and she took pointed notice of the roses—thank God, the box of condoms was in a paper bag, under his elbow—raised one eyebrow, and smiled even more brightly.

"Fancy meeting *you* here, Brody Creed," she said.

Brody laughed. "Fancy that," he replied.

He turned around, walked Tricia to the Pathfinder and waited while she climbed inside. He hoped she wasn't planning on stopping off at the supermarket before she went home, because somebody was sure to tell her about the purchases he'd made there a few minutes before. If word got back to Conner, there would be no end to the ribbing he'd have to endure.

"Drive safely," he told Tricia.

She smiled. "You, too," she answered.

And then she started up the rig and drove away.

Brody watched her out of sight, then took his roses and his box of condoms and headed for Natty McCall's front door.

It opened before he could shuffle the flowers and the paper bag around enough to knock.

Carolyn stood just inside, her eyes luminous, her cheeks flushed. She was wearing jeans, as usual, along with an oversize white shirt with the top three buttons undone.

She was so beautiful that Brody very nearly lost his nerve.

Sure, he hoped they'd finish what they'd started that morning, at Hidden Lake, but before the evening was over, he'd *also* have to explain why he'd gone off and left her nearly eight years before. That was going to be hard, because talking about Lisa and Justin twice in one day was bound to hurt twice as much as doing it once.

And that was a lot.

"Come in," Carolyn said quietly, her eyes dropping to the roses and then rising to his face again. The flush in her cheeks deepened.

The entryway was quiet and cool, and there was a faint, flowery scent in the air, though Brody couldn't tell if it was coming from her or from all the candles and bath salts and stuff she and Tricia sold in the shop.

He handed her the roses but held on to the bag with the condoms inside.

"Thank you," she said, her tone revealing exactly zip about what was going on in her mind. She turned and led the way toward the staircase, and Brody followed.

He half expected that schizoid cat to pounce on him the moment they reached Carolyn's kitchen, but it didn't happen. The feline was on the windowsill, busily snarfing up sardines from a saucer, and he didn't spare Brody so much as a glance.

"Have a seat," Carolyn offered, laying the bundled roses down on the counter. She rummaged through cupboards until she found a plain glass vase and got a pair of shears from a drawer.

"I'd rather stand awhile, I think," Brody heard himself say. At least, he *thought* he'd been the one to say it. He hadn't recognized the voice.

Carolyn glanced back at him, but she didn't reply. Her actions over the next few moments were ordinary enough, he supposed—she filled the vase with water, removed the roses from their cellophane cones, trimmed their stems with the scissors and arranged a fetching bouquet.

And watching her left Brody spellbound.

Even speechless.

When she turned around to face him, he was right there in front of her—he honestly didn't remember the strides that had brought him from one place to another—and he *had* to kiss her.

It was as vital as his next heartbeat, his next breath.

She stiffened briefly, and he felt a tremor go through her, but then she slipped her arms around his neck and kissed him right back.

The floor seemed to pitch under Brody's feet, as if he were out log-rolling on the river or something, and he deepened the kiss, leaning into Carolyn, feeling that free-fall kind of exaltation when she opened for him, responded to his embrace.

"Inevitable," he rasped, when their mouths finally parted.

"Yes," Carolyn agreed.

He scooped her off her feet and kissed her again, this time softly.

It wasn't a big apartment, so he hazarded a guess as to which door led to the bedroom and got it right.

Unfortunately, he'd left the condoms in the kitchen, still in their discreet little brown bag.

Brody swore under his breath, set Carolyn on her feet and fumbled for the buttons on her shirt.

Only her hands were there ahead of his, unfastening the buttons first.

He watched, stricken with need, as she shrugged out

of the shirt, revealing her perfect, lace-covered breasts, her flat, silken stomach, the rounding of her hips. When Brody reached out to unfasten her bra, he felt like a slow-motion figure in a movie, or a deep-sea diver without a tank and a mask.

And then Carolyn's breasts spilled into his hands, the nipples already hard. Ready for him.

She sighed and tilted her head back in surrender as he caressed her, roused her, told her, in all truth, that she was beautiful.

STANDING THERE in her quiet bedroom, Carolyn gave herself up to the commands of her body, gave herself up to Brody.

It had been so long, and she needed him so much.

Tears of amazement burned her eyes when he bent his head to take one of her nipples into his mouth, his strong hands splayed across her lower back, his touch a tacit promise that he wouldn't let her fall.

Staggering sensation rocked her as Brody attended to her breasts, nibbled at her earlobes, traced the length of her neck with his mouth, all the while unfastening her jeans, but, like before, this was something way beyond physical response.

Everything about Brody, from the scent of his hair and skin to the touch of his hands to the warm moistness of his mouth on her, seemingly everywhere, stirred emotions in her that had no names.

He laid her down on the bed sideways, tugged off her boots and, over the tingling flesh of her legs, brought her jeans and underpants down and discarded them. She was completely, wonderfully naked, while Brody, she thought dimly, was still partially clothed.

She groped for his shoulders, his bare chest, heard the jingle of his belt buckle.

"Hold that pose," he murmured, with a hoarse chuckle just beneath the surface of his voice. "I'll be right back."

Carolyn, already dazed, could only moan in reply.

It was a despairing sound, full of yearning.

Brody wasn't gone long, but Carolyn felt his absence as a shadowy chill, his return as the lovely, bone-saturating warmth of a tropical sun.

When he knelt next to the bed and eased her thighs apart, she uttered a sob, not of sorrow, but of wanting and of welcome.

When he took hold of her, she gasped his name, plunging both hands into his hair and gripping his scalp, pressing him closer and closer still.

His chuckle vibrated through her and that—only that—caused her to climax so fiercely that she arched her back high off the mattress and gave a long, throaty cry of pure lusty release.

Brody caressed her hips with his hands as she descended slowly, so slowly, from the heights, but he was still using his mouth on her in an easy, insistent way that immediately sent her rocketing past the last seizures of satisfaction into an even more ferocious state of arousal.

"Brody," she whimpered, when she found the breath to speak at all, "oh, Brody—don't make me wait—take me, *please*..."

She felt him shake his head, felt the silk of his hair brushing the tender insides of her thighs. Felt her need to have him inside her ratchet up to an almost unbearable peak.

And still he drew on her, now nibbling, now flickering her with the tip of his tongue, now sucking without mercy.

She exploded, with a low shout of ecstasy, her body straining like a bowstring drawn tight as volt upon volt of pleasure seared through her.

Brody didn't let her go until she'd given the last, shuddering gasp of surrender. He murmured to her, soothed her as all her muscles melted like wax under her still-pulsing flesh.

He shifted her to the center of the bed, kneeling astraddle of her thighs, and she knew he was putting on a condom.

"Decision time, pretty woman," he said gruffly. "Yes or no?"

"Yes," Carolyn managed to respond. "Oh, Brody—*Yes*—"

He entered her with a long, slow stroke and, that easily, set her ablaze all over again.

They moved in rhythm from the first, pacing themselves, their joining as graceful as a waltz.

Carolyn felt every nuance of pleasure, not only in her body, but also in her heart and her mind and her spirit, as well. She experienced Brody's lovemaking with her entire self, and deemed it sacred.

When she knew Brody was getting close to the pinnacle, she ran her hands over his shoulders and his back and his firm buttocks, whispering to him, comforting him and, at the same time, inciting him to let go.

And when he finally did give in, Carolyn herself was drawn back into the maelstrom of release, as powerless against the seemingly ceaseless, racking joy as a robin caught up in a hurricane.

The sunlight at the window turned pink and then pale

lavender as they lay there afterward, both exhausted, waiting, arms and legs entwined, for their breath to return and their hearts to stop pounding.

The room began to darken.

Winston meowed at the closed door, but neither Brody nor Carolyn moved, except to settle into each other's warmth. When they'd both recovered enough, they made love again, more slowly this time, and less frantically, but with the same shatteringly glorious conclusion.

When it was over, Carolyn was lying on top of Brody, her face buried in his neck, her senses full of him, of his scent and the texture and shape and strength of him. She drifted into a sated sleep and awakened, sometime later, with his fingers driving her straight into the throes of yet another earth-shaking orgasm.

She sighed when it was finally finished. Rolled onto her side, resting in the curve of Brody's left arm.

"Are we going to regret this?" she asked presently.

"Probably," Brody said, in a sexy murmur. "But I'm a great believer in living in the moment."

She giggled at that. Knotted up her fist and thunked him lightly on the chest. "Brody Creed," she said, "you are incorrigible."

He kissed the top of her head. "And hungry," he answered.

"I could whip up some scrambled eggs," Carolyn said, and wondered who this woman was who'd taken her over. The same one, apparently, who had dashed out to the convenience store earlier to buy bread and eggs and milk.

"Sounds good," Brody said. His voice was sleepy now.

Carolyn crawled over him to get out of bed. After a

brief shower, she put the white shirt back on and went into the kitchen.

Winston eyed her reproachfully from the windowsill.

"Don't give me that look," Carolyn told the cat. "You had your supper, remember?"

"Reow," Winston said, and, with an air of elegant resignation, began to groom his right paw.

My cat, Carolyn thought, flashing on her conversation with Tricia that afternoon. *My cat, my apartment, my shop.*

Look who suddenly has a future.

And all I have to do now is find a way to get over Brody Creed before he breaks my heart all over again.

CHAPTER FIFTEEN

DAMN BUT CAROLYN LOOKED GOOD, standing there in her apartment kitchen, cracking eggs into a pan and wearing nothing but some guy's shirt.

Brody frowned. Kim sometimes wore Davis's old shirts to paint or garden or clean house, and Tricia had been known to throw one of Conner's on once in a while, until the baby bulge got away from her. So who was the yahoo who'd left *this* one behind?

"What?" Carolyn asked, with a shy little smile curving her well-kissed mouth.

"Nothing." Brody sighed and hauled back a chair so he could sit down at the table. The lovemaking was over, for now, at least, and maybe forever, once she'd heard what he had to say.

It was past time to set things right between the two of them, though, one way or the other. He owed her the truth about a lot of things—first and foremost, his reason for abandoning her that long-ago night, leaving her with nothing but a brief note, a lot of anger and pain, most likely, and a whole slew of unanswered questions.

Evidently, Carolyn wasn't ready to move on. She peered down at the shirt, then looked up at him with wide, laughing eyes, as though she suspected what was bothering him, but wasn't quite sure. Her eyebrows rose in humorous inquiry. "Why the strange look, Brody?"

"I was just wondering who that shirt belongs to," he admitted, embarrassed but still feeling mighty territorial, too. "I'm over it now."

"It's yours," she told him, taking a mischievous delight in her answer. "You left it behind when you—"

The joy drained out of her eyes as she fell silent, remembering.

"I left it behind when I left *you,*" Brody said quietly, leaning to push back a second chair. "Carolyn, take that pan off the burner and sit down."

She turned away instead, though, shaking her head and shoveling a spatula under those eggs like she was trying to scrape road-tar off a hot surface. "That was a long time ago," she said, her words coming out rapid-fire, seeming to bounce off the cupboard doors and ricochet back at him. "Let's forget it, okay?"

Brody sighed again, shoved a hand through his hair. "If I could forget it," he said solemnly, and in all truth, "believe me, I would."

Carolyn looked back at him then. A scorching smell wafted over from the stove, and she quickly glopped the scrambled eggs onto two plates, brought them to the table, went back to the counter for silverware.

"For God's sake, Carolyn," Brody said, "sit down. Please."

"You *said* you were hungry," she retorted, going bright-cheeked again, but she finally sat down.

Neither of them picked up a fork, or even looked down at their plates. Their gazes had locked, and Brody saw plenty of pain in hers. Maybe, he thought, it was a reflection of his own.

"Her name was Lisa," he ground out. Even that much was damnably hard to say, but it was a beginning.

Bless her, Carolyn didn't come back with a flippant "Who's Lisa?" the way he'd half expected her to do.

"The woman who called that last night," Carolyn said softly. "The one you wanted to be with—"

Instead of me. The unspoken words hung between them.

"Yes," Brody replied, plowing a hand through his hair. "We met while I was rodeoing, Lisa and me, and we had sort of an affair—"

Color flared in Carolyn's cheeks, and her eyes flashed. "How do you have *sort of an affair?*" she asked.

"If you feel some need to make this harder, Carolyn," Brody said, "go right ahead."

She pressed her lips together into a hard line.

He flashed back to the taste of those lips, the feel of them against his.

Hot need struck him like a meteor blazing down from a clear blue sky.

"Lisa and I had an affair," Brody went on, putting a slight emphasis on the last word. "Nothing *sort of* about it. Then we broke up—I wanted to keep on following the rodeo circuit and she wanted to stay put, get married and buy a house, and there was no way either one of us was going to compromise, so we said our goodbyes and I left."

Carolyn waited. She looked pale now, rather than flushed, and very small inside that white shirt. Her throat worked, but she didn't say anything.

"I knocked around the Southwest for a while, then I ended up here. I was going to try and work things out with my family, but, as you know, when I showed up at Kim and Davis's place, they were nowhere around. I think Conner was away, too, at the time. Anyway, once I got that first glimpse of you, standing there in my aunt and uncle's doorway, framed in light, I couldn't think of anything *but* you, Carolyn."

He saw disbelief in Carolyn's face, along with something that might have been hope. Memories haunted her eyes like ghosts and she bit down on her lower lip.

"I wasn't sure what I felt for you was love," Brody went on, "but whatever it was, I'd never come across anything like it before."

She raised one eyebrow, but still held her peace.

"That last night, Lisa called," Brody said wearily. "She told me she was pregnant with my baby, and if I didn't marry her, she was going to put him up for adoption. I freaked right out—everything was going in forty different directions, and I couldn't seem to find the center."

Very slowly, Carolyn reached over and put her hand in his, but her eyes were still watchful, wary.

"Now," Brody said, with a ragged sigh, "I wish I'd *let* her have Justin and give him to some nice family to raise, because both of them might still be alive if I had. Most likely, Lisa would have found a man who loved her in ways I couldn't, no matter how hard I tried, and Justin, well, he'd be seven now. A normal, healthy kid. Starting second grade in the fall."

Carolyn swallowed, squeezed his hand, an I'm-listening sort of gesture. Some, but by no means all, of the ache in her eyes leaked away.

"Instead, they died in a car accident," Brody told her, when he felt like he could go on. After that, it was like somebody else was telling the story, while he stood apart, like a silent witness, listening, watching, remembering.

But detached from the pain.

Carolyn heard him out without interrupting, and, by the time he'd finished, she was sitting on his lap, her arms around him, her head resting on his shoulder.

Brody felt broken inside, torn apart, as though he'd used himself up, not just emotionally, but physically, too. The old grief, which could only be held at bay for so long, washed back over him and a steely force wrenched him back inside himself.

Without a word, Carolyn held him…for a long, long time. Then, presently, she stood up, took hold of his hand and led him back to her bed, where she proceeded to put him back together again, piece by piece.

BRODY LEFT A LITTLE after midnight—he didn't feel right leaving Barney alone for too long at a stretch, he said—and Carolyn, after locking the door behind him, went straight back to bed and slept a deep, healing sleep.

The next morning, yawning, she padded into the kitchen and immediately spotted the two plates of scrambled eggs, now congealed, still sitting on the table.

Making a face, she scraped the food into the sink and washed it down the disposal.

By that time, Winston was making give-me-breakfast-now noises, so she gave him kibble, which he disdained at first, probably angling for sardines.

Carolyn filled a cup with water, dropped in a tea bag and set the works in the microwave. While she was waiting for the timer to ring, signaling the end of two minutes, she thought about Brody. After last night, *not* thinking about him would have been quite a trick.

The lovemaking still reverberated throughout her body, in small, intermittent aftershocks, but that wasn't something to think about, it was something to *feel*. To savor and enjoy, in secret.

No, it was all that Brody had told her about Lisa, about their little boy, about that terrible accident and how he'd lost his way after it happened, that occupied her mind now.

She'd known intuitively that he was telling the truth, so it wasn't a question of believing or not believing what he said. Instead, it was a matter of personal damage.

How could a person ever come back from a tragedy like that?

Could *she* come back from what she'd so thoroughly believed was a cruel betrayal, even knowing the truth?

Some wounds, after all, never healed.

For Brody, the experience was beyond horrific; he'd been on the phone with Lisa when the collision *happened;* he'd heard the deafening crash and then the silence that followed. On top of that, he blamed himself—if only he'd let Lisa put their baby up for adoption, if only he'd been at home on that wintry night instead of riding bulls, he'd have been at the wheel, not Lisa.

He might have been able to steer clear in time to avoid impact.

If only, if only.

Carolyn knew that phrase well. If only her mother had cared enough to stick around instead of dumping her into the foster-care system and taking off for good. If only her dad had been the strong, steady, reliable type, like Davis Creed, willing to raise his child.

If only pigs had wings and chickens could tap dance, Carolyn thought. One of her foster moms had said that every time she dared to express the slightest dream for the future.

Soon, she'd stopped telling anyone what her hopes were.

Emotionally saddened but still jubilant physically, from making love with Brody, Carolyn switched on her laptop so it would boot up while she was in the shower.

Once she'd washed and dried herself off and gotten dressed, the computer was wide-awake, icons flashing, robot voice repeating, over and over, "Somebody likes your friendly face!"

The thing was the auditory equivalent of stone soup, like in the children's story. It just kept right on pumping out noise. So over the whole idea of hooking up online, Carolyn zipped over to the control-panel page and blocked all further communication from the dating site.

And then there was sweet, blissful peace.

"That's better," she told Winston, who didn't offer an opinion, one way or the other.

A few clicks of the mouse took her to the auction site, where she'd posted the gypsy skirt. The bids were still pouring in, and the current number had Carolyn rubbing her eyes, sure she must be misreading it somehow. Nobody paid *that* much for a skirt, however beautiful it was—did they?

She squinted at the high bidder's screen name, in case it was someone she knew, or maybe one of her regular customers, but she didn't recognize the moniker. Still, a prickle in the pit of her stomach insisted that something was amiss.

Carolyn stared hard at the screen, as though that would unveil the mystery, but she remained in the dark.

She was still at the computer, catching up on legitimate email, when she heard the knocking downstairs, at the front door.

Tricia? No, she had a key, and it was still too early for her to be there, anyway.

Brody? A little OMG thrill riffed through Carolyn, but she quickly quelled it. He'd told her he had a lot to do on the ranch, and they'd agreed to take a few days to catch their breaths.

They had a date for Saturday night, dinner and a movie.

In the interim, they'd play it cool.

The knocking continued, polite but insistent.

"Hold your horses," Carolyn muttered grumpily, nearly tumbling headfirst down the inside stairs because Winston ran past her to be on hand for the welcoming ceremony.

By the time she reached the entryway and opened the front door, Carolyn had assembled a smile and pasted it on her mouth.

It fell away when she got a good look at her visitor. Bill Venable was standing there on the porch, looking worried and uncomfortable and, as always, very attractive in his jeans and sleeveless T-shirt. His biceps were almost as impressive as Brody's.

"Bill," Carolyn said, unable to hide her surprise.

"I'm sorry," Bill said. "I know I should have called before I came over."

Carolyn stepped back to admit him. What on earth was he doing there, at that hour of the morning? The newspaper hadn't even been delivered yet.

"Is something wrong?" she asked. "Ellie's all right, isn't she?"

Bill nodded. His beard was growing in, a sign of

anxiety, maybe, since he was normally clean-shaven. "Ellie's fine," he said quickly. "It's just that—well— there's a fire, a big one, down in New Mexico, and I have to leave right away."

They stood in the entryway, with Winston meowing and curling between their ankles, as sleekly sinuous as a snake with fur.

Carolyn waited, still without a clue as to why Bill was there.

He gave a tentative smile. "We were planning on going up in my plane together, sometime soon?" he reminded her. "I didn't want you thinking I'd forgotten. I'm not sure how long I'll be gone, and I'll probably be too busy to call and, anyway, the fire's pretty remote, so there might not be cell service out there—" He appeared to be struggling, and Carolyn felt a stab of empathy for him. When he finally went on, what he said alarmed her a little. "There's always a chance I won't— I just needed to tell you face-to-face that I won't be around for a while."

Carolyn's spirits sank. It was almost as if Bill had come to say goodbye—forever—as he had reason to worry. She'd heard of pilots having premonitions of a crash or some other fatal disaster, of course.

Was Bill telling her that he thought he might be *killed* fighting this fire?

Her eyes filled and, for a crazy moment, she wanted to beg him not to go, to think of Ellie, and of Angela, and all the other people who must have loved him.

"Will Ellie be staying with her grandparents while you're gone?"

Bill shook his head, still looking miserable. "Not for the next few days. A friend of theirs passed away unexpectedly, so they've gone to Houston for the funeral. Ellie's staying with Angela until Charlie and Stella get back."

"Oh," Carolyn said, hopeful that this meant Bill and Angela were reconsidering their breakup. They belonged together, in her opinion.

"It's not what you're thinking," Bill said quickly. "Angela's feelings about my job haven't changed. She hates it, and she's furious because I refused to turn down this assignment." He sighed, thrust a hand through his hair. "But I know she'll take good care of Ellie, and that's what matters most. The two of them are close."

Carolyn thought of her friend soaring above a burning forest in a small plane, spraying fire retardant on flames clawing at the smoky sky like gigantic red-orange fingers, and she was afraid for him. The words *don't go* scrambled up into her throat and got stuck there, making her eyes sting.

Seeing her expression, Bill smiled sadly, gripped her shoulders gently and kissed her forehead. "Think good thoughts," he said hoarsely, in parting, and then he was turning away, walking out, closing the front door behind him.

Carolyn didn't move until several moments after he'd gone.

If only she'd had the power—or the right—to call him back, make him stay right there in Lonesome Bend, where he'd be safe.

But was anyone ever really safe, anywhere?

The answer, unfortunately, was no.

Bill's plane *could* crash, plummet right into the raging, hellish heart of a forest fire, leaving Ellie an orphan and Angela—sweet, well-meaning Angela—in a state of permanent grief. But he could just as easily drop dead from a heart attack, contract some fatal disease, or be run down in a crosswalk by a speeding car.

No one was getting out of here alive, no one had a guarantee that there would be another tomorrow, and another after that.

Living wasn't safe. Look what had happened to Brody's wife, Lisa, and their baby son. They were alive one moment and gone the next.

And as for laying the heart bare by loving another person? Why, that was the biggest, most deadly risk of all.

The starch drained out of Carolyn's knees, and she took a few groping steps backward and plunked herself down on one of the stairs, propping an elbow on one knee and resting her chin in her palm.

Winston approached, purring, and snuggled against her hip, either offering comfort or seeking it—or both.

Numbly, Carolyn stroked his glossy back with her free hand.

Yes, indeed, she'd been right all along—it was downright dangerous to love a person, or a pet, or even a house or a town or a job. Everything could change with a single turn of the steering wheel, or a phone call, or a policeman knocking at the front door.

But in the end, what choice did anyone have?

Could a person choose *not to* love?

They could try, of course, maybe even succeed to some degree.

But they might as well buy a plot and a tombstone, Carolyn reflected, and stretch out prone on the grass to wait for death, while others marched on in the parade of life, laughing and crying, loving and hating, knowing triumph and defeat and everything in between.

She might be able to kid herself that she was safe, but she'd also miss out on the party.

"You're pretty chipper today," Davis observed, that morning, with a slight twinkle, as he and Conner and Brody rode out to mend the broken fence lines Brody had taken note of the day before, while riding the lines. "Yesterday, you were traveling a rocky road."

Brody didn't answer right away, but he was poignantly aware of the value of ordinary moments. Conner was in the back of the pickup, with Valentino and Barney, hoops of new wire and the communal toolbox, while Brody drove and Davis rode shotgun.

They were working together, he and his brother and his uncle, just the way they ought to be.

Another part of Brody wished he was back in bed with Carolyn; it was too bad a man couldn't be in two places at once.

"That was yesterday," he finally replied, "and this is today."

Davis kept his face turned toward the windshield as they bounced and jostled over rough ground, but Brody knew his uncle was watching him from the corner of his eye. "We all racked up a whole lot of 'yesterdays' before you decided to go on ahead and tell me about Lisa and Justin. Why was that, Brody?"

Brody raised and lowered one shoulder, looking not at Davis, but ahead, at the cattle-speckled terrain of the ranch that had been home to generations of Creeds. Some branches of the family tree bore good fruit— solid, honest men and women committed to giving the best of who they were and what they had to building a lasting legacy for their children and grandchildren, right on down. Here and there, though, a rotten apple cropped up, a rascal or even an outlaw.

Most likely, by his own reckoning, he fit into the second category better than the first.

"It was a hard thing to talk about," he finally said.

"Life is full of things that are hard to talk about," Davis countered matter-of-factly. "Seems to me, if a man's lucky enough to have a home and kinfolks who care about him, it would be better to run *to* them when he had troubles, rather than *from* them."

Brody glanced at his uncle, unclamped his jawbones. "What do you want me to say, Davis? That I was wrong to stay away all those years?" A pause. "Well, fine. I was wrong."

"It's not a matter of what's right or wrong," Davis countered quietly. "What bothers me is that you must not have known you'd be welcome here."

"There was that blowup between Conner and me, over Joleen—"

"Don't bullshit me, boy," Davis broke in, sounding gruffer and more annoyed now. "That could have been settled over a couple of beers after supper, and you damn well know it." He gave a deep, ragged sigh. "Here's how I figure it…correct me if I'm mistaken—you were *ashamed* to come home. You figured it was your fault, what happened to the wife and the boy, and you wouldn't *let* yourself turn to your family and your friends."

Again, Brody's back teeth ground together. He had to consciously relax his whole face, and that made it damn near impossible to keep the devil-may-care mask in place.

"I never loved Lisa," he heard himself say, straight out.

It was crazy, because he'd never intended to say anything of the sort.

"You tried to do right by her, Brody. When you found out she was carrying your baby, you went to her. You took responsibility. That might not amount to the kind of love they print up inside Valentine cards, but it *is* love. It's the practical, take-hold, buckle-down-and-get-it-done kind of love that pretty words can't hold a candle to."

Conner thumped on the roof of the cab with one fist, signaling that they'd reached a place where the fence needed mending. Brody stopped the pickup with a lurch that made his brother shout a swear word.

Brody grinned over at Davis. "You missed your calling, cowboy," he said. "You ought to sign on with a greeting card company and write poetry."

Davis didn't crack a smile. "You think about what I said, son. What happened, happened. No getting around it—that kind of loss is an awful thing, but it's over. Your wife and your little boy are gone, and that's a shame, but you're *alive,* and that's counts for something. *Make use of the time you have,* Brody."

Just then, Conner stepped onto the driver's-side running board and banged at the window once, with the flat of his hand. He looked seriously pissed.

"Are you trying to kill me *and* these dogs, driving like that?" he demanded. "First you're doing fifty, then you stop on a damn dime!"

Brody shoved the truck door open, forcing Conner

to scramble clear. "Hell, no," Brody mocked, grinning. "If that were the case, I would surely have succeeded."

Davis rolled his eyes. "Don't start, you two," he warned. "We've got work to do."

THE BIDS ON the gypsy skirt were still climbing, Carolyn learned, later in the morning, when she checked the auction site again. Tricia had a routine doctor's appointment, so she wouldn't be in for a couple of hours.

Meanwhile, Carolyn couldn't seem to concentrate on the task at hand long enough to get anything done.

Ideas for more one-of-a-kind garments had been pouring into her head in such plentitude that she had to keep stopping whatever she happened to be doing at the time to rough out a sketch, lest, in her scatterbrained state of mind, she forget.

A few customers stopped in, and she boxed and addressed several orders for shipping.

Every time she passed through the main part of the shop, her gaze went straight to the large square package containing the Weaver. She hadn't given the batik a thought the night before, for obvious reasons, and Brody probably hadn't, either.

Too bad, because he could have taken it with him when he headed home, and saved her a trip.

On the other hand, Brody Creed had a stubborn streak as wide as the river, and he might have refused to take the piece with him just because he wanted her to deliver it.

Carolyn ran a fingertip over the wrapping, a little smile playing around her mouth but never quite coming in for a landing.

When the time was right, she would take the batik

to Brody's place, as agreed, but there might be more to the delivery than a piece of art.

She was thinking this lascivious thought, and flirting with a few others, when the door of the shop opened, bell jingling, and she braced herself for another on-slaught of unexpected customers.

Instead, Primrose Sullivan swept in, wearing one of her brightly colored caftans and lugging more paintings.

"I've been working like a crazy woman," she en-thused. "Anytime you want me to stop bringing in art-work, you just tell me."

Carolyn laughed, glad to see her friend. And the paintings.

The last batch was selling fast, via the website.

Primrose set down her burden with the gentleness of a mother putting a child down for an afternoon nap and beamed at Carolyn, her blue eyes huge behind the lenses of her leopard-print glasses.

"It's all over town," Primrose announced gleefully.

This was another OMG moment for Carolyn, but not the pleasant kind. She felt her ears burning and her throat closed up tight. Which was a good thing, as it turned out, because she'd been on the verge of blurting out that Brody *hadn't* stayed the whole night, which was true, and that nothing had happened—*not* true—and that, frankly, she was getting sick of being gossiped about.

"You're planning to expand the shop," Primrose rushed on, making Carolyn almighty thankful that she hadn't been able to speak before. "I think that's so exciting! Is it true that you're planning to hire help?"

"Y-yes," Carolyn managed to respond, somewhat

weakly. "It's true. Tricia and I are hoping you might consent to teach some classes...?"

Primrose rubbed her many-ringed hands together in anticipation. "You bet I will," she said. "And you might consider bringing Mavis Pawlings in to teach sometime—she knows everything there is to know about scrapbooking and rubber stamps and all that sort of thing. Then there's Lily Wilde—one of her quilts won best of show last year at the state fair—"

Carolyn smiled, held up both hands, palms out. "Whoa, Primrose," she said good-naturedly, "give me a minute to catch up."

But Primrose was too excited to be still, even for that long. "Scrapbooking is very big, you know," she blurted. "And quilts? Heavens, that's become a regular *industry,* all by itself." She looked around speculatively, a comical sight with her magnified eyes. "Knock out a wall or two," she mused, "and you could sell fabric. This town needs a fabric store—folks have to drive all the way to Denver for a few yards of cotton and spool of thread as it is now."

"Primrose," Carolyn pleaded, grinning, "take a breath."

Primrose *did* take a breath, but the respite was brief. "Handmade items are great," she continued, "but most of your business comes in over the website, doesn't it?"

"Most of it," Carolyn agreed cautiously. "Why?"

Primrose was on a real roll. "The sachets and the doilies and all the rest of it are *fine*—and heaven *knows* I'm grateful to you and Tricia for selling so many of my batiks—but it might be a better use of floor space to display things people would come in purposely to buy. Like quilting fabric. Maybe even a sewing machine or two."

Carolyn smiled. "Primrose?"

"Yes, dear?" The older woman beamed.

"How would you like a part-time job?"

Primrose all but clapped her hands. "Are you offering me one? My friends all say I spend too much time in my studio, and I'm bound to get stale or even burn out, and I'd just love a change of scene for a few hours a day."

"I'll have to double-check with Tricia, of course," Carolyn said, "but I can't think of anybody I'd rather hire to help out around here, and I'm sure she'll agree."

Primrose looked around, her expression dreamy now. "Oh," she said, "I can just *see* it all, in my mind's eye."

"Me, too," Carolyn agreed.

It was then that Primrose noticed the parcel containing the Weaver, still resting on top of a display table. There was something of a caress to the way she touched the wrapping. "I could drop this off at Brody's place on my way home," she offered.

Silently, Carolyn called herself three kinds of crazy—here was her chance to cross an errand off her to-do list *and* a way to show Brody that she wasn't about to dance to his tune—but she shook her head. "He's out at the ranch, working with Davis and Conner," she said. "And the Weaver is much too valuable to be left on his doorstep."

Primrose watched Carolyn closely for a moment, a happy light dancing in her eyes. "You know right where Brody Creed is, at this very minute," she observed, in a teasing tone. "Now, isn't that interesting?"

Carolyn blushed slightly. "I just assumed that's where he'd be," she said lamely.

Primrose chuckled. "It does my old heart good," she said. Like many older people, Primrose didn't do segues.

Carolyn didn't ask what the woman meant, because she already knew.

Segues weren't always necessary, now were they?

Primrose went on to show Carolyn each of the new pieces she'd just brought in, and Carolyn's admiration was sincere.

"What's it like, to be able to bring people and animals to life on cloth or a canvas, the way you do?" she asked wistfully.

Primrose patted her gently on the back. "I imagine it's about the same as being able to sew up something beautiful in no time flat, the way *you* do," she replied. "I've seen your work, Carolyn. You have an eye for line and color and movement—stop being so all-fired humble all the time and own it."

Own it.

What did that mean, exactly?

All her life, it seemed to Carolyn, she'd been trying to prove something—she was a foster kid, *but*— She'd never gone to college, *but*— She'd fallen head over heels for Brody Creed, back in the day, *but*—

But what if everything she'd ever wanted was within her grasp—and all she had to do was own it?

CHAPTER SIXTEEN

Saturday took its sweet time rolling around, as far as Brody was concerned, and staying away from Carolyn in the meantime was only possible because he'd been putting in twelve-hour days on the ranch, along with Davis and Conner. There were fences to mend, strays to round up, sick cows to dose with medicine, stalls to muck out and horses to shoe, deworm and exercise.

A rancher's work is, quite literally, never done.

Since he and Kim and the minidogs were heading out to Stone Creek Sunday morning, Davis whistled a lot, and there was a spring in his step. He was a born grandfather, and Brody knew his uncle could hardly wait for Tricia and Conner's little one to be born so he'd have a Creed youngster readily available for spoiling.

Conner was in a fairly good mood, too, now that Tricia had agreed to stay home, let Carolyn be in charge of things at the shop and take it easy until after the baby came.

As for Brody himself, well, he was as jumpy as ice water on a hot griddle. His moods ran the gamut from woe-is-me to yee-haw, and he never knew when one mood would give way to the other.

He worked a half day on Saturday, appropriated a horse trailer to bring Moonshine back from the ranch to the new barn and, with Barney's questionable assistance, got the gelding settled in his own stall.

To Brody's way of thinking, Moonshine looked a bit on the lonely side, all by himself in that big place, fancy as it was shaping up to be. The stalls were finished and the water and electricity were hooked up, which was more than could be said of the house. The corral fence stood straight and sturdy, too.

"Maybe you and I ought to move in with Moonshine," he told Barney, only half kidding. It wasn't even June yet, and the house wouldn't be ready to live in until mid-August, according to the contractor.

Barney trotted happily at his side, panting, as they headed toward the log cabin where he'd been living since he'd bought the River's Bend property from Tricia.

He hated the lack of elbow room, the counter running through the middle of the building, the jury-rigged bathroom and the borrowed bed and making do with a knee-high fridge and a microwave the size of a shoebox.

Most of all, he hated that he was always alone in the place. That definitely sucked.

But, hallelujah, it was finally Saturday.

He'd had part of the contractor's crew up at the Bluebird Drive-in for a couple of days now, cleaning up the snack bar and hooking up a popcorn machine, rented, like the projector, and he'd hired a caterer from Denver to whip up and deliver a fancy meal for two, complete with wine and candlelight.

Oh, he had definitely outdone himself this time, Brody thought cheerfully. Not that he went around revamping old drive-in theaters for one dinner-and-movie date—there had been a lot of women in his life, and he'd given some of them expensive presents, or paid their bills a time or two, but he'd never done anything quite like this before.

However things shook out between him and Carolyn, when it was all over but the shoutin', he'd have this night to remember, and so would she.

Brody ducked into his makeshift bathroom, stripped off his work clothes and showered.

After that, he put on clean jeans, a pale blue Western shirt, socks and his second-best boots. It was still too early in the day to go with the custom-made pair, the ones he usually broke out only for weddings and funerals with the Creed brand subtly embossed into each shaft.

He ran a comb through his hair—he needed barbering, he guessed, but the more clean-cut he was, the more he could have passed for Conner, and something about that chapped his hide a little. Love his brother though he did, Brody figured it was enough that he and his twin had the same face, coloring and build.

They didn't need the same haircut and close shave, too.

Hungry, but downright averse to the idea of yet another half-assed concoction made up of the strange assortment of stuff in his refrigerator, he decided he'd treat himself to a hamburger and a milk shake for lunch.

With that in mind, he left Barney to snooze on the dog-bed, while he drove over to the Birdcage Café for a generous helping of fat, sugar and preservatives.

The hole-in-the-wall restaurant had been a mainstay in Lonesome Bend since before his dad and Davis were born, and while everybody wondered, nobody recalled why any sensible person would give a food-service

establishment—even a greasy spoon like that one—
such an unappetizing name.

For all that, the Birdcage served a mean burger, made
from scratch, and they grilled the buns in real butter
before slapping a thick patty of ground beef between
them. They changed the oil in their deep-fat fryer once
a week whether it needed doing or not, and the only
thing better than their potato salad was Natty McCall's
secret-recipe chili, available only at the annual rum-
mage sale in late October.

The parking spaces on the street were full, as usual,
so Brody pulled into the dusty gravel lot next to the
café, driving slowly so he wouldn't get his truck too
dirty before it was time to pick Carolyn up for their
get-together that night.

He had some high hopes for the *together* part.

"Way you was drivin' two miles an hour, I figured
some maiden schoolmarm was fixin' to get out of that
truck," boomed Will Carlson, one of several old-timers
who took turns holding down the peeling wooden bench
under the Birdcage's front window, as Brody walked
toward him.

"How many maiden schoolmarms drive extended-
cab pickups, Will?" Brody retorted with a good-natured
grin and a tug at the brim of a hat he wasn't wearing.

Will eyed him from beneath the bill of a ratty old
cap, his face beard-stubbled and loose-skinned. He
shifted his jaw around, most likely in an effort to realign
his ill-fitting dentures. "You come here to see Joleen?"

The old man's question didn't register with Brody
until it was too late—by the time it did, he'd already
pushed open the front door and stepped inside.

And there was Joleen, wearing a waitress uniform

and flirting shamelessly with some out-of-towner in a business suit while she took his order.

Brody briefly considered bolting, but one, that would be a chickenshit thing to do, since this was still a free country the last time he checked and he had as much right to be there as anybody, and two, he wanted a grease-burger.

So he stayed put, feeling his neck warm up as everybody in the café turned to look at him.

Including Joleen.

Brody nodded a greeting to her and took the last stool at the counter, between two grizzled ranchers who'd lived around Lonesome Bend since the fifth day of Creation. That pair of old buzzards hadn't spoken to each other in fifty years, it was said—something about a hand of poker and a girl—which was the only reason there was a single place to sit down.

Joleen, sly-eyed, finished writing up the suit's order and sashayed behind the counter to stand directly in front of Brody.

"Well," she said, almost purring. "If it isn't Brody Creed."

Brody reset his shoulders, set his hands on the counter, fingers interlaced. "Hello, Joleen," he said casually. "How about a burger with everything and a chocolate milk shake?"

Joleen made no move to write down the request or relay it to the fry cook back at the grill. All the chatter had ceased, and even the jukebox fell silent.

Evidently, the folks who patronized the Birdcage had free time aplenty, if they could sit around gawking like they were, with their ears practically tilting forward, like Moonshine's did when he was trying to decide whether or not he ought to spook.

Joleen folded her arms, underscoring her ample breasts. "You probably thought I'd be long gone by now, didn't you?" she asked, with acid sweetness.

"A man can always hope," Brody replied mildly.

This brought a few snickers from the onlookers and made Joleen's green eyes flash with temper.

Brody wondered idly if her eyes were really green, or if she was wearing another set of contact lenses. He didn't plan on getting close enough to find out.

Quietly, he repeated his order.

Joleen turned around and fairly screeched it at Manuel, the fry cook.

Manuel winced, tossed Brody a glance of amused sympathy and commenced to building his famous two-thousand-plus-calorie gut-buster.

After that, Joleen steered clear of Brody to such an extent that Manuel had to bring out the burger and fries himself when they were ready. As for the milk shake—well, Brody decided not to remind anybody of that, because it was too easy to picture Joleen upending the thing over the top of his head.

Gradually, folks lost interest, probably disappointed that there hadn't been some kind of donnybrook, and went back to their own food and the conversations they'd suspended when Brody and Joleen first faced off.

Brody ate most of his meal, though he'd mostly lost his appetite, and he even pretended to enjoy it. When he couldn't face another bite, he estimated the total for his check, since Joleen didn't bring one, and left the money on the counter, next to his plate.

He headed for the parking lot and was just opening

the door of his truck when Joleen shot out of a side door and stomped over to him.

"What about my tip?" she demanded.

Brody grinned affably. "You've got to be kidding," he said.

"It just goes to show I was absolutely right to dump you, Brody Creed, because you have *no class* whatsoever!"

Brody folded his arms. If Joleen wanted to rewrite history, it was okay with him. Especially if it meant she'd let him be from now on. "I guess you did the right thing for sure, that being the case," he said. He set one foot on the running board, fixing to climb behind the wheel. "But since you wanted a tip, here it is, Joleen— move on, find yourself a big city with bright lights, because Lonesome Bend, let alone the Birdcage Café, is never going to be enough for you."

An impish smile played on Joleen's mouth. Some people would have been surprised by that reaction, Brody supposed, but he wasn't. The word *mercurial* didn't begin to describe the woman's temperament.

"I would, if I had, oh, say, five thousand dollars to travel on," she suggested coyly.

"Then you'd better find yourself a sucker pronto," Brody replied easily, "because if I fork over the money, it's going to look like a payoff, and that kind of thing doesn't set well with me."

The smile turned to ice, a thin layer over poison. "Since when do you care how anything looks to other people, Creed?"

Since Carolyn, Brody thought, just then realizing it was true.

He didn't give a rat's ass about the town's opinion

of him, or Joleen's. Never had, really. But it mattered what Carolyn saw when she looked at him—Conner and Davis, too. Moreover, it mattered what he thought of *himself.*

"Well?" Joleen prompted, angered by his silence. *"Since when?"*

"Since now," Brody replied, very quietly.

Joleen blinked. He hoped she wouldn't cry, but if she did, he reckoned he could endure it, since he'd be driving away from here in a minute or so. "It wouldn't be a payoff," she finally said, her voice gone small and a little shaky now. "The five grand, I mean. It would be one friend making a loan to another. And be honest, Brody. Maybe building that big, fancy house and barn at River's Bend is the first showy thing you've ever done, but that's pocket change to you, and you know it."

"Sorry, Joleen," Brody said. "Writing you a check for any amount of money is a message I just don't want to send."

Her shoulders sagged and she scuffed at the gravel with the toe of her white waitress shoe. It wouldn't be white for long, Brody supposed, but, then, Joleen wouldn't be a waitress for long, either.

She had the worst case of wanderlust Brody had ever seen.

"Well, *damn,*" she said finally, and the sorrows gave way to that showgirl smile of hers. "It was worth a try."

Brody laughed. "Good luck, Joleen," he said, "and be happy."

She was still smiling as he drove away, and waving one hand in farewell.

Women, Brody thought. There was just no figuring them out.

CAROLYN ROOTED desperately through her wardrobe for something to wear besides her normal jeans, T-shirt and boots. Bottom line, she'd shot the fashion wad with the cotton sundress she'd worn to Bill's backyard barbecue, and recycling it for a date with Brody just didn't seem right.

"Why don't you wear the gypsy skirt?" Tricia asked. They'd closed the shop an hour early that day, and she'd stuck around to quiz an admission out of Carolyn—yes, she was going out with Brody that night.

It was no big deal, she'd insisted to Tricia.

"Are you kidding me?" Carolyn retorted. "The bid is in four figures. Whoever is so determined to buy that skirt isn't looking for anything that's already been worn."

"They'd never know," Tricia said.

"*I'd* know," Carolyn countered.

"Then maybe they wouldn't care if they *did* know," Tricia said cheerfully.

"Fat chance," Carolyn retorted, unearthing a black sundress with white polka dots and holding it up for a critical examination. When had she made the thing? It had to have been a long time ago, because she didn't remember it at all.

Tricia chuckled. "And yet you would have me believe this date with Brody was no big deal," she teased. "Why don't you just jump in your car and come out to the ranch? We'll ransack every closet on the place if we have to—between Kim and I, we must have *something* you could wear tonight."

"There's no time for that," Carolyn practically wailed, casting a speculative glance at the gypsy skirt, draped neatly on a hanger and suspended from the hook on the back of her bedroom door.

She *couldn't* wear that skirt.

For one thing, it didn't really belong to her.

For another, she might spill something on it, ruin it forever. *Then* what?

And for still *another* thing, Brody hadn't asked her to a formal gala at the White House or a coronation at Buckingham Palace—he'd offered dinner and a movie. She'd look like a fool, getting that dressed up for a blue-plate special at some country café, followed by a flick and popcorn.

She couldn't resist catching one of the ribbons between her fingers, though, and imagining how it would feel to be a princess for just one night.

"Wear the skirt, Cinderella," Tricia said gently.

"I couldn't," Carolyn murmured, sorely tempted to do just that. To be rash and reckless, for once in her life, instead of careful.

To be beautiful.

To be Cinderella.

Oh, but Brody Creed was a cowboy, not a prince.

Lonesome Bend was planted squarely in the real world, not in a fairy-tale kingdom, where fairy god-mothers waved wands and pumpkins turned to coaches, mice to prancing steeds.

She was Carolyn Simmons, an ordinary woman, and she'd better remember it.

Tricia wasn't one to give up. "Well, then, just *try it on*," she said, waddling over to stand next to Carolyn. With a sigh, she stretched to ease the pressure on her lower back and sighed, "I swear this kid is getting ready to audition for *Riverdance*. The way he kicks, he'll be born wearing tap shoes."

Since Tricia and Conner had been closemouthed about the sex of their baby, this was the clue Carolyn had been waiting for.

"Ah-ha!" she cried, jubilant, forgetting the skirt and all its magic for a much greater miracle, the formation of a brand-new human being. "You're having a boy!"

"Don't tell," Tricia said, in a conspiratorial whisper, putting a finger to her lips. "Outside the doctor's office, nobody knows but Conner and me."

"Why the secrecy?" Carolyn asked.

Again, Tricia sighed, but softly, and with an air of contentment. "We're not trying to be mysterious," she said. "It's just that…well, we're both sort of old-fashioned when it comes to having a baby. Not that long ago, nobody knew if they were having a boy or a girl until after their delivery. Now, people have the nursery furnished in either pink or blue and the name picked out months ahead of time. I'd rather have been surprised, and Conner agrees."

Carolyn studied her friend. "You're not superstitious, are you? One of those people who think it's bad luck to buy things for a baby before it's born? In case—in case something goes wrong?"

Tricia smiled. "No," she said. "I'm not. There is nothing wrong with this baby, trust me. He kicks like a mule."

Carolyn smiled back, relieved. "I don't suppose you want to tell me what you're going to name young Mr. Creed, now that the figurative cat is out of the bag?"

"Davis Blue," Tricia answered readily. "We'll probably call him Blue."

"Blue?" Carolyn asked. The Davis part needed no explanation, but—*Blue?*

"For Conner and Brody's father," Tricia said. "Davis's older brother. The story goes that the sky was a knock-out shade of azure when Blue was born—hence the name."

"I like it," Carolyn mused and, for the briefest of moments, she allowed herself to wonder what name she and *Brody* might give a child of their own.

"Me, too," Tricia agreed. "And don't you dare tell anybody. Davis and Kim don't know, and neither does Brody. We want our baby's sex *and* his name to be a surprise."

Carolyn made a zipping motion across her mouth. Then she laughed again, out of pure joy at her friends' good fortune, and gave Tricia a quick hug.

"Now," Tricia said, with a little sniffle, once they'd had their girl moment, "back to the gypsy skirt. *Try it on.* I want to see what it looks like on an actual person, and heaven knows, I'm in no condition to model haute couture."

"Tricia."

"It's the least you can do," Tricia insisted, "after I told you my big secret."

Carolyn sighed, took the skirt from the hook, still on its hanger and held it against her chest, careful not to crush the ribbons. "Oh, all right," she said, starting for the bathroom. "But I'm telling you right now, it's going to look downright weird with a T-shirt."

Tricia went to the bureau, tugged open a drawer and extracted a wispy black silk camisole with spaghetti straps, waving it at Carolyn like a flag. "Wear this," she said.

Carolyn took the garment hesitantly—she'd worn it with a transparent shirt she'd owned, and subsequently discarded as impractical, a long time ago—and gave Tricia a rueful look. "I don't know," she said. "It's pretty skimpy—"

"It's just us girls," Tricia reminded her, almost singing the words and shooing Carolyn toward the bathroom. *"Go."*

STANDING AT CAROLYN'S kitchen door, with the first shadows of twilight falling around him, Brody tried to remember the last time he'd made a fuss like this over a simple date.

Not since his high-school prom, he decided, hooking a finger under the collar of his starched white shirt even though the top three buttons were already undone. Kim had made him wear a penguin suit that night, as she'd done to Conner, too, and Brody had stabbed the girl— Becky? Betsy? Babs?—with the little pearl-headed pin while fumbling around trying to pin on her corsage. He and Conner, along with two of their friends and all four dates, had crammed themselves into the back of a rented limo and thought they were big stuff.

He smiled at the memory.

Remembered that he hadn't knocked.

He rapped his knuckles lightly against the door frame. Through the frosted glass in the door's oval window, he saw Carolyn approaching to admit him, and even before she opened the door, his heart had shinnied up into his throat and swelled to three times its normal size.

Her light hair gleamed around her shoulders, looking soft enough to run his fingers through, and her perfect cleavage formed an enticing V above the black silk of her top.

After her face, though—her shy and lovely and slightly flushed face—it was the skirt he would remember until the end of his days.

It was composed of what seemed to be hundreds of ribbons and beads, and it swayed and shifted around her like a puff of glittering smoke, or shards of glass in a kaleidoscope.

"Wow," he said. He hadn't brought flowers, since she still had the roses from the other night, but now he wished he had. He wished there were a coach-and-six waiting on the street, instead of the car he'd borrowed from Davis and Kim.

Carolyn's cheeks were pink. Without looking down—a skill he'd perfected since puberty—he managed to note that her nipples showed faintly through the black top.

"Wow, yourself," she said, after giving him a flirty once-over. Then she lost whatever bravado she'd summoned up and blushed again. "Do—do you think I'm overdressed? It was Tricia's idea to wear this—she nagged me into it—"

Brody reached out and rested an index finger lightly against her mouth—a mouth he hoped to kiss, and thoroughly, later on in the evening. "It's perfect," he said. "*You're* perfect."

She already had her purse handy, a thin little envelope of a thing she tucked under one arm. Obviously, she hadn't brought her toothbrush and a change of clothes for morning.

He tried not to read that as an omen.

"Thank you," she said, so belatedly that Brody had

to scramble for a moment to recall what she was thanking him for.

Oh, yeah. Saying she was perfect. Well, that hadn't been such a stretch now, had it?

She *was* perfect.

He took her arm as they descended the outside stairs, the skirt whispering like poetry made visible with every move she made.

This time, she noticed he was looking and stopped, when they reached the bottom of the steps, to peer into his face. "Are you *sure* I'm not overdressed?" she demanded.

He chuckled. "As far as I'm concerned, lady, anytime you're wearing more than skin, you're overdressed."

That made her laugh, albeit nervously. But her feet came loose from the ground, where she'd dug them in a moment before, and Carolyn and Brody moved on toward the waiting car.

He might have blown it with the flowers, Brody thought, but he'd gotten this part right. In that getup, Carolyn would have had a hard time getting into the cab of his truck.

He opened the passenger-side door for her, waited while she and that amazing skirt got themselves settled in the seat.

She'd already fastened her seat belt by the time he slid behind the wheel.

He was wearing his best shirt and jeans, and a pair of boots that had cost more than his first car, but now he wondered if he wasn't the one who ought to be fretting about how they were dressed—or *under*dressed, in his case.

Carolyn sat rigidly in the seat, the sliver-thin purse

on her lap, her gaze fixed straight ahead. In a sidelong glance, Brody noticed the pulse at the base of her throat.

He wasn't the only one who was nervous, obviously.

The realization relaxed him a little.

As for chitter-chatter, well, if Carolyn didn't feel like talking, it was okay with him. He was satisfied just to be sharing a car seat with her.

They drove through town and he thought she gave a little sigh of relief when they passed the Birdcage Café without stopping—*as if* he'd take her there—and then the Golden Spur Saloon and Steakhouse, but maybe he imagined it.

When he steered the car onto the bumpy track leading to the Bluebird Drive-in, though, she turned and looked at him with widened eyes. Maybe she thought he doubled as a serial killer in his spare time and he was taking her somewhere remote, so she could be his next victim.

Creed, he thought, *you are losing it.*

Thanks to the generator he'd borrowed from his contractor—it was a noisy piece of equipment, but effective—the building containing the snack bar was all lit up. The ancient movie screen glowed white in the gathering twilight, ready for action.

Carolyn looked around, still wide-eyed, with her mouth slightly open.

"You wanted dinner and a movie," Brody said, watching her.

What if this was the world's dumbest idea? he wondered, while he waited for a reaction.

"You're not serious," she said, but there was a gleam in her eyes now, and that pulse at the base of her throat was beating hard.

Brody said nothing. He just shut off the car, got out and came around to her side to open the door for her.

She put out her hand, and he took it. Helped her out.

She stood there, like a goddess dressed in dancing dreams, looking up at him. Her expression was one of amused bafflement. "I don't understand," she said.

"You will," Brody replied, still holding her hand.

He led her toward the snack bar, which had been filled with the caterer's assistants until a few minutes ago. By now, there was a single waiter, hiding in the back most likely, and he'd be gone, too, as soon as Brody could reasonably get rid of him.

Inside the scrubbed and scoured snack bar, the glass enclosing the popcorn machine gleamed, as did the counter.

A round table sat in the middle of the room, draped with a snow-white tablecloth and set with china and silver. Candles glimmered and flickered in the center and, except for the faint hum of the generator, all was quiet.

Carolyn was speechless. She looked up at Brody's face as though she expected him to say there was some mistake, they'd wandered into the wrong place, whatever.

Brody smiled and cocked an elbow at her so she'd take his arm, which she did after a moment's confusion, and escorted her to the table. He pulled back her chair, waited until she was seated and sat down opposite her.

The candlelight danced across her face and shimmered in her hair.

Right on cue, the rent-a-waiter appeared, with a bottle of French wine and two sparkling crystal glasses.

Carolyn drew in her breath, gave Brody another look of curious surprise and finally smiled back at him.

"When you said dinner and a movie, you weren't kidding," she said, as the waiter poured their wine and scurried off to the back room again, to await his next scene.

Brody grinned, picked up his wineglass by the stem, and waited for Carolyn to do the same. "There are some things," he said, "that I never kid about."

She smiled, and their glass rims made a bell-like sound as they touched them together. "This is like something—well, out of a *movie*," she said.

The waiter returned with salads, set them down with a flourish and immediately vanished again.

The guy certainly knew when to get lost, Brody thought with approval, and his tip was getting bigger with every passing moment.

"This is delicious," Carolyn said, after spearing some salad with her fork and taking a cautious nibble.

Brody laughed. "You sound surprised."

She blushed prettily. God, he loved it when she blushed. "It's… I've never been on a date like this."

"That was the idea," Brody said. "Don't look now, but I'm trying to impress you."

"Well," Carolyn said, "you're succeeding." She looked at him from under her eyelashes, and a corner of her highly kissable mouth twitched. "What comes next?"

Brody pretended to be puzzled. Took another sip of his wine instead of answering. But he was thinking, *You do, if I have anything to say about it.*

Carolyn, so quiet before, in the car, seemed bent on conversation now. "The Bluebird has been closed for years," she said, looking around. Her expression was nostalgic. "Tricia has a lot of old pictures of it. But surely the projector doesn't actually work—"

"We'll see," Brody said.

CHAPTER SEVENTEEN

CAROLYN WAS AMAZED, and not just by the romantic dinner, the delicate dessert to follow, or the way the popcorn machine seemed to come on all by itself, like magic.

That Brody had even thought of something like this, let alone gone to all the trouble and expense to make it happen, blew her away.

They lingered in the candlelight until it was fully dark outside, and then Brody pulled back her chair, waited for her to stand and escorted her grandly back to Kim and Davis's car.

They drove over a couple of humps in the ground and stopped beside one particular rusted post, with a speaker attached.

"Don't move," Brody told her, with a twinkle in his eyes, "I'll be right back."

She turned to watch as he returned to the snack bar.

Sound crackled through the dented speaker on the pole outside the driver's side window, and light spilled across the darkened lot. Once, the Bluebird Drive-in would have been packed with all sorts of vehicles on a Saturday night, every space filled, every speaker clipped onto a car window, but tonight, apparently, it was theirs alone.

True to his word, Brody returned in a couple of minutes, carrying a silver wine cooler overflowing with fresh popcorn in the curve of one arm.

He opened the car door, handed Carolyn the popcorn and got in.

Imagining what buttered popcorn might do to the gypsy skirt, she set the cooler between them, on the console. When she closed her eyes, she felt dizzy, but the instant she opened them again, she was fine.

"I didn't have time to hunt down any of those cardboard buckets they usually serve this stuff in," Brody explained, with a nod at the popcorn, turning and fiddling with the speaker.

Music swelled into the car, accompanied by a few stereophonic screeches, and Brody winced as he adjusted the volume.

Only then did Carolyn look toward the movie screen, now awash in motion and color and light and opening credits.

One name jumped out at her.

Gifford Welsh.

Gifford Welsh, the man who'd single-handedly ended her brief and happy career as his daughter's nanny.

Shock washed over her, like water charged with electricity, stunning the breath from her lungs and making every nerve in her entire body sting like molten wax.

This must be what it's like to be struck by lightning, she thought.

More nausea and another spate of dizziness followed the shock and for a moment, Carolyn was afraid she might distinguish herself by throwing up a *second* time, in front of the same man.

"Oh, my God—" she whispered, incapable of more.

Brody had deliberately chosen a movie starring *Gifford Welsh*.

And why would he do such a thing? Because he'd heard all that stupid gossip about her supposed affair with the actor, *that* was why. He'd set her up, suckered her in with that romantic dinner in the specially refurbished snack bar—maybe the lovemaking had been part of the joke, too—and for what? To play a cruel, sophomoric prank?

"Oops," she heard Brody say, somewhere in the pounding void of furious humiliation that surrounded her. "Carolyn, I—"

Carolyn shoved the car door open, trembling, blinded not by tears but by injured rage. She scrambled out and immediately caught the toe of her shoe in the hem of the gypsy skirt—the *beautiful* gypsy skirt—and heard the fabric give way with a terrible ripping sound.

Over it all, on the gigantic screen, Gifford's face loomed, big as a building.

He was laughing, of course.

Carolyn lifted the skirt in both hands and ran, tripping over the rough ground, finally kicking off both shoes and leaving them behind.

"Carolyn!" Brody shouted after her, his voice gruff. "Wait!"

She didn't, couldn't wait. She couldn't be rational.

This was what she got, she thought hysterically, for believing she could be Cinderella, even for one night.

Brody caught up to her, took a firm hold on her arm, held her up when she would have lost her footing and taken a tumble.

"Listen to me," he said.

Carolyn was breathing hard, coming back to herself, and feeling even more wretchedly embarrassed than before.

Brody used the side of one thumb to brush a tear from her cheek; until then, she hadn't known she was crying.

"Shh," he murmured, and pulled her close to him.

Carolyn struggled at first, but then she clung. She buried her wet face in his once-white shirt, smeared foundation and mascara and lipstick all over the front and let the sniffles turn to sobs.

And still Brody held her. "I'm sorry," he said quietly, his breath brushing past her ear. "Carolyn, I'm so sorry—"

Carolyn, I'm so sorry. The words echoed through her memory, spoken by different voices.

Her mother: *Carolyn, I'm so sorry, but I just can't take care of you anymore...*

Social worker after social worker: *Carolyn, I'm so sorry, but the Wilsons—the Jeffersons—the Crosbys— think you'd be better off in a different foster home...*

And, finally, Gifford Welsh: *Carolyn, I'm so sorry. I thought you felt the same way about me as I do about you....*

"I wasn't involved with Gifford Welsh," Carolyn said now, her voice and her breathing as uneven as the ground around them. "I was *the nanny.* I looked after his daughter, Storm, and I loved that child and *I had to leave her* because he came on to me, while his wife was away, and—and—"

"Carolyn," Brody repeated, gripping her shoulders and resting his chin on top of her head. "Take it easy. It's okay. Everything is okay."

But another wave of fury crashed over her then, and

she pushed back from him. "I can't believe I trusted you again, after what you did before. What am I to you, Brody? Just another notch on the bedpost? Well, here's a flash for you, cowboy—I'm a *real person,* with feelings!"

Brody didn't say her name again. Didn't say anything at all. He just looked at her, his hands hanging loose at his sides, that damned movie looming huge behind him like some Hollywood version of the Second Coming, and odd squeaks of dialogue and music piping from the rusty speaker disintegrating behind them.

A part of Carolyn stood back from it all, detached, silently observing that by now Brody was probably expecting her head to start spinning around on her shoulders or something.

"I want to go home," she said, with hard-won dignity, after a few moments of awkward silence.

"Okay," Brody said, his voice hoarse now. "Let's go."

He took her arm, squired her back to the car and got her settled in the front seat, all without a word.

Getting in on his side, he rolled down the window, unhooked the speaker and gave it a hard toss. Then he started the car and they drove off, leaving the movie playing to an audience of ghosts and the lights burning in the snack bar.

The popcorn spilled into the backseat when they went over a bump, and Carolyn looked down at the gypsy skirt.

It was ruined, of course.

A metaphor for the evening.

A metaphor *for her life.*

So much for Cinderella. Brody wouldn't be around

to try a glass slipper on her dainty little foot anytime soon, that was for sure.

Carolyn waited for Brody to ask if she'd seen her shrink lately, or maybe forgotten to take her medications, but he didn't say anything at all.

"I might have overreacted a little," she finally said, hollowed out by all that searing anger, when they pulled up in front of Natty McCall's house.

"Ya think?" Brody asked mildly, and without a trace of humor.

He got out of the car, walked around to her side, opened her door.

Barefoot, except for her ruined panty hose, she clasped her purse—by some miracle, she'd managed not to lose it—to her bosom and walked as regally as she could across the sidewalk and the grass to the stairs leading up to her apartment.

Brody saw her to her door, but despite the lack of space on the tiny landing, he somehow maintained a little distance between them. A muscle bunched in his jaw, but the expression in his eyes was one of pain, not anger.

"You'll be all right now?" he asked, like he wasn't sure it was safe to leave her in her own company.

Carolyn bit her lower lip, nodded. "Yes," she said.

He held out one hand, palm up, and for just a second, Carolyn thought it was an attempt to make peace. Fortunately, she realized he wanted her house key before she made an utter idiot of herself all over again by giving him her hand instead.

Brody unlocked the door for her, pushed it open. Handed the key back once she was over the threshold, and facing him.

Winston, who'd most likely been watching from the

windowsill, jumped down with a solid *thump* of cat meeting floor, but he didn't hiss at Brody the way he normally would have done, or bristle out his tail.

He actually purred, and looped himself around the man's boots a couple of times in greeting.

Brody didn't acknowledge Winston; he was gazing straight at Carolyn. His throat worked, and the pain in his eyes, visible even though she had yet to turn on the overhead light in the kitchen, matched the dull ache lodged in the center of Carolyn's chest.

"Good night, then," he finally said.

"Good night," Carolyn choked out, with great effort.

Then Brody turned to leave, and Carolyn shut and locked the door between them. Flipped on the lights.

Winston meowed, looked up at her.

She made herself take a good look at the gypsy skirt.

Yep, it was in tatters. A total loss.

Numbly, Carolyn went into her bedroom, exchanged Cinderella's ball gown for jeans and a T-shirt and boots and returned to the kitchen.

"I've done it now," she told Winston, rummaging in the cupboards for the box of ginger tea. Her stomach was doing flip-flops.

Winston leaped back up onto his windowsill. "Reow?" he asked.

She patted his head, smiled sadly. Her eyes felt swollen, though she hadn't cried that much, and she probably had makeup smeared all over her face, and heaven only knew what her hair looked like by now, but none of those things mattered, because it was the same old story. Déjà vu all over again.

She'd been a sucker for a fantasy, allowed herself to

believe in fairy tales. For just one night, she'd wanted to be a princess.

Was that so wrong?

Carolyn forgot about the ginger tea, opened another cupboard door and began taking down souvenir mugs, one by one.

Disneyland. The Grand Canyon. Independence Hall. The Alamo.

She'd never been to any of those places, but she could have described a family vacation to each one of them, complete down to the weather and what meals she'd eaten at which restaurants. There would have been lots of pictures to anchor the memories, and choosing which one to put on the front of the annual Christmas card would certainly be a challenge.

At least she hadn't sent herself postcards, she thought ruefully, her eyes burning with another crop of tears.

In all, there were over two dozen mugs in her pitiful collection.

She'd been—all by her lonesome—to exactly three of the places represented: Boise, Idaho, Virginia City, Nevada, and Reno. Not even Las Vegas, for Pete's sake, but *Reno.*

It was pathetic.

Well, she was through pretending. Through with fairy tales. Through trying to be anybody other than Carolyn Simmons, the foster kid all grown up, with no family and no history and certainly no happy vacations to look back on.

Not that she felt sorry for herself—if anything, she was angry.

Maybe Brody had set her up tonight, and maybe he hadn't.

Either way, she'd acted like a maniac, and he'd avoid her from now on.

Which was probably a good thing.

Carolyn picked up the cup from Disneyland, recalled buying it in a thrift shop somewhere in her totally unremarkable travels and dropped it into the trash can, where it made a satisfying *clunk* sound.

Winston looked at her curiously, but did not seem overly concerned by her strange behavior.

That made one of them.

She dropped in the mug from the Grand Canyon next, and, striking its counterpart from Disneyland, it shattered.

By the time she'd finished, she had three cups to her name.

They were nothing fancy, but at least they commemorated places she'd actually *been to* once upon a time.

She'd always heard that breaking dishes could be therapeutic, and it seemed there might be something to that theory, because she'd begun to feel just a touch better than she had before, even though her head still ached and her stomach was still twitchy.

It was a rite of passage, getting rid of those cups, Carolyn decided, briskly lifting the heavy trash bag out of the bin, tying it closed and carrying it down to the larger bin next to Natty's detached garage.

Step one to becoming the real Carolyn Simmons.

Whoever the heck *that* was.

CONNER WATCHED with a wry expression in his eyes as Brody took a beer from the ranch-house fridge, popped the top and poured some down his throat.

The kitchen was dimly lit—Tricia was in bed, probably asleep, and Conner had answered the knock at the back door muttering, hair all messed up and clad only in a pair of sweat pants.

"What happened to your shirt?" he asked, taking in the large, colorful smudge on Brody's chest. A pensive frown followed. "Or is that *my* shirt?"

"Carolyn's face rubbed off on it," Brody replied, raising the beer can in a grimly humorous salute.

Conner helped himself to a beer of his own and padded over to the table where generations of Creeds, men as well as women, had carried on late-night conversations like this one.

"Sit," he said to Brody.

Brody took time to grab a second beer, for backup, before he sank into a chair.

"How did Carolyn's face happen to rub off on your—my—shirt?" Conner asked mildly. Brody saw amusement in his brother's eyes, along with a generous amount of sympathy. That last part pissed him off.

"It isn't your shirt," Brody bit out. "I bought it two years ago, in San Antonio."

"Whatever," Conner said affably. Then he sighed and went on. "I've figured this much out on my own—the big movie date must have been a bust for some reason," he said, "but you're going to have to help me out with the rest, if you want me to understand."

Brody drained the first beer, reached for the spare, decided to wait until some of the carbonation in his stomach fizzled out and drew his hand back empty. Shoved it through his hair. He'd stopped by the lodge after the debacle with Carolyn to pick up Barney before heading for the home-place, and that poor dog probably thought he'd fallen in with a crazy man.

Not that he seemed particularly shaken up, old Barney, bunking in with Valentino over by the stove as he was. The two of them just fit on the dog bed, and they were both sound asleep.

Must be nice, Brody thought, figuring he'd never sleep again.

Conner snapped his fingers a few inches in front of Brody's nose. "Talk to me," he said. "You got me out of a warm bed, with an even warmer woman, and you owe me a reason."

Brody chuckled. "You want me to tell you what happened," he said.

"Basically," Conner answered dryly, "*yeah*. That would be a start."

"I'll be damned if I know," Brody answered. "One minute, we were having a great time, Carolyn and me. Wine, fancy food, a waiter—we had everything but a string quartet playing smooch music. Then it came time to watch the movie, and all hell broke loose."

Conner's expression was skeptical to say the least. "Come on, Brody. You're not seriously trying to tell me you don't know what happened? You were *there,* damn it."

"Must have been the movie," Brody said, reconsidering that second beer. Might as well down it, he thought. He wouldn't be driving back to River's Bend tonight, anyway. Nope, he and ole Barney, they were spending the night.

"What was wrong with the movie?"

"It starred Gifford Welsh," Brody said.

"Oh, my *God,*" said Tricia, from the doorway to the hall.

She was barefoot, dressed in one of Conner's shirts and pregnant out to here.

"I tried to tell her it was an accident," Brody explained, "but she just *lost it*. Started babbling on about gossip and how she never had an affair with the guy—"

Tricia threw both hands up in the air, for emphasis. "*Honestly,* Brody," she exclaimed. "Do Conner and I have to watch you *every minute?*"

He reddened a little, and stiffened his spine, avoiding Conner's gaze because he knew he'd see laughter there. "How was I supposed to know she'd go off like that? Decide I'd chosen that movie on purpose…?"

Tricia was standing next to Conner's chair now, with her hands propped on her hips and her stomach sticking halfway into next week and her head cocked to one side. "Those lousy rumors have been knocking around Lonesome Bend for *years,* Brody. How can you be the only one who's never heard them?"

Brody swallowed, still careful not to look at his brother's face. "Joleen might have said something about it once, but I didn't take it seriously."

Tricia patted Conner's shoulder and he pushed back his chair a little ways, so she could sit on his lap without being pinned between him and the table's edge. "Carolyn almost left town because of it, several times," she confided. "Between that and the stunt you pulled, it was almost too much humiliation for one woman to put up with. It's a testament to how much she loves Lonesome Bend and wants to make a home here that she didn't bolt a long time ago."

Brody's ears felt hot. "This is *my* fault?"

"Partly, yes," Tricia said. "You were probably one of the first people Carolyn ever allowed herself to trust—

you have no idea what things have been like for her—and you *let her down*."

"Tricia," Conner interrupted quietly, his arm around her, "you know Brody had his reasons for what he did."

Conner was *defending* him? Brody could barely believe it.

"We'll be lucky if Carolyn doesn't pull up stakes and take off for good," Tricia said, though some of the wind had gone out of her sails by then, and she was resting against Conner's chest. "Did you explain that you made a mistake?"

Brody closed his eyes to count to ten, but only got as far as seven before he had to blurt out, "*I* made a mistake? I practically refurbished the Bluebird Drive-in for one date and *I* made a mistake? Hell, Tricia, I didn't even look at the titles of those movies—I just grabbed a DVD and shoved it into the machine, and two seconds after I got back to the car, Carolyn was *freaking out*."

Conner chuckled. "Sounds like most of the drama never got as far as the screen," he observed.

"Hush," Tricia scolded, giving her husband a light jab with one elbow. "This is *serious*, Conner." She turned to Brody. "You've got to talk to her," she insisted, as serious as an old-time preacher describing the torments of hell. "Right now, tonight."

"He's not going anywhere," Conner stated. "He's been swilling beer like his insides were on fire."

"I have not," Brody answered.

"Nevertheless," Conner reiterated, "you're *still* not going anywhere tonight."

Normally, Brody would have argued, just on principle, because he didn't take kindly to anybody—Conner in particular—telling him what to do. Trouble was, Conner was right. He probably wasn't over the legal limit on a beer and a half, but he wasn't exactly in his right mind, either, so why take unnecessary chances?

"You made her cry," Tricia accused sadly, spotting the makeup stain on his shirt. At least, he *thought* it was his shirt. Might be that he had it mixed up with one belonging to Conner.

"She went ballistic," Brody recalled, before finishing the second beer. "Granted," he said, when he'd caught his breath, "I should have checked out the movies before shoving one in the hopper, but it was an *honest mistake,* Tricia. Even if Carolyn *had* had an affair with Gifford Welsh, it wouldn't be any of my damn business, now would it?"

"This is all a big mess," Tricia said despairingly.

Conner gave her a one-armed squeeze. "But it's *Brody's* mess, sweetheart," he reminded her. "And he'll have to straighten it out. In the meantime, let's go back to bed."

That now-familiar sensation of benevolent envy ground in Brody's middle. *He,* of course, would be sleeping alone, in his boyhood bed, unless Barney decided to join him.

And that didn't seem too likely, the way that dog was snoring.

Brody decided he needed a third beer, after all.

Tricia got to her feet, and so did Conner.

While his wife padded back toward the bedroom, Conner paused to lay a hand on Brody's shoulder. "Go easy on the brew," he said. "You're going to have problems enough in the morning without waking up to a hangover."

Brody sighed, too stubborn to agree. "Good night," he said, in a grudging tone.

Conner merely chuckled, shook his head once and followed Tricia into the corridor.

CAROLYN MANAGED TO GET *some* sleep that night, though it was certainly nothing to write home about.

Not that she had a home or anybody to write to.

"Oh, stop it," she told herself, standing straight and tall in front of the mirror over the bathroom sink. "I've had it with your whining, Carolyn Simmons."

For once, there was no snarky answer.

Carolyn lifted her chin, squared her shoulders and critically examined her face.

Her eyes, rimmed with splotches of mascara, put her in mind of a raccoon. And they were puffy, to boot.

What remained of her lipstick was a pink mark on her right cheek.

And was she getting a cold sore, there, by her nostril?

Resolutely, she started the water running in the sink, scrubbed away the remnants of the Cinderella makeup job, and splashed her face with repeated palmfuls of cold water for good measure.

When she'd finished, she still looked bad, but she was clean at least.

She dabbed ointment on the budding cold sore and marched back out into the kitchen, where the gypsy skirt was draped over the back of a chair.

It wasn't a hopeless case, as she'd thought the night before, but it would require fairly extensive repairs. Along with Winston and a week's supply of sardines, she'd pack up the skirt, various sewing notions and her trusty machine to take to Kim and Davis's place, where she'd agreed to house-sit for the next week. Stitch by stitch, she'd put the garment—and the person she really was—back together.

With this mental to-do list rolling around in her brain, Carolyn put on a pot of coffee—she needed *something* to get her going—and decided to reward Winston with his favorite meal for breakfast.

The moment she peeled back the lid on the sardine can, however, the nausea was upon her.

She raced to the bathroom, holding her hair back with both hands as she got very, very sick.

And in the midst of all that, it came to her.

She'd had wine the night before—several glasses of it—and, dazzled by all Brody had done to make the evening special, she'd never given a single thought to her special sensitivity to alcohol.

She *wasn't crazy,* she thought, with a rush of jubilation, even as another spate of retching brought her to her knees in front of the commode.

It was the wine.

BRODY DROVE Kim and Davis's car up to their place first thing the next morning, to swap it out for his truck. While there, he'd feed the horses and have another look at the Thoroughbred, too. With luck, he could cadge breakfast from Kim, or at least a decent cup of java.

Down at Conner and Tricia's place, a man needed an engineering degree to run the damn coffeepot. Marriage and impending fatherhood, it seemed to Brody, had rendered his twin brother a little strange.

He'd been keeping his mind busy with pithy observations like that one for much of the night and all there was of the morning so far, and it wasn't helping.

Thoughts of Carolyn were just beneath the surface the whole time, and they broke through in every unguarded moment.

Even now, he thought a dinner and a private showing of a first-run movie put him in the major leagues when it came to creative dating. He'd seen the look of wonder in Carolyn's eyes when she saw the snack bar decked out for a romantic dinner for two. She'd been charmed, maybe even a little enchanted, exactly as he'd intended.

Okay, so he could have made a more sensitive choice when he chose the actual movie. He'd apologized, hadn't he? Once he understood what the hell she was so upset about, anyway?

He sighed and resettled his hat.

Well, it was actually *Conner's* hat, like everything else he had on this morning.

The question was, how could something so right have gone straight to hell in a handbasket the way last night had?

"Mornin'," Davis called, from the back door, when Brody came out of the barn. "Coffee's on."

"I'll be right there," Brody responded, pausing to watch Firefly at the corral feeder.

Now *that,* Brody mused, was a *horse.*

"Don't even think about it," Davis warned, materializing beside him to set his arms on the top rail of the fence and nod toward Firefly. "He's off-limits, Brody, and that's the end of it."

Brody gave his uncle a sidelong glance. "I can handle any horse," he said evenly. "I've got the championship belt buckles and the prize money to prove it."

Davis narrowed his eyes, and his tone was as solemn as his expression. "Your dad said something a lot like that once," he said. "It was the day I warned him to stay off the stallion we'd roped wild, up in the foothills, until he'd been gelded and had some time to calm down a little. Blue told me he'd never met the horse he couldn't ride, but I thought he was just talking, that he'd seen the sense in what I'd said. Next thing I knew, my brother was lying in the middle of the corral with his neck broken, and that stallion circling him like a buzzard, closing in, fixing to finish him off then and there."

Davis paused, took a ragged breath and gazed off into the middle distance like he could see the scene playing out in front of him, clear as crystal, even after so many years.

"I had the hunting rifle in the truck," he went on presently, without looking at Brody, "and I brought that horse down with one shot, right where he stood." He made a sound that might have been a laugh, but wasn't. "I thought there was still a chance that Blue would pull through," he added. "If I'd seen him tossed by one horse, I'd seen him fly off a hundred, and a couple of those times, he'd even broke a few bones. But Blue didn't move, didn't open his eyes. Kim called the ambulance, and I stayed there with Blue, in the corral, with that dead horse a dozen feet away, telling my brother it would be all right. 'Just hang on, help is coming. I'm here, Blue, right here, and I'm not going anywhere—'"

Davis choked up then, had to stop for a second or two to get a grip.

Brody waited, hot behind the eyes, while his uncle, one of the toughest men he'd ever known, pulled himself back together.

"You know what happened," Davis said, looking

right into Brody's face now. "Your dad never came out of the coma. Six miserable weeks later, he was gone." The older man swallowed hard, and his eyes glistened with rare moisture. "I brought Firefly to this ranch to save his life, Brody. Nobody else wanted him, said he was worthless, nothing but trouble. But you hear me, son, and hear me well... I'll put a bullet in his brain before I'll let anybody—and I mean *anybody*—ride him. Do we understand each other?"

"Breakfast is getting cold!" Kim sang out, from the side porch.

Neither Brody nor Davis moved, or looked away from each other's faces.

"Do we understand each other?" Davis asked, for the second time.

Brody thrust out a sigh. "We understand each other," he replied.

Davis slapped him on the shoulder, and he even smiled a little, but his eyes were as serious as Brody had ever seen them. "I need your word, son," he said.

"You have it," Brody replied. "I won't ride the horse."

CHAPTER EIGHTEEN

CAROLYN HAD JUST RELEASED a very disgruntled Winston from his crate into the wide-open spaces of the Creeds' erstwhile empty kitchen when she heard a vehicle drive up and stop with a squeak of brakes.

She glanced at the clock—it was a little after noon—before peeking out the window, half-expecting to see Kim and Davis, ostensibly well on their way to Stone Creek in the RV, with Smidgeon and Little Bit, returning for something they'd forgotten.

Instead, Tricia, cumbersome, climbed from her Pathfinder, waving one hand in front of her face to dispel some of the dust she'd stirred up arriving.

Heartened, but at the same time feeling like one big bruise, exposed to every jostle and bump, Carolyn opened the side door to greet her friend with a smile and a wave. "You'd better get those brakes checked. I could hear them from inside the house."

Tricia smiled. "Don't worry. Conner made me promise to trade my rig for Kim and Davis's car until the mechanic in town can have a look at it. That's the main reason I'm here."

The *main* reason, Carolyn thought wryly, but not the *only* reason.

By now, Tricia would have at least an inkling about

the things that had happened last night, at the storied Bluebird Drive-in.

"You look like five miles of bad road," Tricia observed bluntly, confirming Carolyn's suspicion and duck-walking toward her. Carolyn wondered idly—and very briefly—if her friend wasn't further along in her pregnancy than everybody thought she was. Tricia looked as though she might deliver baby Blue at any moment.

"Gee, thanks," Carolyn chimed merrily, holding the screen door wide so Carolyn could squeeze past and enter the kitchen. Immediately, she hung the Pathfinder keys from the hook nearby and took the ones for Kim's car.

The car Brody had picked her up in the night before, predisaster.

"But," Tricia went on, dropping into a chair at the table with a relieved sigh and tossing Kim's keys into her purse, "I'm happy to relate that Brody looks even *worse* than you do."

"I guess that's something," Carolyn replied, with a grim little chuckle.

Tricia's gaze had fallen on the gypsy skirt, neatly spread out on the table, awaiting rehabilitation.

"Yikes, Carolyn," she marveled. "What *happened?*"

"You've seen Brody?" Carolyn said, letting Tricia's question ride for the moment. She bit her lower lip and sat down, propping her chin in one hand. "Since last night, I mean?"

"He stayed at our place," Tricia answered, squinting a little. "You really do look awful, Carolyn. You're pale, and there are shadows under your eyes. And the *skirt*—what on earth…?"

Carolyn spread her fingers wide and shoved all eight of them into her hair, along with her thumbs, shaking her head as she recalled the latest calamity to befall her love life.

If it could be *called* a love life.

"I freaked," she moaned. "Lost it. Ruined everything." She made herself lift her eyes to meet Tricia's. "First, I drank wine," she admitted.

"Oh, no," Tricia said.

"Oh, yes," Carolyn responded glumly. "But I've thought about this a lot, and I've decided that's no excuse for the way I behaved. Part of the reason, maybe, but not an excuse." She sighed before going on. "Okay, the few times I've ever indulged in alcohol have all proven...imprudent. I should have anticipated that, and skipped the wine, but I was dazzled, Tricia. Honestly *dazzled.* What *really* went wrong was, I got scared, because nothing could ever be as good as that date was shaping up to be—I'm pretty sure that's how my reasoning went, anyway—and something awful was bound to happen if I let myself believe for another second that—that—"

"That Brody might actually love you?" Tricia supplied gently, with a brief, reassuring touch to Carolyn's hands.

"I made the mistake of thinking he did, once," Carolyn said slowly. "And when I came to my senses, it was like being run over by a freight train. I spent a long time gathering up the pieces, Tricia, and putting myself back together." She managed a thin smile. "Problem is, I think I might have put some of those pieces in the wrong places."

"What happens now?" Tricia asked, after a sigh and a long pause.

"I fix the gypsy skirt and hope whoever's driving the bid through the roof is happy with the results," she said, fairly certain that Tricia had expected her to say she was packing up and leaving Lonesome Bend without a backward glance.

But she'd meant it when she promised herself she was through running, literally *and* figuratively.

Tricia's blue eyes twinkled with a sort of sad mischief. "Oh, I wouldn't worry about the bidder," she said. "She's a very understanding woman. One of *two* very understanding women, actually."

Carolyn felt her own eyes widen. "You know who...?"

Tricia smiled and struck a comical glamour pose without getting out of her chair.

"You?" Carolyn whispered. *"You're* the mystery bidder?"

"Kim and I are going halves," Tricia answered, undaunted.

Now Carolyn was *really* confused. Both Kim and Tricia were beautiful women, and both of them had great bodies—normally—but they were built differently, and Kim was at least three inches taller than Tricia, so there was no possible way they could wear the same garment without extensive alterations.

"Why?"

"Because we've both seen how much that skirt means to you," Tricia said. "We were planning to wait a while, and then surprise you with it—for your birthday, maybe. Or Christmas."

Carolyn knew better than to get her back up and accuse Tricia of joining forces with Kim to offer her charity. They'd done this amazing thing because they were *her friends,* because they had the means and because they cared about her.

Her eyes filled. "Oh, Tricia," she said.

"Don't cry," Tricia said, waving her hand again, the way she had outside, when she was fanning away the dust. "If you do, I will, too, and then my nose will get all red and my eyes will practically swell shut and it *will not be pretty."*

Carolyn laughed, giving her cheeks a swipe with the backs of her hands. "Not pretty?" she joked. "We can't have that."

Tricia smiled and sniffled once and said, "Well."

Winston, having scouted out the new surroundings, returned to the kitchen to wind himself around and around Carolyn's ankles in a figure-eight, purring like an outboard motor.

Evidently, he liked it here, at Kim and Davis's ranch house.

"The auction doesn't end until tomorrow," Carolyn mused aloud, looking at the skirt now. Even bedraggled and in need of mending and some serious sprucing up, it was still breathtakingly beautiful. "Maybe someone has outbid you by now."

"Nope," Tricia replied, with a smug little smile. "Ain't gonna happen. Our ceiling bid is so high, nobody will match it."

With a tentative hand, Carolyn reached out and touched the garment almost as gently as if it were a living thing, and suffering from various painful injuries. "None of it matters, now," she said. "The skirt needs too much fixing to sell to anyone, and I couldn't have let you and Kim go through with your crazy, wonderful and unbelievably generous plan anyway. Not once I found out what you were up to."

Carolyn's natural practicality reasserted itself. She'd call off the auction as soon as she got the chance, she decided, and keep the skirt for herself. Not that she had any more reason to wear it than before, because she didn't, but they shared something now, she and that once-glorious mass of beads and ribbon and fine cloth. They were both veterans of the Cinderella wars.

And they'd both been on the losing side.

A peaceful silence fell.

Tricia broke it with a soft "Come to our place for supper tonight, Carolyn?"

Carolyn grinned wanly, thinking how lucky she was to have friends like Tricia and Conner and Kim and Davis, among others. Not that she could trust either of those women any farther than she could have thrown them, when it came to their matchmaking schemes.

"So you can corral Brody and me in the same room and hope we'll kiss and make up?" she countered, though not unkindly. "No way, girlfriend. I'm not ready to deal with Brody face-to-face quite yet, and I'll wager the reverse is true, as well."

Tricia looked sad, but she clearly understood Carolyn's position, too. "I just wish you weren't all alone, that's all," she lamented. "You'll call Conner and me if you need anything, won't you?"

"You can bet on it," Carolyn promised. "And it's not as if I've become a hermit, hiding out at some robber's roost tucked away in the distant hills, after all. I promised Kim I'd spend the nights here, and basically hold down the fort, but I'll still be going to the shop in the morning, like I do every Monday."

Tricia brightened. "Speaking of the shop—what have you decided? Are you taking me up on my offer or not?"

Carolyn smiled. "I'd be crazy if I didn't," she said. "No matter what happens, Tricia, I'm staying right here in Lonesome Bend. I've had enough of the gypsy life, and I'm through trying to escape my problems. I'm digging in for the duration."

"That's great!" Tricia cried, delighted.

"I thought I'd start by hiring Primrose to work for us part-time," Carolyn said, profoundly grateful for the change of subject. "If it's all right with you, of course. She has some very interesting ideas and, besides, she's a natural saleswoman."

Tricia laughed, getting slowly to her feet. "That she is," she agreed. "Go ahead and offer her a job whenever you're ready. In the meantime, I'll make a preliminary deposit to the business account, just to get things rolling."

Carolyn was teary again. "You're sure you want to do this, Tricia? Really, *really* sure? Because I'd understand if you didn't, and I'd be fine without the shop—"

Well, maybe not *fine,* exactly—she loved the shop—but she'd survive, like always, and eventually thrive.

Tricia gave her one of those impulsive, Tricia-hugs, quick and awkward and wholly sincere. "Well, the *shop* wouldn't be fine without *you,* and neither would I. I'm *having a baby,* Carolyn, not a lobotomy. Before I came to Lonesome Bend to settle Dad's estate, I ran a gallery, remember? I love Conner more than I ever knew it was possible to love a man, and we'll both be crazy about this baby and all his brothers and sisters, but I *need* to be around art on a regular basis—I need color and texture and all the rest."

Carolyn certainly understood; art fed her soul, it was a form of prayer for her, of praise and thanksgiving

She recalled Tricia's arrival in town, a couple of years ago. Naturally, there had been a lot of talk about her when she moved in with her great-grandmother and put the River's Bend Campground and RV park up for sale, along with the ramshackle Bluebird Drive-in. People had claimed Tricia was too citified for a town like Lonesome Bend, even though she'd spent summers there since childhood, and they were sure she'd be on her way back to Seattle and her old life before the ink was dry on the sales agreements for her father's properties.

Instead, Tricia had fallen in love with Conner Creed, married him and fit into the community like the proverbial hand in glove.

After walking Tricia to the garage and watching her drive away in Kim's car, Carolyn went back inside, feeling somewhat at loose ends.

She supposed that house should have felt lonely, as big as it was, with just her and Winston rattling around in it like a pair of pebbles in the bottom of a barrel, but it didn't feel that way at all.

It was a real home, a sanctuary where a man and a woman loved each other, day to day, through thick and thin, working separately and side by side to keep a ranch and an extended family going. There were memories here, practically tangible, and pictures on the walls and mantelpieces full of smiling faces and birthday cakes and Christmas trees and first cars.

In the hallway between the living room and the guest

room where she'd be sleeping, Carolyn paused to look more closely at some of those photographs. One showed Brody and Conner and Steven on what was probably a fishing trip, a blond, sun-burned trio, none of them in their teens yet, beaming and holding up the day's catch.

Next to it was a shot taken on a long-ago Christmas morning—Brody and Conner posing in front of an enormous tree decorated with a hodgepodge of ornaments, each of them gripping the shiny handlebars of a brand-new bicycle. Steven, who had lived in Boston with his mother most of the year, wasn't in the picture, but there was a bulging stocking hanging from the mantel with his name stitched across the top, so he must have been expected to arrive for a visit soon.

Carolyn smiled, touched their faces with a fingertip, lingering a little longer on Brody's image. To look at them, a person would have thought they'd always had it easy, but of course that wasn't true.

Everybody, no matter how fortunate some aspects of their lives might be, had things to overcome. Dragons to face, and rivers to cross.

In Brody and Conner's case, it was a double loss: their parents had both died, in separate accidents, when the twins were just babies. And as much love as Kim and Davis had given these boys over the years, as much guidance and security, they'd still had their battles to fight, not only in the outside world, but also with each other.

Conner and Brody had been on the outs for years and, of course, Brody's wife and child had been taken from him, in a very cruel way.

Carolyn sighed and went on to the guest room, Winston romping at her heels like a kitten, to unpack the few things she'd brought from the apartment in town. Since she'd be going to the shop every day, she didn't need more than fresh underwear, a nightshirt, the usual toiletries and something to wear to work in the morning.

She put things away, closely supervised by Winston, and then decided to take two aspirin and grab a nap, hoping to shake off the last lingering effects of last night's apocalyptic events.

A little over an hour later, she woke up, her headache and the few remaining tatters of nausea gone at last. Feeling quite like her old, best self again, Carolyn smoothed her hair and headed for the kitchen, planning to have a late lunch—something light, like chicken noodle soup—and settle down to work on the gypsy skirt.

And there was Brody, big as life, sitting at the kitchen table, drinking coffee and reading a newspaper.

Carolyn stopped short, just inside the doorway from the dining room.

"I knocked," he said nonchalantly, without looking up from the paper, "but nobody answered."

"So you just walked in?"

"Pretty much, yeah."

"Well, I'll just leave you to your coffee and your newspaper," Carolyn told him hurriedly, turning to march right back out again.

He stopped her with a single word—her name.

She stiffened, but didn't look back at him. "What could you possibly have to say to me, after last night?" she asked, her tone even, revealing nothing of what she was feeling. Not that she exactly *knew* what she was feeling, because she didn't.

She was all a-jumble inside—happy and sad, scared

and excited, angry that Brody was there and, at the same time, deeply, deeply relieved.

"How about 'I'm sorry'?" he suggested, from directly behind her.

How did he *do* that? How did the man cross rooms in the space of a heartbeat, without making a sound? It was uncanny. It was *spooky*.

She swiveled, squaring her shoulders, lifting her chin. He was close enough to kiss her—but he didn't.

"It's *my* turn to apologize," Carolyn said, drawing on all her bravery, and on her new determination to live in the real world like a rational human being with a right to be there, damn it—but not quite meeting his eyes. "You went to a lot of trouble to make last night…special. I should have known it didn't mean anything that Gifford Welsh was starring in the movie, but…well… I didn't, not at first, anyway. I'm not very proud of how I acted, and I am definitely sorry."

"Carolyn," Brody said again, this time with a smile in his voice.

"What?"

"Why won't you look at me?"

Because looking at you makes my clothes fall off, Brody Creed.

Like she'd ever say *that* out loud.

Brody laughed. "Looking at me makes your clothes fall off? Hot damn, that's the best news I've had all day."

Carolyn blinked. Put a hand over her mouth, horrified. Murmured, "Did I actually say…?"

Brody's grin was a mite on the cocky side, and totally hot. "Yeah," he said. "You did."

"Oh, my God," she said.

"That was my reaction, too," Brody said, his eyes dancing as his gaze tripped down the front of her T-shirt. He pretended to frown. "Doesn't look like it's happening, though. Your clothes falling off, I mean."

She felt a surge of heat in her face, knew she was blushing—*again*—and wished she could vanish into thin air, like a wisp of smoke.

She couldn't, of course.

That was one thing about being real. No disappearing allowed.

"My clothes are staying right where they are," she said, with a notable lack of conviction.

"That's probably a good idea," Brody agreed thoughtfully, rubbing his chin, where a golden stubble was already showing. "For the time being, anyhow."

Carolyn tugged hard at the hem of her T-shirt and marched past him, headed for the cupboard. She needed a good, stiff shot of herbal tea, and she needed it now.

Brody watched with amusement as she gathered the necessary stuff.

"It's a damn shame, though," he observed, stroking his chin again.

"What?" Carolyn asked briskly, filling a cup with hot water from a special dispenser affixed to the sink.

"That your clothes didn't fall off," Brody said. "It would have been something to see."

"Would you like some tea?" Carolyn inquired, as though nobody had said anything about anybody's clothes falling off.

Least of all, hers.

"Uh—tea? Thanks, but no. I'm not a big tea drinker."

Carolyn made a face at him.

"Would tequila do it?" he mused, as though talking to himself. "Like in the song?"

"Brody," Carolyn said. "Stop teasing me, will you please? It was a slip of the tongue, that's all."

"Very Freudian," Brody agreed, with mock solemnity. "Especially the tongue reference."

"I did *not* make a 'tongue reference,' as you so crudely put it," Carolyn said loftily, but she was struggling not to laugh.

"There," Brody said, pointing. "You said it again. *Tongue.* You keep bringing it up—definitely Freudian."

"Stop it," she said, choking back a giggle.

Brody's grin broadened and went from sizzle to stun. "Fine," he said. "Build your tea, sit down and talk to me."

Talk to me. Yikes.

"About what?" she asked.

"Yourself," he said. "I told you about Lisa and Justin. Now I want to know what makes you Carolyn, so to speak." She was silent, preparing her tea. Pensive. But she approached the table and sat down, and when she had, Brody sat, too.

Folded his hands loosely and rested them on top of the open newspaper.

"Where should I start?" she asked, thinking aloud.

"Tricia told me you grew up in foster homes," Brody said quietly. "I'm sure that was rough, at least at times, but right now, I'm more interested in knowing why a Gifford Welsh movie would send you over the edge."

Carolyn sighed, took a slow sip of her tea and savored it. Or pretended to, that is. The stuff didn't seem to have any taste at all.

"It was partly the wine," she said.

Brody nodded. "I figured that out later," he said. "Another reason to apologize, Carolyn. I should have remembered that you can't hold your hooch."

She laughed softly, relaxed a little—but not for long. Whenever she thought of Gifford Welsh, she thought of Storm, running behind her car, screaming for her to come back, and the pain was still enough to double her over.

Brody took her hand. "Whatever it is, Carolyn," he said, "it's *okay*. But if we're going to mend fences, you and I, we have to be straight with each other, starting now. No surprises down the road."

Carolyn nodded, swallowed hard, even though she hadn't taken another sip of tea. "I know a lot of people think I had an affair with Gifford," she said, meeting Brody's eyes. "It doesn't happen to be true, but last night—last night, I thought you were…well…throwing him up to me. Letting me know that *you* knew. That's what set me off."

Brody waited calmly for her to go on, his eyes gentle and very, very blue.

Carolyn's fingers trembled when she picked up her cup to drink from it, so she set it down again, without bringing it to her mouth.

Winston, that unpredictable feline, leaped up into Brody's lap, purring and rubbing against his chest.

Brody chuckled and stroked the cat's back, comfortable with the interaction, but made no comment on the animal's apparent new opinion of his character.

The ball was still in Carolyn's court, it would seem.

Slowly, she told Brody what had happened at the Gifford mansion that day, unreeling the memories in her mind's eye as she spoke, reliving them.

She'd been attracted to Gifford Welsh—who wouldn't have been?—but he was *married,* and that meant something to her, if not to him.

She'd fled in a panic—much as Brody had done the night Lisa called and told him she was carrying his child. She'd left Storm behind, unable to explain why she was leaving in such a hurry, and she'd regretted that ever since.

Carolyn had regretted abandoning a little girl, in almost the same way *she'd* been abandoned, and she'd blamed herself for other reasons, too. Had she unwittingly sent Gifford some kind of come-hither message, prompting him to make advances?

Was the whole thing *her* fault?

Looking back, it seemed strange that she'd ever believed such a thing. Carolyn had been his daughter's nanny, his wife had been away and he'd made a move on her.

Gifford, like everyone else on the planet, was responsible for his own actions.

"I shouldn't have left Storm behind like that," she said numbly, when she reached the end of the account. "But I was young and I was shaken up, and I didn't know what else to do but get the heck out of there, fast."

"You did what you thought was the right thing at the time," Brody said. At some point, he'd taken her hand into his.

"So did you," Carolyn said. "When Lisa called that night, I mean."

He raised a shoulder, lowered it again. "I've decided to let myself off the hook for it," he said. "I can't bring Lisa and Justin back, or make things right for them, and it's time I quit trying." He paused, started again.

"I came back to Lonesome Bend to settle down, start a family and build a legacy, and that's what I mean to do."

Carolyn looked at him, thinking how much she loved Brody Creed, how she'd loved him all along, though that love had evolved as she had, as Brody himself had.

He'd been a boy when they met, and she'd been a girl.

Now, he was a man, and she was a woman.

Whole other ball game.

They were at a crossroads, Carolyn realized. They could go their separate ways, sadder but wiser, or they could get to know each other all over again, from an adult perspective.

Carolyn knew what she wanted, but she wasn't at all sure Brody was on the same page, so she kept the words she most needed to say to herself.

Gently, Brody lifted Winston off his lap and set him on the floor.

Carolyn took a big gulp of her tea, just for something to do, and nearly choked on the stuff.

Brody leaned toward her, brushed her hair back off her right shoulder.

"There's one more thing I need to know," he said. "Those foster homes you lived in. Were they good ones?"

Carolyn pondered the question. Finally she sighed. "There were different levels of commitment, but basically I think everybody did the best they knew how," she said, coming to yet another deeply personal conclusion. "Including my parents, I guess."

Brody drew her out of her chair and onto his lap.

It seemed natural to put her arms around his neck and rest her forehead against his.

"I never knew my dad," she confided softly, and then waited for the strength to go on, to say the rest of it.

"Me, either," Brody said. "But we had Davis, Conner and I, and he handled the job just fine."

Carolyn nodded. "You're lucky—that you had Davis and Kim, I mean."

"Yep," Brody agreed. His arms were around her, but loosely, strong but making no demands. "Lucky on all counts, when it comes to kinfolks." He hooked a finger under her chin, lifted, and pulled back just far enough to look directly into her eyes. "And when it comes to you, Carolyn."

She blinked.

"I love you," he said. Just like that.

Talk about things that were too good to be true. "You do?"

He chuckled, and then flashed that dangerous grin at her. The one that made her wish her clothes would fall right off. "I just said I did, didn't I?" he teased. There was heat gathering in his eyes now. "But I don't mind repeating myself. *I love you,* Carolyn."

"Really?"

"Carolyn." Brody tried to sound stern, but the tenderness in his eyes spoiled the effect.

She blushed, confused and joyful and ridiculously shy. "I love you, too," she blurted out.

"Good," Brody said, his mouth close to hers now. "That's good."

"What happens next?" she murmured, as things shifted inside her, finding their level. Her pelvic bones seemed to be melting, along with her knees.

Brody arched an eyebrow. "We go to bed?" He was already slipping a warm hand underneath her T-shirt.

Carolyn gasped. "That's…a given—" she managed to say. "I mean *after*—next week, next month, next year—" He'd unfastened the front catch on her bra, and one of her breasts spilled, warm and ready, into his palm. His thumb chafed her nipple. *"Oh, God—"* she whimpered. He pushed up her T-shirt and then his mouth closed over her. *"Brody—"*

He enjoyed her freely, for what seemed like a deliciously long time, before lifting his head to meet her eyes and offer a belated reply to a question she'd almost forgotten she'd asked.

"I say we let next week, next month and next year take care of themselves and concentrate on what's happening right now," he said. And then he pushed back his chair and stood, lifting Carolyn in his arms. "Which bedroom is yours?"

Brody had barely *begun* to make love to her and already she was limp, completely at his mercy.

She told him where her room was.

And he carried her there, and their clothes fell off, and Carolyn's first orgasm came quickly, fiercely, rocking her very core, wringing a shout of glorious surrender from her.

"Brody!"

He had horses to feed, Brody thought, lying there in the twilight, still partially entangled with a sumptuously naked—and soundly sleeping—Carolyn. Not just Davis and Kim's horses, either, but Moonshine, too, over at River's Bend.

And Barney was down at Conner and Tricia's, awaiting his return.

Brody touched the tip of Carolyn's nose, then her lips.

She stirred, opened her eyes. Blinked, as though surprised to see him.

He grinned. "Gotta go," he said.

Carolyn, still half-asleep, looked immediately alarmed.

"To feed the horses," Brody clarified, placing a nibbling kiss on her mouth, "and collect my dog."

She swallowed. "Then what?"

"Then I'll come back here, if that's all right with you."

Her smile was sudden, a bright flash in the semidarkness of the room. "I have a better idea," she announced. "I'll come with you."

Simple as it was, Carolyn's statement struck at something deep inside Brody. His voice came out husky when he said, "Sounds good."

They shared a shower—somehow managing not to wind up making love again, although the temptation was strong—then got themselves dressed and, after Carolyn had given the cat a fish dinner from a can, headed for the barn.

Together, they made short work of the chores. They rode to River's Bend in Brody's truck, fed Moonshine, fetched Barney's bag of kibble from the lodge and went on to the main ranch house.

Carolyn, evidently suffering a sudden bout of shyness, waited in the truck while Brody went inside, politely refused Tricia's invitation to have supper with her and Conner and reclaimed Barney.

It occurred to Brody as they bumped over the road leading back to Kim and Davis's place that Barney and Winston the cat might not make for the best combination, what with their fundamental differences.

"Winston adores Valentino," Carolyn assured Brody, once he'd expressed his concern. "He'll get along fine with Barney, too."

She was right, as it turned out.

Barney and Winston met up for the first time in the middle of Kim's kitchen, eyeing each other like a pair of gunfighters at high noon.

The cat fluffed out his tail, and Barney sniffed curiously at Winston's nose, and the two of them turned away from each other and casually went their separate ways.

"See?" Carolyn said, taking one of Kim's famous casseroles from the freezer side of the refrigerator. "It's a nonevent."

Brody grinned, looking at the casserole dish in her hands. "You cook?" he teased.

She laughed. "No," she said. "But I do *reheat*."

With that, Carolyn turned her back to him, setting the casserole on the counter and removing the foil covering.

Brody stepped up behind her, slipped his arms around her, and kissed the nape of her neck, delighting in the little shiver of response she gave.

"Speaking of reheating things," he muttered.

"Later," she said. "Supper first. We need our strength."

Brody tasted her earlobe. "Umm," he said.

Laughing again, she wiggled free, switched on the oven and set the temperature. *"Later,"* she repeated.

Later took its sweet time arriving, but eventually, when they'd eaten and loaded the dishwasher, then rigged up a couple of blanket-beds for Winston and Barney, they took a second shower.

This time around, there was no resisting temptation.

There was also no condom.

Hours later, both exhausted, Brody and Carolyn finally slept.

CHAPTER NINETEEN

BRODY'S CELL PHONE was ringing.

Carolyn's heart scrambled into her throat, and as deeply as she'd been sleeping only moments before, she was wide-awake in an instant, if still a little disoriented. Straining for the switch on the bedside lamp while Brody, muttering, groped for his discarded clothes, rummaged audibly and finally got hold of the phone.

"Brody," he answered, his voice raspy with sleep and worry.

Carolyn found the switch, and light spilled into the room. Although she'd slept through that other phone call, on that other night years ago, the similarities were still eerie. She could almost believe she'd somehow blundered into a time warp, and here was Lisa calling to say she was pregnant, and the whole heartbreaking scenario was starting up all over again.

"Conner," Brody said, his gaze locked with Carolyn's. "Stay calm. You have got to stay calm—we'll be right there, and we'll do whatever needs doing, I promise you. In the meantime, *hang up and call 911—now.*"

Carolyn clambered into her clothes, her eyes hot but dry, her throat thick with fear. *Call 911—now.* It was 2:00 a.m.

Dear God.

"Tricia?" she whispered, as Brody clicked the phone

shut and got back into the jeans and work shirt he'd been wearing earlier, when they did chores.

Brody nodded. "She's having pains—bad ones, evidently—and Conner's in a panic."

"What if he's too panicked to call 911?" Carolyn lamented, as she and Brody headed for the bedroom doorway at the same time.

"Conner," Brody said, striding through the darkened house, almost running, "is Conner. He's solid, through and through."

By the time they crossed the kitchen, Brody had his truck keys out. Winston and Barney were both up on all four feet, rising off their improvised beds, watching them.

"You'll have to stay here this time," Brody said to the dog, for all the world as though he expected the creature to understand. "Look after Diablo-cat for me."

Barney lay back down again, with a sigh, and Winston followed suit.

Moments later, Carolyn and Brody were in the pickup, barreling down the moon-washed driveway, headlights slashing the darkness.

Several minutes before they pulled up in front of the main ranch house, they heard the ambulance siren and saw its red light swirling in the gloom as it raced around the far bend and along the county road.

Brody was the first one inside the house, shouting his brother's name.

Conner appeared from the hallway leading to the bedrooms, carrying Tricia, wrapped in a quilt, her face pale as death. The quilt was soaked in blood.

Please, Carolyn prayed silently. *Just...please.*

"They're coming, Conner," Brody told his brother.

"The EMTs are coming—probably turning in down at the gate right now."

Carolyn had never been in such a situation before, would have had no idea what she'd do if confronted with an emergency. Now, she knew—she automatically went straight up to Conner and touched Tricia's wan face.

"Tricia?" she said, firmly, but with a quaver. "Tricia?"

Tricia's head lolled against Conner's shoulder, but she opened her eyes to look at Carolyn. "Don't worry," she said, incredibly, and with great effort. "I'm okay, and so is Blue— This is just— I don't know what this is, but…don't worry…"

Don't worry.

Carolyn lifted her gaze to Conner's face. She'd never seen such fear, such anguish—or such inborn strength. Conner Creed was terrified, but no force on earth could have brought him down as long as Tricia and his unborn baby needed him.

Valentino began to bark hysterically as the ambulance siren grew deafening, and red light flashed against the kitchen windows like fire.

"Shh," Carolyn said, feeling sorry for him. Valentino was Tricia's dog, and his devotion to her was complete. The animal, like Conner, was quite literally beside himself.

Things happened fast over the next few minutes— Tricia was loaded onto a gurney and whisked into the back of the ambulance, an EMT taking her vital signs and starting an IV while Conner crouched on the opposite side of the stretcher, clutching her hand, murmuring to her.

Brody, standing nearby, beside Carolyn, was a living

reflection of his brother's pain. The emergency lights washed over him, in their garish rhythm. Carolyn knew he felt much of what Conner was going through, because of that weird twin-connection, but he was no more likely to buckle under than his brother was.

Around Lonesome Bend, it was an accepted fact that the Creeds were tough, but, slipping her arm around Brody's waist, Carolyn wondered if anybody had any idea just *how* tough.

As the ambulance raced off down the driveway and practically took the turn onto the county road on two wheels, siren screaming now, Carolyn and Brody dashed back to his truck and followed.

Brody's face was grim as he drove, and Carolyn knew he wasn't just sharing Conner's agony now, he was reliving his own. Taking the full weight of the deaths of his wife and child, as surely as if the tragedy had just happened.

It came home to Carolyn then, with cruel clarity, that the accident wasn't just a memory, it was literally a part of him, something he'd have to confront over and over during the course of his lifetime.

The thought was worse than sobering. Something shriveled and shrank inside Carolyn, some hope she'd dared to cherish—again—but she drew a deep breath and refused to give in. If Brody and Conner could hold it together, she would, too, for their sakes, for Tricia's and the baby's, and even for her own.

Courage, like so many other things, was not something one did or didn't have; it was a decision, a choice.

Brody handed her his cell phone. "Davis and Kim will want to know what's going on," he said. "They're on speed dial—zero-eight."

Trembling, Carolyn took the phone, opened it, studied the unfamiliar keyboard briefly and put the call through.

Davis answered after two rings, his voice gruff with sleep and the almost universal alarm of receiving a phone call at that hour. "Brody?" he said. "That you?"

Carolyn found her voice, identified herself and explained what little they knew of what was happening.

"We'll be there as soon as we can," Davis replied, and then she heard him say, "Kim, wake up, it's Tricia—something's wrong…"

Kim must have grabbed the phone from her husband's hand, because hers was the next voice Carolyn heard. "Carolyn? Which hospital are they taking Tricia to? Mercy General?"

Carolyn relayed the question to Brody, who nodded and said, "Probably. Tell them we'll be in touch again as soon as we know anything more." He paused, his profile backlit by the lights of a passing car as they careened along behind the ambulance. "And tell them to *be careful* driving back, because we can't afford to lose them."

Carolyn repeated Brody's words to Kim, and the call ended.

The drive to Mercy General, a small but up-to-date facility that served not only Lonesome Bend, but also four or five small towns around it, was a half an hour away.

It was the longest thirty minutes of Carolyn's life so far.

When the ambulance pulled into the bay outside the emergency room, Carolyn called Davis again, and verified that Tricia had indeed been taken to that particular hospital.

She and Brody ran inside, after parking the truck, but Tricia had been swept away immediately, and Conner, of course, had gone with her.

In a way, it had been easier when they'd had to hurry.

Now, they were just pacing, back and forth, back and forth, high on adrenaline with no way to work it off.

Except for the people at the reception desk, Carolyn and Brody had the lobby to themselves.

Up until Tricia's arrival, evidently, it had been a slow night.

Brody went to the desk every few minutes, asking for news, and each time, the nurses on duty just shook their heads and said they didn't know anything yet.

Brody would pace again, and then return, only to be told the same thing.

Carolyn's heart went out to him, but there was no settling him down. He waved away the cup of vending-machine coffee she got for him, and words didn't help, either. What could she say, anyway—*everything will be all right?*

But maybe it wouldn't.

Maybe *nothing* would be all right, ever again.

Whoa, cowgirl, Carolyn told herself silently. *No news is good news.*

A few minutes later, unable to bear his agitation on top of her own, Carolyn simply walked over to Brody and put her arms around him. He stiffened and then relaxed against her, his face buried in her hair.

"I'm here," was all she had to offer. "I'm right here."

But maybe—just maybe—it was enough, because Brody's breathing deepened and slowed, and she felt his heartbeat against her cheek, gradually losing speed.

He propped his chin on top of her head, and a great, tremulous sigh went through him.

He never cried, not on the outside, at least.

Carolyn, in the privacy of her own heart, cried enough for both of them.

It was nearly 5:00 a.m. when Conner reappeared, looking ghastly pale, shadows etched deep under his eyes—and smiling fit to light up the whole place and the surrounding night, too.

He came straight to Brody, and the two men, virtual mirror images of each other, stood face-to-face. For Carolyn, it was like looking at a pair of exquisite coins, both inscribed with the head of the same noble emperor.

"We got her here in time," Conner said, his voice a broken croak, cracked through with a joy so deep it must have been rooted in his very soul. "Tricia will be fine, and so will our son."

"Your son?" Brody echoed, finally catching up.

"Davis Blue," Conner confirmed proudly. "Six pounds, seven ounces of squalling Creed."

The transformation in Brody's face was a sight Carolyn would never forget. He was positively *illuminated*. "Davis Blue Creed," he repeated, in a tone of wonder.

"You don't mind, do you?" Conner asked his brother. "That we used up Dad's name, I mean, right along with Davis's? We mean to call him Blue, but if that bothers you, Brody, there's still time to make a change—"

"Davis Blue Creed," Brody said again, savoring the name. "It's perfect, Conner. *Perfect*."

"Can we see the baby?" Carolyn asked, her voice small. "And Tricia?" All of the sudden, she was feeling like an intruder, a bystander who didn't actually belong, and she wished she hadn't spoken so impulsively.

She felt like a third wheel—until Brody put his arm around her and drew her against her side.

"Later on," Conner told her quietly, smiling as he registered the couple's body language. "Tricia's sleeping now, and Blue will be in an incubator for a day or two, according to the doctors. Why don't you two go back to the ranch and try to get some sleep?" A wry look moved in Conner's happy, exhausted face. "You could feed the horses in the morning, too, come to think of it."

Brody chuckled, a raw sound, wholly good to hear, and slapped his brother lightly on the back. "Don't worry about the horses," he said. "I'll take care of them, Conner, and Davis's, too."

"And I'll help," Carolyn said.

Conner gave her an awkward hug. "Thanks," he said.

The hug he gave Brody was even *more* awkward, but it was genuine, too.

During the drive back toward Lonesome Bend, Carolyn and Brody were both too emotionally wrung out to talk much, but words weren't really necessary anyway.

Tricia would recover.

Blue would thrive, eventually.

At the moment, nothing else seemed to matter.

A WEEK LATER, Conner brought his glowing wife and his brand-new baby son home to the ranch, where they were greeted with a brief and very low-key family celebration.

There were balloons, a big cake and piles of baby presents, tied up with ribbons the color of Blue's name.

Tricia was practically effervescent with happiness, beaming as friends and family admired the newest member of the Creed clan, but Conner guarded the both of them like a sentinel, and everybody understood when he squired his wife into their room to rest for a while. The diagnosis of Tricia's initial crisis was separation of the placenta from the uterine wall and, while she was fine now, she naturally tired easily.

Blue, meanwhile, remained in the kitchen, holding court and enchanting his grandparents.

Davis and Kim were absolutely besotted with the infant, and Brody looked, to Carolyn, as proud as his brother was. Steven and Melissa and their children would be arriving from Stone Creek soon, for a visit; Melissa and Kim planned to take turns spending nights at the main ranch house, so they could help look after the new baby.

Carolyn, looking on from the sidelines, thought it was a beautiful thing, a family in action, rallying around when their loved ones needed them. *Being there,* at any hour of the day or night, willing to travel any distance, putting personal differences and agendas on a back burner, at least temporarily, to lavish care on one of their own.

It was no wonder, she reflected, sitting there in Tricia and Conner's kitchen, that the Creeds had flourished, not just in this generation, but in all previous ones, as well. In times of trouble *and* times of joy, they stuck together.

Carolyn marveled at that and, silently, she celebrated that such a thing was true.

Every night since Kim and Davis had returned, the day after Blue's birth, she and Brody had shared the three-quarter bed in the rustic cabin he jokingly referred to as "the lodge." The place made her apartment at Natty McCall's look like a palace, with its funny refrigerator and tiny microwave, but she'd been completely happy there, because she and Brody and Winston and Barney were together.

Neither she nor Brody had spoken of love again, let alone marriage, but, for the time being, it didn't matter. The lovemaking was exquisite, and they laughed constantly, she and Brody, and it was all right to live in the moment, because the moment was just fine the way it was.

For the first time in her life, Carolyn didn't have a universal shopping list of things that *had* to happen for her life to work. Just showing up for whatever came next, being present to it, seemed to be enough.

The days had been wonderfully ordinary: she helped Brody with the ranch chores.

She quietly stitched the gypsy skirt back to its former glory.

She took care of Winston and sometimes Barney, and she watched as Brody's big house rose against the sky, more complete with every passing day.

Now, in Conner and Tricia's kitchen, surrounded by friends and family, Brody laid a hand on her shoulder and bent to whisper in her ear. "Let's go," he said. "I have something to show you."

Carolyn nodded, a little flushed, and the two of them said the necessary goodbyes and left, riding in Brody's pickup, with Barney proudly ensconced in the backseat. Winston preferred to remain at the lodge most of the time, not being big on wheeled conveyances of any sort.

Brody drove to the new house, parked out front.

The windows reflected an apricot-and-gold sunset, and the roof and walls looked sturdy enough to weather a century or two of Creeds, being born, growing up, falling in love and marrying and having children of their own, getting old gracefully and, in their own good time, going to their rest.

The thought made Carolyn's heart swell.

Brody opened the truck door for her, and lifted Barney down from the backseat before walking toward the front entrance.

The double doors at the entrance were hand-carved, with the name *Creed* inscribed above them, on a massive lintel.

Carolyn paused to look up, admiring the effect, feeling the impact of that name lodge somewhere deep inside her, become an actual part of her.

Brody used his key, and one of the doors swung open when he gave it a slight push.

He turned to Carolyn, the last of the sunlight shining in his face and hair, and held out a hand to her. "One day soon," he said, very quietly, "I hope to carry you over the threshold of this house as my wife, Carolyn."

She stared at him. "Is that a proposal?" she dared, after a long moment of courage-gathering.

Brody cocked a grin at her, and she took the hand he offered her. "No," he said. "That's a separate thing."

He pulled her into the big living room, and her eyes went immediately to the place above the magnificent fireplace, where the Weaver hung in her fine frame, a monument to grace and wisdom.

Carolyn smiled. In all the excitement over Tricia and baby Blue, and Bill Venable's safe but unexpected return from the forest fire in New Mexico—he'd caught Carolyn during one of her brief stops at the shop and told her he'd had some kind of private epiphany and was now willing to do whatever it took to win Angela back—she'd forgotten about Primrose Sullivan's wonderful batik, awaiting delivery over at the shop.

"Primrose brought the picture over a few days ago," Brody said. "The contractor let her in, and some of the guys on his crew hung it for her, under her close supervision."

Carolyn could just imagine Primrose directing this man hither and that man yon, making them move the Weaver a few inches to the right, then the left, until she was satisfied that its position was absolutely perfect.

"Beautiful," Carolyn said, on a breath.

Brody took her into his arms, right there in the middle of the soon-to-be living room. "Marry me?" he asked, his voice husky.

Carolyn laughed for joy. Reality, as it turned out, was better than any fairy tale ever told. "Yes," she said. "I'll marry you, Brody Creed."

"Soon? So I never have to spend even one night in this house without you?"

Her eyes burned. "Soon," she confirmed. But there was still an element of their relationship that hadn't been settled. "What about Joleen?"

Brody grinned, his hands moving slowly up and down Carolyn's ribs, his head tilted slightly to one side. "Didn't you hear the rumors? Joleen ran off with one of her customers from the café. According to the scuttlebutt, it's love, a match made in heaven."

"You don't say," Carolyn said.

Brody nibbled at her mouth. "I *do* say," he murmured. "What about Mr. Coffee? The hot-shot fire-fighting pilot guy?"

"I knew who you meant," Carolyn answered.

Brody simply raised both eyebrows and waited, but

his hands were still subtly busy at her ribs and the outer rounding of her breasts.

"His name is Bill," Carolyn said, in a coquettish tone, "and he's not a 'hot-shot firefighting pilot guy' anymore. He agreed to take a year off from his job and work out of Denver as an airline executive while he and his new bride, Angela, and his very precocious daughter, Ellie, build themselves a family life."

Brody took a deep breath, let it out as a long sigh. "It seems to be a trend," he said, in a drawl that meant he'd be trying to make her clothes fall off for the next little while. And that he was bound to succeed. "People taking a chance on love, I mean."

"Seems to be," Carolyn agreed, watching his lips.

It was something, what Brody Creed could do with those lips.

He left her, walked over to the fireplace, took something from the high mantel and came back to her.

While Carolyn watched, amazed even after he'd used the words *marry me,* he dropped gracefully to one knee in front of her, held up a little velvet box and popped the lid.

An eye-popping diamond engagement ring glittered inside.

Carolyn gasped and put a hand to her throat.

Brody grinned a lopsided grin. "Here comes the formal proposal," he said. "Will you, Carolyn? Will you be my wife? For better or for worse, for richer or for poorer, in sickness and in health, 'til death do us part?"

Carolyn sank to her knees, so they were approximately at eye level. "Yes, Brody," she replied, "I will be your wife, for better or for worse, for richer or for poorer, in sickness and in health, until death do us part.

I will love you and I will honor you, but you can just forget that part about obeying, because that ain't gonna happen."

He laughed. "Fair enough," he said. "Will you cook my supper every night, and have my babies?"

"I will have your babies," she replied, smiling as he slid the ring onto her finger. "But I'm not much of a cook, so we'll have to work something out regarding supper. Breakfast and lunch, too, for that matter."

Eyes sparkling with amusement, and with love, Brody kissed her, lightly, briefly and with a hunger that aroused a corresponding need in her. "What if *I* make supper?" he countered. "I happen to be a pretty good hand with a skillet."

"I thought you might be," Carolyn said, slipping her arms around his neck and inclining her head toward the kitchen, "when I saw that fancy stove with all the burners."

"I wish this place had a bed," Brody grumbled, kissing her neck.

Carolyn drew him down, onto the floor, urging him on top of her just to feel the weight of him, the promise of his hardness and his heat. "Who needs a bed?" she asked, as his mouth descended to hers.

EPILOGUE

CAROLYN AND BRODY were married in early August at sunset, on the former swimming beach at River's Bend, with the whole town and a good portion of Denver in attendance. Conner was the best man, Tricia the matron of honor and Melissa and Steven's oldest, Matt, proudly served as ring-bearer.

Davis, handsome and comically uncomfortable in his Sunday suit, gave the bride away, while Kim looked on with tears of pure happiness glittering in her eyes.

Carolyn wore the now mended gypsy skirt, with a white camisole and a short silk jacket she'd made to go with the outfit, and Brody looked better than handsome in his jeans, crisply white Western shirt and sport jacket, his concession to formality.

Since it was summer, the sunset lasted well past the actual ceremony, gradually fading as a band struck up a romantic country tune inside the large, rented tent that stood where the lodge used to be.

There was dancing, and there was cake, but the evening was mostly a glad blur to Carolyn—whenever she looked at Brody, which was often, he was all she saw, and she knew by the expression in his eyes that he was under the same spell.

They were surrounded by friends and family, by music and light and love and laughter, but they might as well have been alone on the planet, just the two of them, they were so absorbed in each other. They'd eaten cake, and toasted each other with frothing flutes filled with ginger ale, and posed for endless pictures, images Carolyn knew she'd treasure for the rest of her life.

Davis, with a slight smile, walked up to them, shook Brody's hand and politely asked if he might dance with the bride, since he'd been the one to give her away and all.

Carolyn smiled up at the man she thought of as her father-in-law now, as well as her good friend, and she remembered something he'd said to her, a few days before the wedding, when they'd all gathered at the main ranch house for a family dinner.

"When you marry a Creed," Davis had announced, smiling at her, "you get all of us."

Now, as they danced, as Kim and Brody joined them on the plank floor put down for the purpose, Chinese lanterns casting a multicolored glow, Davis squeezed her hand lightly. "Welcome to the family, Carolyn Creed," he said, in that singular rumble of his. "And I don't mind telling you, you took your sweet time about it."

Carolyn—*Carolyn Creed*—laughed softly. "You sound like Tricia," she replied. "And Kim. Were Brody and I the only people in Lonesome Bend who didn't see this wedding coming?"

Davis grinned, and Carolyn smiled up at him as they danced. "Sure seemed like it," he said. "There were times when I would have liked to thump your heads together. It was Tricia and Conner, all over again. They couldn't see the forest for the trees in the beginning, either."

"You know, don't you, that you and Kim mean the world to Brody and Conner? And to Tricia and me, as well?"

"They're my brother's boys," he said quietly, "and the spittin' image of him, too. There's never a day that I don't miss Blue, and wish he was here with the rest of us, where he belongs, but if he had to go ahead and get himself killed, well, he left a fine legacy behind." He glanced over, saw Conner cutting in to dance with Kim and Brody pretending to protest, and Davis's eyes brightened until they shone. "I love them like my own." He turned his head again, to face her. "And you and Tricia are the daughters we've always wanted."

Carolyn let her forehead rest against Davis's strong shoulder for a moment, overcome with emotion. "Thank you," she whispered.

Davis chuckled and gave her a reassuring squeeze, and then Brody cut in, and she was dancing with her man, her cowboy, her *husband.*

"I love you, Mrs. Creed," he said, smiling into her eyes. "And I'm fixing to kiss you, right here and now, so get ready."

She giggled.

He stopped the giggle with the promised kiss, complete with a pretty flashy dip and some serious tongue-action, and the whole gathering cheered.

"And I love *you,*" Carolyn replied, breathless, when it was over.

Brody curved a finger under her chin and lifted. "What do you say we get out of here, Mrs. Creed," he said, "and leave these good people to party on to their hearts' content?"

"I think that's a fine idea, Mr. Creed," she replied.

He led her outside.

They stood hand in hand in the weighted heat of an August night, watching the light of the moon and a bajillion stars dance on the surface of the river, singing as it passed.

In the morning, they'd be leaving on their honeymoon, location undisclosed, but Brody and Carolyn wanted to spend their wedding night in the new house. It seemed just right, for their life together to begin there.

Brody held on to her hand, and they walked toward home, following a glowing path of silvery moonlight.

It was magical. Something right out of a fairy tale but *better,* because it was real.

To Carolyn's surprise, they passed by the house and headed toward the barn instead.

Inside the entrance, Brody flipped the light switch and Moonshine blinked at them from his stall, sleepily munching on a mouthful of grass hay.

Carolyn smiled and moved to pat the horse's velvety nose, but Brody pulled her on past, stopping in front of the stall next to Moonshine's.

A beautiful, snow-white gelding stood in the center of his space, splendid enough to pull Cinderella's carriage.

Carolyn drew in her breath, laid a hand to her heart.

"He's yours, if you'll have him," Brody said gently. "A wedding present from your lovin' husband. His name's Sugar-man, but you can change it if you want to. He's gentle, but he's spirited, too."

Carolyn, in her shimmery skirt and special jacket, stepped up and clasped the rim of the stall door in both hands, already shaking her head. "I wouldn't change a thing, Brody," she said, turning to look into the face of the man beside her. "Not about him, and not about you."

Brody kissed her gently. "When we get back from the honeymoon, well, I thought you might like to go riding with me. Maybe up to Hidden Lake?"

She smiled. "Brody Creed," she said, "you're the best thing that ever happened to me."

He grinned that megawatt grin of his. "Back at you, pretty woman," he said, bending his head to taste her mouth.

A warm shiver went through her.

"Isn't it about time you carried me over the threshold, like you promised?" she asked, slipping her arms around his neck.

"I do believe it is," he replied, after pretending to consider the matter for a few moments.

With that, they left the barn, walking on that same path of light, and when they reached the house, Brody Creed swept his bride up into his arms, kissed her again and said, "Hold on tight, lady. I think we're in for quite a ride."

Carolyn smiled. She knew he wasn't just talking about their wedding night. He was talking about the rest of their lives.

* * * * *

BLAME IT ON THE COWBOY

Delores Fossen

CHAPTER ONE

LOGAN MCCORD HATED two things: clowns and liars. To-night, he saw both right in front of him on the antique desk in Langford's Interior Designs, and he knew his life had changed forever. He would *never* look at a red squeaky nose the same way again.

Ten minutes earlier

LOGAN GLANCED AT the four signs and groaned.

Marry

Me?

You

Will

It was not the way he wanted to present this proposal to his future wife.

His younger brother, Riley, was carrying the You. His twin brother, Lucky, the Will. Riley's wife, Claire, the Marry. Lucky's girlfriend, Cassie, the Me?

"Unless I want this proposal to sound like Yoda, switch places," Logan insisted.

Since everyone but Logan had clearly had too much to drink in the precelebration prep for this occasion, he took them by the shoulders and one by one put them in the right places.

Lucky. Riley. Claire. Cassie.

"Will you marry me?" Logan double-checked. Then he checked again.

Logan wanted this to be perfect while still feeling a little spontaneous. Just the day before, his longtime girlfriend, Helene Langford, had told him he should be a little more whimsical.

Somewhat wild, even.

Logan was certain most people in their small hometown of Spring Hill, Texas, wouldn't consider him wild even when the expectations were lowered with that *somewhat*. That was his twin brother Lucky's specialty. Still, if Helene wanted something whimsical, then this marriage proposal should do it.

Helene was perfect for him. A savvy businesswoman, beautiful, smart, and her even temperament made her easy to get along with. She'd never once complained about his frequent seventy-hour workweeks, and he could count on one hand how many disagreements they'd had.

She was the only child of state senator Edwin Langford and a former Miss Texas beauty contestant. Her family loved him, and Logan was pretty sure his own family felt the same way about her.

"You got the ring?" Lucky whispered. Or rather, tried to whisper.

Yeah, his siblings, sibling-in-law and future sibling-in-law were buzzed on champagne, all in the name of celebrating the fact that he was finally going to pop the question to the woman he'd been dating all these years.

Logan double-checked the ring. The blue Tiffany box was in his jacket pocket. It was perfect, as well. A two-carat diamond—flawless like Helene—with a platinum setting. It would look just right on the hand of the woman who would eventually help him run Mc-Cord Cattle Brokers.

He took another bottle of chilled champagne from his car. This one he would share with his future bride right after she said yes, and he'd do that sharing without his family around. He wanted to get Helene alone, maybe show her just how spontaneous he could be by having sex with her on her pricey antique desk. The very one she had professionally polished every week.

"All right, no talking once we're inside," Logan reminded them. "No giggling, either," he warned Claire.

It was dark, after closing hours, and any chatter or giggling would immediately carry through the building and all the way to Helene's office in the back of her interior design business. He wouldn't have to worry about other customers, though, since it was Wednesday, the night that Helene used to catch up on paperwork.

Logan eased his key into the lock, turning it slowly so that Helene wouldn't be alerted to the clicking sound. He gave the sign crew one last stern look to keep quiet, and they all tiptoed toward the back. Well, they tiptoed as much as four drunk people could manage, but he wouldn't have to put up with their drunken giddiness much longer. Logan had already arranged for the town's only taxi driver to pick them up in fifteen minutes.

Leading the way, Logan headed to Helene's office. The door was already cracked so he pushed it open, motioning for the others to go ahead of him and get ready to spring into action. They did. Lucky. Riley. Claire. Cassie. All in the correct order, but what they didn't do was hold up their signs. That's because they froze.

All of them.

They stood there, signs frozen in their hands, too.

Logan's stomach went to his knees, and in the split second that followed, he tried to figure out what would have caused them to react like that.

Hell.

If Helene had been hurt, at least one of them would have rushed to check on her, but there was no rushing. Even though it was hard to wrap his mind around it, the freezing could mean they'd just walked in on Helene doing something bad.

Like maybe she was with another man.

She couldn't be, though. Helene had never given him any reason whatsoever not to trust her. Ditto for giving him any reason whatsoever to believe she was unhappy. Just an hour earlier she'd called Logan to tell him she loved him.

Riley looked back at Logan, shaking his head. "Uh, you don't want to see this," Riley insisted.

But Logan did. He had to see it. Because there was nothing in the room that was worse than what he was already imagining.

Or so he thought.

However, Logan was wrong. It was worse. *Much, much* worse.

CHAPTER TWO

LIARS AND CLOWNS. Logan had seen both tonight. The liar was a woman he thought loved him. Helene. And the clown, well, Logan wasn't sure he could process that image just yet.

Maybe after lots of booze, though.

He hadn't been drunk since his twenty-first birthday nearly thirteen years ago. But he was about to remedy that now. He motioned for the bartender to set him up with another pair of Glenlivet shots.

His phone buzzed again, indicating another call had just gone to voice mail. One of his siblings no doubt wanting to make sure he was all right. He wasn't. But talking to them about it wouldn't help, and Logan didn't want anyone he knew to see or hear him like this.

It was possible there'd be some slurring involved. Puking, too.

He'd never been sure what to call Helene. His long-time girlfriend? *Girlfriend* seemed too high school. So, he'd toyed with thinking of her as his future fiancée. Or in social situations—she was his business associate who often ran his marketing campaigns. But tonight Logan wasn't calling her any of those things. As far as he was concerned, he never wanted to think of her, her name or what to call her again.

Too bad that image of her was stuck in his head, but

that's where he was hoping generous amounts of single malt Scotch would help.

Even though Riley, Claire, Lucky and Cassie wouldn't breathe a word about this, it would still get around town. Logan wasn't sure how, but gossip seemed to defy the time-space continuum in Spring Hill. People would soon know, if they didn't already, and those same people would never look at him the same way again. It would hurt business.

Hell. It hurt *him*.

That's why he was here in this hotel bar in San Antonio. It was only thirty miles from Spring Hill, but tonight he hoped it'd be far enough away that no one he knew would see him get drunk. Then he could stagger to his room and puke in peace. Not that he was looking forward to the puking part, but it would give him something else to think about other than *her*.

It was his first time in this hotel, though he stayed in San Antonio often on business. Logan hadn't wanted to risk running into anyone he knew, and he certainly wouldn't at this trendy "boutique" place. Not with a name like the Purple Cactus and its vegan restaurant.

If the staff found out he was a cattle broker, he might be booted out. Or forced to eat tofu. That's the reason Logan had used cash when he checked in. No sense risking someone recognizing his name from his credit card.

The clerk had seemed skeptical when Logan had told him that his ID and credit cards had been stolen and that's why he couldn't produce anything with his name on it. Of course, when Logan had slipped the guy an extra hundred dollar bill, it had caused that doubt to disappear.

"Drinking your troubles away?" a woman asked.

"Trying."

Though he wasn't drunk enough that he couldn't see what was waiting for him at the end of this. A hangover, a missed 8:00 a.m. meeting, his family worried about him—the puking—and it wouldn't fix anything other than to give him a couple hours of mind-numbing solace.

At the moment, though, mind-numbing solace even if it was temporary seemed like a good trade-off.

"Me, too," she said. "Drinking my troubles away."

Judging from the sultry tone in her voice, Logan first thought she might be a prostitute, but then he got a look at her.

Nope. Not a pro.

Or if she was, she'd done nothing to market herself as such. No low-cut dress to show her cleavage. She had on a T-shirt with cartoon turtles on the front, a baggy white skirt and flip-flops. It looked as if she'd grabbed the first items of clothing she could find off a very cluttered floor of her very cluttered apartment.

Logan wasn't into clutter.

And he'd thought Helene wasn't, either. He'd been wrong about that, too. That antique desk of hers had been plenty cluttered with a clown's bare ass.

"Mind if I join you?" Miss Turtle-shirt said. "I'm having sort of a going-away party."

She waited until Logan mumbled, "Suit yourself," and she slid onto the purple bar stool next to him.

She smelled like limes.

Her hair was varying shades of pink and looked as if it'd been cut with a weed whacker. It was already messy, but apparently it wasn't messy enough for her because she dragged her hand through it, pushing it away from her face.

"Tequila, top shelf. Four shots and a bowl of lime slices," she told the bartender.

Apparently, he wasn't the only person in San Antonio with plans to get shit-faced tonight. And it explained the lime scent. These clearly weren't her first shots of the night.

"Do me a favor, though," she said to Logan after he downed his next drink. "Don't ask my name, or anything personal about me, and I'll do the same for you."

Logan had probably never agreed to anything so fast in all his life. For one thing he really didn't want to spend time talking with this woman, and he especially didn't want to talk about what'd happened.

"If you feel the need to call me something, go with Julia," she added.

The name definitely wasn't a fit. He was expecting something more like Apple or Sunshine. Still, he didn't care what she called herself. Didn't care what her real name was, either, and he cared even less after his next shot of Glenlivet.

"So, you're a cowboy, huh?" she asked.

The mind-numbing hadn't kicked in yet, but the orneriness had. "That's personal."

She shrugged. "Not really. You're wearing a cowboy hat, cowboy boots and jeans. It was more of an observation than a question."

"The clothes could be fashion statements," he pointed out.

"Julia" shook her head, downed the first shot of tequila, sucked on a lime slice. Made a face and shuddered. "You're not the kind of man to make fashion statements."

If he hadn't had a little buzz going on, he might have been insulted by that. "Unlike you?"

She glanced down at her clothes as if seeing them for the first time. Or maybe she was just trying to focus because the tequila had already gone to her head. "This was the first thing I grabbed off my floor."

Bingo. If that was her first grab, there was no telling how bad the outfits were beneath it.

Julia tossed back her second shot. "Have you ever found out something that changed your whole life?" she asked.

"Yeah." About four hours ago.

"Me, too. Without giving specifics, because that would be personal, did it make you feel as if fate were taking a leak on your head?"

"Four leaks," he grumbled. Logan finished off his next shot.

Julia made a sound of agreement. "I would compare yours with mine, and I'd win, but I don't want to go there. Instead, let's play a drinking game."

"Let's not," he argued. "And in a fate-pissing comparison, I don't think you'd win."

Julia made a sound of disagreement. Had another shot. Grimaced and shuddered again. "So, the game is a word association," she continued as if he'd agreed. "I say a word, you say the first thing that comes to mind. We take turns until we're too drunk to understand what the other one is saying."

Until she'd added that last part, Logan had been about to get up and move to a different spot. But hell, he was getting drunk, anyway, and at least this way he'd have some company. Company he'd never see again. Company he might not even be able to speak to if the slurring went up a notch.

"Dream?" she threw out there.

"Family." That earned him a sound of approval from her, and she motioned for him to take his turn. "Surprise?"

"Shitty," Julia said without hesitation.

Now it was Logan who made a grunt of approval. Surprises could indeed be shit-related. The one he'd gotten tonight certainly had been.

Her: "Tattoos?"

Him: "None." Then, "You?"

Her: "Two." Then, "Bucket list?"

Him: "That's two words." The orneriness was still there despite the buzz.

Her: "Just bucket, then?"

Too late. Logan's fuzzy mind was already fixed on the bucket list. He had one, all right. Or rather, he'd had one. A life with Helene that included all the trimmings, and this stupid game was a reminder that the Glenlivet wasn't working nearly fast enough. So, he had another shot.

Julia had one, as well. "Sex?" she said.

Logan shook his head. "I don't want to play this game anymore."

When she didn't respond, Logan looked at her. Their eyes met. Eyes that were already slightly unfocused.

Julia took the paper sleeve with her room key from her pocket. Except there were two keys, and she slid one Logan's way.

"It's not the game," she explained. "I'm offering you

sex with me. No names. No strings attached. Just one night, and we'll never tell another soul about it."

She finished off her last tequila shot, shuddered and stood. "Are you game?"

No way, and Logan would have probably said that if she hadn't leaned in and kissed him.

Maybe it was the weird combination of her tequila and his Scotch, or maybe it was because he was already drunker than he thought, but Logan felt himself moving right into that kiss.

LOGAN DREAMED, AND it wasn't about the great sex he'd just had. It was another dream that wasn't so pleasant. The night of his parents' car accident. Some dreams were a mishmash of reality and stuff that didn't make sense. But this dream always got it right.

Not a good thing.

It was like being trapped on a well-oiled hamster wheel, seeing the same thing come up over and over again and not being able to do a thing to stop it.

The dream rain felt and sounded so real. Just like that night. It was coming down so hard that the moment his truck wipers swished it away, the drops covered the windshield again. That's why it'd taken him so long to see the lights, and Logan was practically right on the scene of the wreck before he could fully brake. He went into a skid, costing him precious seconds. If he'd had those seconds, he could have called the ambulance sooner.

He could have saved them.

But he hadn't then. And he didn't now in the dream.

Logan chased away the images, and with his head still groggy, he did what he always did after the nightmare. He rewrote it. He got to his parents and stopped them from dying.

Every time except when it had really mattered, Logan saved them.

LOGAN WISHED HE could shoot out the sun. It was creating lines of light on each side of the curtains, and those lines were somehow managing to stab through his closed eyelids. That was probably because every nerve in his head and especially his eyelids were screaming at him, and anything—including the earth's rotation—added to his pain.

He wanted to ask himself: *What the hell have you done?*

But he knew. He'd had sex with a woman he didn't know. A woman who wore turtle T-shirts and had tattoos. He'd learned one of the tattoos, a rose, was on Julia's right breast. The other was on her lower stomach. Those were the things Logan could actually remember.

That, and the sex.

Not mind-numbing but rather more mind-blowing. Julia clearly didn't have any trouble being wild and spontaneous in bed. It was as if she'd just studied a sex manual and wanted to try every position. Thankfully, despite the Scotch, Logan had been able to keep up—literally.

Not so much now, though.

If the fire alarm had gone off and the flames had been burning his ass, he wasn't sure he would be able to move. Julia didn't have that problem, though. He felt the mattress shift when she got up. Since it was possible she was about to rob him, Logan figured he should at least see if she was going after his wallet, wherever the heck it was. But if she robbed him, he deserved it. His life was on the fast track to hell, and he'd been the one to put it in the handbasket.

At least he hadn't been so drunk that he'd forgotten to use condoms. Condoms that Julia had provided, so obviously she'd been ready for this sort of thing.

Julia made a soft sound of discomfort. He hoped it wasn't from the rough sex because he got a sudden flash of himself tying her hands to the bedposts with the sheets. It'd been Julia's idea.

And it'd been a darn good one.

Ditto for her idea of tying him up, too. He wasn't one to add some kink to sex, but for a little while it had gotten his mind off Helene and what he'd seen in her office.

Clearly, he hadn't known Helene at all.

Logan heard some more stirring around, and this time the movement was very close to him. Just in case Julia turned out to be a serial killer, he decided to risk opening one eye. And he nearly jolted at the big green eyeball staring back at him. Except it wasn't a human eye. It was on her turtle shirt.

If Julia felt the jolt or saw his one-eyed opening, she didn't say anything about it. She gave him a chaste kiss on the cheek, moved away, turning her back to him, and Logan watched as she stooped down and picked up his jacket. So, not a serial killer but rather just a thief, after all. But she didn't take anything out.

She put something *in* the pocket.

Logan couldn't tell what it was exactly. Maybe her number. Which he would toss first chance he got. But if so, he couldn't figure out why she just hadn't left it on the bed.

Julia picked up her purse, hooking it over her shoulder, and without even glancing back at him, she walked out the door. Strange, since this was her room. Maybe she was headed out to get them some coffee. If so, that was his cue to dress and get the devil out of there before she came back.

Easier said than done.

His hair hurt.

He could feel every strand of it on his head. His eyelashes, too. Still, Logan forced himself from the bed, only to realize the soles of his feet hurt, as well. It was hard to identify something on him that didn't hurt so he quit naming parts and put on his boxers and jeans. Then he had a look at what Julia had put in his pocket next to the box with the engagement ring.

A gold watch.

Not a modern one. It was old with a snap-up top that had a crest design on it. The initials BWS had been engraved in the center of the crest.

The inside looked just as expensive as the gold case except for the fact that the watch face crystal inside was shattered. Even though he knew little about antiques, Logan figured it was worth at least a couple hundred dollars.

So why had Julia put it in his pocket?

Since he was a skeptic, his first thought was that she might be trying to set him up, to make it look as if he'd robbed her. But Logan couldn't imagine why anyone would do that unless she was planning to try to blackmail him with it.

He dropped the watch on the bed and finished dressing, all the while staring at it. He cleared out some of the cotton in his brain and grabbed the hotel phone to call the front desk. Someone answered on the first ring.

"I'm in room…" Logan had to check the phone. "Two-sixteen, and I need to know…" He had to stop again and think. "I need to know if Julia is there in the lobby. She left something in the room."

"No, sir. I'm afraid you just missed her. But checkout isn't until noon, and she said her guest might be staying past then so she paid for an extra day."

"Uh, could you tell me how to spell Julia's last name? I need to leave her a note in case she comes back."

"Oh, she said she wouldn't be coming back, that this was her goodbye party. And as for how to spell her name, well, it's Child, just like it sounds."

Julia Child?

Right. Obviously, the clerk wasn't old enough or enough of a foodie to recognize the name of the famous chef.

"I don't suppose she paid with a credit card?" Logan asked.

"No. She paid in cash and then left a prepaid credit card for the second night."

Of course. "What about an address?" Logan kept trying.

"I'm really not supposed to give that out—"

"She left something very expensive in the room, and I know she'll want it back."

The guy hemmed and hawed a little, but he finally rattled off, "221B Baker Street, London, England."

That was Sherlock Holmes's address.

Logan groaned, cursed. He didn't bother asking for a phone number because the one she left was probably for Hogwarts. He hung up and hurried to the window, hoping he could catch a glimpse of her getting into a car. Not that he intended to follow her or anything, but if she was going to blackmail him, he wanted to know as much about her as possible.

No sign of her, but Logan got a flash of something else. A memory.

Shit.

They'd taken pictures.

Or at least Julia had with the camera on her phone. He remembered nude selfies of them from the waist up. At least he hoped it was from the waist up.

Yeah, that trip to hell in a handbasket was moving even faster right now.

Logan threw on the rest of his clothes, already trying to figure out how to do damage control. He was the CEO of a multimillion-dollar company. He was the face that people put with the family business, and before last night he'd never done a thing to tarnish the image of McCord Cattle Brokers.

He couldn't say that any longer.

He was in such a hurry to rush out the door that he nearly missed the note on the desk. Maybe it was the start of the blackmail. He snatched it up, steeling himself for the worst. But if this was blackmail, then Julia sure had a funny sense of humor.

"Goodbye, hot cowboy," she'd written. "Thanks for the sweet send-off. Don't worry. What happens in San Antonio stays in San Antonio. I'll take this to the grave."

CHAPTER THREE

HAVING ONE FOOT in the grave was not a laughing matter, though Reese Stephens tried to make it one.

So, as the final thing on her bucket list she'd bought every joke book she could find on death, dying and other morbid things. It wasn't helping, but it wasn't hurting, either. At this point, that was as good as it was going to get for her.

She added the joke books to the stack of sex manuals she'd purchased. Donating both to the same place might be a problem so Reese decided she'd just leave them all in a stack in the corner of her apartment.

"You're sure you want to get rid of these?" Todd, her neighbor, asked. He had a box of vinyl albums under one arm and a pink stuffed elephant under the other.

Since Reese had bought the vinyls just the month before at a garage sale, it wouldn't be a great sentimental loss. She could say that about everything in her apartment, though.

Now that the watch was gone.

Reese hadn't intended to leave it with the cowboy, but it'd just felt right at the time, as if it were something he would appreciate.

As for the elephant, she'd found it by the Dumpster and couldn't stand the thought of it having the stuffing crushed out of it so Reese had given it a temporary home. Temporary was the norm for her, too, and she made a habit of not staying in one place for long.

"Take them," Reese assured Todd. "I won't be able to bring anything with me to Cambodia."

Reese wasn't sure why the lie about Cambodia had rolled so easily off her tongue, but it did now just as it had the first time she'd told it. So had the other lies needed to support that one because as she'd quickly learned one solo lie just led to more questions.

Questions she didn't want to answer.

As the story now went, she was moving to Cambodia to do a reality show about jungle cooking. She wouldn't be able to communicate with anyone for at least a year, and after that, the producers of the show were sending her to Vietnam. It was surprising that everyone believed her. Of course, everyone wasn't close to her. That was her fault.

In my next life I need to make more friends. And not move every few months.

But with mental memos like that came the depression. She wouldn't cry. She'd already wasted too many tears on something she couldn't change. Though if there was more time, she would have run to the store for some books on coping with grief.

"Knock, knock," someone called out from the open door. "Food pimp has arrived." Jimena Martinelli wiggled her away around a departing Todd, ignoring both the elephant and the heated look Todd gave her.

Jimena was the worst chef Reese had ever worked with, but she was also Reese's only friend. In every way that counted, she was like a sister.

The genetic product of an Irish-Mexican mother and Korean-Italian father, even in a blended city like San

Antonio, Jimena stood out partly because she was stunning. Also partly because she drank like a fish, cursed like a sailor and ate like a pig. Her motto was *If it's not fun, don't fucking do it*, and she literally had those words tattooed on her back.

Reese had first met her when they were sixteen, homeless and trying to scrape by. At various times they'd been roommates. Other times Jimena had stayed behind to be with a boyfriend or a job she particularly liked when Reese had felt those restless stirrings to move. But eventually Jimena had felt similar stirrings—or else had gotten dumped—and had caught up with Reese.

Jimena was also the only person other than Reese's doctor who knew her diagnosis. The sole reason Reese had told her was so there'd be someone to tie up any loose ends in case the last-ditch treatment failed.

Which it almost certainly would.

A 2 percent chance pretty much spelled *failure*.

"I brought the good stuff," Jimena announced. She breezed toward Reese and sat down on the floor beside her despite the fact Jimena was wearing shorts so tight that the movement alone could have given her an orgasm.

Jimena didn't ask what most people would have asked: *How are you feeling?* Nor did she give Reese any sad sympathetic looks. That was the reason Reese had told her. Jimena perhaps wanted to know, but asking Reese about her death diagnosis wasn't *fun*, therefore it wasn't something Jimena was going to do. And that was fine.

Especially since Reese wasn't sure how she felt, anyway.

She'd been drinking too much, eating too much, and she'd had a headache since this whole ordeal had begun. Of course, she wasn't sure how much was because of the tumor, which she'd named Myrtle, or if the overindulgence was playing into this. Reese suspected both.

"Milk Duds," Jimena said, taking out the first item from the bag. There were at least a dozen boxes of them. "Cheetos." Three family-size bags. "Not that reduced-fat shit, either. These are orange and greasy." She pulled out powdered doughnuts next. "Oh, and Diet Dr. Pepper. The store clerk said, 'Why bother?' when he saw it was diet, but I told him I try to cut calories here and there."

Reese wished that all those food items, either separately or collectively, would have turned her stomach. After all, she was a chef with supposedly refined tastes, but she was a shallow foodie.

"I've already eaten so much my jeans are too tight," Reese told her while she was opening the Milk Duds. "At this rate, I won't be able to fit in my coffin."

Jimena started in on the Cheetos as if this were the most normal conversation in the world. "You said you wanted to be cremated, anyway."

"I might not fit into my urn," Reese amended.

"Then I'll make sure you have two urns. Eat up. You can't be miserable while eating junk food."

Well, you could be until the sugar high kicked in, but that would no doubt happen soon.

"Making any more progress with the bucket list?" Jimena asked, taking the notepad that Reese had placed next to her.

Number one was "give away stuff."

Now that the vinyls and elephant were gone, Reese

could check that off. The only things left were the blow-up mattress she used for a bed, the books, her clothes, a box of baking soda in the fridge and a three-month-old tin of caramel popcorn that was now glued together from the humidity. She would toss it, of course, but Reese had wanted to look at the cute puppies on the tin a few more times.

Oh, and there was the backpack.

She'd named it Tootsie Roll because of the color and because it frequently contained some of the candies.

Reese tipped her head to it, the only other item in the living room. "Everything in there goes to you," she told Jimena.

Jimena looked at the worn hiker's backpack as if it might contain gold bullion. Then snakes. "You're sure?" she asked.

"Positive."

Jimena was taking care of her death wishes so it seemed only natural to give her the things Reese had carried with her from move to move. Most of the stuff in the backpack would just disappoint her friend, but there was a nice pair of Shun knives Jimena might like if she ever learned how to do food prep.

"Number two," Jimena read from the list. "'Quit job.' Well, we know that's done after what you said to Chef Dante. I heard the part about you saying you wished someone would crush his balls with a rusty garlic press."

Yes, Reese had said that. And Dante had deserved it and worse. That was the first thing she'd checked off the list, and Reese had done it the day after she'd gotten the diagnosis. Not that she'd heard much of the actual diagnosis after Dr. Gutzman had said the words that'd changed her life.

Inoperable brain tumor. Vascularization. Radiation treatments.

She'd gone in for tests for a sinus infection and had come out with a death sentence.

Those 2 percent odds were the best she had even with intense radiation treatments, and the doctor estimated she had less than a month to live. He'd also explained in nauseating detail what the radiation treatments (the ones that stood almost no chance of working) would do to her body.

Still, Reese would have them, starting tomorrow morning, because an almost chance was the only chance she had. However, she'd wanted this time to get her life in order while she still had the mind to do it.

"Number three," Jimena continued to read. "'Donate money to charity.' You finished that?" she asked, stuffing eight puffy Cheetos into her mouth at once.

Reese nodded. "It's all done. I kept just enough for me to live on…" Or rather, die on. She didn't have much, but she had tried to figure out where it would do the most good. "I divided it between Save the Whales, a local culinary academy and a fund for cosmetology scholarships at a beauty school."

Because on one of her find-the-best-tequila quests, Reese had decided the world needed more beauty, good food and whale protection.

Number four was "find the best tequila."

She'd checked that off only because they'd all started to taste the same.

Number five was dye her hair pink, and number six was eat whatever she wanted and in any amount she wanted. Reese wasn't sure exactly how much weight she'd gained, but she had been forced to wear a T-shirt and a skirt with an elastic waist.

And yet she'd still managed to accomplish number seven.

Have sex with a hot cowboy.

"It's ticked off," Jimena said, looking at number seven. "You actually went through with it? You didn't chicken out?"

Reese nodded. No chickening for her.

"Any, well, you know, bad memories?" Jimena asked. "And sorry if I'm bringing up bad memories just by asking if it brought up bad memories. Because you know the last thing I want is for you to remember the bad shit."

Despite the semirambling apology, Reese knew what Jimena meant and dismissed it. "No bad memories." It was true. There hadn't been, but the bad memories always felt just a heartbeat away. Because they were. "It was nice. *He* was nice."

Jimena smiled, and yes, she did it with that mouthful of chewed-up Cheetos. "So, how nice is nice? Tell me all about it."

"It was good." Reese wouldn't do the tell-all, though. The cowboy was the bright spot in all of this, and the last thing on her bucket list she'd gotten around to doing.

Jimena stared at her. "That's it? *Good?* If you checked it off, it must have been better than just good, or you'd be looking for another one."

It was more than just good, but even if it hadn't been, Reese wouldn't have looked for another one. No time.

After the radiation treatments started tomorrow, she'd be too sick and tired to pick up a cowboy in a hotel bar.

"He was hot," Reese settled for saying, and she showed Jimena the picture she had taken on her phone. Definitely not an Instagram-worthy shot, but Reese had wanted something to look at after she left him.

Jimena squealed. "Yeah, he's hot. Like on a scale of one to ten—he's like a six-hundred kind of hot."

She made a hmm-ing sound, looked at Reese, and even though Jimena didn't say it, she was no doubt thinking how the heck had Reese managed to get him into bed. He was a six hundred, and Reese was a six on a really good day.

Last night hadn't been a really good day.

Jimena took the phone, studied the picture. "You know, he looks kinda familiar. Is he an actor or somebody famous?"

Reese had another look for herself. He didn't look familiar to her, but he was special. He'd given her the best sex of her life. Right in the nick of time, too, since he would be her last lover.

"Are you going to try to see him again?" Jimena asked.

"No. I don't even know his name. Besides, this morning I found an engagement ring box in his pocket so I think last night for him must have been a sow-your-wild-oats kind of thing."

"Ewww." She jabbed the button to close the photo. "Then he's a hot asshole cowboy."

Yes, he was, if that's what had happened. "But it's possible his girlfriend turned him down. I figure there's a reason he was drinking all that Scotch, and he seemed almost as miserable as I was."

At least, that's how Reese was choosing to see it.

"And the watch?" Jimena pressed.

"The cowboy has it."

However, if Reese had seen that ring the night before, she wouldn't have landed in bed with him or given him the watch. Which meant, of course, that she'd given her most prized possession to a potential hot a-hole, but since this was her fantasy, she preferred to believe that he would treasure it as a reminder of their one incredible night together.

"Good." Jimena made a shivery, ick sound. And Reese knew why. Jimena had this aversion to antiques or rather what she called "old shit previously owned by dead people." That's the reason Reese hadn't given the watch to her one and only friend.

"So, what's left?" Jimena said, looking at the bucket list again.

"Nothing."

And no, Reese wasn't counting throwing away the popcorn glue. Since she'd traveled all over the world, there weren't any places left that she really wanted to see. Besides, she'd learned about four moves ago somewhere around Tulsa that, like tequila, places were really all just the same.

So, there it was—everything important ticked off her bucket list.

For the past week there'd been times when it felt as if a meaty fist had clamped on to her heart to give it a squeeze. That fist was doing a lot of squeezing now.

"I started my own bucket list of sorts," Jimena said. "I've decided to sleep my way through the alphabet so last night I had sex with that busboy named Aaron."

Most people put travel and such on their bucket lists,

but this was so Jimena. She didn't have any filters when it came to sex and saw it more as a recreational sport. Unlike Reese. Sex for her was more like forbidden fruit. It meant tearing down barriers, letting someone into her life, and while it had been an amazing night with the cowboy, part of that amazement was that he hadn't known who she really was.

Not exactly a pleasant reminder.

Reese stood to excuse herself so she could go lie down on the air mattress. Jimena wouldn't even question it, thank God, but before Reese could say anything, she heard the movement in the still-open doorway.

"All the stuff is gone," Reese said, figuring this was just another neighbor responding to her "free stuff" sign that she had taped on the side of the apartment complex's mailboxes.

But it wasn't a neighbor.

It was Dr. Gutzman.

Since Reese had never seen the stocky gray-haired man outside his office and never dressed in anything but a white coat, it took her a moment to realize who he was. Another moment for her to think the worst.

"Did you come to tell me there'll be no radiation, after all?" Reese managed to ask.

He opened his mouth, closed it. Then nodded. "You won't be having radiation," he confirmed.

As much as Reese was dreading the treatments— and she was indeed dreading them—they'd been the tiny sliver of hope. Her 2 percent chance of survival. Of course, she hadn't truly embraced that sliver, but now Dr. Gutzman had just taken it away.

"I'd rather not die in a hospital," Reese volunteered.

Jimena stood and took hold of her hand. Reese could feel the bits of sticky Cheetos on her friend's fingers.

The doctor nodded, came in and eased the door shut. He glanced around the nearly empty room and frowned. Perhaps because of the junk-food stash.

"You're not going to die in a hospital," he said. "At least, not in the next week or so from an inoperable brain tumor."

Reese was still on the page of thinking the worst. "Does that mean I'm going to die even sooner?"

He huffed, glanced around as if this were the last place he wanted to be. "There was a glitch with the new electronic records system. Your images got mixed up with another patient. When I realized the mistake, I had a look at yours, and other than an enlarged left sinus cavity, you're fine."

Reese couldn't speak. She just stared at him, waiting for the other shoe to drop. The doctor didn't look like a prankster, but maybe this was his idea of a really bad joke.

"Did you hear me?" he asked.

She had. Every word. And Reese was desperately trying to process something that just wasn't processing in her mind.

"So, there's really nothing wrong with her?" Jimena asked.

"Nothing. She's as healthy as a horse."

Reese hadn't been around too many horses to know if they were especially healthy or not, but she would take the doc's news as gospel.

Right after she threw up, that is.

God, she was going to live.

LOGAN SLAMMED DOWN the phone. Jason Murdock, his friend and the rancher Logan had been buying stock from for years, had just given Logan a much-too-sweet deal on some Angus.

Hell.

Much more of this and Logan was going to beat the crap out of somebody. Especially the next person who was overly nice to him or gave him a sweet deal on anything.

For the past three months since the mess with Helene, nearly everybody who called or came into the office was walking on sonofabitching eggshells around him, and it not only pissed him off, it was disrespectful.

He'd run McCord Cattle Brokers since he was nineteen, since his folks had been killed in a car crash, and he'd run it well. In those early years people had questioned his ability to handle a company this size.

Silently questioned it, anyway.

But Logan had built the image and reputation he needed to make sure those questions were never spoken aloud. He'd done that through ball-busting business practices where nobody but nobody walked on eggshells. Yet, here they were all still doing just that. After three months.

Not just his family, either.

He'd halfway expected it from Riley, Claire, Lucky and Cassie because they'd been at the scene of what Lucky was calling the great proposal fuckup. Logan expected it, too, from his assistant, Greg Larkin, since he was the sort who remembered birthdays and such shit.

But everybody in Spring Hill who'd had a reason to come to Logan's office door had looked at him with those sad puppy-dog eyes. He could only imagine how bad it was when those puppy-eyed people weren't right in front of him. All the behind-the-hand whispers were no doubt mumbles about poor, pitiful Logan and what Helene had done to him.

Logan tried to make a note on the business contract he was reading and cursed when his pen didn't work. He yanked open his desk drawer with enough force to rip it from its runners, and got another reminder he didn't want.

That blasted gold watch.

Why he still had it, Logan didn't know, but every time he saw it he remembered his night with Julia. Or whatever the hell her name was. She should have been nothing but a distant memory now and soon would be once he found her and returned the blasted watch. Until then, he moved it to his bottom drawer next to the bottle of Glenlivet he kept there.

Of course, if it hadn't been for the Glenlivet, he probably wouldn't have slept with Julia and wouldn't have had the watch in the first place.

Logan moved it to the bottom drawer on the other side.

Damn it all to hell!

The engagement ring was still there, too. The bottom drawers of his desk were metaphorical land mines, and this time he made a note. Two of them.

Get rid of the ring.

Find Julia and have someone return the watch.

Logan didn't want the ring around because he was over Helene. And as for the watch—he didn't want it around in case there was something to the blackmail/extortion theory he'd had about her. Even though it had been three months since their encounter, that didn't mean she wasn't out there plotting some way to do something he wasn't going to like. That's why he'd hired a private investigator to find her, but so far the PI had come up empty.

"Don't," Logan barked when Lucky appeared in the doorway of his office.

He hadn't heard his brother coming up the hall, but since Lucky was wearing his good jeans and a jacket, it probably meant he was there for a meeting. Lucky certainly wouldn't have dressed up just to check on him.

"Don't interrupt you, or don't draw my next breath?" Lucky asked. He bracketed his hands on the office door, cocked his head to the side.

"Both if you're here to talk about anything that doesn't involve a cow, bull or a horse."

"How about bullshit?"

Logan looked up from the contract to see if Lucky was serious. He appeared to be. Just in case, Logan decided to clarify. "Bullshit that's not specifically related to anything that involves my ex?"

"Well, unless Helene has started secretly pooping in the pastures, it doesn't," Lucky confirmed.

Logan was almost afraid to motion for Lucky to continue, but he finally did. Curiosity was a sick thing sometimes.

"You haven't been to the house, well, in a couple of months," Lucky went on, "but I had thirty bulls delivered to those pastures and corrals we talked about using."

So, definitely not a Helene problem. And Logan knew which pastures and corrals Lucky meant. The pastures were on the east side of the house, and with

the right mixture of grasses for the young bulls they'd
bought so they could be trained for the rodeo.

"The wind must have shifted or something because,
this morning, all you could smell was bullshit in the
house. Everybody's complaining, even Mia," Lucky
added.

A first for Mia. To the best of Logan's knowledge,
the four-year-old girl never complained about anything.
Unlike her thirteen-year-old sister, Mackenzie. Lucky
and Cassie had guardianship of the pair, but the girls
were yin and yang. If Mia was complaining, Logan
didn't want to know how much Mackenzie was carrying on. Or the longtime housekeepers, Della and Stella,
who also lived at the ranch.

"You're sure it's bullshit and not cat shit?" Logan
asked. Because along with inheriting guardianship of
the girls, Lucky and Cassie had also inherited six cats.
Five of those cats were now at the ranch.

Lucky shook his head. "Definitely bullshit, and I
should know because I'm a bullshit connoisseur."

Since Lucky had been riding rodeo bulls for more
than a decade, that did indeed make him an expert. Not
just on the crap but the bulls themselves.

"That means I'm going to need to move them,"
Lucky went on, "and I was thinking about the back
pastures. But Rico said you were planning on putting
some horses back there."

He was. Or rather, Riley was since he was in charge
of the new cutting horse program that they'd started.
And Riley and Logan had indeed discussed that with
Rico Callahan, one of their top ranch hands.

Logan sat there, debating on which would smell
worse—horseshit or bullshit. It was a toss-up. "Move

the bulls to the back pastures," Logan finally said. "When the horses arrive, I'll have Riley split them in the other pastures for the time being."

It was a temporary fix since Riley would eventually want the cutting horses together so they'd be easier to train, and that meant they needed to prep one of the other two pastures they weren't using. The problem at the McCord Ranch wasn't enough land—there was plenty of that—but with their operation expanding, they needed someone who could manage the ranch grounds themselves. Someone more than just the hands.

"Hire whoever you need to fix this," Logan told his brother.

Whenever he was talking to Lucky, his twin, Logan always tried to tone down his voice. After all, Lucky could have been co-CEO, but in his will, their father had named only Logan. Logan supposed he felt guilty about that, but then until recently Lucky had shown zero interest in being part of McCord Cattle Brokers. Since it was something Logan had always wanted—all of his siblings helping him with the family business— he didn't want to push any of Lucky's buttons that might be waiting to be pushed.

Lucky mumbled that he would hire someone and checked his watch. "Say, it's lunchtime. Wanna go over to the Fork and Spoon and grab something to eat?"

Logan figured that was Lucky's plan all along, to get him out of the office because Lucky could have just called with the bullshit problem. Lucky did have an office just up the hall, but he rarely used it. He wasn't a behind-the-desk kind of guy. Plus, he still had his own rodeo promotion company to run. What with raising two kids and being in a fairly new relationship, Lucky didn't have a lot of free time.

Which meant this was a coddling attempt on Lucky's part.

"No." Lucky held up his hands in defense as if he knew what Logan was thinking. Maybe he did. Logan had never experienced that twin telepathy thing, but it was possible Lucky did. Of course, telepathy wasn't needed since Lucky had seen what Helene had done.

"You're not here to check on me?" Logan clarified.

Lucky shook his head. "Della's on a health kick and is making baked chicken and salad for lunch. I want a mystery-meat grease burger and soggy fries from the Fork and Spoon."

Logan gestured for him to go for it.

Lucky huffed. "The waitresses," he said.

And Logan got it then. Not from telepathy, either. But Lucky had a reputation as a player, and despite the fact that he was now involved with Cassie, the waitresses and some other women in town seemed to enjoy testing Lucky's commitment to Cassie. His brother must want that burger pretty bad to go through another round of that.

"I'm not running interference for you with women," Logan warned him.

"No need. They'll be feeling so sorry for you that they'll leave me the heck alone. The last time I was in there, Sissy Lee spilled ice tea on my crotch and proceeded to wipe it off. Really hard and fast. I think she was trying her damnedest to give me a hand job."

If that had come from any other man, Logan would have considered it an exaggeration, but women did stuff like that to Lucky all the time, and it'd started around the time they hit puberty. Logan didn't get it. Lucky and he were identical, but if you put them in the middle of a bunch of horny women, 90 percent of them would go after Lucky first.

"You won't run into Helene," Lucky continued. "She hasn't come back to town since everything happened."

Yeah, Greg had mentioned that, but when his assistant had tried to give him more details, Logan had told him to get his butt back to work. He didn't need details about anything that involved Helene.

"I don't suppose you've heard from her?" Lucky asked.

Logan managed to stave off a scowl. "No. And I don't expect she'll call because I doubt she'll want to explain what was going on in her office that night."

"Oh, I'm pretty sure I know what was going on."

Yes. Logan was sure of that, too. Helene had been fucking a clown.

In hindsight, it was sort of surreal, like a perfect storm of Logan's nightmares. Well, it would have been if he'd had nightmares about Helene being unfaithful. He hadn't because it hadn't even been on his radar. But the clown nightmares? He'd had plenty of those since he was nine years old and had sneaked a copy of Stephen King's *It* from his dad's office.

"Still no idea who the clown was?" Lucky went on.

This time Logan did give him a scowl and no answer. Because no, he didn't have a clue. Nor did he want to know.

Once you saw your girlfriend screwing a clown, it didn't matter who was wearing those big floppy shoes and was behind the white face, red lips and red squeaky nose.

"So, what do you say about having a burger with me?" Lucky pressed when Logan didn't budge, answer or quit scowling. "I want to talk to you on the walk over. Nothing else about Helene, I promise. This is something else. Something personal."

Since the Fork and Spoon Café was only a block and a half up from the McCord building, it would be a short conversation, but he wasn't sure Lucky was going to give up on this. Besides, Logan wanted a grease burger now, too.

Logan slipped on his cowboy hat, grabbed his phone and headed out. "Don't make a big deal about this," he warned Lucky, and then gave the same warning to Greg when they walked past his desk.

The lanky assistant jumped to his feet as if trying to contain his excitement. Maybe because it was the first time Logan had left the building in more than a week. Easy to stay under the roof of the converted Victorian house when he had a studio apartment on the third floor. It was even easier now that he was having his groceries delivered. The only time he left was for a business meeting out of town.

"Not a word," Logan added to Greg because Logan thought he needed to say something to wipe that gleeful look off his face. And Logan tried not to look too displeased that the guy was wearing a purple suit. Yes, purple. "And do the paperwork to finalize the sale of those cows I just bought from Jason Murdock."

Greg nodded, too eagerly, and Logan was sure he was still eager-ing when Lucky and he walked out the front door.

Logan immediately had to pull down the brim of his cowboy hat to shield his eyes. He'd gone too long without sunshine, and it would continue. The less contact he had with people right now, the better. In a couple more months when the gossip died down, he'd try to get back to normal.

After he learned what normal would be for him, that is.

"Two things," Lucky said as they walked. "How are you? And before you blast me, Della put me up to it. She and Stella are worried about you. I'm not. Because I know if your head was still messed up, you'd tell me."

No, he wouldn't. Logan wouldn't tell anyone, but he was semipleased that Lucky would think that. Or maybe Lucky knew it and was playing a mind game to get him to talk.

"I'm fine," Logan assured him.

That wasn't even close to the truth. He'd had two migraines in six days, and it felt as if another one might be tapping on his shoulder. He wasn't sleeping well, and when he did, he kept dreaming about what he'd seen in Helene's office. Part of him wished he'd asked her for an explanation. *Any* explanation. But then again, what was she going to say? Nothing that would have helped Logan understand, that's for sure.

"By the way, I've never told you this, but before we walked in on Helene, I didn't know what she was up to," Logan said to Lucky. "I had no idea she could, or would, cheat on me."

"Yeah, I figured that out. I read somewhere that repressed people do all sorts of weird sexual things."

Logan waved off anything else Lucky might have added because two women were walking toward them. Misty Reagan and Sandra Morrelli. He definitely didn't want them to hear anything he had to say about Helene so Logan put on his best smile, tipped his hat in greeting and then proceeded to talk to Lucky about those cows he'd just bought. Lucky cooperated, of course, but the conversation must have looked intense enough for the ladies not to issue more than smiles and greetings of their own.

Two bullets dodged.

"What'd you want to talk to me about?" Logan asked.

When Lucky hesitated, Logan thought he knew where this was going. "You want to make things official with Cassie and ask her to marry you, and you're hoping I'm okay with it. I am. You two should be together."

"Thanks for that."

It wasn't a grand gesture. Logan had never believed in the misery-loves-company notion. Besides, he was getting daily calls from Stella about how she didn't think it was a good idea for Cassie and Lucky to be *living in sin*, that it wasn't setting a good example for Mia and Mackenzie.

"When will you pop the question?" Logan asked.

"As soon as I get the ring."

Logan thought of the one in his drawer, the one that no one in his family had seen, and he considered offering it to Lucky. But then maybe it was jinxed or something.

Hell, maybe *he* was jinxed.

"Along with marrying Cassie," Lucky continued, "we've started paperwork to adopt the girls. Surprised?"

"Not in the least." But just three months ago, he would have been. However, Logan had no doubts now.

None. Because his brother was in love, and Logan was completely happy for him.

They were still a few yards away from the Fork and Spoon when Logan got a whiff of the burger that brought in lunchtime diners. Today was no different. Because of the glass front on the café, it was easy to see that the place was packed.

Crap.

He nearly turned around, but Lucky took hold of his arm and maneuvered him inside. The chatter stopped immediately, and the place went silent as a tomb. He should have just ordered takeout and had Greg pick it up.

"They need to see you out and about," Lucky whispered to him. "And it won't be long before they'll have something else to gossip about."

Logan wasn't betting on that. Despite three months passing, Helene was still the most tongue-wagging topic with Logan coming in a close second. The speculation about what he'd seen in Helene's office had probably reached levels of absurdity times ten.

"Hey, maybe I can start a rumor that I knocked up Cassie?" Lucky suggested.

Logan appreciated that, but he thought the offer might have something to do with Sissy Lee Culpepper, who was sauntering over to them. The busty blonde in the skintight Pepto Bismol–pink uniform eyed Lucky. Then she eyed his crotch. She then did the same to Logan and smiled, maybe because she remembered he was the lone McCord male left on the market.

"The only thing open is the counter," she said, "but I can shoo away someone from a booth if you like."

"The counter's fine," Logan insisted. "Could you get us two burger plates and make it fast? We're in a hurry."

"I want a root beer float with mine," Lucky added.

"Sure thing, sweetie."

Sissy Lee called everyone sweetie, honey or darling so it wasn't exactly a term of endearment. More like a ploy to get a bigger tip.

"And for what it's worth," Sissy Lee said, "I think Helene is lower than hoof grit."

That got some mumbled agreements from the other diners. Logan hoped that the conversation would end if he gave a noncommittal nod.

It didn't.

"I got a name for a woman like that," Sissy Lee added in a whisper. "Hick-dead."

Logan wasn't sure if she was attempting pig Latin and was really calling Helene a dickhead. And he wasn't interested in trying to figure it out. He gave Sissy Lee another noncommittal nod. But it was Lucky's wink and smile that got the waitress moving. She added a wink of her own, and using her best femme fatale hip swish, she walked away.

Logan took the stool at the far end of the counter. Not ideal since the grill was just on the other side of a partial wall, and the smoke from the sizzling burgers came right at them.

"Other than a knocking-up rumor," Lucky continued, "you could give them something new to talk about by going on a date."

Logan gave him a blank stare. "There are no eligible women in town that you haven't slept with already. I don't need that kind of gossip. Or that kind of woman."

Lucky shrugged, made a sound as if that were possibly true. "There are always those dating sites."

He'd rather personally shovel every bit of bullshit from the pasture, one cow patty at a time. "No thanks."

"Then what about—"

"No. Thanks," Logan said a little louder than he intended.

It got people's attention. Not that their attention had strayed too far from him, anyway. He could practically feel the sympathy pouring over him.

"Suit yourself, but I was going to say you should ask her out." Lucky tipped his head to the fry cook. "She's new in town, and I haven't slept with her."

Logan looked up, at the veil of greasy-scented gray smoke that was between them and the cook. And his stomach dropped to his kneecaps.

Maybe Lucky hadn't slept with her, but Logan sure had.

Julia Child was in the process of flipping a burger.

CHAPTER FOUR

OH, GOD. THERE wasn't just one cowboy but two. And they didn't just look alike. They were identical.

Now what?

Reese tried not to react, tried not to give in to the gasp that was inching its way from her throat toward her mouth. But mercy, this was gasp-worthy.

She'd come to Spring Hill hoping to find the hot cowboy she had slept with and get her grandfather's watch back. And she'd wanted to do it without attracting any attention to herself—or to him. Especially since he might be engaged or even married by now. She definitely hadn't wanted to intrude on his life, not after that promise she'd given him.

What happens in San Antonio stays in San Antonio. I'll take this to the grave.

Reese had made that promise when she thought the grave was imminent, and she'd wanted to finish that idiotic bucket list. Well, she had finished it, but now she was in the process of undoing it.

But how did she undo this without admitting that she didn't even know which one she'd bedded? And here she had thought this might be the easiest thing left on her undoing quest.

She had finally lost the weight that she'd put on from her carb and sugar binges and had gotten her money back from the canceled cremation. She'd gone through with the charity donations, though, because it hadn't seemed fair to screw them over just because Myrtle the tumor had turned out to be all just a computer glitch.

That left the cowboy and the watch.

"Uh, you're sorta burning those burgers, sweetie," Sissy Lee said, giving Reese a nudge with her elbow.

Reese forced herself out of her panicking trance and looked down at what had been two one-third of a pound patties of prime Angus beef. They now resembled squashed cow dung.

"Sorry," Reese mumbled, and she pushed those aside, scraped down the grill and added two fresh burgers.

She didn't know the owner, Bert Starkley, that well, but it was possible he'd take them out of her pay. That was minor now compared to the fact that everyone in the café was looking at her and the stenchy smoke she'd created.

"No worries," Sissy Lee assured her. The woman got busy making an ice cream float. "Bert'll just give them to his dogs. But you should make the next ones medium rare since that's how Logan and Lucky like 'em."

Logan and Lucky.

So, those were their names, and since it was obvious that Sissy Lee knew them, Reese would be able to pump her for information.

The only other thing Reese knew was what she'd learned from the hotel clerk after she'd hurried back there to find the cowboy. The clerk couldn't give her the cowboy's name, but he'd said that he saw him driving a truck with a business sign on the side, and the only thing he could remember about the sign was that it had Spring "something or other," Texas, on it.

There were a lot of Spring "something or others" in Texas, Reese had learned, and that's why it had taken her all this time to track him down. Her search had left her a little low on money so she'd stayed around and started the job at the café.

While keeping a close eye on the burgers, Reese risked glancing up at the pair. The one at the far end of the counter glanced at her at the same time. Or maybe he, too, was just looking at the smoke because he gave no indication whatsoever that he knew her. It was possible he couldn't even see her, though. Added to that, her hair was back to its natural color now—dark brown. And the final factor affecting this? He could have been too drunk to remember much of anything.

"Lucky and Logan?" Reese said to Sissy Lee. "Twins, obviously."

Sissy Lee chuckled. Not just any ordinary chuckle. "Yeah, all the women in Spring Hill have fantasies about a threesome with those two."

Reese didn't know about a threesome, but her twosome had been pretty amazing.

"You know them well?" Reese asked, fishing while frying. She added some sliced onion to the grill, swirled it around in the grease runoff from the burger—an artery-clogging topping that Bert had told her his customers loved.

"Of course. Everybody does. They're the McCords. And they've got a brother, Riley. He's taken, though. Actually, Lucky, the one on the left, is maybe taken, too. Everybody in town figures he'll be popping the question to his girlfriend soon."

"Oh?" Reese had hoped her noncommittal response would keep Sissy Lee talking, but when it didn't work, Reese had to come out and ask. "What about Logan? Is he involved with anyone?"

"Was," Sissy Lee said, lowering her voice and speaking behind her hand. "I'll tell you all about it later," she added just as another customer came in.

"Carry those burgers out to Lucky and Logan when you're done, will you?" Sissy Lee scooped up some fresh fries and put them on the sides of the plates. "I'll give Lucky his float and take care of Daniel."

Judging from the dreamy way Sissy Lee said Daniel's name, he was a juicy catch. But then Sissy Lee seemed to feel that way about every single guy who came into the café.

Reese finished the burgers, drowning them in the fried onions and thick slabs of American cheese—again as Bert had instructed. Her waitressing skills were a little rusty, but she balanced the plates, along with two glasses of ice water, and made her way to the counter. She set down the food and drinks, thinking it might be a good idea to make a quick exit and watch the McCords from the kitchen.

That didn't happen.

"You're new here," the one on the left said. He flashed her a smile that could have melted heavy-duty aluminum foil. He still didn't show any signs of recognition. "I'm Lucky McCord." He hitched his thumb to his brother. "This is Logan."

No melting smile from him. No sign of recognition, either. She should have asked Sissy Lee if the third brother was their triplet.

"And you are?" Lucky asked.

"Reese Stephens," she said.

Still no signs that they knew who she was, but then she'd used an alias for the hotel. Julia Child. She looked to see if either of them had caught on to the lame joke of her using a superchef's name when she was nothing but a glorified fry cook. But nada.

Logan checked his watch. "I just remembered a meeting I have in Bulverde," he said, standing.

Lucky had just taken a big sip of the float, and he had to swallow first before he could respond. "What meeting?"

"With that seller. Could you please box this up?" he asked Reese after sparing her a glance. "I'll have my assistant come by and pick it up later." Logan dropped two twenties on the counter and walked out. Not in a hurry exactly but not a man who was dawdling, either.

"It's not you," Lucky said, watching his brother leave. "Logan's had it rough lately. I'm sure you've heard." His gaze drifted to Sissy Lee, who had practically put herself body to body with Daniel.

"I only arrived in town yesterday," Reese said. "I haven't had a chance to hear any gossip."

"Trust me, that's plenty of time. Six seconds is enough time." He paused, tilted his head to the side and looked at her. "Say, do I know you from somewhere?"

Reese pretended to study him, too, though she knew every detail because she'd studied the selfie on her phone. Often. Dark brown hair, cool blue eyes, a face not too chiseled. But it was also a face that was a lot more relaxed than the one on her phone.

"I think I saw you driving around town," she finally said. "Were you in a truck with some kind of sign on the side?"

He nodded, tackled a couple of his fries after he dragged them through some ketchup. "McCord Cattle Brokers, the family business."

Reese needed a bit more than that. "And it had Spring Hill, Texas, on the sign?"

Another nod just as he took a bite of the burger.

So, it was Lucky she'd slept with, and since Sissy Lee had already said he would likely get engaged soon, then Reese needed to figure out how to get the watch without messing things up for him. She definitely wouldn't ask about it here. There were at least six customers seemingly hanging on their every word.

"The trucks were Logan's idea," Lucky added a moment later. "Good advertising, he said. That's why we all drive one. Even our housekeepers do."

All? Well, heck. That put her back to square one.

"Man, this burger's good. I think you're the best cook Bert's ever hired."

"Thanks," she mumbled.

Since it was obvious he was interested in eating his lunch and because she didn't want to pique his attention, Reese took Logan's plate back to the kitchen to box it. She'd barely gotten started, though, when Sissy Lee put in another hamburger order.

"Daniel likes his burger still mooing," Sissy Lee added.

Sissy Lee took over the boxing duties while Reese got started. "I didn't figure Logan would stay too long." She shook her head. "It's the first time he's come over for lunch since Helene, that hick-dead girlfriend of his, messed him up."

As gossip went, that was fairly lacking. "How'd she mess him up?"

"Well, that's just it. We're not really sure. The only person who got a glimpse of it was Walter Meekins, the taxi driver. Logan had called him to drive Riley, Claire, Lucky and Cassie back home after Logan proposed to his girlfriend."

Reese didn't have a clue who Claire and Cassie were, but she didn't want to interrupt Sissy Lee. It wouldn't take that long to cook a rare burger, and then Sissy Lee would go back out to flirt with the customers.

"Anyway, Walter didn't see exactly what happened when Logan and the others went into Helene's office," Sissy Lee explained, "but he said he saw this clown running out the back."

"A clown. You mean like something in a circus? Or a horror novel?" Because Reese wasn't sure if Sissy Lee meant that word in a general sense.

"Circus or rodeo kind of clown," Sissy Lee verified. "Walter said when Logan came out he looked like he'd seen a ghost. He's never been the same since."

Lucky had been so sure that the gossips had filled Reese in by now, but obviously the townsfolk didn't know as much as the McCords thought they did.

"Of course, we don't know who the clown was," Sissy Lee went on. "I thought it was Brian, the guy who worked for Helene, but it turns out that he's gay. Of course, I guess he could actually be bi or else—"

"How long ago did that clown stuff happen to Logan?" Reese interrupted.

Sissy Lee shrugged. "This past summer."

That fit with Reese's timeline of her one-night stand three months ago. Maybe.

Sissy Lee put Logan's boxed burger meal aside, and while Reese dished up Daniel's plate, she got an idea.

"Where do the McCords live? Because I'll have a break soon, and I can drop that off to him."

"It's that big house on the edge of town. Can't miss it. Except Logan doesn't spend much time there anymore. You know that Victorian building just up the street? Well, that's his office, and he has a loft apartment there."

Reese had noticed the house. In fact, she was in the Bluebonnet Inn on the same block. She checked the time—still an hour before her break, but maybe Logan's assistant wouldn't come for the burger before then.

Because Reese wanted to get inside that building. She had some spying to do.

"REESE STEPHENS." Logan repeated her name under his breath as he read the initial report the private investigator had just sent him.

There wasn't much info yet, but then when Logan had called the PI the day before, the man had said it might take a while, that the woman wasn't showing up in his usual search engines.

There had to be a reason for that.

Logan didn't know what game she was playing, but she was up to something. No doubt about it. After all, she had that photo of him on her phone, so even if she'd been too drunk to remember, she would have seen it later and then recognized him at the café. Of course, there was the possibility that she hadn't known whether it was Lucky or him who'd gotten into that hotel bed with her, but there was still no reason for her not to fess up.

No good reason, anyway.

So, why was she here in Spring Hill? The private investigator's initial report certainly didn't help with that. Her name was Reese Violet Stephens. She was twenty-nine, single. She'd attended culinary school in New Orleans and worked as a cook or chef at various restaurants all over the US. However, she'd never stayed at any of them for more than a couple of months. No criminal record—under that name, anyway.

And that was it.

She had no social media accounts, no driver's license, no paper trail that people usually left. That only made Logan even more suspicious. The PI, too, and that's why he was digging deeper. Hopefully, that digging wouldn't take too long.

Logan parked in the circular drive in front of his family's home, and he hadn't even stepped from his truck before he got a whiff of what Lucky and he had discussed the day before.

The manure.

Yeah, it was a problem, all right. The bulls had already been moved, but it might take a while for the stench to clear out.

He was about to head up the steps to the porch when his phone buzzed, and after Logan saw the name on the screen, he knew it was a call he had to take.

Bert Starkley, the owner of the Fork and Spoon Café.

Logan had called him the night before, but Bert hadn't answered so Logan had left him a voice mail. Nothing specific and Logan had to make sure he didn't say anything to Reese's employer that would make the man suspicious. Or make Bert think Logan was interested in her. The last thing Logan needed was more gossip about him and a woman. Especially a woman who was almost certainly bad news.

Later, he'd curse himself again for that one-night stand, but now he needed to find out anything he could about her.

"Logan?" Bert said when he answered. "Is everything okay?"

It was a valid question, considering that Logan had never before called the man. "Everything's fine." And he chose his next words carefully. "I was at the café yesterday for lunch—"

"Yep, I heard. Sissy Lee," Bert added as if that explained everything. Which it did. The waitress had no doubt blabbed to everyone that Logan had left the café in a hurry.

"I had to leave for a meeting," Logan lied. He hated liars, but this little white one was necessary. Even if Bert didn't totally believe that lie, maybe he'd still repeat it to defuse some of Sissy Lee's gossip. And he didn't have to think hard to imagine what that gossip might entail. It almost certainly hinged on Helene.

"Sissy Lee mentioned the meeting, too," Bert verified. "How can I help you? Is this about the catering job?"

Logan frowned. "What catering job?"

"Something Della wanted us to do for her."

This was the first Logan was hearing about it, but then he was too busy to get involved with the daily workings of the house. "No. I was calling about your new cook." Logan left it at that, to see what Bert would volunteer about her.

But nothing.

Clearly, Bert was waiting to see what Logan would volunteer.

"Renee?" Logan finally said. "Is that her name?"

"Reese." Again, that was it. Hell, Bert wasn't cooperating with this at all.

"She looked familiar," Logan continued. "I just wondered how you'd found her?"

"She came into the café, asked about the help-wanted sign that I had in the window. I gave her a trial run to see if she could cook. She can, by the way. I hope you enjoyed that burger she fixed."

He hadn't. Logan hadn't eaten a bite of it, so rather than lie again, he just made a sound of approval. "Reese dropped it off at my office after I had to leave. I wasn't there, but she left it with Greg."

Considering Logan had told Reese that Greg would be picking it up in the first place, he was even more suspicious that the woman had personally delivered it.

"You probably heard that Maggie's got to have some surgery," Bert added a moment later.

Maggie, Bert's wife, and yes, Logan had heard. *Female problems*, which was the only thing Logan had listened to after hearing those two words. "I hope Maggie will be okay," Logan said.

"Oh, she will be. Female problems," Bert repeated. "But it means I'll be out of the kitchen for a while. Reese said she'd have no trouble pulling double shifts for me."

Logan was even more leery. Why was she being so accommodating? Of course, the obvious reason might be that with double shifts she would be earning double pay, but Logan wasn't ready to cut her that kind of slack just yet.

"So, Reese had references when you hired her?" Logan pressed.

"Oh, I get it now. You're wanting to make sure she's experienced enough to do the catering job for Della?"

No, that wasn't it at all. "Is she qualified? What did her previous employers have to say about her?"

"Didn't check them out after I tasted a couple of things she cooked for me. The woman bakes, too. Melt in your mouth pies and cakes. She did this lemon thingy that had all the customers going on about it." Bert paused. "But if you're worried about her, I can check her references. Are you, uh, worried about her?"

The question was reasonable, but Logan heard something in Bert's tone. He'd used the word *worried* but what he really meant was *interested*. Hell's bells. Bert thought Logan was looking to hit on Reese.

"I just want to make sure Reese is the right person for the catering job," Logan clarified, though he was dead certain that wouldn't quell any of Bert's *interested* suspicions since Logan hadn't even known about the catering job before this phone call. "If you could follow through on her references, I'd appreciate it."

"Sure. I'll get back to you."

Logan ended the call, ready to go inside, but once again his phone buzzed. Good grief. At this rate, he'd never get in the house, but again it was a call he needed to take.

Jason Murdock's name was on the screen.

Logan and he had been friends since high school, and when Jason had taken over running his uncle's large ranch about thirty miles from Spring Hill, it made sense for them to do business together. Jason had cows to sell, and Logan needed to buy huge herds so he could resell in smaller groups and make a profit.

But there was a problem with Jason.

"If you're going to give me another pity deal," Logan said when he answered, "then I don't want it."

"Good. Because you're not getting pity from me. I don't do pity deals, pity fucks or pity anything else. I needed to unload those cows because I didn't have the room for them."

Logan wanted to believe him, but their friendship might have caused Jason to bend his no-pitying rule.

"I'm calling about Helene," Jason said a moment later. "And yeah, you can hang up if you want, but her mother, Mary, called me this morning. She was boo-hooing all over the place. She wanted me to try to talk you into seeing Helene."

"No." Logan didn't have to think about that, either. "Why would Mary call you?"

"Because she figured you'd just hang up on her. Let's face it, Logan, you're not exactly the forgiving sort."

He wasn't, and Logan liked that just fine. "Why did Mary want me to see Helene?" Logan asked.

"Hell if I know. And she wouldn't say. She just said it was important." Jason paused. "You know if you ever want to talk about what happened that night with Helene, all you have to do is call me."

"Thanks but no thanks." Logan had enough of those images in his head without reliving them through conversation.

Clowns and liars.

"If Mary calls back," Logan told his friend, "have her call me directly." Not that he especially wanted to talk to his ex's mom, but he also didn't want her pulling Jason into this.

Logan ended the call and went inside to ask Della about this catering issue. However, the moment he opened the door, he realized he might not be able to make a beeline for the kitchen as he'd planned. That's because Lucky and Cassie were down on their knees in the foyer. At first Logan thought he'd walked in on something sexual—always a possibility where his twin was concerned—but then he saw that this was something much more intimate.

Lucky was proposing.

He was in the process of slipping an engagement ring on Cassie's finger, and Cassie had tears in her eyes. Judging from her smile, they were tears of a happy variety.

"Crap," Lucky grumbled. "Sorry. I didn't want you to see this," he added to Logan.

Perhaps because Lucky thought it would bring back bad memories of Logan's own botched proposal. It did, but that didn't mean he wasn't happy for Lucky and Cassie. They were suited for each other, though that wasn't apparent to them when Cassie had come back into Lucky's life almost four months ago.

"I didn't like Lucky being on his knees alone," Cassie said, getting to her feet. "I said yes."

She held out the ring for Logan to see. Since he still hadn't closed the door, the sunlight caught the diamond just right, causing it to glint into his eyes.

It was their mother's ring.

Of course, Logan had always known that it was Lucky's to use if he wanted. Despite their mother only being in her forties when she'd been killed, she had made it a habit of saying which jewelry she would leave for each child. The engagement ring she'd wanted for Lucky. The wedding band for their kid sister, Anna. Logan had gotten her pearl necklace and Riley a gold bracelet.

Precious mementos.

But to Logan the most precious thing was his father's pocketknife. That meant as much to him as the engagement ring had meant to Lucky.

Logan gave Cassie a kiss on the cheek and his brother a hug. "Congrats to both of you. It's about time you made it official." He tried to keep his tone light, and he did mean the congrats. Still, that didn't help with the sudden lump in his throat.

"I'm going to tell Della and Stella," Cassie said, glancing at Logan.

She hurried away, probably because she sensed Logan needed some time with his brother. Or time alone. But while Logan would take that time alone, later, for now he needed to do a little business with Lucky.

"I won't keep you," Logan assured him. "I figure Cassie and you will want to celebrate before the girls get home from school." And by celebrate, he meant they'd want to have sex. "I just wanted to make sure the bull situation had been fixed before I leave for Dallas."

The Dallas trip was legit. Logan was on a 3:00 p.m. flight and would be gone at least a couple of days, but considering he was slammed with work and getting ready for several magazine interviews, he was BS-ing about asking about the BS.

Lucky's flat look told Logan he wasn't buying the reason for this visit. "All right, what's wrong with you?"

Logan hated to play the scorned-lover card, but he would this time. "You know what's wrong with me. That doesn't mean I'm not happy for Cassie and you. I am."

Lucky's flat look continued. "Does this have anything to do with the new cook at the Fork and Spoon?"

Either twin telepathy again or a good guess was in play here. "Why do you ask?" Logan settled for saying.

"Because of the way you lit out of there like your balls were on fire. But maybe they were on fire because of the lie you told her. You didn't have a meeting."

"But I did." One that Logan scheduled as soon as he left the café.

Lucky clearly knew he was semilying, again, but Logan didn't intend to let him in on anything. If Reese had meant "what happens in San Antonio stays in San Antonio," then maybe she had a good reason for not wanting the one-nighter spilled, either.

Of course, that good reason might have something to do with blackmail, but for now Logan would use that possibility to his advantage. Besides, he didn't want Lucky or anyone else to know he'd done something so stupid as to sleep with a woman he didn't know.

Lucky kept staring at him. "Reese and I chatted after you left," his brother tossed out there. And he watched, no doubt to see how Logan would respond.

Logan merely shrugged. At least he hoped that was the only thing his body was doing. "Let me guess— she flirted with you?" Easy guess because most women flirted with Lucky.

"No flirting. She asked about our trucks, said she thought she'd seen me driving one."

Logan's stomach tightened. He'd driven one of the

company trucks to that San Antonio hotel, and if Reese had gotten a glimpse of it, then that could explain how she'd found him. Of course, he'd been on the cover of several Texas magazines, too, so perhaps that's how she had made the connection.

"You're not going to tell me what this is really about, are you?" Lucky asked.

Finally a question where Logan wouldn't have to lie. "No. I need to talk to Della," he said, heading for the kitchen.

Logan didn't have to ask if that's where Della was. He followed the scent of something cinnamon-y to the kitchen and found her taking some fresh bread from the oven. Perhaps an attempt to cover up the bull crap outside, and if so, it was working.

"Well, this is a surprise," Della said. It managed to sound like a greeting and a scolding all at once. A scolding because it'd been a while since he'd been home. "Great news about Lucky and Cassie, huh? She went to the garden to find Stella to tell her. You okay with this?"

"Of course."

"Okay with the ring, too?" Della pressed.

"Of course." Logan moved closer and thanked her when Della cut off a piece of the hot bread for him.

"So, was it lucky timing that you were here for the proposal?" Della continued.

Logan took a second, bobbling the hot bread in his hand and blowing on it. "Bert mentioned you were having something catered? Are you doing that for Lucky and Cassie?"

"For Mia. It's her fifth birthday in two weeks, and

she wanted a fairy-princess tea party. I thought I'd have Reese do it."

Reese?

So, they were on a first-name basis. Logan wanted to ask how that'd happened, but Della had an even better radar than Lucky. Logan definitely didn't want her thinking there was something going on between Reese and him.

"She's got experience doing kids' parties?" Logan asked.

"Don't know about that, but everybody in town is talking about what a good cook she is. She made these lemon thingies that folks are going on about."

"Yeah, I heard. But does she have experience doing kids' parties?" he repeated.

"Don't know, but she's obviously got experience baking. I'm having her do a cake and make some party food. She'll be kinda busy what with Maggie's *female problems*." Della whispered those last two words as if it were some kind of secret. It wasn't. Then she paused, nibbled on a piece of the cinnamon bread. "So, any word from Helene?"

Logan had expected the third degree about his own well-being. Not that, though. "No. I won't hear from her, either." He waited, figuring there was more.

There was.

"Her mother, Mary, called me," Della continued. "We've gotten to know each other over the years because of coordinating Helene's schedule for family events and such. Anyway, I thought you should know that Helene had some kind of mental breakdown. She's in a hospital in Houston."

Suddenly, the bread didn't taste as sweet as it had

a few seconds ago. Logan let the news sink in, and he was thankful that it wasn't the heart-crushing blow it would have been just three months ago. Still, he wasn't immune to the news because Helene had been in his life a long time.

"You want to know any other details?" Della asked.

Thankfully, Logan didn't have to make a decision about that because his phone buzzed, and he saw the new text from the PI. The subject was Reese Stephens aka Reese Stephenson.

So, that explained why the PI had found so little on her during his initial search. Stephenson was her real name. But clearly the PI had learned something else.

"I need to read this," Logan said to Della, and he went out onto the back porch.

Reese's age hadn't changed from the original report. Ditto for her going to culinary school and moving around. But there was a whole lot more to the woman he'd bedded in that hotel.

Logan read through the text, and once he got his jaw unclenched, he actually managed to say something.

"Shit."

CHAPTER FIVE

REESE HADN'T COUNTED on being able to make this trip
to the McCord Ranch so soon after seeing the twins,
but she was thankful that their housekeeper Della had
called and asked her to come over and discuss the party
plans. It was the perfect excuse for Reese to get the information she needed about Logan and Lucky.

Well, hopefully it was.

Considering that everyone in town was talking about
Logan's fast exit from the café, it was possible that
Della was going to try to pump Reese for info while
Reese was pumping the woman. Either way, if this
didn't work, Reese was just going to have to come clean
and admit that she did something so sleazy as have sex
with a man she didn't know. Then she could get back
the watch and put this whole mess behind her.

Even if Reese's body wasn't letting her forget it.

Her body didn't have a say in this, though. She'd
learned the hard way that lust often drove really bad
decisions, and it was obvious that sleeping with either
of the McCord twins was a bad decision she couldn't
repeat.

Reese followed the crude map that Sissy Lee had
made for her. It wasn't that long of a walk, less than a
half mile, and the house was so big that she could see
it long before she got to it. Judging from the sheer size

of it and the land surrounding it, the McCords were rich. Of course, she'd already guessed that, but this was rich-rich, and that meant either Lucky or Logan might be especially concerned about having spent the night with someone like her. If so, that could work in her favor because they could be eager to get rid of her.

Part of her wished that wasn't the case, though.

If this had been just another ordinary town, Reese might have considered staying on longer than three months. The pay was decent, and Bert was a good boss. Shortly after he'd hired her, he'd even helped her find a place to live, temporarily. No way could Reese have managed to swing a stay at the Bluebonnet Inn on a daily basis, but Bert had talked the owner of the inn into renting her the converted attic apartment there. It wasn't much, but then she'd never needed much, and this morning she'd learned it had a special view.

Of the McCord Cattle Brokers' building.

She'd yet to see Logan or Lucky come and go, but from everything she'd heard, Logan only left for business trips, and Lucky was only there when he couldn't avoid it. Or when he was checking on his twin. The buzz was that Lucky was still worried about Logan. Everyone in town was.

Logan was Spring Hill's rock star.

And no one she'd encountered so far was taking his ex's side in the breakup. The general consensus was that Helene should be burned at the stake for breaking poor Logan's heart.

Reese walked up the circular drive, and as she neared the house, she caught the scent of poop. She hoped that wasn't some kind of bad omen.

She made her way up the porch, but the door opened

before she could even ring the bell. The outside of the house was so, well, pastoral looking, but that didn't apply to the inside. The tall brunette woman in the doorway looked frazzled. With good reason. There were cats—lots of them—darting around.

Two small children, as well.

There were shouts of laughter. Plain out shouting, too, from a teenage girl on the stairs who apparently wasn't happy about her sister using her makeup on one of the cats. Reese quickly spotted which cat. It was all white except for pink blush on its cheeks.

"I'm Reese—"

"Yes, I know. Della's expecting you. No school today," the woman said as if that explained everything. "I'm Cassie Weatherall. Please come in."

Cassie as in Lucky's soon-to-be fiancée. Reese recognized her from some TV talk shows, the sort where the host and his or her guests attempted to solve some huge problem in the span of an hour. Minus the commercials, of course. There were usually shouts and paternity test results involved.

Cassie looked around outside before she shut the door. "Where's your car?"

"I don't have one. I walked."

She shook her head. "If you need to come out here again, just call the house, and someone can come and get you. Mia, don't touch Mackenzie's makeup again," Cassie warned the younger girl without even pausing to take a breath.

"Sorry," the little girl said as she flew past them. A little boy was chasing her with what appeared to be a magic wand and a chocolate-chip cookie.

The meager apology was apparently enough to get

the teenager to whirl around and disappear into the hall off the top of the stairs.

"This way," Cassie said after she shouted for the children to settle down.

Cassie might look like the prim and proper therapist, but her shout was all mom. According to the gossip Reese had heard at the diner, Cassie had fallen right into that role. Had fallen into the role of being a McCord, too. Cassie had given up her job as a celebrity therapist and had opened an office in Spring Hill. Considering the divorce rate was almost nil, the crime rate as well, it was possible she wouldn't get a lot of business. Then again, there could be a lot of skeletons jangling in closets.

Reese didn't mean to dodge Cassie's gaze, but she couldn't quite look the woman in the eye. She had no idea if Lucky had actually cheated on Cassie, but if so, it was a little stomach-turning to think that Reese could have been the other woman.

Cassie led Reese to the back of the sprawling house to an equally sprawling kitchen where a woman with pinned-up gray hair was at the stove.

"You're here," Della said, smiling.

But she wasn't alone in the kitchen, and the person at the table definitely wasn't smiling. Even though Reese couldn't be certain, she thought this might be Logan.

"You're late," the man said.

Yes, Logan.

The brusque tone caused Reese to freeze. Not Della, though. The woman popped him on the shoulder with a wooden spoon. "What kind of welcome is that?" Della scolded him.

Reese suspected Della was one of the few people

on the planet who could get away with that question. Or the spoon pop.

Cassie shot Logan a glare. "Reese had to walk here," Cassie informed him.

Logan didn't look exactly pleased with that explanation or the spoon popping. Or with Reese.

"Logan's mad because I said I wasn't going to ask you for references," Della explained.

Oh.

Well, that told her loads. He was suspicious of her. Unless Logan was this careful about everyone who crossed paths with his family.

"We need to talk," Logan told her, and he took hold of Reese's arm.

"She's here to go over the party," Della protested, but she might as well have been talking to the air because Logan didn't listen. And he was out of spoon range now.

Reese didn't put up any resistance whatsoever. She'd come here hoping to have a private word with either Logan or Lucky, and she was apparently going to get it. Though it still didn't mean he was the one she'd slept with. This little chat could be a warning for her to stay away from his brother. Or away from his family's kitchen if he was truly concerned about her references.

Logan led her to the side of the house to a sunroom that overlooked one of the white-fenced pastures. Reese hadn't smelled the poop in the main part of the house, but she certainly did back here.

"Yeah, we're working on that," he grumbled.

Until he said that, Reese hadn't even been aware she was making a face. That's because she was focused on the face Logan was making at her. Sissy Lee had said Lucky had a panty-dropping smile, but Logan must have missed out on that particular genetic trait. His abilities seemed more geared toward intimidation tactics.

"What kind of game are you playing, huh?" Logan demanded.

Since that could cover a lot of territory, Reese went with a question of her own. "What kind of game do you think I'm playing?"

Man, he was the rock star of glares, too. "What happens in San Antonio stays in San Antonio?" he tossed at her.

Bingo. So, he was the one. Part of her was relieved that he was the hot cowboy and not Lucky. At least this way Cassie wouldn't be hurt.

"How did you find me?" he snapped.

"Your truck."

He nodded as if no further explanation was necessary. Reese braced herself for the questions that would almost certainly follow.

Or not.

Logan inched toward her, and it didn't appear he had question-asking on his mind. He moved close enough that Reese caught his scent. Very familiar. And as it had done that night in the hotel bar, his scent slid right through her. Pretty amazing considering it wasn't any particular scent and managed to completely erase the bull-poop odor.

For a moment, she thought he was going to kiss her. He moved in as if he might just do that despite the steely look in his eyes. And for a moment it might have seemed to him as if he were going to kiss her, too. His gaze dropped to her mouth before he snapped it away and met her eye to eye.

"I ran a background check on you," he threw out there.

Of course he had. Reese wondered why she hadn't considered it sooner. Oh, mercy. Not this, not now. Had Logan learned what had happened? She hoped not. She hated the thought of anyone knowing how stupid she'd been.

"Are you here to run some kind of con?" Logan added, and his glare didn't ease up one bit.

So, he'd found out about that part of her past. He didn't know about Spenser. Because if Logan knew that, he would have brought it up first.

"I'm not here to con you." Reese was certain he wouldn't believe her, though. And he didn't.

Logan opened his mouth, no doubt to demand that she leave and never come back, but before he could say a word, someone yelled out, "No!" and it was followed by a loud cry.

Logan scrambled around her, running toward the sound of that cry, and when Reese caught up with him, she saw the little girl, Mia, on the floor at the bottom of the stairs. She was sobbing and holding her arm.

"Mia was chasing the cat on the stairs and fell," Cassie explained.

Cassie wasn't sobbing exactly, but she was crying. And looking very much like a concerned mom. So was the teenager who was coming down the steps to her sister's aid. And the little boy she'd seen playing with Mia earlier. He also had tears in his eyes. Heck, so did Reese, she realized.

"I think it's broked," Mia said through the sobs.

Logan was the only one not in the crying/panic mode. He eased Mia into his arms and started toward the door. "Cassie and I'll take her to the ER. Someone call Lucky and have him meet us there."

"Do you need me to go with you?" Reese asked him.

"No, stay here and finish your *chat* with Della."

Della took out her phone, and Cassie hurried to open the door. Logan followed Cassie out but not before looking back at Reese.

"This isn't over," Logan warned her.

REESE DREAMED ABOUT LOGAN. And tonight it was just as good as the real thing had been.

The kiss in the hotel bar especially.

Until that kiss Reese hadn't been sure she could even go through with the last item on her bucket list, but that kiss had pretty much put to bed any doubts she'd had. And it had just been the start.

Logan had initiated the second kiss, in the elevator as they'd headed up to the room. In fact, the kiss had gotten so scalding hot that his hand had ended up under her top, his leg between hers, and there was a whole lot of pressure from his body pressing hers against the elevator door.

That'd been incredible until the door opened, and they'd tumbled out into the hall and landed on their butts.

The clumsiness hadn't stopped there. Nope. They had been so busy kissing and grappling at each other that they'd banged into the wall outside her room, once with such precision that they'd nearly had accidental sex in the hall.

Even now in the dream, Reese could still feel that

hunger. Hunger she hadn't even known was there. And there were sounds that had never been in the dream before, either. Knocking sounds. It was almost as if Logan and she were having sex against the wall, after all.

Or not.

Because the dream changed. Not to sex with Logan but to another part of her life. One she didn't want to remember. But she did.

Spenser.

It was hard to hide from memories in a dream because they chased you down, chewed you up, and there was nothing she could do to stop it.

But the sound stopped it. And the sound wasn't part of the dream this time. Definitely not Logan. That became clear when she heard someone call out her name. Her real name. Logan had only called her Julia that night. And whoever was calling out her name now was also knocking on her door.

Jimena.

For a moment, Reese thought her friend might be part of the dream, as well. She staggered out of bed and went to the door, checking the time along the way. It was close to midnight.

And it was Jimena, all right.

"Food pimp," Jimena said, holding up several large grocery bags. She came in, looked around. Not that she had to look far to take it all in. It was only about two hundred feet of space for the kitchen, bed, sitting area and bathroom.

"Uh, what are you doing here?" Reese asked.

Not that she wasn't happy to see her, but when Jimena had dropped Reese off in Spring Hill four days ago, Jimena had said she was heading back to Houston to see some old friends. When they'd spoken on the phone earlier that morning, Jimena hadn't mentioned anything about a visit.

"I'm here to help you." Jimena handed her the bags of groceries, which Reese was certain contained nothing but junk food. She closed the door, took Reese by the hand and led her to the window.

"See that guy?" Jimena asked.

There were streetlights, but it still took Reese several moments to pick through the night and see the man in the back parking lot of the McCord building. Definitely not Lucky or Logan.

"Who is he?" Reese wanted to know.

"Some guy I met at a bar in San Antonio. His name is Elrond—you know like in *Lord of the Rings*? His dad was a huge fan. I know, I violated my bucket rule of making my way through the alphabet. I was up to the *I*'s, but all the *I*-guys I met didn't do anything for me. Anyway, Elrond's a great kisser, but he's got something even better in his jeans."

Reese groaned. She was so not in the mood for one of Jimena's sex spill-alls. "I have the breakfast shift at the café. I have to be at work in six hours."

"Well, this shouldn't take long at all." She pointed to Elrond again. "He's got a key to the McCord building."

Instant suspicion.

Of course Reese had told Jimena about her Lucky/Logan dilemma, but she certainly hadn't expected Jimena to do anything about it. Especially anything illegal.

"Did he steal the key?" Reese asked.

"No. He was doing some renovations for the Mc-Cords a while back and forgot to return the key. I figured you could use it to look for the watch while no one's there."

Reese was still skeptical. "And how do you know no one is there? Logan has an apartment on the top floor."

Jimena smiled. "He's not there tonight. Don't you ever listen to gossip? The clerk at the gas station said Logan was in Dallas for a meeting and won't be back until tomorrow."

It was the first Reese was hearing of this—and yes, she did listen to gossip. Hard not to hear it in a town this small. But she hadn't been especially listening for gossip about Logan but rather Mia. It turned out that the little girl's arm wasn't broken, after all, just sprained and bruised.

"You said you were anxious to get the watch and then leave town," Jimena reminded her. "So, here's your chance. Say, what made you so eager to leave, anyway?"

"Logan. He ran a background check on me."

Jimena gasped. A reaction that Reese had had herself. Her past had a nasty way of coming back to haunt her. Usually she could outrun it, but this time it'd caught up with her.

"Did Logan tell your boss?" Jimena asked.

"Not yet. But he will." If it hadn't been for taking Mia to the ER and then this trip to Dallas, Logan probably would have already done it.

That meant tonight might be her last chance to find that watch. Bert probably wouldn't fire her on the spot, but that was only because of his wife's surgery. He needed her for both the breakfast and lunch shifts, but he would give Reese her walking papers as soon as he could find someone else. Or heck, maybe he would just close the café for a while.

"I don't even know if the watch is in the McCord building," Reese admitted.

"Elrond said Logan lives there, like all the time. Where else would he have put it?"

Maybe in the trash, but that tightened her stomach just thinking about it.

"If you find it, you won't even have to do the breakfast shift," Jimena said. "You can grab Tootsie Roll and ride back with me to San Antonio."

It was past being tempting, and it wasn't as if she had a ton of options. Now that Logan knew who she was, he might never give her back the watch because he might think she'd stolen it.

"You're sure you can trust Elrond?" Reese asked.

"The man gives multiple orgasms. Of course I can trust him."

There was no correlation to that, none, but Reese decided she had no choice but to risk it. She put the grocery bags on the counter, pulled on her jeans and a T-shirt and followed Jimena out to the stairs and then out of the Bluebonnet. They didn't walk on Main Street but rather on the street behind the inn. Probably because Jimena wanted to make sure they weren't seen.

Reese only hoped she didn't regret this, but she already had a bad feeling about it.

When they made it to Elrond, he kissed Jimena, and they started in on a make-out session while he handed Reese the key. His aim wobbled, because he had his eyes closed while kissing, and Reese finally just snagged them. Part of her almost hoped the key didn't work, that Logan had changed the locks.

But it worked just fine.

She slipped into the back door, the AC immediately spilling over her. The floors were marble, all shiny and cool, and even the walls had some kind of slick finish to them. The bottom floor was dark except for the base lighting around a copper and bronze sculpture of a longhorn. It was large enough to have been a real cow, and Reese dodged the lethal-looking horns as she made her way around it.

She also had to fight back a scream when something went zipping past her. Sheez. It was possibly a raccoon.

Or a very small, hyped-up guard dog.

It shot out of the reception area and disappeared. No growling sounds. No clawing sounds, either, so she hoped it wasn't coming back for her.

Since she wasn't sure how much time she had, Reese went straight to the hall. There were a series of offices, thank goodness with nameplates on the outside. Logan's was all the way at the end.

And locked.

She tried the key, but it didn't work. Sadly, she knew how to pick a lock, but she hadn't brought the old tools of an old trade with her. Elrond probably had something that would work, but judging from the way Jimena and he had gone after each other, he probably had her on the backseat by now for another round of those multiple orgasms.

Instead, Reese went up the stairs. There were more offices here on the second floor, each door indicating the name of another person who worked for Logan and his brothers. She doubted he'd put a watch in any of these offices so she went up the final flight of stairs to the third floor.

There were double doors, wide-open, so she stepped inside.

Whoa.

Unlike her place at the Bluebonnet Inn, this loft was huge. It sprawled over the entire third floor. There were no overhead lights on, but thankfully there was enough illumination coming from the appliances in the kitchen area that she could see well enough.

And what she could see was a mess.

There were gouges in the walls as if someone had punched it multiple times. No, correction. Someone had thrown stuff at it because some of that stuff was still on the polished hardwood floors. Broken sculptures—including what appeared to be a porcelain breast of a woman. Books. Glass. Feathers. Even the remnants of a coffee table.

Had someone vandalized the place? Robbed it?

That caused her to mumble a couple of "Oh, Gods." Because that might mean this was some kind of setup. Maybe Elrond had willingly given her the keys so she could take the blame for this.

Reese turned to run out, but she caught the movement from the corner of her eye. In case the burglar was still there, she picked up the first thing she could grab off the floor. The porcelain breast. Hardly a serious weapon, but she could hurl it at the person if he attacked, and the nipple might put out an eye.

But he didn't attack.

He stepped from the shadows. Slowly. As if he had all the time in the world.

It was Logan.

And he was naked.

No, not naked. He was wearing boxers, but she had

focused on the naked parts because they were more noticeable. He was sipping a drink, also slowly.

"Reese," he said, his voice low and slightly dangerous.

Or maybe that was confusion in his tone because of the porcelain nippled boob she had aimed at him.

"You didn't take this to the grave very long, did you?" Logan asked, and had another sip of his drink, clearly waiting for her answer.

CHAPTER SIX

LOGAN WASN'T SURPRISED to see Reese. In fact, he'd anticipated it. In hindsight, though, he should have coupled
his anticipation with a pair of pants. Greeting a burglar
in his boxers just wasn't very intimidating.

Reese noticed the boxers, all right. Her gaze slid over
him, and even though he couldn't see her eyes that well
in the darkness, he thought maybe she was remembering the night in the hotel.

Logan certainly was.

In fact, when he'd dozed off earlier, he'd dreamed
about it.

"Should I offer you a drink or call the cops?" he
asked. The second one wasn't really an option, of
course. No way did he want to have to explain this to
anyone. But Reese didn't know that.

"You want the cops to find out you slept with me?"
Reese tossed right back at him.

So she did know it was a bluff. She probably thought
that made this a stalemate. It didn't. Because Logan had
something Reese wanted, and it didn't have anything
to do with the part of his body she was gawking at.

To stop the gawking, Logan took his jeans from the
bed and pulled them on. She looked away when he did
that. Maybe because she realized she'd been gawking,
but her attention landed on the porcelain tit she was

holding. She eased it back onto the floor with the rest of the broken clutter.

It wasn't just any old porcelain tit, though. It'd been a "special" gift from Helene. Molded porcelain bookends of her breasts. An inside joke between the two of them. But one of the bookends had gone missing before she'd been able to give the set to him so Logan had instead used it as a decorative figurine.

Logan also took his dad's knife from the nightstand and slipped it in his pocket. Not because he thought he might need it to get Reese out of there but because he didn't want to risk her stealing it.

"By the way," she said. "There's a raccoon or weird dog running around downstairs."

"Cat," he corrected. "A couple of months ago my brother brought three cats here to stay temporarily. He moved the other two, but no one's been able to catch that one."

He could understand, though, how she'd mistaken it for a raccoon because it did look like one. And Reese suddenly looked a little horrified.

"Months?" she questioned. "Please tell me someone's feeding it."

He nodded, not that he wanted to have a conversation about the feline he'd dubbed Crazy Cat. "My assistant, Greg, leaves out food and changes the litter box."

Though Greg had yet to see the cat. In fact, to the best of Logan's knowledge, only he and now Reese had actually seen it since it had been brought to the building.

And this wasn't at all what he wanted to discuss or think about.

"Redecorating?" she asked. She didn't sound concerned that she'd just been caught breaking and entering. But she did look nervous. Reese was rubbing her hands along the sides of her jeans.

"More or less."

Definitely less. The items were all things Helene had given him, and for some reason it gave him pleasure to smash them to bits. And then look at the bits. Strange because usually he couldn't stand clutter or anything out of place, but he had no desire whatsoever to clean up this mess. In fact, he was enjoying watching the fine layers of dust build up with each passing week.

Reese stayed quiet a moment while she studied him. "It really was you with me in San Antonio. After I left your house, I considered the possibility that maybe you were trying to cover for your brother, and that perhaps he'd told you what the note I left in the hotel room said. You could have done that so his girlfriend wouldn't be hurt. But it really was you. I can see it now."

It did sting a little that she hadn't been able to see it right off. He might look like Lucky, but they didn't act anything alike. Of course, he hadn't been acting like himself at that hotel, either.

"Julia Child," he said to remind her that she had been the one to set the rules for that night.

Reese nodded, pushed her hair from her face. "Hot no-name cowboy."

He waited to see if she was going to explain any of what'd happened that night. Apparently not.

"I came for the watch," she said.

Yes, he'd figured that out. But what he hadn't figured out was why. "Was it part of some con?"

Now, most people would have looked shocked and asked, What con? Or seemed outraged at such a suggestion. But because he'd run that background check on her and because she'd just broken into his place, Reese probably knew outrage and surprise would seem as genuine as the name she'd given him in that bar.

"I'd like to have that drink now," she said.

Reese sank down onto one of the chairs in the sitting area. The stuffing was coming out of it, and it was covered with feathers from the throw pillows he'd gutted. Since it was copper colored, it looked like a huge molting chicken.

The drink offer hadn't been genuine, but since Logan needed a refill, he flipped on the lamp and poured them each a glass. He handed it to her and then backed away. Even though he had on jeans now, he was still shirtless, and he was remembering the heated look she'd given him earlier.

A look he'd probably given her, too.

He didn't understand why his body was attracted to this con woman, and he didn't care. The attraction wasn't going to play into this.

"How did you get into the building?" he asked. "Did you pick the lock?"

"Key." She fished through her jeans pocket, came up with a key and dropped it on the small table next to the chair. "And don't ask how I got it."

"How'd you get it?"

She tossed back the shot and made a face just as she'd done after the tequila shots in the bar. "Found it. And no, I didn't steal it. Nor did I steal anything once I was inside." Reese paused. "You found out about my parents."

"Yes," he settled for saying. Logan didn't add more. He wanted to see what spin she would put on this.

But there was no spin. She waited him out, and Logan decided he'd already spent too much time on Reese.

"Your parents, Marty and Vickie, are con artists. Your father died in prison a few years ago, but both have multiple arrests for pulling various scams. Scams in some cases where they used you."

The PI had provided Logan with only one such case, but he figured there were more. In the one that the PI had learned about, Reese had distracted a store owner, claiming she fell and was hurt, while her parents stole items.

"That incident with Mia must have brought back some memories for you," he snapped. "Of course, the difference is she wasn't faking. So, what else did you fake? Did you pretend to be attracted to me—"

She came off the chair so fast that Logan didn't have time to react. Reese took hold of him, jerked him to her and kissed him. It wasn't the first time he'd been forced-kissed. It had happened one other time when he was a stupid teenager and had pretended to be Lucky so he could break up with a girl who was giving him some trouble.

That kiss was nothing like this one.

For one thing, there was some anger involved here. Not on his part. Logan was still trapped between surprise and "what the hell is she doing?" stage. Reese, though, was obviously trying to make a statement, and that statement was that she could make him feel the kiss in every inch of his body.

Every. Inch.

And she succeeded.

By the time she let go of him, Logan had moved on

to the next stage. A hard-on. But since his dick had already caused him to make a bad decision by sleeping with her in the first place, Logan ignored the ache in his groin and stepped back.

"That's why I slept with you," she growled. "It didn't have anything to do with who I am, your bank account, your ranch or your dusty stuff." Reese flung her hand at the damaged items again.

The kiss obviously hadn't affected her the same way it had affected him. Or so he thought. But then Logan heard her uneven breathing, saw the flush in her cheeks. Saw her glance at his hard-on. A long glance. That caused her breathing to become even more ragged.

It didn't mean anything, of course.

So what if they were attracted to each other? It didn't mean he was going to act on it. However, he was going to act on something else—getting her out of his life and away from his dick.

"For the record, I haven't seen my mother in over two years," she finally said, sinking back down onto the chair. "I really am a chef. Went to culinary school. And I wasn't running a con on you."

"Really?" He couldn't have possibly sounded more skeptical.

"Really." And she couldn't have possibly sounded more pissed off. "What else did your spies dig up on me?"

Nothing. But clearly they'd missed something. Something that Logan would have them dig even deeper to find.

"Aren't your con-artist parents enough dirt?" he asked her.

She stayed quiet again for several moments, but

Logan thought she might be relieved. Yeah, there was definitely something else to learn about Reese Stephenson.

"I've done everything I can to distance myself from my parents and the things they did," she finally said. "I never stay in one place for too long because I don't want my mother to find me."

"Then that should fit right into my plans." He nearly brought up that he didn't know what her plan had been, but he decided it wasn't wise to risk another kiss. There were condoms in the loft, and he didn't want that hard part of his body suggesting sex.

"What plans?" she asked.

"For you to leave." He heard the words. The tone. It was probably a tone he used daily to someone involved in his business deals. But it did sound a little Old West, as if he were running her out of town.

Which he sort of was.

"I can't leave," she said on a heavy sigh. "Maggie's got female problems. Her uterus collapsed—"

Logan groaned. "I don't want to hear that. I know you're pulling shifts for Bert, but once that's done, there'll be no reason for you to stay."

"No reason other than that watch."

Logan took the laptop from the floor next to where he'd been sitting and showed her the screen. Footage from the security cameras. "Less than ten minutes ago, I saw you try the door to my office. Were you trying to take something more than the watch?"

She glanced at the screen, then at him. "If you have a security system, why didn't it go off when I came in the building?"

"Because I didn't arm it. I figured you'd come eventually, and I wanted to see what you were going to do."

"The watch," she repeated.

And maybe it only was, but Logan needed more. "If the watch means so much to you, why did you put it in my pocket?"

"I nearly didn't. After I saw the engagement ring."

Yes, that would have been a shock. Well, maybe. If it was a con, then nothing should have shocked her. If he was merely her no-names-allowed one-night stand, then she probably thought he was a sleazebag.

"An asshole," Reese corrected as if she'd known what he was thinking. "But then I didn't ask about your relationship status, and you didn't ask about mine."

"Glenlivet," he said.

"Tequila," she countered.

That was the problem with too much alcohol. It dulled people's minds so they didn't ask the right questions. Well, he was asking them now.

"Why give me the watch?" he pressed. "Was it because it was stolen and you didn't want to get caught with it."

Her eyes narrowed. "Don't make me kiss you again."

His body rather liked that threat. Thankfully, his face scowled instead, as though trying to discourage a reaction. "I thought maybe you were setting me up. Giving me stolen goods that you could use to blackmail me with later."

She looked at him as if he'd sprouted an extra nose. "It belonged to my grandfather."

Logan wasn't sure how to respond to that. "If that's true, then why the hell would you give it to me?"

"I thought I was dying, okay!"

Of all the things that Logan had thought she might say, that wasn't one of them. As cons went, it was darn original.

"I had a bucket list," she added a moment later.

Logan thought about that a second. "And I was on it?"

"Not you specifically, but it was always a fantasy of mine to be with a hot Texas cowboy."

It was a little disarming, and flattering, to think he'd been her fantasy. Well, if he believed her, that is. He didn't.

"If it was so special, why couldn't you tell me apart from my brother when you got to town?" he asked. "Most people can."

"Tequila," Reese repeated. "Trust me, I can tell you apart now. Lucky actually seems like a nice guy. He smiles. And he doesn't bark and growl at people."

Logan hadn't put much stock in the flattering fantasy, but that stung a little. Because it was true. Lucky was a nice guy, and everybody, especially women, loved him. Women had come on to Logan before, even while half-drunk in bars, but it was a rare occurrence. For Lucky, it was an hourly thing.

"I'm the kind of man I need to be to run this business," Logan said, though he wasn't sure why he felt the need to explain himself to her.

"Right. Let me guess. When your folks died, you took it on yourself because you're the oldest. By two or three minutes at most. Or maybe your father—because you were probably closer to him than your mother—asked you to take care of things. And you did. You've devoted your life to taking care of things."

Since that was an eerily accurate summary, Logan just shrugged.

"I'm also guessing that knife you put in your pocket belonged to your father, and you value it so much that you didn't want to risk me stealing it," she continued. "Or maybe you just like keeping it close."

Both. But Logan didn't confirm it. "What does that have to do with anything?"

"Nothing. But you're the one who brought up the kind of man you are."

So he had. "Well, I know what kind of woman you are. I just don't know why you felt the need to tick me off your bucket list that night."

Reese took a deep breath. "I thought I had an inoperable brain tumor and was supposed to start radiation treatments two days after we met. But it turned out to be a mistake. The hospital mixed up my records with someone else. Shannon Satterfield. She did die, by the way."

With any good con, the devil was in the details, and Reese was certainly providing the details. Logan needed to find the devil in them now.

"So, that's why I was in that hotel bar," Reese continued. "And you were there because of Helene."

Reese didn't need any big deduction skills to know that. It was all over town, but no one other than his immediate family had seen exactly what had gone on in Helene's office. In hindsight, Logan supposed plenty would have found it funny, but Logan didn't have that kind of fun meter.

"I'm sorry," Reese said. "I've been cheated on before, and I know it sucks."

He was betting she'd never walked in on her boyfriend having sex with a clown.

She stood, faced him. "Look, just give me back the watch, and I'll leave town as soon as Maggie's uterus is well enough for Bert to return to work."

Most men would have just given her back the watch then and there and made sure she kept her promise to leave town, but Logan wasn't most men.

"Here's how this will work," he said. "You'll do the shifts you promised Bert, then leave. Once you're out of town, you'll call me, and I'll drive to wherever you are and give you the watch. That way, I know you won't stay here and run a scam."

Oh, that did not set well with her. "Fine," she grumbled, and Reese headed for the door. She made it a whole couple of steps before she whirled back around.

She was going to kiss him again. Logan just knew it. And all so she could prove some stupid point that didn't need proving—that they were attracted to each other.

So, he did something about that.

He latched onto the back of her neck, hauled her to him and kissed her before she could kiss him. As ideas went, it was a truly bad one. Because he got a jolt of a reminder of her taste. Another jolt that his hard-on could apparently get harder, after all.

Logan kissed her, deepening it, pressing her against him. And he got another reminder: that he was playing with fire.

The problem with that was the fire was playing right back.

CHAPTER SEVEN

LOGAN FORCED HIMSELF to listen to what was going on in the meeting. Like most of his meetings, this one was important, but he just couldn't seem to process the big picture as he normally could. Too many nonbusiness thoughts.

Many of those thoughts involved Reese.

Because it'd been a week since their kissing session in his loft, Logan had figured this fire for her would have cooled. Or at least Maggie would have healed so that Bert could take over his shifts and Reese could leave town. But apparently Maggie had a uterus that didn't want to cooperate because Reese was still at the Fork and Spoon, and Logan was still trying to get her out of his head.

"Well?" someone said, and since that seemed to be directed at him, Logan looked up to find everyone staring at him.

Lucky, Jason, Riley and Greg. It was Jason who'd issued the "Well?" but Logan didn't have a clue what he was supposed to say. That's because other than that one word he hadn't heard the conversation for the last three minutes.

Possibly five.

"Say, Greg, could you get us some coffee?" Lucky asked the assistant. "I think we could all use a break."

Lucky was clearly looking out for him, probably because he thought Logan was slipping into a depression or something. He wasn't. But Logan didn't intend to tell his brother or anyone else that what was slipping was his sanity. Because he was obviously a fool to be spending this much mental energy thinking about a woman like Reese.

Greg scurried out in that twitchy way he had about him, and that's when Logan noticed Greg had a big red zipper running down the back of his yellow jacket. Probably some kind of fashion statement, but Logan wasn't even going to attempt to figure out what that statement was.

"Doesn't that guy own any normal clothes?" Jason mumbled.

"Apparently not," Logan answered, and his brothers made sounds of agreement.

"You should get a cowboy in here," Jason suggested. "At least one to man the front desk."

Logan huffed. "I tried that once. Let's just say I need slightly better people skills than the cowboy I hired. Greg's good at everything but clothing choices." He paused. "So, what did I miss?"

"You signed over your bank account to us," Riley joked. And he stared at Logan, apparently waiting for some kind of explanation as to why he'd tuned out.

"Headache," Logan said, tapping his temple. Not exactly a lie. He'd battled a migraine just the day before, and he still had traces of it.

Even though he'd never talked about his headaches to anyone but Lucky, Riley and Jason didn't seem surprised, which meant maybe Logan hadn't been as good at masking the pain as he'd thought. He certainly hadn't been good at masking his distraction.

"What's the bottom line here?" Logan asked Jason so he could get back on track and finish this.

To get the blood circulating better, Logan stood from the large oval desk in the meeting room and went to the window. Since this particular room was on the second floor, he had a bird's-eye view of Main Street. And, if he craned his neck just a little, of the Fork and Spoon. If he craned his neck in the other direction, he could see the Bluebonnet Inn where Reese was staying.

"Well?" Lucky asked again.

Apparently, with all that craning, Logan had missed the bottom line.

"Sorry, Jason, but I think we should put off buying the bulls," Lucky said, saving Logan's butt. Logan would thank him for it later. "The price is decent. Not great, mind you. You could do better, but we're heavily stocked at the moment."

Logan nodded and returned to the desk. "Can you hold off another month so we can reassess?" he asked Jason.

Jason flexed his eyebrows, huffed, signs that he didn't want to hold off, but he would. Maybe in a month Logan would have his head back on straight. Except he hoped it didn't take that long.

Greg came back in, scurrying still. The man moved like a cartoon character who drank an hourly six-pack of Red Bull, and he deposited a tray with coffee on the center of the table.

"Thanks," Logan said. "The meeting's done, but could you arrange a cleaning crew to go to my loft and remove everything but the appliances, my desk and my clothes? I also want them to patch up the holes in the wall."

The four men looked at him as if he'd lost his mind. He hadn't. This was the next step to regaining it.

"Anything else?" Greg asked.

"Call Henderson's and see if they can deliver new furniture as soon as the cleaning crew is done."

"Uh, what kind of furniture?" Greg asked.

Since this had always been Helene's domain, Logan didn't have a clue. "You decide."

Despite Greg's questionable taste in clothes, it wouldn't matter. Henderson's was the only furniture store in town, and they didn't have a purple or yellow piece of anything. Whatever Greg picked out would be boring and tasteful.

Greg jotted that down, hurried out. Riley and Lucky mumbled something about getting back to work, leaving Jason and Logan alone. Jason shut the door.

"Trying to rid yourself of Helene?" Jason asked.

"Yes," he admitted. Rid himself of the pieces of her, anyway, since he'd bashed most of the things she'd put in his loft.

Like a moth to a flame, Logan went to the window again and started more neck craning. He'd quit asking himself why he was doing it. "Della said Helene had a breakdown."

"I heard that," Jason admitted, then joined Logan at the window. "Do you still love her?"

"No." Logan didn't even have to think about that.

Jason shook his head, blew out a deep breath. "You two were together a long time. You're sure you just want to throw that all away?"

That was possibly the only question that could have

pulled Logan's attention away from the window. His friend, who was about to cross a line he shouldn't.

"You think I should forgive her?" Logan asked, already knowing that wasn't going to happen.

Jason nodded. "Not for her sake but for yours. Clearing out your loft is a good start. You need to do things like that to get your life back on track. But forgiving Helene is part of that, too." He paused again. "Did you ever really love her?"

Yep, that line had just been crossed, and Logan would have told Jason that if he hadn't looked back out the window and seen something that caught his attention. Reese, coming out of the Bluebonnet Inn. Since it was ten fifteen in the morning, she was no doubt on her way to the café to get ready for the lunch shift.

Logan was suddenly in the mood for a burger.

Which he'd resist, of course.

It was one thing to spy on her, just to make sure she wasn't up to something, but there was no reason for him to spy on her face-to-face. Or eat what she cooked.

Reese glanced around, something he'd noticed that she usually did. It was as if she expected someone or something to jump out at her. Probably something she'd learned from her con-artist past. But she didn't just look around. She also looked up.

Logan stepped back a little because she glanced up at the McCord building. Not at this particular window exactly. She seemed to be glancing at his loft. Reese might have done that because she expected him to be watching her.

Which he was.

He'd warned her that he would be keeping an eye on her. Despite that scalding kiss a week earlier, he had let her know that he still didn't trust her. That made him seem a little off-balanced because why would he kiss a woman he didn't trust? The bigger question, though, was why did he want to kiss her again?

He wouldn't. No way. And he wanted to believe that. Man, did he.

The best thing would be for Maggie to get better so Bert could return to his regular hours. Then he could give Reese the watch and send her on her way. That was the way to ensure there were no more kisses.

"Sorry," Jason said. "I just stepped in shit with that question about Helene. I'll take it back."

Good. Because Logan had no intention of dignifying it with an answer.

"That's the new cook at the Fork and Spoon," Jason remarked. "Have you had one of those lemon thingies she makes?"

"No." But Logan was starting to think he was missing out on something amazing since people brought it up all the time.

"It just sort of melts in your mouth," Jason went on. "She's attractive, isn't she? You know, in a hot unmade-bed kind of way? I know she's not my usual type, definitely nowhere near your type, either, but I was thinking about asking her out for a drink."

Jason was certainly stepping in a lot of shit today, and Logan was about to tell him that it was time for him to leave, but he saw something that grabbed his attention even more than Reese had.

The man following her.

The guy appeared to be in his late forties, thinning ginger hair, skinny, with a face like a rooster. He stepped out from the alley by the hardware store and fell in step behind her.

"You recognize that guy?" Jason asked, following Logan's gaze.

"No."

Reese kept on walking, but when she reached the Lookie Here Thrift Shop, she must have seen the guy's reflection in the storefront windows. She stopped, turned and faced him. Judging from her body language, she certainly recognized him. Logan wished he had binoculars because it was hard to see her expression, but he thought he saw her shoulders go stiff.

So did the man's.

They stood there, staring at each other, reminding Logan of two Old West gunslingers about to draw on each other. They stayed that way for several tense moments before the man reached out and slammed Reese against the door of the Lookie Here.

REESE'S HEAD WAS in the clouds. Or rather her eyeballs were on the window of the McCord building, and that's why she had no idea how long the man had been following her. But after seeing his reflection, she had no doubts that he was indeed following her.

Chucky Dayton.

She so didn't have time for this now. Reese spun around, stopping him in his tracks. He was scowling, but then she'd never seen Chucky without a scowl. She wasn't sure if his face had frozen that way in some kind of weird tic or if he saved those craggy scowls just for her.

"Reese." He said her name as if she were a persistent toenail fungus. "You know how long it took me to find you?"

"I'm guessing here…but about eight months."

Except it wasn't really a guess. He'd found her in Abilene, threatened her, scowled at her and generally made her life miserable until she'd left. Then again, she'd been planning on leaving Abilene that week, anyway. Chucky's arrival had just sped things up a bit.

"Eight months, three days," he corrected as if she'd just made a huge error in her time calculations. "I guess you didn't think I'd find you."

"No. I knew you would. You usually do." It just surprised her that it always took so long. She only used two names—Reese Stephens and Reese Stephenson. A three-year-old with a couple of minutes of internet access probably could have found her.

"And I'll keep on finding you," Chucky snarled, "until you give me what you owe me."

"What my parents owe you," she reminded him.

He didn't listen to that. Chucky never did. And it wasn't as if she could blame him for being angry.

Her parents had indeed conned him out of some money. How much exactly she wasn't sure. The first time Chucky had confronted her five years ago, the amount had been five grand. It had increased each time they met so either Chucky was into embellishment, had a bad memory or he continued to be conned by her mother so the amount was going up.

"You're their daughter," he argued. "And since I can't find your mother, that means you owe me. I want my eighteen thousand dollars, and I want it now."

Reese didn't have anywhere near that kind of money, especially after those charity donations she'd made, but even if she had the cash, she wouldn't have given it to Chucky to settle her parents' debt.

"You're not getting a dime from me," she told him. Maybe she should record that promise because she ended up saying the exact thing to him each time. "I don't clean up my parents' messes anymore."

Chucky wobbled his head, possibly trying to look indignant. He probably didn't know it made him look even more like a chicken than usual. "I can make things real bad for you here."

And then he made a mistake.

A big one.

He caught onto Reese and pushed her against the Lookie Here. Chucky didn't put much muscle behind it, probably because he didn't have much of it in his wormy body. But the slight push brought all the memories ramming into her. Just like that, Reese's breath vanished, and her heart was in her throat.

This wasn't Spenser, she reminded herself. And she repeated it like a stupid mantra.

Chucky's push didn't just get Reese's attention. It also got the store owner's attention, and Gemma Craft, who was Bert's cousin twice removed, came running out with a baseball bat. Both the bat and Gemma looked pretty darn lethal, but Reese didn't intend to let someone else fight her battles for her. She went old-school and rammed her knee into Chucky's nuts.

If he had nuts, that is.

Again, he didn't look endowed in any area except for that beak-like nose. However, even his tiny nuts must have been sensitive because he grabbed his crotch with both hands and howled in pain.

Gemma kept the bat lifted like an ax aimed right at

Chucky's head. "You want me to call the cops?" she asked Reese.

Reese didn't get a chance to tell her no, that she would handle this. That's because she heard the footsteps, and glanced behind her to see Logan sprinting toward her. He made it to her with gold-medal-winning speed.

"What the hell's going on here?" Logan demanded.

"This brainless wonder shoved Reese," Gemma explained. "I saw it with my own eye." Gemma hadn't mistakenly omitted the plural. She really did only have one eye, and she wore a patch on the other one.

Judging from Logan's reaction, he'd seen it, too. With both of his eyes. Probably because he'd been looking at her from his window.

Reese doubted that window-looking had anything to do with the kissing, either. No. He was making sure she wasn't stirring up trouble, and here trouble was being stirred up right in front of them.

"I'm calling the cops," Gemma said, turning to go back inside.

"Thanks, but I can handle this," Reese assured her. Possibly a lie.

Probably a lie, she silently amended.

Reese could handle Chucky, all right. That metaphorical three-year-old with a laptop could handle him, but the old memories were washing over her like acid. Plus, there was the new layer added to this. The mess that Chucky would start slinging that would make her not want to handle it. Because this was exactly the sort of thing Logan had been sure she would bring into his life.

"You want to tell me what's going on here?" Logan asked.

Not particularly, but Reese doubted he was just going to walk away. Neither would Chucky, once he could walk, that is. He was still wheezing and holding his bruised nuts as if they were Fabergé eggs.

"This is Chucky Dayton," Reese explained. "My parents conned him, and now Chucky likes to find me and try to intimidate me. In turn, I end up kicking him in the balls."

Logan didn't roll his eyes exactly, but it was close. And he did groan. It had an "I knew it!" ring to it.

"I do intimidate her," Chucky said. Not easily but he got the words out, and his voice was even more high-pitched than usual. "She always runs from me."

"I always move," Reese corrected. "But then I move for all sorts of reasons." The bottom line was that she moved, period, and it rarely had anything to do with Chucky.

She would in this case, though.

"I'm not gonna let Reese get away with this," Chucky snapped. "She kneed me in the privates."

"Because you pushed her against the wall," Logan snapped right back.

So, he'd definitely seen that, and it had probably looked worse than it was, but repeating the analogy again, Chucky had the strength of a three-year-old.

Logan took a step closer to Chucky. He didn't get in his face. Didn't have to. In fact, he didn't even have to take that step to look intimidating. Simply put, Logan did not look like a friendly sort.

"If you don't leave town," Logan told Chucky, the muscles in his face squirming against each other, "I'll have you arrested."

"And who do you think you are?" Chucky fired back.

"Logan McCord."

It wasn't just the name. It was the way he said it. His tone, narrowed eyes and glare were about a thousand steps past the unfriendly stage.

But apparently the name meant something to Chucky, too. Of course, he would have had to be blind and deaf not to know that the McCords were the big guns in this little-gun town. However, it wasn't just fear that crept into Chucky's chicken eyes. It was greed. It was possible he saw Logan as a source for recouping his money.

Damn.

Chucky wasn't dangerous, but he was persistent and annoying, and he would peck away at her by using Logan. And it wouldn't take much. Just dropping the truth about her parents, and that truth would spread like wildfire. It would hurt Logan's good name just because he was standing here protecting her.

Maybe it was Logan's glare, but Chucky finally turned and hobbled away. Reese wished it was the last she'd see of him, but she knew it wouldn't be.

"I'll leave town this afternoon," she said to Logan. "After I finish the lunch shift."

Logan turned that glare on her, and while it did soften just a smidge, it still let her know that he was not happy about this situation. "You're shaking," he pointed out.

"Nerves." Not a lie. Every nerve in her body was just beneath her skin and was zinging.

"He scared you," Logan added.

It was something a normal person said in situations like this. Perhaps meant to give her some kind of comfort, but it sounded as if there was something more to it.

God, did Logan know?

"I need to get to work," Reese insisted. "My shift starts in a half hour."

That was plenty enough time before the café opened at eleven for lunch. Besides, Reese had finished most of the prep after the breakfast shift when she'd clocked out at nine thirty. The break in between the shifts had given her just enough time to go home and fix herself a bite to eat. Something Reese wished she hadn't done because she could have avoided a Main Street showdown/nut-kicking with Chucky.

Reese started in the direction of the café, fully expecting Logan to follow her. And he did.

"Chucky will be back?" he asked.

She nodded. "But not before he spreads every rumor that he can think to spread. Thankfully, Chucky's not very smart so he might not think to connect the two of us to make the dirt seem dirtier."

Logan stayed quiet a moment. "There's no way he could know about what happened in San Antonio?"

"No. If he had known, he would have blurted it out when you told him who you were. Chucky's not big on keeping secrets. But he probably has heard you and your family have money. That's why I'll leave. When I go, he'll go, too. I'm sorry, though, that you might have to do some damage control."

She wasn't sure what to make of the sound that Logan made or the fact that he followed her all the way to the café. Maybe because he thought Chucky might return for another pushing match.

Or maybe because he wanted to confront her about something else he'd learned about her ugly past.

Reese unlocked the café door and went in. When

Logan continued to follow her inside, she steeled her-self up for the lecture he was no doubt about to give her. Since that would put her in an even worse mood, she went into the kitchen and washed up so she could put the scones in the oven.

Or rather, biscuits.

Bert had assured her that no one would order a scone, but that everyone in town would want to sample a biscuit even if it had berries, cream or other stuff in it.

He'd been right.

"So, are those the lemon thingies everyone's talking about?" Logan asked.

Reese blinked. She hadn't expected that to be part of the lecture or confrontation. "No. These are but-terscotch. I do the lemon ones every other day. If you want, I'll send Della the recipe so she can make some for you."

He mumbled a thanks, watched as she started some dough for the next batch of scones.

"Baking calms my nerves," she explained. "If you were to ever come in and see the counters filled with cakes, pies, scones and cookies, you'll know I've had a bad day."

She meant it as a joke, but her tone must have let Logan know it was too close to the truth. He kept watching, and when Reese could take no more, she whirled around to face him.

"Go ahead," she demanded. "Tell me what a piece of scum I am and that I should stay out of your life and your town." Reese hoped that was all he would tell her, though.

"It seems to me that the scum in this scenario is your parents. Did you help them con Chucky?"

"Of course not." She hadn't helped them since she was a child and didn't know any better. But at least Logan had asked. Most people just assumed she was guilty because of her gene pool.

"Then there's no need for a lecture. Not in this scenario," he added.

"No, but my lack of guilt won't stop Chucky from blabbing. My advice is just to ignore the gossip he stirs up. It'll go away pretty fast after I leave today."

She hoped. But then again, folks were still gossiping about Logan, Helene and the clown.

"You're really leaving?" he asked.

"Yes." Reese didn't have to think about that. It was the only way to get Chucky to budge. The only way she could outrun the memories.

Logan nodded. "I imagine you'll have to work things out with Bert. You might not be able to do that today. He's at a doctor's visit with Maggie in San Antonio. They probably won't be back until late."

True. "I can leave in the morning, then."

Another nod. He checked his watch. Checked the windows behind them. Basically, he was doing something she'd never seen Logan do.

Fidgeting.

"You're doing the dinner shift, too?" he asked.

"No. Sissy Lee's brother's doing it."

A third nod. "All right. I've got to leave for a meeting, but come by my place tonight around eight, and I'll give you the watch."

It was her turn to nod and mumble a thanks. A mumble because she was shocked that Logan was going to carry through on his promise to return it.

Logan didn't say anything else. He just turned and

walked out. But he didn't have to say anything for Reese to know what this meant.

He'd essentially just told her not to let the door hit her butt on her way out. But that was better than the alternative. Logan could have said something worse to her. Much worse.

Logan could have told her that he knew all about Spenser O'Malley. And what Spenser had done to her.

And what Reese had done to him.

CHAPTER EIGHT

THE GOSSIP WAS waiting for Logan when he got back to town after his meeting. And so was the person who'd started the gossip.

Chucky.

The weasel was in Logan's office, and he was leaning back in the chair, hands tucked behind his head as if he were lounging.

Apparently, Greg had found Chucky, invited him in for a chat and made Chucky feel right at home—exactly as Logan had instructed his assistant to do. But judging from Greg's raised eyebrows and under-the-breath mumbles, he didn't think Chucky was worthy of the kid-glove treatment.

"It's about time you got here," Chucky snapped the moment Logan walked in. "When you send for a man to come to see you, you oughta be here to see him. Especially when you send a girlie man to fetch me. Why you got that prissy pants working for you, anyway?"

Logan didn't respond. Didn't care a rat's ass about how long Chucky had had to wait, but he did care about this tool insulting Greg. Keeping that to himself for the moment, Logan went to the side of the room, to the panels that concealed a bar, and poured himself a drink. He sipped it slowly while Chucky cleared his throat.

"I'll take one of those," Chucky demanded.

Logan ignored that, too. "Tell me about this con Reese's parents supposedly pulled on you."

"It's not supposedly." But Chucky pronounced it *sup-bossedly.* "They did it. They got me to invest in some land deal that didn't exist. They took me for twenty grand."

"Funny, the police report you filled out said it was five grand. If you want to look at that report to refresh your memory, I can have Greg bring it in."

Chucky didn't seem especially bothered that he'd just been caught in a lie. "It started out as five grand, but I'm adding interest. And payment for my pain and suffering."

"If you're interested in payment, why not go to the source—to Reese's mother?"

Now he was bothered. "Can't find her or I would. I caught up with her mother a few years back, but she gave me the slip. Her mother is scum, and that scum's rubbed off on Reese. She might claim she's all innocent, but she's not."

The jury was still out on that.

"You've been spreading lies about me," Logan tossed out there after he'd finished his drink.

"Not lies. The truth. I saw the way you came running to defend Reese. My guess is you're doodling her."

Logan figured that was a euphemism for fucking her. He wasn't, but since he had at one time, he didn't deny it. "The lie you told said Reese is running a con on me, and that I'm paying her off so she'll stay quiet."

"So?" said with the arrogance of an idiot who didn't know who he was dealing with.

"So, it's a lie," Logan answered. "The con is on you."

Chucky gave him a blank stare. "Huh?"

"I wanted you arrested and put behind bars in a town that my ancestors built. The police chief is a good friend. In fact, just about everybody in Spring Hill is either a good friend or works for me. I've been waiting for a reason to have you locked up, and you gave it to me today when you pushed Reese."

"What?" Chucky howled, and jumped to his feet. "She kneed me in my privates."

"Only after you assaulted her. I saw it. So did eleven other people. They're all willing to testify against you."

Chucky sputtered out a few syllables. "But she owes me money. Money that either Reese—or you—is going to pay."

Logan tried to rein in his temper. Sometimes, he could put his temper to good use, but there wasn't any reason to bring out the big guns when dealing with a little moron. "No, her mother owes you the money, and neither Reese nor I will pay you a penny."

While Chucky continued to sputter and howl, Logan went closer to him. Too close. He could smell the onions and beer on the guy's breath.

"Here's how this works. I give you a fifteen-minute head start," Logan said, using his low and dangerous voice, "and as long as you leave town and never see or speak to Reese again, I won't have the police chief arrest you."

"You can't do that. Go ahead. Have him arrest me. I'll make bail and be out in a New York minute."

Logan shook his head. "My town. My rules. You'll be lucky if you're out by Christmas."

It was a bluff. It was his town, all right, but Logan had never called in favors like that. So, he added something that wasn't a bluff.

"If you don't leave and if you ever call my assistant prissy pants again, I will destroy you." Since that wasn't a bluff, Logan had no trouble giving Chucky the glare that went along with it.

The man backed away from Logan, and even though Logan couldn't see them, he could practically hear the guy's bruised balls shriveling. He went out in the hall. "I guess you're not worried about Reese getting violent again?" Chucky asked.

Logan tried not to look surprised by that question, but he must have failed because he saw the gleam of victory in Chucky's eyes.

"Reese didn't tell you, huh?" Chucky chuckled. "You should sleep with one eye open when you're around her. And if you don't believe me, just ask her about Spenser O'Malley."

REESE WAS ALL packed up. Not that it was a big deal since all of her belongings fit into the backpack. She'd added a few things during her stay in Spring Hill. She did in most places. In this case she'd bought an old bronze key from the Lookie Here Thrift Shop. It was a silly purchase, but since the initial *R* had been on it, Reese had thought it was some kind of sign.

Perhaps just a sign for her to part with the eight dollars and twenty-five cents it had cost her, but it was something small enough she could carry with her as a reminder of her time in Spring Hill. Of course she'd left enough space for the watch.

She glanced around the room where she'd been staying. Not home exactly, but it had felt better than most places. In fact, it had started to feel, well, good, until Chucky had shown up. She'd told Logan about her con-artist parents, but it was another thing for him to get a dose of what that meant.

In this case—gossip. And lots of it.

According to Sissy Lee, nobody believed the gossip about Reese being there to con Logan, but the buzz was going strong, and with each new buzzing, Logan's reputation and business could be hurt. And here he was finally recovering from the ordeal with Helene.

There was fresh gossip about that, as well.

Gossip about a crew that spent most of the afternoon cleaning out Logan's loft and bringing in new furniture. Reese figured after what she'd seen there, that change was good.

She went out the back exit of the Bluebonnet Inn, making her way to the McCord building. As she always did, she checked around her, but tonight she double-checked just in case Chucky was somewhere nearby waiting to go another round.

There was gossip about Chucky, too.

Sissy Lee had heard that Logan had brought Chucky to his office, but Reese figured that had to be just a rumor. There was no reason for Logan to talk to Chucky since in a few hours Reese would be on her way out of Spring Hill, and Chucky would be gone, as well. There was a six o'clock bus leaving in the morning, and she'd already bought her ticket.

Reese pushed aside the twinge she felt in her stomach and went to the back door of the McCord building. Unlike her other visit, this time it was unlocked, and Greg was still working at his desk.

"Logan's expecting you," Greg greeted. He stood, went closer to her and leaned in as if to tell her a secret.

"Explain to Logan that the brown sofa doesn't work. It's the only one the store had in stock, but it's butt ugly."

Reese doubted she'd be staying long enough for a conversation about sofas, butt ugly ones or otherwise, but she assured Greg she would do just that if it came up. She made her way up the stairs, and like during her other visit, his loft doors were wide-open. Unlike her other visit, though, she smelled chicken, onion and rosemary.

The first thing she saw was the sofa. Yes, it was ugly. The sort of piece that would probably be okay in a family room but not on gleaming hardwood floors against the backdrop of all those windows. It looked out of place.

As did Logan.

He was in the kitchen area of the loft, amid all those high-end appliances, and he was dishing up something from a skillet.

"Della fixed it," he said. "It'll actually be edible."

That's when Reese saw that he had two plates sitting on the new table. She watched, uncertain of what she should do, but then he motioned for her to sit. Apparently, he was sharing his dinner with her. And his wine. Logan opened a bottle that he took from the counter and poured two glasses.

She'd been right about those smells. It was chicken with rosemary and onions, and Della had done a baby potato dish and some steamed veggies.

"The place looks better," she said, and because Reese thought they could use some levity, she added, "I do miss the broken porcelain boob, though. It was a great conversation piece."

"I can have the work crew fish it out of the Dumpster for you."

Good, he was going for levity, too. She hoped. She really didn't want that boob.

"I'm supposed to talk you out of keeping the sofa," Reese said, still aiming for light.

"Greg." He looked over at the sofa. "It's simple, and simple works for me right now."

Reese wasn't sure if they were talking about furniture or life. Or even her. Yes, his life would be simpler when she was gone. Hers, too, she supposed. But she wanted the watch first.

He sat across from her at the bistro-sized table, eating and drinking as if this were a dinner date or something. Reese was instantly suspicious. But she was also hungry. So, she ate. It wasn't just edible, it was delicious.

"Tell me about Spenser O'Malley," Logan said.

Just like that, the food wasn't so delicious anymore. Her stomach tightened into a cold, hard knot.

"Who told you?" But she immediately waved off her question. "Chucky did." Ironic, though, since the man knew almost nothing about it.

Logan didn't press her for anything more, and Reese considered just clamming up, but he'd probably already gotten every last detail from another background check.

"What do you want to know about him?" she asked.

"What do you want to tell me?" he countered.

This was easy. "Nothing. I don't want to talk about him at all, but it's my guess that Chucky told you I was violent and then he dropped Spenser's name."

"Pretty much," Logan admitted. "All the details, though, are sealed in your juvie record."

And apparently Logan's dirt-diggers hadn't been able to get into the sealed record. Which meant she could tell Logan anything. It surprised her that she wanted him to know the truth. Well, what part of the truth she could say aloud, anyway.

"I was sixteen when I met Spenser. He was nineteen. Things were fine between us in the beginning, and then they weren't."

"He was from a good family," Logan tossed out there. He didn't add "like mine" but Reese heard the unspoken words loud and clear.

"He was, but Spenser had anger-management issues. And clout. A bad combination."

A muscle flickered in Logan's jaw. "He hit you?"

Again, there were things unspoken here. Logan had noticed how shaken up she'd been when Chucky had pushed her so maybe he'd put two and two together.

In this case, though, it didn't exactly equal four.

"He did," she admitted. "And that's all I want to say about him."

Reese expected Logan to press for more. He didn't. Maybe because it didn't matter. After all, she would soon be out of his life.

She made the mistake of looking at him, and Reese saw something she didn't want to see.

Sympathy.

Crud on a cracker. Not this. Not from Logan. She needed to get this conversation far away from Spenser, Chucky or anything else in her past.

"Before I forget," she said, and she took out the piece of paper from her jeans pocket. "That's the recipe for the lemon thingies." Reese slid it across the table just as he reached for it, and his fingers brushed across hers.

Good. This was a distraction she actually welcomed.

It felt intimate. Strange. Because this was a man she'd had sex with so a simple touch should have been just that: a simple touch. Of course, maybe nothing was simple when it came to Logan.

"I talked to Della about getting someone else to do Mia's party," Reese explained. Best to keep the conversation moving. "She was a little disappointed but said it wasn't a problem."

Reese hadn't wanted to tell Della that she'd been disappointed, too. She wasn't a kids' party expert, but she had been looking forward to doing the cake and food for the little girl.

"Did you really bring Chucky to your office?" she came out and asked.

He nodded. "I don't think he'll be bothering you again, but I could be wrong. You should be careful just in case."

"Uh, what did you say to him?"

"We just talked." He topped off their wine, and when he set down the bottle, he took out the watch from his pocket. As she'd done with the recipe, he slid it toward her.

No finger graze this time, but the emotions hit her pretty hard when she closed her fingers around it. For such a small piece of gold, it always packed an emotional wallop.

"Thank you," she managed to say, though now there was a lump in her throat.

"The watch is important to you." Not a question, but it was still an understatement.

"Very. It doesn't work. Hasn't since, well, in a long time. But it's still the only thing I actually treasure."

She'd always said she would get it fixed but had never gotten around to it. It didn't have to tell time for her to feel the connection to the man who'd given it to her.

"You loved your grandfather?" he asked.

It took her a moment to trust her voice. More wine helped. "Yes. He was the only sane thing in my life when I was growing up. He died when I was twelve. After that, no more sanity until I was able to escape at sixteen."

"You ran away from home?"

She hoped this didn't take them back to the subject of Spenser. "More like my parents ran away from me. I called the cops on them when they took some things from one of our elderly neighbors. They were arrested, and when they made bail, they didn't come back to the apartment. I figured if I stayed, I'd end up in foster care so I took off."

This probably sounded like a nightmare to someone who'd been raised on that massive McCord Ranch. Then again, Logan had had his own version of a nightmare. "You were...what...nineteen when your parents died?" she said. "So, you weren't much older than I was when you were on your own."

Reese instantly regretted bringing that up. Logan dodged her gaze, and he took a moment before he shook his head. "I wasn't on my own. I had Della and Stella. My brothers and sister. The whole town rallied around us. Plus, I had finished high school and was in my first year of college."

Still, a town, housekeepers and siblings couldn't replace loving parents, and from everything she'd heard, his parents had been exactly that—loving. However, there seemed to be something missing, something he wasn't saying that made her believe their deaths were still a wound that hadn't fully healed.

They finished their meal and gathered up the dishes to take to the sink. "Did my friend Jason say anything to you today?" he asked.

The question was so out of the blue that it threw her for a moment. Good grief. Who had tattled? "He came into the café at the end of the lunch shift and asked me out. I didn't think anyone heard him."

"Word gets around."

That was it. No opinion on how he felt about that. Which meant Logan probably didn't have an opinion. Still, this whole eating-chicken deal seemed as if he did indeed have something to say to her. If he'd just wanted her out of his life, he could have had Greg bring over the watch, and it would have saved him from washing an extra plate and wineglass.

"In case you're wondering, I told Jason no, that I was leaving town," Reese explained.

"And if you weren't leaving?"

Logan didn't seem like the type to pose what-if questions. "What's this all about?" she came out and asked.

He took his time. "Jason doesn't know what happened between us."

Oh, she got it then. "You're worried I'll say something to him. I won't. What happens in San Antonio…" Reese stopped. "Or maybe you're just concerned that I'm not the right kind of woman for him."

"You're not."

Reese pulled back her shoulders, was ready to say a quick goodbye, but then Logan added, "Jason moves pretty fast from one woman to another without thinking things through. He tends to hurt women without even realizing it."

She pulled back her shoulders even more but this time for a different reason. "Are you actually looking out for me?"

He stared at her and leaned against the sink. "I can't get involved with you."

A burst of air left her mouth. It sounded like a laugh, but it definitely wasn't humor driven. "Believe me, I understand."

"No, you don't. You think it's because of what people will say. And that was part of it in the beginning. It's because I'm not ready to get involved with anyone."

"Believe me, I understand," she repeated, this time without the humorless burst of air. "It's only been a couple of months, and you were with Helene for a long time. Plus, there's the whole thing about us not being compatible."

The moment the last word left her mouth, she got a flash of them in bed together. Naked. With Logan's toned and perfect body stretched out over hers. The brief image was more than enough for her to remember everything. To feel everything. And the heat slid through her, settling in her female nether regions.

"Opposites," she amended. Because they had been compatible in bed.

He nodded. Gave her a long, lingering look that singed her toenail polish along with frying some brain cells. The man should come with a warning label attached to his zipper.

She headed to the door, and Logan followed her. Reese turned back around to tell him good, but Logan spoke before she could say anything.

"I want you to stay," he said.

Because she was still dealing with the singeing and frying, it took her a moment to hear him.

"In town?" she clarified. Because her mind was already starting to weave a nice little fantasy where they got naked and landed in bed.

"In town," he verified. Though she thought he might be dealing with his own singeing feelings. Feelings he definitely didn't want to have even though it was just old-fashioned lust.

"You're okay with that?" she asked.

He shrugged. "Sure."

Boy, talk about a conflict in body language so she repeated it. "You're okay with that?"

"Della said I was being an ass," he explained. "She guessed the reason you were leaving had something to do with me. I don't know how. I swear the woman has ESP. So, I told her that I would let you know it was okay for you to stay."

Reese gave that some thought. "If I stay, we'll end up in bed again."

"Yes." No hesitation. Not a drop. And neither was the kiss he gave her.

He didn't linger with the kiss as he had done the look. Just a quick brush on her mouth to let her know that if she stayed, she could have a whole lot more of Logan.

But not without risks.

She figured those risks were too big to take. Not just for Logan but for herself.

"Goodbye," she told him.

Reese walked away and didn't look back. The best thing she could do for Logan and for herself was be on that 6:00 a.m. bus out of town.

CHAPTER NINE

EVEN THOUGH LOGAN knew it was a dream, he couldn't force himself to wake up. Images of the accident that felt so real he could practically feel the cold rain on his skin, could smell the stench of the gasoline spewing from the cars.

Logan didn't remember getting out of his truck. Not then, not now in the dream. He was just there, his feet on the asphalt, running in the rain to get to them in time.

The steam from the radiator had fogged up the windshield and windows, but even through the cloudy glass, he saw Claire. His folks had given her a ride home from a ball game, and she was in the backseat. She appeared to be dazed. Even though she'd been seventeen at the time, she looked much younger in her band uniform.

And helpless.

It seemed to take an eternity to get to the car, and Logan threw open Claire's door first. She tumbled out into his arms, no longer conscious. That's when Logan looked in the front seat.

That's when he knew he'd fucked up.

He hadn't called for help yet. And that skid had cost him seconds. Seconds he didn't have.

His parents weren't moving, though his mother was

making some kind of gurgling sound in her throat. And the blood. God, there was so much blood.

Logan took out his phone. His hands were shaking—costing him even more seconds. And in each of those seconds, his mother was still making those sounds.

No sounds from his father, though.

Logan pressed in 911, and like that night he didn't know who answered or what he said. The only thing he remembered was the emergency operator told him that help was on the way.

Claire moaned, a reminder that she was still alive, and for her to stay that way he needed to get her off the road. Away from that spewing engine, too. There was enough spilled gasoline to start a fire.

"What happened?" Claire mumbled.

He didn't answer. Couldn't. Logan just put her on the gravel shoulder and threw open the front passenger door. His mother's eyes fluttered, threatening to close, but she managed to turn her head and look at him.

Had she said something?

She didn't in the dream. Perhaps she didn't that night, either, but there were times when Logan let himself believe that she had spoken. That she had said the words that he wished she'd said.

It's all right. I forgive you for not saving us.

THERE WERE PLENTY of days that Logan loved his job. This wasn't one of them. He always felt a little like a circus monkey whenever he had to pose for a photo shoot for a magazine. No way could he do this for a living, but a magazine article was always good promo for the business. Considering the crap rumors that were still floating around about Helene and him, Logan figured the family and business could use all the good publicity they could get.

Plus, as bad as this was, it was also a distraction. Something he'd found himself wanting today. And no, it didn't have anything to do with Reese. Or that shit-brown sofa in his loft. Or the paperwork that'd been screwed up on a recent sale. Or the nightmare still rifling through his head.

Okay, maybe it did have a little to do with Reese.

But that was just the tip of this iceberg of a bad mood.

Perhaps Lucky was right. He did need to start dating again, especially since even a seventy-hour workweek wasn't enough to keep his mind off things it shouldn't be on.

Like Spenser O'Malley.

Even though Logan wanted to know what had gone on between Reese and the man, he hadn't asked the private investigator to dig any deeper. Heck, Logan hadn't even done an internet check on the guy's name. It hadn't been easy to hold himself back. Logan preferred to know anything and everything about people who came into his life, but it'd been obvious that the topic was off-limits for Reese.

And for once, he had respected that.

Still, that didn't mean he could stop himself from speculating. The guy had obviously hit her, maybe even done something worse to her. But then Reese must have done something to him, too, to get that juvie record. It was probably a good thing she wasn't around to tell him because Logan wasn't sure he wanted to hear about it.

"Uh, you probably need to soften your expression a

little," the photographer told him. "We've already got enough resting-bitch-face shots."

Logan didn't ease up on his scowl. In fact, he made it even worse so he could let the photographer know he wasn't pleased with that remark. Men didn't have bitch faces. Asshole faces, maybe.

"Why don't you just get your brother to do these photo shoots?" the photographer asked, clicking off some more pictures. "I photographed him at a rodeo last week, and he seemed to like it."

It wasn't the photo session but rather the bull riding that had probably made it enjoyable for Lucky. But the guy had a point. There were some benefits to having an identical twin, and this could be one of them. But he was still walking a fine line when it came to his brothers finally working in the family business. Logan had run the company for a long time, and it was hard for him to give up control. Hard, too, for his brothers to accept him as their boss.

"Resting bitch face again," the photographer grumbled.

Logan gave him a look that could have frozen hell, and the guy must have gotten the message that this was not a good day for a photo shoot. "Maybe we can try this again next week," he said, gathering up his equipment.

Logan didn't stop him, though it would have been easier just to finish this now. The guy left, and Greg came right in and put a small brown paper bag on Logan's desk.

"I popped over to the café and got one of those lemon thingies," Greg said. "Thought you'd like one, too. It's right out of the oven."

Logan glanced in the bag. It didn't look like something that'd caused such a fuss. Then he took a bite, and his taste buds applauded.

Yeah, it was worth a fuss, all right.

"I guess Reese left the recipe with Bert?" Logan asked.

"Nope. Reese baked these herself." And with that bombshell, Greg was halfway out the door.

"Reese baked it?"

Greg stopped, stared at him as if that were a trick question. "I thought you'd heard by now. She didn't leave town, after all. She's staying a while longer so she can do Mia's birthday party."

Logan cursed the flip-flop feeling he got in his stomach and hoped it was from the lemon thingy and not because Reese was still around.

Greg kept staring at him. "Say, you're not going to try to run her out of town again, are you?"

He was about to blast Greg for that, but then Logan had to mentally shrug. He had indeed nearly run her out of town. It hadn't worked, though. Even after she'd spelled it out that if she stayed they'd end up in bed together.

Which they would.

Logan only wondered if it was too soon for them to do just that. Yeah, it was stupid. He needed to stay away from her, but since that clearly wasn't going to happen, he might as well find out what it would be like to be with her when he was sober.

He checked the time. Reese's breakfast shift should be over in ten minutes so he grabbed his cowboy hat and headed for the door. He didn't make it far. Logan got another whiff of lemon, and Jason came in, stuffing his face with one of Reese's tasty pastries.

"Hey, did you hear?" Jason asked. "Reese didn't leave town, after all."

"I heard."

And apparently Jason had not only heard the news, he'd paid her a visit since he was chowing down on the lemon thingy. That visit had no doubt been to ask her out again. Even though this was going to sound like he was calling dibs or marking his territory, Logan figured it was time for his friend to hear the truth. There were man-rules about this sort of thing, and Logan had gotten to Reese first. That meant she was hands-off for Jason.

First, though, Logan shut the door. There was no reason for Greg to hear his dibs-calling. "The night after my botched proposal to Helene, I went to a hotel in San Antonio, met Reese and slept with her," Logan told his old friend.

Jason stopped chewing, his jaw frozen in a twisted angle. Then he laughed. Really, really laughed. "Right. Like you'd go for someone like Reese."

Logan huffed. "It happened."

Jason finally quit laughing and swallowed the rest of the pastry. "Oh, I get it. You were drunk."

"Drunk-ish." Which, of course, sounded stupid. Yeah, he was drunk, but judging from Jason's tone, he was about to dismiss it as something that wouldn't violate a man-rule of a guy going after a woman who'd been his drunk best friend's lover.

Jason kept staring, perhaps processing that, and he shook his head. "I just don't see you two having a one-nighter. *Any* nighter for that matter. So, are you the reason she came to town?"

"Only in a roundabout way. She gave me something and wanted it back."

More staring, more processing. "You didn't knock her up or anything, did you?"

"No. I used a condom." Several of them, in fact, but there was no reason to share that with Jason.

Jason made a sound of amusement. "Well, I gotta say, I didn't expect this. But obviously you haven't picked up where you two left off." He paused. "Have you?"

"No," Logan repeated after a pause of his own.

"Where do you see things going with Reese?" Jason came out and asked.

It was a good question. Logan didn't have a remotely good answer. It would sound shallow for him to say he was only interested in having sex with her, especially when he was still concerned that with her family history she could tarnish the reputation of the company.

"I'm not sure," Logan admitted. "But Reese doesn't tend to stay in one place for long. Six months at most so I suspect in a couple of months, or even sooner, she'll be leaving for greener pastures."

Logan couldn't blame her. It wasn't as if he could offer her anything but sex. Hardly an offer that would tempt a woman like Reese to stay put. As attractive as she was, she wouldn't have any trouble finding another guy to sleep with. One who wasn't accusing her of running a con.

"Until she leaves for those greener pastures, is she hands-off for me?" Jason asked.

"Yes," Logan said without hesitation. It was hard

enough being around Reese, but it would be very unpleasant to see her with his best friend.

"All right." Jason bobbed his head. "I guess this means you're finally getting over Helene. You *are* getting over her, right?"

Logan nodded. It wasn't a lie, either. He was getting over her. He wasn't there yet, though, but this thing with Reese didn't have anything to do with what he'd felt for Helene. It had to do with trust. He just didn't want to put his heart out there for another stomping.

There was a knock at the door, and a second later, Greg opened it and stuck his head in. "Logan, you have a visitor."

"I need to be going, anyway," Jason said, checking the time. "I'll see you at Lucky and Cassie's engagement party next month."

This was the first Logan was hearing of a party, a reminder he needed to get his head out of the clouds and keep better tabs on what was happening in his own family.

"Who's the visitor?" Logan asked Greg after Jason was gone.

"A woman. She says she's a friend of Reese's."

Logan hadn't meant to groan, but he hoped this wasn't another "friend" like Chucky. "Show her in," Logan said.

He wasn't sure what to expect, but at least the woman who came through the door didn't look like a con artist or a rooster. She was in her twenties, tall and looked like a model. Logan figured if Jason had gotten a glimpse of her, then he'd be hanging around for a while longer.

"I'm Jimena Martinelli," the woman said, "the closest thing Reese has to a sister, and I'm here to warn you that if you're dicking around with her, I will cut off that dick and roast it in a fire pit."

Okay, maybe not as normal as he'd originally thought. Logan hoped this woman's idea of dicking around didn't mean just sex.

"Is there something specific I can do for you?" he asked. "Something that doesn't involve my dick?"

"Yeah, you can stop treating Reese like she's a gold-digging slut. She's not." Jimena folded her arms over her ample chest. "The only reason she slept with you was to tick off a box on her bucket list."

Logan nodded. "She told me."

Jimena seemed a little surprised that he knew about the list. "Did she also tell you that she really liked you?"

Now Logan was the one who no doubt looked surprised. "No. But then she hardly knows me."

"Right." Said with all the sarcasm one word could have.

Apparently, Jimena thought a night of sex equaled getting to know someone. And in some ways it did. But there was still plenty Logan didn't know about Reese.

"I just want you to understand that Reese isn't as tough as she looks," Jimena went on. "You were the first man she slept with in nearly two years."

Again, Logan was sure he looked surprised. But then he remembered that might not even be true. Maybe this was Jimena's weird attempt at matchmaking.

"I have several things I need to do," Logan tossed out there. Including a chat with Reese to find out why she'd decided to stay in town, after all. "Was there anything else?"

Figuring there wasn't, Logan took out his phone so

he could make some calls on his walk to the café. But Jimena didn't budge. She also didn't look as much in a dick-roasting mood as she had when she'd first come into the office.

"Was there anything else?" he repeated, sounding as impatient as he suddenly was.

"Uh, I heard about your ex. About you walking in on her with another man. A man who was dressed like a clown."

Logan groaned again. "I won't discuss that with you."

"There's something you should know." Jimena took out her own phone. "I've been seeing a guy. Elrond Silverman. He's not the right letter of the alphabet, but sometimes I let that slide."

Logan didn't have a clue what that meant, and he could possibly be dealing with someone who was mentally unstable.

"Elrond worked for you," she added.

"So? A lot of people work or have worked for me."

She nodded and came closer, holding out her phone screen for him to see. "Last night, we got a flat tire when we were in Elrond's car, and this was in the trunk."

Logan figured there was absolutely nothing on the screen that he wanted to see. But he was wrong. The first thing he noticed was the porcelain tit. One that he recognized because it was a perfect match to the one Helene had given him.

Of her own right breast.

Hell. Had this Elrond stolen it?

Logan tried to remember the story Helene had told

him about it, but all he could recall was that she'd said it had gone missing.

"Does it look familiar?" Jimena asked.

It took him a moment to realize she wasn't pointing to the boob but rather to what was next to the boob.

A clown suit complete with a big red nose.

CHAPTER TEN

REESE FELT THE flutter in her stomach when she saw the man in the doorway of the café. But the flutter fluttered away when after her initial glance she realized it wasn't Logan but rather Lucky.

"Glad I caught you before you left," Lucky greeted.

Since she already had her purse in her hand and had been going to the front door to lock it, he'd barely caught her in time. Even if she hadn't been there, it wasn't as if she would be hard to find since Reese had managed to keep her apartment at the Bluebonnet Inn.

"First, I'm pleased you're staying," Lucky continued. "Logan needs someone to keep him off-balanced a little."

She wasn't so sure of that at all. "There's nothing going on between Logan and me." Something she'd been saying to Bert, Sissy Lee and Sissy Lee's brother when they brought up that Logan was the reason she was staying on a while longer.

Lucky made a sound that he didn't quite buy that. "All right. I'm glad you're staying, anyway. I heard about Chucky. You know if he bothers you again, all you have to do is tell Logan or me."

For some reason that put another flutter in her stomach. Not a sexual one this time but a warm unfamiliar feeling. "Thanks. I'm not used to people having my back."

"Well, your friend Jimena seems to be looking out for you."

No more flutter. Just confusion. "How do you know Jimena?"

"Ah, hell." He groaned. "I just figured Logan had told you that she paid him a visit earlier today."

"I haven't spoken to Logan since last night."

Lucky tried to dismiss her words with a shrug. "I'm sure he'll tell you about it when you see him." Reese wanted to hear about it now, but Lucky just continued talking, and it wasn't about her friend. "Cassie and I are excited about you doing our engagement party."

Reese nodded. "Cassie called this morning, and we talked about that. She said she was looking at the end of next month."

"Uh, could you do it sooner? Like maybe the end of *this* month?"

"Sure. That works out better for me, anyway." In case she decided she needed to get out of town.

The end of the month was only two and a half weeks away, and at first Reese thought the short notice was what was causing that funny look on Lucky's face.

"And maybe don't fix anything with bacon or coffee," he added.

It was a strange request, but maybe Cassie simply didn't like those things. "No problem. Since Cassie wanted a brunch, I could do—"

"We'll need to make it an afternoon or evening party instead. Will that be a problem for you?"

She shook her head, and maybe it was the shaking that caused Reese to connect the dots. "Is Cassie pregnant?" Judging from the deer-caught-in-the-headlights look, Reese wished she hadn't asked.

Or guessed correctly.

"You can't tell anyone," Lucky insisted. "Not yet. Cassie and I need to figure out a way to tell the girls first. And we don't want to do that before Mia's birthday party. We don't want to take anything away from her special day."

"I understand, though in this town nothing stays secret for long," she reminded him.

"Yeah," he said without hesitation. "But don't even tell him." Lucky tipped his head toward the glass front door where Logan was standing.

Reese felt another stomach flutter. Logan had finally come. It was about time. She figured he must have heard by now that she was staying in town, and after the warning she'd given him about them landing in bed, Reese figured he'd either run for the hills...

Or run for her.

She was hoping for the latter.

Reese made a zipping motion across her lips for Lucky. A motion that she prayed Logan hadn't seen because he seemed suspicious when he came in.

"Engagement party stuff," Lucky explained to his brother. "Did you get some of those meetings rescheduled?"

"No. I've got to leave tonight for Dallas."

Reese hated to feel disappointed by that. She should just hit herself in the head with a frying pan. It would be less painful than all this second-guessing, fluttering and fantasizing she was doing about a man she could never have.

"What about you?" Logan asked Lucky.

"I've got to head over to the school right now for Mia's program. Apparently, the pre-K did picture poems complete with painted macaroni borders." He grinned. "Bet you never thought you'd hear me say something like that, huh?"

From all accounts, Lucky had been a serious player so it probably was a surprise that he was now attending school programs and talking about macaroni art projects. Still, it seemed to suit him, and he appeared to be happy. If not a little shaken by the news of Cassie's pregnancy. She wondered how Logan and the rest of his family would take it.

Wondered, too, why Logan was here.

He certainly didn't pull her into his arms and drag her to the floor after Lucky left. Not that Reese especially wanted him to do that...or maybe she did...but it didn't look as if he had kissing, sex, floors or flutters on his mind. And she soon remembered why.

"Did Jimena really visit you?" she asked. She also locked the front door so that no one else would come wandering in.

"She did. She threatened to cut off my dick and roast it."

Reese groaned. "She doesn't mean it. And she had no right. I'll call her and set her straight."

"No need. That wasn't the only reason for her visit." He took out his phone and showed her a picture. "Jimena texted this to me so I'd have a copy."

It took Reese's brain a moment to make sense of what she was seeing A porcelain boob and a clown suit.

"Please tell me Jimena got that boob from the Dumpster," Reese said.

Logan shook his head. "She found this in the trunk of her boyfriend's car."

"Elrond," Reese provided. Then she knew the reason for Logan's look. And the reason he'd come. He wanted to find out if she knew anything more about this. "You believe Elrond was the one with Helene that night?"

"It's not just possible, it's highly likely. After all, Helene was the one who hired him. I didn't have any dealing with him or the rest of the crew who redecorated the building." Muscles flickered in his jaw.

Obviously this was bothering him, and Reese couldn't let it bother her that he was bothered. After all, he had a right to know if this clown had indeed been the one who'd had sex with the woman Logan had intended to marry.

"What will you do if you find out he's the one?" she asked.

He shook his head, put his phone away, and that was apparently the only answer Logan was going to give her. "So, what made you decide to stay in town?"

Reese was thankful for the change in subject but probably not as thankful as Logan was. "I'm surprised you don't know that from the gossip."

"I heard a couple of theories. One was that you wanted to give me food poisoning for trying to run you out of town. Another was that you were too broke to leave. The dark-horse gossip was that you were pregnant with either my baby or the clown's."

Even though she hated to be the center of that much speculation, of any speculation, really, Reese had to laugh. "The clown's? When and where exactly was I supposed to have slept with the clown?"

He lifted his shoulder. "The gossips didn't exactly connect that thread."

And never would because a thread didn't exist. "Well, I'm definitely not pregnant, and I'm not flat broke. And as for the food poisoning, I only do that when I'm really pissed off at someone."

Of course that last statement was a joke, but Logan didn't crack a smile. In fact, it seemed to frustrate him.

"I can't stay long," he said without taking that frustrated stare off her.

"Yes, you're leaving for Dallas. When will you be back?" She tried to make that sound like a casual question. She failed big-time.

"A couple of days. Maybe more. You're not flat broke?" he tacked on to the end of his answer.

She shook her head. "Please don't make me show you my wallet and bank statement." Again, another attempt at a joke, but he still didn't smile.

"Why did you stay, then?" he asked.

Mercy, no matter what she said to that, it would require some soul-baring. Something she wasn't ready to do just yet. Reese couldn't tell him that she'd stayed because of him. That would send Logan running.

"Maggie's uterus," she lied. That poor woman's anatomy was getting a lot of buzz.

He nodded, mumbled something she didn't catch, but Reese certainly *caught* the next thing Logan did.

Logan pulled her to him and kissed her.

It happened so fast she didn't see it coming, but Reese didn't need to see anything to feel it. With just a touch of his mouth to hers, the man could perform some magic, and the flutter turned instantly into a sweet spot of pleasure. She felt as if she were melting sugar in a really hot pot.

He didn't exactly experience the melting, though. Logan seemed to be angry. Maybe with her, maybe with himself. And that anger went into the kiss. He probably soon figured out, though, that when kissing, the anger just made it all seem more intense. More urgent.

Reese figured once they had to break for air that it would be the end of it. That Logan would say he was sorry and that it wouldn't happen again.

He didn't.

He went right back to her mouth for a second round, this one deeper and even longer than the first. The problem with deep, long and intense was that everything revved up. Not just the kissing but the body-to-body contact. Logan snapped her to him, her breasts landing right against his chest.

All in all, a really good place for them to be.

Reese's nipples especially liked the idea because they tightened and hardened. The rest of her body, however, started to soften. Everything below the waist preparing for something it wasn't going to get.

When oxygen became an issue again, Reese was certain it was time for Logan's apology and departure. But no. His arm tightened around her, and with a clever little adjustment, he had their midsections aligned in just the right way for her to feel his erection.

Oh, man.

That wasn't a good thing to feel. Her body was already whining for Logan, and that didn't help. It especially didn't help that Reese already knew that Logan's cleverness didn't just happen with his kisses. He could do marvelous, wonderful things with his erections.

She broke away to give him a second to rethink this. Their gazes met, held, and Reese thought maybe she could regain her footing now that he wasn't kissing her. But without breaking the eye-lock he had with her, he slipped his hand beneath her top and touched her.

Reese made a sound. Way louder than it should have been. All pleasure. It was too schoolgirl for her to react this way to a simple hand on her bare skin, but her sound and reaction were a drop in the bucket compared to what he did next. Logan turned her, lifting her in the same motion, and sat her on the counter.

He probably didn't notice the plate of scones sitting there.

It was incredible what he could do with just a few deft shifts of their bodies. Since this part of the counter was table-high, it gave her the perfect height for him to step between her legs. All the while kissing her, touching her and generally making her crazy.

Of course, she'd felt all of this that night in the hotel, but Reese realized now the tequila had dulled things more than quite a bit. She was getting a full dose of Logan without the boozy haze.

"How far are we taking this?" she managed to ask.

"Not far."

He was lying, delusional or else he had no concept whatsoever of what *not far* actually meant. Because somehow he made their new counter position work so that his erection was now in the V of her thighs. Some well-placed pressure, some more kisses, his hand sliding over her breast, and Reese no longer cared if he took her right then and there.

She didn't even care that she was sitting on a plate

of scones that would give her a greasy stain on the butt of her jeans.

What she did care about was more of everything Logan was giving her. She found herself wiggling to get closer and closer until the only way for more closeness to happen was for her to unzip their jeans and go at it right here amid the scone crumbs.

And that might have happened if she hadn't caught the movement from the corner of her eye.

Logan must have seen it, too, because he let go and moved in front of her. However, he was clearly too late.

Bert, Maggie, Sissy Lee and three people whose names Reese didn't know had their faces pressed against the window. Unless they'd all been struck with a sudden bout of blindness, they'd just seen Logan and her kiss each other's lights out.

ACCORDING TO THE hottest gossip that Logan had heard, Reese was definitely pregnant with his child. Of course, that gossip had been fueled by what folks had seen through the window of the Fork and Spoon. So far, the gossip hadn't made it to any of his business associates, but if it did, well, Logan didn't want to go there. He wasn't exactly a celebrity, but that kind of talk could hurt.

Something he'd known right from the start.

That meant he should just make a clean break with Reese and start dating someone. Someone who could help the gossip die down so he could go back to his normal life.

If his dick could laugh, it would have laughed at that.

For reasons he would never understand, his dick wanted Reese. His mouth, too, and while he hated to let stupid parts of him like that rule his life, it was as if the other parts no longer had a say in it. That's why Logan had decided to go ahead and have an affair with her. That would make his dick and mouth happy, and if he fucked her enough, it might burn this heat to a crisp.

There, that was the plan.

But the plan went a little south when Logan went into the ranch house and saw Reese there in the family room. She was on a stepladder, putting up twinkling lights for Mia's birthday party, and she turned, her gaze connecting with his.

And he forgot how to breathe.

Hell. Now his lungs had gotten in on this stupid attraction.

He could hear chatter in the kitchen. Della, Stella, Cassie. And there were kids running around in the backyard, but Logan's eyes froze on Reese.

"You made it," Reese said as if his arrival were nothing short of a miracle.

In a way it was. Logan had had three days of intense meetings, interviews and the makeup photo shoot, and what he should be doing was heading to the office to clear out what would no doubt be a mountain of work on his desk. But Mia had sent him a personal invitation to her fifth birthday party, and while he often declined personal invites, Logan hadn't declined this one.

He would put in an appearance, and since the party wasn't due to actually start for another half hour, he figured he could also see Reese and the rest of his family. A way of killing three birds with one appearance.

Reese was smiling when she went to him, and she leaned in as if to kiss him. But no kiss. Just a whisper. "Everyone thinks I'm pregnant."

He wasn't surprised the gossip made it to her. The café was usually a hotbed for that sort of thing, but he heard just as much worry and concern in her voice as there was in Logan's head.

"I'm thinking about smoking a cigarette or drinking a shot of tequila in front of them," she added. "Maybe talk about skydiving or some other sport that a pregnant woman wouldn't do."

"It won't help." Then the gossip would be about what a reckless pregnant woman Reese was. "The talk will die down as long as you don't go see the doctor for any reason or if you don't gain weight."

Her eyes widened enough for him to know that those simple instructions were a problem. "I'm guessing that look doesn't have anything to do with any weight gain you might be considering?"

She shook her head. "I went with Cassie to the doctor in San Antonio. Lucky was tied up in a meeting, and Cassie said she wanted to discuss the engagement party on the drive. Cassie didn't tell anyone about what doctor she was seeing or why, not even me, but then she had a script filled at the pharmacy."

Logan picked through that explanation and realized his soon to be sister-in-law was pregnant. For once, he was hearing something ahead of the gossip.

"Prenatal vitamins?" Logan asked.

Reese winced. Groaned. "I'm sorry. I shouldn't have said anything."

It stung that the news hadn't come from his brother or Cassie, but things had been plenty hectic lately. Soon, though, he hoped Lucky would come to him with the announcement.

"I don't think Cassie planned to tell me," Reese went

on. "It was hard not to know, though, when I saw the script. It was written out to Cassie, but apparently everyone thinks she was getting the vitamins for me. But Cassie and Lucky didn't want anyone to know until after Mia's party. They don't want to steal any of the limelight."

Logan was betting if anyone in town suspected that Cassie was pregnant, then the news wouldn't have made it yet to the girls. And even if it did, Mia was such a sweet kid that she wouldn't mind sharing the limelight.

"Lucky knows, though, right?" he pressed.

Another nod. "So do Della and Stella. They guessed because Cassie's been having some morning sickness— apparently whenever she smells coffee or bacon. Lucky and Cassie want to tell Riley and Claire after the party."

And speaking of the party, the room looked great. Very girlie fairy-tale-ish with the lights and the sparkly decorations. Reese had moved a table into the room, and it was filled with all sorts of kid goodies, including a large pink birthday cake.

"How did the meetings go?" she asked.

"They're done." And that was the best thing he could say about them. Logan had been distracted through most of the past three days.

"I talked to Jimena," Reese said. "She won't be threatening you again. And there's been no sign of Chucky." Another pause. "I also talked to Elrond."

"That was on my to-do list."

"I figured it was." And judging from the way she glanced away from him, that didn't please her. Well, talking to the clown who'd screwed his ex probably wouldn't please him, either, but Logan had felt it was necessary.

"Elrond said Helene gave him the porcelain breast, but he insists that he didn't have sex with her."

"He's lying," Logan snapped. "At least about the porcelain breast. Helene had two of them made for me. Bookends," he clarified, "and she told me that one of them went missing before she could give me the pair. Elrond probably stole it."

Maybe it was his suddenly pissed-off tone, but Reese no longer looked so happy to see him. "It's important for you to find out the truth," she said. Not a question. But Logan wondered if it should be.

Was it important?

Hell, yes. But he had no idea what to do with the information once he had it. Clearly, the clown hadn't taken advantage of Helene. Logan had walked in on her at the tail end of an orgasm so this wasn't a situation where he was trying to defend Helene's honor. Or would make sure he got the guy arrested.

So, what was it?

Logan figured it was something he didn't want to examine too closely, and he put it in the guy-thing category. His brother Riley had all kinds of man-rules for situations like these so Logan's new man-rule was that he intended to confront the Bozo who'd contributed to bashing his life to smithereens.

Reese touched his arm to get his attention. "Do you still love her?"

Now, that was a question he seemed to be having to answer a lot lately. "No." And since it wasn't something he wanted to talk about, Logan went with something he did want to say. "I think we should have sex."

She blinked. Obviously, that didn't come out as smoothly as he'd planned.

"Now?" she joked.

Those stupid parts of him wanted to jump at the chance, but Logan figured he had to at least try to act like an adult and not a teenager. "Tomorrow night around eight?"

Reese certainly didn't jump at the invitation.

"I could serve Cheetos and Milk Duds," he joked, too. Except it wasn't just a joke. Logan wanted her to say yes, and he'd obviously botched this.

"Jimena told you about my snack favorites."

He nodded. "She also said you carried a really sharp knife in your backpack."

That got the reaction he wanted. Reese smiled. "Two of them. I'll see you tomorrow night."

However, she didn't get a chance to add more because Della, Stella and Cassie had joined them. Logan got hugs from all three women, and it was from over Cassie's shoulder that he saw Claire, who was standing back from the rest.

"Could you help me with something?" Claire asked.

Logan went to her, but he hoped he didn't have to do anything that required decorating skills. But it wasn't decorating stuff. The moment he made it to Claire, she took hold of his arm. "You think we could maybe go to the sunroom for a chat?"

Uh-oh. She'd heard the rumors about Reese being pregnant. Or maybe she'd guessed about Cassie and wanted him to confirm it.

With Claire's fairly tight grip on his arm, they went into the sunroom on the far side of the house. Away from the playing kids. Away from anything remotely resembling a party. When she stumbled, Logan caught onto her.

"Sheez, are you all right?" He had her sit on the sofa, and he went to the wet bar to get her a bottle of water.

Claire mumbled a thanks, sipped some of the water and looked at him. "What I'm about to tell you stays between us. Sorry to dump this on you," Claire added, "but I thought I was about to pass out. If I'd told Della or Stella that, they would have guessed right off."

"Guess what?" he asked, clueless.

Claire clued him in. "I haven't done the pee stick yet, but I'm pretty sure I'm pregnant."

Oh.

Apparently, he was the only male in the McCord family who hadn't knocked up somebody.

And for some reason, that made Logan feel like shit.

CHAPTER ELEVEN

"YOU'RE SURE ABOUT THIS?" Jimena asked Reese.

Reese looked at herself in the mirror. "Sure about which part?"

Because there were a lot of cogs going right now. Her dress, her shoes, her makeup. The perfume she'd borrowed from Jimena. And, of course, the biggest cog was the reason she was doing all these things.

For Logan.

The new-to-her dress was one that Reese had bought at Lookie Here. It was sunshine yellow, perhaps not exactly her color with her hair, but it'd been one of the few dresses in her size. Reese had been afraid to ask for a larger size for fear it would keep the pregnancy rumors going.

"The sex-date part," Jimena answered after she washed down a mouthful of the scone she was eating.

There was no easy answer for this. No, Reese wasn't sure about it, but yes, she was going to do it, anyway.

It would probably be a huge mistake, something she'd spent her adulthood trying to avoid, and this one had more pitfalls than most. Logan was looking for an affair. That was it. And he'd never tried to make her believe otherwise. Considering their relationship had started with a one-night stand, though, what did Reese expect?

"Whose idea was this, anyway?" Jimena pressed.

"Mine," she lied. It would save time on this conversation. Jimena was worried about her, that was obvious, but her friend would only worry more if she knew Logan had been the one to set this up.

Jimena didn't call her on that lie, but she did stare at Reese from over the top of her diet soda. "Are you even sure he's over his ex?"

"He is." Another lie. If he were over Helene, then why was Logan so insistent on speaking to Elrond? Of course, she wouldn't mention that to Jimena.

"If Logan's over his ex, then why does he want to talk to Elrond?" Jimena added.

Apparently, the woman's telepathic skills were working well tonight because she took that question right out of Reese's head.

"Wouldn't you want to talk to the person if they'd broken up a long-term relationship on the very night you'd planned on proposing?" Reese argued.

Jimena just looked confused. Probably because she couldn't wrap her mind around the long-term relationship part. Jimena didn't stick with men. For her, a week was plenty enough.

Reese checked her hair one last time and hated that she was fussing with it. Hated that she was fussing, period. She hadn't actually had a date in high school, but she remembered the nervous excitement from the girls when they'd talked about dates and such. It'd seemed vain and frivolous to Reese, especially since she was working full-time by then, and yet here she was doing it herself.

Enough.

"You can stay the night if you like," Reese offered.

Jimena shook her head. "I've got a dinner date."

Since the woman had just consumed several pounds of junk food, Reese wasn't sure where she'd put dinner, but she wished Jimena a good night, grabbed her purse and the pie that she'd baked and headed out. It was already dark, but as Reese always did, she stuck to the back street. Old habits. In her youthful con days, it was a way of keeping out of sight, of making herself as invisible as possible.

Tonight, it was so no one would see her going to Logan's.

Of course, the gossips assumed Logan and she were already carrying on a hot affair, but Reese was still mindful of Logan's reputation. Spring Hill wasn't exactly a prudish place, but she was certain the members of the old guard—i.e., those who wanted Logan back with Helene—wouldn't care much for her spending time beneath the sheets with their golden boy.

She spotted Logan's truck as soon as the parking lot came into view, and Reese released the breath she'd been holding. Part of her had worried that he would come to his senses and cancel. Or forget.

Reese went to the back door and was about to test the knob when she glanced in Logan's truck and saw someone. Since the windshield was heavily tinted, she couldn't be sure, but her first thought was that someone had broken into it. She was about to call out for Logan when she realized the person inside *was* Logan.

And something was wrong.

He wasn't just sitting. He had slumped forward, his forehead leaning against the steering wheel.

Reese's heart jumped to her throat because he didn't look as if he were merely in deep thought. He wasn't.

The moment she tapped on the window and he lifted his head, she saw the pain etched all over his face. She threw open the door, and he practically tumbled into her arms.

"Migraine," he managed to say.

She would have been relieved that it wasn't something more serious, but she knew about migraines and how bad they could be. Her grandfather had suffered from them.

"Let me get you inside," she said, trying to keep her voice at a whisper. Logan winced and grunted in pain with each little movement of his head.

She got him to the back door. It was locked. Damn. That meant she had to lean him against the building and go back for his keys. They were still in the ignition. Then she had to figure out which one, all while Logan stood there suffering.

It seemed to take an eternity, and her hands were shaking now, but Reese finally got him into the building. No sign of Greg. Too bad. Because the assistant could have helped with getting Logan upstairs.

"I can walk on my own," Logan said. Each word seemed an effort. "It's okay. You can go now."

Not a chance. Reese didn't argue with him about it, either. She merely hooked her arm around his waist and got him moving. Step by step. There were suddenly a gazillion of them, and both Logan and she had broken out in a sweat by the time she reached his loft.

The brown sofa was gone so she led him to the bed. He eased down onto the mattress and pulled a pillow over his head.

"Meds," he mumbled.

Reese hurried to the bathroom, threw open the medicine cabinet and spotted the prescription bottle of pain pills. Plus, some lavender oil. She grabbed both and a glass of water.

"Don't tell anyone about this," Logan said when she gave him the pills.

"I won't. I'll tell them we had sex instead."

He managed a smile. A very short-lived one that told her how much pain he was in. She put some of the lavender oil on her fingertips and began to massage his forehead, temples and the back of his neck.

"You've done this before," he whispered.

"Yes, for my grandfather. Peppermint oil helps sometimes, too." Though she also knew that sometimes nothing at all helped. Still, the pain didn't seem to be getting worse.

"The grandfather who gave you the watch?"

She nodded. "I lived with him on and off."

"Keep talking," Logan said.

Reese did. She kept massaging his head, too. "He was the night manager of a pizza place so we ate lots and lots of pizza—especially the ones they couldn't sell or the ones customers didn't pick up. I think it set me on my course of the love of junk food."

"Were your parents there, too?"

"On and off," she repeated. "When I was about ten, I think they got fed up and left me with him for good." Or so she'd thought at the time. "Then he got sick and died two years later."

Even though she knew it had to be painful for him, Logan opened his eyes, met her gaze. "I'm sorry."

Yes, so was she. Losing him had crushed her heart. Still did.

"For a long time I blamed myself for his death,"

Reese said before she even knew she was going to say it. And she was instantly sorry. Logan looked at her as if waiting for more.

Reese wasn't even sure she'd ever said this aloud, but she had certainly thought it plenty of times. "When I was living with him, my grandfather started working extra hours to pay for my school things and clothes. I think that's why he didn't go to the doctor right away when he started having symptoms."

Maybe with all the pain, Logan wouldn't even remember her telling him this. It was bad enough that he thought she was beneath him, but now he would know that she had the dreaded emotional baggage. Just what no man wanted to hear.

"Keep talking," he repeated.

She had to pause and take a deep breath. Had to pause again to think about how to say what she wanted to say. Best just to get it out there, and hope that Logan didn't remember.

"He died of lung cancer. I watched him waste away, and that's one of the reasons my misdiagnosis scared me. I didn't want to die that way. Now, see? Aren't you sorry you asked? You should have asked me for recipes or something that didn't involve picking at these old scabs."

"We all have scabs." Logan stayed quiet for several long moments. "I should have been able to save my parents, but I didn't."

Judging from the way he suddenly got so stiff, she was guessing that wasn't something he'd expected to share. However, it was something she'd already heard about.

Gossip, again.

But in this case the gossip seemed to be reliable since it had come from Bert. Logan's parents had died in a head-on collision when he'd been nineteen, and Logan had been the first to arrive shortly after the crash.

"They died at the scene," Reese reminded him, though she was certain he needed no such reminder. "I don't think anyone could have saved them."

He didn't agree. Logan only closed his eyes, and he didn't open them until she stopped massaging his temples. "Thanks, but you really don't have to stay."

She could see him already shutting down, already regretting that he'd let her have a little glimpse of what was in his head. "It's okay. I don't have anything else to do." Reese wiped her hands, took off his boots and pulled the covers over him.

"You're being nice to me because I'm in pain. I don't like that."

"Would you rather I yell at you?" she joked.

"Only if you whisper when you do it." His voice was groggy now, which meant the pain meds were knocking him out. Maybe they would knock out the pain, too. "Will you ever tell me about Spenser O'Malley?"

Obviously, though, the pain meds weren't erasing the things on his mind. "One day." Maybe. Probably not, though.

That wasn't just baggage but rather a mountain of it.

"Is he the reason you're scared of getting involved with me?" he asked.

Definitely not an easy question, and Reese only answered him because she was certain Logan wouldn't remember any of this. "No. I'm scared for other reasons."

She was scared he'd break her heart. And he would. Reese didn't have any doubts about that.

THE SMELL OF coffee woke Logan. Not easily, though. Despite the enticing scent, he practically had to pry open his eyelids. That was thanks to the effects of the pain meds. They'd knocked him out cold, had gotten him through the migraine, but he would pay for the relief for the rest of the day.

It felt as if a bug bomb had gone off in his head.

He finally got his eyes open and came fully awake when he saw how close the coffee cup was to his face. How close Reese was, too. She was standing right over him. A surprise. He'd thought for certain she would leave after he fell asleep. Just because they'd had a one-night stand didn't mean she was obligated to play nursemaid.

Hell. He hoped he hadn't said anything stupid to her, but he did remember a garbled conversation about his parents. Some things she'd told him about her grandfather, too.

Had she mentioned that guy Spenser?

If she had, Logan hoped he remembered what she'd said. From what he could sense, the man from her past was an emotional land mine that he should probably avoid.

"I was going to let you sleep," Reese said. "But Greg slipped a note under your door to remind you about an important meeting you have this morning. The meeting's in thirty minutes, and I didn't think you'd want to miss it."

"I don't," he assured her.

Logan groaned. It was a meeting he had to take, too,

because he'd already rescheduled it twice. A third cancellation could create some ill feelings between him and a seller he needed.

Since Greg usually texted that sort of reminder, it probably meant his assistant realized Logan wasn't alone. Or maybe someone had seen Reese helping him into the building the night before and spread the word. Logan had never told Greg that he had migraines, but the man had no doubt figured it out.

Logan forced himself to a sitting position, took the coffee and gulped as much as he could without burning his mouth. He prayed the caffeine would kick in soon and maybe rid him of the rest of the pain. It wasn't bad now. Just little pinging reminders that he didn't need. Especially because Greg had been right—this meeting was important.

"I didn't open the blinds," Reese said. "It's pretty sunny out there already."

"Thanks." The blinds would stay closed. Ditto for the lights being off. He'd have to ease into the whole light thing unless he wanted the headache to return.

"If you want to grab a shower, I can fix you some breakfast," Reese offered.

She was still being nice to him, and he would have told her to knock it off, but breakfast did sound good. He wasn't even sure the last time he'd eaten, but his stomach was growling.

"Don't you have the breakfast shift at the café?" he asked.

"Not this morning. I can stay a little while longer. If you want, that is."

He did want that. More than he should. And it wasn't all food related, either. Despite what had been a lousy night for both of them, Reese somehow managed to look amazing. Jason had said she was attractive in an unmade-bed sort of way, and while Logan didn't agree with that, looking at her did remind him of bed.

And sex.

Especially sex.

It was her mouth, he decided. Full and kissable. The rest of her body, though, was kissable, too. So that's what he did. Nothing long and deep. Just a taste of her mouth that he'd hoped would tamp down this little fire that was starting to simmer in his body. It didn't. The one kiss only made him want more.

More of something he really didn't have time for.

"Sorry about all of this," Logan said, moving away from her and getting up. "Both the half-assed kiss and the half-assed night. Last night qualifies as the worst dinner date ever."

Reese smiled. "Sadly, I've had worse."

She was probably being nice again, and because the niceness was making him want to pull her back to him, Logan headed to the bathroom for that shower. He didn't take long, mainly because his head was still sensitive, and it actually hurt to have the water hit his scalp. Also because he wanted a chance to say good-bye to Reese before he ate and headed downstairs for the meeting.

His dressing room was off the bathroom, which was a plus. Best not to run around half-naked with Reese still in his house. Well, best not to do that when he had someplace else to be.

Logan finished dressing and hurried back out to find breakfast sitting on the table. Scrambled eggs, and a glass of OJ next to the plate.

But no Reese.

"Reese had to leave," someone said. "She said something about having to go to work."

Maybe it was the fog in his head, but it actually took Logan a moment to recognize the voice. Another moment to pick through the dimly lit room and see the woman standing by the door.

Helene.

CHAPTER TWELVE

SHIT. AND BECAUSE Reese didn't know what else to say, she repeated that a couple more times as she hurried out of the McCord building.

Helene was back.

And Reese didn't know who'd been more surprised about that—Helene or her—when Reese had opened the loft doors. Reese had expected Greg to be standing there when she heard someone knock, and her stomach had landed near her ankles after she saw Logan's visitor.

His *perfect* visitor.

Reese had heard that Helene was beautiful, and it hadn't been an exaggeration. The woman looked like a pageant contestant, moved like a ballerina and smiled like the *Mona Lisa*.

Reese hated her.

But even more than that, Reese hated that she hated her.

She had always known Helene could come back. After all, the woman owned several businesses in town, but Reese hadn't thought her homecoming would have happened with Reese looking and feeling like a piece of gutter trash.

It hadn't helped, either, that Helene had turned that *Mona Lisa* smile on Reese. If Helene had been angry about finding another woman in her ex's loft, she had shown no traces of it. Helene had merely introduced herself and politely asked to see Logan.

Reese had exchanged introductions, shaken Helene's hand and then had somehow managed to rattle off an excuse of needing to get to work. Part of her, the part with a spine, wanted to hold her ground and stay until she could at least say goodbye to Logan. Maybe even kiss him in front of Helene. But Reese had been afraid that any kisses he might have given would have landed on Helene's mouth, not hers.

"Reese?" someone called out.

Lucky.

Definitely someone she didn't want to see right now. Of course, she could say that about anyone. The tears were threatening, and if Reese did disgrace herself by crying, she didn't want a witness. But this was one witness she couldn't avoid because Lucky was running to catch up with her.

"You okay?" he asked.

He stepped in front of her, blocking her path. The question alone meant he no doubt knew about Helene's return, but the look in his eyes let her know that he was also aware that Helene was with Logan right now.

"I'm fine." The lie just sort of stuck in her throat. "You knew she was back?"

"I just found out. Greg told me when I came in for the meeting, and he said you'd left in a hurry."

Reese shrugged. *Don't cry. Don't cry.* Better yet, she told her heart to knock it off. That crushing feeling in her chest was making it hard to breathe.

"I knew she was coming home, though," Lucky continued a moment later. "Her mother, Mary, called me last night to give me a heads-up. She said she tried to call Logan, but he didn't answer."

"Logan wasn't feeling well," she settled for saying.

"Migraine?"

Since Logan had told her not to tell anyone, Reese only shrugged. "For the record, nothing happened between Logan and me last night."

Lucky shrugged, too. Probably because he didn't believe her, and then he huffed. "Look, there's no easy way to say this, but I think you should know. Helene is planning to stay. *Really* stay," he added. "Her mother said Helene is organizing several big charity events and that she's going to donate money to build an addition onto the civic center."

"She's trying to mend her reputation," Reese concluded.

"You bet she is. But Helene's good at this sort of thing, and if anyone can make this shit stink less, it's Helene."

Reese didn't doubt that for a minute. Nor did she doubt something else. "Helene is planning to reconcile with Logan, too."

"She'll try." Lucky pinched his eyes together a moment. "And she might succeed. That'll suck for Logan."

It took some more blinking to stave off those tears. Reese gave up on coaxing her heart out of the crushing feeling and just went with it. After all, she'd known it was coming.

"Helene's perfect," she said. "I mean, I kept hearing people say that, but I didn't know they actually meant it."

"She's not perfect," Lucky argued.

"She certainly looks it. Please tell me she had a boob

job because, in all the gossip, no one mentioned those huge breasts of hers." The porcelain bookends hadn't been to scale at all.

"Funny, it's what most people mention about her first. Guys, anyway," he added in a mumble. "Still, big boobs don't equal perfect."

"She's beautiful, and that outfit she was wearing probably cost more than I've made in a lifetime. Plus, she used a word I didn't even understand. I'll have to look it up to see if she insulted me or not."

"It wouldn't have been an obvious insult. Helene doesn't work that way. She's more the 'silently put a curse on you while conniving to make your life miserable' type."

Reese stared at him. "Did you start to feel that way about her before or after you saw her with the clown?"

"Before." He held up his hands in defense. "But hey, I kept my mouth shut because I thought she was what Logan wanted. God knows Logan never approved of any woman I dated before Cassie."

She didn't know if Lucky was just trying to make her feel better. Reese couldn't imagine anyone disapproving of Helene. Well, not until after the clown incident, anyway.

"Did her mother happen to mention why Helene cheated on Logan?" Reese asked.

He shook his head. "I've got my own theory, though. High-end upbringing and she wanted to sample something down and dirty. Something a little perverse."

"Perverse? I'm not sure you can call it that—"

"You don't know what the clown was doing with his big red nose," Lucky interrupted.

Oh. So, maybe perverse, after all. Perhaps this was

something akin to an heiress sleeping with the pool cleaner.

Or Logan sleeping with her.

Reese hadn't actually wanted to ask him if he'd been playing out a dirty fantasy that night with her at the hotel, but it was possible he had. Maybe Logan had wanted a pool cleaner experience, too.

Mercy. Had that been it?

"Fight for him," Lucky insisted.

Reese wasn't sure she heard him correctly at first, but then Lucky repeated it.

"Fight?" she questioned.

"Not with your fists." He shrugged again. "Though, if I thought it would work, I'd say go for it. I just don't want to see Logan hurt again."

"Neither do I. But he's a grown man, and if he wants to get back with his ex, then it's his decision. I gotta go," she said.

And Reese hurried away so she could get inside her room before the first tear rolled down her cheek. There was only one word she had for herself.

Idiot.

"HELLO, LOGAN," HELENE SAID. She was smiling as if this were a normal visit. It wasn't. Far from it.

Logan felt as if a heavyweight boxer had just slugged him in the gut. Twice. Not just at the sight of Helene but because Reese wasn't there.

"What did you say to Reese to make her leave?" he asked. And he didn't bother to sound even a little friendly.

"Reese?" she repeated.

"Quit the innocent act. You know her name. You know who she is."

No way would Helene not have heard the gossip, especially considering her mother still lived in Spring Hill. Logan didn't want to know the picture her mother had painted of the fry cook at the Fork and Spoon.

Helene's smile faded, and she flexed her eyebrows. "Yes. Reese is an interesting woman. People seem to love those lemon things she bakes. Have you been seeing her long?"

"You know the answer to that, too." Logan would let Helene sort out fact from fiction all on her own.

"You're angry," Helene said, sitting down at the table where his breakfast was waiting. "And you have every right to be."

"You're damn right I do." He hadn't meant to raise his voice and instantly regretted it because it let Helene know that what she'd done had put his heart through the shredder.

"I want you to know that what happened that night wasn't planned," she explained.

"Various parts of a clown just happened to fall into your vagina?" Logan snapped.

Her mouth tightened a little but not for long. She quickly regained her cool composure. "It was a mistake. One I'll regret for the rest of my life, and I'll spend the rest of my life trying to make it up to you."

Even that wouldn't be enough time, but Logan had something more important on his mind right now. "What did you say to Reese?" he repeated.

"I only introduced myself."

Maybe that was true. Helene could intimidate with just a smile. It was one of the things that had actually attracted him to her in the first place. He'd wanted a woman who could hold her ground, go toe-to-toe with him. And Helene had done just that. Or rather had pretended to do it. Like the gossip, Logan didn't know what was fact and what was fiction when it came to his years with Helene.

"I didn't come here to spoil things with Reese," she said, pausing right before Reese's name. There was some disdain in her voice. Maybe some jealousy. Or fake jealousy at least.

"Then why did you come?" he asked.

"Forgiveness."

Logan would have laughed if he could have gotten his jaw unclenched. "Try something simpler. Something you actually stand a chance of getting from me."

In that moment he wanted to ask her why she'd fucked a clown. Why she had betrayed him, but Logan figured there wasn't nearly enough time to get into that. He needed to go to the meeting and then find Reese and discover the truth behind what Helene had said to her while he'd been in the shower.

"All right," Helene finally said. "I don't want you to stand in the way of my return. For the past month I've been in therapy to help me understand why I cheated, and I'm in a much better place in my life now. I want to come home."

"It appears you're already here."

"Yes, and I plan on staying." She took a deep breath, patted her chest as if to steady her heart. Or maybe it was just to remind him of her huge breasts. "I know I have fences to mend, not just with you, but with the entire town. I've already gotten started on that."

Logan didn't ask her how. "I have a meeting. I have to go."

"Greg told me. I won't keep you, but I wanted you to know that I'll be hosting a fund-raiser reception this Friday at the civic center. I'm donating money for the building extension, and this will be a good first step to repairing my image."

The only image Logan had was of a naked Helene on her desk, getting intimate with the red clown nose.

"I hired a publicist, and she's the one who suggested the civic center donation and reception," Helene went on. "She specializes in human branding, which isn't as BDSM as it sounds." She laughed.

Logan didn't.

"Anyway, I'm inviting the entire town to the reception, and I want you to come, as well," she added.

Now he did manage a laugh. He also opened the door and headed out. Helene followed him down the stairs.

"Just think this through," Helene said. "If you don't go, people will say you're too torn up to face me. They'll say your heart is broken."

Hell. The woman knew just how to go after him. Had she always been this way, or had she honed her bitch skills in the past three months?

"Well?" she asked when they reached the bottom of the stairs. "Should I put you down as a yes for the reception?" And Helene made the mistake of smiling at him. An "I've got you by the balls" kind of smile.

But two could play this game. "Yes, plus one. I'll be bringing Reese as my date."

Logan did enjoy the glimpse of Helene's bitch face to go along with her bitch skills. But it was only a glimpse. He didn't wait around to see what else Helene would do or say. He went up the hall to the meeting wondering just one thing.

How the hell was he going to talk Reese into going with him to his ex-girlfriend's party?

CHAPTER THIRTEEN

"No way in hell," Reese told Sissy Lee.

Reese didn't have to think about it, either. If Sissy Lee was right, Helene was throwing some kind of big party on Friday night, and Logan would be expecting Reese to go with him. But Sissy Lee had to be wrong about this.

"You're sure you wouldn't want to show up at Helene's fancy to-do and give her what for?" Sissy Lee asked.

Reese wasn't exactly sure what Sissy Lee meant by that, but if it involved her going to a party as Logan's date, then it wasn't happening. Of course, Logan wouldn't allow it to happen, either.

Probably for several reasons.

When Reese had left Helene in Logan's flat earlier, the woman's smile had made it crystal clear that she was there to reclaim her man. A man Reese was unworthy of. Helene had punctuated her claim with the scalp-to-soles glance she'd given Reese. The woman didn't have to say a word to let Reese know that she wasn't acceptable in Logan's and her social circles.

And Reese didn't want to be acceptable.

All right, maybe she did, but not like this. Not showing up with Logan just so she could rub it in Helene's face.

"What are you going to wear?" Sissy Lee asked.

"I'm not going." Reese finished the burger she was making, plated it and slid it to Sissy Lee, hoping that would put an end to this conversation.

Apparently not.

"I'm wearing the purple dress I wore to my prom," Sissy Lee declared, helping herself to one of the fries on the plate. Since Sissy Lee was in her midthirties, it had been a while since that prom had taken place.

"You might want to take that order to the customer," Reese reminded her when Sissy Lee ate another fry. Much more of this, and Reese would have to make a second batch, and since the lunch shift was nearly over, she didn't want to do that.

Sissy Lee finally headed out into the dining room, but she had no sooner walked out when the swinging doors to the kitchen opened again. At first Reese thought Sissy Lee had forgotten something, but it wasn't the waitress.

It was Logan.

"No, I'm not going to Helene's party," Reese said right off.

He huffed. "I see the gossip made it here ahead of me."

"Hours ahead of you."

Which was her way of reminding him that it'd been nearly half a day since Helene had shown up, and he hadn't called Reese to give her any hint of what had gone on in the loft after she left. Judging from the buzz that Logan wanted to take Reese to the reception, it hadn't gone well.

Reese tried not to smile about that.

Logan opened his mouth to say something, glanced

out at the diners who were watching them and then he pulled her to the side so they'd be out of sight.

"Look, I'm busy," Reese said. "Lucky and Cassie's engagement party is only a week and a half away." Of course, what she wouldn't tell Logan was that she already had everything planned out because then he would argue she was free to go with him to the reception.

But even though she didn't say that, he argued, anyway. "I can hire someone to help you with the engagement party, but if I don't show up at the reception, it'll look as if I'm licking my wounds."

"Are you?" Reese came out and asked.

He made a face. "I hadn't realized how disgusting that sounds. But no, I'm not. And I want you to go with me."

"So you can...what? Show Helene that you've moved on? I'm sure you can find a more acceptable date for that. Besides, I don't have anything to wear."

"I'll take you shopping." Judging from his dour expression, doing that would be about as much fun for him as sliding down razor blades while naked.

"I don't need you to take me shopping. If I were going, I could find something on my own." That was possibly the truth. Possibly.

Logan glanced around, then up at the ceiling as if asking for divine guidance as to what he could say that would make her change her mind. But there was nothing he could say.

Except what he said.

"Please."

That was it. A single word from him attached to a desperate expression.

Reese considered having another go at convincing him to take someone else. Anyone else. Or even his going alone. But then she gave that some thought. Did she really want Logan alone at the party with Helene? Helene might see that as an open invitation to pursue him.

Something she was likely to do, anyway.

Still, why make it easier for her by serving up Logan on a silver platter?

"You're going, aren't you?" Logan asked. He pulled out the big guns. A smile. And a dimple flashed in his cheek.

Good grief. How could she say no to a dimple like that? And the *please*?

Reese huffed first before she answered. "All right, I'll go."

Another smile. Logan dropped a quick kiss on her mouth. "You won't regret this."

He was wrong about that. Because Reese already did regret it.

AND REESE CONTINUED to regret her decision to go.

However, what she regretted even more was that she'd brought Jimena with her on the shopping trip to the San Antonio mall. Her friend and she clearly had different ideas about what constituted a suitable dress.

Jimena studied the latest one Reese had tried on. Electric blue and with enough sparkles to possibly trigger seizures in some people. It was also far shorter and tighter than Reese preferred. Call her old-fashioned, but she didn't like the idea of someone discovering the color of her panties if she happened to lean even an inch in any direction.

"It's not slutty enough," Jimena insisted. "You want to wow Logan's ex when you walk into that party."

She would wow Helene, all right, but not in a good way. The woman already thought Reese was trash, and this dress would go a long way toward proving it.

"In a slut contest, this dress would win," Reese argued. "I'm definitely not getting it."

Jimena looked shocked, though Reese didn't know why. So far, Reese had vetoed every dress that Jimena had chosen for her to try on. In several cases, she had vetoed without even trying on the outfit.

Maybe it wasn't too late to tell Logan to find another date. Or for her to leave town. Of course, that was probably what Helene wanted her to do, and the reminder gave Reese enough of a resolve to go back into the dressing room and try the next one. It was another of Jimena's selections.

Acid green and, yes, sparkles. The back was what Jimena called a crack back. Reese hadn't asked for clarification, but she doubted her friend had meant the dress was suitable for selling drugs or a spinal adjustment.

"So, did I tell you I dumped Elrond?" Jimena asked.

"Really?" She gave Jimena a dose of that same *shock* Jimena had given her with the dress. It wasn't a shock at all. Jimena went through men as quickly as Reese was going through these dresses. "Was it because of the clown outfit?"

"No. I actually sort of got into that. Did you know there's an entire clown fetish thing?"

"Didn't have a clue." She paused. "Did he ever confess if he was the one with Helene?"

"Never. In fact, he denied it all the way up to the

time I dumped him. And you know what? I believe him. Who does Logan think it was?"

"He doesn't know." And this conversation wasn't making her feel any better about any of this. Here she was trying on dresses to go with Logan to his ex's reception, and he was still obviously concerned about the identity of Helene's lover.

Nope, there was no chance of Reese getting a broken heart over this.

Reese put the crack back dress aside and went to the next one. One of her own selections. It was black, plain. And boring. She could be a wallflower in this dress, which was the exact reason she tried it on. She came out of the dressing room ready to hear Jimena make the fake gagging sounds she'd made at all of Reese's selections.

And that's exactly what happened.

"The idea is for you to look good," Jimena pointed out, her voice flat. "So good that the ex will turn green and Logan will want to have sex with you on the hors d'oeuvres table."

Those were high expectations for a mere dress, but Jimena did have a point. As long as she was going to be there at the party, she might as well wear something she knew Logan would like.

With her mission clarified, Reese went back into the dressing room, looked through the choices she had left and came up with a tomato-red dress. No sparkles, but it was silk and had a shimmer to it. That silk whispered over her skin when she put it on, and Reese knew that even without Jimena's approval, this was going to be the one. Not because she loved, loved, loved it, but because she was tired of shopping, and it was on sale.

As she'd done too many times to count, Reese came

out of the dressing room, prepared to twirl around to show Jimena how *enthusiastic* she was with this choice, but her enthusiasm sort of stalled in her throat.

Helene was standing there.

"Well, hello," Helene said, giving Reese another dose of that creepy smile. "What a coincidence, running into you here."

Reese doubted it was anything but a coincidence. Helene was checking her out. Literally. The woman's attention was lingering on Reese's bust area. Reese's B-cups obviously weren't measuring up to Helene's DDs.

Jimena looked at Reese, and she didn't think it was her imagination that Jimena was silently asking if Reese wanted her to punch the woman's lights out. She did, but that wasn't going to happen. If anyone punched out Helene's lights, it would be Reese.

"Is that what you're wearing to the reception?" Helene asked. A glacier wouldn't melt in that cool mouth of hers.

"No," Jimena said at the same time Reese said, "Maybe."

Helene's expression tightened, just enough to show her disapproval. "It doesn't do anything for your skin, does it? It washes you out. May I suggest something in yellow or green?"

Colors that were certain *not* to look good on her. Maybe Reese should put on the electric-blue one and try to trigger a seizure in Helene.

"Then again," Helene went on, tapping her chin as if she were truly giving some input that Reese might take. "This one does make your stomach look flat since it skims over the body rather than hugging it."

Reese figured that was a dig about the pregnancy rumors.

"I think it's perfect," someone said.

Logan.

He wasn't exactly hurrying when he came into the viewing area of the dressing room, but judging from his slightly rapid breathing, there'd been some hurrying involved before his arrival.

"Logan," Helene greeted as if everything were hunky-dory between them. She moved in for a handshake, maybe even a hug, but Logan made a beeline toward Reese.

"Sorry, I'm late," he told Reese.

Reese didn't dodge the hug he gave her. Or even the quick kiss he dropped on her mouth.

Oh, Reese got it then. Logan must have heard that Helene had followed Jimena and her here to the mall, and he'd come to run interference. Or maybe he'd come to give Helene a little payback. Either way, Reese was glad to see him. Glad about the kiss, too, and not because it was possible payback but because a kiss from Logan always made things feel right.

Even when it was a fake kiss.

"There's a purple one in the dressing room that I think Reese should pick," Jimena piped up. She gave Helene some stink eye, and coming from a woman who was even more beautiful than Helene, it was far stinkier than anything Reese could have squinted out.

"Purple, huh?" Logan said. "Maybe I should see it." He took hold of Reese's arm, leading her back to the dressing area.

Thankfully, there were no other customers trying on clothes because this wasn't exactly a man-friendly zone.

"Sorry about that," Logan added once they were in the dressing room. "Greg heard that Helene was coming here to the mall to shop, and I figured it was so she could follow you. I didn't know which store you were in so I had to go to six of them before I found you."

It touched her far more than she wanted that Logan was looking out for her. "Thanks, but it wasn't necessary. Helene is just sizing up her competition, and I'm pretty sure she's decided that I'm not much competition at all."

"You're wrong."

It was one of those perfect things to say. Then Reese realized why he might be saying it. "Don't worry. I said I'd go to the reception with you, and I will. I just won't be going in this."

She plucked out the purple dress Jimena had mentioned. The opposite of a crack back. This was more of a cooch front since the neckline plunged all the way to the navel and then some.

Logan eyed it, not at the absurdity of the design but with an interest that any red-blooded straight man would have. "It would, uh, get everyone talking. And drooling."

"You're not the drooling type. But thanks for coming to my rescue." She was about to usher him out, but Logan didn't budge.

The cooch front must have put some thoughts in his head, or maybe he was still in the "I'll show Helene" frame of mind. Either way, he kissed her again.

"Helene can't see us," Reese reminded him.

Reese had figured that would get that gleaming look out of Logan's eyes. It didn't.

"Good," he said. And he kissed her again.

This one definitely wasn't just some little peck on the mouth to get back at his ex. This was a full-fledged, openmouthed kiss that sizzled in all the right places. Of course, Logan had a way of sizzling just by looking at her.

"So, is this the dress?" he asked. But he wasn't really looking at it. He dropped a kiss on her neck. Then lower.

More sizzling, but Reese knew she had to get some things straight before he sizzled her right out of the dress. She took hold of his chin, lifted it. "What's this really about?"

Logan stared at her. "If you don't know, then I'm doing this all wrong."

"No, it's right." Reese winced at the confession. Best not to bare her soul when the soul-baring needed to come from him. "I just don't want this to be about Helene."

The stare turned a little glare-ish. "Yesterday I invited you to my place to have dinner and sex. The only reason it didn't happen was because of the migraine."

Yes, and then the morning meeting. Then Helene's arrival. Reese was about to remind him of all that, but then Logan pushed away the grip she had on his chin and kissed her again. That caused her breath to vanish, and she couldn't very well give him reminders when she couldn't speak.

But Logan gave her a reminder, all right.

A reminder of just how hot this attraction was between them. Of course, it was just that—an attraction— and Reese should have held back as a self-preservation thing. But then Logan kept kissing her, and thinking about anything except the pleasure seemed to be well beyond her present mental capacity.

Logan kissed her neck again. Then he went lower and used that clever mouth on the tops of her breasts. The dress was cut just so that he didn't have to work too hard to hit his target. However, he did have to work when he dipped lower to catch on to the hem. He slid up the slinky dress, all the while his hand sliding along the outside of her leg.

Then the inside of her leg.

Mercy, that felt good even though his fingers landed against her panties and not bare skin. It rid her of what little breath Reese had managed to gather, but it also did something else.

He's not stopping.

That flashed in her brain along with remembering one teensy little detail. They were in a women's dressing room at a department store while Jimena and Helene were just yards away.

"I don't do things like this," she managed to say.

He didn't laugh, but he could have considering their one-night stand. A one-night stand that had been amazing but was still complicating her life. Like now. Reese wanted him to keep kissing and touching her, but she didn't want him doing it for all the wrong reasons. Considering the timing and the place, it seemed wrong.

But then Logan lowered himself, drawing up her knee to his shoulder, and he gave her such a well-placed kiss that wrong suddenly seemed very, very right.

He slid down her panties and made the kiss even more special.

Reese groaned. Too loud. So she clamped her teeth over her bottom lip in case she did it again.

"Is everything okay?" Jimena called out.

"Fine," Reese answered, her response too fast and clipped. Jimena would certainly know what was going on.

Or not.

"Can I see what you're putting on now?" Jimena asked.

"Not just yet. I'm not ready."

But Reese was certainly nearing the readying point with each kiss. She gasped, then groaned when Logan flicked his tongue.

"That must be some dress," Jimena remarked.

Reese figured if Helene had said anything that would have pulled her right out of the moment. Heck, Jimena might have pulled her out of it, too, but Logan seemed to sense that speed counted here.

"Is Logan helping you?" Jimena again.

"Yes." He was helping. Helping a lot.

Reese pressed her back against the wall to anchor herself. A hanger poked her in the side, and her one foot on the floor was suddenly feeling as it were on the verge of a charley horse. She hung on by latching onto Logan's hair. And it didn't take long for the pressure to build, build, build.

Until the climax rippled through her. Except it wasn't really a ripple. It was more like a tsunami.

"Reese, are you okay?" she heard Jimena ask. Heard the concern, too, in her friend's voice.

But Reese was past the point of answering and worrying about the concern. She just held on and let Logan finish what he'd started.

CHAPTER FOURTEEN

LOGAN GLANCED OUT the window of his office to make sure a real storm wasn't coming. It wasn't. The sky was clear, not even a hint of a cloud. So, the only storm warning was the one inside him, and there was nothing he could do to stop it.

Helene had something up her sleeve.

But what?

Logan hadn't been able to figure it out yet, but he was certain she was going to use this reception tonight as some kind of ploy to do something he wasn't going to like. That concern alone nearly made him want to cancel, but that could be playing right into Helene's hands. If Reese and he didn't show, then Helene could play spin doctor and somehow make herself the victim.

However, he got the feeling that his ex was planning something much worse. And he'd had that particular feeling since she'd followed Reese to the mall two days earlier. Thankfully, Logan had gotten to Reese before Helene could try to sabotage things. Again, he wasn't sure how she'd planned to do that, but he had considered lots of possibilities.

Some stupid.

Like maybe Helene talking Reese into choosing a dress that would fall apart when she stepped into the reception. Or a dress that would turn see-through in the lights Helene was planning to use.

Of course, maybe Helene just wanted to get inside Reese's head. It was that possibility, and the stupid ones, that had sent him running to the mall.

Logan had no idea what had sent his mouth running into Reese, though.

It had started as a way of, well, thanking her. Not just for going to the reception with him but for putting up with all the other shit he'd pulled. Any other woman would have plotted his castration if he'd accused her of conning him and then trying to run her out of town.

In hindsight, though, an orgasm probably wasn't the best way to thank her.

Especially an orgasm in a mall dressing room.

Reese probably wouldn't believe he hadn't planned that down to the final ripple of her climax. He hadn't. She had mentioned something about her not doing things like that. Well, he didn't, either, but Logan hadn't figured out yet why he'd thought it was a good idea.

Why he still thought it was.

Hell, fucking her was an even better idea. But he wanted to make sure that Reese understood that sex between them didn't have anything to do with Helene. First, though, he had to make sure that was the whole truth and nothing but the truth.

Logan signed a contract that he should have been reading just as there was a tap at the door. Part of him expected it to be Reese, coming to cancel out of the reception, but it was only Greg. His assistant was wearing an orange suit with a pink bow tie. Probably the outfit he was planning on wearing to the reception since the event was only an hour from starting.

Greg had some papers under his arms, some in each hand, and he was also balancing a large mug of coffee that Logan figured he would need. He hadn't gotten a lot of sleep the last couple of nights, mainly because Reese had seemed to be keeping her distance. She hadn't called, and Logan hadn't called her for fear of that cancellation thing.

And her dumping him.

Though they'd actually have to have a relationship first before he could become a dumpee.

Greg handed Logan the coffee first. "The McMillian contract," Greg said, placing some of the papers in front of Logan. Then he added another batch. "This is the work contract for the vet you're hiring."

"What vet?"

Greg gave him a blank stare. "The one to deal with the rodeo bulls and cutting horses. Remember, you and your brothers thought it was best if you had a vet assigned just to the ranch."

Logan had some vague memory of that. Hell. He was going to run this business into the ground if he didn't get his mind off Reese and back where it belonged.

"I had your car filled up with gas," Greg went on. "I assumed you'd be using it to pick up Reese. I mean, instead of your truck."

"I'll use the truck." It would seem less of a big deal that way, and he figured Reese wanted to stay as far under the radar as possible. "But there should be enough gas in it." And even if there wasn't, they could walk. The civic center was just a few blocks from the Bluebonnet Inn.

Greg nodded. He had two more sets of papers, and he put one of them on top of the vet contract. This one was in a manila envelope. It was sealed with a large swatch of tape. "It's a report from the private investigator," Greg explained. "He finally managed to get Reese's juvie record."

Logan looked at the envelope as if it were coated with anthrax. He certainly hadn't forgotten about the request he'd made to the PI, but the timing sucked. A couple of weeks ago, he would have been plenty glad to read what was inside.

Not so much now, though.

It felt like exactly what it was—a huge violation of her privacy. Since it was obvious Reese wasn't trying to con or scam him, there was no reason for him to know what she'd done that had caused her to be arrested.

No logical reason, anyway.

Hell.

Logan might have been tempted to open it if Greg hadn't stayed hovered over his desk. "Anything else?" Logan asked.

Greg nodded. "It's about Helene."

"What now?" Logan pressed when Greg didn't continue and didn't budge.

His assistant took a long breath. Then a second one. When he got to the third one, Logan figured this was either bad news or the guy was about to do some yoga or meditation.

"Well, I thought you should know that Helene has been doing some good things," Greg finally said. "Today she paid off a bunch of medical bills for people over at the clinic. And she bought a lot of supplies and even some computers for the elementary school."

Good things indeed, but Logan had to shake his head. "Why are you telling me this?"

For the first time since Logan had known the man, Greg fidgeted. This was different from him twitching and twittering about. He twisted the corner on the final envelope he was holding.

"I think you should give Helene a second chance," Greg blurted out.

Logan had already used his *screw-this* quota for the day. Heck, maybe for the rest of his life, so he just sat there and stared at Greg, daring him to continue with this stupid idea.

"She's trying so hard," Greg went on, "and it's obvious the reason she's doing all of this is to win you back. Do you have any idea how much it'll humiliate Helene to have you bring Reese tonight?" He didn't wait for Logan to answer. "Don't get me wrong. I like Reese, but you and Helene were together a long time, and it seems wrong for you to throw that all away because of one mistake."

It wasn't as if Logan hadn't already considered this. Had dismissed it, too. "It was a *big* mistake," Logan reminded him.

"I know you're thinking this isn't any of my beeswax," Greg continued.

Yes, he was.

"Then why are you bringing it up?" Logan snapped. He stood, went to the bar—not for a drink but so he could check his suit in the mirror.

"Because, well…" After the third time Greg repeated that pair of words, Logan turned back around to face him.

"What's going on?" Logan demanded.

"That." Greg put the last piece of paper he'd been holding on Logan's desk.

Greg didn't offer any explanation to go along with it. In fact, he didn't say anything. The man just headed for the door so Logan went to his desk to have a look.

It was Greg's resignation.

Greg stopped in the doorway. "I figured you'd want that. I've already cleared out my desk, and I've left you a list of suitable replacements to fill my position."

Logan didn't consider himself clueless very often, but this was one of those times. "And why would I want you to resign?"

"Because I was the clown that night with Helene," Greg confessed.

Logan wasn't easily surprised, but that did it. It took him several seconds to get his tongue working, and by then, it was too late.

Like Elvis, Greg had left the building.

LOGAN WAS LATE.

Reese didn't think she'd get so lucky, though, that he would skip out of picking her up for Helene's reception. No. He'd show, but if he didn't make it soon, they were going to be one of the last ones to arrive, which would mean everyone would be there to see them go in. Reese was hoping for the wallflower mode tonight.

The dress might help. Much to Jimena's disgust, Reese hadn't chosen any of the slut-ish dresses but had instead opted for one with more wallflower appeal. A little black number with subtle sparkles. Of course, it wasn't without some controversy.

After giving her that amazing orgasm, Logan had offered to pay for the dress. He probably hadn't meant it as anything more than a nice gesture since she was going to this reception for him, but there was no way Reese would take Logan's money.

No way apparently that she could force herself to calm down, either.

She wasn't a pacer, but that's exactly what she was doing now even though pacing in her small apartment amounted to about eight steps max in any direction. Reese checked her phone. No missed calls or texts, and she was about to call Logan when he finally appeared at her door.

One look at him, though, and Reese knew something was wrong.

"Are you here to tell me you're getting back with Helene?" she asked.

Logan opened his mouth, shook his head and stared at her as if that'd been the last thing on his mind. Reese was so relieved that she kissed him. It wasn't nearly as hot as the ones in the dressing room, and it seemed as if kissing her was the next to the last thing that'd been on his mind.

"Greg was the one with Helene that night," he said.

Reese certainly hadn't seen that coming. Apparently, neither had Logan, judging from the stunned look on his face. She led him into the apartment and shut the door. The walls in the inn weren't exactly thick, and she didn't think he wanted anyone else to hear this conversation.

"How do you know that?" Reese asked, and she was about to launch into a warning for him not to jump to conclusions and believe gossip. Greg seemed like the last person in Spring Hill who'd carry on with Helene.

"Greg told me."

All right, so no warning necessary, though Reese

still couldn't quite wrap her head around it. "I thought he was gay."

"So did most people in town. Evidently he's not." Logan scrubbed his hand over his face, sat on the edge of the bed. "He told me about a half hour ago, gave me his resignation and then walked out. I didn't even get to ask him if it was a one-time thing or if Helene and he had been carrying on for years."

Reese wanted to ask him if it mattered, but obviously it did. Maybe Logan could forgive a single lapse. Maybe that's what was putting those worry lines on his forehead.

"Did I ever tell you that I fucking hate clowns?" he added. "I have since I was a kid."

In the grand scheme of things, that seemed minor, but maybe it was a phobia. If so, that would add a little more salt to an already salted wound. His trusted assistant and his longtime girlfriend together, and now that Greg had just resigned, Logan might never get the answers that he clearly needed.

"Here," he said, handing her an envelope.

She sat down next to him. "Is it Greg's resignation?" Though she couldn't imagine why Logan would want her to see it.

"No. It's the report from a PI I hired. He was able to get into your juvie records."

Her heart flip-flopped. Then fell straight to the floor. Not a good place for a heart to be. Reese's first response was to lash out, to tell Logan he had no right, but then she noticed that the envelope was still sealed.

"I asked the PI to get that before," he added. "Well, *before*. And no, the PI didn't tell me what was inside.

If you want to tell me at some point, then fine. If not, it'll stay your secret."

That was generous, considering that Logan was a cautious man. Also considering that he had to know there was something inside that could possibly hurt his reputation simply because he was associating with her.

"Does this have something to do with what happened in the dressing room?" Reese came out and asked.

"Yes."

So, he was letting his emotions play into this. Reese wasn't sure if she should be flattered or tell him that, in this case, it wasn't a good idea. Nor was it a good idea for her to continue to put her head in the sand on this. She needed to come clean with Logan.

And then find a way to get out of his life.

Reese stood to start talking, but Logan stood, too. "Come on. Let's put in an appearance at this reception."

"You're sure you're up to this?"

"No." He was heading to the door but stopped as if seeing her for the first time. "You look amazing by the way. You didn't choose the red dress."

She shook her head, put the envelope on the kitchenette counter. "This is the 'blend in with the crowd' black one." Not dowdy exactly, but definitely not flashy, either.

He managed a smile and kissed her again. This one was very much like the others that'd started the firestorm in the dressing room. "Thank you for doing this," he added.

Considering the extreme swing of emotions she'd just had, Reese was surprised she was able to get her feet moving. Logan helped with that. He took her hand

and led her down the stairs to the front of the building where he'd parked.

"My advice…" he said as he drove toward the civic center. "Avoid Helene as much as possible."

That had been her plan, but Reese thought of something. "Does she know that Greg told you?"

Logan shook his head. "Like I said, Greg didn't hang around to answer any questions. But I figure he's probably let her know. And she probably told him to lie low to give her a chance to put a spin on the gossip. No one overheard Greg's confession, but it will get around."

Yes, it would. And while it seemed selfish to think it, at least this meaty gossip could maybe finally put to rest the rumors that she was pregnant with Logan's baby. Of course, it would also give Logan something else to get over because he now knew the betrayal had come from someone he trusted.

The parking lot at the civic center was packed, and Logan wound up parking on the street. No one was milling around the building, which meant everyone was already likely inside.

"One drink, a few handshakes," he said, "and we can leave."

Reese wasn't sure if Logan was talking to her or if he'd said that just to steady his nerves. Her own nerves certainly needed some steadying.

As they approached the building, the double doors opened, and Reese saw Jimena step out. A surprise. She hadn't known her friend was coming. Or that Jimena had bought the cooch front dress.

"I came for moral support," Jimena said. "You're going to need it."

That didn't help Reese's already churning stomach.

Hand in hand Logan and she approached the doors. And considering that Reese could see dozens of people inside, she noticed right away that something was missing.

Chatter.

No one was talking, and everyone had their attention focused on the stage area. At least they did until Logan and she walked in. Almost immediately, the whispers went through the crowd like a wave, and the wave didn't take long to make it to the front.

And that's when Reese noticed the person on the stage. Not their hostess, Helene. But rather a clown with a microphone.

If this had been an ordinary situation, Reese would have thought he was part of the entertainment, especially since the clown was onstage with a three-piece band. She wouldn't have given a second's thought to whoever it was behind that makeup, big floppy shoes and the squishy red nose.

However, this situation wasn't ordinary, and she was afraid the clown was Greg.

It was.

Reese got confirmation when the clown spoke, and thanks to the microphone, everyone in the room had no trouble hearing every word.

"I'm here to help mend some fences." Greg raised his glass to Logan.

Until then, everyone had been volleying glances between Logan and the clown, but the volleying stopped, and everyone's gaze now settled on Logan.

"Logan," Greg continued. "When you hear what I have to say, I'm sure you'll be proposing to Helene— tonight. And this time, she'll get the chance to say yes."

CHAPTER FIFTEEN

SHIT ON A STICK.

So much for the quick in and out that Logan wanted.

There was zip that Greg or anyone else could say to make him propose to Helene, and the only *yes* Logan wanted to hear was Reese answering his plea to get the heck out of here. Logan considered just turning around and walking out with Reese, but Greg apparently had something else to say.

"Don't leave, Logan," Greg called out, his voice very loud with the microphone. "This is a public apology to both Helene and you." Greg looked at the people in the crowd who were hanging on every word. "You see, I'm the one who had an inappropriate relationship with Helene."

That started some whispers through the crowd, and Logan heard a couple of X-rated comments about what had possibly gone on during clown sex. The red, bulbous nose came up.

Logan glanced around and spotted Helene. Like him, she was trying to inch her way to the side of the room and out of sight. That wasn't going to happen, though, unless she headed out of the county. With the volleyed glances going on among Greg, Logan and her, the partygoers looked as if they were watching a three-way tennis match.

"It wasn't Helene's fault," Greg went on. "I seduced her, and I caught her at a down moment. She'd just lost a sale on a sideboard. She really wanted that sideboard," he added as if it would help. Ditto for the part about seducing her.

Maybe that's why he'd worn the clown suit, so that maybe people would forget he wasn't exactly the sort of man who could seduce a former beauty queen.

"Greg, please," Helene said, shaking her head. There were tears in her eyes, and even though Logan didn't want to, he felt a little sorry for her.

For a second or two, anyway.

Then he remembered where that red nose had been when Logan walked in on them.

"Anyway, Helene has paid and paid hard for what I did," Greg went on. "Logan, too. And I'm truly sorry for all the trouble I caused both of you. You're obviously meant to be together. Logan used to tell me that all the time, that Helene was the perfect woman for him."

Because Logan still had his arm around Reese, he felt her muscles tighten, and he wished he could tell her that the last part wasn't true. But he couldn't. Because he had indeed said that not just to Greg but to everyone in his family.

"I'm leaving town," Greg went on. "No, it's necessary," he added, though no one had objected. "Once I'm gone, Logan and Helene can find their way back to each other without me around to stir up bad memories."

Greg sniffed as if crying. It was hard to tell because he had fake tear streaks on his cheeks, but his shoulders were slumped when he walked away, his floppy shoes squeaking as he exited the stage. He disappeared out the back door.

No one else moved or said anything. It was as if everyone held their breaths and then released them at the same time. The band started moving, too, and they jumped right into playing a soothing classical tune that didn't go with the tension in the room. Several people rushed to Helene. Riley, Claire, Cassie and Lucky rushed to Logan.

"You knew?" Lucky asked him right off.

Logan nodded. He'd explain more later, but for now he looked at Reese to see how she was handling this.

"I think that went well, don't you?" Reese asked.

Of course, that made Logan smile, but he knew her attempt at a joke wasn't from humor as much as it was from nerves. Worse, some people were now glaring at Reese as if she were somehow responsible for Logan not rushing to console Helene. He'd rather eat the clown nose—and that was after he knew where it'd been—than console his ex.

"Want me to do something stupid to get everyone's attention?" Lucky asked.

It was a generous offer, but considering Lucky and Cassie were finalizing custody of Mia and Mackenzie, it was best if the antics stayed clown-related. Of course, Helene was doing her own antics, too, and more and more people were heading her way to offer hugs and no doubt kind words. Logan got his share of them as well, and not that he was keeping count, but he was getting more than she was.

"Please," Jimena said in an "I've got this" tone. "Wardrobe malfunction," Jimena yelled after she shoved the skinny strap of her dress off her shoulder.

The dress hadn't covered up much before, and now her left breast was exposed. She had a nipple ring and a Lick Me Here tattoo complete with a tattooed arrow that pointed right toward her nipple.

Jimena got more attention than Logan or Helene. In fact, even the band stopped to see her tattooed tit.

"Wardrobe malfunction," Jimena said again.

Jimena paused a couple more seconds before she fixed the dangling boob and dress strap. There were still plenty of dangling tongues, though, and Logan realized that even with Greg's clown appearance, that the gossip about Greg and Helene would be tempered some with the breast reveal.

"Thank you," Logan told her.

"Anytime." Jimena winked at him and Reese. "If that doesn't work, I'll drop something and bend over to pick it up."

"No!" Reese said so quickly that she choked on her own breath. "Jimena only goes commando," she added in a whisper to Logan.

Well, that would definitely be the talk of the town. But Logan didn't think it would be necessary. However, he could use that drink right about now, and he led Reese through the crowd toward the bar at the back. Apparently, Reese needed a drink as well, because she downed the glass of champagne she'd gotten at the bar. Jimena downed two, plus the one she'd already been holding.

Logan wanted to do the same thing. Actually, he wanted a shot of something much stronger, but he sipped the champagne and got to work. His brothers and their partners did, as well. Cassie and Lucky went in one direction. Riley and Claire in another.

Logan greeted all the people he should greet. Bert and some of the town's other business owners. He had to listen to an update on Maggie's uterus. Then more about Walter Meekins's latest gout flare-up. Other ailments included a wart with an infected hair in it and hemorrhoids.

Clearly, the people of Spring Hill knew how to make good party conversation.

Of course, none of the men actually looked Logan in the eye when they spoke to him, and that wasn't because of the clown-Helene thing. It was because all male eyes went to Jimena, perhaps hoping for another wardrobe malfunction.

Reese fared somewhat better with the eyeballing and conversation. She got three requests for the recipe for her lemon thingies, though Elgin Tate, who had been a horn-dog since he'd first sprouted chest hair twenty years earlier, had asked without adding the lemon part.

"I just gotta have that thingy of yours," Elgin had said.

Elgin smiled until he happened to glance at Logan, and then the man scurried off. Logan rarely had to use words to threaten to bust a guy in the nuts.

"Well, of course, I know you'll reconcile with Logan," he heard someone say. Tiffany Halverson, Helene's old college friend.

Somehow, even over the other chatter in the room, that made its way to Logan's ears. To Reese's, as well. And Logan soon realized why.

Helene and Tiffany were inching their way over to them. Logan figured that was by design. Heck, they'd probably rehearsed every word of the conversation, too.

"Logan's the love of your life," Tiffany declared, and she then acted surprised to see him when her gaze landed on him.

"You're sure about that love of your life thing?" Jimena asked. "Because I heard you fucked a clown."

Neither Helene nor Tiffany spared her a glance. Or Reese. Talking to Reese and/or her friend probably wasn't in the script. Yet. But Logan figured Helene and/or her friend had some zingers planned for Reese.

Tiffany did answer Jimena's question, though. "Absolutely, Logan is the love of Helene's life. I look at all of this as just a hiccup, and my prayer is that ten years from now, when Logan and Helene are playing with their children, that this will be just a distant memory. Helene and Logan have both been so hurt by what happened."

This was the first time Logan had ever heard the mention of children, and he had no doubts, none, that Helene had put her up to saying it. Maybe it was the first time he actually saw the woman he'd thought he loved enough to marry. For once he was glad he'd walked in on her with that clown.

"You're smiling," Helene said, but she didn't look especially happy about that. Maybe because he was smiling at Reese. And Reese was smiling back as if they were sharing some kind of secret.

And that didn't please Helene one bit. Logan heard the hitch in her throat and saw just a glimmer of the hurt, and maybe the jealousy, simmering behind those cool blue eyes. However, she concealed it as quickly as it came with a smile of her own.

"Tiffany, I don't believe you've met Logan's date," Helene said. She made the introductions. Polite ones, too, though he was certain that Tiffany already knew who Reese was. "Reese, I'm so glad you could come, and the dress is perfect. Logan helped her pick it out," she added to Tiffany.

No doubt something else Tiffany knew, but the woman smiled as politely as Helene did. "How did you two meet?" Tiffany asked Reese. It was possible Helene had somehow found that out, but Logan had no intentions of confirming it. But Jimena did.

"In a bar," Jimena provided. At least she didn't add anything about the bucket-list one-night stand. Not at first, anyway. "Reese picked him up because he was hot and because she thought she was dying. Logan was a bucket-list thing, but now Reese has to undo all of that."

"Oh," Helene said.

And then she smiled a little smile probably because she quickly put everything together and thought she'd come up with what had actually happened. That Logan had been nursing a broken heart and that's the only reason he'd landed in bed with Reese.

That didn't explain what'd gone on in the mall dressing room. Or all the kisses they'd shared since. It also didn't explain why he had every intention of having sex with Reese again.

Tonight.

Logan glanced around to see if they were the center of attention. They were. Even the band had softened the music, and Logan was betting every word, every expression, was being cataloged and examined so it could be gossiped about later. The trick was not to give them anything more to talk about.

Because if this conversation got out of hand, he might have to ask Jimena to pick something up off the floor, after all.

"So, what do you do?" Tiffany asked Reese.

Again, it would have been a question Helene fed to her friend. Tiffany didn't live in Spring Hill, but Helene had probably filled her in on everything she knew, including the plan Helene had no doubt concocted on how to get back in Logan's good graces. And his bed.

"I'm a cook at the Fork and Spoon Café," Reese answered.

"She's being modest," Helene piped up. "From what I've heard Reese was top in her class at culinary school."

Logan glanced at Reese to see if that was true, but apparently she was still being modest because she shrugged. But Logan didn't shrug. To the best of his knowledge, no one was gossiping about Reese's placement in culinary school. They were only discussing her possible tattoos and the equally possible pregnancy.

So, how had Helene known?

Hell. She'd probably had Reese investigated, and it was hard for Logan to blast her for that since he'd done the same thing. But Helene was almost certainly doing this so she could find some dirt on Reese. Dirt that would send her running.

Perhaps like the dirt in that sealed envelope he'd given her earlier.

Logan wished now that he'd at least gotten a glimpse of the information so he would know how to fight this shit that Helene was no doubt about to sling at her. When he'd been with Helene, he'd seen her make plenty of ball-busting deals, but it was another thing to be on the other side of that.

"I'll see you at Lucky and Cassie's engagement party," Helene said, and she would have just slipped away if Logan hadn't stopped her with a question.

"You're going to that?" He didn't add a "why," but his tone certainly implied it.

"My mother was invited, and I'm her plus-one."

Great. This was Della's doing. Except Della had probably invited her mother more out of a social obligation. She likely hadn't realized that the woman would be bringing Helene. Since it would seem petty to un-invite them, Logan and Reese would be forced into another uncomfortable situation.

"Are you ready to get out of here?" Logan asked Reese.

She was hugging Jimena goodbye before Logan even finished asking. He hated that he'd put her through this, and he had every intention of making it up to her. Jimena didn't seem to mind, either, being left behind, because she started line dancing with the Nederland sisters. Those women were bad news, but Logan figured Jimena wasn't on anyone's good-news list, either.

Logan threaded Reese and him through the crowds, speaking to those that he'd missed, and he made his way to the door. He didn't release the breath he'd been holding until he was outside.

"Are you okay?" Reese asked.

She looked good enough to kiss so that's what he did, and he could almost feel the tension slide right out of him. Whatever this was between Reese and him, even if it was just temporary sex, he was going to take it and not look back.

Logan was still kissing her when he led her to his truck, and it was because of the lip-lock that he didn't see the person leaning against his door until she moved. It was a woman smoking a cigarette, and when they approached, she flicked the cigarette to the ground and crushed it out with the toe of her stiletto.

"Good to see you, Reese," the woman said.

Reese had gone stiff a couple of times in the reception, but it was nothing compared to this. Every muscle in her body seemed to turn to rock.

"You know her?" Logan asked when Reese didn't say anything and didn't move.

"Of course she knows me," the woman purred. She went to Reese, pulled her into her arms. "I'm her mother."

REESE HAD HOPED that the worst part of the night was over, but she'd obviously been wrong. If she knew her mother, things were about to get much, much worse.

The first thing Reese did was untangle herself from her mother's embrace. It was as fake as the smile on her face, and after seeing so many fake smiles at the reception, Reese knew one when she saw it. Of course, anytime her mother smiled, it was likely just to play a con or because she was drunk. Since Reese didn't smell any booze on her breath, it had to be the latter.

"Why are you here?" Reese snapped. She also checked her purse to make sure her mother hadn't already managed to snatch her wallet. It was there, for now.

"Where are your manners?" Her mother turned to Logan, extended her hand for him to shake. "I'm Vickie Stephenson. Reese probably hasn't mentioned me—"

"She has." And he left it at that. His tone, however, implied he knew all about her criminal ways.

"That's a surprise," her mother said. "Reese doesn't

usually tell her…friends about me." And yes, she actually glanced at Logan's crotch.

In addition to being a con woman, her mother slept around a lot. With anybody. One of her favorite things to do was to seduce Reese's boyfriends, and that had started when Reese was a teenager.

"Watch your wallet and your zipper," Reese warned Logan, and she hated that she even had to bring it up. Still, she didn't want him to be robbed. Or groped. Both were possibilities.

"Why are you here?" Reese repeated.

Of course, she could have added a bunch more questions to that including but not limited to, how did you find me and what do you want? Because if Vickie was here, she definitely wanted something.

"Can't I visit my own daughter without my motives being questioned?"

Vickie was using her "high-end" voice tonight. She had many voices and used them to fit the situation. She apparently thought she shouldn't sound like a thug or a hick around Logan. That included dressing high-end. Or her interpretation of it, anyway. She was wearing a black skirt with a leopard print top.

"No, I'll always question your motives," Reese quickly assured her. "Whenever I see you, I know you've brought trouble with you."

Vickie made a sound of frustration that couldn't possibly be genuine because she had to have known Reese wouldn't trust her. Not after their last encounter. She'd taken Reese's keys, broken into the restaurant where she worked and stolen thousands of dollars' worth of knives. Since there probably wasn't a black market for them, Vickie had likely just done it to prove to Reese that she could screw up her life.

Reese had a bad feeling in the pit of her stomach that Vickie was here to do that all over again.

"Can we go somewhere and talk?" Vickie asked. She motioned up the street. "Maybe we can go to that pretty Victorian place where Logan has his office? I'll bet you have some good whiskey in there, and I could use a drink. Could use some other things, too." Vickie glanced at his crotch again.

Good grief. The woman was sixteen years older than Logan, and every one of her forty-nine years showed on her face. She would have had better luck picking up Greg the clown than a guy like Logan.

"How did you find out I was here?" Reese asked.

"Does it matter?"

Well, it mattered even more now that Vickie had dodged the question. "Did Chucky tell you?" Not that Chucky would have just volunteered information like that, but it was possible Chucky had found her and then mentioned it.

"Chucky," Vickie repeated. "Yes. He told me."

For a woman who made her living doing cons, that wasn't a convincing lie. But the problem with Vickie was if she made it seem like a lie, then it wouldn't put the blame back on Chucky, and it didn't let Reese know who'd really ratted her out.

Reese glanced at Logan, and even though he didn't say anything, she thought they might be thinking the same thing.

Helene could have done this.

After all, Helene had known about Reese being number one in her culinary class, and that wasn't even something Jimena would have mentioned—since Jimena had graduated last. It made sense that Helene would have Reese investigated, and if so she could have been the one to find Vickie.

And bring her here to Spring Hill.

Where Helene could see how much trouble she could stir up.

"Can we have that talk now?" Vickie asked. Judging from her tone, the pot stirring was about to start. "Maybe in private? Maybe over drinks? Or would you rather we just chat in front of your friend?"

"I know about Reese's past," Logan volunteered.

"Do you, now?" Vickie said in a tone that implied Logan didn't know everything.

And he didn't.

But her mother did.

Vickie didn't have to mention Spenser's name, but it was there, part of the pot stirring, and it wasn't something Reese was ready to share with Logan. She might never be ready for that.

Reese turned to him, but Logan must have known what she was going to say because he shook his head. "I'm not sure it's a good idea for you to be alone with your mother."

It wasn't, but she didn't have a lot of options here. Reese kissed him but kept it chaste and brief. "I'll take my mother to my place and will call you when we're done."

"I can drive you there," he said, taking out his keys.

But Reese shook her head. "We can walk." She didn't want her mother around Logan for another minute. "Don't worry. This won't take long."

Considering that she'd started out with a string of

lies when she met Logan, Reese hated to lie again, but she was pretty sure this would take more time than "not long."

Reese started the questions as soon as Logan walked away from them, heading for his truck. "Did Helene Langford contact you?"

Vickie made a show of thinking about that. She made a hmm-ing sound and tapped her chin. "Doesn't sound familiar. Refresh my memory."

Reese didn't bother. Even if her mother admitted it was Helene, it could still be a lie, but Reese did need to check with Jimena to make sure she hadn't let anything slip.

"You got a nice thing going here," Vickie said when they reached the Bluebonnet Inn. "Nice dress, and that cowboy you were kissing is dreamy."

Coming from Vickie, it sounded perverse, and it would no doubt lead to demanding that Reese let her in on some of that dreaminess.

"Well, this is a disappointment," Vickie said when Reese unlocked her room and they went in. "I'd have thought you'd be staying in the cowboy's fancy house."

"Even the cowboy doesn't stay in his fancy house. And this place suits me just fine since I won't be in town much longer."

"Oh?" Vickie went to the kitchenette and would have helped herself to a glass of wine from the fridge if Reese hadn't stepped in front of her.

Reese didn't dare move the envelope that Logan had given her. Didn't even glance at it or else her mother might have realized it was something important.

"This isn't a social call," Reese reminded her, "so just tell me why you're here and then leave."

Vickie certainly didn't move any faster. Maybe she would, though, if Reese kept blocking her from getting her booze fix. She would also block the bathroom. And watch to make sure Vickie didn't steal anything. Of course, that was the advantage of not having much because it meant there was nothing much to steal.

Nothing but the watch.

It was the one thing Reese had managed to keep secret from her, and that was in part thanks to her grandfather's warning. "Don't let your mother get her greedy hands on this," he'd told Reese.

Even though she'd been only twelve, she had known it was sound advice. Because although the watch itself probably wasn't worth much, Vickie would want it simply to pawn it for whatever few bucks she could get for it.

Heirlooms had a short shelf life in the Stephenson family.

"You're leaving, you say?" Vickie asked, her gaze combing the room. Thankfully, it was so small the combing didn't take long. "It appears you've got a good thing with the cowboy. Don't know why you'd just give that up."

"I flip burgers at a café, and I live here." Enough said about that. Not a dream job or dream apartment. "The cowboy is temporary just like everything else in my life. You know I don't stay in one place for long. In fact, I'm already antsy."

Reese was afraid that sounded like the huge lie that it was. The not getting antsy was a problem. Because she really wasn't in a hurry to leave. Or at least she hadn't been until Vickie had shown up.

Vickie finally sat down on the love seat. "So, what kind of game are you running on the McCords?"

"No game."

Vickie didn't believe her, of course. "Well, I want a cut of it."

There. It'd taken way too long for Vickie to finally spell out why she was here. "There is no cut because I'm not getting a dime from Logan."

Her mother made a sound of disgust. "That'll have to change. I'll expect payment, and I expect it by tomorrow morning. I have places to be, people to see."

Everything inside Reese went still. "Or?" Because with her mother, there was always an "or."

"Or I'll tell Logan about Spenser."

Reese tried not to react. Was sure she failed. Since she didn't trust her voice, she just stayed quiet and listened as she could feel the proverbial rug being yanked from beneath her feet.

"I know you haven't told him," Vickie went on. "This town is a hotbed of gossip, and I would have heard it by now. By the way, you don't look pregnant."

"I'm not. Hotbeds aren't always accurate."

"That's a shame. You could have gotten a bundle for a McCord heir."

Reese didn't even bother telling her that she would never have a baby just to get money from the father. When and if she had children, it would be for all the right reasons. There wasn't much right about her situation with Logan.

Nothing other than the attraction.

But even Logan wouldn't want to be ruined because of this heat between them. In another month or so, maybe less, he'd find another source of heat.

"So, let me get this straight," Reese said. "If I don't get you some money, you'll tell Logan about my past?"

She nodded. Smiled. Oh, no. That was her snake-oil smile. "And I'll call Logan's business associates. Think how all those ranchers with their down-home values will react to Logan carrying on with the likes of you. I can destroy him."

Reese wished she could argue with that. She couldn't.

Vickie stood. "I'll give you twelve hours," she added. "If I don't have ten thousand dollars by then, I start making those calls and talking to people."

Reese blocked her path when Vickie reached for the door. She knew she had zero bargaining power with this woman. And the calls might not even do the damage that Vickie was claiming they could.

Still, Reese didn't want to take the chance.

"Please don't do this," Reese said, and yes, she was begging.

But got exactly the reaction she expected. Vickie's smile only widened. "All right, I'll give you twelve and a half hours. I'll meet you at the café then. Oh, and bake me something special to go along with the money."

God, Reese couldn't stop this. Well, not without hitting Vickie with a skillet and tying her up in the closet. Extreme, yes, but she was furious enough to want to do it. Of course, she'd been wanting to hit her with something for a while now.

Reese stepped aside and let her leave, knowing there was nothing she could do to stop this train that was speeding right toward Logan.

Nothing she could do here in Spring Hill, anyway.

She grabbed her backpack and headed for the door.

Once she was far away from here, Reese could call the same business associates of Logan's and assure them that she was no longer part of his life.

The first tear slid down her cheek before Reese even made it to the back stairs.

CHAPTER SIXTEEN

LOGAN SAT IN his truck and watched the Bluebonnet Inn. The light was still on in Reese's apartment, but he couldn't see anyone moving around in there from the window. Of course, it didn't take much moving around for Vickie to spell out whatever blackmail scheme she had in mind.

Something that involved him, no doubt.

He'd read her arrest record, and her favorite con was to get friendly with a senior citizen and then rob him blind. The coziness often involved sex, and in many cases, the victim had to be coerced into bringing charges against her because they were either too embarrassed or had fallen for her. Which meant there were likely countless victims out there.

Including Reese.

Reese wouldn't see herself as a victim, though, but she wasn't nearly as tough or guarded as she wanted people to think.

He frowned.

Since when had he become an expert on the inner workings of Reese's mind? Yes, he knew how to bring her to an orgasm, but that hardly made him a Reese expert. Still, he sat and watched, his stomach in knots over the idea that Vickie would use him to get to her own daughter.

His phone buzzed, and Logan nearly sprained his hand yanking it from his pocket. Not Reese, though. Lucky. He considered letting it go to voice mail, but that would only unnecessarily worry his family.

"I'm fine," Logan answered right off to save them some time.

"Good to hear it. Since you're with Reese, I figured she'd kiss any boo-boos you got from Helene's chatter."

"I don't get boo-boos. If you're not calling about my well-being, then why are you calling? And if it's about Helene, save your breath."

"It's about clown shit."

Logan was sure he made a face. "Have clowns been crapping in the pastures, too?"

"No, but one clown crapped his pants. Greg. Apparently, the Nederland brothers followed him out of the reception and gave him a butt-whipping on your behalf."

Hell's Texas bells. The Nederlands were hardly champions of justice. They were three linebacker-sized brothers, probably suffering from some kind of glandular issues because of their size, and they liked to do two things—drink and fight. They had three sisters, same glandular problem, who were even worse than the brothers. Greg was lucky the Nederland males had been the ones to go after him.

"Is Greg okay?" Logan asked.

"Other than crapping his pants, some bruises and a missing tooth, he should be fine. But the Nederland brothers have him pinned down on the ground in the back of the civic center and have said they won't let him up until you give them the say-so."

"Call the cops," Logan instructed. "I don't want to go back to the civic center. I'm tied up."

"Oh, yeah? Didn't know Reese was into that sort of thing." And he probably wasn't joking. "Someone did call the cops, and that's why I'm calling you. Deputy Davy is on the way."

Logan didn't just groan. He cursed. Deputy Davy Devine looked like a zombie and had the IQ of a shrimp. He could start a brawl just by showing up on the scene. Greg could get seriously hurt since he wasn't much of a fighter. Heck, lots of people could get hurt.

But Reese was in the same boat. It was just that her injuries wouldn't be bruises and crapped pants. He hoped.

"Pretend to be me," Logan told his brother. "And tell the Nederlands to back off, that my honor doesn't need defending. Just use small words so they'll understand what you're saying."

"You're sure? You hate it when we've played the switch."

Yes, he did. Mainly because Lucky had used him to break up with girls, and a couple of times it had involved getting smacked upside the head with things that the girls threw at him.

"I'm sure," Logan answered. "The Nederlands are probably drunk enough they won't notice you're not me, and we're dressed almost the same."

Helene would notice, though, but maybe she wouldn't say anything. It did make Logan wonder, though, why she wasn't out there trying to save her clown lover.

Logan ended the call, but the second he did, his phone buzzed again. Speak of the devil—it was Helene—and this time he did let the call go to voice mail. It was probably just her asking him to intervene on Greg's behalf, but Logan had his own intervention right now.

Vickie came out of the Bluebonnet Inn.

She must have recognized his truck because she came his way, and Logan stepped out so she'd be sure to spot him.

"I figured I'd see you again," Vickie purred, and yeah, it was a purr. She was coming on to him, and for some reason she thought it would work. She moved in much too close. Close enough that she brushed the front of her body over his.

Logan took her by the shoulders, lifted her and maneuvered her away from him. And he took back his wallet that she'd lifted.

She smiled, shrugged. "Must be losing my touch with both the wallet and the, well, touching."

"I doubt your touch would have ever worked with me."

"No? Well, plenty of people say that Reese and I look like sisters."

Blind people, maybe, but Logan wasn't here to exchange pleasantries with this turd. It'd been a long night, and he still needed to talk to Reese.

"Here's how this is going to work," Logan started.

But he didn't get to finish because Vickie interrupted him. "You're going to threaten to put me in jail the way you threatened Chucky. Well, that won't fly with me. I keep a lawyer on retainer and will be out in minutes."

Not in the Spring Hill jail, but she was right—an arrest for trying to steal his wallet wouldn't get her much time behind bars. He could goad her into slapping him, but it would have the same results. The only thing he could do is take away what power she thought she had.

"There's nothing you can tell me that will come between Reese and me." That possibly wasn't true.

"Even Spenser?" And she smiled when she asked that.
"Even Spenser O'Malley."

She flinched, maybe surprised that he knew the man's full name, or maybe a gnat just flew in her eye.

"I hired a PI to investigate Reese. And you," Logan added. "I know everything about both of you."

Definitely not a gnat that time. It was a real flinch. "Are you still seeing her because you knocked her up?"

Logan rolled his eyes. He couldn't wait for a couple more months to pass, and then people would see that Reese wasn't showing, and it would put that rumor to rest. Well, they'd see if Reese stayed around, anyway. The jury was still out on whether or not that would happen.

"It's none of your business why I'm seeing her," Logan went on. Good thing, too, since if he couldn't explain it to himself, he damn sure couldn't explain it to this piece of navel lint.

"It'll be my business when I tell your friends about you seeing a criminal."

Now Logan smiled and shrugged. "My friends already know, and just in case you're going to threaten my business associates next, they know, too. I took Reese to a reception tonight where everyone in town saw us. If there was someone who didn't know, they will by morning."

Of course, Jimena's tit slip and the clown crap might take top billing. No way could Reese and he match up to that.

Vickie huffed, glanced around as if trying to figure out what to say to salvage this. "All right. Give me ten grand, and I'll leave town. You'll never hear from me again."

That didn't salvage it. And while she might indeed leave, Vickie was crap. She would just keep showing up. And Logan frowned at all the crap references he was making tonight.

"Listen carefully," he said, making his voice take on that dangerous edge that he liked to have in situations like these. "I didn't give Chucky a dime, and I'm not giving you one, either. Leave town before you see a side of me that most people don't like to see."

That was it. The only warning he intended to give her. It might work. Might not. Which meant Logan needed to be prepared for the fallout. Preparing started with seeing Reese. And he knew where she wouldn't be.

In her room.

Nope, she was probably already trying to outrun the stink her mother was using to smell up her life. And his.

"That's it?" Vickie howled when he got back in his truck. She called him a name, one that questioned his paternity, sexual habits and the size of his dick. Logan didn't care how many names she called him if she just left.

He drove away with her still swearing at him.

Logan went in the direction of Walter Meekins's place first. Since Walter had the only taxi in town, Reese might head there, but no, the taxi was parked right out front and had two cats sleeping on it. So, Logan drove toward the bus station, the only other way for Reese to make a getaway.

Unless she'd called Jimena to pick her up.

That caused his stomach to churn.

Jimena hadn't exactly been in any shape to drive, but that didn't mean Reese hadn't arranged to meet her friend at her car. If so, they could be anywhere by now.

Even though the bus station was only six blocks away from the Bluebonnet Inn, the sidewalks ended after about three of those blocks. And there were ditches. Since there were no streetlights in that section of the road, Reese could twist her ankle. Or get picked up by a serial killer.

And apparently he was imagining worst-case scenarios now.

Logan was about to call Reese, but he spotted something just ahead. At first it looked like fireflies, but then he realized it was his headlights catching the sparkles on Reese's black dress. She had her backpack looped over her shoulder, and yep, she was going straight for the bus station. Except she was limping.

He pulled off the road in front of her, blocking her path.

"I'm leaving," she said, glancing at him.

"I see that." He had to step in front of her when she tried to go around his truck. There was no traffic and probably wouldn't be this time of night, but Logan didn't want to risk her being hit. "Did you hurt your foot?"

"No, these heels are hard to walk in."

They sure looked it, and coupled with the snug dress, she definitely wasn't dressed for a trek to the bus stop.

"My mother's going to ruin you," she added, and that's when the headlights caught something else. The tears in her eyes.

Hell. She was crying.

"Your mother will try," he argued. "But you do know I don't need protecting, right?"

Judging from the tears mixed with a huff, Reese didn't know that. "I can't let her do this to you."

"Leaving won't help. If she comes after me, she'll do that whether you're in town or not. Vickie smells money, and she thinks she can get it from me."

A sob left her mouth, and she sagged against him. "God, Logan. I'm so sorry."

He knew that, and he was also pissed that Reese felt the need to apologize for something she hadn't done. Also pissed that she'd tried to limp her way away from town. And from him. He scooped her up in his arms, kissing her to catch the sound of surprise she made, and he carried her back to his truck.

"At least if I go, you can tell your business associates that you're no longer seeing me," she reminded him when he set her on the seat and then followed in behind her.

Since it appeared that argument might continue, Logan kissed her again. Then he kissed her just because he felt like doing it. The third kiss, though, was all pure lust. That's because kisses one and two gave him a hard-on.

"You're staying," he told her, but it was possible Reese didn't hear that because he was still kissing her when he said it. Possible, too, that she didn't hear it because she really got into the kiss, as well. Not just with her mouth.

But also with her hands.

She took hold of him and yanked him to her.

Logan hadn't expected the kiss to get this frantic and this deep so fast, but heck, he just went with it. In his way of thinking, Reese and he had been to hell and back today, and they deserved this.

But the question was, did they deserve it right here, right now?

Apparently so. Because Reese kissed him as if this were the last kiss she was ever going to get. Not just from him but from anyone. It wasn't true because Logan intended to do a lot more kissing.

And that's what he did.

Her dress was stretchy and clingy, but thankfully stretchy and clingy worked for what he had in mind. He pushed it up, found only a tiny pair of panties underneath, but even the millimeter of silk fabric was too much. He shoved the panties down, too, and kissed her stomach. The inside of her thigh. He would have sampled the part of her he really wanted to sample if she hadn't caught onto his hair and yanked him back up.

"We do this the old-fashioned way," she insisted.

That was fine by him except her idea of old-fashioned and his weren't quite the same. She went after his zipper, and while her frantic hands were giving him some pleasure, there was pain, too. But not enough pain and pleasure to knock the common sense right out of his head.

They were on the side of the road. In his truck. And while he did have tinted windows, anyone driving by could get a glimpse inside if they looked hard enough.

Oh, hell.

She got him unzipped and had him in her mouth before he could stop her.

Logan cursed, all from pleasure this time, and while he did enjoy her particular version of old-fashioned, he couldn't see. His eyes had glazed over. Or so he thought. But they were just fogging up the windshield.

Reese kept him in her mouth long enough to make him want a whole lot more of her. She made a sound of protest when he caught onto her and moved her onto his lap so that her dress was up to her waist and she was straddling him. He made his own sound of protest because this was not the way he wanted to have sex with her. He'd wanted a slower pace. Foreplay.

A bed.

It wasn't the first time he'd had sex in a truck, but the last time had been when he was seventeen. He hadn't realized then just how dangerous it could be. With the steering wheel in the way, Reese and he were teetering between the bucket seats and the gearshift. It didn't help that they were both still jockeying for position. That they were both still trying to kiss each other blind. Or that she had her hands in his boxers.

Or that he had to get a condom out of his wallet.

Getting the condom on was even more of a challenge. He nearly gave her an orgasm just because the back of his hand was moving against her in the wrong place. Of course, it was the right place if he'd been going for a quick end to this. He wasn't. Logan wanted to be inside her this time when they finished this insanity they'd started.

It felt like a juggling act, and when Logan bashed his elbow into the steering wheel, he nearly put this on pause so he could take her back to his place. However, the *nearly* notion went south when Reese lifted herself and then slid right down onto his erection.

Yes, the truck was still uncomfortable, but Logan no longer cared.

He no longer cared that his phone was buzzing, either. Reese started to move, and he caught onto her hips to guide that movement. Not that he had to do much. She'd already found the right pace and angle, and she was working to get him the only thing he wanted right now.

A mind-blowing climax.

She got there ahead of him, which was a surprise considering he'd botched everything about this. Well, everything but the pleasure. Hard to botch that when he was with Reese.

Despite her own orgasm slamming through her, she managed to keep moving her hips. Kept sliding against him to give him exactly what he needed to finish.

Logan let the mind-blowing take over.

Reese collapsed against him, and Logan would have been content to sit there for a couple of minutes to let them both come back to earth. No such luck, though. The approaching headlights caught their attention, and then it did more than just that when the car pulled to a stop ahead of Logan's truck. A car he recognized.

Della and Stella's.

Logan would have rather faced Satan because he wouldn't have been required to explain anything to him.

Seeing the car, and the two occupants inside, had both Reese and him scrambling. Reese crawled off his lap and dragged down her dress. Logan stood no chance of zipping up just yet, but he grabbed his cowboy hat and put it over his crotch. Not a second too soon because the car door opened, and Della stepped out.

"Is everything okay?" she called out. Since she was wearing a party dress, she'd probably come straight from the reception.

Logan lowered his window a couple of inches. "We're fine. I just pulled over to answer a text."

He'd hoped that would satisfy Della enough to wave and get back in her car. It didn't. She came walking toward him, and thankfully at the last second Reese noticed her ripped panties on the gear stick. She grabbed them, shoved them beneath the seat.

"Coming from the reception, are you?" Della asked. She leaned against the door as if this were going to be a long conversation.

It wouldn't be. Not with a cowboy hat on his dick.

Logan nodded. "And now I need to get Reese back to her place."

Della smiled, looked at them. Smiled some more. "It's good to see you two together."

Her smile faded, though, and Logan made sure that wasn't because she'd seen something out of place. Like an open condom wrapper. Logan wasn't sure exactly where that had landed. But then he realized Della wasn't looking in the truck itself. She was dodging his gaze.

"I'm sorry about accidentally inviting Helene to Lucky and Cassie's party," Della said. "Cassie said to do a plus-one—"

"It's okay, really." It wasn't, but at this point Logan would have agreed to a lobotomy to get her out of there. He even moved as if to put the truck into gear.

"Are you okay with it?" Della asked, talking to Reese now.

"Yes, of course." Clearly, she wasn't, but Reese might have agreed to a joint lobotomy at this rate. "But I need to be getting back now."

Della still didn't move. Nor did she make any indications whatsoever that she had immediate plans to do so.

"Is there anything I can do for you before we go?" Logan asked, and he did put the truck in gear while keeping his foot on the brake.

Another smile. "No, but you should probably both

put on your seat belts." With that Della finally headed back toward her car but then stopped. "Oh, and you should probably move that condom wrapper. It's stuck on your shirt." She laughed all the way to her car and was still laughing when she got inside.

At least Della wouldn't gossip about this to anyone but Stella. Stella, however, would probably let something slip so by tomorrow it would be all over town that he'd screwed Reese in his truck. But at least there'd be the mention of safe sex, which might finally dispel the pregnancy rumors.

Reese groaned, and for a moment he thought she was going to cry again. But nope, she laughed, too, and it was a wonderful sound to hear. Not quite as good as her orgasm moan, of course, but it made Logan smile.

Until his phone buzzed again.

That's when he saw he had two missed calls from Lucky. He took this one and put it on speaker so he could start driving back to his loft.

"Anything wrong?" Lucky asked him right off.

"I was about to ask you the same thing."

"Nope. I just wanted to give you an update and got a little worried when you didn't answer. Then I got a text from Della, who said she saw your truck on the side of the road—"

"I'm with Reese," Logan confessed. The confession would save time because Lucky would know exactly what that meant.

"Good. Then I won't keep you. I just wanted to let you know that the switch worked, and the Nederlands let Greg go. We took him to the ER after he changed his pants. You're not gonna believe this, but Greg had that clown nose fixed like a dildo to the end of his dick."

Logan believed it. Tonight, he would believe anything including clown dick dildos. "The doc patched Greg up," Lucky added, "and we're all heading out now. See you when I see you."

Before Logan could even put his phone away, it buzzed again, and he quickly answered it, figuring there was something his brother had forgotten to tell him. But it wasn't Lucky.

"Logan," the woman said, her voice so breathy that it took him a moment to realize it was Helene.

He hadn't meant to groan, but Logan didn't want to go another round with her tonight.

"You have to help me," Helene said. "Please. I need to talk to you right away. Logan, I'm in trouble."

CHAPTER SEVENTEEN

TROUBLE.

Even though Logan hadn't put the call on speaker, the cab of the truck wasn't that big, and Reese had no problem hearing what Helene had just said to him. Since Reese had started this so-called affair with Logan, she had been waiting for the other shoe to drop.

But she hadn't gotten one shoe but rather three.

First Chucky, then her mother. Now this. Of course, the first two shoes had been expected. Not this one, though.

Because *trouble* was a synonym for *pregnant*.

"I'll call you back," Logan told Helene, and he hung up. He didn't say anything for several long moments, but even in the dim light Reese could see his jaw muscles stirring against each other.

Then he cursed.

"Helene isn't pregnant with my baby," Logan said right off. "And she might not be pregnant, in any trouble or anything else. She could be lying to get me to see her."

Yes, she could be, but considering Reese's luck, the woman was in fact pregnant and expecting quadruplets. Even one baby, though, would be more than enough to put an end to whatever this was between Logan and her.

"Just drop me off at the Bluebonnet Inn," Reese insisted. "Then you can, uh, freshen up before you see Helene."

And she was certain he would be seeing the woman tonight. No way would Helene have made that call if she hadn't planned on a face-to-face meeting.

"I haven't been with Helene in over four months," he continued. "If she was really pregnant, she would have told me before now."

It sure seemed as if she would, especially since the woman was trying to win him back. A baby would do that in a heartbeat. Reese wasn't even sure if Logan wanted children, but he wasn't the sort of man to run from fatherhood. And Helene would certainly know that.

"Just drop me off out front," Reese said when they reached the Bluebonnet Inn. She gave him a quick kiss and got out, fast, before he could try to say anything. But there wasn't much he could say, not until he found out what was going on with Helene.

Reese used her key to get in since it was past regular check-in hours. She tried not to look back at Logan as he drove away. And she failed at that. Failed at keeping the sucky feelings at bay, too. It was amazing how good she could feel one minute and how lousy the next.

She made her way toward the stairs, hoping for a quick shower, a drink and then sleep. Maybe not even in that order. However, when she heard the voices out back, Reese knew none of those things would probably happen anytime soon. That's because she heard Jimena and her mother.

"What did you say to me?" her mother snarled.

Jimena repeated it, and from what part of it Reese caught, it was one of her better insults. Something to do with blighted root vegetables and multiple body cavities. Knowing Jimena, though, this—whatever *this* was—wouldn't stop with just bizarre insults. It could lead to a physical fight, and she didn't want to have to bail Jimena out of jail tonight.

Reese went out in the back parking lot, and yes, Vickie and Jimena were there, all right.

"What's going on out here?" Reese asked even though it was pretty clear.

"Your skank friend is trying to run me out of town," Vickie snapped.

"Not trying. I *am* running her out of town," Jimena assured her. "This persistent yeast infection from hell that calls herself your mother has spent enough time ruining your life."

It was true. Except for the *am* part. Vickie outweighed Jimena by a good forty pounds, and Vickie was a dirty fighter. She would bite, kick and pull hair. But Jimena wouldn't go down without kicking, biting and some hair pulling of her own, which meant someone would hear it and call that dorky deputy who kept coming in the diner to chat Reese up.

"Unlike Chucky I don't give in to threats," Vickie said.

"You've seen Chucky?" Reese asked.

Vickie kept her eyeballs pinned to Jimena. "Maybe. But it doesn't matter. I won't tuck tail and run like he did." And because she probably knew it would get Jimena's goat, Vickie smiled. Her smile changed a little, though, when her attention finally landed on Reese.

Reese had no doubts, *none*, that she looked as if she'd just had sex. Plus, she had Logan's scent all over her, possibly a hickey on her neck, another hickey on the top of her right boob, and while her mother didn't have X-ray vision, Reese figured she was standing a little differently since she wasn't wearing any panties.

"You've been with Logan." Her mother touched her tongue to her top lip. "I don't know why we all have to argue about this. We can all share. The man's got enough money and dick to go around and around and around."

"Logan's money's not going anywhere, especially in your pockets," Reese informed her. She didn't even address where his dick wouldn't be going.

Jimena agreed with a crisp nod. "Reese has got a good thing with Logan, and you're not messing it up."

No, she really didn't have a good thing. In fact, Reese might have no *things* at all with Logan if it turned out Helene was indeed pregnant.

"Then we'll agree to disagree," Vickie said, using her best smart-ass tone. "But I'm not leaving."

"Oh, yeah?" Jimena stepped closer and got right in Vickie's face.

Vickie chuckled. "Jimena, are you really going to punch me?"

"No. I'm going to let them do it." Jimena hitched her thumb to the side of the building. "You can come out now, girls."

The Nederland sisters stepped out.

Even though it wasn't very courageous of her, Reese took a step back. Her mother took six.

Reese knew the sisters, of course, because like everyone else in town, they came into the café. The smallest one was six-four. The biggest one could have played starting defensive lineman for the Dallas Cowboys, and with the size of her hips, she could have cleared out the entire football field with just a single shift of position. To say they were intimidating was like saying there was a small patch of ice in Antarctica.

"You talked these thugs into hitting me?" Vickie howled.

The biggest sister shrugged. "She didn't have to talk us into anything. We just like to fight."

Vickie glanced at Reese as if she might intervene, but Reese only gave her a flat look. She certainly wasn't getting between the Nederlands and their intended target, especially for a woman who was trying to extort money and dick privileges from Logan. Vickie must have figured that out right off because she turned and started to run.

The smaller sister moved as if to go after her, but the big one caught onto her arm. "No. Let her have a head start. It's more fun that way." The sisters then began to mosey on after her.

Reese supposed she should remind them not to actually hit—not hard, anyway—but she didn't have the energy. Besides, Vickie was like a cat with thirty-four lives, and she was sneaky. She had probably already scoped out a hiding place before she even let anyone know she was in town.

Jimena, however, didn't hurry to join the potential butt-whipping. "Thank you for trying to help," Reese told her.

Jimena sighed, patted her arm. "You want to talk about it?"

Reese didn't even have to think about that. The answer was no. She just wanted to go to her room and wait for that fourth shoe to drop.

LOGAN DIDN'T EXACTLY hurry when he heard the knock on his loft door. He took his time as he'd done in the shower, as he'd also done getting dressed. Even though he did indeed want to know what Helene considered "trouble," he wasn't sure he was up to dealing with it. Still, it was better than waiting until morning and stewing about it all night.

But when he opened the door, it wasn't Helene.

It was Jimena. And she wasn't alone. She was holding a purring, nuzzling Crazy Cat in her arms.

"Reese wouldn't talk to me about what's wrong so I came to hear it straight from the horse's mouth. What did you do to her?" Jimena quit nuzzling the cat long enough to jab her index finger against his chest. The cat wasn't hissing at her or anything.

Logan hated to be distracted by something like that at a time like this, but it was somewhat of a miracle. "How did you catch Crazy Cat?" he asked.

She looked at him as if his hair had spontaneously combusted. "The cat came to me when I walked in. And that's not an answer to my question. What did you do to Reese?"

Since Jimena seemed to be looking for something specific and wasn't asking in a general sense, Logan went with, "What do you mean?"

"She's upset and won't talk about it. I want to know why."

While Logan admired Jimena for watching out for her friend, he had to shake his head. "I need to have a conversation with someone first because even I don't know what's going on."

"You mean a conversation with Helene. She's sitting in her car in your parking lot. I don't think she saw me when I came in, but I got a pretty good look at her, and I believe she's crying."

Hell. Not tears. He barely had enough energy to deal with the talking.

"Not that I care if Helene cries," Jimena went on, "but I suspect her tears are connected to the love bite on Reese's neck. I've heard a few people say they saw one on Reese, and news like that would have gotten back to Helene."

Mercy, he hoped he hadn't left a love bite. Like his sex-in-a-truck adventure, he hadn't done that since high school.

Logan scrubbed his hand over his face. "Look, I'm not sure exactly what's going on, but when I do know, I'll fill in Reese, and if she wants, she can tell you."

He didn't expect that to work, but Jimena finally nodded. "Deal. Just swear to me you won't pull some shit that gets her hurt."

Logan wished with all his heart that he could promise that, but he figured someone was going to get hurt in this. Maybe Reese. Maybe him. The only thing he was certain of was the shit-pulling wouldn't be done by him.

He reached to pet the cat, but Crazy Cat reacted as if he were coming at her with raptor claws. Full-pitch hissing, and she swatted at him. She started purring, though, when Jimena pulled her closer.

"Well, I'd better leave since someone just opened the back door," Jimena said. "Helene probably."

Logan hadn't heard anything, but then his head was starting to pound. No migraine. Not now.

"By the way," Jimena said, "you know that phone on your reception desk? Well, the lights are all blinking. Looks as if you've got a lot of messages."

He probably had a thousand. In addition to a messy personal life, his business wasn't going so great, either.

"What do you want me to do with Cuddles?" she asked. Apparently, that was the name she'd given Crazy Cat.

And Logan got an idea. A really bad one probably, but then good ideas seemed to be in short supply. "Are you staying in town?" he asked.

"Yeah, sure. For a little while. Reese's place isn't big enough for one much less two so I'm renting the room in that old building across the street from the post office. Wendell Wertz owns it."

Logan knew the building. It had been for sale for five years. "I didn't know there were any apartments in the place."

"Well, it's not actually an apartment. It's what used to be the storage room for a coffee shop."

Yes, back in the nineties.

She shrugged. "Anyway, I'll get something better if I can get hired at the café."

So, she was looking for work. That made his bad idea take even deeper root. "Can you fill in as receptionist until I can get someone in permanently?"

Jimena looked at him with all the suspicion of someone in a police lineup. "Are you offering me a job?"

"A temporary one, starting Monday morning," he clarified. He'd almost said tomorrow, but since that was Sunday, it could wait a day. "It would involve taking care of the cat, too. Oh, and fixing coffee. And answering the phone."

She stayed quiet a moment, giving that some thought. "I'll let you know," Jimena said, and hurried off, meeting Helene, who was coming up the stairs.

Crazy Cat hissed and swatted at Helene, too.

Jimena possibly did also.

Logan wasn't into hissing and swatting, but he wanted to set some ground rules to hurry along this conversation with Helene. At least, that had been the plan, then he did indeed see the fresh tears in Helene's eyes. Instead of giving her a shoulder to cry on, though, he offered her a box of tissues when she stepped into the room. Which she accepted.

"Explain what kind of trouble you're in," Logan demanded.

But Helene didn't jump to answer. Her gaze skirted around the loft. "You've, uh, redecorated."

Hardly the right word for it. He'd replaced the cheap furniture with even worse cheap furniture that'd been delivered earlier, and it now looked like one of those places in need of an extreme makeover. Or a torch. "If that's what you've come to talk about—"

"It isn't." However, that was all she said for a couple of snail-crawling moments. "May I sit? This isn't something I can just blurt out."

He motioned for her to take a seat, but Logan had some of his own blurting to do. "It's been over four months since we've had sex. So, if you're pregnant, the baby's not mine."

Logan had gotten some funny looks over the years—many of those coming this very night—but he had to say that one was the funniest. Helene's mouth dropped open so wide that he could see her tonsils.

"You thought I was pregnant?" she asked in the same tone one might if the world was ending in thirty seconds.

He lifted his shoulder. "You said you were in trouble."

"I said I was in trouble, not stupid. I'm on the pill, and we always used a condom."

"Yeah, I wasn't sure Greg had, though." Or maybe the clown nose had acted as a condom. If so, Logan really didn't want to know the details.

"Wow," she mumbled, and she repeated it a lot of times. "Okay, I'm not pregnant. Have no plans to become pregnant. Have no plans to repeat my mistake by being with Greg again." Another pause. "Is Reese pregnant?"

"No." And he wondered how many more times he was going to have to answer that question. "And I should have said right from the start that I don't want to talk about Reese."

Helene stayed quiet for way too long. "We have to talk about her. Because she's the reason I'm here." Tears sprang to her eyes again. "When I found out you were involved with her, I had Reese investigated. I know, it was wrong, but I needed to know that I hadn't sent you into the arms of the wrong woman."

Since Logan had also had Reese investigated, he decided it was a good time to stay quiet and listen to the rest of what Helene had to say.

"You know about Reese's past, of course," Helene went on. "I'm sure she's told you."

He settled for a nod. She'd told him some of it. Logan figured there was more, and then there was that juvie record he'd managed to get unsealed. Hell, he hoped Helene hadn't managed to get into that because Logan didn't know why Reese had a criminal record.

Helene nodded, too, and he had to hand it to her. She didn't seem disappointed that Reese had come clean. Or at least semiclean. A bitter woman would have probably taken some pleasure in springing the news of her shady past on him. But either there was no pleasure or else Helene was doing a good job concealing it.

"Anyway, I found out about Chucky Dayton." She looked up at Logan. "You know about him, too?"

"Yes." And Logan got a bad feeling in the pit of his stomach. "You're the reason he came to town." He cursed. "Did you contact Reese's mother, too?"

"No." She shook her head. "I mean, I told Chucky where Reese was, but I haven't seen or spoken to her mother. Is she in Spring Hill?"

Logan decided to go with a question of his own. "What does all of this have to do with the trouble you're in?"

"Everything," Helene said on a rise of breath. "Chucky's blackmailing me. He says if I don't pay him twenty thousand dollars, then he'll tell Reese and you that I'm responsible for him finding her. I considered just paying it, but I figured he'd keep coming back for more."

"He would."

Logan suddenly had a flurry of emotions about all of this. Helene had likely started a domino effect what with first telling Chucky and then Chucky had probably told Vickie. Or maybe Helene had been the one to tell Vickie, too. Either way, the domino tiles were already falling, and they were falling on Reese.

"Chucky tried to get rough with Reese," Logan said. "He pushed her against a building, and if I hadn't been there, he could have hurt her."

"Oh, God." More tears.

Logan hadn't told her that to make her cry but only so that she'd understand what a truly stupid thing she'd done. And the only reason Helene had done it was to send Reese running.

It had almost worked.

Heck, it still might work.

"If you stay with her," Helene said, her voice shaky, "you also invite these people into your life. Is that what you want?"

That didn't help with the flurry of emotions, but part of his frustration was that he didn't know the answer. He wanted Reese. For now. He wanted to continue to have sex with her, preferably not in his truck. But Logan couldn't see beyond that.

"It took me eight years to decide to propose to you," he finally answered. "I've known Reese a little less than four months. I don't have to make any decisions about what I do or don't do right this very second."

At the rate he was going, he might never make a decision. Or Reese might make it for him and cut out again.

"Of course," Helene agreed. She stood, looked around again. "You really are moving on with your life." She didn't sound happy about that. Or maybe her reaction was for the decor. His sofa was the same color of vomit.

"You'll move on with yours, too."

"Yes, but not with Greg. I know you wouldn't have asked, but despite the spectacle he put on tonight, there's no chance I'll ever be with him." She paused again. "In therapy I learned what happened with him was just sexual experimentation. Nothing more. It happens sometimes when a woman has my kind of upbringing where people expect her to be, well, perfect."

It sounded as if she wanted him to jump in there with

an "I understand." But Logan didn't jump. Instead, he made the mistake of rubbing his forehead.

"Headache?" she immediately asked.

"I'll take something after you leave." Which was a not so subtle way of telling her this conversation was over.

But Helene didn't budge. She did nod, though. "So, when Chucky contacts me again, I'll just tell him that I confessed to Reese and you, and the two of you are okay with what happened."

"FYI, we're not okay with it. In fact, Reese has a right to be really pissed off at you. But now that we know what you've done, it's taken away Chucky's bargaining power. You don't have to pay hush money."

Another nod, and she finally started for the door. She stopped, though, did another of those annoying looks around before her attention came back to him. "There's no chance of you forgiving me?"

He really did need those pain meds. "Good night, Helene."

Logan maneuvered her out the door and closed it. In the same motion, he reached for his phone and headed to the medicine cabinet. The migraine was chasing him, but if he could drug up in time, he might be able to fight it off. First, though, he needed to talk to Reese. She was no doubt playing some worst-case scenarios about this chat he'd had with Helene.

She didn't answer on the first ring. Or even the second. By the time it got to the fourth ring, Logan was playing out some worst-case scenarios of his own until she finally answered.

"Are you okay?" Reese asked, taking the question right out of Logan's mouth.

"Yes. How about you?"

Judging from the fact that she mumbled some profanity, Logan knew the answer to that. "Look, this would be a good time for you to stay put and not get involved."

"What do you mean?" And Logan really did want to know the answer. Something pretty big had to be going on for Reese not to ask about why Helene had wanted to talk to him.

Reese mumbled more profanity. "Please don't come down here. I'm at the Spring Hill Police Department. I've been arrested."

REESE UNDERSTOOD WHY people called Deputy Davy Devine by the nonaffectionate nickname of Deputy Dweeb. She couldn't figure out how anyone could look so twitchy and yet move so slow at the same time.

People in comas were more active than this guy.

The Nederland sisters were in the cell next to Reese and had said pretty much the same thing. Before they all passed out, that is. Now they were snoring and clearly didn't care about a hasty release. In fact, they seemed so at home in the jail cell that it made Reese wonder how often they had been here.

Unlike Reese. She definitely wasn't comfortable behind bars, though it wasn't her first rodeo, either. But it was her first in a cocktail dress and without panties.

"If I find some firecrackers, I'm going to shove them up that deputy's ass," Jimena mumbled. She was sitting on the floor outside the jail cell where Reese was locked up. "That might get him moving."

Reese doubted it. It had taken him over an hour to read Reese her rights and start the paperwork for the charges against her. Heaven knew how long it'd take for Reese to post bail, though Jimena was there with the cash to get her out.

Of course, Logan was on the way now, too.

Reese had hoped to have all of this resolved by the time he called her but no such luck. At this rate she might not have it resolved before she reached the age of mandatory retirement.

And she could blame her mother for this.

Yet something else on the list of crappy things her mother had done to her and continued to do to her.

Vickie had run from the Nederland sisters, all right. She'd run straight to the jail and had told Deputy Davy that Reese had ordered the girls to attack her. It hadn't helped that the sisters had come into the police station at that exact moment and started punching Vickie. It also hadn't helped that the sisters had verified—in their drunken state, of course—that they were doing this for Reese.

Apparently, the Nederlands failed to remember that Jimena was the one who'd set all of this in motion, but Reese wasn't about to rat out her friend.

Sadly, being in jail wasn't the worst of what she was feeling right now. It was Logan. He would no doubt come down here, get mixed up in all this craziness that was her life, and he'd do that even though he had almost certainly been put through the wringer with whatever Helene had told him.

Of course, the wringer might be better than some of the other things Reese had figured could happen. It was possible that Helene and Logan were back together.

"I went to see him tonight," Jimena said.

Reese lifted her head. "Logan?"

"I know you didn't want me to do that, but I had to warn him not to shit on you."

Great. It was just yet another cog turning in this wheel of a nightmarish night. Reese forced herself to remember that there had been some good parts. Well, one good part, anyway. Sex in the truck. Even though it wouldn't sound like a good part to most people, the sex had been with Logan so that made it a shining spot in an otherwise awful day.

"Logan offered me a job," Jimena added. "A temporary one," she clarified. "He wants me to be his receptionist and take care of the cat."

It was as if Jimena were speaking a foreign language, and that's why Reese just stared at her.

"He didn't say he was offering the job because of you," Jimena went on. "I got the feeling he really needed some help."

"You've never been a receptionist," Reese pointed out.

Jimena shrugged. "I've never bailed you out of jail, but I'm managing that just fine."

Uh, no, she wasn't, and Reese was about to point out why working for Logan would be a really bad idea.

But maybe it wasn't.

After all, Vickie had threatened to call Logan's business associates and try to hurt his reputation. When Reese had told Deputy Davy that, he'd said it was too vague of a threat to have Vickie arrested, that it was a she said/she said kind of thing.

"If you're at Logan's office, you can let me know if Vickie succeeds in turning people against him," Reese suggested.

Jimena stared at her. Though she was staring at

Reese through bars, it wasn't hard to see that her friend was suspicious of that. "Why, so you can leave if it happens?" She huffed and didn't wait for Reese to verify it. "One day you're going to learn that you can't fix shit your mother keeps shitting on. She'll just follow you and shit up the next place, too."

That was a lot of shit to deal with at once, and Reese wished she could disagree, but she couldn't. But if she stayed after such a shit-fallout, then her mere presence would be enough to continue to fuel the gossip.

Reese heard the voices out in the squad room. Two she recognized as Deputy Davy and Logan. She didn't recognize the other man, but several seconds later, the trio appeared. She'd seen the third man in the café—Police Chief Luke Mercer—and he was sporting a scowl that was almost as bad as Logan's.

Almost.

Logan was aiming his scowl at the deputy.

"You're an idiot," Logan said to the deputy, and while Reese had heard him use his badass voice, she'd never heard it this lethal.

"Yeah, he is," the chief agreed. Since it looked as if he'd dressed in a hurry—he had a pajama top hanging out from underneath his shirt—it was likely he'd gotten out of bed to come and handle this.

The chief unlocked the cell door, and Logan immediately went to Reese and pulled her into his arms. "Are you all right? Sorry, bad question," he added when she just gave him a flat stare.

"Something needs to be done about Vickie," Jimena insisted.

Reese was about to say there wasn't much that could

be done, but Logan nodded. "Chief Mercer is arresting your mother for attempted extortion."

Reese gave him a blank stare for a different reason. Because she didn't have a clue what he was talking about. "It'll be her word against mine," she reminded him.

"No, it won't be," Logan assured her. "We're getting some help with that."

"Help?" Jimena and Reese asked in unison. "Who's willing to help me?"

"You wouldn't believe me if I told you." Logan took hold of her and got Reese moving toward the exit.

CHAPTER EIGHTEEN

"DID A CAT eat your homework?" Jimena asked.

Reese was in such deep thought that she heard Jimena's question, but it took a moment for what her friend was saying to sink in. She'd been distracted most of the night before and now the morning since Logan had managed to get her sprung from jail.

"I'm just thinking about what happened," Reese mumbled. Though that was probably as clear as a gypsy's crystal ball.

Logan had been right about Reese not believing who was helping them.

Chucky.

The man who'd been a thorn in Reese's side for years had now apparently decided to grow a pair. Reese only hoped it wasn't a pair that included some kind of backstabbing or scam. She wasn't exactly holding her breath, but it appeared that someone had convinced Chucky to come forward and spell out Vickie's intentions of extorting money from Reese and/or Logan.

And that someone was yet another surprise for Reese.

Helene.

Chucky and Helene seemed an unholy alliance, but from what Reese had learned from Logan, Chucky had tried to blackmail Helene, and Helene and Logan had turned the tables on him. In exchange for Helene not filing charges against him, Chucky would testify against Vickie.

Reese still wasn't exactly clear about how Chucky had found out about her mother's plans, but she suspected that they had had their own unholy alliance before Chucky and Helene decided to do the right thing and go the holy route.

Still, the good news was Reese hadn't had to spend the night in jail, the charges against her had been dropped and Helene wasn't pregnant. The bad news was that her mother was nowhere to be found, and that meant the police chief couldn't arrest her.

"Did the cat shit on your homework?" Jimena asked.

Obviously that was a reminder that Reese's head was still in the clouds. "I left my backpack and panties in Logan's truck." Reese hadn't actually planned to say that, but it was yet something else that had been clouding her mind.

"And you're worried about…what? That he'll keep them? Look inside the backpack? Wear the panties?"

Since Jimena had never actually looked in the backpack, the second question was the only one that was legitimate. Though Reese was worried that one of Logan's brothers or a business associate might see the torn panties. Still, that wasn't her main worry, and Jimena knew it.

It was Logan.

He could tell her a thousand times that he could weather out whatever storms this bad press and her mother might cause, but Reese wasn't so sure. That meant she should be distancing herself from him, or at least thinking about distancing herself, anyway.

But she wasn't.

Here she was waiting for Cassie and Claire to show up to look at the building where Jimena was staying. A building that Cassie was thinking of buying for her new counseling practice. Reese still wasn't sure why the two wanted her in on this look-around, but Cassie had then said they could use the opportunity to go over the final details for the upcoming engagement party.

Instant guilt.

Because Reese hadn't done nearly enough for the party. Worse, less than twelve hours ago, she'd nearly skipped town without so much as a heads-up phone call to Cassie. That did make Reese feel as if the cat had pooped not just on her homework but on her, as well.

Cassie had also invited Jimena because Jimena was already renting a room on the second floor of the building and had a key. Since the owner lived in San Antonio, it would save him a trip to Spring Hill in case Cassie vetoed the place after one look.

Something she just might do.

The midcentury building was definitely nothing special. Gray peeling walls, a warped parquet floor and a trio of short halls off the reception area that led to a number of rooms. There was a metal sign in the corner for watch repair. Too bad that wasn't still there. For years, Reese had promised herself that she would have her grandfather's watch fixed, but with all the moving around, she'd never managed it.

In addition to the repair sign, there were boxes of old books, several industrial hair dryers, a saddle, a masseuse table and plastic riding horses. At least Reese thought they were horses. With the paint peeling off their eyes and faces, they looked like animal zombies.

"Did they used to make porn films here?" Jimena asked.

Reese wasn't sure how Jimena got that from the assortment of things surrounding them, but she supposed it was possible. No, wait. It wasn't. If there'd been a porn industry here, even if it had been sixty years ago, it would have still been gossiped about.

Jimena went to the glass front of the building and looked out, but then she immediately ducked back. Not just away from the window, but she scrambled behind the zombie horses.

"Elrond," she whispered.

Reese had a look for herself and thought maybe from Jimena's reaction that there was more to her friend's breakup than she'd mentioned. Like that maybe Elrond was an ax murderer and was charging toward the building to chop her into pieces. But no ax.

However, Elrond wasn't alone. He was with Helene.

Judging from their body language, they were arguing. At least, Helene was arguing and Elrond was listening. Neither was happy, and Helene stormed off, not even sparing him a glance.

"I'll bet that's because he stole her porcelain titty," Jimena said, still whispering as if they were right beside Elrond and not across the street from him. She pulled Reese back into the shadows with her. "Maybe they'll kiss or something."

Reese had to shake her head. "Why would I want to see Logan's ex kiss a guy who stole her breast?"

"Because then you'd know she's as phony as those tits and that she's still screwing around."

Reese doubted that. Helene was on her best behavior because she wanted Logan back, and no tumble with a boob-stealing clown was worth that. Helene had almost certainly learned her lesson along with sowing all the wild oats she'd ever sow.

As Helene was storming away, Reese finally saw the car pull up in front of the building. Cassie got out from the driver's side, Claire, the passenger's side, and both women immediately stopped, each catching onto the car.

And their stomachs.

Both looked as if they'd been doing some barfing with the possibility of more to come. Morning sickness.

"Sorry we're late," Cassie said, coming in ahead of Claire. Then she stopped, snickered. "And I guess that's in more ways than one."

"Yes, I told Cassie," Claire fessed up. "I'd wanted to keep it a secret until after the engagement party, but it's hard to keep extreme nausea that only happens in the morning a secret."

"You're both pregnant?" Jimena asked, and even though she hardly knew the women she hurried to them for a celebratory hug. It turned into a group hug because Jimena caught onto Reese and pulled her into the mix.

"And are we celebrating your, uh, morning sickness, too?" Claire asked Reese.

Reese shook her head. "Just a rumor."

Claire shrugged as if disappointed by that. "Oh, well. Maybe one day."

It almost sounded like some kind of acknowledgment that one day Reese would be part of this family to exchange such news. But the chances of that happening were akin to gelato freezing in hell.

Or Logan wearing her panties.

"So, I heard about your jail adventure," Claire

went on. "I was arrested earlier this year for a fight at the pub."

Claire looked as sweet as that gelato Reese had just been thinking about, and somehow the arrest gossip hadn't made it to her ears. So, maybe Jimena had been right about the porn thing, too. Maybe gossip in the town was selective.

"And I was committed to the loony bin," Cassie volunteered.

Reese had heard mention of that but only in whispered tones the way a person would mention yeast infections. In other words, something unpleasant but not serious.

But Reese knew where they were going with this. They were trying to make her feel better about what'd happened. Of course, the difference was neither Cassie nor Claire had a real police record. They were still suitable mates for the McCord men.

Reese wasn't.

"Thanks for being here to let us in," Cassie told Jimena, and she started to look around. "I haven't been in this place in ages." Judging from the sound Cassie made, she was seeing something Reese hadn't.

"Over the years, it's been a bookstore, a beauty salon, a jeweler's and a day care," Claire remarked.

That explained the zombie horses.

"When it was still a day care," Claire went on, "I used to bring over the lunches from the café. I was a waitress there," she added to Reese.

Claire was still trying to make her feel part of the group, but Reese felt herself pulling further away.

"Look, what you're doing is nice," Reese said. "In fact, you're both very nice, but the only reason Logan slept with me at that hotel in San Antonio was because of what happened with Helene. And the only reason I slept with him was because I thought I was dying."

No surprise whatsoever on their faces. Zilch. And that's the reason Reese looked at Jimena.

Jimena shrugged. "So, I might have mentioned it to them, all right? But for the record, you've been with Logan since then, and it didn't have anything to do with mistaken brain tumors and clown sex."

No, it hadn't, but that didn't mean it was more than just sex.

"So, you really thought you were going to die?" Cassie asked. She no longer sounded just nice now. She sounded like a therapist.

"I did." Since Claire and she seemed to be waiting for more, Reese added, "I did a whole bucket-list thing. Ate what I wanted, gave away my money, quit my job."

"And Logan was on that list?" Claire said.

"A hot cowboy was." Sheez, Reese suddenly felt like a slut. A hot cowboy—*any* hot cowboy.

"Wow." Claire again. "So, it was like fate when you met Logan. I mean, what are the odds that you'd be looking for a hot cowboy—which he is—at the exact moment he was nursing a broken heart?"

Cassie nodded. "Logan's not the one-night-stand type."

Heck, he wasn't the broken-heart type, either, so Reese wasn't going to read much into this. For her own self-preservation, she needed to get her mind on something else.

"Let's look at the rest of the place," she insisted.

They got moving, but she also heard Jimena whisper

to Cassie and Claire. "Reese has a tough time trusting men. Old man-baggage stuff."

Great. Now they'd moved from bucket lists to man-baggage. With all this revealing going on, she might as well strip down and show them her tattoos.

Cassie made a sound of agreement. "It's hard not to have man-baggage once you're past twenty-one, but all it takes is one good man to help you put that baggage away for good. Did you have to deal with any lingering depression after learning you didn't have a tumor? I mean, did you have survivor's guilt?"

"Yes," Reese admitted.

Jimena admitted even more. "Reese didn't know the other woman who really did have the tumor, but she was worried she might be a mom or someone who'd be missed."

Reese was still worried about that.

"That's a natural reaction," Cassie went on. "But you seem to be handling it well now."

Reese ignored them and started opening doors. Some contained even more bizarre collections of building memorabilia. White foam wig heads. Disassembled cribs. The only reason Reese spent even a second glancing at them was so she wouldn't be looking at the other women. Eye contact might just encourage them to keep talking. All she needed to do was finish this tour and then get the heck out of here.

She opened one of the doors and had a serious wow moment.

"It's a kitchen." Reese went in, her gaze taking in the very high-end appliances.

"That's right," Cassie said. "About ten years ago, it was a bakery." She pointed to the sign that was propped up in the corner. Shirley's Sweets. "But it didn't last long. Only a couple of months."

Claire nodded. "That was the baker from Abilene, but she wasn't very good at business. One day she just up and left."

"You sure she wasn't murdered?" Reese asked. That got their attention. "I mean, because this isn't the kind of kitchen a baker would just leave behind. There must be twenty grand worth of appliances and equipment in here."

At the mention of that, all of their shoulders straightened. Because maybe there was a body in the oven. As if to prove that theory wrong—hopefully it was wrong—Reese opened the oven door.

And burst a lung screaming when spiders came scurrying out.

The four of them went scurrying out, too, some faster than others. Claire practically sprinted out of the room.

"Maybe that's why the baker left," Claire said, shuddering.

Cassie shuddered, too, and Reese was shuddering right along with them. Finally, this was something she had in common with the pair.

But Jimena didn't leave. She squished a few spiders, and as if this were the most mundane part of her morning, she strolled out of the kitchen. "I can clean that out for you if you decide to buy the building," she offered.

The spiders seemed to be the least of the problems, or maybe they were some kind of omen. Still, Cassie continued to look around as if she hadn't completely gone off the notion of putting her office in here.

"I have an idea," Cassie finally said. "I could buy the building, and the two of you could rent space from me."

It took a moment for Reese to realize Cassie was talking to her. "What?"

"You could open a bakery, and Claire could use a couple of these rooms for a photography studio. That'd still leave plenty of room for my office and for the apartments on the second floor," she added to Jimena. "Which I'd redo, of course. The whole place needs a face-lift."

"And a good exterminator," Claire added. She was still shuddering.

"Yeah, it sounds great," Jimena piped in. "You could call the bakery Reese's Lemon Thingies."

"No, it doesn't sound great." Reese hadn't meant to say that so loud—it was practically a shout—but she was still stunned that Cassie was making plans. Long-term plans. Plans that included her.

"I'm not the 'opening a bakery' kind of woman," Reese explained when they all just stared at her.

"So, you want to keep working for other people?" Jimena asked. But she didn't just ask it. She was on board with this, too, though Reese wasn't sure how.

"You know I move at least every six months," Reese reminded her.

The three women made varying sounds that they did know that. And that they disapproved. Worse, they looked at her with those looks of disapproval.

It was Claire who broke the silence. "You've been seeing Logan." Then she held up a finger. "Excuse me a sec." And she hurried to the bathroom. A few moments later, Reese heard a different kind of sound—retching.

"Anyway," Cassie said, picking up where Claire had

left off. "If you want to have a fighting chance with Logan, then at least consider my offer. You wouldn't have to put up any cash until you actually opened Lemon Thingies."

"Or you could call it Queen of Tarts," Jimena suggested. She snapped her fingers. "Or how about Dough Play?"

"Or Wants and Kneads?" Cassie added. "Or Sweetie Pies?"

"For Goodness' Cakes would work," Claire put in as she came out of the bathroom. "Or Sugar Mama's."

Jimena did more finger snapping. "Or instead of Lemon Thingies, it could be Reese's Thingies."

For Pete's sake, that sounded as if she had testicles.

"Or Reese's Sweet Spot and Thingies," Cassie went on.

That sounded as if she were horny and testicular.

Reese groaned. Not only were they planning her future, they were planning it with really stupid names.

"I don't fit in here," Reese yelled. "And I don't fit into Logan's life. For Christ's sake, I have tattoos."

"Are they spelled correctly?" Cassie asked, and she appeared to be serious. "Because my grandmother had misspelled tattoos, and it drove Lucky nuts."

Reese tried not to groan again. Failed. "They aren't words but a rose and rosebud."

"Sounds tasteful," Claire remarked. "I remember my mother had tats that weren't tasteful at all. Snakes and a spider." Another shudder.

Of course, Reese had heard bits and pieces of Claire's and Cassie's not-so-perfect upbringings, but at least they'd had some semblance of a normal childhood.

"I was raised by con artists. We would have had

to come up in status to be called trailer trash." Reese shook her head. "I'd never fit in here."

Cassie and Jimena opened their mouths, no doubt to argue that, but both their mouths stayed open. And Reese soon saw why when she followed their gazes and saw what had captured their attention.

It was Logan.

He was across the street in front of the post office where earlier she'd seen Helene and Elrond. Elrond wasn't there.

But Helene was.

Reese watched as the woman put her hand on Logan's chest, leaned in and whispered something to him. He didn't back away. In fact, Logan leaned in and whispered something right back to her.

Before both Logan and Helene exchanged a very intimate-looking smile.

LOGAN SCOWLED.

First at the stuff the guy had just put on his desk. Then at the guy himself. Logan couldn't remember his name, but the person he was scowling at was someone Lucky had hired to do maintenance on the company trucks and other vehicles.

The stuff the man had put on Logan's desk was Reese's backpack and panties. Red panties that had been visibly ripped.

"Found these when I was cleaning out your truck," the guy said, and he made the mistake of smiling.

Logan's scowled deepened. "Shut the door on your way out," he snarled.

That didn't lessen the guy's smile, and he added a knowing wink. A wink that Logan couldn't deny because he had indeed done some winkable stuff with Reese that had resulted in those torn panties, but there was no reason for someone he barely knew to point that out.

He pressed the intercom button to call Jimena, who should be in reception. Whether she was there was anyone's guess and whether she was working was another guess entirely. Since it was her first day, Logan didn't even know if she was at her desk.

And she wasn't.

That's because at that exact moment Jimena came in the door carrying a cup of coffee, something he was about to request she bring him. She also looked reasonably dressed for the job.

Of course, he was grading on a curve here since Greg had often been unreasonably dressed.

Jimena was wearing a tiger print dress that fit her like a sausage casing and purple glitter shoes. And she smelled like Cheetos. Since there were some yellow stains on her fingers, Logan doubted the finger stains were a coincidence.

Logan figured the sausage-casing clothes would impress Delbert Clark, his ten o'clock appointment. Delbert had an eye for good Angus cows and questionably dressed women. Since Logan had been doing business with the man for nearly a decade, he didn't exactly need to impress Delbert, but it was always good to start with a happy client.

"Your coffee," Jimena said, putting the cup on his desk. "Beans are ground fresh. Two sugars, a teaspoon of half-and-half just the way you like it. Greg left notes about things," she explained. "Building temperature, how you like your coffee, litter box cleaning, your somewhat persnickety personality. Had to look up *per-snickety*, but I gotta say, I agree with him."

"I have to say I don't care for being called persnickety." Or having his coffee mentioned along with kitty litter maintenance.

"Greg said in his notes that you'd say that if I brought it up." She slid some papers his way. "That's the contract for those ugly bulls with the humps. The ones that the fella sent pictures of this morning."

"The Brahmas," he supplied. So, evidently Jimena could print out a contract and make coffee even if she didn't know squat about livestock and referred to him with insulting labels.

She scowled, too, when she saw the panties and backpack, and Logan quickly shoved them under his desk.

"You didn't give those back to Reese yet?" She sounded more like his sister than his employee.

"I haven't seen her since Friday night when I got her out of jail." And yes, it was Monday, three days later. But he'd had meetings most of the day on Saturday, had gotten a migraine and had spent a good chunk of Sunday in bed.

"You haven't spoken to her?" Another snap.

"Only for a couple of seconds. I called her, told her I wasn't feeling well and that I'd go by the café today for lunch."

She huffed. "Turd on a tire iron," Jimena grumbled. "I had a date yesterday and didn't check on her because I thought she'd be with you."

"Uh, why would you need to check on her?"

"Because of what she saw, you idiot."

Logan scowled again. There was no reason for her to call him an idiot. Was there? "What did she see?"

Jimena's hands went on her hips, and either the sausage casing was causing her eyes to bulge, or else she was truly pissed off. "You and Helene carrying on in front of the post office."

He had to shake his head, and Logan was certain he looked as confused as he felt.

Jimena made a "duh" sound. "Cassie, Claire, Reese and me were all there Saturday, looking at that building Cassie wanted to buy. Did you know it used to have a bakery in it?" But she waved off that question and continued. "Anyway, we saw you getting cozy with Helene."

"Cozy?" Logan wanted to throw up his hands. "What are you talking about?"

"Post office. Saturday. You. Helene. Whispers. Smiles. In-your-face contact." She spoke slowly as if he were mentally deficient.

Heck, maybe he was because Logan didn't remember…wait…yes, he did. "That wasn't cozy. Helene was just thanking me for getting her out of a sticky situation." The one with Chucky that could have ended up costing her a fortune. "And I thanked her for getting Chucky to testify against Reese's mother."

For all the good that'd done. The police chief had yet to find Vickie, which would only be a good thing if the woman stayed away from Spring Hill and especially from Reese. Logan figured a swarm of bees would have an easier time staying away from something sweet than Vickie did of staying away from Reese.

"You smiled at Helene," Jimena said like an accusation.

Yes, he had. He remembered that now. Logan also remembered why he'd done it. "Because people were watching, and I didn't want to seem petty."

"Well, Reese thought it was more than that. You should have seen the look on her face. I thought she was going to throw up." She lifted her shoulder. "But that could have been because Claire just threw up, and that was making us all a little queasy. Plus, Reese was spooked because of all those spiders in the oven."

Logan hadn't known any of this was going on. And some of it, he just didn't understand. But one thing was clear; he needed to talk to Reese if she believed he was getting *cozy* with his ex.

He thought about calling her, only to realize she was working and wouldn't be able to answer. However, she should be finished with the breakfast shift in thirty minutes or so, and he could see her then in person.

"When Delbert Clark gets here, show him in right away," Logan instructed.

Jimena didn't acknowledge that. Didn't move. "Uh, about that," she finally said.

The *uh* couldn't be good, and the gloom-and-doom look on her face supported that notion. "What's wrong?"

She took several deep breaths, which no doubt tested the stretch of the dress fabric. "Delbert Clark called about fifteen minutes ago and canceled the meeting."

"Why didn't you put his call through to me?"

More deep breaths. "Because he said he didn't want to talk to you. He said he didn't want to do business with a man who was boinking a convicted felon."

Hell. Logan just had to sit there a couple of seconds and take that in. Vickie had obviously gotten to Delbert, but what surprised Logan was that the man had put gossip over business.

Of course, maybe it wasn't just gossip.

Maybe Vickie had shown Delbert some kind of proof to back up her claims. Then again, Vickie was a con artist so perhaps she was able to use those conning skills to convince the man.

"I told him no one uses that word—*boinking*—anymore," Jimena added. "And then I called him a jackass. Trust me, I could have come up with something much worse to call him, but I kept it PG-rated for your sake."

"Thanks," Logan grumbled, and he wasn't the least bit sincere. He didn't want his receptionist calling an old business associate any names since this was something Logan was sure he could smooth over.

He scrolled through his numbers and pressed Delbert's, and the man answered on the first ring. "I told your girl that I didn't want to talk to you," he said before Logan could even get out a greeting.

Several different emotions hit Logan. First the shock, then the hurt. Followed by the anger. "She told me that, but I didn't believe her. I just figured after all the business we've done together that you owed me a personal explanation."

"Well, I don't," Delbert snapped. "I don't care where you dip your wick as long as it doesn't come back on me."

Logan had to get his jaw unclenched to speak. "How would that come back on you? And please don't use any other reference about wick-dipping."

"Huh?" He sounded surprised that an outdated comment like that would offend Logan. "All right. Then what should I call her—your convicted felon of a lover?"

"You could just call her Reese since that's her name."

Delbert mumbled something that Logan was glad he didn't catch. "I don't plan on calling her anything because there'll be no more business between us unless you dump her. The woman… *Reese*…is a con artist, and I don't want to risk her getting hold of my bank account number and shit like that."

"Her mother's a con artist, not Reese," Logan corrected, "and her mother is no doubt the one who told you these lies."

"Lies aren't lies if there's proof to back them up," Delbert snapped.

Logan tried again to explain, but he was talking to the air because Delbert had already ended the call.

"Now can I come up with something worse than jackass to call him?" Jimena asked.

Even though Jimena only heard Logan's end of the conversation, she'd no doubt figured out the direction it had taken. Logan would have said, "Sure, why not?" but he saw Reese standing in the doorway.

Crazy Cat was at her feet, coiling around her ankles.

Logan wasn't sure how much she'd heard, but she had an even more troubled look on her face than Logan was sure he did. He immediately changed his expression because Reese would feel bad enough about this without his rubbing salt in the wound.

"I called her and told her about Delbert," Jimena volunteered, scooping up the cat. "Reese asked me to spy and find out if your business was getting hurt because of her."

Hardly an admission an employee should make, but

in a way Logan was glad Reese was here. He could try to make her see this really wasn't her fault and explain that cozy smile that had apparently made her look as if she wanted to throw up.

Jimena sniffed her. "You smell like bacon."

Reese gave herself a whiff, too. "I didn't have time to shower after breakfast shift."

That was probably the reason the cat was stretching and arching to get closer to Reese. But Reese had her attention nailed to Logan.

"I'll leave you two alone," Jimena said, but she stopped after she was in the doorway with Reese. "Buns in the Oven," Jimena said.

"Uh, what?" Reese asked. Logan mumbled the same.

"That's the name I thought of for your bakery. Of course, most people would think you were naming it that because you're pregnant, which we know you're not, but it's a great name."

"You're opening a bakery?" Logan asked. Sheez. For a gossipy town, he hadn't heard a peep about this.

"No, I'm not." Reese huffed, gave Jimena a frustrated look that Logan was betting she had to use frequently when it came to conversations with the woman. "There's a kitchen in the building Cassie's thinking about buying—"

"Cassie bought it this morning," Logan interrupted. "She asked to use some of the ranch hands to help clear out the place." What Cassie hadn't mentioned, however, was anything about Reese and a bakery.

Jimena got moving again but stopped once more, this time in the hall. "I still think you should consider Cassie's offer." She snapped her fingers, obviously way too gleeful considering that Reese and he had something not so gleeful to discuss. "You could name it Stud Muffins."

Reese shut the door in her friend's face.

"Cassie's offer?" Logan asked.

Reese gave a weary sigh, shook her head. "Cassie said I could rent the space from her. But I'm not going to do that because I'm not opening a bakery. Especially not one with a name like Stud Muffins."

She probably couldn't help herself—she smiled. Not all from humor, though. Logan could also see the frustration.

"I'm sorry about that business deal with Delbert," Reese said. "I should have already left town."

Because this might require more than just words, Logan got to his feet and went to her. Yes, she did smell like bacon, and while it wasn't exactly a turn-on, it sure wasn't a turnoff, either.

"I'm not ready for you to leave," he told her.

They weren't words of gold, and it sounded selfish. Because he was. Despite the mess that had just gone down, he really wasn't ready for her to leave town. Of course, that wasn't fair to her because that meant he wanted to talk her into staying around…until he was ready for her to leave.

Hell. It wasn't just un-golden words; it made him feel like the names Jimena was no doubt thinking of to call Delbert.

Still, that didn't stop him from kissing Reese. Or rather trying to kiss her. He got a quick brush of his mouth on hers before she eased back.

Oh, *that*.

"You didn't see what you thought you saw between

Helene and me," he explained. "I'm definitely not getting back together with her."

"It'd be less trouble for you if you did."

"You're wrong. That would be the worst kind of
trouble." Because if he were with Helene, he'd be with
a woman he no longer wanted. A woman who didn't fire
up every inch of his body. A woman he couldn't trust.

Ironic, though, that he could trust Reese. And the
firing-up part was a given anytime he was within six
miles of her.

Like now.

Logan kissed her again, and this time he made it
more than just a brush of the lips. He drew her to him,
hoping for something long, deep and satisfying, but
she pulled back again.

Reese fumbled in her purse that she had hooked
over her shoulder and came up with an envelope that
she handed him. Logan instantly recognized it because
it was the report from the private investigator that he'd
given her. It was still sealed.

"Read it," Reese said, putting it in his hand. She told
him the rest of what she had to say from over her shoulder as she was walking out. "And then you'll know why
we can't be together."

CHAPTER NINETEEN

REESE WALKED. SHE DIDN'T know where she was going. She just put one foot ahead of the other and kept moving. Because if she stopped, she would fall apart for sure. That still might happen, but it was harder to break down sobbing if she kept moving.

God, what had she done?

She didn't regret giving Logan that report. It was something she should have insisted that he read when he'd first gotten it. That way, they would have never had sex for a second time. They wouldn't have made out in the dressing room at the store. They wouldn't have kissed.

That didn't help her mood.

Neither did thinking about what she had to do next. She had to leave town, of course, and she would do that right after the engagement party. It would be the first time she'd left a place not because of the wanderlust stirrings inside her but because she'd made a mess of Logan's life.

She cursed her mother. Cursed this bad hand of a life she'd gotten. But it wasn't just the life she'd been born into, though. It was some of the bad choices she had made on her own. That wasn't on her mother or Chucky. Reese could put that right on her own weary shoulders. She had been the one to get involved with

Spenser O'Malley. She was the one with the police record.

"Reese?" someone called out. Summer Starkley. A college student who was also a part-time waitress at the Fork and Spoon. Thankfully, she was on the other side of Main Street so she probably couldn't get a good look at Reese's face. "I heard about the bakery idea. Love it. I'd be one of your first customers."

Reese just smiled, hoped it looked genuine and didn't show too much of the frustration over hearing about that damn bakery. Talk of it was probably better than the pregnancy rumors, but still, she might scream at the next person who brought it up or suggested some stupid name for a business she wasn't going to own.

"You're here," she heard someone else say. Cassie this time, and that's when Reese realized she was walking right past the building in question. "I was hoping I'd run into you today."

Cassie was in the doorway of the building, and she caught onto Reese's arm and tugged her inside. "Can't you just see a sign with Sweet Tooth on it?" And, God forbid, she was pointing to the kitchen.

Reese didn't scream, though, it took some effort to hold it back. "Cassie, I can't open a bakery here." Best just to set her straight once and for all. "In fact, I'll be leaving in seven days."

No way could Cassie miss the timing. It was the day after the engagement party. "Did something happen between Logan and you?"

Not yet. "I'm just ready to move on," she lied.

Cassie didn't exactly call her on that lie, but she made a sound that reminded Reese that the woman was a therapist. A sort of "oh?" sound that was probably a prompt for Reese to continue.

She didn't.

"Well, at least you're staying to do the engagement party, right?" Cassie asked.

"Of course."

Cassie blew out a breath of relief. "Good, because it's really going to be more of an engagement party–adoption celebration combined. The paperwork went through, and the girls are officially ours."

Cassie dragged Reese into her arms for a hug while she made excited squeals of joy. Reese was happy for her. She truly was, but Cassie seemed to be taking on a lot right now what with getting engaged, the baby and a new business.

Reese glanced around at that new business venture in progress. Even though Cassie had just bought the place, the reception area had already been cleared of the debris, and Reese spotted cleaning crews in the other rooms, including the kitchen.

"The place already looks much better," Reese said.

"Thanks." Cassie led her to the first room. "I thought this could be Claire's studio. Lots of light and space. Of course, she'll only be here a couple of hours a week what with her son and the new baby on the way. Plus, she'll still do wedding photos with her business partner, Livvy. But Claire wanted a local place to do portraits and such."

It was a good space, and a good idea, too.

"I'm having that wall torn down," Cassie said, showing her the next two rooms. "That'll give me an office and a private waiting area. A private entrance and exit, too, in case the clients don't want people to know they're in therapy. Not that something like that would stay private in this town, but still…"

It was another good idea.

The next two rooms were his-and-her public bathrooms, and they'd also been cleaned. And that left the kitchen. Reese didn't want to glance in there, but she found herself doing it, anyway. It was akin to an alcoholic eyeing bottles of booze. Too much temptation to tell the crew not to use those steel scouring pads on a wooden butcher's block. It would leave scratches. But she held her tongue. If she said anything, it would appear she had an interest in it.

"Can you keep a secret?" Cassie asked. She lowered her voice, though there was no way the cleaner could have heard her. Not with the way they were scraping away at those tables.

"As long as the secret doesn't involve me opening a bakery," Reese countered.

"Oh, it doesn't. I figured if you didn't want to open it, then I'd offer it to Jimena since she went to culinary school, too."

Reese hadn't meant to look horrified by that idea. Again because it would make her appear interested, but she felt she should warn Cassie. "I love Jimena. She's my best friend. But she's a horrible cook."

Apparently, that hadn't made the gossip mill yet, but it would if Jimena ever flipped a single burger at the café. However, there were no worries with this particular kitchen and its restaurant-quality equipment. Jimena would never figure out how to turn any of it on. Her forte was making coffee and opening a bag of Cheetos without getting a paper cut.

"Well, maybe I can entice someone else," Cassie

went on. "And now to the secret. Lucky and I are getting married right after the engagement party."

"Married?" Again, that wasn't in the gossip chain so it was an honest to goodness secret.

"I know. It's crazy, but we just wanted to say 'I do' and get on with our lives. Anyway, we're having the justice of the peace come to the house after all the guests have left. It'll be just family and close friends. And Lucky and I wanted you to be there as one of the witnesses."

Reese felt as if someone had punched her, and worse, it was hard to think of how to tell Cassie no what with all that scouring going on.

"One second," she told Cassie, and went to the door of the kitchen. "Uh, you don't want to use those steel wool pads on wood. It'll make it easy for bacteria to get into the scratches." Or in this case, into the gouges they were creating. "Just use a soft cloth."

Of course, Cassie was smiling when Reese turned back around. The woman was sneaky. But it wasn't going to work.

"I just don't want you to have to replace that particular prep table," Reese explained. "As big as it is, a replacement will run you close to a grand."

Cassie didn't smile at that. "Thanks. I had no idea. I guess I have a lot to learn about going into business."

Yes, like maybe it wasn't a good idea to have a photography studio, a therapy office and a bakery all in the same building. The smell of the baked goods would be everywhere.

But come to think of it—maybe that wasn't a bad thing.

Fatty, sugary things tended to cheer people up and

make them happy. Happy people smiled, and that would make it easier to take their pictures. It would also help with those in therapy.

"This was always a dream of mine," Cassie went on. "Not to buy a really crappy building that needs a lot of work, but to be part of this town."

Reese had to shake her head. "You grew up here."

"I didn't feel part of it, though. My father owns the Slippery Pole Strip Club. Hard to fit in with DNA like that."

"But you were a celebrity, a *somebody*," Reese reminded her. "I saw you on TV."

"There's that old saying—when the gods want to punish you, they give you what you wish for. I wished to be somebody, to be important and away from this messy life, and I got exactly that. Except the other life was just as messy, and I was miserable. I'm not miserable now. I'm exactly where I should be. Very, very happy."

Cassie moved closer, looped her arm around Reese. However, before Reese could say anything, not that she had a clue what to say, Cassie lifted her hand in a wait-a-sec gesture. "Bacon. You smell like bacon. I need a minute. I'll be right back." And she ran off to the bathroom to deal with what appeared to be another round of morning sickness.

"Sorry," Reese called out to her.

Apparently, morning sickness didn't mind intruding on something *very, very happy*.

Reese didn't doubt that Cassie was telling the truth, though. This probably was her dream, and she was probably happy with a couple of *very*'s thrown in. But telling Reese all of that was probably another sneaky therapist ploy to make Reese see that she, too, could have a life here.

But she couldn't.

Because once Logan read that police record, it wouldn't matter. He would be more than ready for her to leave.

LOGAN PUT THE envelope on the center of his desk and stared at it. Something he'd been doing since Reese had left it with him and then disappeared. Obviously, she hadn't wanted to wait around and see his reaction.

Because his reaction would be bad.

He had no doubts about that. After all, it was a police report, and even though what was inside had happened over a decade ago when Reese had been just seventeen, she must have thought it would still send him running for the hills.

Or in this case, send *her* running for the hills.

She probably wouldn't leave town immediately. Not with the engagement party coming up. But she was likely off somewhere, planning her escape so that she wouldn't have to deal with whatever fallout that police report would cause.

He decided to buzz Jimena first and have her bring him a fresh cup of coffee, but the moment he reached for the intercom, there was a knock at the door, and when it opened, Jimena was there, coffee in hand.

She put both the coffee and some papers on his desk. She also eyed the envelope and then cursed. "Is that what I think it is?"

"If you think it's Reese's juvie record, then yes, it is what you think it is. Reese gave it to me to read."

She blinked. "I thought you were firing me."

"Not at this moment." They stared at the envelope together. "Do you know what's in it?"

Jimena nodded. "Reese and I met right after it happened. We were in the hospital together."

"Hospital? What does that have to do with her being arrested?"

The woman looked around as if deciding what to say or do. "How much do you want to know?" Jimena finally asked.

"Everything," he insisted, though he wasn't sure that was true.

One second he hated the idea that something could come between Reese and him, and the next second he thought he might as well get it over and done. After all, no matter what happened between them, she would still leave.

"The police report won't have the backstory," Jimena said. She went to the door and closed it. "So, here's the skinny. When I met Reese, I'd just fallen off a two-story balcony because I was drunk. I had three broken bones, sixteen stitches, a dislocated shoulder, and I was still in better shape than Reese was."

Hell. Logan couldn't breathe. It felt as if someone had sucked all the air out of the room.

"Spenser O'Malley?" he managed to say.

"Oh, yeah. There are tools in the world, but he was a sick fuck of a tool. He beat her, and I don't think it was the first time. Then, after he beat her, he dumped her at the ER, went to the police station and had charges filed against her for theft and assault even though the cops never found the money she supposedly stole from him."

Logan could possibly see the theft charges since

Reese had admitted to doing some cons. "Assault? But he's the one who beat her up."

Jimena rubbed her middle fingers and thumbs together. "Spenser was rich. Well connected in that hick town, so the cops believed him, and they arrested Reese while she was still in the hospital bed."

Unfortunately, Logan had a much too vivid imagination and could see her there. Could feel it, too. And worse, it explained why Reese had been so hesitant to get involved with someone else who was well connected. Like him. Except he would never do that to a woman.

Something about this didn't make sense, though.

"Reese could have told me what happened," he said, talking more to himself than to Jimena, trying to work it out in his head. "She was a victim here..."

He looked up, his gaze connecting with Jimena's. "Reese went after Spenser when she got out of the hospital?" he asked.

"We both did. He stole Reese's grandfather's watch, and Reese wanted to get it back."

Logan had no doubts about that. After all, Reese had broken into his own loft to retrieve it. But he never would have assaulted her as Spenser had done.

"We were going to threaten to beat him up if he didn't give her the watch. By then, Reese was my friend, and I wasn't going to let that dickweed get away with what he'd done."

Logan agreed. If he'd been around, he would have done the same thing. In fact, he still wanted to do the same thing. And worse. Logan wanted to hurt the guy the way he'd hurt Reese.

Jimena tipped her head to the envelope again. "The rest of the details are in there."

"Accurate details?" he asked.

"We didn't lie to the cops. Guess whose idea that was?"

He didn't have to guess. It was Reese's. "Is Spenser completely out of the picture now?" And if he wasn't, Logan wanted to know where the guy was.

"He's out. Way out. Only because he's dead."

Good. Logan wasn't in the habit of wishing ill will on people, but he did in this case. In this case, dead wasn't even enough.

"Just know this," Jimena went on. "It took Reese a long time to be with another man. A *long* time. And you know what she called her night with you in San Antonio? Nice and good," she answered before he could decide if he wanted to know. "*Nice and good* might not sound like much to you, but it's the best thing she's ever said about any guy."

That didn't make everything he was feeling any easier.

"If you hurt her, as a minimum I'll brew cat shit in your coffee," Jimena added. And she walked out, leaving Logan to curse again.

He quit arguing with himself and tore open the envelope. It wasn't the actual police report but rather a summary from the private investigator. There it was— the details Jimena had just given—and more.

It was the *more* that got Logan's attention.

Hell.

Spenser O'Malley was dead, all right. He'd died the night that Reese and Jimena had gone to threaten him to give Reese back the watch. And Spenser had given it back in his true asshole kind of way. He'd tossed it on the ground, breaking the crystal watch face. Before Reese or Jimena could even lay a hand on him—or in Jimena's case, a bat—Spenser had run away.

Right into the street.

Where he'd been killed by the Houston-bound, 8:00 p.m. bus.

REESE HAD TO get out of the building. She needed to get moving again. If she didn't, she was going to think about what Logan was reading in that report. And right about now, he had probably already read it, and he was cursing himself for ever getting involved with her.

Her breath caught in her throat. Her heartbeat started to race. And the memories came. Memories that she didn't want to discuss with Cassie.

"Cassie, I have to go," Reese called out to the woman while she was still throwing up in the ladies' room. "Something important's come up."

Reese hurried out before Cassie could stop her.

Since she felt all clammy and sick, she headed in the direction of her apartment. Of course, it was a people minefield along the way, and it seemed as if everyone in town was suddenly out for a stroll. Reese had to smile again. Had to pretend nothing was wrong all the while she was falling apart inside.

How could she have let this happen?

And she wasn't just thinking about Spenser now but Logan. How could she have let herself fall this way? She wasn't a faller. Spenser had taught her that lesson, but here she was with her heart aching and the sick feeling that she had lost something that she could never get back.

By the time she made it to the Bluebonnet Inn, her face was hurting from the smiles and the too-tight muscles. Reese hurried up the stairs, hoping she wouldn't encounter anyone else along the way. And she didn't. Not until she reached her apartment.

Logan was sitting there on the floor with his back resting against her front door. It was such a relaxed pose, for a split second she thought it was Lucky. But it was Logan, all right.

"I called around," he said. "Various people saw you walking so I decided to head here and wait for you."

He stood slowly, met her eye to eye. He knew. She could tell. He'd read the secret that had put her stomach in knots.

Since Reese didn't want to air her dirty laundry in the hall, she unlocked the door, and Logan followed her inside. He didn't say anything until he shut the door behind him.

"Jimena said if I hurt you that she'd put cat shit in my coffee," he said. "Anything you can do to make sure that doesn't happen?"

That certainly wasn't the conversation starter she'd expected, but Reese nodded, anyway. "It's just an empty threat."

Logan lifted his shoulder as if he might not believe that. "We have a lot of cat shit she could use, and she's convinced I'm going to hurt you."

He came closer, and each step seemed to cause her heart to skip beats. However, there was no anger in his eyes, in his tone, not in any part of his body. It stayed that way when Logan slipped his arm around her and kissed her.

Oh, my.

It was a nice kiss, one that untightened those stomach knots and eased away some of the tension in her shoulders. It would have been so easy just to melt into that kiss, maybe melt into some sex, too, but Reese knew that kisses and sex were a temporary fix. And it would only postpone the conversation they had to have.

"Didn't you read the report?" she asked.

He nodded, tried to kiss her again, but she stopped him.

Oh, she got it. "These are pity kisses, aren't they?"

His forehead bunched up. "I don't pity-kiss, have pity sex or really anything else that has to do with pity."

That was probably true, but it didn't explain why he was trying to kiss her again when he should be telling her they were all wrong for each other. So, Reese was the one to say it.

"I could mess up everything for you and your family."

Logan gave a fake yawn. "Old news. We're rich. It's hard to mess up really big trust funds."

"You're making light of this?" she snapped.

"No." And he suddenly got very serious. "I'm just trying to make you understand I'm sorry for what happened to you."

"Aha! I knew it. Pity."

"No. Sympathy and understanding."

"Pity," she grumbled. Reese groaned. "Why don't you ask me why I was stupid enough to get involved with a man like Spenser?"

"You were seventeen. All of us are pretty much stupid at that age."

"I'm betting you weren't."

"Then you'd be betting wrong. At seventeen, I was

doing dumb things like switching places with Lucky so he'd take English tests for me. In exchange, I'd go on dates with very sexually aggressive girls who thought they were getting Lucky. Literally."

He was still trying to make her feel better, but it wasn't working. Nothing could. "The only reason I wasn't charged with manslaughter was because there were witnesses who said neither Jimena nor I forced Spenser into the street. But the bottom line is that I'm responsible for a man's death."

"How do you figure that?" he challenged.

"Spenser ran out of the alley because he was scared of me."

Logan shook his head. "I'm thinking that had more to do with Jimena's bat and a scary threat she probably made to go right along with it."

"No. It was me. Spenser could see in my face that I wasn't going to take any more of his punches. He knew I would fight back, and since he was basically a coward, he ran."

"And he ran into a bus, which I think is some kind of cosmic justice."

It sounded, well, forgivable the way Logan put it, and it wasn't. He pulled her to him again. Kissed her light and soft.

"What happened to you sucked," he said. "You didn't deserve it, but you were ready and willing to get out of a bad situation. And you did. You went to culinary school, got jobs. You made a life for yourself, and you did all of that without the benefit of a trust fund or a family who would walk through fire for you."

Reese dismissed all of that because of what'd happened to Spenser. But to say that to Logan meant she'd just have to keep reopening this wound she didn't want opened. It was a wound that hurt less when it wasn't discussed. And when no one else knew about it. Reese could keep it covered with thick imaginary bandages.

Since she thought they both could use some levity, Reese gave it a try. "You really had sex with Lucky's girlfriends?"

"It's how I lost my virginity. That wasn't a proud moment for me. I was ashamed. Very ashamed."

He was smiling so the levity worked. Or maybe he was just reliving that *ashamed* sexual experience.

"Are you being nice to me so I'll tell Jimena to cancel the cat-shit coffee plans?" she asked.

"In part. In part, too, because I want you in my bed later."

Oh, that got her toes curling. Probably her eyelashes, too, since Logan added a kiss to it. "How much later?"

"Tonight, maybe? I've got meetings stacked up for the next few hours. In fact, I'm running late for one now."

She stepped away from him. "Go. Don't be late." Reese didn't want to do any more damage to his business.

"He can wait. I just want to make sure you're okay."

"I'm fine." It wasn't a lie exactly. She was as fine as she could ever be considering she would always be broken. And that's why she had to tell Logan this now. "I still plan on leaving soon."

He took one short breath. "I figured as much. But I still want to make sure you're okay."

"I am, really."

Logan stared at her as if trying to figure out if that was true. "All right. I'll see you later, then." He moved to leave, but his phone buzzed. "Probably Jimena." But he shook his head when he looked at the screen. "It's the police chief."

Reese automatically moved closer to the phone because this could be about her mother.

"Please tell me you arrested Vickie," Logan greeted.

"No. Haven't found her yet, but we have a problem. By any chance have you spoken to Chucky in the past couple of hours?"

"No," Logan answered, and Reese shook her head, too.

"That's what I figured. Well, Chucky just called here, and he said he's no longer cooperating, that he's withdrawing his complaint. Sorry, Logan, but that means I can't arrest Reese's mother, after all."

CHAPTER TWENTY

LOGAN FOUND A spot out of the path of the other guests. He went to the corner of the sunroom so he could sip his drink and hoped it looked as if he were having fun. After all, this was his twin brother's engagement party, and fun and celebration should be at the top of his to-do list. For the next couple of hours, anyway. But it was hard to think of fun and celebration when Reese was so miserable.

She was trying to hide that misery, of course, and for most of the guests, she was succeeding. Reese was all smiles and friendly conversation as she chatted about the food all laid out on the table. Some of the stuff Logan recognized—various finger foods—but Reese had also included some fancier things, too, like pâté-wrapped brie cheese. All served with champagne, of course, and nonalcoholic sparkling cider for Mia and Mackenzie.

For Claire and Cassie, too.

Everything was picture-perfect. Which in his mind was different from ordinary perfect. It just meant everything looked the way it should. People smiling, having fun. Even Helene was working the room and pretending to be happy that she was there. Logan was pretending as well, but he was certain he failed big-time when he saw Lucky making his way toward him.

Lucky handed him a fresh glass of champagne. "As my late business partner used to say, you look lower than a fat penguin's balls. I'm guessing all that lowness has something to do with one of them." Lucky tipped his head to Reese and then Helene.

"Reese," Logan readily admitted.

For just a second, Logan had considered lying, but it was hard to get away with lying to an identical twin. Probably something to do with sharing the same quarters and food source for the first nine months of their lives.

Lucky made a sound of agreement. "Is Reese still planning on leaving?"

"She says she is." And since leaving was exactly what she'd done all her adult life, Logan had no doubt she would do it now.

"And you can't change her mind? You must be losing your touch."

The little dig was mandatory between brothers. Logan suspected it was to mask the emotional core of this conversation. If it got too much more emotional, one of them would have to curse or add some crude reference regarding dicks since a ball reference had already been used.

"I tried to convince her that it didn't matter about her juvie record or what had happened in her past, but I don't think I got through." Hell, Logan knew he hadn't. "Of course, it didn't help that Chucky reneged on his deal and that now Vickie is free to do what she wants."

"Yeah, that sucks donkey dicks."

The fact that Lucky had gone to the D-word so soon meant he was feeling a lot of this dark-hearted crap that

Logan was feeling. And it was something he didn't want to feel.

"Has the police chief arrested Chucky yet for trying to extort money from Helene?" Lucky asked.

"He would arrest him if he could find him. Vickie and Chucky are nowhere to be found."

That wouldn't last. Those two smelled money the way sharks smelled blood, and they would be drawn right back to the McCord bank accounts.

Logan watched as Helene reached the table where Reese was standing. He couldn't hear what they said to each other, but it was all smiles. And brief. The briefness brought on an even more genuine smile from Reese.

"I don't want to hurt her," Logan went on, and that didn't have anything to do with Jimena's cat-shit threat.

"Reese?" Lucky asked.

Logan frowned. "Of course."

"Just checking. Come on. Take a walk with me. I want to show you the new rodeo bull I bought."

It didn't seem like a good time for that, what with the party in full swing, but Lucky led him outside, anyway.

"A lot of changes going on," Lucky said once they were in the backyard. "I've already talked to Riley and Anna about this, but I wanted to get your opinion about Cassie, me and the girls staying on here at the house permanently."

Logan was sure he looked surprised. "I thought that was already a done deal. Why, were you thinking of moving elsewhere?"

"No, we all love it here, but I wanted to make sure it was okay with you. It's your home, after all."

True. Home, in name only. Logan rarely stayed there anymore. He'd moved to his town loft because it was easier for work purposes, but he'd also done that because after Lucky, Riley and Anna moved away, it just hadn't felt much like home. It was starting to feel more like it now, but his loft wasn't that far from the ranch. Plus, the house was huge so he would always have his suite there. Well, unless Cassie and Lucky had a houseful of kids, that is.

"Riley's okay with it, too," Lucky went on. They continued walking toward the barn and that attached corral. "Claire and he are planning an addition to their house, though, so they can have a playroom for Ethan and a nursery."

So many changes, and while Logan didn't feel left out exactly, he was the oldest. Okay, he did feel a little left out, but that didn't mean he wasn't happy for his siblings.

"Anna gave it her blessing, as well," Lucky said. "If she decides to move back after finishing law school and getting married, she said she wanted to build a house by the springs, anyway."

Logan knew the exact spot. In fact, his kid sister had talked about having a house there since she was in first grade.

"I think it's all great," Logan assured him. "The ranch and the house will be a great place to raise the girls and a baby."

Lucky stopped for a second, laughed. "*A baby*. Now, that's something I'll bet you never thought you'd say when it came to me."

Logan would have liked to say he'd expected it, but

it hadn't been anywhere on his radar. Until Cassie came back in his life, Lucky's longest track record with a woman was less than the same amount of time Reese stayed in one place.

Not very long at all.

"Fatherhood will suit you," Logan assured him. "Riley, too. I can't wait to have more nieces or nephews." He already thought of Claire's son, Ethan, as family. Also thought the same way about Mia and Mackenzie.

Logan spotted the bull when they reached the corral. It was a beauty and would no doubt earn them a pretty penny once it was trained. That was yet something else Lucky had added to the ranch—the rodeo bull training program. It was as successful as the cutting horse operation that Riley had started.

All the pieces were falling into place.

"Dad would have loved this," Logan said.

It was something he hadn't intended to say, though. It'd just slipped out, and while it was true, it was also a downer because it was a reminder that their folks weren't here to share any of it.

"They're here," Lucky whispered, seeming to know exactly what Logan had been thinking. He blinked hard as if blinking back tears and then shook it off. "No fat penguin balls today. I'm getting married." He pointed to the trees in the backyard. "Right there." He checked his watch. "In an hour or so."

All in all, it was the perfect way to elope.

"Why don't we go back in?" Lucky suggested. "I can tell some off-color jokes to get some of the crowd heading out. Of course, it might cause others to stay."

"You should make some dick jokes," Logan advised.

"Absolutely. Balls and dicks. My preferred way of going off-color."

They'd reached the porch when the sunroom door opened, and Helene stepped out. She didn't seem surprised to see them. Just the opposite. Of course, with all the windows in the sunroom, she had perhaps been watching them.

"Any chance we can talk?" she asked Logan.

This wasn't the time or the place, but then that applied to all times and places when it came to Helene. It was probably best to talk to her in a public place, though, than have her come to his office. Which she would. It was clear she had something to get off her chest. Probably something to do with the Vickie-Chucky mess.

Lucky waited until Logan gave him the nod before he gave Helene a warning glance and then went inside. Logan appreciated the warning; it was good for his twin to have his back, but it wasn't necessary. Logan no longer felt the punch of emotion, either good or bad, when he looked at Helene.

"Thank you for seeing me," Helene said. "I wanted to let you know that I'll be filing charges against Chucky, after all, since he didn't go through with our bargain. Of course, he'll probably just disappear."

Probably. And that was the best-case scenario in this—that the man would disappear and take Vickie with him.

"I don't like all the gossip it'll create," Helene went on. "I was just starting to restore my reputation, and here it'll come out that I told Chucky where Reese was."

"Are you trying to back out of filing charges against Chucky?"

Her hesitation let him know that she was. "I'll do it. For you. I know you're still upset with me, and this might help mend the rift between us."

"No, I'm not upset, not anymore. I wish you only the best."

And he meant it. Even more, Helene knew he meant it. But as for that rift, well, Logan figured her idea of rift-mending meant getting back together. That wasn't going to happen.

Unlike him, there was plenty of emotion on her face. He saw the hurt and knew there was nothing that could be done about it. Nothing that he could do, anyway.

"Can we talk about what happened that night?" she asked.

He lifted an eyebrow. "Are we going to discuss clown noses?"

"No. God, no." She shuddered. "All of that was just a fantasy. I couldn't bring myself to ask you to dress up like a clown."

"Then that should have been your cue to break up with me. Because if your boyfriend can't fulfill your fantasies, then he shouldn't be your boyfriend."

Helene nodded, paused, nibbled on her bottom lip. "And now you have someone else in your life to fulfill your fantasies."

"No clown stuff, though," he said to add a light touch. It didn't lighten anything, though, because it basically confirmed to Helene that Reese and he were indeed into some fantasy-fulfilling. Of course, right now the sex was enough of a fantasy.

"You don't feel it's too soon?" she asked.

"For what?" he asked right back.

Helene lifted her shoulder as if the answer were obvious. "To be involved with someone. I mean, I can't even think of being with anyone else yet. After all, we were together for eight years."

She seemed to be implying that this was some kind of rebound relationship between Reese and him. Was that what it was? Helene was right about it being soon, only four months now since the clown incident, but Logan wasn't at all certain that it was *too soon*.

But that did get him thinking.

If it was too soon, then Reese would be the one to get hurt. Maybe that's why she still seemed so hellbent on leaving. And the problem with that? Logan couldn't even guarantee her that she wouldn't get a broken heart from this.

"No word about Chucky or Vickie?" Helene asked.

It took Logan a second to switch gears and remember that he was still having a conversation with Helene. "Nothing. You?"

"Nothing," she repeated, then paused. "Have you seen Greg?"

Logan shook his head and caught a glimpse of Reese walking past one of the windows. She didn't exactly look out at them, but he figured she'd seen them talking.

"I haven't seen Greg, either," Helene went on, "but I heard you hired Reese's friend to replace him. I suppose she has a lot of office experience?"

"None whatsoever."

Added to that, Jimena had a smart mouth, vile threats and dressed like a call girl. Still, she could handle Crazy Cat, and other than the threats, she hadn't done too much to get on his bad side.

"I see," Helene said, which was probably code for *I can't believe this shit. You hire someone with no experience. You sleep with a fry cook, one with a police record. And you haven't been flossing regularly.*

Logan decided to skip the code and go with a direct question. "Did you give Elrond one of your porcelain boob bookends?"

Clearly, she hadn't been expecting that question. "Wh-what?"

"Porcelain boob bookend," he repeated even though Logan doubted repetition was necessary in this case. "Because he had a boob identical to the one you gave me, and he also had a clown suit. I just figured that wasn't a coincidence."

Her mouth tightened a moment. "I didn't sleep with him. Not after Greg decided he'd fulfill the fantasy for me."

There it was again. Fantasies. And clown suits. No doubt lies, too. Logan was almost positive she wasn't telling the truth about being with Elrond.

"I didn't sleep with him," Helene repeated, and this time she had a bite to her tone. "I'm not a whore."

Logan shrugged. "Even if you'd had sex with both of them, it wouldn't have made you a whore. Just a liar and a cheater." There was no bitterness in his voice, but she probably would have preferred it if there had been. Because it would have meant he was still emotionally invested in her.

"There you are," Jimena said, opening the back door. "Cassie and I were talking about litter boxes and cat, um, droppings, and then I looked up and saw you out here, with Helene."

Logan scowled at her. "No threat necessary. Helene and I were just having a friendly chat, but we're done now."

"Good, because the party's wrapping up, and I thought you'd want to say goodbye to the guests especially since three of them are business associates. One of which you have a meeting with in two days."

That was code, too, for *get your ass inside before you hurt Reese's feelings*.

Helene quickly picked up on the code because she got moving. Jimena would have followed her, but Logan stopped her by stepping in front of her.

"One question," he said.

"Yes, I have been stockpiling cat shit," Jimena answered right off.

He made sure his scowl deepened. "That wasn't the question. I want to know if Reese packed to leave."

Jimena suddenly didn't look so smart-assed. "She's always packed and ready to leave. Now, if you're wanting to know if she *will* go, that I can't say. You should ask her. Then you should ask her to stay."

He already had. Apparently, he was a lot better with business deals than he was with Reese.

"By the way, should I bring Crazy Cat back here since she belongs to Cassie and Lucky?" Jimena asked.

They already had Crazy Dog, five cats, two kids and another on the way. It seemed cruel to add another fur-critter, especially one with the worst temperament in the kitty kingdom. Still…

"Keep that cat at the office as long as you're working for me. But when you leave, part of your clearing-out duties will be to bring the cat here, understand?"

Jimena nodded, turned, but then as quickly turned back around. "Is it okay if I have sex with your friend Jason?"

Logan was about to groan, then say okay, but he rethought that. "Only if Jason agrees." Which he would. Jason liked the call-girl-looking, smart-mouth type.

Jimena gave a fake laugh, shot him the bird and went inside. Just as Reese was coming out.

"Is everything okay?" Reese asked. She had no doubt heard and seen the interaction between Jimena and him, but Logan figured her question had more to do with his earlier interaction with Helene.

"Helene and I were just talking," he explained. "I suppose you could say Jimena and I were just talking, too, but it never quite feels like conversation with her."

"I know what you mean." She stayed back. Again, probably because she'd seen him with Helene and wasn't sure what was going on. Reese looked as if she were debating either fight or flight.

"Helene thinks it's too soon for me to get involved with you," he relayed. "I believe she's wrong."

"And if she's not?"

Because she still wasn't coming closer to him, Logan went to her. He slipped his arm around her waist, brushed a kiss on her forehead. "We don't have to push things between us. There's no timetable. We could continue to see each other, and if it's too soon, then it shouldn't take us long to figure that out."

He figured this was the part where she would just remind him that she wasn't a stayer but rather a leaver.

But Reese made a sound that could possibly be of agreement. Good. He was making some progress even if, in the back of his mind, he was wondering if progress was just a mistake.

"I should go back in," she said. "Lucky and Cassie want to say their vows as soon as the guests clear out. I can help with that. Better yet, Jimena can help with that."

She kissed his cheek. So chaste. The kind of kiss that longtime couples gave each other, but it still packed a wallop. Maybe Reese wasn't capable of giving him chaste kisses.

Logan followed her in, but he didn't get far when he spotted the guest who was coming into the sunroom. Delbert Clark. Since Delbert was no longer doing business with McCord Cattle Brokers, Logan didn't have a clue why he was there. He certainly hadn't been invited.

"I need to talk to you," Delbert said the moment he laid eyes on Logan. But Logan realized Delbert wasn't just looking at him. He was looking at Reese.

Hell. What now? If Delbert was going to demand that he break up with Reese, then it was going to be a very short conversation. Logan didn't usually dig in his heels when it came to repairing a business relationship, but in this case he'd make an exception.

"This isn't a good time," Logan said, stating the obvious.

Delbert glanced around as if seeing the party food and guests for the first time. Clearly, he had something else on his mind. "Sorry. I didn't know, but this can't wait. Can we go somewhere and talk in private?"

Logan wanted to say no, but it was Reese who motioned for him to follow her into the family room. It wasn't exactly private since someone could walk in at any moment, but maybe that meant Delbert would say his piece and leave. But he didn't jump right into anything. He just stood there, sweat popping out on his forehead and the veins bulging on his neck.

"You need to call off your mother," Delbert told Reese.

Reese shook her head when he didn't add more. "I haven't seen my mother in days," she said at the same moment Logan asked, "What are you talking about?"

"I'm talking about your mother screwing me over, that's what, and I want it to stop."

"You think I can control what my mother does?" Reese asked. "What *did* she do?"

Still nothing from Delbert to explain. He didn't start talking until after several huffed breaths and some pacing. "You know she called me and said I should quit doing business with Logan because you're bad news, because you could end up hurting me and my own business."

Reese nodded. "And you did break ties with Logan."

Now Logan huffed and folded his arms over his chest. "I'm guessing Vickie did something else. Something more than just bad-mouthing me and playing on your narrow little mind."

A flash of anger went through Delbert's eyes, but it cooled as quickly as it had come, and he cursed. "She's blackmailing me."

Logan glanced at Reese to see if she had any idea what was going on, but she just shook her head again.

"I had sex with Vickie," Delbert finally said. "I

didn't know who she was, but she came on to me when I was in a bar. I made the mistake of leaving that bar with her." He groaned, scrubbed his hand over his face and then looked at Logan. "She said I was to do what she told me to do, or else she'd tell my wife."

"Let me guess—Vickie filmed your one-nighter?" Reese asked.

"Filmed with audio," Delbert explained. "And the images aren't blurry, either. Vickie said she'd give me the video if I severed business ties with Logan and told him I was doing that because of you."

"And Vickie wanted even more after that," Logan finished for him.

"Yeah. She wanted me to contact even more of your business associates and get them to blackball McCord Cattle Brokers. She must have a hard-on for you, Logan, to want to screw you over like that."

"She wants money," Logan corrected. "Vickie figures if she hurts my business enough that I'll pay her off. I won't." He was also guessing that this was Vickie's way of punishing Reese, of showing Reese who was in charge.

And it was working.

The color had drained from Reese's face, and she was probably about to launch into some apologies. "This isn't your fault," Logan told her, not that she would believe him, but he had to try. "But this is *your* fault," Logan said to Delbert.

"I know." Another groan. "I just need you to help me. Maybe Reese can help me get that video."

"Vickie probably made multiple copies and has stashed them in hard-to-find places," Reese said. "This is one of her favorite cons, by the way, and it won't end with these first demands. She'll want money from you and lots of it. And she'll keep wanting money."

"So, how do I stop her?" Delbert asked.

Logan and Reese exchanged glances, and since he figured Delbert was going to need it, he gave him a pat on the arm. And he told Delbert exactly what he was going to have to do to make this mess, and Vickie, go away.

CHAPTER TWENTY-ONE

ONCE AGAIN HER mother had ruined things. Not just for Delbert, either. And Vickie would keep on ruining things because that's what she did. Heck, she'd even ruined Cassie and Lucky's wedding for Reese since Reese hadn't been able to think of much else other than their conversation with Delbert.

Thankfully, Cassie and Lucky hadn't seemed to notice. Hard to notice anyone being distracted, though, when they were clearly so much in love with each other.

The informal wedding itself had gone off without a hitch. The rain had held off. There'd been a cool breeze, and the only talk had been of the happy couple and the life they were building together. Perfect, in fact.

There it was again. *Perfect.* The word that seemed like a pipe dream to Reese. Perfection just wouldn't happen with her mother around and her own past always haunting her.

"We won," Logan said, pulling her out of her thoughts.

For a second, Reese thought she'd missed something he'd said, and maybe she had, because that's when she realized Logan had pulled to a stop not in front of the Bluebonnet Inn but in the parking lot of the McCord building. The rain that had held off all day was now sliding down the windshield.

"We won," she agreed. "But this won't be the last of it."

"It will be if Delbert goes through on filing those charges against your mother."

Yes, and while Delbert had hesitantly agreed to do just that, he might change his mind when he realized this would cost him his marriage. Of course, it would end up costing him that, anyway, because even if he paid and paid and paid, Vickie liked to tear apart people's lives.

"Even if Vickie's locked up, she'll find a way to cause trouble," Reese continued. Mercy, she was pure gloom and doom, and here less than an hour after attending a wedding.

"Tell you what," Logan said. "Let's quit thinking about Vickie right now, and get out of this truck before it starts raining any harder. It'd be nice to get inside and stay put while this storm moves through."

"Does this mean you want me to spend the night here with you?"

"Is that a trick question?" he asked.

"No. We just hadn't discussed it, and I thought with everything going on—"

Logan put an end to what she was saying with a kiss. He managed to rid her of her breath and her doubts in one swoop.

Apparently, she was staying the night.

"Wait here for just a couple of seconds until I get the back door unlocked," he told her, and he hurried out of the truck. There was a small awning just above the door, but he still got wet. Logan didn't hurry to unlock the door, though. Instead, he must have gotten a call because he looked at his phone screen.

Reese got out, too, and ran toward Logan just as he opened the door and got them inside.

"It's Chucky," Logan mouthed, keeping his phone pressed to his ear so he could hear whatever the man was saying.

Of course. There was no way Chucky was just going to slink away from this.

Logan continued listening on the way up the stairs, turning on lights as they climbed, and by the time they made it to the loft, Reese didn't have to ask if it was bad news because she could tell from his face that it was. Logan confirmed that by not saying anything until they were inside.

"You're sure you want to do that?" Logan asked the man, but she couldn't hear Chucky's response.

Several seconds later, Logan hit the end-call button, put his phone back in his pocket. He also poured them drinks and had a long sip before he continued.

"Chucky says if Helene files charges against him that he'll copy old newspaper articles about Spenser O'Malley and plaster them all over town."

Her breath vanished again, but this time it wasn't from one of Logan's kisses. Chucky really knew which wounds to go after so he could hurt her the most. And what with her mother trying to ruin Logan, it pretty much killed what little festive mood she had left from the wedding.

"Spenser." Reese sank down onto the nearest chair. She really didn't want all of that brought out in the open again. Especially since it would be gossiped about.

"I think Helene was having second thoughts about those charges, anyway," Logan commented. "She's worried how it'll look when everyone learns she told Chucky you were here."

"Is that what she said to you when she was talking to you on the porch?" she asked.

"Among other things." He had more of his drink, handed Reese hers and sat down across from her. "Helene and I are not getting back together. Ever. You don't have to worry about that."

Good. Because she had enough to worry about, and apparently so did Logan.

"What else did Chucky say?" Reese pressed.

Logan took a long, deep breath. Probably not a good sign. "Chucky says he'll start rumors that I could have saved my parents but that I was drunk when I got to the scene of the accident."

The profanity flew out of her mouth before Reese even knew she was going to say it, and she slammed her glass on the coffee table. "That little shit. I want to go after him. I want to rip off his dick and beat him senseless with it."

She was halfway to the door before Logan reached her. He caught onto her arm and whirled her back around. Reese was certain that the anger was visible in every part of her body, but Logan managed to look a lot calmer.

"Dick-ripping?" he questioned. "A little extreme, more like something Jimena would do, but thank you for the offer. I did notice, though, that you didn't get pissed when Chucky threatened to slime you, only when he turned that potential slime on me."

"Because he's going after you because of me." She still didn't have control of her voice. It was too loud, too shrill.

"No, he's going after me because he's greedy and wants money. And he believes this is the fastest way to get it."

That was true, but it didn't help that situation. "So, what do we do?"

He kissed the tip of her nose and stepped away so he could get her drink. "We wait him out. Chucky wants money, and he loses the chance of getting that money if he spills all."

Reese knew that was true, but the idea of waiting sickened her. "This is such a mess. Not just what Chucky is trying to do to us, but what Vickie's trying to do to Delbert." She sighed. "At least Delbert and I did something to get ourselves into hot water. You didn't."

She saw Logan flinch just slightly, and the only reason she caught it was because Reese had her attention nailed to him. It was still a sore subject after all these years, but she hadn't heard any gossip about the accident.

"It's ironic that a vehicle killed both your parents and Spenser," she threw out there. Reese went with a hunch. "You think you should have been able to save them?"

He turned now, avoiding her gaze. "Do you think you should have been able to save Spenser?"

"Of course. In a perfect world, Spenser would have lived, redeemed himself and went off to live a happy life." Reese paused. "I'm sorry. I shouldn't have brought it up."

The words had hardly left her mouth when Logan turned, slid his hand around the back of her neck and dragged her to him.

"I'm tired of talking," he said, and he crushed his mouth to hers.

LOGAN HADN'T INTENDED for the kiss to be foreplay. He'd just wanted to end the discussion, and the most pleasurable and fastest way to do that was just to kiss Reese. Of course, anytime he kissed her was pleasurable, but this particular kiss did double duty.

He didn't want to think about his parents' car accident, Spenser O'Malley, Chucky or anybody else. He only wanted to be with Reese tonight, and if he kept kissing her, that just might happen.

Outside, the storm kicked up, the wind and rain slapping against the windows. Since the back wall of his loft was about 70 percent windows and glass, it seemed as if the storm was right inside. Inside him, too, but Logan put all of that raw emotion into the kiss.

Reese staggered back, and for a couple of really bad moments, Logan thought she was calling a halt to this so they could keep on talking. But she was only catching her breath. Once she'd gulped in some air, she came right back to him, and she kissed him with as much emotion and intensity as he'd kissed her.

Maybe they both had some things to work out tonight, and Logan was thinking the bed was a good place to do that. Of course, that was his hard-on talking again, but for once maybe that idiotic part of him was actually making sense. At least this couldn't complicate things because their lives were already beyond complicated.

Logan pushed that thought aside, too, and pulled her to him. Not that he had to do much pulling. Reese was already in the mode of having her body pressed against his. His hard-on thought that was an excellent notion, too, but there was something in his brain that kept telling him to slow down, to enjoy the moment, because with Reese he never knew how many more moments like this he was going to get.

So, Logan slowed the pace. Since it was already at frantic, it wasn't easy. Still, he took his time, savoring her taste and the way she felt in his arms. Savoring her.

Man, she fired up every inch of his body, and he'd quit trying to figure out why. It probably didn't make sense to her, either. He wasn't the perfect man for her because she would always be worried about what people thought. About what people would find out to hurt them. But for this moment, it was perfect.

She was perfect.

Logan brushed some kisses on her neck, then lower to the tops of her breasts. It did exactly what he'd intended it to do. It got her hotter. Did the same to him as well, and without breaking those kisses, she started maneuvering them toward the bed.

He didn't resist, but he continued to keep things slow. Tiny steps. Big, long kisses. So that by the time they did tumble onto the mattress, Reese knew that he meant business. A different kind of business since it was usually a frantic grab-and-get when they were with each other.

"You don't have to make it nice for me," she whispered.

"I'm not. This is for me," he whispered back.

Reese stopped a moment, her gaze meeting his. The lights weren't on, but a well-timed lightning bolt let him see her face. She was questioning this. And Logan knew why. For lack of a better word this was intimate, and they weren't just swept up in the moment. They could decide whether to stop or not, but the decision would be made not with hard-ons and arousals but with their heads.

Scary shit.

Logan braced himself for Reese to cut and run, and she probably thought about doing that. But she didn't. Her mouth came back to his, and she kissed him. Long, slow, deep.

He eased up her loose cotton dress, slipping it off. Her bra, too, so he could lower those kisses to her breasts. She made a silky sound of pleasure, took what he was offering, and she slid her fingers into his hair. He stayed there a moment, pleasuring her. Pleasuring himself, too, before he took the same slow pace to remove her panties.

His hard-on made itself known then. The brainless wonder wanted to dive right in, but Logan fought the urge and did something else he'd been wanting to do. He kissed every inch of Reese. By the time he worked his way back up to her mouth, she was panting. And grabbing at his clothes.

Logan let her grab, and he tried not to wince when she fumbled, and fumbled, and kept on fumbling with the zipper of his jeans. Since he didn't want this to be a hand job, he finally helped her. Got his eyes uncrossed, too.

The condom was an issue since Reese tried to help with that, as well. Obviously, she'd reached her threshold for long and savoring and just wanted him inside her. Logan and his hard-on were all for that, but he still tried to hang on to the moment by entering her slowly.

That lasted a heartbeat.

Reese turned, flipping him on his back, and she got on top of him. The pace was anything but slow. It didn't take her long to find the right rhythm, and since she was clearly hell-bent on finishing this too fast, Logan caught onto her hips to help her.

She looked amazing on top of him. Not like something from a porn movie, more like one of those sensual scenes where everything seemed graceful and choreographed. Of course, that was probably influenced by the fact she was fucking his brains out.

Thanks to some more lightning, Logan was able to see her face when she climaxed. Amazing. Watching her was almost better than having a climax of his own.

Almost.

Logan would have liked to watch a little while longer, but his hard-on had had enough. He caught onto Reese, pulling her down to him, and he let his hard-on finish what it'd started.

LOGAN FIGURED IT was the sound of the storm outside that triggered the storm in his head. The dream came just as real as it always was.

He was on the mental hamster wheel again, going through images so familiar that he didn't need the dream to see them. Just like all those other times, he fought the skid on the road, fought everything inside him that tried to claw its way to the surface.

The fear.

The sickening dread of what he would see as he ran to the tangled wreck.

Tonight was no different. He pulled Claire to the side of the road. Protecting her. And then he was on the hamster wheel again, hurrying back to his parents. Realizing he'd made a mistake by not calling for help the second he'd spotted the wreck.

Just like every other dream, his mother turned and looked at him, the life already leaving her eyes. But she said something. This time, though, it was different. Logan didn't just hear the words in his head; he saw them form on her lips. Barely a whisper. But it was more than loud enough for him to hear.

I love all five of you.

"Logan?" someone said.

Since he was still in the dream, it took him a moment to realize it wasn't his mother calling out his name. It was Reese. She was shaking him, and she sounded very concerned.

Logan forced his eyes open, and just like that, the dream vanished. He hadn't wanted to hold on to those images, anyway, but he wanted to hold on to those words.

"I love all five of you?" Reese questioned.

Obviously, he'd talked in his sleep. "The dream," he managed to say.

"I suspected as much. I didn't think you were talking to me and four other women."

Good. Reese had kept it light. Not quite a joke, but it batted away some of the dark cobwebs.

"One of your parents said that?" she asked.

Logan sat up, nodded. "My mother. But I'm not sure she actually said it. Sometimes, in the dream she doesn't say anything. Sometimes, she says what I want to hear her say."

Reese stayed quiet a moment. "What do you want to hear her say?"

Logan stayed quiet a moment, too. *"It's all right. I forgive you for not saving us."*

He figured Reese was going to be surprised by that,

but she didn't seem to be. She made a sound of understanding. "I do that with my Spenser dreams. I rewrite what happened so that it has an ending I can better handle. It doesn't help."

"Then what does help?" And he was serious. Because while Reese was still troubled by what'd happened to Spenser, she wasn't the one having nightmares or migraines.

"Accepting it," she said.

"You're able to do that?"

"Most days." She settled against him. "It's not a perfect solution, but I don't think we ever get perfect when it comes to our past." She groaned softly. "Sorry, that's probably too deep for a postsex chat."

Only if they were trying to make sure the postsex chat didn't mean anything. This conversation meant something. On the surface, they didn't have a lot in common, but beneath the surface, that was a whole different story.

"Jimena said you were always packed and ready to leave," he threw out there.

"I am. Though I can't imagine why she'd tell you that."

"Because I asked her. I figured now that the engagement party was over, you'd be looking to move." Logan adjusted his position so he could look her in the eyes. "Give it at least another week."

Reese certainly didn't jump to agree to that. "And then?"

"And then give it another week after that."

She smiled. Barely there and brief. But it was still a smile. "I'll think about it, but Jimena doesn't believe this will turn out well between us."

No, she didn't. Most people probably felt that way including members of his own family. Thankfully, they hadn't voiced those concerns to his face.

"Get some sleep," she said, brushing a kiss on his cheek.

"You, too." But Logan thought he should add one more thing. "Don't let Jimena put cat shit in my coffee."

Not just a smile this time but also a chuckle. Logan suddenly wasn't sleepy at all and wondered if he could cash in that laugh for another round of sex. But he must have tempted fate with that thought because his phone buzzed.

He checked the time. It was just past midnight. Way too late for someone to be calling him about business so that meant it was some kind of emergency. He got a slam of instant memories. Of another storm. Of the car accident. And Logan grabbed his phone so fast that he nearly dropped it. He didn't even check the screen before answering.

"McCord," the caller said. Definitely not family, but it was a voice that Logan recognized.

Chucky.

"What the hell do you want?" Logan greeted.

"Just thought you should know that I worked out a deal with your lady friend, and I'll be leaving town."

By lady friend, Chucky was no doubt referring to Helene. "She paid you off?" Logan countered, and he put the call on speaker so Reese could hear.

"Just in case you're recording this, let's just say we came to a mutually satisfying agreement." Chucky mispronounced *mutually*.

Yeah, Helene had paid him off.

"Then why call me with all of this?" Logan asked.

But as soon as the question left his mouth, he got a really bad feeling about this.

"Because I didn't want to leave without telling you about Vickie." Chucky cleared his throat. "Your lady friend probably doesn't know it, but Vickie broke into her office. Vickie's sneaky like that. Anyway, Vickie found something that she might try to use against your lady friend. Something Vickie can use as blackmail."

Logan dragged in a long breath. "Let's just cut the lady-friend crap and tell me what Vickie found in Helene's office."

"Not Helene," Chucky corrected. "Your other lady friend, the one who works for you now. Jimena."

CHAPTER TWENTY-TWO

Jimena was late for their meeting, and Reese figured that was exactly what her friend wanted to be. Because Jimena was avoiding this conversation.

Reese didn't need any special powers to determine that.

When Reese had called Jimena immediately after Chucky's bombshell news, Jimena hadn't been asleep—because she was with Jason—but after Reese had told her it was important that they talk, Jimena had said she'd meet Reese at the Bluebonnet Inn at eight the following morning. That way, they could chat before Jimena had to go to work. Well, Reese was here.

But Jimena wasn't.

It was only ten past eight, which meant Jimena was hardly late enough to start thinking about her friend being hurt and lying in a ditch or something, but Reese had to know what Vickie had found in Jimena's desk.

Of course, this all could turn out to be some kind of con on her mother's part. Maybe on Chucky's part, too. Because maybe there'd been nothing to find, but this could be a way of stirring up Reese. If so, it had worked.

It had worked for Logan, too. He was at the McCord building with a team that was installing a security system. One that would no doubt be top-notch and would prevent future break-ins. It was too bad they didn't have a time machine to go back and undo the break-in her mother had supposedly done.

Reese prayed this didn't end up hurting Jimena in some way.

Her phone rang, and Reese was ready to chew out Jimena for being late, but it wasn't Jimena. It was Helene. Good gravy. She hadn't had enough caffeine yet to deal with Helene. Reese answered, anyway, because she was still worrying about the "Jimena in a ditch" theory, and Helene might know something to dispel that.

"Sorry to bother you so early," Helene greeted, "but I knew you were up because I saw you leave Logan's about an hour ago."

Reese didn't ask how she'd seen that, but Helene did have an office just up the street from the McCord building so it was possible the sighting had been accidental and that Helene wasn't spying on her. From everything Reese had heard about Helene, the woman worked long hours and was often in early enough to have seen Reese leave.

"I was hoping we could meet for coffee and a chat. I called the café," Helene said, "but Bert said this was your day off."

"It is, and I'm kind of busy right now. Besides, I'm not sure we actually have anything to discuss. Unless it's about you not filing those charges against Chucky."

"You heard. Yes, it's true. I'm not filing charges, and he's agreed to leave town."

"You paid him?" Reese asked.

"I'd rather discuss that in person," Helene answered. "I'll tell Logan this, of course, but I also wanted you to know that Delbert called me last night. He said he wasn't going to have charges filed against your mother, either, that he was going to take care of the matter himself."

That meant Delbert was going to pay Vickie off. Reese didn't especially care if a rich, cheating man was willing to pay hush money, but it wouldn't be the last of her mother's demands.

"I know it's hard for you to understand," Helene went on, "but a reputation is a delicate thing, and sometimes it's worth any price. I understand why Delbert's doing what he's doing."

That might have prompted Reese to say something along the lines of wishing them both luck and that there was no need for a chat over coffee, but there was a knock at the door, and when Reese threw it open, Jimena was standing there.

"I have to go," Reese told Helene, and she ended the call before the woman could say another word.

Jimena did something similar to Reese. She started talking before Reese could get out her first question. "I had the hottest night with Logan's friend Jason. Can't wait to tell you all about it."

Reese was well aware that Jimena had left the engagement party with Jason. Was also well aware they'd started groping and kissing each other before they even made it to his truck. Under normal circumstances, Reese would want to hear a few PG-rated details but not now.

"Your date update can wait," Reese told her.

"And so can a few other things."

"No. I need to tell you about Chucky."

"Later. For now, get your grandfather's watch and come with me," Jimena insisted. "We can talk while we walk. And hurry. I have to be at work in an hour. I have an asshole for a boss who'll fire me if I'm late." Jimena chuckled as if this were some kind of joke. Well, the asshole for a boss part was a joke, but the rest of this wasn't.

Reese shook her head. "Where are we walking, and why do I need to bring the watch?" She froze. "Oh, God. Does Vickie know about the watch?"

"If she does, she didn't hear it from me. Just get the watch and come on. I have a surprise for you. And FYI, I'm not going to spill anything juicy until you get it so the longer you fart around, the longer it'll take for you to hear what you want to hear."

Reese doubted that was a bluff, and since she really was anxious to hear what had happened between Chucky, Jimena and Vickie, she hurried to the coffee bag where she'd hidden the watch after wrapping it in foil.

"Is someone going to try to steal the watch?" Reese asked.

Jimena shrugged, and with that as her only explanation—which, of course, was no explanation at all—she started out the door and down the stairs. Reese put the watch in her jeans pocket, grabbed her purse and hurried after her.

"All right, start talking," Reese insisted the moment they were outside. "Did you really pay off Chucky?"

"I did," Jimena readily admitted. "I figured it was time you had one less dickwad in your life. Can't do anything about the mother-dickwad, but you'll never have to see Chucky's boney ass again."

Reese was stunned. "You paid off Chucky? Where did you get the money?"

"From Elrond," Jimena said in a discussing-the-weather kind of tone. "I blackmailed him. Told him I'd give Logan pictures of Helene and him having clown sex."

"But Helene had clown sex with Greg," Reese pointed out.

"Well, she had it with Elrond, too. He let that slip when he was talking to me." Jimena stopped, paused. "Do you have any idea what they do with those big red clown noses?"

Reese huffed. "No, and I don't want to know." She had to lower her voice when she realized this wasn't a conversation she wanted others to hear, and they were passing people on the street as Jimena led her heaven knew where. "Where did Elrond get the money to pay you off?"

"From Helene. He blackmailed her, and he stole my threat. Sheez, the man can't even come up with his own blackmail idea."

Reese's head was hurting now, and she rarely got headaches. "So, let me get this straight. You blackmailed Elrond. He blackmailed Helene, and you gave the money to Chucky to get him to leave? Why didn't you just spend the money on yourself?"

Jimena looked at her as if she'd laid an egg. "I couldn't let Chucky keep pestering you, and besides, it wouldn't have been right to keep dirty money."

It was hard for Reese to fault that logic, especially since it might work. *Might*. And that *might* was only temporary. "Chucky will just be back when he runs out of money."

Jimena smiled. "No, he won't, and here's the kicker. I altered copies of the clown sex photos. I erased Elrond's face and put in Chucky's to make it look as if Chucky's got his nose where it doesn't belong—if you get my meaning." She winked.

Yes, Reese did get her meaning. "So, you're blackmailing Chucky because if he comes back, you'll give those pictures to his wife."

"Yep. Easy peasy, huh?"

Nothing about this was easy or peasy—whatever the heck that meant. Jimena might need a flowchart to keep up with who was blackmailing whom and why. Plus, there was the other matter that Reese wanted to discuss.

"Chucky called Logan last night, and he said Vickie stole something from your desk," Reese put out there. "Chucky thought it was something she could possibly use to blackmail you."

Now it was Jimena who stopped. "Hmm. Well, I did have both sets of the clown sex pictures in there. Copies, mind you. I have the originals in a password-protected storage cloud."

Sex pictures that wouldn't shed good lights on Helene or Chucky. Her mother could be planning to blackmail both of them.

Again, a flowchart might be needed.

"Are you sure Vickie couldn't have taken something else from your desk?" Reese asked. "Maybe something she could use to hurt you?"

Jimena paused a second, giving that some thought, and shook her head. "There were some other sex pictures of Elrond and me, but if she plans to blackmail me with that, she's barking up the wrong tree. I don't care who sees my sex pictures."

Reese put herself in a con-artist frame of mind to see if she could figure out how this might work for her mother. It didn't take her long to come up with an angle. "Jason. If Vickie thinks you're trying to have a relationship with Jason, she could hold on to the pictures to try to cause some trouble between you two."

"Oh, you mean because Jason wouldn't go for sleeping with a woman who had sex with the man who had sex with his best friend's ex."

Heck, they needed a flowchart for that, too. "I don't know Jason that well, but it could be an issue for him. He could see being with you as some kind of disloyalty to Logan."

Jimena made a sound of agreement. Followed by a sound of annoyance. And that's when Reese knew that Jimena did indeed have a thing for Jason.

Damn.

Reese wasn't sure how her mother pieced together stuff like this, but Vickie always seemed to be one step ahead of them. And speaking of steps, Jimena quit walking, and she pointed to the sign in the front of the jewelry store.

Watch Repairs.

"I called ahead," Jimena said. "They don't usually open until ten, but we've got an appointment. Don't worry about the cost. I milked a little extra money from Elrond."

It was a wonderful gesture. Not milking money from Elrond—Reese didn't care much for that. But with everything going on, she was surprised, and pleased, that her friend had thought of this.

So, why couldn't Reese make herself go into the shop? She held her ground even when Jimena opened the door and tried to usher her in.

"All right," Jimena finally said. "What's this about?"

Reese shook her head. "I'm not sure I can put it into words."

"This is about Spenser. He broke the watch, and you don't think you deserve to have it fixed because of what happened to him."

All in all, that was an accurate assessment. Was that it? Reese did a quick soul-examining and realized that it might be.

"Of course that's malarkey," Jimena went on. "You love that watch, and it should be fixed so that it's the way it was when your grandfather gave it to you."

Reese did a little more soul-examining and realized Jimena was right. A broken watch wasn't doing service to her grandfather's memory. The brokenness was only a reminder of Spenser, and that was something Reese could do without. Or rather it was something she *wanted* to do without.

They went inside, and the repairman, Jeff Latchwood, motioned for them to come to the back counter where he was working. Reese knew him from the café. He was a "well-done burger, no cheese, with pickles on the side" kind of guy.

He took the watch from her, holding it with what she thought might be reverence, and he gave it a good examination. "Yep, I can fix it, but I'll have to order a crystal to replace the broken one. It might come in right away, or it could take up to two weeks. I'll give you a call as soon as it's done, and you can come in and pick it up."

Reese's heart sank. Not the feeling she'd hoped to get so soon after all that soul-searching and the revelation of why she did indeed want this fixed.

"While I'm waiting on the crystal," Jeff went on,

"I'll give it a cleaning and make sure nothing else is broken inside."

"Sounds good," Jimena declared, and she got Reese out of there probably before she could change her mind. Which she was about to do.

"Two weeks?" Reese repeated. "I wasn't sure I'd be in town that long."

"Well, now you have to be." And Jimena smiled.

Reese frowned. "Did Logan put you up to this?"

"No." She seemed sincere about that. "Why?"

"Because he asked me to stay."

"Then maybe he's not an asshole, after all." Jimena's gaze flew to the time on her phone screen. She took off. "Shit. Gotta go. I don't want to give Logan a reason to fire me. Bye!"

That sounded as un-right as something could sound coming from Jimena. To the best of Reese's knowledge, Jimena had never cared whether or not she got fired. And she'd never before sprinted toward work even when there was imminent threat of being fired. Reese hoped that didn't mean Jimena had gotten her heart set on keeping this job because Logan would almost certainly hire someone more qualified.

Reese looked back at the jewelry shop, considered returning to say she'd changed her mind, but then she saw Helene walking toward her.

Apparently, Logan's ex wasn't giving up on having that chat with her because Helene waved and called out to her. "I'm so glad we ran into each other. I really do need to talk to you."

Reese got that, which made her believe this wasn't "running into each other" coincidence. Helene had probably tracked her down, and that meant Logan had perhaps told her about Vickie's latest break-in, the one that might or might not involve clown sex pictures of Helene.

"I need to get back to my apartment," Reese said. That was a polite way of saying she really didn't want to talk to her. But Helene was evidently determined to do this because she fell in step alongside Reese.

Because Reese wasn't sure how much the woman knew about Vickie's theft, she just stayed quiet and let Helene take the lead. And Helene jumped right in.

"For the record, I didn't cheat on Logan because I was dissatisfied with the sex," Helene blurted out. "I wasn't satisfied with *me*. Strict upbringing, always following Daddy's rules. Everything I've done in my life was for someone else." She shrugged. "Well, except for having sex with a clown. I did that for me."

"All right," Reese said because she didn't know what else to say. It seemed creepy talking about sex with Logan's ex. Actually, it seemed creepy talking about clown sex, period.

"I hate that I hurt Logan," Helene went on. "If I could go back and undo it, believe me, I would."

Reese did believe her. Those minutes of pleasure—if that was the right word—had cost her a good man. Of course, it had likely been more than mere minutes since Helene had been with both Greg and Elrond.

Helene stayed quiet a second while the Starkley twins walked past them. The twins noticed, though, and judging from the lingering looks they gave Helene and Reese, it would soon be all over town that she and Logan's ex were having a discussion. In the gossip mill, that would turn into a heated discussion. By the end of the day, it would be a catfight on Main Street.

"I'm just going to come out and say this," Helene continued after dragging in her breath. However, she didn't just come out and say whatever was on her mind. She took so many breaths that she sounded asthmatic. "I want to offer you the chance of a lifetime."

That got Reese's attention, though—as the daughter of con artists, she was always skeptical of chance-of-a-lifetime offers. Usually they were meant to screw the offeree while benefiting the offerer.

"I want to set you up in your own restaurant or bakery," Helene went on. "Your choice. I'll front all the money, build it to any specs you want. I'll even pay your employees until you start to turn a profit."

Reese stopped in her tracks so she could look at the woman to see if she was serious. She was. And because Reese was the daughter of con artists, she followed this through to the most obvious question of all—what was in this for Helene?

And the answer to that was Logan.

"That's very generous of you." Reese started walking again because she figured this conversation wasn't going to last much longer. "And the only condition… wait, there are two conditions. One is that the restaurant and or bakery can't be anywhere near Spring Hill. The second condition you want is for me to agree to never see Logan again."

Judging from the way Helene suddenly got very interested in studying the cracks on the sidewalk, Reese was spot-on. "It's a really good offer. It could set you up for life."

"Yes, it could set me up to be the kind of woman who accepts bribes," Reese argued. "Not exactly what I'm going for in life."

Helene stayed quiet a moment. "So, your answer is no?"

"No times a gazillion."

"I see." More of those quiet moments while she looked at anything and anybody but Reese. "I guess this means you're in love with Logan, then."

Reese opened her mouth to answer another "no times a gazillion," but she suddenly found herself studying sidewalk cracks, too. She couldn't be in love with Logan.

Could she?

But then she remembered this chat had zilch to do with love. It was about Helene trying to control a situation she'd lost control of months ago.

"It means I'm not for sale," Reese settled for saying. "When and if I leave Spring Hill, it will be my decision and under my own terms."

Oh, mercy. She'd actually used the *if* word when it came to leaving. In the past, there'd definitely been no ifs involved. And Reese could thank Logan for that.

"Well, I had to try, didn't I?" Helene said.

Now Reese used her "No." And then she added some more. "Do you really think you can win Logan back by getting me out of the picture?"

Helene shrugged. "I suppose you're right. I could just wait this out since I believe this is a rebound relationship for Logan."

The rebound comment felt like a sucker punch, but since it might be doused in truth, Reese stayed quiet. Helene didn't.

"But waiting's not exactly my style, you know?" Helene added.

Reese had to shake her head. She didn't know. Helene had dated Logan for eight years. That was a long time, and it had no doubt included plenty of waiting to see when they were going to the next level.

"Does that mean you're giving up?" Reese asked her, but figured she wouldn't get a straight answer. That's why it surprised her when she did.

"Yes," Helene said. "I think I need to do something drastic with my life to make some changes. I have a bucket list. I think it's time for me to start checking things off. I've always wanted to have a one-night stand. A no-names-allowed kind of thing."

Reese nearly choked on her own breath, and at first she thought this was Helene's way of getting in a dig at her, but the woman didn't give any indication that she'd just summarized Reese's life four months ago.

They finally reached the Bluebonnet Inn, and so that Helene wouldn't follow her in, Reese stopped and turned to her. "I wish you the best."

Helene blinked as if surprised by that. "Logan said pretty much the same thing. I thought he was lying. *Hoped* he was lying, because saying that meant he no longer had feelings for me," she amended.

The look on Helene's face implied she'd said too much. She checked the time on her phone. "I have to run." She turned as if to do that, but then stopped, as well. "You won't mention our chat to Logan, will you?"

"No." Reese didn't have to think about it. Logan didn't need to know that his ex had tried to pay her off.

Helene made a sound as if she didn't quite buy that, but she headed off, anyway. Reese didn't waste any time going into the Bluebonnet Inn and up to her room. She didn't want anyone seeing her watch Helene make her exit because the gossip would spread about that, too.

By the time the story was done, Reese would have been rushing to call Logan to tell him about the encounter.

Reese would call Logan but not about that.

There was still the whole issue of clown sex pictures and how they might be used. The whole question was if Reese would really wait two weeks for the watch to be repaired. And the biggie question...

That whole L-word thought she'd had about Logan.

With that question staring her smack-dab in the face, Reese opened the door to her room and came smack-dab in the face with someone else.

"Reese," her mother purred. "I've been waiting for you."

CHAPTER TWENTY-THREE

LOGAN SMELLED HIS coffee before he sipped it. No cat shit, or if it was in there, it hadn't altered the taste. However, he was concerned that he'd done something to put that pissed-off look on Jimena's face.

"Did another seller cancel business with us?" he asked her.

Jimena shook her head. "No, but you do have a visitor. I told her you were really busy, but she insisted on seeing you. She would have just charged back here, but I'm bigger than she is and threatened to put her in a headlock. That's okay to say that, right?"

"Depends on the visitor. Is it Vickie?"

"Helene."

Logan thought about it a second and decided the headlock threat was still all right. If he could live with the cat-shit threat hanging over his head, then Helene could manage this.

"What does she want?" Logan asked.

Jimena rolled her eyes. "To talk to you privately. And yes, she emphasized the *privately* part."

If this had something to do with the clown-sex photos, then it was possible Helene didn't know they'd been stolen from Jimena's computer. Or maybe she did know and that's why she'd insisted on a private conversation.

"Show Helene in but also call Reese for me and see if

she can come over for lunch." Logan had been swamped all morning with meetings and paperwork, but he really did need to talk to her about these blackmail attempts.

"I'll make sure she comes." Jimena turned to leave, but Logan thought of something else.

He took out the blue boxed ring from his desk. The ring that was supposed to be Helene's. "Could you take this over to the jewelry store and return it?"

"Sure. Is this what I think it is?"

"It is, and yes, I should have returned it months ago, but I kept forgetting. Just ask for Jeff."

"I've met him. Reese and I were there earlier. She's finally getting her grandfather's watch fixed." Jimena leaned in closer as if telling a secret. "Jeff said it'd take two weeks for the repair. Two weeks," she emphasized, and waggled her fingers at him. She had on polka-dotted nail polish. "A smart man would use those two weeks to sweet-talk Reese into staying even longer."

Yes, a smart man would, and Logan would try, but with Vickie breathing down their necks, Reese might just run and then sneak back later to get the watch.

"Logan?" Helene called out from the hall. "I really need to see you."

Jimena's eyes narrowed. "I told her to stay put. Can I headlock her now?"

While the petty part of him might have found that satisfying, there was no need. "Just do that errand for me. I'll answer the phones while you're out." That was something Helene probably wouldn't appreciate, but she'd appreciate a headlock even less.

Jimena glared her way out as Helene slunk her way in, and Helene closed the door behind Jimena as soon as she could.

"You know I can recommend some qualified office help," Helene started.

"No need." Best to get right down to business. "What can I do for you?"

Considering that Helene had been so darn anxious to get in to see him, she still took her time answering. "I came by to say goodbye. I'm leaving town for a while. Hoping to regroup my life."

He nodded. "Good luck with that." The phone rang, and Logan held up his hand in a "wait a sec" gesture and answered it. Delbert.

"Logan, we have to talk," Delbert blurted out.

"Apparently, there's a queue for that. Is this about that personal matter?"

"It is. I gave that woman money to keep quiet, and she wants more."

"Of course she does." Logan didn't want to mention names because even though Helene appeared to be studying some new artwork, she also appeared to be listening in. "There's only one way to fix this. You know what you have to do. Come clean." And with that, Logan hung up and moved on to the second cog in this blackmail wheel.

"Do you want to talk about those photos that Vickie has?" Logan asked.

Helene seemed to release the breath she'd been holding. "You know about those." She sighed, sank down in the chair across from his desk. "She's blackmailing me."

"Of course," Logan repeated. Now he sighed. "There's only one way to fix this—come clean."

She glanced at the phone, probably putting the pieces together. Helene likely didn't know that it was Delbert who'd called, but now she had an inkling that someone else was in the same leaky boat that she was.

"That's hard to do." Her voice was whispery, the sound of a woman on the verge of tears. "I could hurt you and your business."

He lifted his eyebrow. "If anything, people will just feel sorry for me. I hate pity business more than pity sex, but I won't be the one hurt in this."

She conceded that with a soft sound of agreement. "So, how would I go about coming clean?"

Logan had a few suggestions. Helene wasn't going to like them, though. "You could just tell one of the town's bigger gossips that there are sex photos. Or print an apology in the newspaper along with enough details to defuse future threats from Vickie. Or you could record Vickie blackmailing you and use it to have her arrested."

The last one, though, wouldn't stop the threat because Vickie would just continue the blackmail when she got out of jail.

Helene nodded. Stood. Whether she would do any of those things, he didn't know. But this was a case of not his bull, not his bullshit. Logan already had enough of his own he had to shovel.

"Oh," Helene added. "I tried to bribe Reese into leaving town. I figured I should tell you before Reese does."

"She won't tell me," Logan assured her.

"Of course she will." Said like gospel coming from a woman who clearly didn't know squat about Reese.

The phone rang again so Logan motioned for Helene to close the door on her way out. He figured it was

Delbert again, calling to whine about the mess of his own making. But it was a different whiner.

Chucky.

"Have you seen Vickie?" the man greeted.

"No. Why? What's going on now?"

"She's gone bat-shit crazy, that's what." Chucky was talking so fast that his words ran together. "She hired some thug to bust my nut, and the only way I got out of it was to pay the guy off."

"Maybe that was her plan along—to have you pay the guy so she could split the profit with him?" Logan suggested.

Judging from the long pause, then the profanity, Chucky hadn't considered that. "Vickie," he growled, and he made the woman's name sound like profanity, too.

"Look, I don't know what you expect me to do—"

"I want to leave the country and start a new life," Chucky readily answered. "I got dreams of owning a beach house in Hawaii."

Logan wasn't sure if he should point out that Hawaii was part of the country. "And you expect me to help you with that?"

"Yes, I do," Chucky verified. "I told you about Vickie taking stuff from Jimena's computer. Well, I took stuff from it, too. Pictures. And I know a lot of other stuff that could ruin you."

Hell. Not another round of this. "Are you blackmailing me?"

Chucky hesitated. "No, of course not." Yeah, he was blackmailing him. "Wouldn't want to say anything in case you're recording this. Let's just say I expect you to help me make my dreams come true because you're a generous person."

"I'm not generous," Logan reminded him. "And neither is Jimena. Do you remember that she can make things difficult between you and your wife?"

"Let her try. My wife will come back to me when I'm richer than you. I'll meet you at your office first thing in the morning to discuss this. I'll see you at 8:00 a.m. sharp. Be there and be prepared to make my Hawaii-house dream come true."

Logan would rather eat Hawaii than pay off this turd.

The moment Chucky ended the call, Logan took out his phone and pressed Reese's number. If Vickie was hiring thugs—even conning ones—to threaten Chucky, she could do the same to Reese, and Logan needed to warn her.

Her phone rang but then went straight to voice mail. Logan left her a message to call him ASAP and then got busy thinking up a plan. He had to do something to put an end to Chucky's and Vickie's threats once and for all.

"How did you get in here?" Reese asked her mother once she got her mouth working. She cursed the jolt of surprise and knew she had let down her guard. Not a good thing to do around Vickie.

"The door was unlocked so I decided to come in and wait for you."

That might be true. Reese had left in a hurry with Jimena so it was possible she'd forgotten to lock up. Just as possible, though, that her mother had picked the lock. Vickie was good at that.

"Well, you can just un-wait," Reese told her. "Because I have nothing to say to you." However, she did have something to do. Reese started checking around the room to make sure her mother hadn't stolen anything.

"I have something to say to you," Vickie answered. "I'm tired of being messed over by life. By you. By everybody."

Reese didn't bother to give her a flat look for the "by you" comment. She just kept checking to make sure everything was there. Things were okay in the kitchen so she went to the small closet.

"You might have heard," Vickie went on, "that I happened to come across some interesting photos and information."

"I heard." Since she didn't have much stuff, it didn't take Reese long to go through the closet, but that's when she saw that her backpack was unzipped. She laid it on the bed so she could go through it.

"You're pretending not to be interested, but I know you want to know what I have."

"Sex pictures that you stole from Jimena's computer." She rummaged through her things and found the chef's knives. It was the only thing that mattered to her now that the watch was at the jeweler's. For the first time, Reese was actually glad it hadn't been in the room for her mother to find.

"And do you know what I can do with those sex pictures?" Vickie asked like a greedy dog over a coveted bone.

Now Reese gave her the flat look. "Blackmail people." She used her Captain Obvious voice.

"Yes," Vickie answered as if it hadn't been so obvious, after all. Clearly, she wanted to play a game here, but Reese wasn't in a playing mood. "I have sex pictures I can use to blackmail that uppity bitch Helene. More sex pictures to blackmail that trashy bitch Jimena. More sex pictures to blackmail that hound dog Delbert."

Reese continued her flat look. "Is that all?"

Vickie's eyes narrowed. No, this game wasn't going her way, but then Reese saw something she didn't want to see. A gleam in those beady-rat eyes. Her mother had something else.

"I have something else," Vickie verified a split second later. "I got copies of the old newspaper articles about Spenser O'Malley. How do you think your hot cowboy will react when he sees those?"

"Hot cowboy?" someone said from the doorway.

Logan.

Reese wasn't sure she wanted him here for this conversation, but her mother smiled, thinking she was about to drop a bombshell.

"You don't know what Reese did," Vickie said.

"Yes, I do. I read the entire report on Spenser O'Malley. I personally think he got what he deserved, and Reese was in no way to blame for that."

If her mother's eyes narrowed any more, she'd look as if she had straight lines where her eye sockets should be. "Well, the town might not be so forgiving," Vickie spat out.

That was true, but then Reese had never stayed around a town long enough to know how they reacted to news like that.

"Plus, there's Jimena," Vickie went on. "I can mess things up between her and her cowboy lover boy. I can show him those sex pictures of Jimena with another man."

"Please." And Reese didn't say it as a plea, either. "Jimena will probably show Jason the pictures herself. She uses them as foreplay." That was possibly true, anyway.

More eye narrowing from Vickie. Reese wished she had some superglue to squirt on them so they'd stay shut that way.

"Fine. But you're not going to blow off the rest of what I've got." When Vickie opened her eyes again, she didn't look at Reese but rather Logan. "I've heard plenty of stories about the night your folks were killed. Word is you blame yourself."

Everything inside Reese went still, and she thought she might permanently shut her mother's eyes without the use of superglue. A couple of punches might do it.

"You stay away from Logan," Reese warned her. Then she instantly regretted it. Because her mother smiled again, and Reese knew she'd given her exactly what she wanted.

A way for her to manipulate Reese.

"Those stories are old news," Logan explained.

"Yes." Vickie could have won a smugness award with the tone slathered on that one-word response. "But it's another thing to see those stories in print. Think of how painful it would be for your family to read them. Oh, did I mention that I'd be going to the newspaper with all of this?"

Reese wanted to believe the newspaper wouldn't touch it, but they actually had a gossip section under the general label of "What's Going on, Y'all?"

"So, basically you're trying to hurt Logan, Delbert, Helene, Jimena and me?" Reese asked. She didn't have to ask why. "How much?"

Still smiling, her mother stood. "I'm still considering that, but I thought you could talk to all parties involved, and you could find out what they'd like to do to make me go away."

"If I bargain with you," Logan said, "will you give me dirt to put Chucky away? I only want to deal with one of you."

Vickie's smile widened. "Well, of course. I have… things on Chucky, too. I'd be glad to give them to you for, well, let's just say services rendered."

Logan nodded. "I'll meet you later with my answer."

"Wonderful. Just know that if you double-cross me, I have those photos and articles hidden away. They're with a friend, and if I get arrested or if I disappear, the package will be delivered not just to the local newspaper but to everyone in the tricounty area."

With that threat still hanging in the air, Vickie turned and walked out. If Reese had thought it would do any good, she would have gone after her, but her mother's favorite things were steak and desperation. Reese didn't want to give her either. So, she did the only thing she could do even though she knew it would do no good at all.

"God, Logan. I'm so sorry," she said.

Reese could have added a whole lot more to that apology if Logan hadn't kissed her. Not a little peck, either. He really kissed her. When he had robbed her of her breath and seemingly the cartilage in her kneecaps, he pulled back.

And he was smiling.

"I have a plan," Logan announced.

CHAPTER TWENTY-FOUR

6:00 p.m.

LOGAN SUSPECTED THAT some wars had been launched with fewer working parts than this plan, but if it worked, it would solve all their problems. Well, it would solve everything for everyone but Vickie and Chucky.

Of course, there was a big-assed "if" attached to all of this, and it was possible it could blow up in his face. He didn't mind some face-blowing every now and then but not when Reese could be hurt. And his family.

Hell, lots of people could go down if he screwed this up.

That probably explained why his stomach was doing some twisting and turning. But it wasn't all bad. He got that feeling a lot right before he closed a big sale. Maybe it was a good sign now, too.

Logan opened the back door to the Fork and Spoon, and once he made his way into the dining area, he spotted Chucky right away. The weasel had taken the far corner booth, and he was already doing that rat-twitch thing with his face. The twitching eased up just a little when he saw Logan. Probably because Chucky was relieved that he'd actually shown up.

Chucky was perhaps smiling about something else, too. He could see Vickie pacing in front of the grocery store across the street. That wasn't by accident. The woman was exactly where she was supposed to be, and she was waiting for Logan to show. Of course, she hadn't seen Logan go into the café because he'd been sure to use the back door.

"I made sure Reese wasn't here," Chucky said right off while Logan was still standing. "Bert said it was her evening off. I also checked the table and booth to make sure it wasn't bugged. Now you gotta empty your pockets just like you said you'd do."

Logan had indeed agreed to that since Chucky was afraid that Logan would record him saying something to incriminate himself. But that wasn't Logan's plan at all. He took out his wallet, phone, the small tape recorder, the pocketknife and his keys. Chucky didn't pat him down exactly, but he did motion for him to turn. Logan had purposely worn a tighter fitting shirt so the man would be assured that he wasn't wearing a wire, either.

"Okay, no recording anything until we finish the first part of this," Chucky stated. He glanced out at Vickie again, who was now checking her watch.

Logan nodded since that was the deal. Chucky and he would work out blackmail payments from everyone involved, and then in turn Chucky would spill the dirt on Vickie.

"You made a smart choice dealing with me instead of that crazy she-bitch Vickie," Chucky said as Logan sat across from him.

"Now you empty your pockets," Logan insisted.

That was part of the deal, too, but in hindsight he wished he hadn't. There was no reason for Chucky to record this, especially the parts where he was going to say how much he demanded and the names of the people he'd be demanding it from. But Logan wanted to make it look as if he was being thorough.

He should have known, though, that abnormal people might have abnormal pocket contents.

A wallet. Keys. Phone. Handkerchief—well used. Two malted milk balls—unwrapped. A breath mint—unwrapped. Turtle decal stickers. Two wads of what appeared to be lint. Or perhaps fungus. A stick of gum also seemingly coated with fungus/lint.

Chucky checked the time on his phone—6:05. "We don't talk until Vickie's given up on you and leaves," Chucky insisted.

Since that was part of the deal, too, they just waited. Vickie paced while she waited, and she was clearly on edge, her gaze darting to her phone and then all around. A couple of seconds later, she disappeared into the grocery store.

"Why's she going in there?" Chucky asked.

"Who knows? Now that she knows I'm not going to show, she might be buying rat poison or something."

Chucky made a sound of suspicion. "Don't think you can cook up something here with me and then head over there and do more cooking up with her."

"Huh?" That was the best Logan could do with the info Chucky had just given him.

"I don't want you double-crossing me by meeting her after you meet with me. That's why I'll be following you when you leave here, and I'll keep right on following you until I got my money."

Logan simply nodded, though he was slightly impressed that Chucky had thought to take such measures.

Chucky popped the breath mint in his mouth. "All

right, now let's get down to business. I want twenty-five thousand each from Delbert and you. Another twenty-five from Helene. Another twenty-five from Reese and ten from Jimena. Now, I'm figuring Reese and Jimena haven't got that kind of money so you'll have to pony up for them." He grinned, revealing a piece of lint on his teeth, probably from the breath mint.

Logan rubbed his forehead and appeared to be distressed about that amount. One hundred and ten grand. It was a lot of money, but Logan was betting it wouldn't buy much more than some sand itself on a Hawaiian beach. Apparently, Chucky's big ideas weren't so big, after all, but Logan wasn't going to point that out to him.

"And how did you want the payment?" Logan asked.

Chucky slid the stick of gum closer to Logan, and that's when he saw the email address written there. "For my PayPal account. Make sure y'all send it as a gift so I don't have to pay fees."

In addition to teeny ideas, Chucky was also an idiot since the account could be traced. Of course, Chucky was counting on them never turning any of this over to the authorities or he would release all the crap he was holding over their heads.

"The money's gotta be in my account no later than 8:00 p.m.," Chucky added.

Again, Logan pretended that would be a problem. It wasn't. Those kinds of payments could be made in under a minute.

"Now, to your side of the deal." Logan turned the tape recorder. "Tell me everything I'll need to have Vickie arrested and put behind bars for a long, long time."

Chucky smiled. A second piece of lint was now on his teeth. He started talking. And he talked and talked and talked. When he was done, Logan motioned toward the kitchen where Deputy Davy was waiting.

Davy didn't waste a second hurrying out to use his handcuffs on a gob-smacked Chucky.

VICKIE COULD ALMOST feel that money in her hands, but she didn't like this little twist that Logan had added to their arrangement. For one thing, he was late, and that was going to cost him. It would continue to cost him for every minute he kept her waiting.

The second thing she didn't like about this was the meeting place. What the hell was a shitake mushroom, and why would Logan tell her to meet him there? Maybe because that's where he'd planted some kind of bug. Well, this wasn't her first rodeo, and they wouldn't be standing anywhere near the shitake when he arrived.

She meandered her way through the vegetable row and found something that wasn't spelled at all like it sounded. Still, this had to be it. There were no other mushrooms with a name that came close.

Vickie waited some more, glanced around to make sure Logan hadn't hired a stock boy or something to use some long-range recording device. But the only person who appeared to be in the entire store was a clerk and a teenager mopping up a spill in the milk aisle.

6:16.

Yeah, being late was going to cost him.

She pulled out her phone, ready to call Logan and blast him a new one, but then she finally spotted the devil himself. Too bad that he hadn't shown any interest in her because she wouldn't have minded a tumble in his hay.

"Give me your phone," she insisted as he approached her. "And anything else you could use to record this."

He obliged and gave her a small tape recorder. He also showed her the contents of his pockets—keys, a wallet and a pocketknife. That wallet, or rather his bank account, was going to be a whole lot lighter before this was over.

"I'll keep this simple," she said, and Vickie handed him the routing numbers for an offshore bank account. "I don't care how you, Delbert, Helene, Jimena and my daughter divvy it all up, but in the next twenty minutes I want five hundred thousand dollars added to that account. In exchange I'll give you the password for the storage cloud where I'm keeping all the pictures, reports and such."

"Does that include the dirt on Chucky?" he asked.

"No. As soon as you agree to the money, you'll hear all you need to arrest Chucky."

Shit, she would have given him that for free. Anything to make Chucky fry, but it was a nice touch to tie it to their business deal. Except she had her own twist to add to the deal. One that these marks wouldn't know about until, well, until she ran out of money and needed more. Yes, she'd give him the copies of stuff she had in the storage cloud.

But there were three clouds.

Good thing she'd learned all about computers during her last stint in jail.

"So, do we have a deal?" Vickie asked.

Logan nodded.

That was a half-million-dollar kind of nod. So,

Vickie decided to help him out a little. She turned on the recorder for Logan and started telling him all the dirty little secrets that she knew about Chucky.

When she was done, Vickie heard the footsteps and saw the chief of police making his way toward her.

"Vickie Stephenson," he said. "You're under arrest."

"What the hell do you think you're doing?" Vickie howled.

Logan smiled. "Double-crossing you." He handed the recorder to the cop. "Thanks, Luke," he told him.

"Anytime, Lucky," the cop answered, and he hauled Vickie away.

Reese had no idea how the rest of the plan was going, but she felt as if she were juggling cats. Everyone was talking at once, and the poor newspaper editor, Marlene Holland, was trying her best to write everything down.

Operation Dirt Sweep was in full swing.

For Marlene, it had to be like Christmas, her birthday and Fourth of July all rolled into one. She'd have enough stories for the newspaper to last for weeks. Maybe months.

"Everybody get quiet for a second," Marlene finally shouted. Surprisingly, everybody did. "All right, now let's do this alphabetically so I'll make sure to get it all down." She looked at Cassie. "That means you go first."

Cassie pushed her way through the others to get to Marlene's desk. The editor's office was the size of a broom closet so it took some doing.

"I'm two months pregnant," Cassie announced. "So yes, that means I got pregnant before getting married and before Lucky and I got custody of our girls."

All in all, it wasn't big news, but it was something

Cassie probably would have preferred to spill at a family gathering rather than to the town's biggest blabbermouth. Still, it needed to be said so that it couldn't be used as gossip fodder against her.

Claire was up next, and Riley was right by her side. "I'm pregnant, too, and I was trying to keep it a secret so I wouldn't steal Cassie and Lucky's thunder what with their wedding."

Again, not a big revelation, but judging from the dog-with-a-bone look Marlene gave her, it was still news that Marlene could use.

"Delbert?" Marlene called him up.

Unlike Cassie and Claire, he didn't charge forward. He stayed in the corner. "I slept with her mother." He flung a finger at Reese. "Vickie." Said like venom. "And now she's blackmailing me."

Surprisingly, Delbert had managed to get through that with only mumbled profanity, but no matter how he went with this, it was going to cost him. This way, he would just pay money to his wife in a divorce settlement rather than paying it to Vickie as hush money. Either way would eventually bleed him dry, but Delbert had been the one to cheat, and he wasn't exactly blameless in this.

Reese motioned for him to finish up. It wasn't called Operation Dirt Sweep for nothing.

"I, uh, told Logan I couldn't do business with him," Delbert went on, fessing up to Marlene, "but that's because Vickie told me to say that. I'll keep doing business with Logan if he'll let me, and I'll tell everybody to do the same."

Reese wasn't sure how much clout Delbert would

have with those friends after this. Then again, maybe the publicity would actually help.

Helene was up next, and this was where Reese held her breath. Unlike Cassie and Claire, whose secrets would have soon "shown," Helene could have kept hers buried if she'd wanted to keep being blackmailed.

"There are sex pictures of me with two different men," Helene finally said after a long silence. "Greg and another man who worked for Logan."

"Elrond, my ex," Jimena piped up.

Helene gave her a sharp look. "He was only your ex after he was my ex."

It was a valid point, and Jimena shrugged, nodded.

"I also located a man, Chucky," Helene went on, "and told him that Reese was here in town. And I did that with the hopes that he'd pressure her into leaving. I also tried to bribe her to leave. I'm really sorry about that."

Reese hadn't expected the woman to confess that last part since only Helene and Reese knew about it, but maybe Helene had thought it would come back later to bite her in her perfectly shaped butt.

"One final thing," Helene went on, "I paid off Elrond because he was blackmailing me with those sex pictures."

Marlene looked up from her writing. "Is that everything?" she asked when Helene hushed. "Nothing about Logan and you maybe having some ex-sex on the side?"

"No. Logan's choice, not mine. Trust me, I've thrown myself at him enough times, and he's turned me down. That's why I'm leaving town and finding some new adventures."

Reese and she actually shared a smile. She wanted

to tell Helene that she was proud of her for doing this, but the words weren't necessary. Helene appeared to be proud of herself.

Jimena went closer to the desk when it was her alphabetical turn. "I blackmailed Elrond because of his clown sex fetish so I could pay off Chucky so he'd leave Reese alone. Do you want to hear about the other men I've had sex with while I've been in town?"

"Of course," Marlene said.

"Even if one of them is someone close to you? As in very close?" Jimena's gaze lingered on Marlene's wedding band.

"No, what you already gave me is fine." Though Marlene did narrow her eyes at Jimena.

Reese knew Jimena hadn't slept with Marlene's husband, Roy. Roy was in his sixties, chewed tobacco and was missing several teeth. Still, it had given the town's biggest gossip a small dose of her own medicine.

It was finally Reese's turn, and she was dreading it. No way could she back down when the others had been so brave, but she suddenly wished Logan was there with her.

And he was.

At that exact moment Logan came through the door, Lucky behind him, and even though there was no room for them, they made room. Lucky went to Cassie, pulling her into his arms, and Logan went to Reese.

"How'd it go?" Reese asked, afraid of the answer.

He gave her a thumbs-up and a kiss. Both were exactly what she needed.

"Is it finished?" Delbert asked. "Did you get Vickie and Chucky?"

Helene asked a variation on the same question except she added, "Are they rotting in jail?"

Logan and Lucky nodded.

"I got Vickie to rat out Chucky," Lucky continued, "and Logan got Chucky to rat out Vickie. Both have been arrested and will face multiple charges."

That caused some whoops of joy and some hugs throughout the room. Sometimes, like now, having an identical twin brother came in handy. But Logan and she weren't out of the stew pot just yet.

Reese handed the PI's report to Marlene. "I have a police record, and the details are all in there."

Marlene didn't exactly start drooling, but it was close.

"What Reese's not saying is that the charges were trumped up," Logan explained. "Also, she wasn't responsible for Spenser O'Malley's death. He was an abusive dick who got hit by a bus. It was an accident and not her fault."

Reese felt it again. The L-word. Other than Jimena, people didn't usually stick up for her, and here Logan was doing it even though it could cost him plenty.

But his next admission would cost him even more.

That's why Reese knew she wanted to stick up for him. "My mother tried to blackmail Logan by saying she'd have you print gossip about his parents' death. Gossip and rumors," Reese emphasized.

Somehow, Claire, Cassie, Lucky and Riley all worked their way to the desk and joined Reese and Logan in hovering over Marlene.

"I'm sure everyone here wishes they could have saved the McCords," Reese added. "But since it was an accident, no one had control over that. What happened happened, and it's certainly nothing to be gossiped about."

"Understand?" Jimena added.

Despite barely having her face squeezed between three lethal-looking cowboys and the three determined women with them, Jimena's expression was somehow more fierce than all of theirs combined.

Jimena mumbled something about cat shit in coffee.

And Marlene nodded. "Understood." She glanced down at the all the notes she'd made. "Plus, I have enough here to last me until I retire." She paused. "Why exactly did you tell me all these things?"

"So that Chucky and Vickie can never use any of this to blackmail us," Logan answered, and one by one, they all gave a confirming nod.

The cons had been conned, and when the McCords, Delbert, Jimena, Helene and she all walked out of the newspaper office, they'd be doing it with something they hadn't had when they came in.

A clean dirty slate.

CHAPTER TWENTY-FIVE

LOGAN WASN'T SURE Reese would show. Even though Chucky and Vickie were in jail, the whole town of Spring Hill would soon be talking about the tell-all gossip. That could send Reese running for the hills, but Logan was hoping it would send her running for him.

A lofty wish.

He sipped his Glenlivet, not at the "make me forget this shit" pace he'd had the last time he was in the Purple Cactus hotel bar. Tonight, there was nothing he wanted to forget and plenty that he wanted to remember. His family had stood by him and Reese, and while they had personal motives for what they'd done, Helene and Delbert had come through, too.

His phone dinged, and he saw the new text from Lucky. Anything yet?

As Logan had done with Riley's, Claire's, Della's and Jimena's texts, he answered no. He'd told them all what his plans were for the night. In hindsight, that had been a mistake, since they were collectively texting at a pace greater than that of a teenager. But as corny as it sounded, Logan had wanted their approval.

And he'd gotten it.

Well, he'd gotten it from everyone but Jimena, but Logan was hoping she'd come around if and when

Reese came around. And if and when he could put his family's approval to good use.

Logan frowned.

There were a lot of ifs and whens in all of this, and he always liked to deal in sure things. Especially when it was something this important.

He had all the arguments worked out in his head. If Reese said this was a rebound relationship, he could argue that four months was plenty enough time to get over a woman he'd never actually loved. He could admit that to himself now. He'd never been in love with Helene. She'd just been part of that perfect plan he'd had to make that perfect life.

Of course, Reese's other argument would be the effect she could have on his business, and Logan had a comeback for that, too. He could give her data and examples of other storms the McCords had weathered. He had all his ducks and stats lined up. And forgot every single duck and stat when Reese walked in.

Even though his back was to her, thanks to the bar mirror their gazes connected, and she made her way to him. No turtle shirt tonight. She was wearing jeans and a snug red top that he wished he could take off her.

In the privacy of a bedroom, of course.

She slid onto the bar stool next to him. "Jimena dropped me off. If I hadn't agreed to come, I think she would have kidnapped me and brought me here, anyway."

Logan made a mental note to give Jimena a raise. And offer her the job permanently. He didn't like the idea of living with the cat-shit threat, but Jimena's pluses outweighed her minuses.

Most days, anyway.

"How much tequila is it going to take to make you stay?" Logan asked. And he ordered her a shot.

"To stay here tonight or to stay in Spring Hill?" she clarified.

"Both."

Reese shook her head. "Tequila won't do it tonight. If I stay in Spring Hill, it could still hurt your business."

It hadn't taken her long to bring that up. "Business might fall off with the cattle, but Lucky seems to think it'll help with the bull sellers. They tend to prefer selling to someone with a little mud in their past."

Judging from the look she gave him, he hadn't convinced her, so Logan kissed her. He made it French, and even though it still might not have convinced her, he thought maybe he left her with a nice buzz, one not caused by the tequila, either.

"Let's play the word-association game we played the last time we were here," he said when he eased back from her. "I'll start. Family."

Another flat look, but she did respond. "Good."

Logan smiled and wondered if she knew that four months ago that wouldn't have been her answer. She probably would have said, "Shitty."

"Sex?" he continued. And he slid her his room key.

She angled her eyes at him. "Isn't it early for that? We went a couple of rounds with the game last time before I offered you sex."

"True, but you were easing into things." Clearly, though, he needed to do some more easing.

"All right. Here's another word. Watch?" he continued.

"Grandpa." Reese drank more of her tequila. "You do know this game sounds like caveman talk?"

He took out the pocket watch and placed it on the bar next to her shot glass. "Jeff from the jewelry store checked the antiques shop, and they had a crystal that was the right size. He fixed it and gave it to Jimena to give to me."

Reese opened it as if she were handling the queen's jewels. Of course, this was even more valuable to her than an entire treasure trove.

"It's perfect," she said, and he didn't have to see her eyes to know there were tears in them now. Logan hoped those were happy tears and that seeing the watch fixed and whole didn't trigger any memories of the person who'd broken it.

She kissed him.

So, no bad memories, after all.

"Thank you." Reese eyed the watch, the room key. His mouth. His crotch. "You're not about to offer me a white picket fence, are you?"

"We're not really the picket-fence types. Actually, I'm just offering you, well, me. You can take that on whatever terms you want. You can keep having sex with me. Or not. You can keep working at the café…"

"Or not?"

He nodded. "You can take Cassie's offer to open your own bakery. Though I'm kind of hoping that won't be an 'or not.' You could probably get a good deal on that Shirley's Sweets sign."

Ah, that got a smile from her.

"You could put down roots in Spring Hill," he added. "Or not," he mumbled.

She stayed quiet a moment. "You're really offering me just you?"

"Darn tootin'." Of course, he'd never actually used

the term *darn tootin'* before, but he hoped it showed his playful side. "Seems only fitting since I want you to be my…"

Now, here's something Logan had given much thought.

"Lover?" Reese supplied.

"Definitely that, but I'm thinking more. Maybe the right word is *woman*. I want you to be my woman."

"Sounds a little caveman-ish." Reese smiled again. "But I like it. After all, we're not the white-picket-fence type as you pointed out." The smile didn't last long, though. "What I'm about to say is terrifying for me," Reese continued, "but I love you."

Yes, that fell right into the terrifying territory for him, too, and it was something he'd never said to a woman other than his mother.

"I hate you for it," Reese went on before Logan could get his tongue untangled. "In fact, when I first realized it, I called you some really bad names and considered letting Jimena put a voodoo curse on you."

"Minus the voodoo curse, I had the same reaction." He let that hang in the air for several seconds before he eased his gaze to hers. "There are a lot of things that can make my life easier, Reese. You're not one of them."

"Gee, thanks—"

"But there's only one thing that can make my life happier," Logan interrupted. "And that's where you come in."

The smile returned, soft and sweet, and then not so sweet when she kissed him. She slipped the watch into her pocket and eyed the key card. "You really got a room?"

"Yep. Two-sixteen. The room we were in four

months ago." Which suddenly seemed like a lifetime ago. It also suddenly seemed as if it'd been a lifetime since he'd had sex with her, and the stirrings behind his zipper reminded him of that.

The stirrings in his heart did, too.

It was good to have a second opinion from two different parts of his body.

They finished their shots together, got off the bar stools, also together, and Logan picked up the key card. In the same motion, he slid his arm around her waist to get her moving. Not that he had to add one bit of pressure. Reese kissed him all the way to the elevator. Groped him part of the way there. Talked dirty to him for the last few steps.

Then blew his mind on his last step. Not with her mouth or hands but rather with something she said.

"By any chance do you love me?" she asked in the same tone of the most skeptical question that'd ever been asked.

"I thought you'd never bring it up." He flipped over the room key where he'd written, "I love you, Reese." Except there must have been some water or something on the bar, and it now looked more like "I *blob* you, Reese."

"That's supposed to be *love*," Logan clarified, and he kissed her again just in case she had any doubts about that.

They kissed the rest of the way to the room, which made it sort of difficult to get the door unlocked. It also didn't help that she was already trying to unzip him. Logan let her do that while he kicked the door shut and maneuvered them to the bed.

"What if three months from now, my wanderlust kicks in and I decide to leave town?" Reese asked.

Since she now had her hands in his boxers, it was a little hard for Logan to think. "Then I can go with you. Or you can promise when the wanderlust runs out, that you'll come back to me for another round of regular lust."

Her hand froze, and she looked up at him. Logan decided while she was mildly thunderstruck that he would try to get some even ground here. He shoved down her jeans and panties to her knees and kissed his way to the part of her that he'd just uncovered.

She cursed him, but this time he thought it was because she wasn't pissed off about falling in love with him. "If you're going to do that, let's do it together."

All in all, it wasn't a bad idea. But there was something Logan wanted to do first. No, they weren't the white-picket-fence type, but he wanted Reese to have something to make her understand just how much she meant to him.

He took it from his pocket and slipped it into hers.

"A condom?" she asked.

Logan shook his head. "My father's knife. I want you to hold on to it for safekeeping."

If he'd offered her the world, Reese couldn't have had a better reaction. Her eyes filled with tears, and she kissed the living daylights out of him—which was the way Logan preferred to be kissed, anyway.

"I really do love you, hot cowboy," Reese said.

If she'd offered him the world...wait, that *was* the world. "I really do love you, too, Julia Child."

While Reese blinked back tears and kissed him,

she fumbled with his jeans, and for a moment Logan thought she was trying to turn this into a hand job.

She wasn't.

"For safekeeping," Reese said.

Logan felt around his pocket, and there it was. Her grandfather's watch. A knife and a watch.

Yeah, Reese had given him the world, all right. The only world that Logan wanted, anyway.

* * * * *

SPECIAL EXCERPT FROM

HQN™

*Lawson Granger thought he put his past behind him…
until his first love, Eve Cooper, returns to Wrangler's
Creek, Texas, with a baby on the way and a teenage
daughter with questions about her real father…*

*Enjoy a sneak peek of TEXAS-SIZED TROUBLE,
part of the **A WRANGLER'S CREEK NOVEL** series
by* USA TODAY *bestselling author Delores Fossen.*

She was dying. Eve was sure of it.

The pain was knifing through her, and the contractions were so powerful that it felt as if King Kong were squeezing her belly with his hairy fist. Her breathing was too fast. Her heart racing.

And now she was hallucinating.

Either that or Lawson Granger had indeed slipped in the puddle where her water had broken and was now dying from a head injury. Great. If it wasn't a hallucination, it meant she'd returned to Wrangler's Creek after all these years only to cause the death of her old flame.

Her old flame grunted, cursed and maneuvered himself onto all fours. So, not dead, just perhaps with critical internal injuries. Of course, anything she was thinking or considering right now could be blown out of proportion because of the god-awful pain that was vising her stomach.

"My water broke," she managed to say. "And my phone." She'd dropped it when one of the contractions had hit, and the phone was now scattered all over the stone entryway and hardwood floor.

Eve wouldn't mention that the reason her water had broken right by the door was because she'd been trying to hear who was talking outside the guesthouse. She'd thought it was another of her *fans*. Apparently not though.

"This is too soon," she muttered. "I'm not due for three and a half weeks. A baby shouldn't come this soon, should it?" Eve knew she sounded frantic, perhaps even crazy, but she couldn't make herself stop babbling. "Please tell me the baby will be all right."

Lawson lifted his head, making eye contact with her. Yes, he possibly did have a head injury because he looked dazed.

Oh, God. There was blood.

It was on his head and on the butt of his jeans. Eve saw it while he was still on all fours and trying to get to his feet.

"You're hurt," she said, but it was garbled because another contraction hit her. For this one, King Kong had brought one of his friends to help him squeeze her belly. Because Eve had no choice; she dropped to the floor.

She was sinking onto her knees just as Lawson was getting to his. He caught on to the wall and, grunting and making sounds of pain, he got to his feet. He glanced around as if trying to get his bearings, and he growled out more of that profanity. Some of it had her name in the mix. It definitely wasn't the sweet tone he'd used when they were teenagers and he'd charmed her out of her underpants.

Where will this unexpected reunion lead?
Find out in TEXAS-SIZED TROUBLE by
USA TODAY *bestselling author Delores Fossen, available now.*

PHEXPDF0218

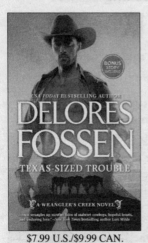

$7.99 U.S./$9.99 CAN.

EXCLUSIVE
Limited Time Offer

$1.⁰⁰ OFF

USA TODAY bestselling author

DELORES FOSSEN

returns with a gritty
Wrangler's Creek novel

TEXAS-SIZED
TROUBLE

*Available January 23, 2018.
Pick up your copy today!*

HQN™

$1.⁰⁰ OFF the purchase price of
TEXAS-SIZED TROUBLE by Delores Fossen.

Offer valid from January 23, 2018, to February 28, 2018.
Redeemable at participating retail outlets. Not redeemable at Barnes & Noble.
Limit one coupon per purchase. Valid in the U.S.A. and Canada only.

52615447

Canadian Retailers: Harlequin Enterprises Limited will pay the face value of this coupon plus 10.25¢ if submitted by customer for this product only. Any other use constitutes fraud. Coupon is nonassignable. Void if taxed, prohibited or restricted by law. Consumer must pay any government taxes. Void if copied. Inmar Promotional Services ("IPS") customers submit coupons and proof of sales to Harlequin Enterprises Limited, P.O. Box 31000, Scarborough, ON M1R 0E7, Canada. Non-IPS retailer—for reimbursement submit coupons and proof of sales directly to Harlequin Enterprises Limited, Retail Marketing Department, 225 Duncan Mill Rd., Don Mills, ON M3B 3K9, Canada.

U.S. Retailers: Harlequin Enterprises Limited will pay the face value of this coupon plus 8¢ if submitted by customer for this product only. Any other use constitutes fraud. Coupon is nonassignable. Void if taxed, prohibited or restricted by law. Consumer must pay any government taxes. Void if copied. For reimbursement submit coupons and proof of sales directly to Harlequin Enterprises, Ltd 482, NCH Marketing Services, P.O. Box 880001, El Paso, TX 88588-0001, U.S.A. Cash value 1/100 cents.

5 65373 00076 2   (8100)0 12337

® and ™ are trademarks owned and used by the trademark owner and/or its licensee.

© 2018 Harlequin Enterprises Limited

PHCOUPDFHI0218

INTRIGUE

EDGE-OF-YOUR-SEAT INTRIGUE, FEARLESS ROMANCE.

Save **$1.00**

on the purchase of ANY
Harlequin® Intrigue book.

Available wherever books are sold,
including most bookstores, supermarkets,
drugstores and discount stores.

- ✂

Save **$1.00**

on the purchase of any Harlequin® Intrigue book.

Coupon valid until April 30, 2018.
Redeemable at participating outlets in the U.S. and Canada only.
Not redeemable at Barnes & Noble stores. Limit one coupon per customer.

52615476

Canadian Retailers: Harlequin Enterprises Limited will pay the face value of this coupon plus 10.25¢ if submitted by customer for this product only. Any other use constitutes fraud. Coupon is nonassignable. Void if taxed, prohibited or restricted by law. Consumer must pay any government taxes. Void if copied. Inmar Promotional Services ("IPS") customers submit coupons and proof of sales to Harlequin Enterprises Limited, P.O. Box 31000, Scarborough, ON M1R 0E7, Canada. Non-IPS retailer—for reimbursement submit coupons and proof of sales directly to Harlequin Enterprises Limited, Retail Marketing Department, 225 Duncan Mill Rd., Don Mills, ON M3B 3K9, Canada.

U.S. Retailers: Harlequin Enterprises Limited will pay the face value of this coupon plus 8¢ if submitted by customer for this product only. Any other use constitutes fraud. Coupon is nonassignable. Void if taxed, prohibited or restricted by law. Consumer must pay any government taxes. Void if copied. For reimbursement submit coupons and proof of sales directly to Harlequin Enterprises, Ltd 482, NCH Marketing Services, P.O. Box 880001, El Paso, TX 88588-0001, U.S.A. Cash value 1/100 cents.

5 65373 00076 2   (8100)0 12340

® and ™ are trademarks owned and used by the trademark owner and/or its licensee.

© 2018 Harlequin Enterprises Limited

HIDFCOUPBPA0118